WARRIORS OF THE DRAGON GOLD

WARRIORS
OF THE
DRAGON
GOLD

RAY BRYANT

MILDMAY BOOKS

LONDON

Mildmay Books Limited
Venture House
29 Glasshouse Street
London W1R 5AP

First published 1987

Copyright © Ray Bryant 1987

Typeset by Input Typesetting Limited, London SW19 8DR
Printed in Great Britain by Redwood Burn Limited, Trowbridge, Wiltshire

British Library Cataloguing in Publication Data

Bryant, Ray
    Warriors of the dragon gold.
    I. Title
    823'.914[F]   PR6052.R9/

ISBN 1–869945–08–5

FIRST BOOK
THE DAY OF THE RAVEN
1013–1035

SECOND BOOK
THE DAY OF THE DRAGON
1036–1049

THIRD BOOK
THE DAY OF THE LEOPARD
1052–1066

TANGLED PATHWAYS TO THE
ENGLISH THRONE, 1013–66

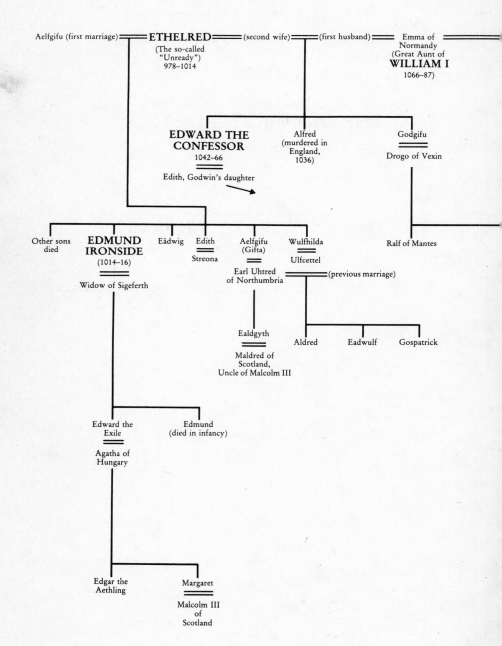

Aelfgifu (first marriage) ═══ **ETHELRED** ═══ (second wife) ═══ (first husband) ═══ Emma of
(The so-called
"Unready")
978–1014

Normandy
(Great Aunt of
WILLIAM I
1066–87)

**EDWARD THE
CONFESSOR**
1042–66

Alfred
(murdered in
England,
1036)

Godgifu
═══
Drogo of Vexin

Edith, Godwin's daughter

Other sons
died

**EDMUND
IRONSIDE**
(1014–16)
═══
Widow of Sigeferth

Eâdwig

Edith
═══
Streona

Aelfgifu
(Gifta)

Wulfhilda
═══
Ulfcettel

Ralf of Mantes

Earl Uhtred
of Northumbria ═══ (previous marriage)

Ealdgyth
═══
Maldred of
Scotland,
Uncle of Malcolm III

Aldred

Eadwulf

Gospatrick

Edward the
Exile
═══
Agatha of
Hungary

Edmund
(died in infancy)

Edgar the
Aethling

Margaret
═══
Malcolm III
of
Scotland

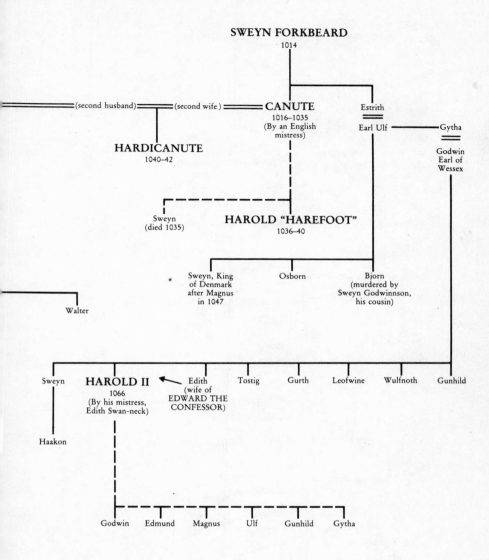

SWEYN FORKBEARD
1014

═══(second husband)═══════(second wife)═════ **CANUTE**   Estrith
                                               1016–1035 ═══
HARDICANUTE   (By an English   Earl Ulf ──────── Gytha
1040–42   mistress)   ═══
                                                                              Godwin
                                                                              Earl of
                                                                              Wessex

         Sweyn   **HAROLD "HAREFOOT"**
         (died 1035)   1036–40

              Sweyn, King   Osborn   Bjorn
              of Denmark   (murdered by
              after Magnus   Sweyn Godwinnson,
              in 1047   his cousin)

Walter

Sweyn   **HAROLD II** ←── Edith   Tostig   Gurth   Leofwine   Wulfnoth   Gunhild
         1066   (wife of
         (By his mistress, EDWARD THE
         Edith Swan-neck)   CONFESSOR)

Haakon

         Godwin   Edmund   Magnus   Ulf   Gunhild   Gytha

Order of rule: Ethelred, Sweyn Forkbeard, Edmund Ironside/Canute, Harold Harefoot,
        Hardicanute, Edward The Confessor, Harold II, William.

═══ Marriage lines

─── Blood lines

─ ─ ─ Illegitimate lines

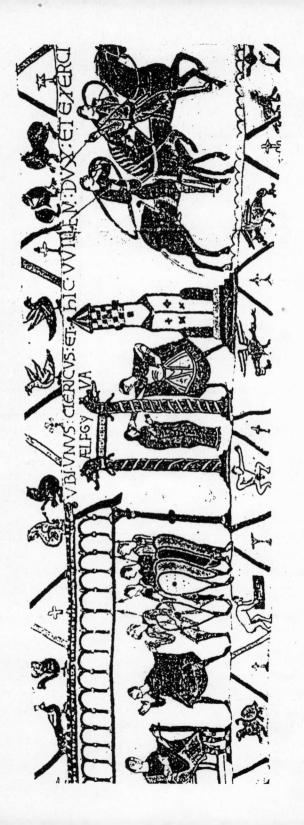

THE MYSTERY LADY OF THE BAYEUX TAPESTRY

Why did Earl Harold and Duke William, at the height of their urgent preparations to take over the English Kingdom, take considerable time off to journey all the way to Brittany on a costly campaign, ostensibly to put down a rather unimportant Count in an unimportant province?

Why, at around that same time, was a northern English nobleman called Gospatrick Uhtredsson murdered at the court of Edward the Confessor, apparently on the orders of Queen Edith?

Why is there just one year's records missing from the Anglo-Saxon Chronicles, so meticulously compiled for centuries? That year is the very year in which Harold made his historic journey to meet William – 1064.

But the most intriguing question of all, who is the mysterious lady Aelfgifu, who makes a sudden appearance in the Bayeux Tapestry, then vanishes again just as quickly?

She appears just at the point where Harold and William meet for the first time, in Normandy.

In the panel on the left William is seated in his court, as visitor Harold seems to be telling him of something interesting at another place.

In the margin below – the only point in the entire tapestry margins where such symbols appear in the place of animals or rural scenes – there is depicted a naked man (a hint at some obscenity?) putting an axe into or taking it out of a box, certainly a symbol of treachery.

Now, in the centre panel, there emerges for the one and only time in the tapestry the lady Aelfgifu.

In England, Aelfgifu is both a proper name and a title for a queen. This Aelfgifu is shown being fondled by a monk, secretly perhaps, because he is apparently reaching through a window or doorway. In the margin below there is again a nude man, in a lewd pose, again suggesting scandal. The unfinished caption over this panel says only: 'Where a certain cleric and Aelfgifu . . .'

No explanation of who the cleric is, what they are doing, where they are or what significance they have in the otherwise perfectly chronicled story – it is simply broken off there, and the pair are never mentioned again.

Then why does Harold seem to be pointing them out to William?

Whatever the reason, in the next panel on the right, William and Harold set out with a great band of William's soldiers to Brittany . . . Merely to deal with little Count Conan, as an amusing diversion for guest Harold? Or for some other sinister purpose lost to historical record – something to do with Aelfgifu and a certain cleric?

It is as though an innocent tapestry worker had started to include Aelfgifu in her rightful place in the tapestry text, and then someone in authority happened along and said: 'Oh no, no more mention of Aelfgifu. Now that William the Conquerer is King, there will be no more talk of Aelfgifu and her kind.'

In the nine centuries since the tapestry was woven, historians have failed to identify Aelfgifu. Many have thus dismissed her as unimportant, others have offered explanations that were not too serious.

This book suggests for the first time just who Aelfgifu was, and the very important role she played in the Conquest. She could have upset the plans of both Harold and William to sieze the English throne, and she had a stepson called Gospatrick Uhtredsson who had to be dealt with for the same reason.

After the Conquest Aelfgifu disappeared, so did mention of her in the tapestry, so did the cleric, so did all records of the year 1064 – the year in which William and Harold caught up with the dangerous lady Aelfgifu under cover of a campaign in Brittany.

This book also questions the accepted fact that the English crown had been promised to William by his cousin Edward the Confessor. The promise was supposed to have been given during a visit William made to England early in the 1050s, while Harold's family were in exile following various conflicts with King Edward.

Nonsense. Norman propaganda – so brilliantly contrived that the lie has endured as the official version of events for more than 900 years. At the time the promise was supposed to have been made, Edward the Confessor had many potential heirs far more highly qualified than William (and bear in mind also that English Kings at that time were elected. A King could nominate his heir, but the final choice from among suitable royal candidates was left to the Witan).

First and most important of all, there was the son that Edward himself might have had by Queen Edith, Harold's sister. There were reports that Edward was impotent, or that Edith was barren, or even that the marriage remained unconsummated through Edward choosing to be celibate. However, none of these rumours were ever substantiated.

It is also worth mentioning that, despite impotence or barrenness or whatever, the people of those times still had sufficient faith to believe very firmly in miracles. But there were others Edward would have chosen above William, to whom he owed nothing.

There was his nephew Edward the Exile, son of Edward the Confessor's half-brother Edmund Ironside and grandson of Ethelred the Unraed. Edward had been in exile in Hungary since the usurper Canute had sent him there, but that did not preclude him from the succession.

Later there would be another highly qualified heir in Edgar the Aethling, son of Edward the Exile. Some historians have it that Edgar was passed over simply because he was too young. But could Edward the Confessor have predicted the date of his own death? He would at least have kept Edgar's options open.

Candidate number four was Ralph of Mantes. He was the son of Edward's sister Godgifu, and he held an Engish earldom. Being of royal blood on his mother's side, Ralph could certainly have been considered – and certainly above William.

There was even another nephew of Edward, Count Walter of the Vexin. He was imprisoned by William, and died in captivity in 1063. Does that sound the kind of act for which Edward the Confessor would reward William with the English Kingdom?

And candidate number six, better placed than William, was Earl Harold Godwinsson. Edward thought so highly of Harold he treated him like a son, and raised him up to the position of second highest in the land. Harold was not of royal blood, but then neither was William. There were witnesses when Edward, on his death-bed, apparently consigned the Kingdom into Harold's care; and Harold was duly elected as King by the Witan, albeit a Witan consisting mainly of his family and friends.

William stole the English crown. He had no right to it whatsoever. And yet, it was partly Harold's fault for getting himself involved in an intrigue with such a man . . . an intrigue concerning the mysterious lady Aelfgifu.

R.B.

FIRST BOOK

The Day of the Raven

1013–1035

PROLOGUE
1013 A.D.

IN Denmark the banners of war were raised. A thousand feast fires burned along the coast from the Frisians to the Skaggerak. Beacons flared out a call to arms from cliff to cove to wide salt marsh, luring men from their homes with a promise of plunder and glory. Warriors young and old gathered up axes, swords and shields, and joyfully set forth for the dragon ships with never a backward glance at homes, herds or wives. The ships, like wild-eyed beasts, raised rigid heads above the smoke that rolled out across the water, and strained at their moorings like leashed hounds, while on the blazing shores their masters chanted and feasted the hours away in drunken, boastful companionship, content to spend the eve of conflict in ritual preparation. They drank potent beer and gorged themselves on black-roasted meats in the thundery summer night, clashed blades and hilts on hard leather shields as though they would rival the thundering of Thor's hammer. They laughed and sang, and cared not that this might be their last great earthly celebration before the voyage to Valhalla, while their fierce-proud women fed the flames, and cheered their men to battle on love and ale.

And all through that night of fires rode King Sweyn Forkbeard, savage old ruler of the Danes, and with him went his eager young son Canute. They passed from camp to camp, and with each fresh burst of cheering that greeted them, the King assured his heir that never before had such a mighty force gathered for the invasion of England. Many times that night did Forkbeard stand on a high place and speak encouragement to his warriors, and none listened more enthralled than Canute. The boy could scarce contain his eagerness as he watched his father harangue the vast crowds, brandishing his heavy sword westwards at the distant isles of Britain.

'Danes, hear your King!' Forkbeard roared. He waited for a thousand cheers to die away, and repeated: 'Hear your King, who goes now to his last great battle!'

'No!' shouted the ranks of rough warriors, but Forkbeard raised his arms to quiet them.

'Yes, this will be my last fight,' he said. 'This I know, for it has been told in the runes. But this is no reason for sorrow; it is a reason for rejoicing! I ask you, what more worthy cause could take me back to the hated shores of England? I go to slay Ethelred, to wrench his kingdom from his dead hands for my sons, and for my grandsons!'

To silence the deafening approval that greeted these words taxed even the authority of Forkbeard. The Vikings yelled themselves hoarse. When at last the King regained the attention of his men, he spoke more quietly, yet with no less force.

'Many times, through many generations, we have warred in England,' he told them. 'We have come home the richer for each voyage. We have taken their gold, their silver, their animals, their women, their children, and even their lands. What man here does not have a kinsman among the people of the English Danelaw? But this time it will be different! We go not merely to fill our ships with treasure. This time, when we set foot on English soil, we shall burn our ships. This time, England itself is the prize!'

Again Forkbeard had to wait for silence.

'This time,' he continued, raising his voice above the dying shouts, 'this time we will finish once and for all our war of vengeance against the despised Ethelred. Now he shall pay for the foul slaughter of our people!'

There could not have been a single soul in all that great crowd who did not know that Forkbeard was speaking of the St. Brice's Day massacre in 1002. King Ethelred of England, fearing a Danish plot to overthrow him, had listened too readily to those who advised him to kill certain Danes living in the Danelaw. The King's executioners had carried out his orders with zeal, and had gone much further. Innocent men, women and children had died, some of them second or third generation settlers in England. Eleven years later, reminded of that cruel deed, Forkbeard's followers were all the more inflamed. Once more the cries of war were hurled up into the crackling night air, and each earl and chieftain urged his men to shout the loudest for blood and for revenge.

'My own sister was murdered by Ethelred!' Forkbeard bellowed above the roaring. 'Will you forget your sisters, your brothers, your cousins? No, you will not! This time there will be no turning back. This time Ethelred and his kin will be destroyed. The English crown shall be our prize! England will be a spoil of war to be divided up among those bold enough to sail with me this dawn. Who follows Forkbeard?'

The howling warriors fought among themselves to be first aboard the longships. They wrestled free of the arms of their women, and plunged into the waves like lemmings, wading out to the vessels in their hundreds, in their thousands, with banners and swords and spears held high.

At dawn the ships sailed out before a blood-red sun. There were more of them than any man had ever seen in one place before. Each was crowded to the gunwales with warriors, who sang lusty songs and beat their shields to the rhythm of the oars. A host of dragons dipped and rose with the swell as if questing for prey, and the swish and slap of six thousand oars sounded across the water like the flurrying of ravens' wings.

I

IN the streets of York there came sounds that spoke of terror, noises of carts rumbling by, the shuffling of hundreds of feet through the mud, and the urgent murmurings of frightened people.

The citizens of York were leaving. They had packed their belongings on to hand-carts or ox-wagons, and great processions of them were jostling each other to leave the city in all directions. There were women and children and old men and goats and dogs, all moving as quickly as the slowest of them would allow, yet none of them knowing where it was safe to go – to the north, the south, the east or the west – or even if there were anywhere safe at all.

Through the stout walls of her house, Gifta could feel the fear in them, a fear she could well understand. There was no shouting or screaming, but she knew it was only a matter of time before they would panic.

'The Northmen are coming, the Northmen are coming,' the frantic whispers ran through the streets. 'Dear God,' was the prayer ever on their lips, 'from the fury of the Northmen, Good Lord, deliver us!'

However, there would be no leaving from Gifta's house yet. A girl of just seventeen she might be – and certainly as frightened as anyone else in York – but she was mistress of a noble household, and she was determined there would be no desertion of duty at home while the men were bravely fighting the Viking invaders out in the fields and hills. Gifta must set an example, even if others were too cowardly to follow it, for she was a princess, daughter to King Ethelred. Her full name was Aelfgifu – Noble Gift – a name borne by Saxon queens for more than five hundred years. She was also the wife of Uhtred, Earl of Northumbria, who at this very moment was leading the struggle to save his earldom and to support his King's stand against the Danes.

'My lady, you must not let the Northmen take you,' her handmaid Constance had pleaded, when news came that the Danes had beaten back Uhtred's men so close by at Helmsley. 'They must not take the daughter of Ethelred!'

'So, would you have Earl Uhtred return to his home and find it empty?' Gifta scolded Constance, but her maid's words had struck coldly at her heart. She, like all the poor trembling women around her, had heard stories of how the merciless Vikings snatched up English women, tore off their clothes and threw them naked across their horses to be taken to their ships. The Northmen pulled babies from their mothers' breasts, impaled them on spears. Such terrible tales made Gifta think of her own child now growing within her. She felt sick to think what would happen when the Vikings reached Earl Uhtred's hall. Her ragged little bodyguard could not hope to hold them off for long. There would be a brief and bloody battle at the stockade gate, the dwindling defence force would fall back to the doors of the hall itself, and then the Vikings would stampede in, rape her and her women, carry them off to slavery, perhaps torture and kill them.

The eyes of the household were constantly upon Gifta, seeking help and encouragement, although she was the youngest of the women. She busied herself with the running of the household, as though nothing untoward was happening, and hoped that her own fear would not show. She listened to the squealing and groaning of wagon wheels outside and thought they sounded like tormented souls. In the crackling flames of the log fire she saw more destruction, and heard the Vikings laugh, as they would laugh when they came to drag her from her hall.

She had dreamed many times lately of the fall of the house of Ethelred, and dreaded that her nightmares would come true. Only last night, she had dreamed that a flock of evil-eyed ravens had ravaged the land and stripped it bare. She had seen a golden dragon, the ancient golden dragon of Alfred's Wessex and now of Ethelred's England. The ravens had siezed upon it with great savagery; the dragon had fallen, and the ravens had picked its flesh to the bone even as it died. Gifta herself had taken up a knife, and all alone had tried to beat off the dreadful black horde, but a suffocating darkness had fallen over her, and she had woken sweating and gasping for air.

She knew she could not bear to see her nightmare played out in reality. She fingered one of the long bone needles on her sewing board, and wondered if she would have the courage to plunge it into her heart when the Northmen appeared at her threshold. She had been taught it was sinful to take one's own life. But would it not be more honourable for a daughter of Ethelred to die thus, rather than submit to humiliation at the hands of her father's enemies, or be taken for ransom? Or was it the greater sin to kill her unborn child?

Suddenly the big double doors of the hall were pushed open, bringing a gust of cool air that brought Gifta back to the present.

Her stepson Gospatrick came running in, and Gifta drew her hand back from the needle like one caught stealing.

Gospatrick was only six years younger than Gifta, the last of Uhtred's three sons by his first marriage. Gifta and Gospatrick had grown very fond of each other since her marriage to his father a little more than a year ago, and they were more like sister and brother than stepmother and stepson. Gospatrick, in his father's absence, had decided that he would protect Gifta from the Vikings. For hours each day he stood with the bodyguard outside the house, gripping the hilt of his knife, waiting for the attack. Now he came running in to Gifta in great excitement, stumbling and almost falling headlong among the floor rushes.

'They're back! Father, and Aldred and Eadwulf, they're back. A lot of the men are wounded. Father is hurt, too! He's got a wound, from a Viking! He's bleeding!'

Gifta leapt to her feet.

'Merciful God!' she shouted. 'Is he in pain? Constance, fetch hot water and cloths and the herb salves. Quickly!'

'Don't worry, it's not serious, it's only a cut on the arm,' Gospatrick tried to tell her, 'But just think, a Viking did it! They've been fighting hand to hand with the Vikings!'

Gifta felt faint. She pressed her hands together, striving to stay calm. Her husband had been wounded in close combat with the Danes! That brought home to her the reality of the war, more vividly than the sight of frightened citizens fleeing York. She could feel her fear growing into the terror she had tried to deny, and for a moment wanted to faint away and blot out the horror of it all. But she heard the sound of horses' hooves out in the yard, and the voice of Uhtred shouting to his men, and recovered her composure. She heard herself snapping at Constance for taking so long with the hot water.

Earl Uhtred entered his house unsteadily, weary from many days of hard riding and fighting. His face was grimed with sweat and dirt, and his shirt was stained with blood. He had not even paused to take off the crushing weight of his chain-mail coat. He looked older than his forty-two years, for in the dim indoor light his tired eyes were hidden in shadowed sockets, his brow lined with worry and fatigue. His shoulders, usually proud-squared, now drooped as if to match the slant of his long, fair moustaches. For the first time in his life, he looked unsure of himself, defeated. He felt as dispirited as the people of York for whom he had been fighting – those same people who had almost unseated him in the crowded streets in their haste to be away.

Uhtred put his good arm round his wife, but brushed aside her efforts to tend his wound until he had drained a beaker of ale. He slumped into a high-backed chair, managing a smile at Gospatrick's boyish eagerness to inspect the gash. Gifta knelt beside Uhtred and pushed up the damaged sleeve. She gasped at the sight of the swollen, blood-caked cut on his forearm.

'An axe splintered my shield,' Uhtred explained. 'It was the splinters that did the hurt, not the blade. I killed the fellow before he could try again, praise be to God.'

'You killed a Viking?' Gospatrick cried. 'How did you kill him, father? Did you stab him with your sword?'

'Sliced him with it, boy,' Uhtred corrected his son. 'You don't jab about like a peevish girl when a man's swinging a double-bladed axe at you. You take your sword in both hands, wounded or not, and you slice him down the middle with it. Aye, and he's not the only one I've slain these last few weeks. I can't count how many, yet still the devils came!'

'No one has ever seen so many Danes,' Aldred confirmed. 'Men who've been fighting them for years, they all say it. They all swear this is the most enormous army the Northmen have ever raised. I don't know how in God's name we can stand against them.'

'I'm not so sure we can,' muttered Eadwulf. He, like his elder brother, had just fought the first battles of his life. The boys had been in the field for a matter of weeks only, but already they were seasoned fighting men. Now it seemed to them that they had been warriors for long seasons past. Both were as downhearted as their father.

'Does it pain you?' Gifta was asking Uhtred, as she carefully washed the mess of torn flesh.

'No. Don't fuss so; I'm all right,' Uhtred said. 'There are many worse off than I. Some of those we brought back will not live through the night. It's their wives you should think of, my love, trying to patch up men who are chopped up like meat on a butcher's stone.'

'If their wives are still here,' Gifta sighed.

'Aye, we saw the great exodus. You have probably felt much afraid, seeing them all leaving like this. But they are right, Gifta. Time is running out. There is nothing to do now but flee – for the women and children, anyway. The Danes will be here again in two days or less, and this time we have little to stop them with. The King wants you to go back to Winchester to be with your family, and I agree with him. I am sending you there as soon as you are ready to go, this very day.'

'But are you coming too?' Gifta asked.

'No,' Uhtred said. 'I must stay here with my sons and try to keep the army together. The King and your brothers are going south again to gather yet more men. You'll see them at Winchester, like as not.'

'But I cannot go without you!' Gifta protested. 'I would die of worry, being so far away! I want to stay. Is there nowhere nearby where I would be safe?'

'Do you think I would leave my wife, a daughter of Ethelred, within reach of the Northmen?' Uhtred took Gifta's hands in his. 'No my love; with you in their hands the whole kingdom would be held to ransom . . . and there's no knowing what they might do to you. No, there is no choice. You must leave for Winchester while we can still hope to get you there. Gospatrick will go with you,' he added, ruffling the boy's hair. 'You will protect your stepmother, won't you my son?'

'I'm not going,' Gospatrick declared. 'I'm staying with you. I'm old enough to fight.'

'You'll do as you're told, boy,' Uhtred said sternly, 'like any good soldier. Your turn to fight will come. And who else can I trust to guard Gifta, if you won't go with her?'

Gospatrick attempted to argue further, but was silenced with a look.

'Is it really so hopeless, then?' Gifta asked. 'Are the Northmen stronger than us?'

'At this moment, yes. As Aldred says, they are stronger than they've ever been. And this time they show no signs of withdrawing for the winter. Far from it. They've burned their ships.'

'You can feel their determination this time,' contributed Eadwulf. 'They are not offering to take tribute for a truce as they have so often done in the past. They want more. They want it all, the whole of England.'

'A prisoner boasted of that to us,' Uhtred added grimly, 'before we slit his throat.'

'It disgusts me to think of the numbers of English who have sided with them,' said Aldred. 'Perhaps they are not all actually fighting alongside the Danes, but they're certainly doing nothing to help us. You can no longer tell friend from foe. There are English on the Danish side, and Scandinavians fighting for the English. Some Norwegians have come to help us, but not many.'

'They know that Forkbeard's ambitions stretch to Norway as well as to England,' said Uhtred. 'Forkbeard has said he will make England part of a Danish empire. It's obvious that Norway would be next.'

'Then he reckons without the spirit of Ethelred's house!' the Princess Aelfgifu insisted desperately. 'My father and my brothers will never sacrifice their kingdom! God willing, they will throw out these Viking swine. Oh please, Uhtred, tell me there is hope! I am more afraid than ever now that you are sending me away. Will I ever see you again?'

Uhtred placed his hands on her shoulders and leaned forward to kiss her.

'Of course there is hope,' he answered, with a conviction he could hardly feel himself. 'You have said as much, haven't you? Your father and brothers, descendants of Cerdic and of Alfred the Great, are not easily cowed by a band of cut-throat Danes. And you will see me again, I promise. All the armies of the Northmen could not keep me from my dear wife nor from the child you carry for me. Now, you must start packing. I want you away from here within the hour. Just take what you need for the journey. If I have time I will send on the rest of your things.'

There was a smile on Uhtred's face, but a great sadness in his heart. He saw in the eyes of his wife and his youngest son a trust and confidence that made him proud, yet he could not banish the memories of the Viking hordes, wave upon wave of them, bearing down on him. Sometimes it had seemed as if he alone stood between them and defeat. Could he possibly keep his promise to these two trusting people, if it meant he must brave that ocean of death again? It was only by a miracle that he was here with them now, he knew. Lost for a moment in a waking nightmare, he felt himself once more among the heaps of slaughtered English on the windswept moor, heard his men screaming like children as they ran. He saw again the shield-wall of the Danes advancing relentlessly as a thunderstorm, recalled the murderous light in the faces of those dark-souled warriors who moved to surround him and hack him down in a rain of steel. A hideous forest of axes and spears had sprouted out of the bare landscape to surround him, the helpless leader of a vanished army. A berserk chieftain had come charging out from the chanting ranks, his axe whirling high above his head. All that Uhtred could remember were the Dane's clenched teeth, his bristling black beard and burning gaze, the cruel humming of the axe as it hurtled towards him, and the shock as it struck his shield. By instinct, he shook his numbed arm free of the broken shield and took a double grip on his sword hilt. The Dane was preparing to strike again. Uhtred must have raised his sword; afterwards he would swear that he knew nothing of the broad blade's light until he saw it cleave the Dane from neck to breast.

Aldred and Eadwulf brought in more men, and he turned and ran, sickened by his fear and ashamed of being forced into a cowardly retreat. He heard the Northmen shouting insults, jeering at them, daring them to go back and stand like men, instead of scuttling away like scalded curs.

Even back in the land of the living, in the warmth of his home and the precious company of his wife and sons, Uhtred could still hear the mockery of the Vikings, still feel the cold stab of terror in his guts. God alone knew how much he wanted to escape to the south with Gifta and Gospatrick, far away from the enemy at his threshhold – but he had vowed to serve his King and to do all he could to save the kingdom. He would not run away from that duty as he had run away from the recent battle, even if it meant his death.

Uhtred hid his doubts behind a show of courage. He stood up and for a moment took his wife and youngest son in his arms.

'So, Gospatrick,' he said. 'Will you stop sulking and help your stepmother pack? Only children sulk, and you are not a child any more.'

'But I still have to go with the women,' Gospatrick grumbled.

'Aye, and I have told you why. I need a trustworthy man to look after my wife on a dangerous journey, that's why. Listen to me, Gospatrick Uhtredsson. You are a good lad, and a brave one. I mean it when I say I can trust you to care for Gifta, not just in the next few days, but always. Promise me you will stay by her side, if anything happens to me and your brothers. She and the baby are the only family you will have, and I can do all I have to do with an easier mind if I know you two will stay together. She is a fine woman, Gospatrick. It has been a great joy to me, to know that you and she have come to love each other. Think of her as your true mother, then, and accept her guidance as you would mine. Will you promise?'

'Of course I will,' Gospatrick said tearfully, 'you know I will. But nothing is going to happen to you! You're great warriors. Those Vikings can't kill you!'

'Of course not,' Uhtred smiled. 'I was speaking only of what I would like you to do if there was an accident, that's all. Believe me, I'll be coming to Winchester to see you both as soon as we've sent those Danes back where they belong.'

'Then we'll all come back here?'

'Naturally. Could we live anywhere but our splendid city of York? So run along now, and help Gifta. The sooner you get going, the sooner you can write and tell me how Wessex compares with Northumbria, eh?'

Gospatrick felt that Wessex was bound to be a horrible place, full of strangers and with nothing to do. Nevertheless, his father's praise and reassurances had all but reconciled him to being sent away.

Not as much could be said for Gifta, however. Her husband's talk of what might happen had deepened her fears, and it was with a renewed foreboding that she went about her preparations for the long journey south. With each piece of jewellery or clothing that she placed in the hastily gathered boxes and bundles, she took a longing look around at the big timber hall. It was her home; she had made it her own, and she felt a fierce resentment of the intruders who had come to take it from her.

The last year had been a wonderful adventure for Gifta. Suddenly, she had been treated like a grown woman and a responsible wife, rather than as just another child of the royal household. She had constantly marvelled at the happiness of being mistress of her own house, first lady of York, virtually queen of Northumbria.

At first she had faced the prospect of marriage with trepidation. But Uhtred had feted her fondly and, after growing accustomed to the husband her father had chosen for her, Gifta realised that she actually did love him. In his house she had given up her virginity, and had learned to share his bed with pleasure and pride. Here she had hoped to bear their first child, the first of a whole new family which would transform Uhtred's womanless hall into a warm and proper home. Here she would have delighted in entertaining her father and brothers and sisters, and all the nobility of the land.

Everything she touched, everywhere she looked, reminded Gifta of some moment from the past year. There, in the centre of the hall, they had played childish games after the Christmas feasting. By that fire one glowing winter evening, with the snow deep outside, they had listened to a honey-voiced bard from Iceland who sang in praise of her father and her father's fathers. The huge doors reminded her of the day last spring when both her sisters had arrived unexpectedly, allowing her to play host for the first time. And Uhtred had been sitting there, in that chair, when she had whispered to him that she was with child; he had been so surprised, he leapt up and spilt his wine over Gospatrick's head, and shouted to the world the news that she had tried to pass on so secretly.

There were happy memories at the long oak table, too. The first night she had come to her husband's hall, she had sat there mute under the gaze of Uhtred and his sons – all strangers. Not one of them knew what to say, until the innocent Gospatrick, confused by the relationship between Gifta and his two brothers who were older than their stepmother, asked in a nervous voice: 'If you have a baby, will they be its fathers?'

He had meant to say 'uncles'. For a moment Uhtred had looked outraged, then realising it was no more than a slip of the tongue, they had all burst into helpless laughter.

'Half-brothers, Gospatrick,' Aldred spluttered, 'we will be the child's half-brothers, just as you will!'

Gifta thought she heard again, just for an instant, the echoes of that night's laughter, faintly, somewhere high up in the rafters. She looked up at the familiar pattern of stout black beams and dark brown thatch, but never had it looked so sombre.

But there was no more time now for memories. Two covered carts stood in the yard, each with four mules in harness. The women respectfully waited for the Princess Aelfgifu to get in first. A few servants and their children were already inside the second cart. Gospatrick sat astride his pony at the head of a dozen armed and mounted men, all that Uhtred could spare for a bodyguard.

Gifta could not go without one last look back at the sprawling, barn-like building. She threw herself into her husband's arms and wept upon his chest.

'Courage, wife,' Uhtred murmured. 'Gospatrick will have need of your strength.' He pressed a hand to the slight swelling of her belly, adding: 'And so will this one. Don't forget, if it's a boy, his name is to be Waltheof after my father. If a girl, her name must be Ealdgyth.'

'You don't expect to see our child born.' Gifta wept.

'If it is God's will, I shall,' replied Uhtred. 'We must trust in Him. But remember, whatever happens to me, you are carrying the first grandchild of King Ethelred, one who must be kept safe at all costs. Remember who you are, Princess Aelfgifu. No more crying now; just thank God that we have had one year together, and that because of it, Cerdic's line lives on in you.'

Gifta nodded, and wiped away her tears. She got up on the cart without another word. Gospatrick waved to Uhtred, Aldred and Eadwulf until the carts had left the stockade, when their view was blocked by the close-set stakes. To Gifta, that symbolised the end of all hope. While she was able to see Uhtred there had always been a chance that something miraculous might happen to prevent their parting – news might come that the Danes were falling back, or that her father had ordered Uhtred to travel south with her – but now it seemed certain that God's will was that she should go and Uhtred stay.

Gifta repeated over and over to herself the words she could have spoken to Uhtred before leaving him. If he must die, she realised, she should have let him know how much she loved him. She should have told him that his gentleness and generosity had made him a noble man in all senses of the word, and that she could not have hoped for a more loving husband if she had chosen one for herself. She could have told him that she was proud to be carrying his baby, not because it was a child of Cerdic's and of Ethelred's line, but because it was his. There was so much she should have told him, and the unsaid words weighted her down.

II

THEY were at Wallingford, about to cross the Thames, when a young thane rode up with an escort to meet them. He looked greatly relieved at having found them; it was obvious he and his men had been searching for them for many days.

'My lady Aelfgifu!' he cried, reining in beside the wagon, 'Thank God I have found you!' Then, looking at her pitiful entourage – a single wagon with a few women, a boy on a pony and no mounted escort – his expression became one of astonishment. 'But where are your guards?'

'The cowards fled within a day of our leaving York,' Gifta explained. 'Some of the servants, too. They even took one of our wagons one night while we slept.'

'It's a miracle that you should have travelled this far unharmed, lady.' the young man said. 'The King has sent me to meet you. He and all your family are in London. He wants me to take you there.'

'But I was told to go to Winchester!'

'They have gone to London for the protection of its walls and larger numbers of fyrdmen, lady. And also because the fleet is there, should the King need it. Since you left York the Danes have taken most of Mercia and East Anglia, and seem to be marching on Oxford now. There is very little time to get you to your family safely . . .'

'Dear God,' Gifta breathed, 'but what of Northumbria?'

The thane hesitated, avoiding her gaze.

'I'm sorry to be the bearer of bad news, lady,' he answered quietly, 'but your husband has conceded all of Northumbria to the Danes. They say he had no choice. His army was overwhelmed. Earl Uhtred himself surrendered to Forkbeard.'

'But what has happened to him?' she pleaded.

'He lives, and is quite well – the last we heard.'

'And my brothers?' Gospatrick interrupted anxiously. 'Are my brothers all right? Aldred and Eadwulf – they were with my father . . .'

'Yes, they are both alive, but prisoners of Forkbeard. Please, we must be going now! Each moment we delay we risk running into the Danes. We know they are at least as close as Northampton, perhaps even nearer.'

The young man had to choose whether to take them to London along the north bank of the Thames, where they might get trapped by the Danes with no escape across the water, or whether to take the longer route south of the river. He chose the northern way, and they spent two days and nights hurrying through Oxfordshire and Buckinghamshire. They reached London safely, but in an exhausted and nervous state.

Gifta was first of all taken to the royal house by the Fleet River, where her father and her brothers were holding a council of war with the few generals they had left. The men had not even taken off their travel-stained mail coats, for they had only recently returned from a series of bitter, last-ditch battles. They bore a beaten look. In the last few months they had been outnumbered and outmanoeuvred by the Danes at every turn and they had lost much. Today they were discussing not so much where to meet the Northmen next, but whether they could afford to meet them at all without more fighting men. Shortly before Gifta and Gospatrick entered the chamber, it had been suggested that all the English could do now was wait for the Danes to storm the walls of London. They would make their last stand there, or surrender the kingdom entirely. The terrible knowledge that it had come to this showed clearly in their faces, and none looked more grim than Ethelred, their King.

Ethelred was forty-three years old. For thirty-five of those years he had been King, and for long periods of his reign he had been harried by Viking invaders and betrayed by ambitious men at his own court. With each passing year he had become less resolute, until this autumn when the last of his diminishing will drained away. His fair-bearded face was etched with the worries that had beset him since early summer. He stood limply, like a man whose only desire was to go to bed and sleep away his troubles. He brightened at the sight of his daughter, and hurried to take her in his arms.

'Thank God you are safe!' he cried, 'I've had men out searching for you for days. So much has happened since I told Uhtred to send you home. Are you well? Is the child all right?'

'I am well, father,' Gifta assured him, 'and I believe no harm has come to the child. But what about you? You look so tired! Can you not rest a while?'

'There is no rest for me, not any more,' Ethelred sighed. 'You have heard how the Danes have advanced?'

'Yes, I have. Father, please do not despise Uhtred for surrendering! He fought so hard. I know he would never give up unless there was nothing else left to do.'

'Hush child, I do know,' the King calmed her. 'I bear him no ill-will, believe me. He got a message to me only two days ago. He promises he will fight again when the chance comes.'

'What has happened to him? Do you know?'

'He is quite safe for the moment. Forkbeard has appointed his own earl to run Northumbria, and Uhtred and his sons are prisoners in their own house. Uhtred has been told he will be allowed to keep certain property and lands if he will swear allegiance to Forkbeard, but I don't think your husband will ever swear such an oath. He is biding his time.'

'I thank God that they are alive,' Gifta said. 'But what will you do now? What will happen to us?'

'Nothing will happen to you,' promised Ethelred. 'That I have sworn. I have decided to send you all, daughters and younger sons, to your stepmother's home in Normandy. Edmund and Eadwig and I will stay for as long as we have an army, but I think it may not be long before we follow you.'

'Then it's all over,' Gifta murmured, bowing her head.

'Not yet, little sister,' said her elder brother, Edmund, putting an arm around her. 'Father believes there is little hope now. But I shall go on fighting until the day Forkbeard wears the crown of England on his scruffy head, and has me splayed out in the blood-eagle'.

Gifta shuddered at Edmund's words. The blood-eagle was the traditional way in which Vikings dealt with those they wished to send to a slow and tormented death. The victim's ribs were cut from his backbone and splayed out like wings while he still lived. It was the vilest form of death men could devise.

Gifta flung her arms about her brother as though to reassure herself that he was still in one piece.

'Don't say such things! I can't bear it!' she begged.

'Don't worry, little sister,' said Edmund. 'I want to live, to see England free of the Danes. I want Father to name me his heir; I want the Witan and all England to choose me for their King. No, Forkbeard shall not have my crown! I shall fight, little sister, I shall fight!'

'Edmund thinks I have given up too soon,' Ethelred said patiently. 'I have not. Rather, I am staring truth in the face. The Danes control most of the kingdom and we have too few men to stop them taking the rest. If we cannot win now, we must be prepared to run, to fight again another time.'

'There are some things I will not prepare for!' declared Edmund, who had no time for the policies of caution his father had adopted throughout his reign. 'You've been listening to cowards and women, father. And look where their counsels have led us! Unraed, men call you: the poorly-counselled! A king need listen to no such warnings. A king should decide for himself!'

Indignation flickered in the older man's eyes; the barb had struck home. Edmund had reason to be cocky, for his bravery in battle had earned him a nickname too: Edmund Ironside. Ethelred did not want to be drawn into more argument just then – let the boy revel in his glory while he might, the King was thinking, and God forbid he should ever become as weary as I – but he could not let pass the public rebuke from his son.

'If I have made mistakes,' he told Edmund coolly, 'it has been in underestimating my friends. What I have never done is underestimate my enemies, which is what you advise me to do, Edmund. I have ruled this Kingdom since long before you were born, boy, and I believe I have one or two things to teach you still.'

Edmund shrugged carelessly, and said no more. Ethelred turned his attention to Gifta. He took her to one side then, out of the hearing of young Gospatrick, who had faithfully followed Gifta since their arrival at the palace. 'It hurts me to tell you this,' Ethelred said more quietly, 'but Gospatrick cannot go with you to Normandy. When Uhtred heard of my plans, he begged me not to let the child leave the country. I think he fears he will have little enough chance to see his son again as it is. But don't worry; Gospatrick will be safe. Uhtred has arranged for him to stay with friends, well out of reach of the Danes. Uhtred also asked your forgiveness, knowing how you love the boy. You do understand don't you?'

Gifta nodded, but it was a gesture of resignation rather than one of obedience. She was tired and hungry and changes were happening faster than she could keep up with them. She felt let down by the people she trusted most. Both her husband and her father had sworn that they would never surrender their heritage, yet in so few days Uhtred had already done so, and now Ethelred was all but following in his footsteps. Uhtred had but a short while ago entrusted Gospatrick and Gifta to each other's care, had made them swear to stay together, yet now he was snatching the lad away from her again, and sending her to a strange country virtually alone and friendless.

Her love for Uhtred and Ethelred was as strong as ever, but she was beginning to resent the fact that she was the one who had to sacrifice everything, who was being hustled out of the way with the children, but who was given no chance to play her own part in saving all that was dear to her. Suddenly, exhaustion and unhappiness overwhelmed her, and the proud wife of the Earl of

31

Northumbria broke down and wept, feeling as helpless as her own unborn child.

'I curse the Northmen!' she sobbed. 'And I curse England's traitors! If it weren't for them, I wouldn't be taken from my home and my husband, from my family, even from my country. I may be only a woman, but I swear, father, I will strike a blow to hurt them, even if I have to live a hundred years to do it!'

Ethelred took his daughter's face in his hands, and wiped the tears from her cheeks. He bent forward to kiss her.

'Spoken like the daughter of a king! But, Gifta, remember you may yet be the mother of a king. You know you must go. I wish Gospatrick were going with you, but Uhtred wants him to stay.'

'I do not know how I shall tell him that he cannot come with me,' she whispered, choking back tears. 'Dear God, he's been the bravest of them all, protecting me on the way here. He would have given his life for me without a pause for thought. The day after we left York, someone called that the Vikings were coming, and our brave bodyguards were the first to go, riding for their lives. But do you know, Gospatrick drew his knife and stood by my wagon, ready for the Danes if they came. As it happened they turned out to be Englishmen, but it made no difference. Gospatrick Uhtredsson, my eleven-year-old stepson, was the bravest man in sight!'

'There is nothing to be done about it,' Ethelred said, tiredly. 'You must be strong, both of you. Go and see your sister and stepmother now. We still have much to talk about here.'

Yes, I must be strong, Gifta thought bitterly – strong enough to stifle my misery, but weak enough to do as I am told.

In the great hall she found her sister Wulfhilda, who had been married for only a few weeks to Ulfcettel of East Anglia. With Wulfhilda was their stepmother, Emma of Normandy, and the children Emma had borne to Ethelred, Edward and Alfred and their daughter Godgifu.

Gifta's greeting for Wulfhilda was a joyous one, but she was cooler towards Emma. Gifta's relationship with Emma had always been strained; she had never been able to forgive the proud Norman noblewoman for taking the place of her beloved mother. Emma, in turn, tended to look upon Gifta as an arrogant and unapproachable young woman.

From the start, Gifta had been suspicious of the Normans' motives for arranging a marriage between Ethelred and their most prized daughter, sister of the Norman ruler Duke Richard II. England had hoped that the chief benefit from the alliance would be a strengthening of her hand against the raiders of the North, who frequently used the ports of their Norman kinsmen for their attacks on the English. The marriage had made scant difference, though. Still the Vikings came, more viciously than ever. Normandy had so much more to gain than England from the match, Gifta believed. Ever ambitious to gain more land, the Normans must be rubbing their hands gleefully over the wealth that was promised by the birth of two sons to Ethelred and Emma, for those sons might one day be kings of England.

Thus Emma was, for Gifta, the very symbol of a foreign threat to her beloved England.

She could not even feel much affection for her half-brothers and sister – although they were of her father's blood, and Edward was only eight years old, Alfred six and Godgifu five – because they were Emma's brood, and had already inherited some of her less pleasant Norman traits.

To Gifta, those children were the living proof of the Norman desire to control England. She could not help treating them at best with a detached forbearance, and it showed. And by way of revenge, Emma made it perfectly plain that she regarded Gifta's stepson Gospatrick as an insignificant provincial lout, compared with her own sons. She had referred to Gospatrick, within Gifta's hearing, as 'that poor motherless whelp dear Gifta looks after.' It was not clear whether the use of the word 'whelp' was meant to imply that Gifta was a bitch, but Gifta certainly took the remark as an insult to her stepson if not to herself, and that was insult enough.

'Good evening, stepmother,' Gifta formally greeted Emma, 'I expect you, at least, are pleased to be going back to Normandy?'

'Yes, Aelfgifu dear, for a time,' Emma smiled. 'Try not to be so downhearted, child. Think of it as an opportunity to learn something of our Norman way of life.'

Conceited cow, thought Gifta. She really does think that her damned Normans are God's gift to mankind! There was nothing that Gifta wanted to learn from the Normans, but she was too tired to draw claws with Emma tonight.

'Where is Edith?' she inquired of Wulfhilda.

Wulfhilda looked embarrassed, as if the answer she had to give was a shameful admission to make in front of Emma.

'Streona has refused to send her back,' she stammered. 'Father's furious, didn't he tell you? He believes he's hidden her away. But he's got no men to spare to go and force Streona to let her go.'

Edith was their elder sister, and her husband Streona the worst friend Ethelred had among many untrustworthy courtiers. Many times Streona had made himself a profit, or had got out of a tight spot, by selling out to the king's enemies, yet somehow Ethelred had always forgiven him and restored him to trusted positions, only to be let down again.

'Does that mean we must leave her behind?'

'It grows more likely with every day.'

'Dear God, why did father let Edith marry him?' Gifta exclaimed. 'You can see why he wants to keep Edith locked away, can't you? He may need to change sides again. Poor Edith is his hostage!'

'Streona is not the only one,' Emma contributed smugly. 'So many of your father's thanes have deserted him, he no longer knows who are his friends and who are not.' There was a mischievous gleam in her eyes then, as she looked to Gospatrick. She reached out and gently lifted the boy's chin, as if to cheer him up, and told him in a patronising manner: 'But Gospatrick, dear child, you must not think of *your* father as one of those disloyal thanes. I'm sure he did not *want* to give Northumbria to the Danes.'

Gospatrick angrily pulled away from her.

'He did not *give* it to them!' he snapped. 'I would never think my father a traitor, never!'

'No, Gospatrick, you are right. He isn't!' Gifta said hotly, no longer able to restrain herself. 'There is no more loyal man in the kingdom than Uhtred, and don't you ever listen to anyone who says anything against him – not even your Queen!'

'Do calm down child,' Emma said easily, 'I said nothing of the sort. People will think you feel guilt for Uhtred, if you cannot control that temper of yours.'

'I know what you meant, and Uhtred gives me no cause for guilt at all. Sometimes you can stoop very low in your eagerness to strike at me, stepmother.'

Emma remained composed, but her eyes flashed a warning.

'Guard your tongue!' she ordered. 'I believe I am entitled to some respect from you.'

'Father once told me that respect is earned, not commanded,' said Gifta. 'He also said it should be offered in return.'

'Oh yes, your father has said many wise things,' Emma sneered. 'It's a pity he is so willing to credit others with the same cleverness. See where his wisdom has brought us all today.'

The outburst against Ethelred astonished Gifta, who looked desperately to Wulfhilda for support.

'Now she insults our father! Is there anyone in England you approve of, stepmother? Why did you ever leave your precious Normandy!'

'Enough!' Emma demanded. 'One more insult from you, and I'll have your father argue it out with you!'

'Are you sure you can trust him to do it?' was Gifta's final taunt.

The irate Emma drew herself up, searching for more suitable rebukes, but the quarrel was interrupted by the timely arrival of Gifta's brother Eadwig, Wulfhilda's husband Ulfcettel, a few slaves, and a young monk whom Eadwig introduced as Father Theobald.

'You must board your ship at first light,' Eadwig told them gravely. 'We've just heard that Oxford has surrendered to the Danes.'

It was Gifta who broke the stunned silence.

'Are they coming here now?' she asked.

'Forkbeard is probably on his way to Winchester, expecting to find us there,' he said. 'But it won't be long before he makes for London. We're getting you out while there's time. These slaves will help you get your things together. Father Theobald has been appointed your confessor. Father did not want you to lack spiritual guidance. That's all – except that father says he's very sorry he can't come to you tonight. He's very tired. He will see you in the morning, before you get on the ship.'

'If there is any service I may render tonight, I shall be pleased to do so,' said Theobald quietly.

Gifta declined with a polite shake of her head. She felt numbed, knowing there were only hours left before she must step aboard that ship and go far away across the Channel, leaving England for the first time in her life. There was no guarantee that she would ever come back to the country and the people she loved. All the spiritual guidance the entire Church of Rome could offer would not help her in this terrible time, she thought. All she wanted was the strength to say: 'No, I will not go, you cannot make me!' Failing that, she longed for the courage to make light of her parting with Gospatrick, and the ability to convince him that it was for a short time only. None of this could Father Theobald nor any other churchman give her, for she had asked it of God many times over and he had not responded.

'Goodbye, my little flower,' Ulfcettel was saying cheerfully to Wulfhilda. 'Don't fret so. We'll have you back here by Christmas. . . .'

Ah yes, Gifta thought, watching them, that is how it is supposed to be done. That is how the last farewell is said, if you are a man and war is the very stuff of life, like drinking wine and singing songs of heroes. That is how the men do it, for it is they who shape this life to their liking, and accept separation as just another price to be paid for glory. For them, to leave a loving wife and a

35

comfortable home and go off to war is merely to put down a bridge between one joy and the next. And if life and wife and home are all to be gambled away? Well, that too is part of the game. Would the stew have flavour without the spices? Without the tusks of the boar, would there be any thrill to the hunt?

The Devil take men and their careless farewells!

Gifta took Gospatrick to a quiet corner, and held him close while she explained that they could no longer be together. Gospatrick cried, and caused her more pain by gazing at her as though he'd been sorely deceived.

'Father said we needed each other!' he sobbed. 'he said I must always protect you! Why did he lie to me?'

'He didn't lie,' Gifta said, choking on the words. 'He could not see what would happen. You must not blame him for this.'

'But what am I going to do?' the boy pleaded. 'I'll have no one now. You can't leave me!'

'Of course you will have someone. Your father's friends are to look after you, and I am leaving Constance with you. And isn't it better if Uhtred can come for you as soon as he is ready? It would be so much more difficult if you were in Normandy.'

'That's only an excuse,' said Gospatrick resentfully. 'It's just because Queen Emma hates me. She doesn't want me in her rotten country. Father doesn't want me either, because he thinks I'm not good enough to fight.'

'Please, Goose,' Gifta begged, using her special nickname for him. 'Don't talk like that. Please don't let us part with tears!'

Gospatrick made a brave attempt to stop crying. He tried to disguise his grief with haughtiness.

'It's not your fault,' he conceded. 'I won't ever hate you for it. You have to do as your father tells you, too. Fathers just bully us; whatever we want to do, they just bully and push us about. But one day I'll be old enough to fight. Then I'll kill every Dane and every traitor I can find. I swear it!'

Gifta remembered her own vow to her father, and pressed Gospatrick's head to her breast.

'Aye, and I shall feed them to your sword, dear Goose!' she laughed, 'like the cook feeds bad cuts of meat to the hound!'

III

Before the New Year, the dreaded news reached Ethelred's family at the court of Richard II in Rouen. The Danes were victorious, and all of England was theirs.

Soon Ethelred himself arrived in Normandy, in exile from the kingdom that his ancestors had ruled for five centuries. Edmund and Eadwig had stayed on, still determined to fight, but their father could see no point in it. He sat staring into the flames of the great hall fire, a man dazed, who had given up all hope, relating to a hushed audience how he had so nearly triumphed at the last.

'We knew they were marching on London from the south,' he told them. 'They knew we could defend London Bridge easily for as long as we wanted, so they tried a ruse. They halted a little to the west, at the Lambeth shore, and built rough bridges. They meant to surprise us with an attack around to the north of the city. But it all went wrong for them, for once. Their bridges broke, and spilled scores of them into the river. We saw their bodies floating past the city walls. We guessed their plan then. Instead of them surprising us, we surprised them.

'We lay in wait for them, at the Aldersgate and the Ludgate, with every man we could muster. In God's name I swear to you, we made great slaughter that day, greater than I have seen in all my years of fighting Northmen. It seemed that victory was in our grasp at last!'

'Then what happened?' asked the disillusioned Emma, impatiently.

Ethelred sighed, shaking his head. He stared into the dark red wine in his goblet, as if seeking the answer there.

'God forgive me, I don't know. I watched the great victory march through the streets of London, saw my men holding aloft flaming torches and the heads of Vikings on high poles, and thought this must be the time to spur them on, to fight back, to strike the death blow at Forkbeard. But suddenly, that was it. They all gave up. They would fight no more, they said. Our Norwegian friends told me then and there they were going home. And as they went, the London fyrd dispersed like shadows. One moment jubilation and boasts of heroes, the next . . . silence. Oh, dear God, why? Why did you do this to me?'

Emma made no move to comfort him. Gifta shot her an icy look, and herself went to put an arm around her father's drooping shoulders.

Ethelred remained in a state of depression for days, until better news came unexpectedly from England. The triumph of King Sweyn Forkbeard had been short-lived. Within a short time of crowning himself King of the English, the old Viking caught a severe chill, and was dead almost as soon as his victory march through the country ended.

His son Canute was quickly crowned in his place, but some of the English thanes who had accepted Forkbeard's rule were less sure about the untried youngster.

As those men wavered, Edmund Ironside and Eadwig took advantage of the split in the ranks to rally men to Ethelred's cause once more.

They called a hastily-convened meeting of the most trusted men of the Witan and urged a swiftly-organised winter fight before Canute could become accustomed to leadership. The Witan earnestly debated the question for hours. Most were reluctant to engage in winter battles with insufficient forces, but they agreed to send for Ethelred to return. Ethelred must agree to pardon all those who had sided with the Danes, they insisted, and must promise to rule more justly than in the past.

In Normandy, Ethelred received the Witan's summons with mixed feelings. He was overjoyed that some of his wayward thanes wanted him back, but from previous experience he was doubtful about how long they could be expected to remain loyal. Leaving England with his tail between his legs once was enough for him. He did not want to have to do it again.

'I would agree to their terms,' he told his brother-in-law, the Duke. 'But should I go?'

Richard gave it careful thought.

'It is probably your last chance to win back your kingdom,' he said. 'Give Canute long enough, and he'll win their fickle hearts. Of that you can be sure, knowing your English lords.'

Ethelred nodded.

'I shall go back to England,' he declared.

Gifta was in the women's quarters with Wulfhilda when Emma came to tell them of Ethelred's decision. They had been learning French from an elderly priest, but Gifta had long ago grown bored with his droning voice. She sat at the stone sill of the window high in the castle, staring out over the rooftops of Rouen to the mist-hazed fields, dreaming of her beloved Northumbria. When Emma cut short the lesson to give them the news from England, Gifta forgot that she was eight months pregnant and went dancing round the room.

'We'll be going home!' she shouted, 'Wulfhilda, this means we shall be going home!'

'I am afraid not,' Emma said airily. 'Not for a while, anyway. There is still danger.'

Gifta stopped dancing.

'When, then?' she demanded. 'For the love of God, when? I have been shut up in this cold stone prison long enough! I shall go mad if I have to stay here much longer!'

'You will go back when your father says it is safe, I would imagine. Really, Aelfgifu, you will never gain peace of mind until you learn to accept your lot. No sooner do you receive good news, than you want more. At least you are comfortable here, and protected – in this cold stone prison – while you wait for your husband's child to be born. Are you not a good deal more fortunate than the women who could not escape?'

'Wait for my husband's child,' Gifta repeated impatiently. 'Men make us pregnant, then go away and fight wars and leave us to wait about like . . . like huge waddling cattle. Why don't you preach peace of mind to them, stepmother? They are the ones who need it.'

'That is a task beyond me,' Emma smiled. 'A woman can give a man peace, but only God can give him peace of mind.'

'Then I wish he would!' Gifta said through clenched teeth. 'There are times when I think God sleeps.'

'Gifta, you should not say such things,' whispered Wulfhilda, shocked by her sister's blasphemy. 'God never sleeps!'

'Does he not, Hildy? Then why does he allow such evil things to happen? Why is it that what happens seems to be different from all we are taught? We are told to believe that our father, as King, is God's own representative on earth. So why does God allow murdering heathens to come along and steal his kingdom? Does it make any sense?'

'You forget that the hand of God has already fallen,' Emma chided her. 'Forkbeard is dead. He was struck down before he had time to enjoy his spoils.'

'But now his son takes his place. And he is a young man. We have yet to see if God will strike him down – he has a whole lifetime to enjoy his spoils.'

This apparent mockery of the Lord's works offended Emma. She thought it was time she put her stepdaughter in her place. 'It is not only heathens who must fear being brought to account, Aelfgifu. Even your father – God's representative on earth, as you say – has sins for which he must answer. Perhaps he must even answer for sins committed in his name by his friends. You know what some holy men have said, that your father's reign has been cursed since that day many years ago when he became King, after his half-brother Edward was murdered and buried without royal honours. It was men of your father's household who committed that crime. The scholars say that was why a bloody cloud kept appearing in the sky after Ethelred was crowned, often even at midnight. The anger of God was revealed in that fearsome sight. They also say that it is why so many of your brothers died young. It was God's punishment on the house of Ethelred.'

'You are repeating old gossip,' Gifta told her angrily. 'My father had nothing to do with the murder of Edward the Martyr. I cannot believe God would be so unjust as to punish him for something he did not do. Neither should you believe it – if you have any loyalty as a wife.'

'Well he had everything to do with the slaughter of St. Brice's Day,' argued Emma, 'the year he married me.' (Perhaps he wished he could have murdered you instead, thought Gifta, but she resisted the temptation to say it aloud.) 'That was just as tragic. Poor Ethelred listened to bad advice and he's paid dearly for it these last twelve years. He ordered the death of the Danes, and none was spared. Men, women and children, Christian and heathen, nobles and slaves, all died together. The land ran red with the blood of even those Danes whose fathers and grandfathers had been born in England. It was enough that they had Danish names. Were not the perpetrators of that crime as evil as Forkbeard? Have you not considered that Forkbeard may have been an instrument of God, an evil set loose to atone for another evil?'

'You speak more like an enemy than a wife,' Gifta said, furious.

'You questioned the ways of God,' Emma accused her in return. 'I, as a devout Christian woman, suggested some answers. If to hear the truth causes you such distress, I can only advise you not to ask again.'

'Oh don't worry,' Gifta retorted. 'If I do ask again, I shall ask one less prejudiced, such as Theobald.'

'Ah yes, Father Theobald,' Emma nodded, still with an accusing look in her eyes. 'We have noticed that that young man is always around when you call. He seems quite devoted to you.'

'Well, at least he is agreeable company,' Gifta snapped, and flounced out of the room as well as her awkward condition would allow.

In desperation, she sought somewhere comfortable and private, but she found her stepmother's castle a cold, crowded prison.

This home of Emma's summed up the Norman people, Gifta thought.

It was cool, pretentious, arrogant and domineering, bestriding the land like a feelingless master, so different from the warm and earthy nature of the timber and wattle and daub halls to which she had been accustomed all her life. Like the Normans themselves, the castle was rough-hewn and immovable. Emma's brother, Duke Richard, and his sons Richard and Robert, had all offered her adequate hospitality, yet she could not help seeing them in that light. The Normans were a race so distant in both customs and manners, they might have evolved on the other side of the world rather than on the other side of the Channel.

It was difficult for Gifta to believe that these people were of the same stock as the Northmen who had long since settled in England within the confines of the Danelaw. These Anglo-Danes had lost their raiding instincts and had turned into industrious and contented farmers, yet they had not shed their love for heroics and poetic saga, nor the zest for hard living that had inspired their forefathers to brave the elements and conquer all across the known world, from Scandinavia to places east of the Holy Land.

The Normans, however, were descended from the very worst of Danes. Even though they covered their brutish coarseness with fine clothes they remained, even the powerful lords, low-born and unlettered, with manners no better than those of the native peasants over whom they ruled.

They had no respect for the dignity of poor people, as Englishmen had, and even among themselves they squabbled like dogs over the tattiest stretch of territory.

Normans looked down on the English custom of keeping slaves, saying it was barbaric. And yet, as far as Gifta could determine, the slaves in her father's house were treated much better than the so-called free peasants of Normandy. An English slave might not have the choice to go where and how he pleased, but he was well fed, sheltered, cared for and often treated with affection, and he could be made a freedman with his own smallholding as a reward for good service.

No Norman could hope for similar treatment, Gifta had argued with her hosts, during those embarrassing occasions when the Norman court amused itself by teasing the English guests.

In Normandy, she said, the peasants worked crippling hours for no reward. All the fruits of their labours were claimed by their lords, and the poor people of the fields subsisted on the meanest of charity. The peasants Gifta had seen had seemed close to starvation, their faces and bodies ravaged with toil, and they lived in hovels.

The indignant Normans denied all that, of course, accusing her of prejudice and exaggeration. When Gifta challenged them to show her a happy peasant, they merely resorted to mocking laughter.

'A happy peasant?' cackled Richard, the Duke's older son, 'what, do your English slaves pass their time in feasting and dancing then, princess?'

Their mockery could not shift Gifta from her stand. She continued to insist that the English system was preferable to the Norman, and that the Norman peasantry was but one example of a brutal and confused method of government (if it could be flattered with that description, she added beneath her breath) which could benefit none but the richest and most powerful, and perhaps the most treacherous.

It was not the fault of the Normans, Gifta conceded, loftily. England had the advantage of a system that had been developed over five centuries, which had regard for the rights and interests of all men and women.

No one man could sway the Witan except the King, and even he was elected from among the eligible royal candidates. Earls, reeves, thanes of boroughs and aldermen of towns all enacted the laws and duties agreed by the Witan, all answered to the Witan, and through the Witan's counsellors to the King or, if necessary, to Mother Church. Even a woman had a right to her own property in England. She could speak in the courts, make her own will, could even refuse to marry the man chosen for her by her parents. Normans, Gifta pointed out, had no more respect for their own noblewomen than for their peasants.

If a Norman master said a woman would marry the man selected for her, then God help her if she refused. She would either have to go through with it or spend the rest of her days in a nunnery. The Norman way refused a choice to any but the chosen few. There was no flexibility or forgiveness in Norman government, no course between unquestioning obedience or outright treachery, no encouragement of loyalty for its own sake, without reward, so that the only way to achieve personal advancement was to betray one master to gratify another.

It was not only the manner of governing that Gifta had come to despise in Normandy, however. Before she had grown very big with child, the men of Duke Richard's court had found her most attractive, and some had tried to make her forget her marriage to faraway Uhtred. Gifta, by receiving their advances coldly, had made it plain that she did not like Norman men, and found them conceited, unromantic and pretentious. They treated their women too roughly for her liking, and she considered that to be courted by a Norman must be more like rape than seduction. Where an Englishman would woo his lady with poetry and song, making her feel like a prized flower to be plucked delicately from among all the blossoms of May, a Norman would go right ahead and drag her up by the roots and expect her to wilt in his hands. The Normans might consider themselves charming, but they were as clumsy lovers as they were heavy-handed masters, Gifta thought, and it angered her all the more that the Normans tended to look upon Englishmen with contempt.

She knew it was whispered around Richard's court that the duke had condemned his sister to life in a pig-sty by marrying her to Ethelred. Oh, it was a rich sty, they giggled, but a messy one. All English, from highest to lowest, lived, sustained and gratified themselves like hogs, at home, in bed, at the table or anywhere else. They ate too much, drank too much, and lived in the same squalid conditions as their servants. Normans, on the other hand, had moderate habits and kept themselves reasonably clean. For years it had been a popular but irreverent joke in Normandy that Emma had more gold at her disposal than any other Queen in Christendom – as long as she did not mind grubbing through the palace swill to find it. Most Normans knew what an outlandish distortion of the truth that was, but still maintained that the differences between the two races were vast.

Had Gifta been less determined to find nothing good in Normandy, she might have conceded that despite their coarseness and pretensions, the Normans had some habits and customs that the English would do well to copy.

Norman men were accustomed to cutting their hair short, shaving their faces and occasionally taking a perfumed bath. They were often offended by the wild and unkempt aspect of their English neighbours, who went hairy-faced and rarely freshly-clothed. They wore rounded cloaks over shirts or belted tunics, and had forsaken the heavy cross-gartered trousers of the north in favour of the slender hose preferred by the French and Italians. They had also cast aside their thick tweeds for the lighter woollens and linens of warmer climates. While they retained the same love of elaborate jewellery and weaponry as their northern cousins, they had long since abandoned the Scandinavian passion for tattooing the body, plaiting and adorning the hair, and decorating helmets with animal horns, feathers, complete animal heads or gruesome masks. These changes had given the Normans a neater appearance – or a more monkish look, as Englishmen preferred to describe it.

Gifta was not impressed by their elegance and thought their sober appearance did nothing to improve their dispositions. Give me a rough Englishman with a poetic heart, she said, rather than a sleek Norman with a heart of stone. If, God forbid, she were to find herself widowed, and faced with the prospect of a Norman for a husband, she would have no hesitation in taking herself to the nearest nunnery.

'Norman men have a great sense of responsibility,' Emma had preached. 'Such a husband would give you security.'

'Aye, in a dungeon, like as not,' Gifta muttered.

She tried to avoid the company of her stepmother and other Normans as much as she could after her father had gone back to England, certain in her own mind that it would be only a matter of days before it was her turn to take ship for home. Then there would be no more talk of Norman husbands, no more taunts and mockings; she would be back in her own home, in England.

IV

THE long winter days passed with a scarcity of news from England. February gave way to March, and on the night Gifta went into labour she still had not heard the words she longed for.

It was a difficult birth, but Gifta and her baby daughter Ealdgyth were attended by all the midwives Duke Richard could muster, and they both came through it well. The two of them were fussed over by everyone at court for a few days, so that the proud mother had something to think about other than her longing to go home.

Then, a week later, a close friend of Uhtred came to Gifta with two letters. One was from the Earl himself, the other from Gospatrick. It was the first word she had had from either of them.

She opened Uhtred's first. He began with affectionate words, and assurances that he and his sons were safe and well. He went on to apologise for taking Gospatrick away from her, and to explain his reasons.

'I am no longer a young man,' he wrote, 'and there is no telling how long this war will last. Sending you away was hard enough for me; once I had surrendered Northumbria, I could not let Gospatrick go away too.

'As long as he is in England, even though I be dying, I know I will see him again.

'God willing, you will soon be at my side again. There is great excitement here now that Forkbeard is dead and Ethelred returned, and men are beginning to talk of victory over the Danes once more.

'However, it must be said that Canute is supremely confident. He has kept some hostages, but has gone away to Northampton leaving Aldred, Eadwulf and me here with not a single guard over us. He feels he can trust the oath of allegiance we gave to Forkbeard!

'Canute has also taken an English wife, as if to prove that he is here to stay. She is a girl you will have heard of. Her name is Graciousgift. You will remember that many years ago her father was executed and her brothers blinded on your father's orders, for plotting with the Danes. I suppose she sees this marriage to Canute as a kind of revenge against Ethelred.

'You will remember, too, that my family were also supposed to have been involved with the death of her father, so maybe I should expect little mercy if she does indeed become Queen.

'However, the young lady will be fortunate if she gets a crown. They are calling it a marriage, but it is strongly rumoured that the only service she saw was between the blankets. She is no more than his mistress, and some who know Canute well are saying that he looks for a more noble wife than this little slut to rule his conquered kingdom at his side.

'Still, I cannot believe that Canute will rule for long, with our dear King returned to us and ready to fight afresh!'

Gifta laughed aloud at Uhtred's rude reference to the marriage of Canute and Graciousgift, and repeated it to her sister, who was holding Ealdgyth while Gifta read.

'Does he mention Ulfcettel?' Wulfhilda asked anxiously.

'Yes. He says to tell you your husband is also safe, and longing to see you. He writes about Edith, too. I have not seen your sister Edith, he says, for Streona keeps her firmly under guard. But I have heard that she is in good health.'

'Poor Edith,' Wulfhilda sighed. 'If only she could be here with us.'

'You mean we there with her,' Gifta was in higher spirits now. She picked up the shorter, but no less loving, letter from Gospatrick.

'Dear Gifta,' it said, 'I am happy now because father sent me a message saying he is coming to see me soon, but I wish I could see you as well, because it has been such a long time and I am fed up with being away from you all.

'What is it like in Normandy? Are you happy there? Has my new little brother been born yet? I saw the whole Danish army pass by here the other day, but they took no notice of us. Father says not to tell you where I am, in case the Danes get hold of this letter, but I am all right. Constance is looking after me as you told her to, but she fusses a lot. Can you please write and tell her not to be so strict? I have enough to put up with. She is even stricter than you were, and I am not a child any more. I have tried to explain to her that she is only your maid, but that makes her cross.

'She has been a bit better lately, though. I think she has fallen in love with a man called Cedric. He lives here with his parents and his brother Oswald. Cedric and Oswald take me out hunting and teach me how to trap animals and birds and all that. I won't mind if Constance wants to marry Cedric, will you? She gets all moony-eyed about him sometimes, enough to make you sick. I don't know what he sees in her.

'Well, that's all for now, as I have some lessons to do, but I do hope we will be back together soon.

> All my love,
> Goose.

Gifta was crying as she put down Gospatrick's letter. The tears came from a sense of loss, but also from happiness, that her stepson had been able to express such love for her in his own childish way.

She immediately took up her pen and wrote her replies. She tried hard not to say a word of her misery in Normandy, but concentrated instead on telling them of the baby and how she was growing every day. When she had finished writing Gifta's throat was sore with the effort of holding back her sobs. If they looked hard, Uhtred and Gospatrick might see that the parchment had been stained with tears. She took her baby back from Wulfhilda, and gave the child her breast.

'Shall I fetch Theobald?' asked Wulfhilda, who knew how her sister was best comforted these days. At a nod from Gifta, Wulfhilda went off to find the monk.

Theobald arrived just as Gifta was moving Ealdgyth across from one breast to the other.

To Gifta it meant nothing to expose her body in the quite natural act of feeding her baby. Mothers often did so in the company of an entire hall full of people; and anyway, since Theobald was a priest, she saw it as no different to receiving the attention of the holy men physicians when she was ill. In her innocence, she failed to consider the sensitivity of Theobald. He was not a physician. He was a young and chaste man who had never before seen the naked bosom of a woman. At first he was deeply embarrassed, then alarmed at the sudden desire he experienced, to caress those milkful mounds where the baby was suckling. He said a silent prayer, and tried not to look at her as he sat down before her.

'Father, help me please,' Gifta pleaded. 'How am I to find peace of mind as long as I stay here? I cannot rest. I am so tired and depressed. Some of the time I cannot attend to Ealdgyth properly . . .'

Theobald's mind was wandering. He could think of nothing other than the usual platitudes.

'You must have faith in God,' he said, stumbling over the words. 'You must put your trust in him. You must never feel he is working against you . . .'

'I have tried, I really have,' Gifta assured him. 'But somehow, every time I tell myself I have much to be thankful for, I know I am lying to myself. Oh, dear Mother Mary, help me. There is such a raging hate inside of me. I should not hate, when I have this child to love, should I?'

'Perhaps it is only frustration, not hate. It is only natural you should be upset, forced to part with your loved ones, for so long. Do not feel such guilt. You are a good woman, my Lady Aelfgifu. There is so much love inside you, you may mistake it for hate. So powerful are these emotions in us, sometimes they are indistinguishable, one from the other.'

Gifta managed a smile.

'Dear Theobald,' she said, 'I know I can always rely on you to say the right words. I wish I could believe I am worthy of them, that you don't just say them to make me feel better . . .'

The baby had had her fill. Gifta eased her away from the breast and up on to the opposite shoulder to wind her. The princess's wet nipples were revealed again, but still she was unaware that she was tempting the monk. Theobald could restrain himself no longer. He reached out a trembling hand, and pressed the palm over one gloriously large tit.

'Be at peace, my child,' he mumbled, the words rolling one over the other in his excitement. 'Lord, give tranquillity to this aching breast . . .'

Gifta should have been shocked, but she was not. With Theobald sitting there speaking his fervent request to God, she could not think it sinful that he was touching her, no more so than if he had placed his hand on her head, as he usually did in moments of prayer such as this. Certainly she drew a much-needed solace from his gentle caress.

She had felt Theobald give her one brief caress, then quickly take his hand away as if it had been burned. When she looked at him again she saw a manly lust in his perspiring face, an expression far removed from the pure, priestly ministration at which they had both been pretending. Even so, she still did not feel the slightest indignation. On the contrary, she was grateful for the few seconds of pleasure he had given her.

'I am sorry,' murmured Theobald, hanging his head in shame. 'I fear I must do painful penance for this.'

Gifta laid the baby in her lap and carefully covered herself.

'No, father, please do not take it so,' she begged him. 'The wrong was mine, for forgetting that a priest is still a man. There is no harm done. I asked you for peace, and you gave it. Can there be any evil in that?'

Her forgiveness helped Theobald, but he suffered the self-inflicted penance anyway to salve his troubled conscience, and for some time afterwards he devoted himself to his scriptural studies in a bid to rid himself of the memory of Gifta's nakedness.

That was a useless exercise. Neither he nor Gifta could forget that tender incident. Never again would they feel quite the same way in each other's company. Gifta could see that the monk was disturbed, and sympathised with him, so much so that once or twice she wanted to suggest he embrace her again if it would console them both and lead to nothing more, but she never dared to speak her thoughts. That was just as well, for despite all Theobald's efforts to ignore her sexuality, he could no longer regard her simply as his spiritual charge.

He was in love with her, and trying to decide what to do about it became a daily trial. He considered putting aside the Cloth, and declaring himself hers. He had no idea how she would react to that, though, and he could not bring himself to speak of it for fear of making a fool of himself, and making worse the mistake of that one careless occasion.

He also tried staying out of her way, but that upset her, and her genuine need for him as a guiding light soon brought him back. Finally, Theobald decided to spend as much time with Gifta as she needed, and to do his best to behave towards her as one would a helpless child, rather than as an attractive woman. He thought he might be able to work it out of his system in that way, but he was wrong. In fact, he made such a show of his detachment when he was with her, Gifta thought he was being deliberately cool, and became anxious that she might have hurt him.

There seemed no answer until one night when, after a trying dinner with Duke Richard and his family, Gifta had need of Theobald's physical closeness once more.

'I spoke today with some merchants recently arrived from London,' the Duke had told Gifta. 'It would appear, from what they say, that all is not well between your father and Edmund. Apparently they had quite a quarrel over some woman Edmund decided to take as his wife – much against your father's will.'

'A woman?' echoed Gifta, frightened by this talk of a rift in the family, 'what woman?'

'I think she is called Algith,' Duke Richard said. 'As I heard it, Ethelred grew short-tempered with some rebel nobles in the north, and ordered Streona to have them executed . . .'

'Streona! Surely he has not taken that traitor back yet again?'

'Perhaps he had no choice. After all Streona holds your sister prisoner, I hear. So Streona has changed sides again, and no doubt will again if it suits him.'

'I'm sure he will. But what of this quarrel . . . ?'

'Well, I don't know how reliable these gossiping Jews are, but according to them, Streona obeyed your father's orders and put the northern rebels to death and Edmund, for some reason, was outraged. This Algith had been wife to one of the rebels, and Edmund said he would take the woman and her lands under his personal protection. Ethelred told him to think again, how unwise it would be for the King to be defied so openly by his own son, but Edmund told your father to stop interfering. Now they have gone their separate ways, and by all accounts they are fighting their own separate wars against Canute.'

'Merciful God!' Gifta breathed. 'As if they can afford to . . .'

'Quite. And Canute mocks them both. He took time during the war to visit Denmark. And he gave your father a grisly warning that he intended to be back. He took some English prisoners aboard his ship, cut off their hands, ears and noses, and threw them overboard along the coast.'

'Your beloved England does not sound a pleasant place to be Princess,' young Robert teased her.

'I am sure Aelfgifu still thinks it more civilised than our barbaric Normandy,' Emma contributed.

Gifta ignored them both.

'Is there no better news?' she asked the Duke. 'No sign that England is growing stronger?'

'The war goes on,' he answered simply, 'and to everyone's cost. Both English and Danes have been laying waste the country, trying to deny each other sustenance. Wait, there is one interesting thing . . .'

'Yes?'

'Graciousgift has given Canute a son, Sweyn. But rumour says it is not Canute's child at all. Graciousgift is said to be a lady easy with her favours. Nevertheless, Canute is delighted with his offspring. Perhaps no one has told him of the rumour. I wonder if the man lives who would dare?'

Gifta sat in silence for the rest of the meal, mulling over the significance of the row between her father and brother, and the birth of an heir to Canute. The rest of the company left her to her own thoughts; by then they had grown all too familiar with her tantrums and complaints, and it was only Theobald who saw how sad she was. Quietly, he went to her after supper and escorted her back to her room. She went straight to Ealdgyth's cradle to look at the sleeping child, and as she turned back to Theobald to thank him for his concern, she burst into tears. She startled him then by throwing herself into his arms.

'Oh, Theobald, I cannot stand it any longer!' she cried. 'I cannot stand this place a day longer! Why have I had no news? No letters from Uhtred, or Gospatrick, or anyone, for months. Have they forgotten me? Has something happened to them? Dear God, help me. Help me, Theobald. Please, help me . . .'

'You mean . . .' Theobald stuttered.

Gifta did not wait for him to finish. She took his hands and held them to her breasts, hugging him close to her, crying into his chest.

Never in his life had the poor man been so terrified. As soon as he was able to pull away from her, he made his excuses for leaving. He ran away from that room as though the avenging Lord himself was breathing angrily down his neck. It was much later, when he'd had time to think rationally, that he vowed not to torture himself any more. If the woman wanted him he would have her, he swore, and the david take him if that was how it must be.

V

IN a great hall in Yorkshire, the tables were richly laid for a feast. English hosts and Danish guests mingled together in easy conversation. The air was thick with the smoke of cooking fires and servants moved through the crowds with huge platters laden with roast meats, and wine and ale flowed freely. It was a scene of merriment rare in England since the start of the Viking wars, and yet, to the careful observer, just the hint of a sinister undercurrent might have been evident in this spring evening of celebration. While the English thanes were dressed in their finest tunics and cloaks, many of the Danish warriors were garbed in full battle gear of chain-mail coats and iron helmets. They were also armed, and idly handled axe or sword hilts as they talked boastfully to the wives and daughters of their hosts, while in one corner of the hall near the big double doors there was, beneath the hum of small talk and the lilting music of the minstrels' harps, a low murmur of conspiracy.

In that corner stood Lord Streona, arguably the most feared of Englishmen, and beside him the Danish earl Eric Longaxe, who had proved himself an equally brutal lieutenant of Canute. The two men stayed apart from the rest of the throng and spoke in low voices, for what they planned for that night had nothing to do with the jollity that most of the feastmakers expected.

'To be honest, Streona,' Longaxe was saying, 'Canute wonders if he dares trust you. No, don't be angry – those are his words, not mine. You must admit you have changed colours often. He sees you as a powerful ally, but he is a cautious man. And he has time only for those who are scrupulously loyal to him alone.'

'Then we must reassure him, mustn't we?' replied Streona evenly. He was a big, bluff man, with fierce-red hair and beard, and he bowed to no one. 'That is why I am here tonight, to prove my support of him as King of the English.'

'All right,' Longaxe nodded. 'You see I have brought all the men you asked for. Now perhaps you'll explain to me exactly what this is all about.'

Streona gave the mysterious smile he loved to affect in moments of drama, and tipped his head back to drain a goblet of wine, carefully wiping red dribble from his beard.

'Tonight,' he said, 'we are going to remove a man from Canute's path. One who, more than any other in the North, is capable of preventing his final bid for the throne.'

Longaxe looked around the hall with interest.

'And who is that?' he asked.

'He isn't here yet. But he will be soon. He believes he has been invited here to form a new alliance to help Ethelred. His name is Uhtred, once Earl of Northumbria.'

'Uhtred?' Longaxe repeated sceptically. 'But he has done nothing since he surrendered Northumbria to Forkbeard. Canute let him and his sons go free because they had been so quiet!'

'Ah, but he is a cunning one, is Uhtred,' Streona grinned, 'a man after my own heart. He has been deliberately lying low, waiting his time. He has been sending messages to Ethelred. Now they think the time is right, just when Canute thinks he has all but won. A double attack on Canute at Northampton is their plan, Uhtred from the North and Ethelred from the South. They intend it to be their supreme effort, the death blow.'

'I see. So our placid Uhtred is dangerous, is he?'

'He is. There is not a man in this hall who will not follow Uhtred, once it is known he is taking up his sword again. That is why he must be killed in sight of them all, as a sharp warning to them.'

'But does he have the strength to rally them?'

'He does. For more than two years he has been working quietly. I hear his army is back to easily the strength it was before your first invasion.'

'And he hopes to make more allies here tonight, you say?'

'That is why he is coming. Or at least, he thinks so.'

'Does he believe you to be among those allies?'

'Oh no, he doesn't know I'm here, or he would not even come near the place. He has no more desire to strike a bargain with me than I have with him.'

Longaxe nodded again, thinking deeply.

'If he is as cunning as you say,' he offered at last, 'surely he will not be unprepared for trouble?'

'He will have a company with him,' Streona agreed, 'but you have enough men here to deal with them.'

Eric Longaxe the Viking gazed hard into the cold eyes of Streona the treacherous English lord, searching for the hint of an untruth.

'And how am I to know that this is not a trap for me, instead of for Uhtred?' he demanded softly, with a warning in his voice. 'You are both sons-in-law of Ethelred, kinsmen by marriage, are you not?'

'Really,' Streona laughed, 'would I be standing here defenceless, if I planned to have you killed? I value my life too much to stand with the hares when the hounds are loosed. That is one thing you know about me for sure, Eric Longaxe.'

Longaxe smiled humourlessly, and inclined his head in acceptance.

'Besides,' Streona went on, 'you may also have heard that Uhtred and I have old family wars to fight. There has been a feud between his kin and mine for generations.'

'Very well, I believe you,' Longaxe said. 'Let us both await the coming of Earl Uhtred.' He looked once more at the press of people, most of them standing in groups, drinking and talking. Some were already sitting at the tables, others were throwing dice, a few joined the balladeers in song. Longaxe added: 'Do our hosts know that their feast is to be spoiled with blood and slaughter? Or are they in for as rude a shock as Uhtred and his men?'

'The master of this house knows,' Streona said. 'I had to have his assistance for what must be done. But few others have guessed what entertainment we have for them. It will make a change from tumblers and magicians, eh? But listen, choose a good man to strike at Uhtred, won't you? He is an old fighter but a good one, not a man to be underestimated. That is a tribute I pay him gladly.'

'I have just the fellow,' Longaxe declared. He beckoned across to them a young man in war dress, blond and handsome and with the fluff of a new beard on his cheeks. There was a keen light in his eyes, and a fresh-sharp axe in his hands. 'This is my son, Olaf,' Longaxe told Streona, 'as strong a lad as you'll ever meet. I swear he can fell a tree with a single sweep of that axe.'

'A big lad, aye,' Streona said doubtfully, 'but inexperienced?'

'Yes, but that is why I choose him. He is eager to blood his blade, and tonight he will have a chance to prove himself. There is no surer killer of a man than an unblooded Viking, Streona. I speak as one who has seen it many times.'

'If you say so, I would not dare to argue,' Streona said. Turning to the young man, he challenged: 'So, you are ready to do this thing for us, are you, boy?'

'No man calls me boy,' Olaf Ericsson coldly corrected him. 'Not after this night. Point out the prey to me, and I will show you why Eric Longaxe and his kin are called the Hawks of Hjorring.'

Longaxe slapped his son on the back, smiling proudly.

'You see!' he chuckled, but then the smile faded. 'But mark you well, Streona, that my own son will stand first among my warriors when the deed is done. Any treachery, and I shall gut you like a fatted bullock!'

'You need fear no tricks from me,' Streona assured him. 'Canute has shown himself the strongest man in England. And I follow only the strong.'

Streona left the Danes then, and returned to his place at the main table, confident that his scheme was destined for success.

There would be a great deal of property and power for the taking when Uhtred was out of the way, and Streona knew that Canute was generous to those who served him well. Streona reckoned that he might even acquire the whole of Northumbria, for Canute would surely see how close to disaster his entire English campaign had been once he learned of the plot laid by Uhtred and his father-in-law. It could be said that Streona had saved nothing less than the life of Canute this night.

Streona sat down beside his wife, Edith, Ethelred's eldest daughter. Edith observed his self-satisfaction as readily as she had recognised his mood of secrecy earlier.

'What is happening?' she pestered him. 'There is something wrong; I can feel it.'

Streona poured himself more wine.

'What are you going on about now, woman?' he mocked her. 'You are always moaning about something. Enjoy yourself.'

'You know what I mean. What are all these Danes doing here, so heavily armed? What have you been muttering about with them over there? Are we all to be massacred, as you had those thanes killed last year?'

'Last year, my dear, I was only carrying out your father's orders, had you forgotten? Come now, surely you don't think that your beloved father and I would want to be rid of you?'

'You have turned against father again. That is obvious, since you are consorting with the Danes tonight. How can I ever be sure what you're up to?'

Streona leaned towards her, to all the world like an affectionate husband whispering to his loved one.

'Dearest wife,' he hissed, 'princess you may be, but you ought to know better by now than to get up on your high horse with me. Shut up, and fill your babbling mouth with this good food. Or I just might be tempted to throttle you myself!'

The feasting gradually became more riotous as more guests crowded into the packed hall, and Streona ate and drank as though that were his only reason for being there. It pleased him that the racket of music and laughter and excited voices had grown so loud, for he thought that if Uhtred arrived uncertain of what to expect, the noise would entice him inside without fear.

Streona was right in that. When Earl Uhtred and about forty of his Northumbrian thanes dismounted outside the house an hour later, they heard the merry-making and felt easy. All the same, Uhtred was a warrior, with twenty-five years' experience in all manner of double-dealing as well as clear-cut battles, and he was taking no chances.

'Look around the house before we go in,' he ordered a few of his men. 'If you catch the sniff of a Dane, come back here fast.'

After a few minutes the men were back.

'There's no one out here,' their leader reported. 'Everyone is inside.'

Uhtred gave a short nod of satisfaction. They had taken quite some steps into the hall before they realised that the armed men in there were Danes. Uhtred saw at the high table his sister-in-law Edith and her turncoat husband Streona.

'Streona!' Uhtred roared, his hand flying to his sword hilt, 'you deceiving dog!'

Streona leapt to his feet.

'There is your prey!' he bellowed to Olaf Ericsson.

Edith stood up too. In an instant she knew what her husband planned, and screamed a shrill warning. Streona swung round and hit her across the mouth, knocking her to the floor. But no warning could have come quickly enough for Uhtred. Olaf leapt out from the crowd, his axe whirling high, and on his trembling lips was the war cry of his family:

'Follow a Hawk of Hjorring!'

Uhtred's sword was only half out of its scabbard when Olaf's blade hewed into his chest, splitting him from throat to stomach. The great warrior of Northumbria fell back among his men without a sound, dead as he hit the floor.

The Vikings broke out from the ranks of guests and charged Uhtred's men. Some of them panicked and tried to get back through the doorway, hampering those who were willing to stand and fight. The attackers made the most of the chaos, and the killing was swift and thorough. The thanes, like terrified sheep in a slaughterhouse, trampled one another to cower away in corners; the Danes despatched them as methodically and impassively as butchers, moving determinedly among them, slicing one even as they singled out the next. The screams of the dying men rose high above the howling of the women, who watched in terror as the rushes and timbers of the hall were washed crimson. Only half a dozen men escaped out into the yard, and they were soon hunted down, to be hacked to death in barns and hedgerows.

In the hall, Olaf Ericsson stood astride Uhtred's body with feet planted wide, holding his bloody axe high above his head. His face was flushed, and his eyes wild-white with the thrill of what he had done. Eric Longaxe went to his son and hugged him hard, then the Danes heaved the youth up on their shoulders and carried him out in a chanting procession of torchlight and waving swords, around and around the house.

Edith ran to her brother-in-law's body, her hands outstretched as if to help him. When she saw his dreadful death-wound, she fell to her knees in his blood and covered her face, sobbing.

'Traitor!' she shrilled at Streona, as he came to gloat over his fallen enemy, 'murderous traitor! Can no one trust you? Oh dear God, my poor sister! What have we done to her?'

●

Gifta gave little thought to Edith, or to Edith's feelings, when she heard of the death of her husband. After the first terrible shock, the first shriek of anguish, she lapsed into silence. She watched little Ealdgyth, toddling about and playing happily with her dolls; how Uhtred would have loved to see his child! She thought of young Gospatrick and of how the news would wound him, and of her other stepsons, Aldred and Eadwulf. Were they to be murdered in the same foul manner, or would they risk their lives in revenge? She felt cold, helpless, bitter, empty. The happy days of York were done with, gone forever. Now, even if she returned to England, their lives would never be the same again. For the first time, it no longer mattered whether or not she ever went home.

'I knew it would come to this,' she whispered, through salt-wet lips. 'I knew I would never see him again. I knew . . .'

Wulfhilda tried to comfort her.

'Courage, Gifta,' she said, taking her sister's hand. 'Let your sorrow out; don't hold it back. God will sit in judgement of this evil deed. He will punish the guilty.'

'Will he?' Gifta laughed coldly. 'I would like to think so. No, I believe he has forsaken me.'

'No, you must not think that way,' Theobald gently scolded her, 'God does not forsake the faithful. You must keep your trust in . . .'

'Theobald, for pity's sake stop your preaching, will you?' Gifta rudely interrupted. 'This is one time when your pious prattling does not help!'

He was deeply hurt by her rebuke, and she could see it. She could have cut out her tongue for those few cruel words. Later, when some of the pain within her had eased, she apologised profusely, and he found it easy to forgive her because he had long ago fallen in love with her. He had desired her ever since she had allowed him to touch her body, and although there were times when he despised her for giving him that and nothing more, he had always tried to understand that she was a married woman faithful to her husband. This was a virtue to be admired, and respected. Now, however, she was free, and when she came to beg his pardon for her outburst, he could no longer resist the temptation to court her seriously.

Within a few weeks, the setting for it was right. They were sitting in the castle garden, breathing in the scents of the May blossoms and the grass, wet after a recent shower. Gifta, dressed in a long, close-fitting gown of mourning purple, and a round white hood, looked like a wistful little girl lost, and so much in need of love.

'Gifta,' Theobald began cautiously, 'for a long time now I have cared for you, as would a father, or a brother . . .' and there followed a long pause, in which it seemed to him that even the birds stopped singing and held their breath, before he went on: 'Of course, I've been honoured so to do, but . . . but I feel I could serve you better yet, now that . . . now that you are alone. I mean, if you would allow me . . .'

It was obvious what he was trying to say in his own clumsy manner, and Gifta was taken by surprise. She blushed, and turned her head away.

'I'm sorry, have I offended you?' asked Theobald, alarmed. 'Please, princess, do not think ill of me! I know I am only a poor monk, and I know that as one who has taken holy orders I should not speak or think of these things, but I cannot help myself. I must say what it has been in me to say these two years past. And I will gladly face any punishment that God or his church thinks fit, if . . .'

Dear Theobald, Gifta was thinking, he understands so much about morality, and faith, and good and evil, and yet so little about people, least of all women. His timing was atrocious. When she had wanted physical comfort, he had run away from her. Now that her desire for his manliness had passed, and what she really needed was a father-figure, here he was offering himself as a lover. Not since the night that Uhtred had taken her as a bride had she been so afraid of giving herself to a man, for her experiences had left her wary of further emotional involvements. How could she hope to explain that to the innocent Theobald? She did not want to upset him again, but she needed time.

'I know what you are trying to tell me,' she said softly, still not meeting his gaze, 'and I am flattered – truly I am. But what would people think of us, Theobald? A widowed princess, and a holy man?'

He was silent for so long after that, she wondered if he had taken it as an insult. She risked a look at him. He had accepted her words in the spirit she had intended, she observed, and he was merely thinking it all over.

'We would be outcasts,' he admitted at last.

'Criminals, even.'

'I would be careless of it. I would like to think that you would be, too.'

'You would have destroyed your career.'

'Perhaps I am not strong enough to be a good churchman, anyway. We could go and live somewhere where it would not matter.'

'And how would we live?'

'I could work. I am a fair scholar. There are libraries, translations to be written, books to be copied, letters to be written and read . . .'

'But I have responsibilities still, Theobald. I have my daughter, and my stepsons in England, whom Uhtred would not want me to forget. My father will expect much of me, too, when this war is done. There will be new alliances to set up. I shall probably be married again, to a Norman or a Flemish prince, or a Scot. Our lives are not our own, Theobald.'

'Would you want to be married off like that?'

'No, but is the choice mine?'

'If we ran away to another country, there would be nothing they could do about it. We could go to Paris, or Rome, or even Barbary, and hide ourselves.'

'And if you were caught "abducting" me, you would be put to death, most painfully.'

'I would take the chance gladly, Gifta.'

Gifta was trying not to cry.

'Please, dearest Theobald,' she begged, 'do not speak of running away, not now. There is so much I've run away from already, so much that I had loved.'

'I'm sorry. I am being presumptious.'

'No, not at all. I appreciate your thoughts, honestly I do.'

An awkward silence between them seemed to transform the warm air of the garden into a suffocating blanket of unease. Even the sounds of coming summer were apparently muted by the atmosphere of guilt. They sat there as if conscious that they should be far away from each other, removed from temptation, but neither of them had the courage to move. Eventually, Theobald could put up with the tension no longer. He had to insist on talking this matter out, here and now, today.

'If the Danes did win England,' he said, 'and you could never go back – I'm sorry, I do not mean to distress you by talking this way – but if it did happen, would you consider my offer then? Or am I being a fool to believe that you could think of me as anything but a friend and confessor? Please tell me, honestly . . .'

Gifta sighed and bowed her head, fidgeting with the jewelled rings on her slender fingers.

'I loved Uhtred very much, Theobald,' she reminded him. 'I have not begun to forget him yet, nor am I sure that I will. Please give me time.'

He was about to assure her that he did understand, but he was not given the opportunity. A page came hurrying through the garden with a message from Duke Richard, to say that Gifta's presence was needed in the great hall immediately. The boy wore a nervous look, and Gifta guessed that something was wrong. She clutched at Theobald's hand as they rose from the bench.

'Merciful God,' she breathed, 'what is it now?'

'More news of the war, perhaps,' Theobald suggested.

'No,' said Gifta, clutching at the sickness in her stomach, 'it is more than that, I feel it . . .'

Her fears were confirmed the moment she walked into the hall. The duke was walking to and fro with solemn countenance, and Emma, sitting in a tall-backed chair, was equally grave. Her children stood beside her with eyes downcast, and it looked as though young Alfred was fighting to hold back tears. Wulfhilda was slumped at the table, shaking with sobs. The duke ceased his restless pacing and came to place a hand on Gifta's shoulder.

'It's your father, princess,' he said quietly, 'King Ethelred is dead.'

Gifta's feelings emptied out of her like a rush of air. She felt faint, and Duke Richard helped her to a chair. She had no more tears to weep, she had wept them all for her husband and for herself. There were none left for her father. She fought to find her voice.

'How?' she croaked at last, 'how did he die?'

'Peacefully, in his sleep,' Richard answered gently. 'Doubtless fatigued by all his gallant efforts to save his kingdom. It happened on the twenty-third day of last month, April. Messengers brought the news to Rouen today.'

Gifta looked up at Emma. There were no tears in those cold eyes, she noted with bitterness. Oh yes, thought Gifta, that hard-faced crow looks concerned, but only for herself. She is wondering what is to happen to her, now that she is no longer queen.

Emma, seeing Gifta's gaze, gave a disapproving stare in return. She did not care for the way her stepdaughter was sagging down in her chair like a common serving-woman, and she proudly raised her chin as if to set Gifta an example as to how to bear loss with dignity.

'He was an ageing man,' Emma said, with resignation. 'It was inevitable, and we should have been prepared for it. He is worthy of our respect for never giving up until the end of his life. We may lessen our grief by thinking of him thus.'

Gifta could have knifed Emma for those smart, dismissive words. Instead she did no more than utter a tiny snort of contempt, which Emma might or might not have heard. And yet, for the time being, Gifta did try to put her own sorrow aside, but only because she did not want to give her ice-hearted stepmother the satisfaction of watching her break down again.

'How do things stand in England now?' she asked the duke.

'The same. Some have declared your brother Edmund King, others have sworn for Canute. It goes on.'

'You have not told Gifta of her new nephews,' said Emma.

'Ah yes,' Duke Richard remembered, 'as life ends, so it begins again. We heard by the same messengers that twin sons have been born to Edmund Ironside. He has named them Edward and Edmund.'

Gifta nodded dumbly. How pleased her father would have been to have grandsons at last, she was thinking, and to have known there was fresh hope for England. Her brothers, Edmund and Eadwig; her half-brothers, Edward and Alfred; and now her nephews, Edward and Edmund; there were plenty of princes yet to bear the ancient golden dragon banner and to make all of Ethelred's struggles worthwhile, if only they could clear the land of those accursed Danes.

'Please, Duke Richard,' she pleaded, 'can you not send some men to help Edmund, before it is too late? Before my brothers die too?'

A few months earlier she would not have dreamed of asking the Normans for aid, but with her husband and father so recently dead, she was growing desperate. Richard's response, however, did nothing to encourage hope.

'My dear princess,' he said, much as he would to a child, 'I assure you, nothing would please me more – but at this time I cannot. I have troubles here in Normandy, as you know. It leaves me few men to spare . . .'

Robert had entered the hall as his father was speaking. The young man strode across to them, and butted in cheerfully:

'Were you asking my father to help England, princess? Good idea, I'm all for it! Just what I've always said, father. After all, we do have a treaty with King Ethelred, and . . .'

'King Ethelred is dead, Robert,' Duke Richard scowled, annoyed as much by the youth's insolence as his lack of tact. 'I have just broken the news to his family.'

Robert blushed furiously, and bowed to Wulfhilda and Gifta: 'Oh, forgive me! God rest his soul.' He waited for what he considered a decent pause before adding: 'But I do believe we should send an army into England. I have said so before. Perhaps now the need is greater than ever, and the time more opportune.' He went to his little cousin Edward and ruffled the boy's hair, saying: 'After all, here is a kinsman of ours who may one day inherit Ethelred's crown, if he is given the chance. If it would help him, I would gladly lead an army to England myself. What about that, Edward?'

Edward's tear-filled eyes brightened. He worshipped his cousin who had been teaching him and Alfred how to fight and become Norman knights. Edward had tried his best to learn the lessons well, but he was a weak, pale child who was really better suited to the religious studies to which he gave so many hours. Nevertheless, he did not want to disappoint his hero Robert, and stood up straight and tried to stop crying.

'That would make me very proud, Robert,' he said, in a tremulous voice. 'I want to go with you, and avenge my father. May I?'

Duke Richard was listening to the exchange with growing anger. He took Edward's arm, to guide him away from Robert.

'Forgive me, Edward,' he said, 'but I cannot embark upon an invasion, not just now. One day, when you are old enough to understand more of politics, you will know why . . .'

'Politics, father?' Robert sneered. 'Is it not *politic* to assist our allies when they need us most?'

Richard wanted to slap Robert for the embarrassment his son was causing him. He knew only too well why the young man was showing such interest in England. Robert was wildly ambitious. He had covetous thoughts, not only about a large slice of Norman territories for himself when his father died, but also of gaining considerable English property through his family's connections with Ethelred. What better way to secure that than to take an army to England, help drive out the Danes, and then sit waiting for the rich rewards to follow? This was not the time to argue about it, Duke Richard felt, but he could not let his insolent son have the last word. So, while his answer was directed at Edward, in the tone of it there was a very clear warning for Robert, if Robert had the sense to hear it.

'It is a complicated matter,' he told Edward. 'You must believe me when I say it is not just a question of wanting to do these things, or not wanting to. You see, for many years I have worked to establish peace treaties with the Scandinavians. At one time I offered your mother into marriage there, before she wed your father. It's all to help guard my lands against the French, or Flemish, or anyone else who tries to attack them. When you rule a province as turbulent as this one, you cannot afford to have enemies outside your borders as well as inside them. Do you understand? If I deliberately went out to make war on the Danes, Normandy would be in chaos within weeks.'

'It's all right, Uncle Richard,' Edward said sadly, looking away in case he should start crying again, 'I understand.'

'He may, but I don't,' Robert scoffed. 'Are Normans such mice? The only way to show the world we mean to be a power to be feared is to go out and pit our swords against upstarts like Canute!'

'Robert!' the duke snapped, 'I think we have heard enough of your advice for now!'

Gifta had heard enough, too. She clapped her hands over her ears and ran out of the hall.

'Damn you, stop it!' she screamed back at them from the door, 'I don't want you all squabbling over my father's very grave!'

When Theobald went to her room a few minutes later he found her playing with Ealdgyth, and in a mood which suggested she no longer cared what befell her. Theobald stooped to join in the game with a wicker ball, and chose his words carefully.

'They squabble because they are afraid, princess,' he said. 'Do not despise them for it – we are all afraid, in one way or another. With them, it is a case of how they are to hold on to the power they have. It does not affect you alone that your father's world has gone. It grieves you, but it frightens them greatly. Who shall be next? That is their fear.'

'I was not thinking of them,' Gifta moaned. 'The Devil take them all, for all I care.'

'But you seemed deep in thought. I wondered if their argument had disturbed you.'

'It did, but it doesn't now. I was thinking of this dear child of mine. I used to imagine what a fuss would be made of her, by her father and grandfather, when we got her home. It seems so wrong that neither of them will know her.'

Theobald wanted to take her into his arms, so pitiful and appealing did she sound.

'You have had such a hard time, Gifta,' he began, but he broke off in puzzlement as she suddenly got up and walked to him. She placed her hand on his head, smoothing the palm across the tonsured scalp.

'In the garden,' she said softly, 'you said you needed me.'

'Yes . . .'

'Do you really? Do you need me more than the solemn promise you made to God, to be chaste?'

'Yes.'

'I feel honoured, deeply.'

'It is I who is honoured, to have been so close to you.'

'Theobald,' Gifta said, almost inaudibly, 'now I need you . . .'

He was staring into her thighs, his face close to her gown where it ran down into a soft curve at the base of her belly. His cheeks were on fire with the knowledge of his closeness to her.

'I . . . I . . .' was all he could say.

She leaned down and held his face, and kissed his forehead.

'Please, Theobald,' she implored him, 'I need you right now. Come to the bed . . .'

He stood up to be led there, as submissive as a little boy. There was nothing he could say. He watched her undress, and felt as if he was seeing it all from far off in another world, a dream world he had thought would never be his to experience.

VI

GOSPATRICK had come to love the rolling downs of Berkshire, but the call of the Yorkshire moors was irresistible. On his last day in the south he went out into the hills for a long ride and, looking out across those wide, gentle acres, he thrilled to the knowledge that soon he would find air and freedom and space like this in his own homeland in the North. At last he was going home. He galloped his horse madly across hillside and through dale, as if he were already on the road to York. By the time he got back to the big house of the shire-reeve in Wantage it was nearly mid-day, and both he and his horse were muddied with sweat and dust.

'Gospatrick, really!' Constance fussed, 'How can you travel like that, all mucky and tired out? You had better rest. You can leave tomorrow, there is no hurry . . .'

The boy gave a careless laugh, and poured himself a cup of wine.

'You are only trying to delay me as long as you can, Constance,' he accused her affectionately, 'and I will not be delayed longer. You know that. Have you packed my food and clothes?'

Constance nodded, pointing to two bundles by the door.

'I try to delay you,' she admitted, 'because I dread to think what Princess Aelfgifu will say when she hears you are gone. Her very last words to me were that I should not let you out of my sight until she returned.'

Gospatrick assumed an indignant air.

'That was three years ago,' he reminded her. 'I am older now. Does Gifta expect you to look after me all my life?'

'You are not yet fifteen,' scolded the princess's faithful maid.

'Near enough. And it is my brothers who have called me back to York. They should know what they are doing, shouldn't they? Aren't they as capable as caring for my welfare as you or Gifta?'

Constance went to him and fondled his hair. He detested people doing that to him now, as if he was still a child, and she was upset when he pulled away from her slightly.

'Gospatrick,' Constance said earnestly, 'I know you can't wait to see your brothers again – that's understandable – but I'm worried about what they may drag you into . . .'

He was buckling on his sword, gazing with pride at the carved scabbard and jewelled hilt. It was only a small sword, but he had always regarded it with affection. His father had given it to him, telling him he could wear it when he reached manhood at fifteen years, and it meant more than ever to Gospatrick since Uhtred's death.

'Revenge, do you mean, Constance?' he said, through clenched teeth. 'As God is my witness, I hope they *are* planning revenge! I pray that they are going after my father's murderers and that they will wait only for me to join them before they do. It is my right, to be there when the sons of Uhtred avenge their father's death.'

Constance wiped at a tear on her cheek.

'They've no right to ask you to fight, my lamb,' she argued. 'You are much too young.'

'Better too young than too old,' Gospatrick laughed harshly, 'and I shall be too old if I wait for you to let me go.' Then his manner softened and he put his hands firmly on her shoulders, adding with sincerity: 'Dear Constance, I hate to leave you, truly I do. I can never thank you enough for all you've done for me, all your patience and kindness these three years. You can be sure my stepmother is grateful too. Thank you, a thousand times, thank you. I hope you marry Cedric. And I hope you will be very happy. I must go now. Goodbye.'

Constance could only sob her farewell. Gospatrick went to pick up his supplies, then turned back.

'Say goodbye to Cedric and Oswald for me, and to their mother and father. Tell them I'll never forget all they have done. God willing, I'll see you all again one day.'

He rode as quickly as he could without pushing his animals too hard. North of the Thames at Wallingford he headed east for his first night's stop near Wycombe, staying well clear of Canute's main stronghold at Northampton. After that he went on through Hertfordshire, Cambridgeshire and Lincolnshire, never once encountering a Viking force. It was a peaceful journey. The summer trees were just paling to soft yellows and browns, as they had been on those days three years before when he and Gifta had fled from their home. Now the difference was that there was a false calm over the land, belying the torments its people had suffered for so long.

The feeling of peace dissolved some days later when he reached the Humber, where the ravages of three years of merciless warfare were more apparent.

Time and again, determined armies had scorched meadows and crops to a blackened desert, and now it was a dark, weed-strewn wilderness. The hedgerows were fallen, the trees gaunt, the land laid waste and lifeless. The farms were abandoned, their herds scattered or slaughtered, their soil ruined for years to come.

No man or woman moved in all that burned-out land, a land denied the mellow golds and reds of autumn that had so pleased Gospatrick's eyes in the south. Nothing had escaped. Whole hamlets were deserted, their little houses standing empty with doors swinging broken and vegetable plots trampled. Churches stood silent. Shallow, hastily-dug graveyards had become overgrown in two or three years, but not enough to deter the scrawny dogs that scratched hopefully through them, smelling out bones.

Gospatrick, remembering the lovely Yorkshire of his childhood, wept openly as he rode through the wreckage of it.

Near Goole, he encountered the Danes at last. Some three hundred of them, fresh from a recent skirmish, had gathered in one of the few villages where the inhabitants had doggedly stayed on. The Northmen were rolling drunkenly in the streets, gorging themselves on the peasants' precious food supplies, pawing at the women. The few old men and boys, all that were left of the male population, could do nothing but stay hidden away. The Danes did as they pleased, without hindrance. They beat down doors and looted the houses, defiled the church and cemetery. They galloped horses through the crops, and set light to barns to watch them burn. They had rounded up pigs and sheep, and were roasting them on spits in the wrecked meadows.

Gospatrick rode into the main street and saw them too late to avoid being seen. A bearded monster of a Viking spied him first, and called out, laughing, to the nearest of his friends.

'Hey, look!' he cried, 'here's the English army, come for us again. They're stronger this time. A boy and two horses!'

The men guffawed, and began to gather around. Gospatrick knew he should have wheeled his horse round and got away at the gallop, but pride held him in check. He would not run from the first Danes he had ever met face to face, no matter what might befall him. He halted his horse and waited, sick to the pit of his stomach with a terror he tried hard to conceal.

The Viking who had mocked him now snatched hold of his reins and stood staring up at him with threatening eyes.

'Who are you, boy?' he demanded. 'What are you doing here? Come to spy on us, have you?'

'No,' said Gospatrick, ashamed of the nervousness in his voice, 'I am just a traveller going home.'

The Danes laughed, looking to their leader to continue the torment. He did not disappoint them. He made an exaggerated study of Gospatrick's clothes and jewellery.

'Just a traveller? No, lad; I think not. You look like a nobleman to me. Doesn't he look like a fine young nobleman, men? You've come to fight us!'

'Help, he's come to kill us all!' called another.

'Get him down!' several more shouted. 'Get the little Englishman down off his high horse! Lay him out in the blood-eagle! Let's have the blood-eagle!'

They looked as though they meant it. They were crazed with drink, brutal from constant warring. Gospatrick's legs trembled against his saddle. He was terribly afraid he might be sick.

'Kill me then, you cowardly curs!' Gospatrick screamed at them, covering his dread with defiance, 'kill me as you killed my father!'

He reached for his sword. The big Viking chuckled at the puny threat. He grabbed the boy by the clasp at his throat with one hand and by the belt with the other, and dragged him from the saddle. He stamped around in a wide circle, easily swinging Gospatrick high above his head to the uproarious applause of his companions.

'Look out, everyone!' the Viking bellowed, 'this terrible foe will slay us all! Stand clear, get back all of you!'

Gospatrick was lowered, dizzy and with stomach heaving, into the rough crowd. They pushed him, staggering, from one man to the next, in a hail of thuds and buffetings, belted him across the rump with the flats of their blades. He fell face down, and was pulled up and knocked down again. One Dane gave him a hefty kick as he lay there, forcing the wind from his lungs in raucous gasps. His purse spilled open, loosing coins into the dirt, and his tormentors fought for the money, ripping the whole purse away from his belt. Some tore the bundles from his horses; others went for the animals themselves. The big Viking violently pulled off Gospatrick's cloak and clasp, sending him rolling over and over. They fell on him again like vultures, tearing at his trousers, shoes, tunic, shirt, his crucifix, bracelets, rings and sword belt, until he lay bruised, dazed and naked by the roadside.

Still they ridiculed him. They prodded him and pricked him with their swords, and some even poked at his genitals. Two took hold of his feet and hauled him on his back across the sharp ruts in the road. Two more took his arms, and they swung him between them like a sack of grain. Laughing uproariously, they hurled him into a stand of nettles, then, finished with their fun they went back to their feastings. Gospatrick crawled out from the nettles, pitiful as a savaged rabbit, whimpering with rage and pain. A small group of villagers watched him, unwilling to come near him until the Danes had gone. Later, two of the women came and helped him up and half carried him into a poor little house, where they gave him a cup of water and bathed his wounds. When he was able to sit up, they dressed him in a coarse cloth smock, and all the while Gospatrick wept softly, not so much from pain, though that was hard enough to bear, but from humiliation. To be thrashed in battle was an ordeal he thought he could have borne, but to be bullied and tossed about like a little child, without being given a chance to fight like a man, was an unbearable disgrace.

'They even took my sword,' he mourned. 'My father gave me that sword. I was so proud of it. Oh God, if I could have used it on just one of the pigs!'

'Never mind, my pet,' one of the women said soothingly, dabbing with a damp cloth at a cut on his forehead, 'God will punish those heathens one of these days, be sure of that.'

Gospatrick eased himself off the cot where they had laid him. He ached from head to foot, but he would lie down no longer.

'I will punish them for Him,' he swore. 'Have you any weapons in the house? A knife, an axe?'

'Now don't be a little fool! You can't fight them. They'll chop you in pieces in a moment!'

'Let them. They have forced me to it. I'm a man, not a baby to be played with. I can't live with the shame of it!'

'It's no shame. They were far too many for you. It could have happened to any man.'

'Anyone they considered a man they would have killed. That would have been an honourable defeat. Not this. Please, may I take this knife?'

The woman spread her hands in a gesture of resignation.

'Do what you will, then, foolish boy,' she said. 'I cannot stop you.'

Gospatrick took a battered knife from a hook on the wall, and hobbled out of the cottage. The big Viking and some of the others who had beaten him were sitting around a fire in a field, their thirst for sport sated. They gazed at Gospatrick with amusement as he limped towards them. The big man hauled himself up to his feet, and stood with legs astride and huge arms folded on his chest, grinning at the boy.

'By Odin, he's back again,' the Dane taunted. 'What is it, boy? Haven't you had enough?'

'Give me back my sword,' Gospatrick demanded, halting a few yards away. 'My father gave it to me. Put it back in my hand, and I will fight to the death for it. Or are Danes nothing but thieves and murderers?'

For an unnerving time the big Viking studied Gospatrick with piercing eyes.

'You have the makings of a fine warrior, lad,' he grunted eventually. 'You're brave. Your father should be proud of you, so go home . . .'

'My father is dead,' Gospatrick cut in, 'murdered by you Northmen. The least you can do is let me honour him by granting me a warrior's death.'

The Viking's face grew grim, and his hand went to rest on his sword-hilt.

'Not murdered, boy,' he said sternly, 'we Danes do not like to be called murderers. Say to me that your father was killed in battle with us, and I'll respect his memory with you. But tell me again we murdered him, and I'll thrash you like . . .'

'He *was* murdered! Betrayed, trapped, and *murdered!*'

'By the gods! I'll . . .'

'Go on then, fight me! Man to man. That's all I ask!'

The Viking shook his head in disbelief, and turned away. He singled out the man who had taken Gospatrick's sword, and held out his hand for it.

'Give it to him,' he ordered.

The other man leapt up and dropped into a fighting crouch. In one hand he brandished his own axe, with the other he clutched the sword belt to his side.

'No, I won it!' he snarled. 'It's mine. You give him back what you took from him, if you want to.'

'Give it to me,' his leader warned, 'or I'll take it and slice your ears off with it. Maybe I'll give those to the boy, too.'

The sword thief considered his chances, and did not care for them. He swore angrily and threw the sword down at the big man's feet. The Viking chieftan picked it up and strode across to Gospatrick. He held out the sword, but silently requested the knife in return. Gospatrick surrendered up the weapon. The Viking threw the knife far into the field, then strapped the sword around the youngster's waist.

'You have earned it with your boldness,' he said. 'Now be on your way. The mule over there, you can take it in exchange for your horses. I do not refuse your challenge – a Dane never does. Just be satisfied that we may meet again one day, then you might kill me, or I might kill you. But not today, lad. Today you have fought well enough to be allowed an honourable retreat. Now go.'

Gospatrick was lost for words. Danes were nothing but cold-hearted rats, he had always heard, yet this man was showing a compassion as sincere as his earlier malice and, more surprising, a sense of justice. Gospatrick felt like crying again, but this time simply out of confusion.

'You are worth better than the company you keep,' he said, with a contemptuous nod towards the others. 'I shall be proud to do battle with you. Thank you for my sword. The rest of it I care not a spit for. You can keep it.'

He stalked away towards the mule, but stopped and looked back.

'Do you know one called Olaf Ericsson?' he asked.

'Aye,' replied the Viking. 'Everyone knows the son of Eric Longaxe. Why?'

'When you see him,' Gospatrick said, 'tell him that the sons of Uhtred of Northumbria will not rest until they have cut him down, him and the English traitor Streona together. I pray I will meet them before I meet you again, for they are more deserving of death.'

The Viking tilted back his hairy chin and shook with a loud merriment.

'Damn it, boy,' he shouted. 'I swear you are the most courageous fellow I've come across, in this land of mice. You almost make me sorry I gave you a walloping! Now get out of here!'

Gospatrick rode slowly the rest of the way to York, mulling over his suffering at the hands of the Danes. They were vermin, he told himself, as inner rage brought out the heat of shame and pain. Lord help the English, they must settle with the Danes one day. Mice, did that great oaf say? He dared to suggest the English were mice, men like Gospatrick's father, who had been slain without a chance to defend themselves? No, it was the Danes who were rats. They fought only when they had the advantage of larger numbers or surprise, and at other times ran away or tried to buy their way out of trouble. Such were the men responsible for the sad state of England, the burned earth and the empty villages, the weeping women and the fatherless children.

He entered York and found it torn and barely alive. The Danes were to blame for this ruin, too, he thought bitterly.

Many of the city's houses had been reduced to blackened shells. Churches had fallen victim to the same desecration he had seen in other parts of Yorkshire and north Lincolnshire, and shops and ale-houses were boarded up or ransacked down to the last crumbs. Rubble and rubbish were strewn everywhere, hungry cats and dogs prowled the streets, and the few people who were still there moved listlessly, as though there were no more to do than get through the day searching out scraps.

Gospatrick urged his mule to a trot, concerned for the condition of his own home.

Uhtred's hall was still there. He paused at the stockade gate to survey it thoroughly, hardly able to believe the evidence of his own

71

eyes. It was undamaged, yet strangely different. It took him some moments to realise that the difference was its eerie quietness. Never before had he seen the place without at least a dozen people and scores of animals in it. The dusty yard, once constantly alive with activity, contained not a single chicken, goose, dog or horse. The stables and outhouses were deserted, the vegetable plots overgrown, the sties and paddocks empty of livestock. There was a ghostly silence over all, and he felt like an intruder, as though he had no right to be there.

The last time he was here, three long years ago, he and Gifta were preparing to leave. He remembered his father as well, through a mist of sorrow. So strong were the memories in that second or two, that he almost felt he could see his family as they were then.

Gospatrick dismounted and walked across the yard, the cool wind blowing the dust of yesterdays in his face. At the doors he hesitated, without knowing why, then manfully pushed them creaking open.

Aldred and Eadwulf raised their heads from a meal, and wondered at the sight of the scruffy figure in the half light of the threshhold. Aldred had partly raised himself from his seat, to shoo away the beggar, when recognition lit up his face.

'Gracious God, it's Gospatrick!' he yelled. Both he and Eadwulf knocked over their benches in their eagerness to greet their brother, and Gospatrick ran to them. The three met in a hugging dance in the middle of the rush-covered floor. They bellowed greetings and questions at each other so rapidly that no-one had time to answer, and so noisily that much of it could not be heard anyway.

'Lord, it's good to see you, little brother,' Aldred exclaimed, when some of the excitement had died down. 'But what on earth are you doing in those rags?'

Gospatrick told them about his beating at the hands of the Danes, and lifted the smock to show them his grazes and bruises.

'Vicious dogs,' growled Eadwulf, 'Is that how they fight now, beating boys?'

'I am only amazed they did not kill him,' said Aldred. 'Gospatrick, I'm sorry. It was wrong of us to encourage you to come back here. Dear God, we could have lost you. Why didn't you bring a bodyguard?'

'A bodyguard?' Gospatrick laughed, 'Like the one that deserted us the day after we left here? There is no-one left, Aldred. Constance is the only link with Northumbria I've had, these last three years. But you were not wrong to ask me back, never. I could not be happier, Danes or no Danes. How goes the fight? Can we still raise an army?'

Aldred laid a comforting hand on Gospatrick's shoulder, knowing the news he had to give would disappoint the boy.

'You won't have heard,' he sighed. 'We lost another battle, Gospatrick. Just days ago. It was the worst rout yet. All the leaders we had left were killed. Ulfcettel, the husband of Gifta's sister Wulfhilda, he died there. All is lost. Even King Edmund has accepted defeat, his brother Eadwig too. They have disbanded their armies. Edmund has signed a pledge to rule jointly with Canute.'

'Edmund Ironside,' Gospatrick gasped, 'giving half his kingdom to a Dane? I can't believe it!'

'It's true. I'm as sorry as you are, but it's true.'

Gospatrick had lost his appetite. He sat staring round the gloomy hall. It was a dark, miserable place now, nothing like the warm and happy house he had known. Only the people who had lived in it had made it a home, and nearly all of them were gone. His father had given it life and purpose, and without him the hall sagged like a battered old war tent from which the pole had been dragged out. Gifta had given it light and warmth, and without her it was stark and unwelcoming. Friends had come to eat and drink and talk; without them, it might as well be closed up like a tomb. Without the servants and slaves who had heated it in winter, cleaned it in summer, cooked and washed and sewn in it, the hall had begun to gather the dank smell of death. It would never come to life again. Gospatrick wanted to take a torch and burn it down, to spare it this awful emptiness, this slow and miserable death.

His brothers could guess what he was thinking.

'Aldred is right,' said Eadwulf. 'We should not have let you come back here. We have grown used to it, but it must be a shock for you to see it like this.'

Aldred fetched fresh clothes. Gospatrick changed into them, and in the process had to unbuckle the sword he had so nearly lost to the Danes. He handled the weapon thoughtfully.

'The Northmen who killed our father, and our King, and our uncle Ulfcettel, they must all die,' he said resolutely. 'Every Dane who came here must be killed, or sent back to Denmark. Father vowed it, and so do I. If King Edmund has given up, does that mean we have to? Surely there are men who will still fight?'

Aldred and Eadwulf exchanged glances, wordlessly asking each other how they could convince the boy that it was hopeless. He had not seen the death and devastation with which they had lived for so long. He had not been made weary by endless conflict. He could not understand.

'There are no men, Gospatrick,' Aldred said patiently. 'There are no thanes left to rally them. They are dead, crippled, exiled, imprisoned, or just exhausted. And without the thanes, the fyrd will certainly not come out.'

'We are thanes,' argued the boy. 'We are fit and free. So what if there are but three of us? Should we not try until there are none?'

Aldred thumped his fist on the table, angry at being preached to by a fourteen-year-old boy who'd suffered little.

'Damn it, do you think we are happy with it?' he shouted. 'Do you think we *want* to be slaves of the Danes after all these years of fighting, of watching our friends cut to pieces? You have no idea what it's like!'

Eadwulf, seeing Gospatrick taken aback by Aldred's outburst, tried a kinder approach.

'It's not so easy, little brother . . .' he began, but Gospatrick cut him short with a sudden tantrum of his own.

'For the love of God, stop calling me *little* brother! I've waited years to be a man; I've grown tired of waiting for my fight and being told I can't have it. Don't treat me like a child any more, please!'

'All right, all right, I'm sorry,' Eadwulf apologised, 'But listen to me, will you? It is not so easy to take up arms again, much as we would like to, and not just because the King has ceased to fight. Look, you've seen the condition this country is in, haven't you? You've seen the fields without crops, without herds, the empty granaries. Men cannot fight without food, Gospatrick. This threatens to be the worst winter we have ever known. People will die of starvation, in their thousands, unless something is done quickly. Merchants must be allowed to fetch food in from wherever they can buy it – Scotland, Ireland, France, even Denmark if necessary. They must have freedom to travel, which they can't do as long as a war is raging . . .'

'That's right,' Aldred confirmed. 'Cattle and sheep must be bred up once more. The bridges have to be repaired so that men and beasts can get to market. Shelters have to be built for the winter. Our people need help to organise all this. We have no time to fight while the people are dying for want of bread. Who would there be to fight for?'

Gospatrick thought it over in silence for a while.

'You can build bridges and houses. I am going to fight,' he said at last. 'And I want Gifta back in this house.'

'Oh, dear God, Gospatrick.' Aldred slapped the table. 'Can't you see? Gifta will never come back here, no more than father will. It's done, brother; it's the past. She has her duties as a princess that have nothing to do with us or our lives any more. She's Ethelred's daughter, Edmund's sister. She will be married again to someone

Edmund wants to bind to him. The world has changed. We have to make a new life, not hanker after the old. That's why we wanted you back here, to be a part of it with us. We've sorrowed too, Gospatrick. Don't stand off from us, as though we've felt nothing. We want you back. The three sons of Uhtred must stand together!'

Gospatrick was still shaking with anger and helpless rage. He hid his face from his brothers, moving away from them into the shadowed corner by his old cot. Still he fidgeted with his sword, running a finger along its edge.

'And what of father?' he muttered. 'Is he to lie unavenged? Are we never to seek out Olaf Ericsson, or Streona?'

'What are you suggesting now, that we are cowards?' Aldred asked hotly. 'Yes, of course we are going to avenge our father. We are going to kill Streona and every member of his family who was in the least way connected with the massacre. But we are not going out against him, weak as kittens as we are. When we have the strength again, then we will strike. And on that day, Northumbria will be washed from east to west with the blood of his kin.'

'And have you warned Streona of our vow, as tradition demands?' Gospatrick inquired.

'Gospatrick,' Aldred sighed, 'we have been rather busy, you know.'

Then I will do it myself, Gospatrick swore to himself.

The following day he made an excuse to leave the house at first light.

He combed York until he could find a piglet to buy, and then set out by fast horse across the moors. He carried the squealing animal in a sack on his saddle to the nearest stronghold of the Streona clan, and boldly cantered in through the stockade gates. Only one old yard slave watched, puzzled, as Gospatrick pulled the piglet struggling from the sack. He drew his knife, slashed the beast's throat, and hurled it bleeding on the threshhold of the house.

'Streona swine!' he yelled. 'Come and tend your brother!'

A group of astonished people collected in the doorway, a frail old man, two children, a youth not much older than Gospatrick, a war-crippled young man and a middle-aged woman. They looked from the dying piglet to Gospatrick, haughtily walking his fine horse to and fro in their yard, insulting them for a reason they could not understand.

'I am Gospatrick Uhtredsson,' he shouted down at them. 'My father, Uhtred, Earl of Northumbria, was killed by your craven kin. Know that the sons of Uhtred will not rest until every one of the name Streona lies at his threshhold, like the bloody swine you see there!'

Some younger and stronger menservants came running from the house. Gospatrick threw the stained knife down after the pig, reined his horse about and galloped away. He did not stop until he reached a moorland stream, where once he had gone fishing with his father and brothers. There he sat beneath the same old, stunted oak tree, watching the water gurgle over the stones while he thought out his future course.

He would die of impatience if he stayed with Aldred and Eadwulf to restore the farms. That was not what he had waited for all this time. If he made no effort to fight, he would be failing in his pledged duty to Gifta, and she deserved better than to be left in exile for the rest of her life, whether or not she could ever live in his house again.

Thus resolved, he returned to York. He had his speech ready for his brothers when they returned home that night.

'Where is King Edmund?' he asked, as they ate supper.

'In London, I think,' answered Eadwulf. 'Why?'

'Because where he is, that is where I am going.'

Aldred lowered his goblet.

'Oh,' he said. 'For what purpose?'

'To offer him my sword.'

'Living in the south so long must have affected your hearing,' Aldred said sarcastically. 'Did you not hear us say the war is over?'

'He will fight again when he is ready. I know it.'

'It's a long way to go to waste your time and his,' Eadwulf joined in. 'He will probably tell you to go home again.'

'You're talking to me like a baby again,' Gospatrick accused them.

'Baby or not,' Aldred said firmly, 'we will not let you go.'

'You can't stop me. In a few weeks I shall be fifteen. You will not be able to stop me then, so why try to stop me now?'

'Gospatrick, why must you be so damned stubborn?' Aldred stormed. 'There is no war! Can't you get that through your head? Learn patience, boy, as we've had to! If Edmund does take up sword against the Danes one day, then you can join him. And we'll come with you. Until then you simply have to accept there is nothing to be done in London, or anywhere else.'

'I am going anyway,' Gospatrick declared. 'I can't stay here and run a farm. I haven't the slightest interest in cows or goats, thank you. But perhaps if enough people like me go to the King and swear to raise armies for him, he will listen.'

'By the blood of Christ,' Aldred breathed, 'I'm beginning to wish we'd left you in Wessex, until you were old enough to see sense.'

'Maybe I wish that, too,' Gospatrick retorted, sulkily. 'I would not have had so far to go to London.'

Over the next few days Aldred and Eadwulf realised that Gospatrick could not be swayed from going to London, so they provisioned him and saw him off and wished him well.

Gospatrick left York only a month after returning there, on a cold November morning with the first of the winter snows building up in a heavy sky. This time he deliberately refused to look back at the house as he rode away. Much later he would reflect that perhaps he should have done, for time and circumstance had yet more changes to make to his life, and would destroy some of the most precious things he left behind there.

His childish action at the house of the Streona clan had helped worsen a lifelong blood feud. The family had not taken his challenge lightly. On a day to come, one that would cause Gospatrick agony all his life, his eldest brother Aldred would be lured into a woodland with a false invitation to a hunt. There, like his father before him, Aldred would be hacked to death.

VII

LONDON was in a worse state than York. It was not so heavily
damaged, but was crowded with homeless thousands who had
walked in to the city from the desolate countryside in the hope of
better pickings. Whole families, in pitiful rags and gaunt with
hunger, sheltered under makeshift lean-to sheds in the narrow
streets, which ran with vermin and stank with filth. Their only hope
was to beg from passers-by. It was impossible to move through the
city without being constantly accosted by them. Bands of cut-
throat thieves took advantage of the breakdown in law and order,
and no one went out by night or along side alleys by day, even if
they had nothing of value. Disease was rife, too. Many poor people
in the dirty hovel encampments were lingering on the edge of death.
The city had given up trying to bury its dead. These days the carts
rumbled down only as far as London Bridge, where the corpses
were tipped into the mud as the tide was going out.

Gospatrick rode through the miserable thoroughfares, saw this
picture of Hell, and thought that here was yet another account the
Viking invaders must pay.

At the stockade gate of the royal house, he climbed down from
his horse to explain his visit to the captain of the guard.

'I am Gospatrick Uhtredsson,' he proudly introduced himself,
'adoptive nephew of King Edmund. Will you take me to him?'

The captain laughed, and nodded at his men. When he spoke, it
was with a distinctly Danish accent.

'Here's another of them. They keep crawling out from under
stones.' The guards moved out to surround Gospatrick. 'Hand me
that sword, lad. And any other weapons you have. Then you'll be
taken inside, right enough.'

Gospatrick was dumbstruck. In his worst imaginings he had not
expected to arrive here and find Danes as guards outside the King's
house.

'What is this?' he blustered, 'where are King Edmund's guards?'

'Same place he's gone, I'd hope,' the captain laughed. 'Not heard
the news, boy? Your Edmund Ironside is as dead as that gatepost.
It's King Canute you bow to now.'

Escorted across the courtyard by two Danish warriors, Gospatrick felt a chill that had little to do with the November weather. It was as if he were walking to his execution.

'Was he jesting?' he asked. 'Is Edmund really dead?'

'He is,' was the careless answer.

'How did he die?'

'Easily,' the man chortled, 'like all the English.'

They took him into the great hall. There was quite a gathering of England's diminished nobility there, cheerlessly huddled around the large central fire. At the heart of the group were Prince Eadwig, and King Edmund's widow Algith and twin baby sons, Edward and Edmund. Gospatrick thought he recognised some of the others, but most were strangers to him. He stood, regarding them all with the same helpless stare which they in return afforded him, as the great doors boomed shut behind him and were locked.

Eadwig beckoned to his adopted nephew to join them. The young prince had aged considerably since they had last met, his eyes all but lost in darkened sockets, and his brow deeply furrowed. He was still garbed in prince's finery, but looked as dispirited as the hapless beggars in the streets.

'Come in, Gospatrick,' he said. 'I will not say "welcome", only that I'm sorry you should be caught here as well. How are my sisters? Have you heard from Gifta?'

Gospatrick warmed his hands by the blazing logs.

'I had a letter from her in September,' he answered numbly. 'She was well then, and the child too. So was Wulfhilda, though of course that was before she heard of the death of Ulfcettel . . .'

Eadwig nodded.

'And now this,' he finished.

'Is it true, uncle? About King Edmund . . . ?'

'Yes, I'm afraid it is.'

Algith started to cry. She made an effort to cease her weeping when she saw that it disturbed little Edward. Gospatrick waited a moment before asking:

'Did the Danes kill him?'

'I believe so. They claim he died a natural death, but I knew my brother too well to accept that. He was as fit and strong as ever. It is rumoured that Canute had Edmund poisoned by one of his own servants. I don't doubt it.'

'Merciful God, is there no end to their evil?' Gospatrick whispered. His brothers had been right, he feared. There was no hope now, no more prospect of a fight. Here in this hall were the last, sad remnants of a once-mighty leadership. At one time the English nobles had been as numerous throughout the land as the towns, hamlets and villages. Today, even gathered together in Edmund's hall, there were not fifty left.

Ethelred, Edmund Ironside, Uhtred, Ulfcettel, all the magnificent names of three years ago, all were now no more than that, just names, and not even carved in stone for men to remember.

'What will happen to us?' Gospatrick asked Eadwig.

'Canute is deciding that now, I would think. He ponders over how important we are now. While Edmund lived we always had a chance of rallying the people once more, and Canute knew it. Now he has won the last victory. The very last. I don't suppose he will want us to stay as thorns in his side.'

'You mean he will kill us?'

'Possibly. Or exile us, one or the other.'

Gospatrick went to look at the two babies, who lay in a cradle close to their mother. He gently touched the cheek of tiny Edmund, son of Edmund Ironside. But this Edmund looked sickly, much the weaker of the twins.

'He will not murder babies, surely?' Gospatrick whispered.

'They are of the English blood royal,' Eadwig stated simply.

At that moment a tall man with greying hair and moustaches stepped out from the depths of the hall, and took Gospatrick's arm.

'You are Gospatrick Uhtredsson?' he asked.

'Yes . . .'

'I am Orm Osricsson. You have heard of me, perhaps?'

'No, sir; I'm sorry . . .'

'Ah well, you would be too young, I suppose,' Orm sighed, in the manner of one formerly famed, but now fading from recognition. 'I was a good friend of your father,' he explained, 'and as such, I am pleased to meet his youngest son. We fought many a battle together, your father and I. A greater warrior never lived, believe me.'

'I do, sir. I thank you for your tribute.'

'Ah, and to think of the manner of his dying . . .' Orm added sadly, shaking his head.

'Were you there?' asked Gospatrick urgently.

'Aye, much to my shame. I was there, and could not raise a hand to help him. My dreams of it have tormented me many a night since.'

It was the first time Gospatrick had met anybody who had actually seen his father's murder. He stood open-mouthed, staring at Orm as if he were a god arrived among men, wanting to ask him so much, yet wondering if he could bear to hear the answers. Orm understood, and eased the way for him.

'Here,' he said kindly, 'come and sit down with me, and I'll tell you of it, if you wish. You do? Well, it was a shameful business, shameful . . .'

'Was he really killed with his sword still in its sheath, as I heard?'

'Yes, he was. He died with his hand upon the hilt, ready to fight to the last, as he'd always been – if only the swine had let him. Oh, what a dreadful night that was. We had all gone there, thinking ourselves among friends, as your father did. Once there we were trapped inside, outnumbered by Danes and Streona's men. We had to make the best pretence of it even then, as if we desired nothing but friendship and peace. Several of us thought we were the ones who'd been drawn into the web, to make a meal for the spider. But when your father stepped into the hall, it was plain to see that he was the fly. Dear boy, I know your grief has been great, but can you imagine how it is to see the murderer's axe fall on your lifelong friend, and to be helpless to do anything but watch? God knows, I have seen it often enough in battle, but never like that, so suddenly, in the midst of the feast . . .'

Gospatrick bowed his head. He would not cry again, he told himself. He would never cry again.

'It all happened so fast. Even as we opened our mouths to shout a warning, I saw young Olaf Ericsson step out of the crowd, yet still he had struck before my voice came to me. It was Princess Edith who managed to call to Uhtred. That foul husband of hers struck her to the floor. Do not think ill of her for what Streona did, Gospatrick. She risked her own life to try to save your father.'

'What else happened? Were many others killed?'

'Oh, everything went mad then. The Danes hacked the rest of Uhtred's company to death right there in the doorway, friends of mine among them. The women were screaming, fainting, throwing themselves down, imploring everyone not to kill them. Everyone was trying to get out, trampling each other in their terror. I just stood and watched, I felt so helpless. I have never known anything like it, and I never want to again. And at the end of it, Streona stood there laughing at us, and told us to go home and remember what we had seen – as if we could ever forget.'

'Laughing, you say?'

'Aye, laughing, the devil.'

Gospatrick took a deep breath.

'We have sworn to kill him, my brothers and I,' he said. 'He and Olaf Ericsson. They will both die.'

'A bold vow.'

'I mean it. I have never meant anything so seriously.'

'But I beg of you – as your father's friend – do not be rash. Do not think of Olaf Ericsson as any ordinary man, for there are many who swear he is not. They say he is a demon in human form.'

A chill ran through Gospatrick and the hall seemed very dark and cold suddenly.

'And what do you say, Orm Osricsson?' he asked hoarsely.

'By all the saints, I do not know. Men swear he is indestructible, an evil born of Ethelred's sinful deeds. He has slain many men since he murdered your father. He is the most feared of Canute's warriors, so much so that Canute has chosen him to command his personal bodyguard. He is completely without fear, as though he knows he cannot be harmed. In that last battle, when so many of our nobles died, he was seen to slay fifteen men with as many strokes, never once moving from the one spot.' Orm leaned forward and his voice dropped to a reverent murmur. 'Some have sworn upon oath that they have seen Satan himself appear at Olaf's shoulder in such moments, when his blood lust is at its highest.'

Gospatrick's mouth was dry. He could scarcely swallow down the lump in his throat.

'Demon or not,' he said with difficulty, 'there must be a way to kill him, just as there must be a way to rid England of the Danes.'

Orm shook his head.

'Patience, boy,' he replied gravely. 'Patience and faith in the Lord, those are the only weapons we have left. But be of good hope. In my shire there lives a wise old monk well known for his visions and prophecies. He saw all our sufferings in a dream, long before the Northmen came. The Devil is at work in this land, he says, and will not be cast out until a day many years hence, when a godly one shall come from across the sea to rule us. On that day, Canute and his sons will be long dead.'

'Another invader?' Gospatrick said with contempt. 'Is that what we must wait for?'

'Do you forget there are sons of Ethelred in exile?' Orm chided him. 'It might mean Edward, or Alfred. Who knows? The workings of God are not for us to know, nor to question.'

'You're right, of course. But it seems unjust that we should have to wait for Canute's evil brood to live out their lives when we could be fighting them. Even if it means being cut down to the last man.'

Orm smiled.

'You are a brave lad, a son worthy of your father,' he said. 'All you lack is patience. I think I owe it to Uhtred to try to teach it to you. Come, let me show you something.'

He got up and went to a corner where he kept a few possessions.

He returned with a chequered board and chess pieces, which he placed between them.

'Have you seen the hawk searching for its prey?' he inquired, setting out kings and queens, rooks, bishops, knights and pawns. 'He hovers on high, as silent and motionless as a cloud. When the moment is right, he swoops. Have you watched the cat, stalking a bird? Though that tasty morsel may fly away at any moment and he hungers madly for it, he does not rush in. No, he moves a muscle here, a sinew there, quietly, slowly, inch by inch nearer, until the prey is his. Man can learn the skills of the hawk and the cat, and put them to good use. This game can put your idle moments to good use, and teach you the patience, the cunning and the tactics of the wild ones. Have you seen it before?'

'No. Did you invent it?'

'No, no,' Orm laughed, 'it comes from the East, from Persia, they say. Emma and her Normans brought it to England, and of course it became fashionable among our thanes. I think it has lessons for us. No one knows craftiness better than the Normans, eh? Now, let me show you how to move the pieces . . .'

Gospatrick concentrated hard, and tried the game several times before he got the idea of it. Eventually he was able to play against Orm, and did quite well for the first dozen or so moves. Then he thought he saw a means of trapping Orm's king and shot his queen across the board with a cry of triumph. Orm casually picked off the piece with a knight that the boy had overlooked.

'Too eager, my friend,' he said. 'Now do you see what I mean by striking out too soon? Your most valuable fighter has gone.'

Gospatrick sat back with a grunt of exasperation.

'I would have had your rook in the next move,' he declared. 'Then you would have been checkmated.'

'Ah, but between a man's intention and his act there is often that fatal slip of judgement. It is the same in war.'

'You say that everything happens according to the will of God,' Gospatrick grunted. 'So what's the good of patience?'

'You still don't understand, do you?' said Orm, replacing the chessmen in their ranks. 'The Lord decides the destiny of man, but that does not mean we need do nothing to help achieve his purpose. Here, try again. And this time remember that caution, as well as valour, wins wars.'

VIII

O RM should have remembered that the fates also play a part in the affairs of men. While they were imprisoned in the royal manor, there came a fresh turn of events that was finally to cause King Canute to make up his mind what to do about his hostages.

Streona, confident that he had served Canute well enough to earn some high rewards, travelled to London to see the king. He had in mind nothing less than the earldom of Northumbria, and perhaps even the regency of all England when Canute went to Denmark to consolidate his kingdom, as he had stated he would.

Nothing troubled Streona as he rode into the city and made his way to the house of a friend. Everything had happened just as he had planned. He had removed some of Canute's most dangerous enemies, and he had his wife, the princess Edith, to offer Canute as an extra hostage, to help ensure that the rest of King Ethelred's family behaved themselves. The country was secure at last under the hand of a strong leader, and Streona was very much in that leader's favour.

The sun was shining brightly on his fortunes as well as on stricken London, the arrogant Streona congratulated himself. But shortly before he reached his friend's house, he was recognised by a group of London fyrdmen.

'That's Streona,' one man said resentfully. 'He's one of the traitors that handed us to the Danes. Look at him, all dressed up in his finery and fat as a prize calf!'

'Yes. He's done well out of it,' growled another.

'He won't have to go hungry, or watch his family die.'

'King Ethelred would be alive today, if it weren't for the likes of him.'

'Aye, and Edmund Ironside.'

'Swine! He ought to be strung up!'

Their mutterings developed into angry ranting as news of Streona's arrival spread quickly through the neighbouring streets. Small gatherings of idle men at ale-houses and street corners gradually became a single mob. The bitterness of months of starvation and fear was all brought boiling to the surface and directed towards one man, the hated Streona, until, just before dark, one of the ringleaders suggested they were all loud-mouthed cowards if they were going to do nothing but stand there complaining, and the challenge was taken up. Men drunk with fury and frustration snatched up torches, clubs, knives, axes and stones, and marched to where Streona was staying. They surrounded the house, chanting insults, cursing Streona and all his clan.

'Send the traitor out!' they screamed, 'or we'll burn this house down!'

The owner came to the door and tried to reason with the crowd, but he was shouted down. A stone was thrown, narrowly missing his head as it thudded into the heavy oak door. He ducked back inside. More stones rattled against the walls. A torch was hurled up on to the thatch, but rolled down again before it could do any damage. By this time, Streona's friend was pleading with his guest to try to calm the mob. Streona, conceited enough to think that he had sufficient authority to quell any collection of ruffians, opened the door just wide enough to be seen.

'Go away, you fools,' he blustered. 'Stop this nonsense and go home, or I'll fetch the soldiers to you!'

'Aye, *Danish* soldiers!' came a venomous retort.

'Homes? We've got no homes to go to, thanks to you!' shouted another.

Streona laughed harshly at them.

'You blame me for everything?' he taunted the mob. 'What have I done? I've helped get you a strong king, that's all.'

'A foreign invader! And you're a traitor!'

'England had no need of traitors. It had all the cowards it needed. Where were the brave men of London when Ethelred had Forkbeard retreating, when he needed them most, eh?'

A dozen men rushed the door. They crashed it wide open and grabbed Streona before he could turn back into the house. He was bundled out into the yard, screeching threats, and in seconds he was lost in the press of enraged people. The owner sent his servants out to help, but they were easily pushed back. Soon Streona's indignant warnings gave way to pleas and promises of justice, but there was no mercy for him there. He was jostled, pulled about and punched, his clothes ripped, and his cries were drowned beneath the howls of the crowd.

Two servants ran to the stables and mounted horses bare-back, hoping to reach a military patrol, but they were dragged down and thrown to the ground.

It was too late to help Streona anyway. He was knocked down, kicked and crushed beneath scores of stamping feet. Finally he was clubbed and stabbed again and again as he lay like a heap of torn rags in the mud.

He was dead long before the ringleaders pushed their way through the mass to take him away for public punishment. Cheated of their entertainment, they lifted up the broken body and carried it by torchlight to London Bridge, lustily singing that this was the fate of all treacherous noblemen. At the bridge, they sliced off the head and limbs, kicked the whole bloody mess into the river, and watched it drift away on the filthy brown water.

When there was no more to see there, they continued their march of vengeance back through the London streets, abusing those householders who had taken in Danes and traitors, hurling stones as well as insults at their homes. During that night of violence, two houses where Danes were known to have lived were burned down, and five Englishmen were dragged out and hanged from the beams of their own homes. The mob celebrated with songs and mocking verses, and calls for the house of Ethelred to be restored. Not once were the Danish warriors sent out against them, while the city rang to chants of: 'Long live Eadwig! Eadwig, son of Ethelred, is our King! Throw out the Dane!'

At the royal house, the captives heard the shouting. News of Streona's death came through to them, and they knew it was they who must fear the consequences of this night.

Gospatrick, at first, did not understand what the riot meant. He was delighted that Streona had met an even more bloody and ignominious end than Uhtred, but at the same time angry that the right to deal with his father's betrayer had been taken from him.

'Now there is only Olaf Ericsson to deal with,' he told Orm.

But Orm was a worried man, and had no time for the boy's wild boasting.

'Just pray that you will live through this day yourself, lad,' he snapped.

Gospatrick could not fathom the mood of Orm and the other men until later in the morning, when the captive company received the visitation they were dreading.

The doors of the hall were thrown open, and King Canute strode in, followed by some advisers and guards. The great room fell silent, and all eyes were on the conquerer. He stood with arms folded across his chest, his hard young face expressing contempt and pity as he surveyed his hostages one by one. He was no longer an uncertain youth, brought to England in the train of his legendary father Forkbeard, but a war-wise and determined ruler whose sharp stare was usually sufficient to put down dissent. He knew that within moments of entering that hall he had sewn the seeds of fear in his audience, without speaking a word or displaying any sign of anger. With careful timing, he started to stride among them, his brawny arms still firmly placed across his chain-mailed breast, as though sorting out those who must be punished as an example to the others.

'You have heard of the happenings of this night,' he said, simply as a matter of fact.

'We have,' agreed Prince Eadwig.

'You know that Streona and others were torn to pieces by the mob'

'Yes.'

'Englishmen tearing apart Englishmen . . .'

Gospatrick could not keep quiet.

'Streona got what he deserved!' he piped up. 'He was a murderer, and a traitor to . . .'

His voice faded away to a whisper as Canute's cold stare fell upon him. The king approached the boy and stood over him. Gospatrick held his ground, but felt that he was shrinking to half his size.

'Who are you?' Canute demanded.

'My name is Gospatrick Uhtredsson.'

' "My Lord King!" ' Canute bellowed, 'when you speak to me . . .'

Gospatrick complied, resentfully: 'My Lord King.'

'And how old are you?'

'Fifteen years . . . my Lord King.' I . . . I am stepson to the Princess Aelfgifu, adopted nephew of Prince Eadwig. I came to offer King Edmund my sword. . . .'

'Did you indeed?' Canute growled. 'Well, listen to me, young Uhtredsson. Now that you have reached manhood, you should know better than to be insolent to your superiors. This time I will pardon your youth and inexperience – and be sure that I care not a piss for the fate of Streona or any like him. Had he been a Dane, however, let me assure you I would have hanged half the men of London by now.' With that he turned his back on Gospatrick and addressed the rest of the prisoners. 'Streona's death is nothing to me. What does concern me is that this proves there is still resistance in England. That resistance must be stamped out!'

'Resistance!' Eadwig laughed without humour. ' "Englishmen tearing apart Englishmen . . . "?'

Canute shot him a warning look.

'Your name,' the King told him, 'and the names of others here, were called out by the mob last night. They still regard you as their leaders. So we had a few of them arrested this morning. They confessed under torture, that you were still plotting a war against me even after Edmund Ironside and I had signed our pact to rule jointly . . .'

Eadwig knew his fate was decided. He had nothing more to lose by showing his contempt for Canute.

'Is that why Edmund died so suddenly?' he sneered.

'Your brother died because it was his time,' Canute said. 'Now it is your time.' He reached for a scroll of parchment, which was handed to him by one of his men, and purposefully unrolled it. 'The men named on this list are those betrayed by the informers . . .' he began.

'Informers?' Eadwig echoed. 'A few miserable beggars picked off the streets at random? Oh, my friends,' he turned to the imprisoned nobles around him. 'How sorry I am that the great Canute has reduced you from warriors to mere scapegoats!'

Canute waited patiently until the interruption was done. No English prince was going to upset his awesome oratory.

'Prince Eadwig,' he continued, 'Shire-Reeve Godric of Cheshire, Alderman Osric of Doncaster, Orm Osricsson, Waltheof Gamelsson, Egbert of Wolverhampton, Osgod Edgarsson, Egbert of Gloucester and Egfrith of Northampton. You are to be executed. You will be given one hour for your shriving. Then the sentences will be carried out.'

There were murmurings of sympathy and mutterings of anger. Those named stood mute with shock. Gospatrick went to Orm, but could say nothing; the elderly warrior put an arm around the boy's shoulders as if it were he, not Orm, who needed to be given courage.

'Ah, even in death Streona wins,' Orm sighed.

Edmund Ironside's widow broke down completely. She had not heard all of Canute's words, and thought they were all to be killed. She clutched her babies to her, and rushed to kneel wild-eyed before the king.

'Please, spare these innocent ones!' she sobbed.

Eadwig, stunned by the fate awaiting him, nevertheless had thought for his tiny nephews.

'What of Edmund's sons?' he demanded of Canute. 'Will you kill them too?'

Canute had already given consideration to the problem of Edward and Edmund Edmundsson, but pretended to think it over.

'You need not worry about them,' he said at last. 'I shall send them into the care of my kinsman, the King of Sweden. Their mother can go with them.'

Eadwig was in no position to ask for more.

'Can I die sure of that?' he begged.

'I swear it,' Canute said.

'And all these other loyal men of mine. What will become of them?'

'They will stay here under close watch, until I feel they can be trusted to try my patience no more. They know now how I deal with rebels. Before they are freed, I will expect promises from them all that there will be no more plotting against me, or my heirs.'

This was too much for Gospatrick.

'I will never swear allegiance to you . . . !' he cried angrily.

Canute turned to him, towering over him like an angry father about to slap the disobedience out of a troublesome child.

'You dare speak to me like that, boy?' he roared, 'God's blood, I'll . . .'

'Gospatrick!' Eadwig called sharply.

'Yes, uncle?'

'You will apologise, and say no more!'

'Apologise . . . ?'

'Yes, Gospatrick, apologise. I order it. Do you go against my wishes?'

'No, my lord . . . !'

'Then do as I say. Now!'

Gospatrick, bewildered, looked up at the hated Canute. He wanted to put a sword through the man, yet his hero Prince Eadwig had ordered him to humble himself before him. There seemed to be no end to the humiliations he must suffer at the hands of the Danes.

'My Lord King, I ask your pardon for my words,' he muttered.

Canute nodded, but was not yet satisfied.

'But you refuse to swear allegiance?'

Resentful silence was all he was offered. He repeated, a shade more menacingly: 'You refuse to swear allegiance?'

'Gospatrick,' said Eadwig, tiredly. 'You will swear for Canute.'

'I swear to serve King Canute,' said Gospatrick, and he thought that if he had that sword now, it would be his own body he ran it through.

IX

CANUTE went back to the riverside house he had commandeered, the house that would serve him until he had built the big new timber palace he planned to erect near the village of Charing. He was in a sour mood when he reached there, for executing men was not a task he cared for. It should not be necessary to dispose of warriors in that way once they had been beaten in battle, he believed, and he cursed the English for persisting in their petty hedgerow warfare.

Needing to drink heavily, he took one goblet of wine after another, irritably pacing about the hall, watched with worried eyes by his sister, Estrith, who had come from Denmark to join in his victory celebrations, and her husband Earl Ulf. Canute's English bed partner Graciousgift was there too, but on sufferance. These days she was treated more like a favoured servant than a privileged member of the king's household, and she was coming to realise it.

She had given him a second son. The birth of Sweyn had been followed barely a year later by the arrival of another boy, Harold. But rather than strengthening their love, the coming of the new baby had fuelled Canute's doubts about his common-law wife.

No-one had actually told him that Graciousgift was unfaithful, and as yet he had not accused her, but he was an observant man, and was not deaf to the suppressed giggles that rippled among the women of the household. Those silly whisperings seemed to arise whenever Graciousgift was absent on some supposed errand, and for Canute, who trusted no-one too far out of his sight, they were enough to arouse his suspicions. He would have tackled Graciousgift with it, had it mattered all that much to him. But as it happened, there was no place for her in the future he saw for himself. He did not even care a great deal whether Sweyn and Harold were his sons or not. God willing (for Canute was, like many another modern Viking, a devout Christian), there would one day be heirs of more certain and noble parentage.

For the time being he saved the news he had for Graciousgift, and addressed himself first to Estrith.

'I have decided to stay in England for a while after all,' he told his sister. 'There's still too much trouble here. I want you to go back and look after Denmark for me – as my regent.'

Estrith lowered her head in assent. There were niggling doubts in her mind. Ulf, her husband, was an ambitious man and had already given her cause to wonder if he was as loyal to Canute as he pretended. Was it only by chance that Ulf consorted with just about every Danish noble who was most dangerous to Canute? Also he had been a little too eager to gain favour with the late Edmund Ironside, in the early days of their joint kingship.

Estrith was a beautiful woman, small, yet with a strong will and extraordinary energy. Her brother greatly respected her for her political ability and so far she had always been able to keep the heady schemes of her husband in check. Now, however, she was with child for the first time, and she was not so sure that in her present condition she could deal with both the regency of Denmark and the manoeuvres of her husband.

'You should not stay away too long,' she warned Canute. 'Denmark has its troubles too. Each year you are absent, someone else there grows a little bolder.'

'I know. But it's these damned English who give me the most headaches still.'

'Yet you hang their heroes,' said Estrith, cleverly in tones that made it sound less like a criticism than a gentle reminder, that perhaps his judgement was not always of the best. 'Are you sure it is right to kill Eadwig today – the last of the sons of Ethelred?'

'No, I'm not sure,' Canute admitted miserably. 'But it's done now.'

'Not yet.'

'It will be, within the hour. When Canute passes sentence, Estrith, he does not rescind it shortly afterwards. I could hardly maintain discipline like that.'

'You are too good a man to let pride stand in the way of second thoughts, brother.'

'I have no second thoughts. Eadwig must die. Like his brother before him, he's too much a symbol of what used to be. With all of Ethelred's sons dead, the line is seen to be finished. The English will finally have to accept me. Besides, there is another good reason why I must stay here after these executions, not only to hold on to control . . .'

'What else, then?'

'When the fighting is all done, there comes consolidation. A king must find a queen who will help make his rule secure, and I have one in mind . . .'

Graciousgift had been taking no interest in the conversation until then. She looked up sharply, astonished by Canute's casual words, uttered as though she were sitting there deaf as a piece of furniture.

'A queen?' she repeated, shrilly. 'But am I not . . . ?'

'No. You are not, and never have been,' Canute cut in, 'whatever else you are. There is no advantage to being married into a defunct English nobility now. I must have a queen who strengthens my position, helps show my power and influence to the world.'

Graciousgift was white with fury and fear. To be cast aside by Canute was insult enough, but to be humiliated in front of his family was intolerable.

'You are throwing me out!' she cried. 'Dear God, what have I done to deserve that?'

'I am not throwing you out,' the king irritably corrected her. 'You will be well looked after. You can even carry on as my mistress.'

'Mistress!' Graciousgift shrieked. She turned to Estrith and Ulf, but saw no offer of sympathy there. Desperately she looked to Canute again. 'But what of our sons? Do they mean nothing to you either?'

Canute was losing patience.

'My sons and their future,' he told her coldly, 'are no concern of yours. I know what I want for them. They will go to Denmark with Estrith, and so will you. You are their mother after all. Estrith will be responsible for teaching Sweyn to act for me.'

Graciousgift was speechless. Not only pushed aside like a plaything, she thought, but banished from her own country! Her sons given into the care of their aunt! Why, she wondered, did kings single her out for such unkindness? She had thought no-one could have caused her more pain than had Ethelred, who had destroyed her family by murder and mutilation. What Canute was doing to her, however, was even worse. He had led her to believe there was a place for her in his world, but all the time he had been merely using her. She would admit that she had not been a virtuous woman, but this punishment seemed needlessly cruel. She did not try to say any more, but left the hall without waiting to hear who was to replace her.

Earl Ulf had been itching to know. He leaned forward in his chair.

'This queen,' he prompted. 'Who is she?'

Canute laughed, savouring their surprise.

'Emma of Normandy,' he announced.

Estrith and Ulf exchanged glances, open-mouthed.

'Emma?' Ulf repeated. 'Ethelred's widow?'

'Yes, if it can be arranged.'

'Isn't this another slap in the face for your English subjects?'

asked Estrith. 'You take their king's throne, then take his widow
to wife?'

'The English will take as many slaps as I care to give them,'
declared Canute. 'It will prove that I mean to carry on exactly
where Ethelred left off. More important still, it continues the treaty
Ethelred had with Normandy. And Emma still has friends,
influence and property here in England. It consolidates everything
nicely. Don't you think it a perfect choice?'

Estrith rapidly turned over the plan in her keen mind, as was her
habit.

'There are advantages,' she agreed. 'But I can see problems, too.
What about the succession? If the choice ever falls between the
sons that Emma gave Ethelred, and the sons that she may give you,
the Normans could support either one to their own benefit. Then
things may not work out as you would wish.'

'True,' Canute shrugged. 'But all that's a long way in the future.
Meanwhile I have Sweyn and Harold to follow me. If I say so,
they can take precedence over any sons Emma gives me.'

'That sounds the best plan to me,' rumbled Ulf. 'Let the Normans
get too near the hen-house, brother-in-law, and they'll leave you
with feathers and bones.'

'It will be a foolhardy Norman who tries to steal Canute's meat,'
Canute boasted. 'Anyway, I have made up my mind. Emma it will
be. I shall send a messenger to Duke Richard at once, proposing
the marriage. But there's another match I want to discuss with you,
Ulf.'

'Yes?'

'Your pretty sister Gytha.'

'Ah! And whom do you want her to marry?'

'An Englishman. But one who's done me far greater service than
Streona ever did. He's got greater strength, resolution, cunning,
and courage – all that Streona had and more. His name is Godwin.
I'm going to appoint him Earl of Wessex. How does that sound to
you?'

Ulf liked what he heard. One earldom in Denmark and another
in England were powerful possessions indeed for any family. This
would be a valuable stepping stone in his own career, he recognised.

'That sounds fine to me,' Ulf said eagerly. 'I have met this
Godwin, and you speak truly of his qualities. Gytha will marry
him if you wish it. But is he not of – ah – fairly humble birth?'

'A farmer's son,' Canute confirmed; he held in contempt anyone
who respected another's breeding more than the man himself. 'But
the farmer's boy who raises himself to the company of kings must

have much to recommend him, don't you think? If his lowly origins offend you . . .'

'Oh no, no, no . . .' said Ulf hastily.

'Good. Then perhaps we will have a double wedding feast to celebrate. Now, until then, we have earldoms to bestow. Mercia, East Anglia, Northumbria. . . .'

Soon after the wall torches had been lit, the officer in charge of the executions came in. Canute had drunk himself into a jovial mood, but with the coming of this fellow his face reverted to its earlier grimness.

'Is it done?' the king inquired.

'It is, my Lord King,' the soldier said. 'They are dead.'

'So,' laughed Ulf, who was deep in his cups. 'You have struck off all the heads of the English serpent. Well done!'

'I have destroyed a family that has reigned for five hundred years!' Canute snapped back at him. 'That is no cause for mockery!'

'I have brought the woman and her children, my Lord King,' the soldier interrupted. 'They are outside.'

'Bring them in.'

Edmund Ironside's widow entered with head bowed low, her buxom frame sagging like a half-empty sack. Another woman was with her; they each held one of Edmund's baby sons who were now a year old.

'You are taking ship for Sweden tonight,' Canute told Algith. 'Is there anything you want?'

'I have my children,' she whispered. 'There is nothing else, no-one. You have slaughtered my entire family.'

'Your family should have known the value of peace treaties,' Canute answered shortly. 'Now listen to me, carefully. Do not try to return to England, nor to send your sons back here, no matter how much pressure is put upon you to do so by Ethelred's family in Normandy. The safety of your children is in your hands. Do you understand?'

The sorry little group were ushered out, but after they had passed through the door, Canute beckoned to the old warrior to come back. He handed him a scroll of parchment.

'Be sure you give this to the King as soon as you reach Sweden,' Canute ordered. 'It must be given to him, and no one else. Do not fail me.'

Estrith eyed Canute accusingly.

'Those little boys will not live long in Sweden, will they?' she challenged him. 'Your letter has ensured that.'

'I have fought for too many years for this kingdom,' he muttered angrily, 'to have it all undone by people warring in the name of

Ironside's sons. Since I have set out to destroy Ethelred's line, I must destroy it completely.'

'Then you should not have promised their safety to a man going to his death,' said Estrith. 'You have brought evil upon yourself with that false pledge.'

'I promised Eadwig they would be sent to Sweden, and they are being sent to Sweden. I have told our cousin to let them live long enough for people to forget they are there – then to dispose of them as quickly as he can.'

'There are some who will not forget,' his sister insisted. 'Ethelred's sons, Edward and Alfred, will not forget. And they will constantly remind the Normans of such a bloody deed. That would harm the treaty you want with Normandy. You are a bold man and a wise one, brother, but a little too hasty at times. There is still time to get your letter back.'

Canute paced about the hall for some minutes, considering her advice.

'No one could prove that I ordered it,' he said at last. 'And I will be married to Emma long before it is done.'

He made no attempt to reach the ship before it left port. The little family sailed, ignorant of Canute's plans for them, to Sweden where the sick twin, Edmund, soon died. The King of Sweden read Canute's letter, and thought hard about it. He was no killer of children, he decided. In time, he would send the outcasts to Hungary, where not even Canute could find them.

X

THE peregrine falcon soared on high, blue-grey wings spread like cloaked swords. She spied her prey, and briefly hovered, poised upon the air as still as a stitch on a wide blue tapestry, as quiet as the summer breeze.

A tiny lark had flown up from a distant meadow. The falcon's gaze had fallen upon the smaller bird, as surely as a sunbeam must strike to earth. The hunter swooped, scarring the sky with her flight, flowing along the treeline of a sharp green escarpment, and shooting like an arrow across the mirroring silver of the Seine. The lark vanished beneath its talons.

As the falcon struck, the brilliant gathering of noblemen and noblewomen scattered across the broad slopes cheered and applauded Duke Richard, as flatteringly as if he had brought down the prey with his own hand.

'An excellent catch, my lord!' they cried. 'What a splendid bird!'

'She's come down on the far side of the river, my lord,' said her handler, worried.

'Then you had better go across and get her, hadn't you?' the Duke laughed. 'Lose me the best falcon I've had in years, and I'll hang up your ears in my hall!'

The falconer hastened off, calling his men to go and help him, not realising that the Duke was really in a grand and forgiving humour. Richard was in his element, this glorious day, out in his beloved Norman fields, without a care, showing off his treasured hawks, and glorying in the admiration of his nobles. The scents of horses and fresh grass were sweet to him as the smiles of the slender beauties in their elegant gowns. Later they would feast on the cold joints of fowl and beef and fruits and wines from the south, all spread on white cloths in the shade.

He reined his horse about, and rode up beside his sister, Emma, who was looking quite demure for a woman well into her thirties and a mother of three. Emma wore a gown of turquoise embroidered with gold, from which showed delicate ankles in white stockings and gold and blue slippers; her cream-white wimple was of silk secured by a circlet of gold. She sat her gleaming black mare like a statue, and Richard thought her a desirable prize for any man.

'Did you see it?' he enthused. 'A thousand yards, I swear, and straight as a javelin. That's an idea. I'll call her Javelin, if I get her back.'

'A fine bird,' Emma complimented him, though her thoughts were elsewhere.

He noted her distraction, and grinned approval.

'Well, you are giving it the most thorough consideration, I'll say that for you. Have you decided yet?'

'Is the choice mine?' she countered.

'Oh, come! Have I commanded you to marry him?' Richard responded. 'You have a choice, although you know how pleased I will be if you accept.'

'And how angry you will be if I refuse.'

'Now please, Emma, don't make me out to be a bullying big brother. I shan't close my ears to your wishes, you know that. You have always done your duty for Normandy most faithfully, and you could be excused for bowing out gracefully this time – if the prospect was really so repugnant to you.'

Yes, Emma thought, she had always carried out her duties. She'd been bartered about Europe like a prime heifer; first offered to some rough Scandinavian, rejected and sent home in humiliation, only to be married off to the second choice, a single-minded and blundering English king. And, when he had thrown away his kingdom, Emma had been sent home yet again, then widowed. Now she was being put up in the marriage market once more, for another brutish Dane to paw over and bid for. Sometimes it seemed her duties consisted of little more than spreading her legs like a harlot for the gratification of kings. One would have thought that now, at her age, she would have been offered more dignified responsibilities.

Still, she consoled herself, at least she would be able to retain her English position and properties, which were worth a degree of suffering. If she stayed here in Normandy, what would she be? An encumbrance of a sister, an ageing aunt, a testy old widow disregarded by everyone, expected to do nothing more than oversee the making of tapestries and the tending of kitchen gardens.

'I will marry Canute . . .' Emma announced.

'Good girl!' roared Richard.

' . . . if he will renounce that woman Graciousgift, and put her sons out of his will.'

'Denounce his so-called sons as heirs, in favour of any sons you may give him? Of course,' Richard said airily.

'That condition may be more difficult to impose,' Emma warned.

'It can be done. We can get the consent of the Church for that.

Sweyn and Harold are no more than bastards of doubtful parentage. It has been suggested that, not only is the brat Harold no son of Canute's, he's no child of Graciousgift either. They say he was put in her confinement bed to hide the loss of her own child. How can anyone support the case of such mongrel whelps to be Canute's heirs?'

'No. You are right. Any son I bear Canute has to be the next King of England.'

Richard, highly satisfied with the conversation, stopped to find out whether his falcon had been recovered. His idiot servants were still trying to wade across the river, hand in hand, clinging to overhanging branches. The bird would probably have flown by now. Richard determined to keep a tighter leash on his English pets.

'That means you must renounce those sons of Ethelred,' he reminded Emma.

Emma looked to where Edward and Alfred were learning about falconry from their cousins Richard and Robert. The boys were happy here, their mother knew, and had doubtless all but forgotten England. Edward was such a pale and thin child, too, better suited to the warmth of Normandy than to the chill damp of England and happier to wield a scholar's pen than a soldier's sword. Edward would never make a strong ruler, so who else had she to worry about? Her daughter, Godgifu, was playing at making flower chains with Gifta's little daughter Ealdgyth. There was Gifta herself, strolling deep in conversation with the monk Theobald as usual. These girls Emma looked upon only as chattels, like herself, to be married off some day to the best political advantage. She had done her duty by all of them. They were all safe and secure in Normandy. She owed nothing to them, nothing more to the memory of Ethelred.

'The house of Ethelred has fallen,' Emma said. 'The house of Canute is in the building. I can share that house, but they cannot. Their future lies in Normandy, not in England.'

'And if they dispute the succession, later?'

'Then we'll worry about it later.'

'So be it,' consented Richard. 'You've made a wise choice, Emma. I am proud of you. I suggest we send you to Canute at the earliest opportunity, before he finds himself another wench.'

Gifta had been watching the confidential exchange with interest.

'Emma is looking more like a cat than ever today,' Gifta giggled to Theobald. 'But Duke Richard looks cheerful enough. I wonder what they are talking about?'

'Please, Gifta,' Theobald sighed, 'it isn't what they're talking about that's important. It's what we must discuss. Please try to help me.'

Gifta sat down in the shade of a stout Lombardy poplar, and rested her head back in one of its fluted folds. She plucked a long strand of grass and chewed on the stalk, and lazily viewed the broad sweep of the Seine below. The river looked as drowsy as she felt today, too tired to flow along the course it knew it must take.

'I don't know, my dear Theobald,' she sighed. 'What can you do? What can we do? We have been very wicked, and God will probably consign us to Hell. Perhaps I should have entered a nunnery, like poor Wulfhilda.'

'That does not help,' Theobald complained.

'Well, what can I suggest, for Heaven's sake? Either you give up the Cloth, or you don't. It is a matter for your conscience alone.'

'If I do, people will suspect what has happened between us. They will know I have forsaken my vow of celibacy.'

'Then don't.'

'Which means I can never marry you. But if I could marry you, it would at least atone for our sin of adultery.'

'You are the priest,' Gifta said carelessly. 'You tell me which is the greater evil.'

'Oh, dear Lord,' Theobald prayed, 'why did you let me give in to the temptation of the flesh?'

'That does not say much for your love for me.'

'I do love you, Gifta . . .'

'Then do you think you are the only man of the Church ever to couple with a woman? Don't be a fool. Most of them do at some time, I shouldn't wonder.'

'That does not excuse me.'

Gifta was becoming irritable.

'Oh, do what you must!' she told him. 'Go to confession again. Do whatever you have to do. If it troubles you so much, perhaps you should stop making love to me.'

'Would you not care?' asked Theobald, alarmed.

'I care so much, I want you to do it again now,' she teased him. 'Over there, in the trees. Shall we?'

Theobald coloured up and looked around, as though convinced that the whole company around them had heard. He angrily shushed her, and pretended to be thumbing through his prayer book. Her attitude these days worried him. She seemed to be growing ever more indiscreet, more apathetic, but, worst of all, more careless of criticism. It was only he who was taking care to keep their secret. Gifta sometimes behaved as if she did not care who knew, and perhaps she did not.

He could hardly blame her for her loss of sensitivity, he supposed, looking more on the generous side. She had come through so much these last few years, and had kept much of her sorrow bottled up inside, trying not to be constantly miserable in his company.

In quick succession, she had lost her husband, father, brothers and brothers-in-law. She had no idea what had happened to her sister Edith in England, and her younger sister Wulfhilda had been so distressed at the death of Ulfcettel, she had committed herself to spend the rest of her days in a convent. In addition, Gifta's little nephews she had never seen had been exiled to Sweden, and her favourite stepson Gospatrick was a prisoner of Canute, his fate uncertain.

All Gifta had left were her daughter Ealdgyth and her nervous lover, Theobald. Her indifferent manner must be a shield to conceal what were really very deep feelings, Theobald understood, but he did wish that she could afford him a little consideration. He loved her and wanted to do right by her, but could she not see his dilemma? Did she expect him to disregard his vows as though they had never meant anything to him?

Of course other Churchmen took women sometimes, but for many of them it was a momentary lapse of discipline, quickly atoned for and forgotten. Not many of them had to face such a difficult decision as confronted Theobald. It was time to be more firm with her, he realised.

'Gifta!' he whispered harshly, 'don't treat me as nothing more than a sinful diversion, someone to take your resentment out on whenever the world hurts you. If you do, I shall have to go away. I cannot bear to live like this any longer.'

Gifta sat upright, like one arising startled from sleep. Theobald had never spoken to her so sharply before, and she did not know if she was more offended or frightened.

'You make me sound like a whore!' she hissed back. 'How dare you speak to me as if I need nothing but your damned body!'

'Then stop treating me this way. Stop taking me into your bed and sending me away in the morning like . . . like some special kind of servant. Stop talking about my problems as though they are nought but a nuisance you cannot bother yourself with. I am a man. I have a man's feelings. I want to stay with you. Help me to!'

Gifta saw the hurt in his eyes, heard the heartfelt plea in his voice, and softened.

'God forgive me, I've been unfeeling,' she admitted. 'I have been selfish.'

'No, just not concentrating enough on the future, that's all.'

'Is there a future?'

'You still think it impossible for a princess to marry a monk?'

'No, I did not mean that. I meant, is there a future for any of us? Our way of life has gone, so much has changed, forever. I'm confused.'

'But you think you could marry me?' he prompted.

'Must you press me? You seem no surer yourself.'

'But that is what we must discuss. That is what I have been trying to say to you, all day.'

She shook her head in bewilderment and made to get up. He gave her his hand to help her to her feet, and for a brief time it was one of those rare occasions when their fond touch could be in public. They strolled along the edge of the meadow in the quiet, dappled shades, staying beneath the overhanging branches that so closely resembled flimsy curtains; curtains they wished they could pull down to hide their guilt, to protect their privacy while they struggled to know what to do with their lives.

'Once, I hoped that we could go back to England,' Gifta said. 'Now that dream is dead. Perhaps now I can start to think about a different kind of life, instead. Give me time, Theobald. That's all I ask. We will work it all out in time.'

'Perhaps. But time grows short. I'm sure some people suspect us. Your stepmother, particularly. Emma gives me some peculiar looks, sometimes. If your family took it in mind to have us punished, they could ensure the Church did it well. What would they do to me, for ravishing the Princess Aelfgifu, as they would claim? Priests have been tortured to death for less.'

'Please! Don't talk that way. I cannot bear to think of losing you as well. We will go away before there is ever any danger of anything like that.'

'Then it is time to start thinking where to go.'

'We will think,' promised Gifta, but her mind was no longer on their conversation. Her attention had been distracted by the large crowd that had gathered around Emma and Duke Richard, chattering excitedly. There were ripples of applause, and Emma was smiling modestly. The duke had his arm round his sister's waist, and was beaming as if she had done something he could be mightily proud of.

'What is going on?' Gifta asked Theobald. 'Perhaps she flew up and caught a bird, all by herself.'

The crowd drew back, expectantly, as Gifta walked over to Emma, and fell silent as though they sensed that shortly there would be a terrible scene. It was an embarrassing moment, not least for Gifta, who at first could not imagine why so many eyes were suddenly upon her.

'Congratulate me, Aelfgifu,' Emma invited her stepdaughter sweetly. 'I am to be married again.'

'Oh,' Gifta responded icily. 'To whom?'

'I have received a proposal from King Canute. Richard and I have decided it is desirable I should accept.'

'King . . . !'

Words failed Gifta. At once, there raged between them a silent storm, of accusation on the one side, of cool defiance on the other. Gifta's hands were clenched at her sides, but her anger was an invisible dagger that she raised to Emma's heart. Emma was aware of it, and her defence against it was her customary arrogance, her conviction that she was beyond reproach, particularly as far as her insolent little stepdaughter was concerned.

'Don't let us have one of your tantrums, Gifta dear,' she warned. 'It would be most unbecoming.'

'Canute!' Gifta spat out, hardly hearing Emma's rebuke. 'You call that monster king! You're going to marry him!'

'Aelfgifu . . . !'

'I knew you were capable of anything – *anything* – but, dear Mother of Christ – *this*. I would never have believed it, even of you!'

'Silence, girl! If you don't still that poison tongue of yours . . .'

'Are you really telling me that you are going to marry the man who stole your husband's kingdom, broke his heart, murdered his sons? The one who made widows of us all? It's unbelievable!'

'The war is over!' Emma snapped back. 'It's in the past, gone . . .'

'You may think so!'

'Duty does not die. That is the difference between you and me, Aelfgifu. I know my duty when I see it, and I do it, no matter what my feelings . . .'

'Perhaps that's because you have no feelings!'

Emma was about to raise her hand to the girl, but restrained herself in time.

'Think of me what you like,' she said levelly, 'It matters not. I am going to marry Canute. We will all be going home . . .'

'Home? Ha! Speak for yourself, stepmother. Do you think I could go back to the land where my brothers were done away with like common criminals – to be ruled by their murderer? To wonder if every mouthful of food is poisoned? To lie awake at nights, wondering if I was going to be strangled in my bed . . . ?'

'You are a fool, Aelfgifu.'

'. . . And do you think,' Gifta persisted, 'that I would take Ealdgyth back to live among Danes? You must be mad. What of your own children, *Queen* Emma? Will you take them back to that murdering swine you intend to rut with? Or will you leave them here to rot, while you give Canute a new litter of brats?'

Still Emma kept her temper in check, aided by the knowledge that, before all these witnesses, she looked the more dignified. Noticing Theobald, she saw a way to hit back at Gifta.

'Well, we all build new nests, don't we, Aelfgifu?' she sneered, 'however distasteful they may appear to others.'

There was no mistaking the unspoken ultimatum. Stop harassing me, Emma was saying, or I will make public this unsavoury liaison you have with the monk. Gifta knew she should tread more carefully, but she would not be cowed.

'Then go to England and bed your Danish pig,' she muttered. 'And praise God, you'll never interfere with my life again.'

'Agreed, if you will leave me alone.'

'Oh, I shall indeed.'

'Good. Then you will stop urging Robert to take a Norman force to fight Canute, against his father's wishes.'

'Oh yes,' Gifta laughed humourlessly, 'that would worry you now, wouldn't it? It would spoil everything. Well, let me tell you, stepmother – I swore to my father that for as long as I live, if there is anything I can do to injure Canute and his rabble, I shall do it! There is *my* duty!'

It was a declaration of war, and Emma took up the challenge.

'So be it,' she said, turning away. 'But you *are* a fool, Aelfgifu. Choose to draw daggers with me, and you will suffer a thousand cuts before I am done with you.'

Theobald watched Emma go, feeling like the mouse that has been shown the cat's claws, then seen the cat lose interest for a while. His tormentor would return, he feared.

'Lord have mercy on us, she knows' he whined. 'She knows about us, and you have made an enemy of her. We're done for unless we leave here!'

Gifta was keeping a tighter rein on her own fear. She was well aware that she had chosen to fight alone and virtually defenceless against powerful foes, but she had built her confidence up with that plucky argument with Emma, and already she was beginning to map out her own schemes for the future. There would be allies she could find and trust, somewhere. There would be friends who would help her bring down Canute and Emma. The day of reckoning would come, and in her triumph she would spit upon the graves of all those who had so cruelly wronged her and her family.

'All right,' she soothed Theobald, 'we will go away. It does not matter to me any more, where we live. I hate this place and these people. I would live in purgatory to be rid of them.'

They started making inquiries about places where a monk's work might be needed. Theobald used the slow and complicated ecclesiastical channels of communication, but Gifta played the more risky game of trying to sweet-talk her way around a brother of Duke Richard – the Archbishop of Rouen, no less. Theobald had devoted himself to the Church in England most commendably, and since then in her personal service, the princess told the Archbishop, and she wanted to see his conscientious work rewarded with a position where he could serve God as he really desired to. The Archbishop promised to find a suitable post for Theobald. After that, Gifta could only pray that the Archbishop would not mention the matter to Emma.

The weeks passed and Theobald daily grew more anxious. Even when Emma had sailed to England for her marriage to Canute, Theobald continued to worry in case she decided to write home to Duke Richard and reveal all.

Nothing happened, though, as the weeks became months, and soon it was obvious that Emma had plenty else to occupy her mind. Less than a year after her departure, news came that Emma had given Canute a son called Hardicanute, the heir that the Norman court had hoped for. Emma's family in Rouen were too busy with their celebrations to bother with Gifta and Theobald.

So far, Canute had made no proclamation that this latest son would take precedence over Sweyn and Harold, but the Normans were content to wait. There was plenty of time for Emma to use her undoubted powers of persuasion on the king. The one certainty was that Emma would now have ruled Edward and Alfred out of the succession. Young and inexperienced in politics though they were, the boys grasped that much as soon as they heard of the birth of their half-brother in England.

'This means I can never wear my father's crown, doesn't it?' Edward asked Gifta.

'Not unless you fight for it,' Gifta said. 'Make the right friends, people like your cousin Robert. Show them your determination; build up an army, bit by bit, and wait for your day. Show you are a true son of Ethelred, and one day Ethelred's line will be restored.'

'Yes, Gifta, you're right. I will.'

'And I will help you, little brother.'

A few days later, Theobald went to Gifta in a high state of excitement, to tell her that their long search for somewhere to go was over.

'It was your word with the Archbishop that did it!' he babbled. 'I have been appointed to the library at Dinan, in Brittany. It's just what we wanted, somewhere far from Rouen. But that isn't all. There are rooms above the library where we can live, almost completely isolated from the rest of the town. Hardly anyone will know we are there. I have spoken to a very understanding old monk who is responsible for the library. He said just pretend we are brother and sister, and no one will trouble us at all!'

'That's wonderful, Theobald,' Gifta complimented him. 'My, you've been so patient! And to think that we can live in peace now, away from here!' She threw her arms around him and kissed him, adding: 'Yes, it's wonderful. How soon can we go?'

'I am leaving at once, to get things ready. I want it to be a home for you and Ealdgyth, when you get there.' Then, looking around at the grandeur of Duke Richard's castle, he said: 'Oh, Gifta, my love, it will be nothing like the palaces you have known all your life . . .'

'That's just what I shall love about it,' she laughed. 'Yes, go as soon as you're ready. We'll come immediately.'

Before setting out on her long journey to Brittany, Gifta went to see Edward, Alfred and Godgifu. She found herself growing more fond of them since Emma had gone away, and now that they were growing up she realised that they could be useful allies in the battles that still lay ahead.

'Never forget, any of you,' she told them, 'that Canute is our enemy. His father murdered our father as surely as if he had held the knife himself. The Danes murdered my husband and brothers and robbed us all of our homes and our country. One day we will have our revenge. I will write to you regularly. Will you promise to write back, and let me know all that happens here?'

Like Gifta, the children had said too many goodbyes over the years to be affected by one more. Gifta did not mind that they were not grieved at her going. Her chief concern was that she should not lose touch with the politics of the Norman court, and through them the latest developments in England and the rest of Europe. She had no intention of cutting herself off from events to come. In her half-brothers and half-sister, the children of Emma, she had the perfect spies close at hand.

XI

I T had been a long and exhausting journey from England, across tempestuous seas, then through the sleet-blown flats of Denmark. Canute had not seen his homeland for years, but this was no sentimental journey. He had been brought hurrying back here by a rebellion led by none other than his brother-in-law Ulf, and in his heart there was room only for revenge.

He rode like a man possessed, in defiance of fatigue, uncaring of the screaming gale that blew out his useless cloak behind him, as violently as it shredded the clouds across the sky. With him rode an army of Englishmen and Danes come to fight side by side against Danes and Norwegians. At Canute's left hand was the English Earl Godwin, leading his fyrdmen of Wessex through a country as distant and strange to them as the moon. At Canute's right rode his demon shadow, Olaf Ericsson, the Hawk of Hjorring, leading a body of Norsemen who had almost forgotten this land of theirs. Together they travelled in the teeth of the white-specked wind, fierce and grim of countenance, to face enemies who had once been friends.

The old hall of the Danish kings loomed up before them, a great and ugly pile of tight-knit timber, dark, ancient and weather-beaten, its beams leaning in one upon the other like stout old warriors tired of battle and resting against each other's shoulders. It was warm and welcoming and held the promise of safety within its ring of spear-like stakes.

Canute swung down from the saddle as his horse slowed down. The stable hands were slow to come out into the storm and when the first of them appeared, an old man and a young boy, they felt the full force of the king's fury. Canute grabbed the boy by the front of his coat and pushed him back, slamming him hard into the old man's chest. Both fell into the mud, and Canute kicked at them to be up.

'Move yourselves, damn you!' he raged. 'My horse is not a worthless dog, to be left out in this weather!'

The King stamped into the hall, followed by Godwin and Olaf. His sister Estrith and his sons Sweyn and Harold were there to greet him, but he strode straight to the fire, brushing at the freezing wet on his clothes. When servants brought meat and wine, Godwin and Olaf snatched at them hungrily; Canute shoved aside the platter of food and took only a silver goblet, from which he drank rapidly. Then he turned upon Estrith.

'So, where is this cursed husband of yours?' he demanded.

Estrith remained calm.

'In Zealand, the last I heard,' she answered. 'Camped close to his longships, ready to come to the mainland.'

'How many men?'

'A good four thousand.'

'Ha! They'd better be good! I've got three thousand who are better, and I'll have more tomorrow. But what in the name of God is he up to, Estrith? Why has he done this?'

'If I told you,' Estrith said, 'I expect you'd hit me.'

'I shall hit someone before this day is out, if anyone else hinders me. Answer me, woman!'

'Ulf thinks he is the most poorly rewarded of all who helped you take England . . .'

'He thinks what?'

' . . . He says you have overlooked him, shut him away here like an outcast, while others enjoy their English spoils.'

'Shut him away?' echoed Canute, incredulous. 'I give Denmark into your care, and he calls that shut away? Has the man forgotten the gold I near drowned him with? What in the name of Christ does he want?'

'He wants to rule Denmark in his own right. He says England is enough for you and your sons. He wants Denmark for himself, but more, for Sweyn, Osborn and Bjorn when he is dead. Ulf believes our sons have more right to the Danish kingdom than yours.'

Canute eyed his sister meanly.

'And do you believe that, too?' he asked her.

Estrith lost her temper. She could be as fiery as her brother when provoked and for a moment the impetuous offspring of the pirate Forkbeard squared up to each other like angry, spitting cats.

'How dare you accuse me!' she cried. 'Have I ever deceived you? I am the one who called you from England. And how many times have I warned you about Ulf's ambitions? Yet you insist on heaping responsibilities on him that only make him greedy for more! *You* put Denmark in his hands, not I!'

'I thought you had the strength to restrain him!' Canute roared back. 'All right, if I even suggested I couldn't trust you, I'm sorry, but I expected you to know better than to let him draw his knife at my back!'

'What should I have done?' Estrith mocked him. 'Knock him down? Chain him? Cut off his head while he slept?'

Canute hurled his goblet to the floor, and kicked it into a corner. He slumped into a tall chair, and stared sullenly into the fire. He was tired of war, and it showed. He had been content to build up his rich English kingdom to his liking, with new ways of government, new laws; this rebellion of Ulf's in the old land was more than a betrayal and an insult, it was an intolerable disruption of the life Canute had made for himself.

'I must make a widow of you, Estrith,' he sighed. 'I must make your sons fatherless. Godwin, the man is brother-in-law to both of us; we have to kill him, you and I.'

Estrith was resigned, in the manner of war-hardened Viking women who bore, lay with and buried a warrior breed, with a sad but sure acceptance of fate. Such women heard a war-cry in the first wailing of a boy child, felt a suckling son pawing at the breast as if grasping for a sword.

'I must lose either husband or brother,' Estrith answered. 'Don't you think I thought of that, when I sent word to England?'

Canute took her hand.

'I asked too much of you,' he admitted. 'It's work enough for a man, running this country. No woman should be asked to do it.' Looking at his eldest son, he added: 'I would have been as wise to put Denmark in the care of young Sweyn. The question is, what do I do with it now?'

'I have no idea,' Estrith sighed.

'Perhaps Godwin can advise me?'

Godwin, the Danes' Englishman, stepped out of the shadows like a great bear lazily ambling out of the woods at the call of spring. He was a large-built young man, slow of movement but vigorous of mind, and quick to sieze an opportunity. No one knew yet the qualities that had brought Godwin to the top, so fast had been his rise. Even Canute knew little more than that his Earl of Wessex was of humble origin, the son of a tenant farmer, but a man who had soon proved he was a capable military commander with a crisp understanding of politics. Loyalty was not a word Godwin would have used to describe his attachment to the king. He served the strongest, because it was unrewarding to support the weak. Sentiment played no part in his designs. Unlike others of his countrymen, Godwin had not switched from side to side during the wars. He had been Canute's man from the first, because Canute had been quite clearly the most purposeful and the man most likely to succeed. Godwin had become a Dane as easily as he changed his shirt, and with no greater pull of conscience. He looked and behaved like a Dane. He wore his hair in the old Viking way, parted in the middle and falling in two long plaits to his chest, and his long, fair moustaches drooped below his sturdy chin. He decorated himself elaborately with tattoos, gold bracelets and torque, jewelled clasps and buckles. A huge bearskin cloak hung to the ground from the broad sweep of his shoulders.

'A man's best friends are his blood-kin,' Godwin told Canute. 'He should trust them above all others. They will draw strength from his trust. I think you can do no better than to make Sweyn your vassal king, with Estrith to help him as regent. No one will serve you better than they.'

'Thank you,' Canute said simply, and to Estrith he said: 'So, sister; will you do this thing for me?'

'I will try to contain these hot-blooded people of ours for as long as you ask me to,' Estrith said. 'But I think it would help to have Sweyn as a figurehead. Ulf is no-one. Give them your son as their King, and it may be better here. One of the chief troubles is this; there has been a feeling among the people of Denmark that they are leaderless.'

Canute pushed himself up from the chair.

'Then let us show them they are not,' he said. 'Let us show them that, though I may be in England, I still have eyes and heart in Denmark.' He turned to Olaf Ericsson, the Hawk of Hjorring, or as lesser men had named him, the Devil's axeman. 'How many of the best men can you find me,' the king asked him, 'ready to travel at once?'

'Tell me a number, and they will be brought here,' answered Olaf, smiling his cold, cruel smile. 'I will drag them from their beds and their women, if need be.'

'Get me a thousand then,' Canute ordered. 'Let me be at least as strong in numbers as Ulf. That is all I need to deal with him.'

There was one more question Estrith had to ask Canute, although the time was not well chosen.

'Canute, one more thing . . .'

'Yes?'

'Hardicanute . . .'

'What of him?'

Estrith beckoned to a servant to take Sweyn and Harold out of hearing distance, before continuing:

'They are saying he will succeed you.'

'Are they?' Canute responded coolly. 'And how do they know, before I myself have decided? Why does it concern you, Estrith?'

'It does not concern me, but you know the Danes. They are

grumbling here that it would be unfair to Sweyn and Harold, the only sons of yours they know.'

'They must grumble on then,' Canute shrugged. 'When the day comes, I will tell them the name of my successor. And by God, they will accept him, whatever his name.'

Canute set out with his army the next day and travelled to the east coast, where he gathered a fleet. He crossed into Zealand by night in the hope of surprising the rebels, but Ulf was warned of his approach and escaped to the north.

Ulf deliberately avoided a meeting with his king, and instead raided the villages along the shores of Zealand and the mainland, killing, looting and burning, trying to force as many Danes to his side as he was able to reach before the inevitable clash of the two armies. Finally, Ulf fled with his forces into Sweden.

Once more Canute pursued his former friend across land and sea, and this time caught up with him on the broad, sloping plains near Skene. Here, on a calm morning in summer, they faced each other from opposite ridge tops, with nothing more than a narrow brook to separate their apprehensive forces.

The sun struck gold and crimson fire from eight thousand shields, set patterns of silver and bronze dancing through coats of chain-mail and iron-studded leather, and flashed upon a host of spears. The lovely valley was carpeted with white and yellow flowers, and many of the men turned their faces to the sun, feeling that it was the last warmth they would know, and heard the untroubled song of the skylark.

'Ulf looks unhappy,' observed Godwin, shading his eyes against the glare. 'Maybe he regrets coming against you now.'

'It's too late for regrets,' Canute murmured.

'All the same,' said Olaf Ericsson, 'it looks as if he's sending out his emissaries.'

It was true. Two of Ulf's noble followers had stepped out hesitantly from the ranks and were walking down into the valley. They came self-consciously, like boys who knew they had done wrong but were pretending it was all an innocent mistake. Their uneasy looks started a sardonic chuckle in Canute's throat.

'If they come to beg, I have no time for them,' said the king. 'If they come to threaten, they'd as well save their breath. Go and meet them, Olaf. Give them my answer before they put the question.'

Olaf roared his delight, and pushed a pathway through his men eager to be at the foe. Mighty and frightening in both appearance and reputation, he had only to be seen by Ulf's army for them to realise there was no mercy in Canute's heart. He went down from the ridge strutting like an eagle, slowly, firm-footed, teeth bared in a ghastly grin and eyes glaring out malevolently from under his hawk's-head helmet. His great axe he swung straight-armed, forward and down, up and back, from side to side in powerful strokes, its blade humming, beating through the air like eagles' wings. Terrifying, Olaf advanced directly upon Ulf's messengers, and they stopped in mid-stride at the sight of him.

'I am Olaf Ericsson,' the great warrior boasted. 'The first I killed with this axe was the famous English warrior Earl Uhtred of Northumbria. At Ashingdon I slew fifteen men with as many blows. I am a Hawk of Hjorring, and I can lay low any man here. I am better than any fifteen of you, and you send out two? What have you to say to me, miserable fleas from the treacherous dog Ulf?'

Whatever Ulf's emissaries had to say was never heard, for as the two men backed away, hands raised in appeal, their voices were drowned by the mocking laughter of Canute's soldiers. Olaf, now at the foot of the hill, joyfully turned and waved the axe at his men.

'Follow a Hawk of Hjorring!' he bellowed, and made for the enemy lines without waiting to see them respond to his cry.

The two armies rushed down to meet at the stream, and Danes, English, Swedes and Norwegians were thrown together in bloody battle. Axes and swords clashed on shields and helmets, and thousands upon thousands of shouting men met and tangled themselves in ash pole and blade, pushing, pressing, yielding, striking out like maddened beasts. The narrow vale echoed to the beating and clanging of steel and leather, the yells of the blood-maddened and the screams of the dying. One whole army forced itself foot by foot through the other, broken yet relentless, like persistent waves around moving stones. Then those who had given way summoned up new strength, re-formed, and heaved back. The flowers and the grass were crushed into mud, and the brook ran crimson as the corpses piled up along the marshy banks. The conflict swayed first one way through the valley and then the other, leaving in its wake an awful mess of begging, wounded and formless dead, discarded shield and shattered shaft, shapeless helmet and mangled limbs. The sun ascended and descended through its broad arc unheeded, and when shadow dulled the hills ready for night, three thousand men lay blind in death's eternal dark.

Still the fighting raged, with Ulf's two thousand survivors struggling in untidy clumps up and down the valley, desperate not to be surrounded and overwhelmed by Canute's now-greater numbers. The shouts of the triumphant grew more hoarse, the wailing of the weak more pitiful, the strokes of sword and axe

111

more weary, and the steps of exhausted warriors less steady, in the ghostly dusk. At last night called an end to this short but bitter war.

There had fallen Thored Widepaunch, his notorious great belly slashed wide open by a fellow Dane's axe. There died Thorkel One-Eye, his famous half-sighted face crushed by a heavy blow from a sword. There, almost sunk from sight in a morass of other men's blood, was Einar the Jester, his merry tongue silenced forever, and near to him lay Eric Longaxe, father of Olaf. Among three hundred English dead was Cedric, younger son of the Shire-Reeve of Berkshire and husband of Constance, waiting-woman to the exiled Princess Aelfgifu. To Cedric's weeping brother Oswald would fall the task of telling the widow and her son that Cedric was buried in a faraway land called Sweden.

Ulf was brought out from among the rebel prisoners to face Canute, his hands lashed before him. The earl stood with his head slightly lowered in the flickering flamelight, within smelling distance of the slaughtered.

'You cause me great grief, Ulf,' said Canute, shaking his head at the waste. 'I never thought we would meet like this.'

'It might have been a happier meeting for me, too,' argued Ulf, 'if you'd listened to my messengers.'

'You thought to make your own terms?'

'Well, call them suggestions. Whatever name you give them, they might have helped avoid all this bloodshed.'

'Tell me of them now.'

'Why? The damage has been done.'

'Tell me anyway.'

'I had thought we might come to an agreement,' said Ulf, the faintest renewal of hope in his eyes. 'My messengers were first to beg your pardon on my behalf, for presuming to oppose you. That much still stands. Then they were to ask, if there was any hope that we could make peace, and . . .'

'And?'

' . . . And perhaps look again at the distribution of power in Denmark . . .'

'Aha. And what had you in mind?'

'I have been little else but henchman to my wife,' complained Ulf. 'I deserved more honour. A man cannot control a nation when he is nought but a woman's shadow.'

'So you wanted to be king?'

'I would not have called it that. Regent, perhaps. It was Estrith I wanted to rise above, not you. I only wanted all Danes to know that here, at least, I was second only to Canute.'

'That is not quite what I heard from Estrith,' said Canute. 'She told me you wanted a crown, not only for yourself, but also for your sons rather than mine. To me that sounds like a kingship, a new line.'

'By all the gods, how can a woman betray her husband so?' he protested, with a commendable show of hurt. 'I swear that is not so. I have always served you faithfully, my Lord King. I will again, if you offer me the chance.'

Canute slowly shook his head.

'I could never trust you again, Ulf.'

Ulf shivered, and his eyes dulled. He knew from long experience how Canute dealt with those whom he would not trust.

'I made a mistake,' he tried. 'All these years we have been friends, fellow warriors. I am married to your sister. Does all that mean nothing to you? One mistake!'

'A costly mistake,' came the pitiless answer. 'A thousand of my warriors are dead out there; scores more are crippled. I came here to kill you. What you have done today can hardly persuade me to mercy.'

'It was your battle, not mine.'

'But it was your rebellion.'

Ulf shrugged. He had done with pleading, and he refused to die like a coward.

'Kill me then,' he said. 'Don't leave me standing here hoping any longer. Grant me one favour, though . . . ?'

'What is that?'

'Will you tell my sons that I died as a warrior should – bravely?'

'Yes, that is only the truth,' Canute nodded. 'It's a small enough thing to do for my own nephews. But I will not allow more memory of you than that. From this day your sons will be called Estrithsson after their mother. Not Ulfsson.'

'Ah, you punish severely indeed,' Ulf groaned. 'To wipe out an enemy is one thing; but to wipe out his name! How you must hate me!'

'There can be no greater hate than for a friend turned foe,' Canute said. 'The hate is not of my making. I gave you my sister in marriage. I gave you wealth and power. But most of all I gave you my trust. All this you threw back in my face. Could I still love you as a friend after that?'

Ulf nodded acceptance of Canute's words. There was nothing more to say. His misting gaze sought out Earl Godwin.

'Does my sister know why you came to Denmark?' he asked.

'She does,' Godwin confirmed.

'Poor Gytha,' Ulf sighed. 'Another woman split between husband and brother. Tell her I asked her forgiveness, will you?'

'I will,' Godwin promised, 'and I think she will forgive you. She almost convinced me this must all be a foolish misunderstanding, such is her love for you.'

Ulf gave him a small smile of thanks, but it was matched by a scowl from Canute, who wanted no more delay. The King beckoned to Olaf Ericsson, and the axeman promptly stepped forward.

'Behead him,' Canute ordered, with an almost inaudible catch in his voice.

Olaf felt no pity for Ulf. He had seen his father killed this day, and no revenge could be sweet enough to atone for the death of the only man he had ever respected or loved.

'Let us see if his head falls as easily as his kingdom,' Olaf laughed viciously. 'Make him kneel.'

Two men forced Ulf to his knees, and a third took him by the hair and exposed his neck to Olaf's blade.

Olaf made his aim, and raised the axe high. Canute's hand jerked slightly at his side then, as if he was about to stay the sentence, but it was as soon still again.

'God, what a cursed people are the Danes . . .'came the muffled last words of Earl Ulf.

Olaf swung the axe in a perfect flashing crescent of silver, and one sickening thud saw the work completed. A gasp of admiration and approval soughed through the assembled host as the bloody trophy was lifted up.

'Here's Earl Ulf,' announced Olaf, walking it through the throng. 'Anyone feel like rebelling now?'

Canute was silent for a long time after the death of Ulf. His face was impassive while he sat probing the depths of the fire with almost unblinking gaze, but plainly he was disturbed. Eventually he brought his head up in a sudden, small movement, as if coming out of a waking dream.

'Your men fought well for me today,' he praised Godwin. 'For the first time in all these years, I felt I was really King of the English.'

'King of the English you are, my Lord,' Godwin smiled. 'None of us doubts it.'

'Is it not strange,' Canute mused, 'that a man should find friends so far from home, and at home find that his friends have become enemies. Tell me, then, how is it that men whose land I have conquered can be so loyal to me, and a Dane whom I raised up from nothing be so false?'

Godwin thought about it for a while.

'Loyalty is to the man, not the land,' he said. 'A man may love the land he lives in, but he must have respect for other men. Take me, for instance. I know that Northumbrians are Englishmen, just as I am. But I know no more about Northumbrians than I know about Norwegians, or Swedes. Why should I favour Northumbrians above the Danes I live with?'

Canute recognised the truth of those words, but still he looked worried.

'So,' he said, 'can I not hope to hold on to two lands, so far apart?'

'Perhaps you can, if you choose your counsels carefully. Ethelred's kingdom fell not because he himself was weak – he was not – but because he was incapable of distinguishing between wise man and fool, loyal man and traitor. You are a better judge of men. With Ulf you were merely unlucky. Why, you've done more to knit the English together and earn their respect than Ethelred achieved in nearly forty years. Choose the right man here in Denmark, and I believe you can hold both countries.'

'Thank you. It is not easy to see deep into a man, is it?'

'A man like Ulf, no.'

'Nor a man like you, come to that.'

Godwin looked up quickly to see if the king was suggesting he might turn out to be treacherous, too, but Canute was studying him quite openly, with a measure of curiosity.

'You are a remarkable man, Godwin,' Canute told him. 'You are a natural leader yourself, yet you reach no higher than you think you should hold. You are ambitious, yet you know just how much to take and where to stop. I wonder, what drives you?'

Godwin grinned. They were two shrewd men together, and heedful of it. They were both born masters of men, thankfully with a common cause. Godwin was content to take second place, and as long as he remembered it and Canute knew it, they would get along nicely. In those last words of Canute, Godwin heard the gentle reminder of the commander saying to the liegeman: 'I like you because you do not over-reach yourself, so let us hope it always stays that way.' Godwin was intelligent enough, too, to know when his advice began to border on the presumptuous, when his praise was turning to idle flattery, and such had been the case tonight. Not for the first time, Godwin pulled back comfortably before the brink.

'Reward, simply,' he answered unashamedly. 'But I respect strength and loyalty too. I think of it like this. To get reward, you must first have a master. To get good reward, you must have a strong master, and to be sure of continuing reward you must help make him stronger yet. That's wisdom, I would submit, rather than ambition.'

'I see,' Canute laughed. 'To the leader goes the labour. The second-in-command gets the spoils!'

'Something like that,' Godwin confirmed.

'You are honest, too.'

'It pays, when one's master is not a fool.'

'No, I am not a fool. Perhaps I was where Ulf was concerned, but never again. Does it not frighten you, Godwin, that I shall now test every blade I use – every day of its life?'

'No,' said Godwin unhesitatingly. 'I am no fool either. I shall not be found wanting. And you will be sure of me.'

Both men went home happier for each other's words.

Canute took Godwin's counsel, and made his son Sweyn King of Denmark, as his vassal, under the regency of Estrith. On his return to England he explained to Emma that it was unlikely that their son Hardicanute would succeed him, if Sweyn carried out his duties in Denmark satisfactorily. Emma paid suitable lip-service to Canute's wishes, but secretly promised herself the succession would be open to change when the time came.

Godwin, meanwhile, rejoined Gytha and his family confident that he had consolidated his position as the second most powerful man in England. He was well aware that Queen Emma viewed him with distrust, and he knew she was a force to be reckoned with, but he was certain that he and Canute together were cunning enough to foil any of her devious plotting on behalf of her Norman kin.

XII

EMMA needed new allies in England if she was to prepare the way for Hardicanute. Canute still had ambitions for his sons in Denmark, and set at nought the pact which had led him to marry into the Norman ducal family, so that Emma's persuasions fell on deaf ears. Where the building of the empire was concerned, Canute gave most attention to the counsel of the crafty Earl Godwin, who believed in the supremacy of the Danes.

Baulked of her ambition, Emma fell prey to fears for the future which were heightened by the death of her brother, Duke Richard II. He had been a tower of strength to her, and for a time the loss of him looked like a death blow to her plans. Nevertheless, as soon as her elder nephew took over in Normandy as Richard III, Emma petitioned him to maintain close diplomatic ties with Canute and to champion Hardicanute's cause, as his father had done.

But the younger Richard's reign was short-lived. He died within a year, and it was strongly rumoured throughout Europe that he had been poisoned by his brother, the energetic and impulsive Robert. Whether or not that accusation was justified, Duke Robert of Normandy soon gained the reputation of being an adventurous ruler, and an immoral one.

Robert the Devil, as he came to be called, set about a policy of expansion. Between lusty forays in the beds of his several mistresses, among whom was the tanner's daughter Herleva who gave him a bastard son called William, Robert eagerly went to war with numerous rivals, and became a feared soldier. His greatest triumph was to convince Henry of France, both by force of arms and strength of will, that he, Duke Robert, should have dominion over the territory of the Vexin.

The Norman realm was growing profitably, and Emma began to see in her bold nephew Robert a potentially more useful helpmate than even her brother had been. Excited ambassadors and messengers scurried between England and Normandy. Emma gave Robert her blessing, and pledged him her whole-hearted support in all he did. She also gave her daughter Godgifu in marriage to Count Drogo of the Vexin, thus helping to set the seal on Norman interest in that region.

Duke Robert appreciated his Aunt Emma's efforts, but made it plain to her that Edward and Alfred were still his favoured cousins. They, not little Hardicanute, were his choice to rule England. They would have plenty to remember him for, plenty to thank him for, if ever they were in a position to hand out favours; Hardicanute would not.

Emma was disappointed once more. Hardicanute was the bright light in her firmament; the sons she'd had by Ethelred were mere memories. It was difficult enough to arouse Canute's interest in his own youngest son; it would be impossible, she knew, to talk him into accepting Edward or Alfred, children of the hated Ethelred, rather than his own Danish sons, Sweyn and Harold.

Yes, she needed friends, but was hard-pressed to know where to look for them. Then, as she awoke one morning, inspiration came to her. Emma remembered her stepdaughter Aelfgifu.

Gifta was an unlikely conspirator at first sight, after all their mutual distrust and dislike, but Emma knew herself to be artful enough to persuade her stepdaughter into a new, useful relationship. Gifta was still quite close to Edward and Alfred, and therefore had access to Duke Robert. And then there were Gifta's stepsons in England, Gospatrick and Eadwulf, who still had many old family friends and allies among the thanes of the North. If they could be persuaded to forget old differences, she had something to offer all of them. There was not the least reason at present to suppose that any of these people would lend their weight to Emma's efforts to have Hardicanute made heir to the throne, but Emma was not, this time, thinking along logically straight lines. Her ideas, however, were slowly hardening into possibilities. She alone had the reasons and the authority to bring Gifta back to England with all the honours due to her, if she wanted to come. To Gospatrick and Eadwulf could be restored some of the northern possessions stolen from their father, and that in turn would give them more of a voice in the Witan.

Likely ally or not, Gifta held the keys to some useful doors, Emma realised. With ideas yet half-formed in her mind, she invited Gospatrick to the palace in Northampton.

Gospatrick, deeply suspicious of his stepmother's stepmother, at first considered ignoring the invitation altogether. To one who had lost both father and eldest brother as a result of treacherous hospitality, it seemed foolish to go. On the other hand what had she to gain by drawing him into a trap? His small properties would not yield a decent day's boar hunt for the likes of Canute or Emma. He was involved in no politics, and indeed had done nothing of note since being released from Canute's custody, many years before.

Still wary, Gospatrick arrived at the palace and was taken before the awesome woman he had not seen since Ethelred's family had fled to Normandy in the bitter winter of 1013.

'You asked permission to leave England, to visit your stepmother,' Emma reminded him.

'Yes,' Gospatrick confirmed. 'That was many years ago.'

'Well, now you may go,' the Queen said expansively. 'I put your case to the king, and he agreed. I pointed out that you'd never been any trouble to him.'

Gospatrick did not know what to say, or even what to feel. It was fourteen years since he had seen Gifta. He had been a boy of eleven, she a girl of seventeen. He had long ago given up hope of ever seeing her again, and he wondered whether he really wanted to. Would they have anything in common, after fourteen years? Or would it be just an embarrassment to them both, stirring up unhappy memories for no better reason than curiosity? There had been a time when this offer of Emma's would have had him leaping for joy. Today it brought a sadness, as would a reminder of an old bereavement one had tried to forget. That former life was gone, buried; it had died the day Earl Uhtred stepped into his friend's hall to be cut down by Olaf's axe. He had a new life in Northumbria now. He had a wife and a son, to whom all his affections had been transferred these last few years. Besides, he sensed that some cunning lurked behind Emma's change of heart, and her purpose worried him. She had never before shown any consideration for Gifta, and certainly none for him.

'You don't seem very pleased,' said Emma.

'Your pardon, my lady. It is . . . a surprise.'

'Of course. Anyway, you can go if you like.'

'Thank you. I am most grateful.'

'You will, of course, convey my affectionate greetings to my stepdaughter. It's so long since I've seen her. Though not nearly so long as you've waited. It would be nice to have some of the family back together again, would it not? Tell Princess Aelfgifu this from me – it is no longer unsafe for her to come home to England, if she wants to. The fighting was all over long ago. My husband mellows as he grows older. He is no longer the impetuous young warrior who executed her brothers, or sent her nephews away to Sweden. His worst instincts burned out a long time ago. So, you can tell her . . . what a wise ruler he has become.'

'You want her to come back?' Gospatrick asked carefully, wary of the unusual frankness of Emma's conversation.

'It is true,' Emma said coolly, 'that we did not exactly get along with each other in those early days, but that's all in the past now.

119

I will be honest with you, Gospatrick. I miss my family very much. Edward, Alfred . . . I feel that if your stepmother were to come home and see for herself that all is settled and calm here now – no danger any more – then in time my dear sons might also feel safe, and come back. Now do you understand?'

Gospatrick's fears had not been allayed. He thought this might be some kind of trap for Gifta, not for him, and he did not intend to be the bait. However, it would be a bold man who dared be too blunt with Queen Emma when she was in this mood of feigned magnanimity. He decided to find out a little more, and said, in an easy conversational tone, 'I must say it surprises me that King Canute would tolerate the return of any of Ethelred's family. But then, as you say, he has become a very wise ruler. He demonstrated as much when he sat on the shore and showed his courtiers that not even he could hold back the tide.'

Emma had always felt that Canute had made himself ridiculous that day, and that altogether too much importance had been attached to this so-called display of sagacity.

'Gospatrick,' she snapped, 'I know very well when someone is being facetious with me.'

'Forgive me lady; I did not mean to be.'

'Canute has nothing to fear from a daughter of Ethelred. As for my sons, they have already accepted that their half-brother Hardicanute has gone ahead of them in the line of succession. Canute knows he need not fear them, either. He is a generous man, Gospatrick, as well as a wise one. He regrets destroying so much of Ethelred's great family – he always did. Having Ethelred's daughter and sons back in England will help make up for that, he feels.'

'Are you saying, then, that it is at King Canute's own wish I can ask Gifta to return?'

'The invitation is mine, with Canute's approval. That is enough.'

'Again, I apologise.'

'Learn some diplomacy, Gospatrick. Perhaps you will not have to apologise so often. Well, will you go to Brittany or not?'

'Yes, I will go.'

'Good. On your way through Normandy, you can personally deliver a letter to Duke Robert for me.'

'I will.'

'Oh, and one other thing – my advice to Aelfgifu if she does decide to come back is to leave behind that monk of hers. Will you tell her that?'

That angered Gospatrick. He knew all about Theobald, for Gifta had confided in him long ago, writing of her loneliness and grief, her need for someone to turn to, her guilt and agonising over the sin of it. She had begged Gospatrick to forgive her for replacing his father with someone else. Gospatrick had done so, realising that she had to make a new life, just as he had. What right, he thought, had this evil woman to sit in judgement on Gifta, when she herself had married the murderer of her husband?

'That monk,' he said, with unmasked disdain, 'was all Gifta had, after the Danes had finished their slaughter of her family. I don't suppose she will leave him behind. She is too loyal.'

'Dear God, you say that as if you accuse me of disloyalty. You not only lack diplomacy, you're an insolent fool. I could have you flogged within an inch of death, if the mood took me. Get out of here. Go to Brittany, deliver your messages. And Gospatrick, when you come home, with or without Aelfgifu . . .'

'Yes, my lady?'

' . . . guard your tongue more closely. Your poor stepmother has suffered so many losses over the years.'

XIII

GOSPATRICK reached the valley of the Rance on a scorching afternoon in July. He stood with his horses, staring across the river at the town of Dinan, he studied the tall, dominating timber fort on its grassy knoll, and watched the handful of Breton soldiers who lazily walked its ramparts. He picked out each little house of wood and stone, and thought that the occupants must be dozing away the day, so silent were they. A few peasant cottages were almost concealed on the wooded slopes, and below the narrow, stout-beamed bridge some fishermen were preparing their nets.

The church stood a short way up the hill, near the fort, and Gospatrick knew that Gifta would be somewhere in the untidy clutter of timber outbuildings behind it. They were just like the old barns at the back of his father's hall in York.

What a place for an English princess to live in, he thought. Could she really be happy here, as she had told him in her letters? Gospatrick had always had doubts about making this journey and now it occurred to him more strongly than ever that the woman he was about to see might be a total stranger, a tired old housewife, a mockery of the pretty, lively young stepmother he remembered.

'Oh God,' Gospatrick prayed, 'we have lost so much. Please grant that our memories shall not be destroyed, too!'

He crossed over the bridge and went into the town. The children soon noticed the curious Englishman, and ran on ahead of him, shouting. He was only half-way up the hill when he saw a woman, a monk and a young girl coming to meet him.

He stopped and they stopped, staring at each other the length of the dusty street, viewed by an interested gaggle of townsfolk, who had appeared from nowhere. Gospatrick recognised Gifta at once, and felt his heart leap; the years had not been cruel to her. Certainly she was a little fuller in the cheeks and a shade rounder at the chin, and there were lines in her face where none had a right to be, but it was his Gifta right enough. He had only to look into those deep, feeling eyes of hers to be sure. Age had done nothing to dim the beauty nor cool the warmth there, and he thought that even if he could see nothing but those eyes, he could still have picked her out in a crowd.

'Gospatrick!' she called, 'it is you!'

Gospatrick forgot instantly that he had ever had doubts about coming here. Gifta came to him with arms outstretched, and he met her with a passionate hug. They stood for some time like that, speaking their thoughts and their pleasure only in sighs and tiny laughs and tears and kisses. The warm-hearted Bretons applauded them, but they were hardly aware of it. When eventually they eased away from each other, Gospatrick turned his attention to the slender girl of fourteen. To him, she was more than just a pretty child. She was the very image of Gifta in her youth, a living memory.

'Is this my little sister?'

'Yes, this is Ealdgyth.'

Gospatrick put out his hand smiling, and the child took it with an endearing shyness.

'Ealdgyth,' Gospatrick said, lightly kissing her forehead, 'how lovely you are. What a pity I had to wait so long to see for myself.'

Ealdgyth was overcome with embarrassment. Gospatrick, seeing her blush to the roots of her golden hair, left her alone. He noticed the monk Theobald as though for the first time. Towards this man he still felt a sort of curiosity. He would not begrudge Gifta her need for love, yet he could not help feeling resentful that this tainted priest had moved into his father's bed.

'We met once,' Gospatrick politely acknowledged. 'On the night you left England with Gifta.'

'We did, sir,' Theobald nodded, as wary of Gospatrick as Gospatrick was suspicious of him. 'I am honoured to meet you again.'

Gifta was quick to see that it would take time for the two men to trust each other. She moved in and took Gospatrick's arm.

'Good Lord, how you've changed,' she told him. 'From a boy into a tall, handsome young man. Oh, my darling Goose! There's so much to talk about, but all I can do is cry!'

'Cry?' Gospatrick laughed, 'No, the time for crying is long past. It's time we had some merriment in our lives! Look, are we to stand in the middle of the town blubbering at each other, or are you going to invite me home for supper?'

'Of course. You must be starving, and tired. We'll feed you full, and talk until you fall asleep.'

Gospatrick walked through the town like a conquering hero, with Gifta on one arm and Ealdgyth on the other. Theobald discreetly walked behind leading the horses.

'Have you been well?' Gifta chattered. 'Are your family well? You told me you've a wife and son. What is your boy like? Does he take after you?'

He chuckled at the hail of questions, and sought to slip in an answer or two.

'Yes, yes, we are all in fine health. And Eadwulf does look a little like me, I suppose. He's a splendid lad; full of mischief, as boys are . . .'

'How lovely. I'm so glad you've found happiness at last. You deserve it so much.'

'Not as much as you do,' responded Gospatrick, and restrained himself from glancing back at Theobald as he inquired: 'And what about you? Are you happy here?'

Gifta was no longer sure about that herself. She did not often think about it any more.

'Reasonably,' she affirmed, quietly, so that Theobald would not hear. 'Yes, I suppose that is the right word for it. We make the best of what we have. And, thank God, I have Ealdgyth and Theobald. And now, you again!'

'But you would still like to come back to England?' Gospatrick prompted her.

'I don't know. I honestly don't know any more.'

'I have a letter for you from Emma. In it she invites you back.'

'Goose, what is she up to? Why should she want me back?'

'I'm not sure. I've thought about it a lot, these last few months. She may really want you to go home. She is short of friends, that is certain. Canute does not take enough notice of her wishes. She's not as powerful as she thought she was going to be when she married him. They say Canute has now practically discarded Hardicanute as a likely heir.'

'But how on earth does she think I could help her?'

'Who on earth knows what that woman thinks? I'd like to see you back in England, Gifta, but for the love of God be careful of Emma. I wouldn't trust her further than I could throw a horse.'

'You forget I know her even better than you do.'

Gifta led Gospatrick into her home somewhat self-consciously, as if expecting him to be shocked. He could understand why. First they had to pass through the library, laden with dust and dampness that smelt of many ages. The rooms, up some ancient and narrow stairs, were cleaner, but they were held together with rickety old timbers and leaned at a distinct angle under the burden of time. The main chamber was a long gallery barely high enough for Gospatrick to stand up straight. Gifta and Theobald had done their best with some new furniture and bright hangings, but Gospatrick still felt it wrong that a daughter of Ethelred should be reduced to living there. He hid his distaste, however, and sincerely praised what she had made of it.

'It's a home,' she said simply. 'Perhaps one day we will find something better.'

Gifta had food brought for Gospatrick, and while he ate she sat beside him, reading her letter from Emma.

'Oh yes,' she said, after a few lines. 'She's certainly worried about her precious Hardicanute, isn't she? Listen to this: "I trust you not to repeat a word of what I say to you, Aelfgifu, but I think you will agree that we who care about England's future must try our hardest to dissuade Canute from handing over rule to his rough Viking sons." What a nerve the old hag has! As if she hasn't done as much as anyone to perpetuate Viking rule! She knows what dangerous ground she's treading on, too. She implores me not to write back, but to send my answers with you, Gospatrick, by word of mouth, and . . . oh, merciful God!'

'What's wrong?'

Gifta was scanning the lines over again, not believing what she had read the first time. She slapped the parchment down into her lap, white-faced with indignation.

'Now,' she said slowly, 'she has the gall to offer me . . . a marriage between Hardicanute and Ealdgyth!'

'Ealdgyth?' Gospatrick was outraged.

'Yes. She says "it would help the English nobility accept Hardicanute, and would mean both a continuance of the Danish and Norman alliance, and the revival of Ethelred's line." The perfect match, she calls it!'

'Mother, no!' Ealdgyth interrupted. 'I don't want to marry him!'

'Nor shall you!' Gifta said firmly. 'We have our own plans for you, don't we, my love? The granddaughter of Ethelred can do better than marriage to a filthy Viking!'

Reassured by Gifta's words, Gospatrick went back to his meal.

'Well,' he asked, 'does your dear stepmother have any more surprises for us?'

'No, but what do you make of this? She urges me to keep in touch with her nephew Duke Robert, my brothers Edward and Alfred, and my nephew Edward in Hungary. Oh Gospatrick, I wish I knew what was going on in that devious mind of hers. She frightens me, even at this distance.'

'Don't let her. She is a frightened woman herself. There is no harm she can do you while you're here. Let's talk of nicer things, shall we? You said you had plans for Ealdgyth. What are they?'

Gifta gave her daughter a fond smile. Ealdgyth, bashful again, played with the rings on her slim fingers.

'We think we have a splendid bridegroom for her, and Ealdgyth thinks she agrees, though she can't be sure until she's met him.'

'Who is he? Out with it!'

'I have had much correspondence with the Scottish royal family. They have even sent out ambassadors to me – although I have always ensured we met them in Rouen or Paris, never here. It's fairly certain that Ealdgyth will marry Prince Maldred, grandson of King Malcolm. You see what an opportunity it is for her, an alliance worthy of a granddaughter of Ethelred? More than that, it's an alliance too between England and Scotland if ever descendants of Ethelred regain the English throne. They might even help us do it.'

Gospatrick put down his knife.

'Gifta,' he breathed, 'For one thinking of returning to Canute's England, you're playing dangerous politics!'

'I know it.'

'An English-Scottish pact to restore Ethelred's line! Canute would have you slain in an instant.'

'Perhaps I ought not to consider going back, then.'

'You're quite determined on this, then?'

'I swear by the cross of Christ, I will do *anything* to pull the throne out from under those murderers! I swore it once, and I swear it still. You don't approve?'

'Of course, but . . .'

'Does it scare you?'

'Frankly, yes. I admit it. Unless you have lived as an English thane under Canute, you cannot imagine how you live with fear all the time, in case someone betrays you to save himself, be it truth or falsehood. But I will support you, you know that. I, too, remember the vow I made over my father's grave.'

'I never doubted it.'

Gospatrick turned to Ealdgyth.

'But your mother is right,' he told her, 'it's a wonderful opportunity for you, nonetheless. Are you happy with her choice?'

'If mother says it is right,' Ealdgyth whispered, hardly raising her head.

'Ah, but you must look at it more broadly than that. Think of the pride you will restore to your family. You never knew our father, but I can tell you he would have been very pleased and proud at this news. Earl Uhtred worked all his life to end the feuding between the English and the Scots. He knew it would be for the good of Northumbria, and of all England.'

Gospatrick had aroused Ealdgyth's interest. She got up and went to sit by his side as if already feeling, through him, nearer to the father she had never known.

'They say our father was an extraordinarily brave man,' she said urgently, 'the bravest in England. Is it true?'

'Every word of it,' Gospatrick confirmed. 'He was the bravest warrior and the finest man I ever knew. To be a son of Uhtred was to know that not a man in the world dared threaten you harm. It would have been the same for you, if you'd grown up in Northumbria. It would have been a foolish man that dared touch the daughter of Uhtred.' He took her hand, adding: 'But fear not, little sister. You still have a big brother, who has taken on the mantle of our father. No one will ever offer you hurt, not while I live.'

Gifta, watching the tender exchange between her daughter and stepson, clapped her hands and uttered a cry of delight.

'Oh, Gospatrick,' she said. 'You make me so happy. You have brought England here with you. I did not know until now how much I missed hearing an Englishman making his bold boasts beside the fire! You've brought memories flooding back. All we need now is a singer and his harp, and the telling of the sagas. Do go on, let's talk of all the people we knew. Your brother, Eadwulf; how is he?'

Gospatrick's smile faded. He had hoped that Gifta would not ask.

'Eadwulf,' he repeated, quietly. 'Yes, Eadwulf. I pray for him.'

'Why? What's wrong?'

'He shames me and all our family, Gifta. We have all had to make our peace with the Danes – there has been no choice – but he has gone much further. He has even married a Danish woman, a cousin of Earl Godwin's wife.'

It was a story Gifta had grown accustomed to hearing over the years. All the people she had known, if they had not been killed by the Danes, had made friends with them.

'Do not be too hard on him,' she sighed. 'Perhaps he truly felt there was no choice.'

'Well, if he had done it because he wanted to live in peace, I could understand it. But I'm afraid it has been to advance himself. He has a good position as Reeve in Norfolk, and he is vying for the Earldom of East Anglia. He told me he could get me a post too, but I told him I spit on such favours. I would never serve among Canute's bullies. As a son of Uhtred, I consider it my duty to win back the Earldom of Northumbria one day, and I'll kill a Dane before I grovel to one. Oh, it's sad to see it, Gifta, I can tell you – so many of our great men have done more than accept Danish rule; they've fallen in with it, even my dear friends Cedric and Oswald. You remember, I lived in their house for years after you left? Cedric was the one who married your waiting-woman, Constance.'

'Oh, dear Constance! How is she?'

'She is well, the last I heard, but widowed. Cedric was killed fighting Canute's war in Denmark, like many other Englishmen, I'm ashamed to say. Constance bore him a son he never saw.'

'Poor Constance. But as a widow she's in plentiful company. Do you think she needs help? Money, perhaps?'

'No, Oswald looks after them very well. He is Shire-Reeve of Berkshire now. Constance and little Cedric live very comfortably, you can be sure of that.'

'Well, that's some good news. Don't you have any more? We mustn't be so gloomy this first evening together.'

'Not really,' Gospatrick answered, with a wan smile. 'There has been little cheer for Englishmen living in England, unless they have grovelled to Canute.'

He eased Ealdgyth's hands from his arm and went to the table to pour himself more wine. He tried hard to think of something cheerful to tell Gifta, but the effort only served to remind him how much out of touch he had become where the daily happenings and current politics of England were concerned. These days he was a simple family man, content to stay within his own small circle. He was an earl's son turned farmer, and he realised he made a poor courier for Gifta, who wanted to know so much.

'Canute's power grows, year by year,' he tried, helplessly. 'Everyone speaks of him as a wise and just ruler, a man of tremendous energy and intelligence. They've forgotten that not so long ago he was a bloody pirate.'

'Yes, we have heard the legends,' Gifta said. 'How his court tried to convince him that he could stay the tide, and he sat on the beach and proved to them that he could not. It's a pity he didn't drown doing it. Mother of God, to think it's fifteen years since he set foot on English soil . . .'

'Don't speak of it. It cuts me to the quick, every time I remember that he won, and how he won.'

'But there is still time to rectify it.'

'You're thinking of your little plot with the Scots?'

'That is not all we have to hope for. Duke Robert is trying to persuade Edward and Alfred to take an army to England the moment Canute leaves it, either in death, or the next time he visits Denmark. He has promised them men and arms.'

'What do you want me to do?' Gospatrick laughed. 'Stand on the beach alone to welcome them?'

'There is much you could do, if you are willing,' Gifta gently chided him.

'Oh? Tell me.'

'I can't ask you to raise armies in England, but you could recruit some agents. I shall be doing what I can to encourage support for Duke Robert's plan in Normandy and Hungary, and Scotland, but I need friends in England. People who can tell me what is happening at Canute's court, people who perhaps will give me practical help when the day comes.'

'I have told you there are few. If I cannot trust my own brother, whom can I trust?'

'There must be some. Please try, Gospatrick. Talk discreetly to old friends of your father, and mine. Just because they are living peaceably it does not mean their fervour is dead forever. Talk to churchmen in the Witan. Try to make them see what an abomination it would be if Sweyn Canutesson became King of England. What I need from you most, though, is information. I have spies in Duke Robert's court, but you are the only man I can trust to do the same work for me in England. Will you?'

Gospatrick could not refuse her, although he was thinking of that terrible day when he had watched Canute single out for execution nine men whose only crime had been to have their names called out by their faithful followers. The memory gave him cold shivers down his back.

'Yes, I will do it,' he said. 'But writing to you about it will be dangerous.'

'I know. I don't want you to risk your life, God knows. We must use other names. You call yourself Goose. It's a name known only to us . . .'

'And Eadwulf,' Gospatrick corrected her.

'Yes, but it is hardly likely that he will see our letters. And even if he did, would he betray his own brother to the king?'

'No, I don't think he would do that to me. All right, I will use the name Goose. What name will you use?'

'You remember my favourite horse in York?'

'Butterfly?'

'Yes. I will write under the name of Butterfly.'

'You've given it a lot of thought, haven't you?'

'I've had a long time to think about it,' Gifta replied grimly. 'Thank you for this, Gospatrick my dear. I know what I am asking of you, but please don't take any unnecessary risks. If I lost you as well, I think I would take no more interest in this life. It's for you as well as for us I want this done, believe me. I long for the day when I shall see you Earl of Northumbria, as mighty and

129

worthy an earl as your father. And then I could come back to my old home to see you . . .'

'Yes, and me!' Ealdgyth piped up. 'Mother has told me so much about your house. Is it still there?'

'Aye, it's there,' Gospatrick said sadly, 'but neglected now. But don't worry,' he added, seeing his sister's look of disappointment, 'I shall do it up grandly to welcome you.'

'But right now,' Gifta told Ealdgyth, 'you'd better dream of it in your own bed. It's late, and we've had a busy day. Do you mind if I retire, too?' she asked Gospatrick. 'There is still so much to talk about, but I think we'd better leave it until tomorrow.'

'Tomorrow, and the next day, and the next,' Gospatrick agreed. 'I shan't be long awake, either.'

Gifta and Ealdgyth went to bed, leaving Gospatrick to his wine and Theobald to finish his day's work in the library.

Gospatrick waited for a while, then upon an impulse went downstairs to join Theobald. He found the monk listing some parchments by the light of a solitary candle. The man hardly looked a fit lover for a princess, Gospatrick mused, standing there at the tall desk with his head bowed, his tonsured head shining in the dim glow.

The monk glanced up at his guest's approach, but said nothing. Gospatrick, feeling equally awkward, made a casual study of the bending shelves laden with dusty scrolls and bindings. What on earth, he wondered, could be the point in keeping all these laborious works, copies of copies, comments on copies, copies of comments, the dry remarks of generations of priestly scribes, and devoting one's life to nothing other than their preservation?

'I want to thank you,' Gospatrick said, 'for looking after my stepmother and sister all this time . . .'

Theobald did not pause in his task. He seemed puzzled, however, that Gospatrick should take the trouble to come and thank him for doing what was, to him, quite natural.

'It has been my honour, and my joy,' he answered. 'But thank you for your words. Earlier, I felt that you did not. . . . approve of me.'

'I'm sorry. I did not mean to imply that. It was just that I remember how happy my father was with her, that's all.'

'I understand.'

The silence that followed felt to Gospatrick as oppressive as that of a tomb. Never had he felt so enclosed, so unnerved, as in this eerie place. Did the spirits of all the holy and wise and learned men tarry here, to watch over their recorded words for all time? It was like one of those dark dells in the forest where one could feel the gaze of gnomes and elves – and yet it was worse than that, for here

130

there was no comforting glimpse of sky and stars and clouds, no link with the real world. Yes, he had heard that libraries were the homes of ghosts, and now he could believe it.

'You probably know Gifta better than I do now,' he continued, dry-mouthed. 'Is she really so determined on vengeance still? I had thought she would have forgotten over the years.'

Theobald rolled a parchment and re-tied its ribbon. There was a slight, sardonic curling at the corners of his mouth as he returned the document to its place on the shelves.

'Forgotten?' he said. 'How? You did not see her in those early days, when news of the death of one after another of her family reached her. It was terrible. Every few weeks, one more name, so that she began to expect that each month was bound to bring another loss, until no one was left at all. She has been set on vengeance ever since, and frustrated that she has been able to do nothing about it. She has kept it to herself, for Ealdgyth's sake and mine. It has been heart-breaking to watch it, for fifteen years.'

'Yes, I suppose it has. You must have been very patient.'

'Oh, I have patience in plenty,' Theobald assured him. 'It is important for a man of the Church. And anyway, I love her deeply, and I could forgive her anything. Come, let us walk outside for a while. I want to talk to you about this, now that you have mentioned it.'

Gospatrick was glad to get out into the fresh air. The night was soothingly warm and calm, and brilliantly set with stars. Bright moonlight had transformed the town and the valley into a gently shaded picture in black and white. They walked among the plane trees and the poplars on the hill above the church.

'Are you afraid,' Theobald asked, 'of what Gifta asks you to do?'

'Yes, I must admit that I am.'

'So am I.'

'For Gifta, or for me?'

'For all of us,' said Theobald, and raising his head to Heaven as if to seek inspiration, he went on: 'I had a dream, the first night I heard you were to come here. In this dream, a great wind blew open the door of my library, and fire began to consume the books. I held Gifta close to me, and as we watched the flames, two fearsome creatures came in. One was a bird with the head of a dragon, the other a huge cat. Their mouths were covered in blood, and we watched them spit human remains out on to the floor. Those remains were you, Gospatrick. Then they came for us, and I awoke sweating and screaming.'

Gospatrick's flesh crept cold.

131

'What does it mean?' he whispered.

'Such visions, I believe, are a warning from the angels, who see all that is to happen. Those creatures, are they not the symbols of England, Denmark and Normandy? The English dragon, the Danish raven, and the Norman leopard. They are going to destroy us one day, those who struggle for kingship. This was a warning to us, to take no more part in their unseemly wars. They will kill you, Gospatrick. And then they will kill Gifta.'

'You are saying I should refuse to help her?'

'Ah, I know you cannot, and I know it is hopeless trying to dissuade her. I have tried myself, many, many times. I only wanted you to know of the warning with which I have been blessed – or cursed, I know not which.'

'Have you told her of this dream?'

'Yes.'

'What did she say?'

'She said if we took heed of all the warnings our dreams gave us, we might as well lie down and die anyway.'

'She has not changed,' Gospatrick laughed. He sat down on a fallen tree, and stared out across the peaceful moonlit river and forest. 'I hear your warning,' he said more seriously, 'but she is right, my friend. Even when we know our likely fate, can we change the course that life leads us on? One day we will die. Does it make much difference when that day will be? Better to die striving for what we want, than overcome with regrets in our old age.'

Theobald nodded.

'So be it,' he said. 'I will pray for us. That is all I can do.'

XIV

'WELL Gospatrick,' said Queen Emma, with false interest. 'Did you enjoy your visit to your stepmother?'

'Thank you, my lady; I did.' Gospatrick said carefully. 'It was good to see her looking so well.'

'And?' Emma demanded, her patience already fading.

'Gifta thanks you for your kind consideration, but she feels this is not the right time to come home. And honoured though they are by your offer, she does not wish a marriage between your son and her daughter. She asks me to apologise on her behalf for refusing you.'

Emma's face revealed nothing other than its customary coolness.

'Princess Aelfgifu is a fool,' she said. 'She always was. She has rejected her one chance for reconciliation. Still, I'm not entirely surprised. I hear something about negotiations with King Malcolm. A marriage between Ealdgyth and his grandson?'

'I know nothing about that.'

'Gospatrick, why do you bother to lie to me? Do you think I really believe you spent three months in Dinan without talking about your sister's proposed marriage?'

'I'm sorry. Perhaps I should have said I don't wish to discuss it. It's none of my business.'

'And none of mine?'

'I didn't say that.'

'Well, it is your business, you'll find – and mine, and everyone else's. If your stepmother thinks this pact with the Scots will bring her any gain, she's very foolish. When Canute hears about it, it will be very obvious to him what she's hoping to do . . .'

'Which is?'

'You know as well as I do, fool! Aelfgifu's playing a very dangerous game, you know. Give Canute the slightest excuse to go into Scotland, and he'll have an army across that border like lightning!'

'Perhaps you're making more of the marriage than there is in it. My sister has to have a husband from somewhere. And as a grand-daughter of Ethelred, she is a most suitable bride for any prince.'

Emma gave him a dismissive wave of her jewelled hand.

'Don't play Innocence with me,' she said, with mock pleading.

'I have seen the best of the cunning ones in my time, Gospatrick Uhtredsson, and you and your stepmother are not among them.'

Gospatrick shrugged carelessly, bowed politely, and turned to leave. Emma halted him with: 'Gospatrick . . . !'

'Yes, my lady?'

'I have no more to convey to Aelfgifu, but I have no doubt you will be writing to her again?'

'Of course.'

'Then please tell her what I have said.'

'Certainly.'

'And remember it yourself. Your brother Eadwulf, you know, has been very sensible. He does what pleases the king. When you get back to your beloved Northumbria – so near Scotland! – do not do anything to oppose Canute or me, will you?'

'I really cannot imagine, my lady, what I could do to upset you,' Gospatrick said, with mocking politeness. 'You surely don't fear a fool like me?'

●

They came for him one evening in early summer as he was riding home alone through a stretch of woodland. He knew as soon as he saw the dozen chain-mailed soldiers ahead of him that they had been waiting for him, and he knew he had no hope of escape. He sat and waited, preparing himself for death, but their weapons stayed sheathed as they drew up around him.

'Gospatrick Uhtredsson?' demanded their leader.

'I am.'

'You're to ride with us. Now.'

'Where to?'

'You'll see when we get there.'

'And what have I done?'

'You'll find that out, too.'

They offered him no information at all on the long ride south. At night they bound him and stood guard over him; during the days they ignored him as if he did not exist. He gave up asking questions after the first day. It became obvious they were going to London, and it was not difficult to guess who had sent them.

But why? And why now?

He was certain his latest letter to Gifta had been intercepted, and that they knew who were the two who used the names Goose and Butterfly; he tried desperately to remember exactly what he had written . . .

'How long the peace will last is not easy to say. As Canute grows older, there are clouds gathering. No one here has ever seen Sweyn, but we hear stories from Denmark that he is a man who rules by cruelty, and badly at that. Better known here is Harold (they have nicknamed him Harefoot because of his short legs, and he does look like a hare standing on its hind legs!), but he is not held in high regard. He is a loutish, drunken womaniser, the most arrogant and empty-headed youth you could imagine. As for their little brother Hardicanute, he is closeted up with the queen so much that few have had a chance to assess him, but by all accounts he is a spoilt and feckless boy, as you might expect of one whose chief company is a mother like Emma. I think even those who sing the praises of Canute now recognise that he has no worthy heir, and there is just the faintest suggestion that they are beginning to argue about who should succeed. I trust this gives you a little more hope for Edward and Alfred.'

. . . Dear God, there was enough in that to hang him a score of times. If they had gained possession of it, he would spend a few moments of utter humiliation before Canute or Emma or both, and then it would be over.

●

Gospatrick got a few glimpses of Canute's magnificent new palace by the Thames before he was thrown into a small, dark, damp cell somewhere beneath it.

Still no one told him what was happening to him. His gaoler could not because in that charming way Canute had of ensuring that his prisoners learned nothing, the man's tongue had long ago been cut out.

The days passed, the weeks went by and became uncountable, and soon all time was just an endless procession of days in which Gospatrick was brought food and drink, slept fitfully, at one moment felt certain he had been completely forgotten, and in the next was sure that execution would follow instantly. He shouted, banged on the door, he pleaded, he cried, but none of it had any effect. Only silence answered him from the darkness of the corridors outside his cell, or occasionally the miserable creature who guarded him would shuffle in to replace one plate with another, or to hurl a bucket of water into Gospatrick's latrine corner.

Then one day he heard marching feet approaching along the corridor. Even as he stood up the door was thrown open, and two soldiers stormed in. They took his arms and pinned them back, twisting them painfully. A big man of awesome aspect strode into the cell after them.

'Gospatrick Uhtredsson,' the warrior boomed. 'I hear you have waited many years to meet me. I am Olaf Ericsson.'

The Hawk of Hjorring, the demon warrior, the murderer of Gospatrick's father, killer of many, many more. Gospatrick at last faced the living legend, and was as helpless as all those who had gone before. His guts were a void, his body frozen with fear and yet, he thought, it was only fitting that he should die by this man's hand. It was as if he had been seeking death all his life, and now here it was, come for him in person, as it had come for his father Earl Uhtred that night so long ago in Northumbria.

Olaf was smiling the smile he always wore when he was going to kill.

'So,' he said. 'You have met me. Now what do you think?'

'I am thinking,' Gospatrick grunted, 'that it is a pity you will not give me a fair chance to kill you, to avenge my father.'

Olaf laughed. He drew his sword, and pressed it to Gospatrick's chest, just hard enough to penetrate the cloth of his shirt and open the skin. Gospatrick felt a tiny trickle of blood, and prayed for courage.

'Your father,' said Olaf, 'was easy to kill. As you will be. But you have things to tell me first, Gospatrick Uhtredsson. You are an enemy of King Canute, and you must tell me who your friends are.'

'I am not an enemy of the King.'

Olaf deliberately made a deeper, longer gash, in the soft flesh beneath Gospatrick's left collar bone. Gospatrick groaned this time, as his torturer moved the sword point down menacingly to rest over his heart.

'You are an enemy of the king,' Olaf repeated. 'You were with the king's enemies before, and he let you go. You swore allegiance to him then, didn't you?'

'I did, and I have never broken my word.'

The blade moved over and made a burning scratch across Gospatrick's ribs.

'My father, when he was young, sailed to the Barbary coasts,' Olaf related, with pride. 'Such stories he told me, of those lands! They have there something called the death of a thousand cuts. That's how many it takes, before a man dies. I have never tried it . . .'

'If you are going to kill me, just get on with it . . .'

He cried out again at the fourth cut.

'First I must know who your friends are,' Olaf reminded him. 'People are plotting against King Canute, and he must know who they are. What are their names?'

136

'I don't know . . . oh, God!'

'God it is you will cry to, many times tonight. But he will only help you when you have given me names.'

'I know no names, I swear it!'

Olaf motioned to the two soldiers. They released Gospatrick. He slumped to his knees, and Olaf reached down and hit his victim hard across the face with his studded hunting gauntlet. Gospatrick spun down to the floor. At another signal, the soldiers picked him up again and held him between them.

'You hate the king, don't you?' Olaf accused.

'No . . .'

'Yes, you do; you hate him. And you know the names of others who hate him. Who are they?'

'I don't know! I'm only a farmer . . .'

Olaf sighed, and for a moment appeared to be deep in thought, as if considering what to do next.

'I have heard,' he said conversationally, 'that Oswald, Shire-Reeve of Berkshire, is a traitor to Canute.'

'No,' Gospatrick begged. 'That is not true. Oswald is the king's faithful liegeman. He fought for Canute at Skene.'

'I know that. I was there, too. It was there that I beheaded Earl Ulf.'

'Then you must know that Oswald is true to Canute.'

'No, I don't know that. I think we'll have him arrested just the same.'

'I don't know what you want of me, Olaf Ericsson, but I cannot betray innocent people. Just kill me and have done with it.'

'What about your brother Eadwulf?'

'Eadwulf is a good servant of Canute!'

'How do you expect me to believe that, when you're not?'

'Why am I not? What have I done to harm the King?'

'You beg me to kill you. You must be guilty!'

'I don't know why I was brought here, but if you're going to continue this torture, I'd rather die quickly.'

'You went all the way to Brittany to see Princess Aelfgifu.'

'She is my stepmother.'

'But she has married her daughter to a Scottish prince.'

'The Scots are not enemies of Canute.'

'That's not what we've heard. We've heard that Ethelred's sons want to come back from Normandy, and that the Scots might help them.'

'Why should they?'

'You must know lots of people up there in Northumbria who

would love to see Canute dethroned, who'd let the Scots pour across the border whenever they wanted . . .'

'I don't. I don't know any such . . . ah! Merciful Christ . . . !'

'You are stubborn, Gospatrick Uhtredsson. When I come back, I think I shall probably kill you.'

Gospatrick lived in terror after Olaf and his bullies had gone. But he was left alone to lick his wounds, returned to the silence and darkness once more. His next visitor, a week later – or two weeks, he could not tell – was a priest.

'I have come to hear your confession,' the priest explained. 'Be at peace, my son . . .'

'I have no confession to make,' Gospatrick groaned. 'Go away. Tell them to come and kill me . . .'

'My son, you must not succumb to the despair of . . .'

'Get out! God deserted me and mine years ago. I don't want him now!'

In the lifeless days that followed, Gospatrick thought he would go mad. He tried keeping a tally of passing time by making marks on the wall, but he slept frequently, and could never tell whether it was night or day when he awoke. His imagination began to tell him he had been there for months; his hopes tried to insist it was merely weeks. And all the time he lived with one dread, that Olaf Ericsson would appear once more at his door.

In a corner of his cell he found a loose rock, just the right size to fit tightly into his clenched hand. If Olaf did come back, he swore to himself, he could make one bold effort to smash Olaf's head in with that precious piece of stone.

XV

THERE came the sound of the key in the lock, the door creaked open, and a figure stood framed in the gloomy light. Gospatrick strained his eyes to see who it was, wondering if he still had the strength to attack Olaf.

'Gospatrick . . . ?'

Eadwulf's voice? No, it couldn't be. It was a cruel trick, like sending the priest to make him feel his end was near. But it did sound like Eadwulf. Gospatrick struggled to his feet, and staggered towards the door.

'I've lost my stone . . .' he wailed.

'Christ's blood, Gospatrick, what have they done to you?'

It was Eadwulf. Gospatrick burst into tears and threw himself into his brother's arms. Gently, Eadwulf eased him out of the cell and up towards the light of day.

'Come on, old fellow,' Eadwulf encouraged. 'We'll get you some clothes, and a decent dinner . . .'

'I never thought I'd come out alive,' Gospatrick said later in the ale-house, his eyes still watering in the brightness of day. 'What in God's name has been happening, Eadwulf?'

'You don't know what's been going on?'

'Not a damned thing. I don't even know what year it is.'

'Canute is dead.'

'What?'

'Yes, King Canute has died. Now all Hell has broken loose . . .'

'How did it happen?'

'Quite naturally, after an illness, at Shaftesbury last month. The Witan is in an uproar. No one knows what to do. Emma panicked the moment she realised Canute wasn't going to recover. She had everyone rounded up who she thought might be an enemy . . .'

'You mean, this was all her doing?'

'Yes, it was she who had you imprisoned, along with others. We had no idea what had happened to you. Your wife, Gifta, me; all we knew was that you'd vanished from the face of the earth. Once I learned where you were, I begged Emma to let me get you out, and she relented. I think she's so afraid now of having no friends, she'll do virtually anything anyone asks her to . . .'

'But who is to succeed Canute?'

'No-one, yet. That's what all the fuss is about. Not only Canute, but his eldest son . . .'

'Sweyn, also dead? How?'

'Who knows? Does it matter? There are rumours from Denmark of assassination, but we think it more likely he poisoned himself with his drinking. But you haven't heard all of it yet. Duke Robert has also died, on his way back from a pilgrimage to the Holy Land. They've made his little bastard brat William Duke of Normandy – at eight years old, mind you! – and the place is almost in a state of civil war. I tell you, you've never seen anything like the royal courts at London, Winchester, Northampton – they're buzzing like wasps' nests!'

Gospatrick's thoughts were racing, trying to grasp all the news as well as his sudden freedom. If there was war in Normandy, he was thinking, would Gifta be safe? Should he go to her?

'Canute, Sweyn, Robert, all dead,' he repeated, shaking his head. 'How the Devil has reaped his harvest!'

'Aye, and it means trouble for us all, if power falls into the wrong hands,' agreed Eadwulf. 'We could be at war here within days.'

'What is happening, then?'

'Harold Harefoot is preparing an army at Northampton. He could be moving on Winchester already for all I know. Emma's there, screaming at the Witan to accept Hardicanute as king. She's turned to Earl Godwin for help, but no one knows yet which way he will step. There's talk that Edward and Alfred are about to invade from Normandy . . .'

'What, even without Robert to back them?'

'Oh, that doesn't mean they haven't still got Norman support. The uncles gathered around little William can see that a victory here could strengthen their interest at home. In fact, there's never been a better time for the nobles of Rouen to make a show of power. If Edward and Alfred could take England now, we could find ourselves being ruled from Normandy before we realise it.'

'So who gets your sword, Eadwulf?'

'It has to be Harold,' Eadwulf declared.

'Why?'

'Why? See reason, can't you? He's the natural successor. He's now the elder son of Canute, and he's the strongest. If Hardicanute, or Edward or Alfred, take what he believes is rightfully his, we'll have the Danish wars all over again for years to come!'

'He's a drunken Danish pig,' said Gospatrick, causing Eadwulf to cast anxious glances about the ale-house. 'Being ruled by that ill-mannered, whoring Viking will be no better than war.'

'Damn you, what an obstinate mule you are!' Eadwulf growled. 'You've never learned, have you? I should be sitting with the Witan now, instead of chasing around London trying to get you out of prison. Look, please come to the Witan with me. We could have Northumbria back, the two of us; Northumbria and East Anglia! I need your vote!'

'You will not get my vote for Harold Harefoot.'

'Who then?' Eadwulf cried, exasperated. 'Who do you think should be king?'

'Does it make any difference who votes for whom?' Gospatrick almost shouted. 'The strongest man will take England! The Witan is a gathering of straw men, Danish playthings. Don't worry, Eadwulf, you'll get your Harold. I doubt that anyone but Emma will have the guts to stand up to him for long.'

'Then come and help make it legal. At least you will get some reward for it. You'll be in a position worthy of a son of Earl Uhtred, instead of just being a humble farmer.'

Gospatrick gave his brother a look suggesting he should be ashamed.

'Worthy of Uhtred?' he echoed. 'Do you know who came to torture me at sword-point in that prison? Olaf Ericsson, that's who. The man who murdered our father. Now talk to me about "a position worthy of a son of Earl Uhtred," eh?'

Eadwulf was speechless.

'Go to your Witan, Eadwulf,' Gospatrick quietly told him. 'Do what you have to do, but leave me out of it.'

'Do I have your word you won't support any of the others?' Eadwulf asked at last, with genuine concern for his brother as well as for himself.

'No, you don't.'

'You would go to war against me? Is that what you want: brother against brother, as it used to be?'

'What is Harold against Hardicanute, or Hardicanute against Edward and Alfred, except brother against brother? It's not my doing.'

'Just because those brothers fight, it does not mean we have to. Gospatrick, I appeal to you...'

'And I should be appealing to you,' Gospatrick said softly, sadly, 'to take the one chance we have had in twenty-two long and bitter years to rid ourselves of the Danes. But I'm not going to. I'm not going to appeal to you, because you long ago made it plain; it doesn't matter to you any more, what they did to us.'

'You speak as though you're ashamed of me.'

'Not of you, Eadwulf. Of what you've become.'

'It's the same thing.'

'No, you, my brother, I love. You, the Danish follower, I can never understand.'

'Then perhaps you had better not try any more,' said Eadwulf, rising from the table. 'At least I am a practical man, Gospatrick. A tree bends with the wind, or it breaks. I saw you break and crash to the ground long ago, and it saddened me. The worms of resentment have been eating at you ever since, and now I must watch you just rot away. Your England is a dream; it has nothing to do with reality. The England you long for was dead by the time you were old enough to take up a sword for it. That was what you could never understand. Goodbye, dear brother. I wish you well.'

Perhaps he is right, Gospatrick thought, when Eadwulf had gone and left him staring into his ale. Perhaps he was trying to fight for a long-dead cause. Well, it did not matter. He would fight for it all the same. Better to strive for a lost cause than an evil one.

XVI

EDWARD, son of Ethelred, raised an army and crossed the Channel to win back the kingdom stolen from his father. It was the signal that a handful of men in England had been waiting for. Gospatrick at once got together all the fyrdmen he could muster, and left instructions for others to follow, before riding to the south coast.

He did not need to ask the way to the battleground once he had reached south Hampshire. The signs were all too familiar. There were shuttered villages, frightened and miserable people streaming away from their homes, distant palls of smoke, blackened fields and starving animals.

He stopped an old man who had been hauling a few salvaged possessions in a barrow, followed by a group of weeping women and children.

'How goes the fight?' Gospatrick asked. 'Who is winning?'

'Are you jesting?' the old man spat. 'Who's winning, indeed? We don't even know who's fighting! Our homes are ruined, that's all we know.'

Southampton seemed to be the centre of the fighting. Gospatrick led his men there, and saw a dozen ships at anchor. A running battle between invaders and fyrdmen was raging through the streets of the little port. Families had fled, though a few had left it too late and were cowering in their homes. Many buildings were ablaze, and the combatants choked in the thick, black smoke from thatch and timber. The cold morning air rang to the sounds of steel upon steel and the cries of the wounded.

The English appeared to be regaining ground lost earlier, slowly forcing their Norman and Breton foes foot by foot back towards the water. As Gospatrick watched, a Norman knight stood in the doorway of a ransacked church and tried to whip his wavering men back into order, but the sullen company deserted him, scampering away down narrow alleyways, and he went down alone under a great weight of English axes.

On a hillock near the beach, the golden dragon banner of ancient Wessex fluttered above English soil for the first time in nearly twenty years, but now it flew not proudly, but forlornly at the rear of an ignominious retreat. Gospatrick took his little force of forty men directly there. Far from being welcomed by a would-be monarch as he had hoped, he was greeted with angry words by a petulant and irresolute prince.

'Gospatrick, about time!' were Edward's first words to him. 'Where in God's name are my Englishmen? Are those all you've brought me? I lost that many before we set foot on shore!'

Gospatrick took one look at his leader, and was no more impressed than Edward seemed to be with him.

Prince Edward had never been of strong or warlike appearance, despite all the efforts of his Norman cousins to make a knight of him, but today in his chain-mail he looked more like a sallow scholar dressed unwillingly for war. He was a man of thirty, but his pale, almost feminine complexion looked uneasy behind the helmet with its heavy noseguard. Some would have said he had the countenance more of a misplaced divine than of a soldier. Perhaps it was this which gave the impression that he had come into the war half-heartedly, and was seeking a way out almost before it had had time to get started.

'More will be here,' Gospatrick promised. 'They are following on . . .'

'Thank Heaven for that!' Edward snapped. 'I thought I was to get none at all. I have already lost the Flemish. They took their loot and stole three ships almost without drawing sword. How soon will your men get here?'

'By tomorrow morning at the latest, I pray.'

'Tomorrow? By all the saints! Earl Godwin's army will be here long before that. Our prisoners tell us Godwin would have been here sooner, but he held back to stop Harold Harefoot sacking Winchester and stealing the treasury. No one over there knows who they're supposed to be fighting for. If only we could have won ground faster . . .'

'Perhaps it's not too late.'

'Yes it is. If I cannot get reinforcements today – this very hour – we're lost!'

'You must hold on!' Gospatrick pleaded. 'This is your one chance for the kingdom! Disengage now. Fall back to your ships, and stay off shore until my men and others arrive.'

'You forget the English fleet,' the prince snapped back. 'We've already had to run before them, and they're three times as many as us. I lost them in fog this morning south of the Isle of Wight, but it can't be long before they find us again.'

'No, not with all this smoke clouding the sky like a great beacon!'

'When you have to rely on an army of mercenaries,' Edward sneered, 'that's the kind of blundering you can expect.'

They watched the untidy battle for Southampton creep steadily nearer. A knot of defenders was placed around Edward and his standard as the invaders continued to fall back, and it would not be long before they would have to fight to hold even the little hilltop where they stood. Many of Edward's troops were fighting not so much to win or even to hold ground, but to keep open means of escape with the booty they had taken in the first onslaught. Close to panic, they were dodging from house to cottage to barn, encumbered by sacks of stolen property, using each bit of cover only briefly before abandoning it for the next, and always working to keep themselves between the enemy and the ships. The English had sensed victory and kept up their attack, shifting their assault from one group of intruders to another with swords and shields swinging, while triumphant cries came hoarsely from their throats. They flushed Normans and Bretons out from burning barns with as much zeal as if they were securing splendid palaces, and went into the fray with a will even when they were six against a dozen.

'Call them back,' repeated Gospatrick, disgusted with Edward's sorry efforts. 'This is useless. You are wasting men and time. I entreat you, my lord; wait for more men!'

'My mother could have sent help,' Edward wailed.

'Queen Emma wants Hardicanute on the throne,' Gospatrick told him bluntly.

'I know. She cares nothing for me, or for Alfred.'

Gospatrick could no longer bear to stand idly by, listening to the prince's self-pitying. He drew his sword, and called his men to go with him into the mess of smoke and running men. It might inspire Edward's ranks to fresh courage, he thought, if he were seen to lead a charge against the fyrd. He ran like a bull, shield held out before him and sword raised high, straight for the nearest knot of his countrymen.

The first man he met was the first man he ever killed in his life, but he smote down the young serf with a slashing sweep to the neck without regret, and hurtled on over the crumpled body to face the next. He did not know how close behind him his Northumbrians were, nor did he much care in those moments of wild and murderous ecstasy. His eyes blazed with madness; ages of dormant frustrations were set free at last, to fuel his impetuous attack. Powerfully swinging his sword to the right and to the left, he slew two more men before his run faltered. He searched for more victims, the desire for blood now coursing through him like a boiling flood – but suddenly there were no more to be found.

The battle was done. The English had withdrawn to the town square, cheering and dancing in a victory celebration, as the

Normans and Bretons finally straggled back to the beach. Looking north, Gospatrick saw the reason for the abrupt halt to the fighting. Earl Godwin's huge army had appeared, oozing out from the forest as steadily and relentlessly as a spilling of treacle from a cask. The earl himself, riding a big white horse, called his warriors to a halt, and sat surveying the scene. He made no move to attack, but waited for Edward's next move.

Gospatrick returned to the prince.

'They outnumber us,' mumbled Edward numbly, like a man in his sleep. 'They outnumber us five to one, I would say. Shall we wait for your men to arrive tomorrow, Gospatrick?'

'He's not coming at us,' Gospatrick said, ignoring the limp jibe. 'Perhaps he would be prepared to talk?'

'About what?' Edward was in despair, as his father had been, a generation earlier.

'I have heard that he's not yet declared for one side or the other. Why shouldn't he throw in his lot with you, as well as any other?'

Edward snatched off his helmet and tiredly ran his fingers through his whitish fair hair.

'I have no doubt that Harold Harefoot is not far behind him,' he sighed. 'Do you honestly think Godwin will go against him, for my sake? He does not even know me. No, the Danes have given Godwin too much. I have heard all about him. He is the Danes' man through and through.'

'What will you do, then?'

Edward looked longingly out to sea. Some of his soldiers were already making their way back to the ships, wading waist-high through the waves.

'Go back to Normandy,' he replied quietly, 'before those scoundrels steal every last boat from me and leave me here. I was ill-advised to undertake this expedition, unready. Had Duke Robert lived, he could have equipped me better than this. But that is the will of God. I have been happy in Normandy. I may as well go back there.'

Gospatrick, head bowed, sheathed his sword with a slam.

'Gifta, forgive me,' he whispered.

'You had better come with me,' Edward suggested. 'They will probably deal with you most harshly.'

For a moment, Gospatrick was tempted to accept the prince's offer. He glanced up at the might of Earl Godwin of Wessex, then at the ships, and decided that if he could not live with his family in England, he would rather not live anywhere at all. He no longer cared what became of him.

'No,' he said. 'Please tell Gifta I send my undying love, and – well, just tell her I tried.'

'So be it,' Edward shrugged. He motioned to his bearer to take up the golden dragon standard, and without another look back at Gospatrick or England, walked eagerly down to the sea.

As Edward's fleet departed, Earl Godwin's army began to advance upon the lone figure on the shore. Then a single rider broke out from the mass, and approached at a canter. It was Eadwulf, whose presence seemed to indicate that Godwin was acting for Harold Harefoot after all.

'You're mad!' he stormed. 'A deceitful fool! Is this what you've been plotting behind my back all the time? And you had the nerve to speak to me of shame! God alone knows what they'll do to you now, and this time I can't stop them!'

'I'm sorry,' Gospatrick said sincerely. 'If I'd known what a feeble effort Edward would make, I wouldn't be here.'

'Feeble or not, you're a fool to be here anyway. Why did you tell me nothing of what you planned? Have we drawn so far apart that you can no longer trust me?'

Gospatrick shook his head, having no more to say. Godwin sat high before him, his horse stamping and snorting, cheated of a battle. He looked up at Canute's feared and powerful commander and waited, shivering in the biting wind, for what he had to say.

There were others with Godwin whom Gospatrick knew. Olaf Ericsson was there, cruel-eyed as ever, mocking his erstwhile victim with a chilling smile. Also with Godwin were his two elder sons. The first was a churlish youth called Sweyn, as Canute's eldest son had been; the second was a boy, not quite fourteen years old, named Harold, just as Canute's second son was named. Unlike his elder brother, young Harold Godwinsson was a tall, handsome boy.

Godwin was staring hard at Gospatrick, and was a long time making up his mind how to treat him.

'You are a brave man, Gospatrick Uhtredsson,' he acknowledged eventually. 'In that you are like your father, although they tell me he was wise as well.'

'Wisdom is born of experience,' Gospatrick answered, as steadily as he could. 'It seems my experience of war came too late to teach me much of value.'

'So it would appear,' Godwin agreed. 'Have you really waited all these years to bring Ethelred's brats back to England?' And with a nod at the ships sailing off into the distance, he added: 'Now you see what you waited for. You didn't really think Edward would have the wits or the guts to rule a country such as this, eh? Think

147

no more of those sorry exiles. Normandy's the best place for them. Harold Harefoot is to be our king, and no Norman rabble is ever going to force its way into Canute's domain. Go home, Gospatrick. Go and till your land.'

Gospatrick raised his head in surprise.

'You mean I'm not to be killed?' he asked.

'I'm not a vengeful man,' replied Godwin. 'You have done me no harm, yet. And we've all been somewhat confused as to where we stand, these last few months. I suggest we all go home.'

And Earl Godwin wheeled his horse about and rode away. Gospatrick and Eadwulf stayed where they were, silent in disbelief. Finally Eadwulf got down from his horse, and the brothers hugged each other thankfully. They had no need to speak of apologies or forgiveness. When they broke away from each other, Gospatrick gazed out far across the sea, to the unseen land for which those tiny specks of sail were heading.

'She'll be grieving again,' he said, and Eadwulf knew he could only be speaking of their stepmother.

'She's strong. She'll get over it.'

'Will she? Oh Lord, Eadwulf – what did we do wrong? All I ever wanted was to take my place as a warrior, and today I killed innocent men trying to do just that. Yet it seems each time I have stood up to fight, someone has slapped me and sent me away like a naughty child. Sometimes I think my whole life has been wasted.'

'You have no need to feel like that. It was your bad luck to be in the wrong place at the wrong time. We who had the chance to do our share of the fighting were content to put down our swords when we knew the battle was done. You and Gifta were never given the chance to do any of it. It is no fault of yours that only the phantoms were left to do battle with.'

Gospatrick nodded, thanks in his eyes.

'Phantoms,' he said, 'yes, you're right. A thousand nights, I've wrestled with phantoms.'

'But now we've got problems to wrestle with instead,' Eadwulf smiled. 'The Witan's about to meet. We'd better get ourselves there.'

The sons of Uhtred walked to their horses with their arms across each other's shoulders, and behind them the fires died down.

XVII

THE Princess Aelfgifu stood at the balcony of her chamber, staring across the valley of the Rance. She was looking north, as if seeing England. Her face was a mask, but in one hand she held the key to her thoughts, a letter from her stepson Gospatrick, explaining what had happened at Southampton when her half-brother Edward had attempted to recapture the English crown.

'Gifta,' Theobald called gently, coming to stand at her shoulder, 'It's a cold night. Do come in . . .'

'I feel so sorry for Gospatrick,' she murmured, not turning away from her vigil. 'He apologises so much, as if it's his fault.'

'You should both try to put your minds at rest. It's over now.'

'Yes, it's over.'

She scanned the letter once more, however, as though unable to believe it. Gospatrick's words seemed to be sentencing her to exile forever more.

'It's the fault of all of us, for trying to make a soldier of Edward,' she sighed. 'He's better off buried away in his books – like us. Oh, Theobald, all these years, all the waiting, the hoping, and it all comes to nothing. We've failed my father, and my brothers.'

'No . . .'

'Yes, we have. We've let them down. Their lives were given up for their kingdom, they thought, but it was all for nothing.'

'You did what you could. It was not God's will . . .'

'God's will. God's *cruel* will, that I should lose every one I loved! There's nothing more for me to do now. My daughter is married; Gospatrick has his family; Heaven knows what Edward will do now. There's nothing left.'

She did not realise how her words hurt Theobald. Nevertheless, his voice was even as he answered:

'There is plenty left. You must not give way to despair. It's wrong for you to be cooped up here, in this stuffy old library. You should go to Rouen, or Paris, or Scotland, or visit your nephew in Hungary, even. It's wrong of me to expect you to stay here, in this dull little backwater . . .'

Gifta managed a grateful smile. They went back into her chamber, and closed out the night, and she put the letter firmly into her box, symbolically shutting away the sorrows of the past.

'Well, perhaps I will do that,' she said. 'After all, I must not lose touch with everything, must I?'

The tone in which she spoke made Theobald suspicious.

'You're not thinking of continuing your intrigues?' he worried.

'Canute is dead,' she replied. 'But his evil brood lives on.'

'Oh, Gifta! Why . . . ?'

'Do I frighten you, dear, timid Theobald? I'm sorry. I can never stop. You must know that by now. I don't know what can be done now, but you've just said yourself, I cannot waste away here and mope for the rest of my life. I shall go to Rouen, and talk to Edward and Alfred. Perhaps we'll think of something, one day.'

'Gifta, Gifta, my love – why can't you accept . . .'

'No, don't say it. Don't say "what must be". I do not believe it must. I do not accept my lot as easily as you do, Theobald. I shall fight, until the day I die. It's my nature.'

'Yes, it is the nature of you. But would that God could give peace to your soul.'

'He will do that,' Gifta said, 'when he metes out to Canute's breed the justice that they deserve. Pray for that day, my love. That is the day you will see my soul at peace.'

And Theobald went down on his knees and prayed, and Gifta leaned across and kissed his tonsured head. She went to bed then, and slept soundly.

SECOND BOOK

The Day of the Dragon

1036–1049

I

Four boys crouched at the edge of the haunted meadow, perfectly still. A fly settled on the face of one of them, and crawled there undisturbed. For an hour, none of them had spoken or moved.

It was the youngest, Heca, who first dared a whisper.

'What does a Shin look like?' he squealed. 'I've never seen one.'

Cedric Cedricsson, at fifteen years old the only man among them, put up a hand to silence Heca.

'If you *had* seen one, I doubt you'd be alive today,' he whispered. 'Be quiet, will you? If it makes any noise, I want to hear it.'

Heca, Guthrum and Elfric looked expectantly at Cedric to see what he would do, if anything. Already they were regretting this expedition to the notorious Shin Field, in the hills a few miles south of Reading. If Cedric was going to back out of fulfilling his boast, to enter the field armed only with a sword, then they would rather be on their way back home.

'A Shin is the most evil of demons,' Cedric went on, doing his best to terrify the younger boys. 'This one has killed two people at least. It tore them to shreds. So don't go speaking of it with disrespect. I tell you, we are in the company of the Devil himself today!'

The Shin had come to this field in the time of their grandfathers, Cedric had heard, and had made its vile presence known one stormy evening to several villagers on their way home from planting crops. They had seen a huge ball of fire floating slowly across the meadow. Its fierce brightness and the way it moved so silently had sent them mad with terror, and just as frightening had been the way it vanished, as suddenly as it had appeared. That same year the crops had failed and the cattle had fallen sick, obviously the work of the Shin.

A few years passed without incident, and everyone hoped that the demon had departed. Then a young girl was found, mutilated, torn to pieces by some wild and furious thing, in the same place.

The Shin was seen again later, this time in the form of a naked man with the head of a bloody-mouthed wolf. Few people went near the meadow after that, until a foolish woman wandered there in search of blackberries. She was found in the woods nearby, murdered as cruelly as the first victim.

Priests went to the field to exorcise the evil, but they could not tell whether their ministrations were successful. As a precaution, they forbade their people to approach within sight of it, adding the dread warning that salvation would be denied to souls of those killed by Satanic powers. A stone cross was put up to warn off strangers, and these days the meadow and surrounding woods were a tangled wilderness. Even the cross was completely overgrown with moss and brambles.

'Well, are you going in?' Guthrum asked. 'If you do you're a fool; if you don't you're a coward. So much for your boasting!'

He and the other boys were jealous of Cedric. Cedric had reached his fifteenth birthday, and had been declared a man by his elders, whereas they had still at least a year to wait before they were entitled to the same privileges that he now enjoyed. Cedric was allowed his own property; he could wear his hair long and put on a sword, and speak at meetings of the town council. Best of all, he could make his boasts without being ridiculed by the older men, provided he was prepared to match words with deeds. Another cause for envy was that, even when they reached adulthood, they would not acquire his status. Their clothes would not be as fine as his, and because they were not sons of thanes their hair would have to be cut short. Only noblemen could grow their hair long and affect long moustaches. Cedric was entitled to these signs of rank since he was the son of the late Cedric, a tenant landowner of some standing, a warrior in the service of the king and one-time Alderman of Reading. Cedric knew how the boys regarded him, being merely the sons of craftsmen and merchants and he knew that they would force him to act upon his stupid boast. It was obvious they would show him no mercy now.

Suddenly Elfric siezed Guthrum's arm. 'Look,' he gasped. 'See what has come to torment us! The Devil's bird!'

A magpie had flown to a bough nearby. It perched there studying the boys with a mischievous eye. Until that moment the meadow had been utterly silent. No insects hummed there; there were no small rodents rustling in the undergrowth, and no other birds sang or fluttered through the branches. The place was as still as a graveyard. The sudden arrival of a magpie must surely prove that the Shin still lived here, shunned by all creatures except for those which were themselves accursed.

'I want to go home,' Heca whined, and he started to crawl back towards the tethered horses. Briefly Cedric hoped that the others would also want to leave, but Guthrum snatched Heca's sleeve and dragged him back.

'No you're not! you'll go when we go! Come on, Cedric, don't keep us waiting in this horrible place. For the love of God, do what you said you'd do, and let us get away from here!'

There was no hope of backing out. Cedric took a deep breath. He stood up, drawing his sword, and with his left hand he fingered the crucifix around his neck.

'Dear Jesus,' he muttered, as he crossed the track. 'Keep me from the clutches of the Shin, and I promise to guard my stupid tongue in future. I will also give my gold goblet to your church.'

Slowly he stepped across the low brambles and into the long grass, wondering how quickly he would be able to run through it should the Shin appear. Would he be able to run at all? His legs seemed to flutter like leaves in the breeze.

He looked back and was dismayed to see how little distance he had covered. He had thought he must be at least a quarter of the way into the meadow, yet the track was a scant twenty paces behind him. He prayed that would be enough. He could see that the others were as anxious to be done with this adventure as he was. In their eyes, he had fulfilled his boast.

A tiny sound rooted Cedric to the spot with fright, and his stomach started churning. A desperate prayer formed in his mind, but refused to be voiced.

The rustling noise was repeated, a breath louder, a shade closer. The other boys had already fled. Cedric swore at their heartless cowardice. Again the leaves moved. It was a strange sensation, to be ready to run yet unable to.

The undergrowth parted and a scruffy mongrel dog appeared, sniffing with deep interest at the grass.

'Are you the Shin?' Cedric stuttered, and he raised his blade to strike off the animal's head before it could change into a more deadly guise.

The little dog afforded him a puzzled look, wagged its tail, and trotted away to continue its exploration of the meadow.

Cedric took a corner of his cloak and wiped the sweat of panic from his face. Then casting aside all pretence at dignity, he ran back to the path bounding like a grasshopper through the brambles.

'Cowards!' he yelled at his companions, who were hiding behind the horses, 'Babies! I went into the Shin Field alone, and you ran at the sound of a leaf!'

'You had your sword,' Guthrum mumbled. 'We had nothing.'

'We thought we could get help for you,' Elfric added weakly.

'Was it the Shin?' Heca cried.

'It could very well have been the Shin,' Cedric said, trembling. 'And who were you going to get to help me, eh? Those swineherd girls we saw? By the saints, if you are to fight with me in battle one day, I hope you'll get bolder. I want men at my side, not babies!'

Cedric's anger served to conceal his own fear, and his shame at having been scared by a little dog. He swung up on to his horse and, without waiting for the others, urged it into a canter. His nerves began to steady after a while, and his thoughts turned to the reputation which he would now enjoy.

Men would call him Cedric the Bold from this day on, or Cedric Shin-Taunter. Poets would sing songs about him, as they had sung them about his warrior father, at the feasts on winter evenings. Perhaps he ought to start making up some lines himself, and pay the minstrels to sing them, just in case no one else thought of it. He tried out a few as he rode, but under his breath so that the others would not hear.

> 'They say that Cedric the Bold
> taunted the devilish Shin in his lair,
> and the demon dared not venture out . . .'

No, that wasn't thrilling enough. So:

> 'They tell how Cedric, Taunter of Shin,
> boldly walked into the demon's lair
> and challenged the unseen one to fight . . .'

Well, Cedric considered, perhaps it was best left to the poets, who would not approach the task as modestly as he. Cedric didn't want to be a poet, anyway. He wanted to be a warrior as his father had been, to serve his king as the elder Cedric had served Canute. King Canute had been dead this last year, but Cedric had vowed to follow whichever king succeeded the old Danish conquerer. He might one day hold his father's position as Alderman of Reading, which would mean leading the townsmen to war in the army of Godwin, Earl of Wessex.

Cedric told himself that he should perhaps view today's adventure in the Shin Field as a turning point in his life, a last boyish prank. Tempting demons was a childish and foolish pursuit. Grown men should no more waste their time and skill on that kind of silliness than they should play with wooden swords. It was time to stop playing games with mere boys, Cedric decided, as he went down through the forested hills to Reading.

It was a Sunday, and most people were in church, leaving the streets to the chickens and dogs. Nearly every day in Reading was quiet like this, though. The town was a small collection of timber and thatch houses, hovels and cattle sheds, with a small stone church, no more than fifty buildings in all, nestling beneath the wooded Chilterns where the Thames and Kennet met. South of the town, where narrow plank bridges crossed a pattern of seven streams, a solitary watermill stood in reed-grown marshland.

The rest of the borough was constructed on firmer ground between the streams and the Thames, its homes huddled together within the remains of an ancient stockade like a flock of tired sheep in a cramped pen.

Nearly two hundred years before, Alfred the Great had fought the Danes for possession of this little river-bound encampment, and twenty-three years ago the place had been sacked by Canute's father – the Viking Sweyn Forkbeard – in the wars against Ethelred. Otherwise, nothing much had ever happened here. Today, above the bee-hum of a summer afternoon, there occasionally rose the chanting of the priest in the church, and the half-hearted crowing of a cockerel.

Cedric rode alone to the house – the largest in Reading – where he lived with his mother. Cedric's family was among the most notable of Berkshire, their reward from Canute himself for good military service. Cedric's uncle Oswald was Shire-Reeve of the county, and his cousin was Alderman of Reading. Cedric himself had lands of his own under tenancy to Earl Godwin, which he was entitled to manage now that he was fifteen years old and had become the head of his small household. No longer did he help his mother, Constance, to run the house and the farms, it was her place to help him.

It was because he enjoyed his new adult standing that he was able to feel free of worry about having absented himself from church to go to the Shin Field. His mother might be cross with him for his sinful lapse, but there was little that she could do about it other than chide him.

As Cedric rode into the yard of his home, he saw another horse in the stable, one he recognised at once as belonging to his uncle Oswald, who was making one of his infrequent visits from Wantage. Cedric loved and respected his father's brother, for Oswald had cared for Cedric and Constance ever since the death of the elder Cedric in Sweden. Cedric ran eagerly into the hall, where Oswald and Constance sat together at the head of the long table conferring quietly. Oswald had been eating, but he threw down his knife to greet Cedric. He was as fond of his nephew as Cedric was of him.

'Well, look at you!' he roared, clapping his hands upon Cedric's shoulders to hold him at arms' length. 'God's word, what a man you've become since I saw you last!'

Oswald was a big hearty man, an impressive figure with a mane of yellow hair, and broad shoulders filling his wine-red cloak like two hills of solid bone and muscle. Cedric, though, was much too delighted with his uncle's greeting to feel dwarfed by him. At that moment he wanted to blurt out the story of his Shin Field feat, and win praise from Oswald, but he hesitated to do so in the presence of his mother, who might spoil everything with her fussing when she learned what her son had been up to.

'Aye, I'm fifteen now, uncle,' Cedric responded proudly. 'Old enough to honour my father's memory by becoming a warrior at last. You are staying tonight, aren't you? Can we talk about your battles? There's so much I want you to tell me!'

Oswald let the boy go with a sad smile. He had known that Cedric would clamour to hear his tales again; it was the same every time they met. Uncounted nights, they had sat in the firelight while Oswald related how the fyrdmen of Berkshire went to Denmark and Sweden with King Canute to put down the rebel Earl Ulf, how bravely they fought, how so many, like Cedric's father, never returned to their homes. It did not matter to young Cedric that he had learned the story off by heart, and could even correct Oswald on tiny details when his uncle's memory failed him; he still wanted to hear it from Oswald's lips because Oswald had been there, had seen it all. In the early years Oswald had enjoyed repeating the saga as often as Cedric wanted, but age must be turning him into a sentimental fool, he thought, because he could no longer speak of it without a mist coming to his eyes. In the old days he was full of the glory and the pride of it, but the older he got the more he thought what a waste of life it had all been. They had been Englishmen fighting to save Denmark for a Danish king, and since Canute's death those Danish lands had been taken by King Magnus of Norway. So his brother Cedric had died for nothing. Constance obviously thought so, too, because she tried sharply to dampen her son's enthusiasm.

'You should not worry your uncle for that story every time he comes to see us,' she told the boy. 'He must be getting tired of it. Perhaps he might come more often if you did not pester him so!'

'No, no, I don't mind at all,' Oswald lied. 'I can understand the lad's eagerness. He's waited a long time to be a man. Now you are one, Cedric, so we'll have that story once again, as a celebration.'

'Oh, thank you uncle. And do you also remember your promise, that you would take me to the Witan when I came of age?'

'And so I shall, when next the Witan meets,' Oswald confirmed. 'And it will be meeting soon to talk of the succession. You'll hear some very wise men speak important opinions there. Here, come and sit with me. It's something like that I have to speak with you about . . .'

'What, the new king?'

'Mmm,' Oswald mumbled through a mouthful of food. 'In a way, yes. I've got a very important task for you, nephew, your first public duty as a grown man. And I am telling you of it on the order of none other than Earl Godwin himself.'

Cedric was struck dumb. He looked at Constance in amazement as if he expected her to laugh at the joke Oswald was playing on him. But she only smiled as if she already knew all about it.

'Earl Godwin?' Cedric echoed. 'How does the earl know of me?'

'How does he know of you? Now what kind of a question is that for a new-grown man?' Oswald laughed. 'Don't you think he makes it his business to know what young men he has in his service? He asked me if I could recommend a reliable fellow who would perform a duty for his lord, and I mentioned your name. Good, says he, this Cedric Cedricsson sounds just what I'm looking for, if he's as good as his father was. He remembers your father, you see. Wasn't it Godwin who led the Wessex fyrdmen to Denmark and Sweden?'

'Yes, of course. But what is this duty? What do I have to do?'

'It's a most important errand,' Oswald said gravely, 'and a great honour for you. You've heard of Prince Alfred?'

'The son of Ethelred?'

'Himself. Well, he's coming back from Normandy before the year is out, to set before the Witan the claim he and his brother Edward have to the crown.'

'What claim? I thought Harold Harefoot was to be king, or Hardicanute.'

'Aye, those two certainly have more hope, for between them they have the support of most of the Witan, but Edward and Alfred still think it worth a try.'

Oswald took a few minutes to explain to Cedric the vexed question of the succession. Edward and Alfred, the sons of King Ethelred and Queen Emma, had gone into exile in Normandy after the Danish invasion which established Canute as ruler. They had been welcome there because Emma was sister to the duke of Normandy. Harold Harefoot was Canute's son by his first marriage to an Englishwoman. After Ethelred's death, however, Emma had returned to England to become Canute's second wife, and Hardicanute was the son of that union.

'Alfred will argue that Harold is of doubtful parentage,' Oswald continued, 'since even Canute himself could never be sure who else served that whore he took as his first wife. He'll also point out that Hardicanute is half Danish, half Norman, no more English than Emma his mother, even if he is the most natural heir to Canute. Alfred will try to persuade the Witan – but more particularly the Church – that it would be a good thing for Christendom if the English crown were restored to Ethelred's line, now that the Danish conquest is so much history.'

Cedric was only half listening. He was itching to know what part he had to play in all this.

'But what do I have to do?'

'You are to command the guard sent to greet Prince Alfred at Dover, and escort him to Winchester.'

That silenced Cedric again. The whole house had become so quiet that he could even hear the birds in the rafters. It was just like that moment when he had gone into the Shin Field, and the whole world had held breathlessly still.

'Cedric,' Constance prompted, 'Are you pleased?'

'Pleased? Of course; but . . .'

'But what?' Oswald asked. 'Worried?'

'Well, just a little, I suppose. I don't understand. Why has Godwin chosen me?'

Oswald could not make that out, either, but he did not reveal his doubts to his nephew or to his sister-in-law. In fact, he was disturbed by Earl Godwin's insistence that Cedric should lead Alfred's bodyguard. It was not unusual for a young man just grown up to be given some great task, in order that he could quickly prove his worth, but this did seem an extraordinarily large responsibility for someone as untried as Cedric, especially as the return of Prince Alfred had aroused deep-seated feelings and harsh political clashes among the Witan.

The young prince had many enemies in England, men who had prospered and grown powerful under the Danes and would stop at nothing to prevent either Alfred or Edward from succeeding Canute. Not least among them was Earl Godwin himself, who had reached his exalted rank purely by virtue of his services to Canute during nearly twenty years of Danish rule. Did Earl Godwin intend to insult Prince Alfred, Oswald wondered, by sending a boy of no rank or title to meet him? If so, Oswald could only hope that Cedric would not be humiliated by realising that he had been used as a political pawn.

There was another thing which troubled Oswald, and that was the stance that the prince might adopt upon his arrival. Was he really coming in peace, or would he be determined never to leave his father's kingdom except in death?

Since Canute had died, Alfred's brother Edward had already tried to take the throne by force. He had led an invasion of the south coast with ships and men drawn from Normandy, Brittany and Flanders, but it had failed miserably because Edward got the support of far fewer English than he expected. The attack could have been the headstrong act of Edward on his own, or he might have had Alfred's approval; no one in England was sure. But the fact remained that Alfred's intentions would remain a mystery until he actually set foot in England. It was unlikely that he would make another attempt at conquest, as the visit had been so carefully arranged through the Witan and the Norman court, yet still there was room for doubt.

Could it be right, then, that an unproven youth such as Cedric should be sent to meet the prince?

All these questions Oswald kept to himself. He did not dare defy an order from Earl Godwin, but he could at least try to put Cedric on his guard without worrying him with details.

'Your humility does you credit, Cedric,' he said. 'It shows how suitable you are for the task. But I want you to understand what a serious undertaking this is. You know it won't be easy to carry it out absolutely correctly, don't you?'

'I know!' Cedric exclaimed. 'I've never met a prince before. I've never even met an earl, or anyone more important than you. I didn't mean it quite like that . . .'

'Cedric, Cedric,' his mother laughed. 'Don't get into such a flurry. People of royal blood are not ogres; you will find that deep down they are just like you and me. As long as you treat them with proper respect, you need have no fear. You know that I speak from experience . . .'

'Yes, mother,' Cedric interrupted impatiently. 'You've told me many times about the Princess Aelfgifu, daughter of King Ethelred. It's all right for you to be so calm about it, though. This is all new to me!'

'Well, just remember what I tell you,' Oswald reminded him. 'You will be acting directly upon the orders of Earl Godwin who is in charge until a new king is elected, in Wessex at least. Therefore you will have all the authority you need to carry out your instructions and they will be most thorough.'

'You mean I will be completely in command?'

'Completely. You must allow no-one to over-ride the decisions you make. Do you understand that? No-one, not even Prince Alfred. If the prince questions your authority, you must remind him as tactfully as you can that his safety depends on the arrangements Earl Godwin has made for him. Now, don't worry, you'll have plenty of time to prepare. I'm going to give you all the help you'll need. I'll teach you how to command a bodyguard, how to greet the prince, how to arrange for his comfort, everything. And I'll give you a hundred of the best fighting men in Berkshire to ride at your back. You see? You won't need to feel afraid, will you?'

Afraid! The very word was enough to fill Cedric with indignation. No longer could he resist singing his own praises.

'Uncle,' he said, smugly. 'You are talking to a man who went alone into the Shin Field but an hour ago, and came home to tell the tale!'

His mother was horrified. She made the sign of the cross and reached for his arm, as if to protect him from further harm.

'Cedric!' she gasped. 'The Shin Field? How could you do such a foolish thing? And on the Sabbath, too!'

Oswald was hiding a smile. He was no less superstitious than other men, but he had never believed the Shin story. He and his brother had taken girls to that field long ago, as it was such a delightfully isolated spot. They had never encountered a demon there, but it had been tremendous fun 'protecting' the girls from it.

'A bold gesture, Cedric,' Oswald said, as if deeply impressed. 'But your mother is right, you know. A man has no need to tempt the fates in order to prove himself. He faces enemies enough as he goes through life – unscrupulous neighbours, fire, flood and famine, sickness that steals his children and murrain that kills his cattle, crops that fail, storms, droughts – he does not have to challenge the Devil as well. You have your chance to show your mettle now, doing a real man's work.'

II

OSWALD was as good as his word, and spent many hours of that summer teaching Cedric court manners and the skills of organisation. He also gave him a few lessons in skirmishing and the tricks of evasion and escape, just in case. Cedric learned quickly, and began to feel quite confident when the autumn came and it was time to lead his men to Dover.

The day the prince came, the weather was cold and drizzly. The sea was a heaving mass of grey swell and white caps. The welcoming party stood on a short timber jetty, hunched amid piles of crates and casks and fishing nets, and wrapped themselves tightly in their cloaks and stamped their frozen feet as they watched the ten awkward little boats from Normandy pull into the shore. It was hardly an occasion of great ceremony, Cedric thought. The ships, sails down and oars away, wallowed in the troughs and slid back over the crests of the waves like beached whales trying to regain the deep sea. Most of them dropped anchor when they were close enough in for the men to leap over the gunwales and wade ashore, but the flagship – flying the old Wessex banner, a golden dragon on a white ground – laboriously pushed on dipping and rising and fighting the choppy sea, right up to the jetty, until it bumped against the stanchions and was secured.

The passengers crawled off, sick and thankful to be on dry land. A nobleman with a serious face stepped out from the crowd, followed by a dozen Norman spearmen. He went directly to Cedric.

'I am Gilbert de Bernay, Prince Alfred's aide,' he announced. 'You are in command?'

'I am,' came the proud reply. 'My name is Cedric Cedricsson, the appointed representative of Godwin, Earl of Wessex. It is my honour to escort you to Winchester, where Prince Alfred will meet his mother and Prince Hardicanute.'

De Bernay glanced briefly at Cedric's followers, and was disturbed by what he saw.

They had sent a mere slip of a boy and a handful of soldiers to guard the prince! To de Bernay this was proof enough that the road from Dover to Winchester would be the most dangerous the prince had travelled since he had fled England twenty-three years earlier.

'Prince Alfred thanks you for coming,' de Bernay said with a shallow smile. 'He will come ashore in a moment.' He took Cedric's arm and guided him a short distance away from the others. 'I'm afraid the Prince will need some assurances about his welcome here,' he went on. 'We were attacked by English ships out in the Channel, a force twice our size. But we were lucky. They could not turn against the wind and tide, and we escaped them.'

Cedric was outraged at the suggestion that Englishmen would attack a guest of the Witan.

'It could not be so!' he protested. 'You must be mistaken.'

'No, I am not. The ships were full of spearmen, but they did not get close enough to throw. I advised Prince Alfred to return to Normandy, but he insisted on coming here.'

'Perhaps they thought you were pirates.'

'With the prince's banner flying at the masthead?'

'Well, an invasion then. After all, Prince Edward tried to invade only a few months ago.'

'Could ten ships and fifty soldiers be mistaken for an invasion? I'm sorry, my friend, but I do not think it was fear of an invasion that led to that assault. It seemed to me that they had been waiting. What is happening here, Cedric? Is the prince's life in danger? If I thought that, I would untie his ships and set sail for Normandy before he could step ashore!'

'The prince is in no danger from me or my men,' Cedric answered hotly. 'As I told you, I am here by order of Earl Godwin, and my orders are to get Alfred safely to Winchester. I will tell the earl you were attacked, and I am sure he will punish those responsible.'

Gilbert de Bernay made a careful appraisal of the boy.

'I believe you, and I trust you,' he declared at length. 'I only hope that what you tell me is right.'

There was no time to discuss the matter further. Alfred had left the ship, and was coming to join them. He was a man of nearly thirty, richly dressed and wearing his hair short in the Norman style. His cloak was of purple velvet, and around his head was a single band of gold set with amethyst and garnet, like a modest crown. He was extravagantly bedecked with glistening brooches and buckles, with silver bracelets and rings. The man behind the clothes, however, sparkled less royally than his jewels. His face was pale and drawn, either from sea-sickness or from the shock of being attacked by the countrymen he hoped to rule. Nevertheless, Cedric was awed by this son of the legendary Ethelred, and he hardly knew where to find his voice when Gilbert de Bernay presented him to the prince. He did remember, though, to bow and kiss the hand that was extended to him.

'If you would care to follow me, my lord,' he said, 'you may rest and refresh yourself at the Alderman's house.'

On the way into the town, Gilbert rode close beside the prince.

'My lord,' he whispered. 'I beg you, let us go back to Normandy now, today, before it is too late. You saw what happened in the Channel. Now we have only a pimply boy and a few armed farmers to guard your life. This is a trap, I am sure of it!'

'There is no turning back, Gilbert,' Alfred answered calmly. 'I have sworn to regain my father's crown, and that is what I am here to do. It is my duty to God, and to my father's memory. Stop worrying. My mother is in Winchester, and she has strong allies here.'

'And many say that Queen Emma would rather see your half-brother Hardicanute on the throne,' Gilbert reminded him. 'I beg your pardon for speaking so plainly, my lord, but it is only out of loyalty that I do so. Queen Emma thought nothing of leaving you and Prince Edward in Normandy when she came back here to marry Canute, and she has shown little regard for you since.'

Alfred gave his aide a hard, sideways look.

'My mother left us in Normandy to keep us safe,' he said sternly. 'Would Canute have let us live, as rivals to his own sons? It is true that mine is not the most loving of mothers, but she would not have me harmed.'

'Perhaps not,' Gilbert agreed. 'But even if you have nothing to fear from Queen Emma or Hardicanute, there is still that bastard son of Canute, Harold Harefoot. He is the greatest threat. They also say that Earl Godwin is thick as thieves with Harold, and here we are, right in the midst of Godwin's territory. This whole business smells rotten to me.'

'You worry without cause,' Alfred scorned him. 'Come, compose yourself, before they hear your mutterings. I do not want anyone here to think that I am coming home without a shred of confidence in my own claim.'

Gilbert resigned himself to Alfred's decision, but remained uneasy throughout the night and on the journey out of Dover the following morning. The column of two hundred riders – soldiers, servants and clerks – made its way across Kent and into the gentle autumn woodlands of Sussex, and met with no signs of hostility. Gilbert began to relax for the first time as they halted for the second night at a large farm near Horsham.

'You see, Gilbert?' Alfred said cheerfully, fully recovered now from the Channel crossing. 'Everyone knows we have come in peace. What could anyone gain by fighting me? If too few of the

Witan vote for me, I shall return to Normandy. It is as simple as that, and Harold must know it.'

Prince Alfred was given a private room, while the rest of the company were accommodated in the few curtained cots that lined the walls of the hall or in the stables, according to their rank. The prince retired early, but his followers mingled with Cedric's men and the rest of the household in an evening of feasting to the sound of harp and pipes and song. The big cruck-beamed house offered meagre comfort, and this indulgence in ribald jests and drinking helped put off for a time a draughty and uncomfortable night. Supper was eaten at three trestle tables around the central fire. Swords, shields and spears were hung on the walls or pillars, well away from their owners, as a gesture of peace and goodwill.

Cedric, using the house of another man as if it were his own, played the host with boyish enthusiasm. He directed some men in the care of horses and supplies, others in the preparation of table and bedding, gradually growing more at ease as he became accustomed to his position.

He also drank too much, and being unused to strong ale, was quickly affected by it. By eight o'clock he was beginning to teeter as he walked, and to giggle stupidly.

Cedric found Gilbert sitting on a stool near the fire, alone with his thoughts amid the raucous merriment. Taking a goblet of wine for each of them, he pulled another seat up beside the Norman. He nearly missed it at his first attempt to sit down, but the second time he placed himself more carefully.

'You look very serious,' Cedric slurred. 'Aren't you enjoying yourself?'

'Don't worry about me,' Gilbert answered, with a smile for the boy's tipsiness. 'Better look after yourself. Too much of that stuff will knock you out. Your head will be ringing like a blacksmith's anvil tomorrow.'

'I'm all right,' Cedric frowned, not terribly sure that he was. 'What's the matter? Not still worried about the prince, I hope?'

'I shall be happier when we get him to Winchester,' admitted the Norman.

Cedric studied Gilbert with as much concentration as his condition would allow.

'You're very fond of him, aren't you?' he said.

'Yes, I am,' Gilbert agreed. 'He's a good man.' He smiled again, as he watched the crackling flames, and the smoke drifting up to blacken the stout rafters and the hanging sides of pork and mutton, eventually escaping through the hole in the thatch. The noise of feasting washed over him easily, almost unheard. 'I have known

Prince Alfred and his brother and sisters ever since their mother took them to Normandy,' he continued. 'Alfred and I are exactly the same age. His family stayed at my father's house for a time. We had great fun together, riding, hunting, chasing the girls. It was he who taught me English. He always said he would take me to England one day, when he came to take revenge on Canute. He did not know then he would have to wait all these years for Canute to die.'

'So, are you going to stay here with him?'

'If he decides to stay; so shall I. Whatever he does, I am happy to serve him.'

'It is good to be loyal to your king,' Cedric nodded wisely, but he spoilt the effect of his words with a violent hiccough. 'I like Alfred, too. I shall also serve him when he is king.'

'There is no guarantee that he will be, none at all,' Gilbert sighed. 'Even if the Witan elects him, which seems unlikely considering the support that Harold Harefoot has, he must face the danger from Canute's family. But he is determined to try. He longs to rule, and to rule well, jointly with his brother Edward. Alfred says that was the wish even of Canute in his last days.'

'What, that Alfred and Edward should share the throne? What about Canute's own sons?'

'Harold and Hardicanute deny that their father ever said it, of course,' Gilbert acknowledged. 'But it is possible that that is what Canute wanted, out of remorse for what he had done to the family of Ethelred, perhaps. It is well known that, in his later years, he regretted many of his early excesses. It is also well known that Canute did not think too highly of the intelligence, or the capabilities, of his own sons. He is reported as saying once that, if ever Harold or Hardicanute ruled England, all his life's work would be undone in a night. I can believe it. Canute was a very wise man, and a good ruler for one brought up in the Viking tradition. I believe most people would own to that.'

'He was,' Cedric confirmed, speaking with difficulty. 'England was very happy when good King Canute was here. Very happy, very happy . . .'

'You've had too much,' Gilbert gently scolded the boy. 'A warrior should never drink too much, especially when he is guarding a prince. Why don't you get some sleep? We have another hard day tomorrow.'

Cedric felt slighted then, but the advice had a mildly sobering affect on him. He wondered why it was that one moment his elders would tell him he was a man and must act like one, and the next moment treat him like a boy. He thought he was no more the worse for drink than any other reveller in the hall, but because he was so much younger than they, they felt entitled to put him in his place. Here he was leader of a hundred men, carrying out an important duty, yet still he had to prove himself.

'I'm no child, Gilbert,' he insisted. 'I have shown I am a man. I went alone into the Shin Field. There are not many who would do that!'

Gilbert was merely amused by Cedric's petulant outburst.

'The Shin Field?' he repeated. 'I don't understand.'

'No, I don't suppose you would. I suppose Normandy doesn't have any Shins, eh? I'll wager it's all so goodly and God – so good and Godly – the way you Normans behave. Ha, you've even turned our Prince Alfred into a Norman . . .'

'These Shins,' Gilbert interrupted, now trying to placate him, 'what are they? Something dangerous, hmm?'

'Very, very dangerous,' Cedric told him. 'They kill people, horribly. They are just about the most dangerous kind of thing you will ever find in England . . .'

Cedric was soon to learn how wrong he was. He was not given a chance to explain the nature of a Shin. At that moment there was a loud commotion outside the hall which made itself heard above even the laughter and singing. First came shouts, indicating that something had alarmed the English and Norman guards out there, and then followed the tramping and neighing of a large number of horses.

'What is that?' Gilbert whispered, and his hand moved to the hilt of his sword.

'I will see,' Cedric bravely offered, and he prepared to draw his own blade as he left his stool. He had taken no more than two steps when the great double doors crashed open. Twenty heavily-armed soldiers in chain-mail coats and iron helmets strode in. Many more could be seen outside in the yard, still astride their horses, surrounding the little band of guards. They looked menacing, these intruders, and the hall fell deathly silent. Gilbert had leapt to his feet, his hand still upon his sword, but the rest of the men in the hall stayed at their benches. They knew there was nothing they could do but watch and wait, for the newcomers could be on them and hacking them down before they could struggle free of the tables and reach their weapons. They were at a further disadvantage through being quite drunk and they realised it.

'Hold!' Gilbert yelled. 'What is this?'

Most of the men who had burst into the place paused, but one – obviously their leader – never faltered. He was a huge warrior, fierce of countenance, with bushy beard dyed black and plaited in forks in the old Viking style. His cold eyes glittered malevolently from behind the long nose-guard of his helmet as he advanced upon Cedric and Gilbert. His weathered face bore battle scars, and there were more on his large, horny hands, made bolder by the firm grip with which he held his axe and shield. Cedric thought he knew now how a mouse felt when cornered by a cat.

'Where is Prince Alfred?' the big warrior demanded, and there was a deliberate sneer in the way he pronounced the word prince.

'Who wishes to know?' Gilbert countered, with commendable courage.

'Olaf Ericsson,' came the reply, 'a name well known in this land, Norman. Who are you?'

Olaf Ericsson, the Hawk of Hjorring! Cedric quailed at the sound of it, and so did many of his countrymen. Well known! This man had been the most feared warrior in England since the Danes had run riot through their conquered country more than twenty years ago. There had never been a more merciless killer than Olaf, the Devil's axeman. The very mention of this, the most dreaded of all Vikings, was enough to send brave men running. Through battle and through political intrigue he had served Canute like a mad executioner, as if to murder and maim was the sole aim of his life, and his prowess had earned him the high rank of Captain of the Housecarls, Canute's personal bodyguard of professional fighting men. In all that crowded hall, Gilbert alone appeared to be either unaware of his reputation or uncowed by it.

'I am Gilbert de Bernay, Prince Alfred's aide,' he stated evenly, trying to match Olaf boast for boast.

'Then I would speak with the master, not the servant!'

'My master is resting. He cannot be disturbed.'

Olaf took another step forward, towering over Gilbert in a manner which suggested that he was in no mood for argument.

'Even the rest of princes must sometimes be interrupted,' he said. 'My orders are to take him into my safekeeping, and escort him to Guildford.'

Cedric at last found his voice.

'Whose orders are these?' he asked Olaf, feeling ridiculously small. 'I am the leader of the prince's guard, and Earl Godwin's orders to me are to take him to Winchester.'

Olaf glanced down at the boy and uttered a snarl of derision, like a lion irritated by a yapping pup.

'Your orders have been superseded, little fellow,' he said. To Gilbert he added: 'I, too, have orders from Earl Godwin. You will fetch your prince. We must be on our way at once.'

'You expect us to leave now, in the night?' Gilbert argued. 'Why? What is the meaning of this?'

'You test my patience too far,' Olaf snapped. 'Do as I tell you, and fetch your prince!'

'The prince is here,' said a quiet voice, and the silent gathering turned to see Alfred walking steadily across the hall. He did not look worried, merely annoyed at having his sleep broken. He came face to face with Olaf with the dignity of a king receiving a subject, but the Viking made no attempt at a bow, nor any other mark of respect. Alfred, unperturbed by this rudeness, politely continued: 'I am Prince Alfred. Perhaps you would care to tell me what you want?'

'You are to come with me,' Olaf declared confidently. 'Earl Godwin has decided to change his instructions, to fool anyone who knows of your destination and thinks to waylay you. It is a precaution, that is all.'

'Very thoughtful of him,' Gilbert contributed suspiciously. 'But what proof do you have that he sent you?'

Olaf ignored him, and addressed himself to Alfred.

'Earl Godwin himself is waiting to meet you at Guildford. He wants to entertain you personally. Then, when you have been to Winchester and seen your mother, he will take you to meet the king.'

Alfred affected not to understand.

'The king?' he inquired of Olaf. 'And who is the king?'

'Why,' grinned the Viking, 'Harold Harefoot, of course. I thought you would have known.'

'We have not heard that Harold has been made king.'

'Well, he has not been crowned yet, but with most of the Witan preparing to give him their votes, he's as good as on the throne. Now, will you come with me to Guildford?'

Alfred took his aide to one side.

'I think this crude fellow is trying to tell me that I am nothing but an unwelcome guest,' he said, 'to be treated with a little rough courtesy and then sent home. What do you think is happening? Is Harold really all but crowned?'

'I would not be surprised, my lord. I have urged you to turn back all along, and now I am sure I was right. In particular I do not like this sudden change of plan, especially as that insolent brute is in charge. Continue on to Winchester if you must, and see your mother. But then, for the love of God, get out of this damned country as soon as you can!'

Alfred considered the advice, aware that behind him Olaf was impatient to be on his way.

'No, we will not upset them,' he decided. 'We will go to Guildford. I welcome the chance to talk to Earl Godwin. And Harold, too, if necessary.'

'My lord, I beg of you, think again,' Gilbert pleaded. 'This could be a trap!'

'How so?' Alfred shrugged. 'If they wanted to kill us, they could do it here. And could we prevent them?'

'Very well,' conceded Gilbert. 'We will go, if that is what you want.'

They rode for long hours through the night, with Alfred's Normans and Cedric's fyrdmen herded together between two troops of housecarls. Through the green-black of the great Wessex forests they hurried, along lanes scarcely wide enough for four horsemen abreast, and over broad heathlands tangled with bracken and brambles. The four hundred men and mounts moved like a roll of thunder across the moonlit countryside, the rumble of hooves and jingling and rattling of saddlery and weapons striking terror into the hearts of those who heard them pass. In a dozen or more hamlets, behind the barred doors of wattle and daub cottages, frightened rustics whispered warnings to each other and huddled protectively over their sleeping children. The simple folk told each other that only ghosts or demons would ride like wild things through the witching hours. They prayed and made the sign of the cross, and did not dare peep out lest the evil spirits should attack them, or enter their bodies through their eyes and ears.

They could not know that some of those who rode past were as terrified as they. Cedric, for one, was certain that the night would end in disaster. The rough journey had painfully sobered him, and he was feeling angry and unsure of himself. He still considered himself responsible for the prince's safety, yet he knew there was nothing he or his poor fyrdmen could do against the might of Olaf's housecarls. Even if he was able to help Alfred escape, where could they go? Miserably, he reflected that he had failed to carry out the most important instruction his Uncle Oswald had given him, not to let anyone over-ride him, but he had no idea what other course he could have taken.

'Please believe this is none of my doing,' he apologised to Gilbert. 'I had no knowledge of it. I promise you, if we are being led into a trap, I will gladly die fighting for the prince.'

No attack was made on them, however. The cavalcade arrived in Guildford in the early hours of the morning, and made its way to the house of the Alderman. The moon had gone by then, and the horsemen clattered through the sleeping town in the utter blackness before dawn. The last of them were still entering the gates as the leaders reined in outside the Alderman's home.

While the men fought their restless mounts into stables or paddocks, Cedric siezed the opportunity for a council of war with Alfred and Gilbert.

'What do you want me to do, my lord?' he asked the prince.

'I don't know,' Alfred said tiredly, seeming resigned to whatever fate had in store. 'Do not concern yourself so, Cedric. Your loyalty heartens me, but I think we shall be all right now we are here.'

Gilbert disagreed.

'Perhaps Cedric should try to slip away and ride to Winchester,' he proposed, 'to let Queen Emma know what is going on.'

Alfred pondered over the idea. He saw how worried Cedric looked.

'I don't think that plan pleases our young friend,' he said.

'I would rather stay with you, as I was told to do', Cedric said. 'I have already disobeyed orders in straying from the road to Winchester. But, if you want me to go . . .'

'No, it does not matter. If anything is going to happen to me, there would be plenty of time for it before you could get to Winchester and back.'

Cedric was about to point out that Reading was nearer and that he knew people there who might be able to help, when Olaf came over and ordered rather than invited them to go into the house.

Four men waited in the hall to greet the travellers. They were Earl Godwin of Wessex, his eldest son Sweyn, Eadwulf, High Reeve of the Danelaw, and Lyfing, Bishop of Worcester. At the sound of their names, relief washed over Prince Alfred. Earl Godwin really was here, which must prove that this was no trap, but more reassuring still was the presence of the bishop who surely would not be a party to any treachery, and that of Eadwulf, whom Alfred knew of old and to whom he was related by marriage. Eadwulf was a son of Earl Uhtred of Northumbria who was killed in the Danish wars. Uhtred had taken as his second wife Alfred's half-sister Aelfgifu, who was therefore stepmother to Eadwulf. As Alfred remembered, Eadwulf had had two brothers. The youngest of these, Gospatrick, had always been Aelfgifu's particular favourite, and she still wrote to him regularly even though she had lived for many years in exile.

Alfred was then able to turn his interest to Godwin and his son. Sweyn was a sallow, strutting youth of about seventeen, unsuccessfully trying to emulate his father's proud stance, but the famous Godwin was a very impressive figure.

Godwin stood above his companions, both in height and by the sheer power of his presence. To see him was to recognise instantly the man of ambition, cunning and ruthlessness he was reputed to be. Those were the qualities which had enabled him to rise from a humble tenant farming family to become, by favour of King Canute, overlord of an enormous earldom that stretched from Kent to Cornwall, from the Thames to the south coast. He ruled the ancient Anglo-Saxon kingdom of Wessex with almost as much authority as had Alfred the Great, but because he had been virtually right-hand man to Canute, his influence stretched far beyond the Wessex borders.

Godwin's career had been furthered by his marriage to the Danish woman Gytha, whose brother Ulf had married Estrith, Canute's sister. Although Canute had later executed Ulf for leading a rebellion against him, no stain of this treachery had fallen upon Gytha. She was still high in the regard of the Danish court, and she was aunt to the royal princes of Denmark, Sweyn, Osborn and Bjorn Estrithsson, who were fighting to wrest their kingdom from the grasp of Magnus of Norway.

Small wonder, then, that Godwin had no desire to see Danish power in England fade with the death of Canute. He was English by birth, but wholly Danish in his loyalties. He had been Canute's man while the old conquerer had lived, and now he was committed to the interests of Canute's sons. His love of all things Danish showed clearly in the way he lived. He had named his first two sons Sweyn and Harold, as Canute had, and he had given Danish names to others of his eight children. He spoke Danish as fluently as he spoke English, furnished his home with Danish goods, and even bore the scars of battles fought for the Danes. A fit man in his forties, he even managed to look like a Dane. His long yellow hair and beard were plaited in forks, his pale blue penetrating eyes and ruddy complexion resembled the cold-weathered countenances of the old Vikings. He wore clothes and jewellery worthy of the greatest Norse nobleman, a scarlet cloak embroidered with silver, leather tunic studded with bronze, tweed trousers cross-gartered to the knees, cap trimmed with more silver. His sword was set with precious stones; his bracelets, torque, brooches and buckles of gold were set with garnets, emeralds, rose quartz and amethyst – indeed he was more brightly decorated than Prince Alfred. He was also more lordly in his greeting, so that a stranger could have been forgiven for confusing the two men and believing Godwin to be the future King and Alfred his subject.

'Ah, my dear prince!' Godwin bellowed, striding across the hall with arms outstretched. 'Come in, please, and make yourself at home. You must be tired and thirsty after your long ride. May I offer you some wine?'

'Certainly I am tired,' Alfred said coldly. 'I hope soon to resume the rest that has been so rudely broken. Perhaps you will explain why I was forced to come here in such haste, in the middle of the night?'

Godwin smiled broadly.

'I have been asked to look after you, my lord prince,' he answered jovially. 'And that is what I am doing, in the way I think best. It was better for you to come by way of Guildford. There are many dangers in the Wessex forests.'

Alfred sat down and began wearily rubbing his eyes.

'I see,' he commented sourly. 'A pity, then, that no such protection was available when English ships attacked us in the Channel.'

'You were attacked? By the English? My lord, you must be mistaken.'

'I admit that I have not lived in this country since I was a child, but I do know Englishmen when I see them.'

'Then whoever they were, they shall be brought to trial. I'm afraid it cannot be denied, though, that you do have enemies here.'

'Not least of whom is Harold Harefoot. Is it true that he is now called King Harold?'

'He is not king yet, but he fully intends to be.'

'Are those ships in the Channel an indication of what he intends for me?'

'Harold wishes you no harm,' Godwin said. 'But he does want you to renounce your claims – yours and Prince Edward's – and return to Normandy in peace.'

'And if I refuse?'

Godwin shrugged. 'That is for you to discuss with Harold, if you wish to see him. But I would advise you that he is well supported. I'm afraid some of the Witan misjudged the mood of the others when they invited you here, and so did your lady mother.'

'I am fully aware that you are against me, Godwin, but I cannot help wondering just how many others are, if the truth be known. What about you, Eadwulf?'

'My lord, I am for Harold,' his adoptive nephew admitted.

Alfred sadly bowed his head; Eadwulf's betrayal was a bitter blow. Yet, he told himself, he and Eadwulf had been separated for many long years. Why should the man have retained any loyalty to him?

'And the other earls?' he inquired.

'Leofric of Mercia and Aldred of Northumbria are with us,' Godwin told him.

'And what of the Church?' Alfred asked Bishop Lyfing.

'Well, my son,' Lyfing hedged, with a little cough of embarrassment. 'Of course the Church upholds the principle of Christian rule by one devoted to God and the doctrines of Holy Rome . . .'

'Yes, of course,' Alfred snapped, 'I respect those principles myself, as I am sure you know. From what I have heard of Harold Harefoot, however, it hardly seems likely that he fulfils those conditions! Perhaps I should discuss that with the Archbishops of Canterbury and York, just as I should be discussing all these things with the Witan. Unless, of course, you have been appointed by the Witan to act as their spokesmen?'

'Not by the Witan,' Godwin admitted, his smile turning cool.

'By Harold, then?'

The earl avoided that issue.

'We understand' he said slowly, 'that your claim, quite apart from the fact that you are a son of the deposed Ethelred, rests upon a promise that Canute is supposed to have made? You insist that he made you and your brother Edward his chosen heirs?'

'That is true.'

'Do you have evidence of that? Harold has a document in which his father names him heir.'

'And I have heard that Harold, in addition to his other failings, cannot read.'

'He has people to read it for him.'

'And write it for him, I shouldn't wonder,' Alfred said drily. 'But curse it, I am too tired to argue tonight. Will you allow me to sleep now? And please, send your wolfish housecarls away. They make my men nervous. I myself will rest more easily without their protection.'

Godwin, with a grin, gave Olaf Ericsson a sign of dismissal.

'Take your men and go,' he commanded. 'We must allow the prince to sleep soundly.' No-one else saw the tiny wink of understanding that passed between Godwin and Olaf. The captain left without a word, and in a moment they heard his horsemen depart.

'You will continue your journey tomorrow, then?' Godwin suggested to the prince, pleasantly.

'Today,' Alfred corrected him. 'It must be nearly daylight already.'

'Then we wish you goodnight, my lord. Or good day, whichever you prefer.'

Only when Godwin and his men had gone did Alfred permit himself to look downhearted.

'You were right,' he told Gilbert. 'Our journey is wasted. The Witan is no longer the voice of the English elders, the Danes have made it their gaming-board. Men like Godwin rule England now, and they are Danes at heart.'

'Then you will go back to Normandy?' Gilbert urged.

'Yes, but not until I have seen my mother. I will not let them think they have frightened me away. For now, I am going to bed. As God is my witness, never have I known a more tiring day than this!'

The prince chose one of the cots in an alcove at the side of the hall, and was asleep almost as soon as he had thrown himself upon it. Gilbert prepared for bed, too, but he was still on the alert.

'We cannot drop our guard, Cedric,' he said. 'You had better go out and make sure our men are still awake.'

'But Earl Godwin is close by,' Cedric protested. 'Surely we are safe now?'

'Please, do as I bid you. I'm afraid my trust in Godwin is not as firm as yours.'

Cedric went out, to find his soldiers and Alfred's grumbling bitterly as they paced about in the cold morning air. Most of the servants and clerks had found places to sleep in the stables and barns, but the English fyrdmen and Norman spearmen had faithfully remained at their posts. They were watching the first streaks of light appear above the eastern horizon, and wondering how much longer they would have to stand around. Cedric surveyed the ramshackle stockade gates, leaning open on worn hinges, and decided it would serve little purpose to close them. He was less worried about an attack now, however, and considered his guards defence enough.

'What is happening, young Cedric?' one of the Berkshire men asked grumpily. 'Do we get some rest this night, or not? All the housecarls have gone to their beds. Why shouldn't we?'

'You can,' Cedric relented, 'But at least a dozen must stay on watch. No, two dozen. Share out the hours as best you can. Call me if there is any sign of trouble, but call me anyway at the eighth hour.'

Leaving the men still grumbling, he went back into the house. He found himself a cot near to Alfred and Gilbert, and collapsed thankfully on to the straw mattress. He barely had time to unbuckle his sword belt and pull his cloak tightly about him before he fell into an exhausted sleep.

Those left on duty had started a small fire in the yard. They were sitting outside the main doors of the house, dozing, or complaining to each other about the discomforts, when they heard once more

176

the drumming of hooves. At first the sound was faint, but it gradually grew louder. One or two of the men stood up, as if that would help them hear more clearly.

'Can that be the housecarls again?' wondered a fyrdman. 'What are they up to now?'

'Better close those gates,' suggested another. 'I don't care to meet up with that lot again!'

'Do this, do that,' grumbled the first man, making his way towards the gates. But it was too late. The riders were indeed the housecarls, returning with Olaf Ericsson at their head. With chilling war-cries they came through the open gates at the gallop. The man on his way to the gates tried to run, but was trampled beneath the pounding hooves like a sack. His companions shouted in alarm, leaping to their feet and snatching at weapons they never had a chance to use. They were cut down by a storm of spears and axes in the first few seconds after the housecarls reined in, sprang down from their horses and savagely went in for the kill.

Having dealt with the watch, the housecarls split into two groups. The first company went to the stables and barns. Some pulled brands from the fire and threw them on to the thatched roof of an outhouse. They barricaded the doors, and laughed and howled insults as the men trapped inside struggled to get out. More raiders surrounded the stables, waiting for their victims. When the English and Normans came running out, dozily fumbling with sword belts and shields, the housecarls dashed among them like wolves scattering a flock of panicking sheep. Some they slashed down immediately, others they took prisoner.

It was these, more than one hundred of them, who were to suffer the worst fate. The bloodlust of the housecarls had been brought to the boil, and they were out to make a night's sport of the attack. They dragged the pleading captives out into the yard, and there began an orgy of torture and murder such as Guildford had never seen before. Some of the men they blinded with swords. Others they spreadeagled over the fire until their clothes caught alight, then sent them running around the stockade to fan the flames into a blaze. A score or more they mutilated by chopping off hands, feet, ears or scalps, and some they impaled on the stockade stakes, leaving them to die an agonised death. Others they lashed behind horses to be dragged at speed around the yard. The crazed laughter and shouts of the housecarls and the screeches of the dying rent the dawn air and awoke the whole town, but no-one ventured out.

Meanwhile, a dozen of Olaf's men had made straight for the house, swarming over the stricken defenders, and hacking to death the few left alive after the first onslaught. They axed down the doors and stormed into the hall, searching among the cots for Prince Alfred. The noise had startled Cedric out of his sleep, but in the first few moments of hearing the racket outside and the smashing of steel upon timber, he had thought himself in the midst of a nightmare. When he realised what was happening he leapt from his bed, scrabbling among the covers for his sword.

'My lord, wake up!' he screamed.

In the same instant he saw the housecarls with the yard-fires behind them, charging down the hall like enraged giants.

'Kill the brat!' he heard Olaf order.

One of them made for Cedric while the others went on to take Alfred. Cedric raised his sword, but the ferocity of the man intimidated him. The housecarl rushed at him, swinging his axe in a vicious arc, intending to split the boy in two at a blow. Cedric dodged and dropped into a timid crouch, but without thinking he swept his sword up to fend off the axe. The blades clashed violently, and Cedric's arms shuddered as the sword was torn from his hands. The axe swept sideways and the housecarl stumbled under his own weight. Cedric, defenceless now, moved quickly in a last effort to save himself.

He hurled himself at his attacker. Their bodies collided sharply, forcing the breath from them both in loud grunts. Cedric desperately clung to the housecarl, pinning his arms to his sides. They shuffled and stumbled like drunks through the thick rushes on the floor.

'Help that fool with the boy!' Olaf shouted.

Cedric knew he had little time. He pressed hard against the floor and pushed the housecarl off balance. Together they crashed down, and Cedric rolled aside and scrambled away on hands and knees. He ducked under a table and toppled it over as he got up, putting a barrier between himself and his pursuer. Desperately he looked around for a weapon. He ripped up a heavy turning iron from the roasting spit, and swung it threateningly at the three men who were clambering over the table.

The soldiers were undeterred. Cedric hurled the iron at the nearest of them, but did not wait to see if it hit him. He dashed out of the hall through a narrow door into a pantry. There he found a large knife, and turned about with his back to the wall, prepared to fight to the death.

His luck held good. Even as the housecarls reached the door they were called back by Olaf, who had achieved the most important thing in capturing Alfred. Olaf wanted to be away, and the fate of the boy no longer interested him. Cedric crept back into the hall just in time to see the housecarls manhandling the prince out of the house. He ran to peep through the hinges of the great doors. He watched as the housecarls stripped Prince Alfred naked, rolled him in the dirt and the blood of his companions, and bound him hand and foot across a horse. They were gone, riding away into the early morning mist, yelling insults, laughing uproariously, dragging behind them a score of men taken as slaves. The crippled, the dead and the dying they left where they had fallen.

Sickened and ashamed, he ran back to look for Gilbert. He found the Norman lying at the foot of the prince's bed, where he had made a brave bid to save his master. Gilbert lay doubled up, gurgling through a mouthful of blood, his hands clutching at a spear thrust deep into his belly.

Cedric sank to his knees beside his new-found friend, wanting to do something for him, yet knowing there was nothing to be done. Gilbert, recognising him, made a pitiful attempt to raise his head.

'Cedric,' He moaned. 'Help him, please . . .'

'How?' Cedric wept, 'What can I do?'

Gilbert tried to say more, but choked on the words. The blood spilled down his chin, and his head rolled to one side.

Cedric knelt there for what seemed an age, powerless to do anything except close his friend's eyes. He felt as if every sinew had been cut, as if all will had been drained from him. He had failed the prince, failed Gilbert, failed Oswald, failed himself. The hall was deathly silent; he was the only one left alive in it.

Suddenly he snapped out of his trance. Groans and sobs of agony came to him from the yard, where those who still lived were begging for death.

Cedric stood at the door, gazed at the carnage, the filth of human remains spread all over the yard, and doubled up vomiting. When that fit was past, he gave way to uncontrollable weeping. He beat his fists upon the hard earth, shrieking out his grief and shame until there was nothing left inside him.

III

SHORTLY after the massacre at Guildford, Godwin and Sweyn were summoned to Northampton by Harold Harefoot. Sweyn, who had never before met the infamous son of Canute, went with some trepidation, but his wily father set off jauntily. He was quite used to handling kings and princes, and he foresaw no problems with Harold.

The house that Harold liked to call his palace was built, like a Viking longhouse, of stout fir beams cemented with straw-bound mud, and had a steep log and thatch roof with gables and eaves bearing carvings of dragon heads and the old Norse gods. The main house and its sprawling outbuildings were protected by a high fence of sharpened stakes and patrolled by housecarls. The inside of the great hall was arranged as a Saxon dwelling, comprising one huge main room with a fire pit, and tables on low platforms around three sides. Between the two outer rows of heavy wooden pillars were rows of beds and cots.

Harold did not care to hang his wall with tapestries and silks, as did some of the English lords who had been influenced by the fashion from Europe. He preferred to follow the traditions of the Norse warriors and hunters; his hall was hung with the skins of wild bears, bulls, boars and stags, and an armoury of spears, axes, swords and shields.

Half-a-dozen lean and almost savage hounds snuffled about the floor for tit-bits from the tables, and lifted their legs against the pillars. The place stank of stale food, human sweat and dog excrement, but Harold and his wild young Danish friends spent most of their time there, attended by an abundance of servants, slaves and whores. Often there came poets, eager to make their reputations with flattering songs about the bastard son of Canute, who actually delighted in his uncertain ancestry and encouraged the minstrels to make as much play upon it as they liked.

It was an assumed Norseness, done to excess, from the pretended worship of pagan gods to the gilded drinking horns used by Harold and his friends. The young man was trying to convince everyone that this was a Viking stronghold like those of one hundred years ago and more, but no-one saw through it all more surely than Earl

Godwin, the Englishman who knew the Danes better than any son of Canute.

'The scruffy little idiot thinks himself a Viking,' Godwin whispered to Sweyn as they entered the hall. 'Skinny, pox-ridden little weed! He wouldn't make a decent mouthful for a real Viking.'

The young prince was surrounded, as always, by hangers-on. He had been drinking steadily for hours, and was slumped in the high-backed chair that passed as his throne. His right arm was thrown around a nervous young girl, who was squeezed into the chair beside him, an unwilling player in the endless pretence. Bishop Lyfing and Eadwulf were also there; they had already taken a verbal beating from Harold. The bishop was pale, and he was dabbing at the perspiration on his cheeks, while Eadwulf's face was as long as a bloodhound's. Harold turned his attention from them on seeing Godwin and Sweyn enter, and fixed a stern eye on the newcomers.

'Godwin!' he barked. 'Come here, man. We've been waiting for you!'

It was difficult for Godwin to conceal his distaste for this unworthy offspring of the great Canute. At nineteen Harold was a thin, greasy-complexioned youth, dirty and unkempt, a drunken lout whose body was riddled with the diseases of whores. But worse, in Godwin's eyes, Harold was stupid and boorish and a disgrace to his father, the man whom Godwin had admired above all others. Still Godwin managed to greet him with a smile of deference.

'My lord Harold,' he called back genially, 'It's good to see you again. I trust all is well with you?'

'No, all is not well,' Harold grumbled. 'I have just been demanding to know of these bungling friends of yours what in Odin's name went wrong. Now I ask the same of you!'

The Earl of Wessex deliberately glared at Eadwulf.

'Well might you ask,' he responded calmly. 'Is it true, what I am told, Eadwulf? That Prince Alfred is dead?'

Eadwulf nodded dumbly.

'Olaf's wolf-pack killed him,' he said desperately. 'Don't ask me why; I never told them to. All I did was tell them where to take him in Norfolk. But they tortured him. They blinded him. They injured him so badly, he died.'

'A pity,' Godwin said coolly. 'We all knew Lord Harold wanted him for a hostage.'

'Of course I did!' Harold raged. 'Those were my instructions, weren't they? Didn't I make that clear? A hostage, I wanted. What good is a dead hostage? Can I force Edward and Hardicanute to withdraw their claims, by brandishing their dead brother at them?'

Harold's companions laughed loudly at that, and their flattering mirth dissolved his anger. He basked in their applause.

'Well, it's not my fault he's dead,' Godwin was saying. 'Eadwulf should have kept control of Olaf's stupid mob.'

'Do you think I wanted Alfred dead?' Eadwulf shouted furiously. 'He was my own stepmother's brother, you know! Almighty God, if I had known this was going to happen I would never have had anything to do with it!'

'It was a perfectly laid plan!' Harold snapped indignantly. 'With Alfred in my hands I would have had them all where I wanted them: Edward, Hardicanute, Emma, all of them! I could even have made Emma go back to Normandy and take her brat with her. Now what am I going to do?'

'There is much you can do,' Godwin assured him. 'It would be a fool who dared threaten you, knowing what happened to Alfred.'

'You think so? That no-one will oppose me now?'

'Certainly you don't need to worry about Edward. He won't come near England again. All you need do is make Hardicanute a fair offer, to keep him and Emma quiet.'

'What do you call a fair offer?'

'Half England. Give him everything north of the Humber. He can call himself king there, but he'll only be your vassal. You will still have by far the richer slice of the meat.'

'But suppose he really tries to make himself king, and comes against me with the Northumbrians?'

'That's a chance you have to take. I don't think he will. He's more likely to go to war against you if you leave him nothing. He's afraid of you. Play on that fear. Leave him a way to step down with honour.'

Harold mused it over.

'You may be right,' he conceded, 'that might be the right way to deal with Hardicanute. But what of Edward? Will he do nothing? He'll want revenge for his brother's death. The Normans will be angry, too; so many of their people died.' Harold's well-known temper flared suddenly. He leapt from his chair, fists clenched, screaming: 'Those men should not have been killed! Whose idea was it to kill them?'

Godwin answered with a placid smile.

'You did say, my lord,' he replied carefully, 'that the fewer the witnesses, the better. I don't think we can blame Olaf for that.'

'But, by all the gods, the Normans might even decide to support Edward's claim, help him invade England!'

'Don't worry,' Godwin insisted gently. 'The Normans will do nothing of the kind. A year ago, when Duke Robert was alive, they might have, but not now. Look what a state they're in themselves. Their nobles are all at each other's throats, and what do they have for a duke? Little bastard William, not ten years old! Are they really likely to cause us trouble?'

Harold nodded, his rage dying. His vacant gaze fixed itself somewhere beyond Godwin.

'Then I am king?' he queried, like a small child wanting reassurance.

'You are king,' Godwin told him. 'All you need is the crown to prove it. Most of the thanes support you, and they control the Witan. However, there is one more force you should have on your side, to be certain . . .'

'Who?'

'The Church.'

Harold laughed aloud.

'The Church?' he scoffed, snapping his fingers in the face of Bishop Lyfing. 'What good is your Christian Church to a man who calls upon the warrior god Odin?'

Godwin waited until the applause for Harold's childish gesture had died down.

'Do not dismiss the Church so lightly, my lord,' he warned. 'It's all very well to have the strength of your warriors behind you, but the Church can be a formidable enemy, or a powerful friend. With the English Church behind you, you will find favour with Rome. So the Pope is not going to give his blessing to any war which Edward may try to wage against you. Put a stop to the rumours that you worship the old gods. Show that you are a Christian . . .'

'A Christian!' Harold snorted. 'Me, a Christian!'

'Yes, you! You must accept the Church as a counsellor, to be consulted about every important decision you make, even if you take no notice of what they say. Am I not right, Bishop?'

Lyfing recognised the threat in Godwin's voice. Godwin was actually reminding the Bishop that he was very much at Harold's mercy now, having got caught up in the Guildford massacre and the murder of Prince Alfred, and that he had better state right here and now where he stood, whether still for Harold or against him. Lyfing was already regretting coming under Godwin's influence, and it occurred to him that Godwin had deliberately entangled him in Alfred's murder without warning, but he knew it was too late to turn back.

'Make your peace with the Church, my son,' he told Harold with an edge of bitterness. 'I will do all I can to help you.'

'All right, all right, so I'll be a Christian,' Harold surrendered with a laugh. 'In public anyway. I'll also give the Church some gold. That will prove my devotion, won't it?'

'It will help,' Godwin agreed.

'What a man has to do, to be king,' Harold sighed. 'This will ruin my reputation. But I'll do as you say, because I think I can trust you, Godwin, you evil man! Go on, get out of here, before you have me taking holy orders!'

So loud were the laughs from Harold's cronies that Godwin had difficulty making himself heard.

'Shall I go to Hardicanute with your offer?' he called.

'Yes, offer him what you like,' the prince said airily. 'Tell him he can be Archbishop of Canterbury as well, if you like!'

The raucous noise of their drunken jokes followed Godwin and Sweyn some way down the road to Winchester.

'I don't understand you, father,' Sweyn said. 'I thought you had sworn for Hardicanute. Everyone did. You certainly convinced Hardicanute of it. Why have you turned against him?'

'You don't understand politics, my boy,' Godwin laughed. 'Be a friend to everyone, until you see which way the wind blows. At first I thought Emma's influence would be enough to put Hardicanute on the throne, but then I saw how much support that snivelling little sot had. Now the wind swings Harold's way, and shrewd old Godwin is suddenly his trusted advisor. You wait and see; there'll be some choice pickings for us out of this. I fancy we'll have earned an earldom for you by the time Harold Harefoot is king!'

'An earldom for me? Which one? Where?'

Godwin had already started to plan that.

'A new one, I think,' he said. 'Leofric is always complaining that he can't contain the Welsh all along his Mercian border. Perhaps we can take a slice of it off his hands. Say, Herefordshire? And Gloucestershire too, perhaps?'

'Will Leofric let you get away with that?'

'Oh, he'll not have much choice, if King Harold agrees. It will be our reward for services rendered. Yes, that will make a nice addition to our estates in Wessex. But,' he added, suddenly stern, 'you will have to show Harold that you are better at keeping out the Welsh then Leofric.'

'Of course,' said Sweyn, with all the assurance of a seventeen-year-old who had yet to experience failure. 'I'll handle the Welsh all right.'

'Good. You worry about that, and leave Harold and Leofric to me.'

'And Hardicanute? And Emma?'

'They will be no trouble, believe me.'

An early sleet was blowing in when they reached Winchester a few days later, and the sudden turn of the weather put Godwin in a bad mood. He did not relish travelling home to Bosham in such conditions, but much worse was the prospect of staying at the home of Queen Emma. She, with her correct Norman manners, would feel obliged to offer him hospitality, despite her ill-concealed dislike of him and the bad news he was bringing. He, with his hatred of all things Norman, would feel equally ill at ease.

'I don't want to be trapped in this tomb,' Godwin told Sweyn at the gate of Emma's house. 'I'd rather go home through all the snow that ever fell.'

Emma had built herself a Norman keep within the ruins of a Roman villa. She had even imported some of the stone from Caen, so that she might feel closer to home. It was Sweyn's first sight of the strange house, and the boy gazed about him in wonder as the servants led them along a torch-lit passage, into the soaring, white-stone hall with its huge canopied fireplace and extravagant tapestries and silks. Godwin had been there several times before, and regarded it all with contempt. In his opinion the heavy oak table built of planks from mature trees was ostentatious, and so was the coloured Italian glass in the narrow windows, which gave the place the appearance of a church rather than a house. Least of all could he understand Emma's latest and most prized acquisition, a brilliant carpet on the stone-flag floor the like of which, she had been convinced by a Persian merchant, would soon be adopted in all the fashionable European palaces. No one else in England or Normandy had one yet, and Emma was very pleased with it.

Godwin, warming his backside at the fire, stared down at the carpet and shook his head, tut-tutting to himself.

'Look at that,' he scoffed to Sweyn, 'Tapestries on the floor! What extraordinary folk these Normans are. They build stone vaults to live in, they eat the hind parts of frogs; their men look more like monks than warriors with their silly short hair! Now they put tapestries on the floor for people to walk over!'

Sweyn was still chuckling at his father's grumbles when Emma and Hardicanute appeared on the stone stairway at the far end of the hall. He had to raise a hand to hide his smile, but Godwin had not finished yet. The sight of Hardicanute leading his mother down the steps, one hand lightly touching hers, was more than the rough-and-ready earl could stomach.

'Prancing little pansy,' Godwin growled. 'He's even worse than Harold. Can you imagine *that* stepping into Canute's shoes?'

Sweyn, however, was paying no attention to the object of

Godwin's scorn. Hardicanute was merely an unimpressive youth of his own age, thoroughly put in the shade by the overbearing presence of the legendary Emma.

Everything about the slender and upright queen had an air of severity, from the glistening, hawk-like eyes and close-lipped mouth down to the thin hands, which she clasped before her. She was dressed, like all women of her class, in a loose-fitting gown and overmantle of modest green, held by a thin golden girdle, a wimple encircled by a jewelled band, and soft leather slippers, yet somehow the elegance and simplicity of her attire added to the air of command that lay over it all like an invisible shroud. Emma radiated pride and dignity and confidence. Little wonder, when one considered that for most of her life she had helped influence the rulers of three nations. Her father, brother and two nephews had all been Dukes of Normandy, and she was great-aunt to the young Duke William. She had been the second wife of the English king Ethelred, then the second wife of the Danish conqueror Canute. To Ethelred she had borne Edward and Alfred, and to Canute she had given Hardicanute. Despite the power wielded by Harold Harefoot, Canute's son by his first marriage, Emma was still a force to be reckoned with in both England and Normandy and a serious threat to Earl Godwin. Certainly Godwin did not frighten her. That was plain from the way in which she advanced upon him today, like a woman intent on murder. Her eyes were ablaze, her body taut with inner rage.

'So, at last you have had the manners to come here!' she rapped. 'Now perhaps you will have the decency to tell me; who murdered my son?'

Her display of fury did nothing to unsettle Godwin. It even amused him, for it was strongly rumoured that Alfred's death had been most opportune for Emma, who now saw the way clearer for Hardicanute. Indeed, some people had gone so far as to say that Emma had urged her son to come to England knowing full well that his life would be in danger.

'Some overzealous housecarls, lady,' Godwin answered. 'The fools thought they were protecting Harold.' He added the lie: 'They will be suitably punished.'

'Damn you,' Emma snarled, 'you know what I mean. I'm not talking about the vile little savages with the blinding irons.' Her voice faltered at that, but she recovered to continue: 'It's those who ordered Alfred's death I want to see punished. Who were they? That swine Harold? You, perhaps?'

Godwin stood his ground.

'Prince Alfred's death was an accident.'

186

'An accident!' Emma echoed harshly. 'A very convenient accident, for some. And who will be the next to suffer an *accident*? Hardicanute? Me? You had better tread carefully yourself, Godwin, if you are as innocent as you pretend. A man who will murder two hundred men to get his way will not tolerate too many people of your standing.'

'Oh no, mother,' Hardicanute spoke up. 'I'm sure Earl Godwin has taken all necessary steps to ensure his own safety. Haven't you, Godwin? Is it true, what we hear: that you have switched your loyalties to Harold's camp?'

Again the earl lightly sidestepped the insult.

'I have been asked to bring you a message from Harold, if that is what you call switching loyalties,' he said. 'He offers you a portion of the kingdom, from the Humber northwards.'

'He offers what?' Emma demanded indignantly. 'What right has he to make offers? My son is Canute's natural heir. Harold Harefoot is nothing but a mongrel upstart!'

'But he has the support of the Witan, and he will be crowned king next year. There is no longer any doubt of that.'

'No, thanks to the traitors we called friends,' Emma hissed. 'My God, if Canute could see what was being done here! If he could see how all that he built is being torn down by the pack of wolves who called themselves his friends!'

Hardicanute laid a hand on Emma's arm.

'Do not distress yourself so, mother,' he pleaded. 'I suppose we must count ourselves lucky that I have been offered something better than my poor brother's fate. I will accept the North, if that is all I can achieve for now. But I warn you, Godwin,' he went on, 'there will come a day when justice will be done, when I shall have what is rightfully mine. And on that day, Alfred will be avenged.'

'He will be avenged, by God,' Emma vowed. 'If it takes me forever, I shall see that his murderers do not go unpunished. Harold himself must know that that desire beats in my breast stronger than any other.'

'Then may I suggest that you would be wise to go a very long way north of the Humber?' Godwin said, 'Or better still, return to Normandy?'

That rendered Emma speechless, but not for long.

'How dare you!' she gasped. 'How dare you tell me to leave the country where I have lived as queen to two kings?'

'For your own good,' Godwin shrugged. 'Would you care to live in England when your stepson is king?'

'Is that a threat?'

'Not from me, lady.'

'But from Harold? Is that another message he has asked you to bring?'

'To my knowledge, Harold has made no threats against your life,' Godwin told her. 'But you are the best judge as to where you will be safest.' He beckoned to Sweyn, indicating that they should be on their way. As a parting shot at Emma, he added: 'Do let me know if there is anything I can do to assist you – before you leave.'

'Damn you, Godwin,' Emma said through clenched teeth. 'Tell me, do you sleep soundly at nights after you have betrayed your friends?'

For a long time after Godwin and Sweyn had left, Emma stood in silent fury gazing around her grand hall, the last remnant of an empire she had helped to control for nearly twenty years. This would not be the first time she had been exiled from England, but it would come so much harder now because she had fought so tenaciously to rebuild it all following her first downfall, when Ethelred had lost the kingdom. She had still been a young woman then. Since that time she had devoted the best years of her life to Canute, all in vain.

'If ever you are king of this cursed country, Hardicanute,' she advised her son, 'do not be so foolish as to think that you can govern it alone. I hate to admit it, but no king can rule without men like Godwin at his side, whether he be a good king or bad, strong or weak. I know; I have seen it all too often. Ethelred was destroyed by his own courtiers. Canute was a strong man, and no fool, but he succeeded as much through choosing the Godwins of this world as by his own efforts. Even sheep may command the flock, as long as the dogs are there to hold off the wolves. Know your friends. Be sure they are tough, and not too highly principled. Knowing your friends is more important than knowing what they do in your name, as long as it is you they do it for.'

'Such friends must be hard to find,' Hardicanute sulked. 'I thought Godwin was mine, but look what happened. If you must trust men who are unprincipled, how can you trust them to be loyal? That is a contradiction, isn't it?'

'You hold on to the strong men by offering them greater rewards than your enemies do. It is an art you will have to learn. Did you offer Godwin anything but your gratitude? That is not enough. With men like him, loyalty is bought and paid for. Remember that, and survive!'

'If ever I get the chance!'

'You will,' Emma promised. 'Your day will come. Use your time well in the North, and prepare for that day. I shall go back to

Normandy. Perhaps it will be for the better. Little William will need a strong friend to guide him. I shall try to teach him the lessons we have learned here the hard way, and hope that one day it will be of some benefit to him.' She kissed her son's cheek, concluding: 'We must console ourselves that, out of every evil, a little good may be born.'

IV

M AY blossomed gloriously after the hard winter, like a sudden
burst of sunlight out of black clouds. The acres of varied
green along the Thames Valley exploded into yellow, white, scarlet
and violet, urging to life a vast new population of bees and tiny
flies. Birdsong piped and whistled along the broad river, which was
swelled by heavy rains and snows melting in the Cotswolds and
Chilterns. Again the forests teemed with beasts. Wolves and boars,
the smallest mice, all hunted and foraged, mated and marked out
territories, filling the dark green glades with snorts and squeals and
the rustlings and whisperings in the undergrowth.

In a marshy meadow by the Thames, a mile outside Reading,
two men, one very young and the other rather older, met each day
to the ringing noises of steel upon steel as they fought out mock
wars with sword, axe and shield. Forward and back they stepped
and stumbled through the soggy grass, swinging, thrusting,
dodging, their heavy breathing broken now and again with sharp
exclamations. Their faces and hands were wet with sweat, their
cloaks slapped out behind them with the tugging of the breeze, and
their teeth were firmly set in grim concentration.

'Guard, Cedric, guard!' Oswald shouted as he had countless
times before. 'Keep your guard up, boy!' He halted his axe in mid-
swing and thudded the blade into the gluey ground, flexing his arm
to stretch the muscles. 'You threw your shield halfway back around
your body,' he criticised the boy, his words coming in short, harsh
gasps. 'I could have cut you in two then. How many times have I
told you about that? Can't you get out of the habit?'

Cedric, leaning on his sword, bit his lip.

'I'm sorry,' he panted. 'Sometimes I think I have you beaten, I
suppose.'

'Never think it, not until your man is lying dead. That is when
you have him beaten,' Oswald said. He flexed his fingers once
more, and drew his sword. 'Look,' he went on encouragingly. 'You
seem to do much better sword to sword. Perhaps you're not ready
yet for the axes. So, let us work on the best of your skills for now.
Ready?'

Cedric nodded, and took up his stance. Slowly they circled each

190

other, slightly crouched, their shields held across their bodies and their blades at knee-height, watching each other for the first move.

'Uncle,' Cedric asked, as they crab-walked round. 'Have I improved at all?'

'You have improved, but you are not ready yet. Not for Olaf Ericsson.'

'Then how much longer?' the youth wanted to know. He was tired of the endless waiting. All through the winter Oswald had trained him like this at indoor tournaments, gradually perfecting this move, improving that one, progressing week by week with an art that had amazed Cedric with its intricacy. Before that dreadful night in Guildford, Cedric had thought he knew how to handle a sword. Now here he was, eight months later, still begging for more knowledge. The answer, as he expected, differed not at all from the answers he had been given since he began.

'You will be ready when I tell you,' Oswald said.

'You'll never tell me!' Cedric yelled. He leapt forward, swinging the sword around his head, shouting: 'Not tomorrow, next week, next year, never! Because you don't want me to fight Olaf!'

Oswald only chuckled. He stepped back, easily parrying with sword and shield each blow from the youngster's humming blade.

'Wait, hold up!' he ordered. 'Don't attack in a rage. I've told you that, too.'

Once more they paused. Oswald shook his head and smiled as he watched his nephew's temper cool.

'No,' Oswald said, 'I don't want you to fight Olaf, not until you are able to kill him. Is that so surprising? I don't want to lose you, you know.'

'All the same, I will,' Cedric vowed. 'And soon. Whether he kills me or I kill him, it doesn't matter as long as we fight. That's all I want.'

'I know,' Oswald told him. 'You're possessed by the idea. You have been ever since . . .'

He hesitated, not wanting to hurt Cedric's feelings by mentioning Guildford. Tiredly, he threw down the stout wooden shield and sat on it, tracing with one finger the patterns on the embossed bronze overplate, and the dents left there many years ago by Viking axes in Sweden.

'Your father was a great warrior, Cedric,' Oswald said quietly. 'He was better than me, by far. But in the battle of Skene he died, and I lived. I have often wondered why, and the only answer I can come up with is that he was unlucky enough to encounter a man who was better still, and I was more fortunate and did not. No man is ever fully ready for war or death. There is always one small thing he may have overlooked, or forgotten. All right, perhaps you are as ready as you'll ever be, but I still don't want you to go. Even if you were the best fighter I'd ever seen I wouldn't want you to go, because Olaf has experience on his side. Also, he has the killer instinct, something you have not. I could train you for another year and he would still kill you. Do you understand? I can teach you so much more, yet I can teach you nothing more. I can teach you to kill, but I cannot teach you how to kill Olaf Ericsson.'

Cedric had been listening to Oswald, but his uncle's voice sounded far away, like the soft humming of insects on the river. He was trying to imagine what it would be like to meet Olaf again, but somehow the man's face would not form in his mind.

'You are saying that if I am going, I may as well go now,' Cedric suggested. 'As a matter of fact, I had decided to. I'm leaving today. I had meant to tell you, once we'd finished here. I suppose I was hoping you'd say I was ready. I wanted to hear you say that.'

'Today, eh?' Oswald said expressionlessly, pulling himself to his feet. He picked up the shield and began strapping it back on his arm. 'Today,' he repeated, pretending to be busy with the ties. 'I wish you wouldn't, nephew.'

'I've told you how I feel. You and mother, you're the only ones I've told. I can't wait any longer. I've lived with it all this time, since that night in Guildford, and I cannot hold back for another day. Now I want everyone else to know how Cedric Cedricsson punishes traitors, especially that pig Olaf.'

'That pig Olaf happens to be the most dangerous and merciless warrior in all England.'

'It doesn't matter, don't you see?' Cedric declared passionately. 'It doesn't matter, because Prince Alfred and Gilbert de Bernay and a hundred good Berkshire men died at Guildford. Because of that I can't wait any more to take revenge on Olaf. It's the only way I can get back my honour. It doesn't matter if Olaf kills me. If he does, he'll only be finishing what he started at Guildford. I'll be dead, like the others, but at least I won't be shamed any more.'

'You are not shamed. I have tried to tell you that.'

'I *am* shamed, shamed and disgraced. Do you think I don't know what people have said about me since that night? They laugh at me, uncle, and not always behind my back. They make jokes about me, except the ones whose husbands and sons and brothers did not come back, and they hate the very sight of me. They hate me because I was the only man to survive the slaughter. I was the one who took their men away, and I was the only one to come back. Oh God, they despise me. I even despise myself! The nightmares I've had! Night after night, I've seen the faces of the dead, the maimed and the blind, and Olaf laughing as he murdered my friends . . .'

'And fighting Olaf is all that will ease the pain,' Oswald said with understanding.

Cedric was pressing at the bridge of his nose, where a burning swell was pushing unmanly tears into his eyes.

'Yes,' he gasped. 'That is all I live for.'

'Where will you start?'

'At Bosham. I'm going to see Earl Godwin.'

'Godwin? Why?'

'It's my duty. I should have done it long ago, but I was too afraid. I have to explain myself to him, and beg his pardon for my failure. If he decides to punish me, I shall have to accept it. Besides, he is the best man to help me find Olaf. If Olaf has not been punished already, I can offer that service to Earl Godwin and thus prove my loyalty to him.'

Oswald did not know what to say in the face of such simple faith. He had decided long ago that Godwin must be as guilty as anyone of the murder of Alfred. After the massacre, Oswald also understood at last why poor Cedric had been chosen to lead the escort party.

What a cunning plot, Oswald thought. First, try to sink Alfred with an attack in the Channel, or send him scampering back to Normandy. Then, if that doesn't work, greet him at Dover with a fresh-faced boy and a band of rustics who obviously could do him no harm. Then lure them inland, and there let the assassins take over and do their evil work unhindered. He hated Godwin for the cynical and ruthless manner in which he had used Cedric, and he cursed himself for a fool because he had taken an unwitting part in the plot and had allowed Cedric to go. Oswald did not know how to explain to Cedric that he had only been a piece in a deadly game. Cedric had been proud to serve Earl Godwin, and it would shatter the boy's pride still more to learn that he had been tricked by the very man who had employed him. Cedric, untried and gullible, still believed that the slaughter was the work of Olaf Ericsson alone, perhaps in the interest of King Harold, but certainly against the wishes of Earl Godwin. But Cedric was a man now, and Oswald could not stop him going where he wanted to go, but he prayed for a way of warning the lad of the dangers he faced without making him feel a fool.

'Earl Godwin would have punished you by now, had he considered you to blame,' Oswald tried.

'That may be so, but it doesn't excuse me from going to him. I must beg his forgiveness, and I want his consent to what I intend to do.'

'All right, by all means speak to Godwin before you fight Olaf. He will probably forbid it. After all, Olaf must have been acting on someone's orders. Most people think King Harold decreed that Alfred should die. You realise what that means, don't you? In trying to kill Olaf, the king's man, you will be attacking the king himself.'

'Be that as it may, Olaf deserves to die.'

'But you will ask Earl Godwin's advice first?'

'I will.'

'Good,' Oswald said. With luck, he told himself, Godwin would tell Cedric to go home and mind his own business, and in time the boy's wounds would heal.

'You are a wise young man, Cedric, and a brave one. No doubt about that.'

'*I* doubt it, sometimes,' Cedric sighed. 'I did not feel wise or brave when Olaf forced command of the escort from me. Had I been more resolute then, Alfred and Gilbert and all the others might be alive today.'

Oswald laid a comforting arm across his nephew's shoulders.

'No, no, you blame yourself too harshly,' he said. 'There was nothing more you could have done. It is simply hard for a young and eager one like you to accept that old warriors are the best, because they have survived longest. They have the instinct to kill, and that is something you can't be taught; it has to come with experience. Remember, the longer a man survives, the more battles he wins. The more he wins, the more deeply the killer instinct is graven upon his very nature. Bravery and boldness are not everything, Cedric. We are all brave, we are all cowards, depending upon the circumstances. We are all wise, we are all fools. Look at the river there. Is it broad, or narrow?'

'I don't understand,' Cedric confessed.

'Well, is it not both? When it freezes in January, you can walk across it. Now, when it is in full flood, you can hardly cross it with the help of a boat. Men are like that. One day at peace, the next enraged. One day shallow, the next too deep to plumb. You are no different from any other man, my boy, but you seem to mistake what you expect of yourself for what others expect of you. Be like the river. Do what the season and the conditions demand of you, no more. Do you understand?'

'I think so.'

'Good, for words are all I can give you now, and I pray they will be some use. Go, seek your dragon. And God be with you!'

The way south from Reading was a series of winding tracks. Often scarcely more than footpaths, they wound through the endless slopes of oak and beech, ash and elm, thicket and heathland that were part of the great Wessex forests stretching from Dorset to Kent, from Essex and Oxfordshire to the coasts of Hampshire and Sussex, with only a few small towns and villages thinly scattered. The difficult way was made more hazardous by outlaw bands who would appear suddenly on the road and kill and strip a traveller for a few pennies. There were wolf packs, wild boars, feral cattle and occasionally a bear, and many pretty glades and dells were the known abodes of fairies and elves, demons and goblins.

When the rains were heavy, as they had been this year, the streams and marshes swelled into enormous swamps which caused a good deal of casting about for safe roads. On some days a rider might progress only seven or eight miles towards his destination; he could cover twice that distance looking for a way through the forest, or for the nearest settlement where he could stay at the home of an ale-wife or in a religious house. It was easy to get hopelessly lost and ride for hours in the wrong direction if the sun was hidden in cloud. Then the traveller had to seek for some habitation and ask the local people for guidance, only to find that most of them had never ventured beyond the village, and knew nothing of other places no more than a few miles away.

Cedric pressed southward through these lonely wastes for three days, growing more tired, filthy and short-tempered with every mile. Late on the third afternoon, when he rode out of the trees and across a few unfenced meadows to the sea, it was like leaving the wilderness for the Promised Land. He dismounted and got down on his knees, and gave thanks to God for his deliverance.

Before him the fields gave way to the coarser shore grass, then to a wide and stony beach. Black rippled mud flats were left exposed by a low tide, and noisy gulls were scavenging and squabbling in the shallows. There were no buildings to be seen, not even fishermen's huts. He knew he must be somewhere in the region of Chichester or Bosham, for he had been pointed this way at the last hamlet, but he had no idea whether he should now turn right or left. He allowed his weary horse to graze while he pondered over the choice.

He had been standing there for only a few minutes when another rider appeared out of a copse, and made towards him. At first Cedric was pleased to see the newcomer, for the man could surely direct him, and yet, as the horseman drew nearer, something about him made Cedric uneasy.

The rider was a youth of about Cedric's own age but of much

nobler rank. He sat astride his splendid bay with the arrogance of one early accustomed to command, instantly recognising in Cedric a person of lower birth. His handsome young face held a challenge in the coolness of his blue eyes and the firm set of his mouth. His dress and adornments marked him out as rich too. His cloak and tunic were of the finest cloth and delicately embroidered. He wore a beautifully engraved silver torque in the shape of a snake, long silver bracelets and glittering brooches, and his sword hilt was decorated with garnet and turquoise. As further marks of his high standing, the boy wore his hair flowing freely below his shoulders, and on his throat and right wrist were tiny tattoos depicting the rampant Wessex dragon. He regarded the dirty figure of Cedric with scorn as he reined in a few yards away, and sat silently as if waiting for an introduction. It was this authoritative air, visible even at some distance, which had disquieted Cedric. Without a word being spoken, Cedric had been made to feel as though he were trespassing on hallowed ground.

'Am I near to Bosham, sir?' Cedric asked politely.

'Who are you?' the proud youth responded. 'What are you doing here?'

'I go to see Earl Godwin.'

'Do you indeed? That remains to be seen. I did ask your name which you have not yet told me, unless my hearing fails me.'

'I am Cedric Cedricsson, of Reading.'

The grand one gave a sarcastic laugh.

'Oh, really?' he said. 'And where might this Reading be?'

'It is in Berkshire, sir; by the Thames. I'm sure you have heard of the Thames?'

Cedric had not meant to be insolent, but that was how it sounded. The youth flushed angrily, and leaned down from the saddle with eyes narrowed.

'Do you jest with me?'

'No sir, I only wished to make myself clear. Forgive me if I sounded rude; I had not intended it.'

The boy made a thorough study of Cedric's face, trying to detect traces of mockery or a lie. Finally he seemed satisfied that his apology was genuine.

'This message that you have for Earl Godwin,' he said, 'who sent you with it?'

'No one sent me, sir. It is personal business I have to discuss with him.'

'Is that so? Well, you will have to discuss it with me first, or you will never lay eyes on Godwin. Do you think my father sees every scoundrel that happens to come to his door?'

Ah yes, Cedric thought, the likeness is obvious now. Here was the same immovable confidence Cedric had seen in Godwin and his eldest son Sweyn at Guildford. It must be true, what they said of this family, that they considered themselves the true masters of England, and so behaved towards English subjects as would kings and princes.

'Pardon me,' said Cedric, with due deference, 'but you are Lord Godwin's son?'

'I am Harold Godwinsson, second son to the Earl of Wessex,' the youth confirmed. 'So, now that we know each other, am I to wait much longer for you to state your business, Cedric of Reading by the Thames?'

Pride began to surge through Cedric's veins. He'd be damned if he'd let this lordly pup bully him. He had come to see Earl Godwin, and he would talk with no one else.

'I'm sorry,' he told Harold. 'What I have to say to Earl Godwin is for him alone to hear. I cannot speak of it to you.'

Harold was taken aback by this show of defiance. He slid down from his horse and drew his sword. He assumed a thin smile of bravado, and pointed the blade at Cedric's throat.

'You will talk to me,' he ordered. 'Or you will fight me for the right to see my father.'

Into Cedric's mind there came a memory of himself nearly a year ago, trying to assert his manhood with some foolish adventure in the Shin Field. Harold, he realised, was attempting a similar show of courage and manliness.

Harold had not yet progressed beyond what Cedric now called his 'Shin Field age,' but understanding that did not make the situation any the less delicate for Cedric. Harold might be merely playing at manhood, but it was a dangerous game. Surely he must know that a man did not draw his sword upon another unless he was prepared to use it?

'I cannot fight you,' Cedric said firmly, and made to remount.

Harold skipped around to stand between him and the horse, his sword still held threateningly.

'Why?' he jeered. 'Are you a coward?'

'No, my lord, I am not a coward,' Cedric replied patiently. 'I cannot fight you because I am a faithful liegeman of the Lord Godwin. So, can I kill his son?'

'Ha! You need have no fear of killing me. The best of warriors have taught me my skill. I'm more than a match for you!'

'That may be so, but we are not going to put it to the test. A fine choice I have, don't I? Either you cleave me in two, or I kill you and finish this day dangling at the end of a rope. A man needs better reason to fight than that, Harold Godwinsson. Now, will you let me pass? I have travelled a long way, and I'm too tired for more of this game.'

Harold was annoyed. He shrugged in a gesture of resignation and sheathed his sword.

'Wrestling then,' he insisted. 'I suppose you are allowed to wrestle with me?'

'No. I have no desire to wrestle with you, or run a race, or throw dice, or answer riddles. I want food, drink and rest, and I want to speak with Lord Godwin.'

'I was right,' Harold grumbled. 'You are a coward. Well, I'm afraid you have no choice. For all I know, you could be an outlaw, a poacher, or an assassin. It is my duty to learn your purpose before I allow you near my father. So, state your business, or fight me.'

He shed his cloak and sword-belt and threw them to the ground. He dropped into a wrestler's crouch, swaying easily from side to side as he edged closer to Cedric.

Seeing that he had no hope of simply riding away from this irritating lordling, Cedric gave in and wearily stripped to his trousers and shirt. When they squared up to each other, shuffling slowly about in the low tangle of weeds, Cedric saw that Harold was the taller of the two by a couple of inches, and more heavily built. He was probably the stronger, therefore, and Cedric braced himself for a difficult contest. He prepared himself just in time, for Harold launched himself forward without warning and crashed shoulder first into Cedric's chest.

The blow might have sent Cedric sprawling had he not been ready. As it was, he had just time to step back and ride the main force of the charge. Nevertheless, it was a painful thump to take so early in the bout and it shook Cedric's confidence, as it had been meant to do. Cedric, his chest sore, dodged out of range while he recovered his breath.

'Is that how you always fight, going backwards?' Harold mocked him. 'Come on, I'm waiting to fight!'

Cedric lunged into the attack. They became locked together in a pushing, shambling dance, hampered by the grass clinging around their feet. Cedric found now that Harold's strength was indeed greater than his own. He soon found himself in trouble, gripped tightly in Harold's powerful arms, and his fatigue did nothing to help. It was as much as Cedric could do to keep his feet on the ground, and air in his lungs, in those long seconds they spent staggering back and forth, striving to push each other down.

'You see?' Harold panted. 'The best of wrestlers have taught me, too. Now tell me your business, eh?'

Cedric shook his head and struggled valiantly. He tried to press upon Harold and slide free of his hold, but instead he unbalanced himself. Harold, quick to take advantage, placed one long leg round behind his opponent's knees and shoved hard. Cedric collapsed and fell on his back, then Harold was astride him pinning one of his arms down with a knee and the other with a vice-like hand. With his free hand Harold spanned Cedric's throat and pushed back his chin, so that his victim's head was pressed firmly and uncomfortably into the ground.

'There now!' Harold exulted. 'Now you will talk to me, you cowardly dog!'

Cedric could hardly draw breath, let alone speak. His chest and throat were crushed under Harold's weight, and Harold's knee against his arm was sending spasms of pain up to his shoulder. All he could manage was another slight movement of his head.

'A brave one, if not much of a fighter,' Harold mused. 'How long are you prepared to stay there? It would be easier to talk.'

He loosened his grip on Cedric's neck then, giving him a chance to say something. Cedric coughed harshly, and tried to blink tears of pain from his eyes.

'Is this how the Godwins treat their guests?' he choked.

'Watch your tongue, dog!' Harold snapped. 'What right have you to consider yourself a guest at the house of Godwin?'

'I am a thane, a man of property, and your father's liegeman!' Cedric rasped. 'I had heard that even the meanest serf could expect to be received with courtesy by Earl Godwin! Perhaps I was misinformed.'

'By God, you're a cheeky one!' Harold laughed. 'All right, thane, get up. I'm sick of your whining!'

Harold got up and went to sit on a low hillock. Cedric made no effort to rise but lay there miserable and ashamed, hating Harold for this humiliation and wondering why he must always be the loser. Exhaustion had at last overtaken him. He would gladly have stayed there in the mud to sleep, if he could expect no better welcome than this at Godwin's house. Harold, puzzled by his sullen silence and reluctance to get up, came to kneel beside Cedric.

'Hey, come on,' Harold said not unkindly, as though feeling some remorse. 'What are you worried about? There's no disgrace in being beaten, you know. The only disgrace is in refusing to fight. But you fought. You did your best.'

'Who said I was disgraced?' Cedric answered sourly. 'There is certainly no disgrace in losing a fight when you're hungry and dead tired from three days' travelling. I'll fight you again, Harold Godwinsson, any time, when I am as fit and fresh as you are!'

'All right,' Harold smiled. 'But I'll still beat you. I've never been beaten yet.'

Harold extended a hand to help Cedric up. Cedric reluctantly took it.

'What happens now?' asked Cedric, dusting himself down. 'Are you still not going to let me by?'

'You've earned your right to pass,' Harold condescended. 'I'll take you to my father myself.'

'Thank you,' Cedric said acidly, as they put on their cloaks and weapons. 'I shouldn't think he has many guests, if you afford them all this kind of welcome!'

Harold laughed, a carefree and attractive laugh that Cedric found strangely comforting after the boy's earlier hostility. Much to his surprise, Cedric realised that it would not be impossible to like this arch young nobleman.

'Come on,' Harold was saying, 'I can't wait to hear this secret you have guarded so fiercely. I warn you, though, there are no secrets in our house. Talk to Godwin, and you talk to the whole clan. That's the way we are.'

He led the way along the beach, riding at a canter with scant regard for Cedric's weariness.

After two miles they came upon Bosham. It was a bustling little town, standing on a flat promontory that stretched out across the muddy creeks and channels of the harbour. A large fleet of fishing boats and three merchant vessels were presently stranded there, the larger boats busily loading and unloading cargoes with tackle and hoist along the wooden quayside while they waited for a high tide. Beyond the wharf stood a church with a stone tower, a big timber hall that was doubtless Godwin's house, and numerous smaller buildings of wood and some of stone, consisting chiefly of the remains of an old Roman settlement. Beyond the town, across the fields, was the little Benedictine monastery famous for a visit by St. Wilfrid hundreds of years before.

Harold, crossing the flat plank bridge that ran over the widest of the creeks to the town, here assumed the role of guide. He pointed out some of the more interesting remnants of the Roman villas upon which generations of Saxons had since built their timber and turf cottages, but in particular he drew Cedric's attention to the church. Like some of the houses, it had been put together with many of the slabs and age-stained columns from the Roman ruins.

'A daughter of Canute lies buried in that church,' Harold told him. 'She was only eight years old when she died. This place meant a great deal to the old king. He did my father a tremendous honour when he gave him this house and estate.'

Encircled by a tall fence of sharp stakes, Godwin's hall stood like a massive barn amid a number of smaller outbuildings, which huddled up to it like cubs suckling at a fierce old she-wolf. It was the biggest house Cedric had ever seen, bigger even than his uncle Oswald's in Wantage. Like Godwin himself, it dominated everything around it, including the church, with an almost frightening air of authority. Either Godwin had imposed his personality on this huge hall, or the house had shaped him, it was not easy to say which. It was large, down-to-earth and square-cut, solid and practical. And, also like Godwin, Cedric noticed, it was well protected. In addition to the sturdy stockade there were half-a-dozen housecarls in chain-mail standing at the gateway. As if they were not enough to frighten off intruders, the yard was also patrolled by a pack of savage-looking hounds.

'You see?' Harold grinned. 'You're lucky you met me. They would have given you more trouble than I did.'

Cedric felt inclined to agree. He was chilled by the sight of the housecarls, but he looked closely at them as he rode by hoping, yet at the same time dreading, to recognise Olaf Ericsson among them. He was not there, however, and Cedric was ashamed at feeling relieved that his meeting with the murderer was not to be just yet.

'What's the matter?' Harold asked. 'Never seen housecarls before?'

'Oh yes,' Cedric replied bitterly. 'I've seen them before. More of them and closer than I ever want to see them again!'

'Oh, you and your mysteries. Now what are you talking about?'

'You'll find out, since you are to share my secret, as you call it.'

They halted before the second largest building in the compound, a two-storey Roman granary with offices over the ground floor. It had been converted into stables below, with timber stalls fixed in between the columned archways. Grooms hurried out to take their horses as they dismounted.

'I've often thought that would make a splendid house,' commented Harold. 'But father doesn't like stone buildings. He prefers that draughty old pile of logs we live in over there. Stone is for tombs and churches, he says. If ever I own Bosham I'll make this my house, and give that timber barn to the pigs and cattle. I think the Romans had the right idea, don't you? Did you know that in Rome everyone still lives in stone houses? My tutor told me. He's been there.'

'It would be a strange sort of house,' said Cedric, who thought that only priests and monks lived in chilly vaults like that. Touching the weather-beaten facade he added: 'Too cold for me.'

'You think so, do you?' Harold scoffed. 'Well, I'll take you upstairs tomorrow, and perhaps you'll change your mind. The windows let in an amazing amount of light, and you'd be surprised how warm stone and plaster can be when you've got a fire going – not that there's much ventilation, mind you. But there are so many rooms up there, everyone could have one to himself. You wouldn't have to live in the crowded market place of a house that we do. Come on into the hall; you'll see what I mean.'

Dusk was making a pale gloom of the spring evening. They walked across the yard and entered the stout double doors of Godwin's hall, and Cedric saw at once what Harold had meant by living in a crowd. The house swarmed with people, and at first sight they were a bewildering Babel of bustle and noise. An army of servants and slaves were darting about, far outnumbering Godwin's large family. Some were lighting candles of peeled reeds soaked in animal fat, and the fat was melting and spluttering and smoking black in the flickering flames. Others fussed around the central fire, where pots boiled and meats roasted on the iron griddle and spits, and a thick column of yet more smoke rose up to the hole in the high roof. Dozens more attended the tables which lined three sides of the gigantic room, and those tables bore an array of dishes such as Cedric had never seen gathered together in one place before. Girls carried plates from the fire to the table, and empty platters out to the cleaning room at the back of the hall. Matronly women pummelled at mattresses on the cot beds behind the tables; men raked over the cinders of the fire pit, and boys turned crackling joints on the spits, while clusters of women chatted as they sat and sewed.

Godwin's younger children ran around everywhere, shouting and screaming as they played, chased by yapping dogs. In one corner, a solitary harpist tried in vain to hear the notes he was playing. Silk hangings fluttered in the breeze from the open doors, and tapestries flapped against oak pillars. Burning logs spat, crockery and knives rattled, benches and tables creaked beneath the shifting of arguing guests. A dropped cooking iron clanged on the hard earth floor, earning a careless scullion a cuff on the ear. In the rafters, roosting birds chirped and fluttered, and occasionally spattered the noisy gathering below.

Harold, though quite used to the din, turned to Cedric and said: 'I told you so.' He then shouted the length of the hall: 'Father! I have a visitor for you!'

Only then did Cedric's attention move to the top table, where two men sat whom he recognised at once, though they were barely visible in the leaping light of the wall torches. One was unmistakably Earl Godwin, seated in his great oak chair like a king on a throne, and the other was his son Sweyn, newly created Earl of Hereford and Southern Mercia. They had recently returned from a day's hunting, and were gorging themselves like hogs at the plentiful table. At the sound of Harold's voice, Godwin put down his food and peered through the smoky gloom. He took a few moments to lick his greasy moustaches and fingers.

'Who is it?' he bellowed back down the hall. 'Come here, will you?' He scanned the room for his wife and spying her, bawled: 'Gytha! Shut these damned people up, will you? I can't hear myself speak!'

Gytha did not have to utter a word, however. Silence followed Godwin's order immediately. The chattering and the clattering of dishes, the high-pitched squeals of children, even the barking of the hounds, all ceased as though cut through with an axe. No one dared move a muscle, it seemed, except for the two very smallest children who ran to their mother and hid their faces in the folds of her dress.

Cedric was not suprised that Godwin's voice was enough to quell the storm that had raged moments before. Even when sitting deep in the shadows, Godwin the king-maker looked every inch the tyrant he was. Fierce blue eyes gleamed out from darkened sockets like sapphires, and the spread of his horny hands on the table was a challenge to all not to advance beyond their mark or speak out of turn. Cedric, approaching the table with Harold, felt his legs quiver. In trying to avoid Godwin's gaze, he looked up and saw the Golden Dragon of Wessex waving gently above the earl's head.

Cedric recognised it as the standard that Prince Alfred's party had carried to Guildford and fear struck at his breast like a spear. For the first time it occured to him that Godwin might not have been innocent of the massacre. He had walked into the lion's lair, and the lion was breathing in his face. Suddenly he was very frightened, and angry with himself for coming here. He also felt a deep sorrow that his liege lord had apparently tricked him into leading the prince to an ambush, and he wanted nothing more than to turn and run away.

'I know you, don't I?' was Godwin's curt greeting.

'Yes, my lord,' Cedric spoke up. 'We met at Guildford. I am Cedric Cedricsson. I led Prince Alfred's escort from Dover.'

Godwin's eyes narrowed.

'I had heard,' he said slowly, 'that all those poor souls perished . . .'

'Not all, my lord. A handful escaped unharmed. I was fortunate to be among them.'

'Ah, well done,' Godwin nodded, and went back to his meal. There was no sign of guilt or embarrassment in his silence. He grunted at last: 'Well, what are you doing here?'

Cedric watched himself scuffing the rushes from one foot to the other. The presence of the dragon banner in this house had changed his whole view of Alfred's death, and he hardly knew what to think.

'I came here for two reasons,' he shakily explained. 'First, to ask your pardon for failing to prevent the murder of Prince Alfred, and accept the punishment you think fit . . .'

Godwin's face remained inscrutable. He picked up a big drinking horn, a beautiful piece made from African ivory with a rim of beaten gold, and slopped wine into it from a flagon. He drank slowly while Cedric waited, breathless and cold.

'You were a long time coming to me,' Godwin remarked at last. 'It happened – what was it – seven, eight months ago?'

'For a long time I did not know whether I should come or not,' Cedric stammered. 'I was ashamed. I wished I had died at Guildford.'

'Well, I suppose it's noble of you to come now. But have no fear, boy, there's no punishment for you. When Godwin punishes, he does not wait a year to do it. It was not your fault. There was nothing you could do.'

'Thank you; you are most gracious, my lord,' Cedric said, hoping the earl could hear no edge of sarcasm in his voice.

'Yes I am; I'm noted for that, and for the generosity of my table. Are you hungry? Find yourself a place. Eat!'

Cedric gazed again at the banquet, and marvelled at the fare although his appetite was gone. It was always dinner-time at Godwin's house, men said, and the earl always insisted that any and every dish he might fancy should be ready for him whenever he wanted it. Even the house servants were said to be the best fed in the country. Each night, after the family had left the tables, they were allowed to take their pick from what was left, which probably explained why they all worked so hard to get the chores done, and why poor folk had been known to sell their children into the earl's service.

'No, thank you,' Cedric said politely. 'But there is the second purpose I spoke of . . .'

'Yes?'

Cedric took a deep breath.

'I want the head of Olaf Ericsson,' he declared.

Godwin nearly choked on the piece of bread he had been stuffing into his mouth. Tears came to his eyes, and he wiped them away to gawp at his young visitor.

'Well, you won't find that at my table!' he roared.

Sweyn, seated at Godwin's right, threw back his head and screeched with laughter, rather too loudly as though only to please his father. Harold also laughed, but quietly. There were a few hesitant giggles through the hall, but when Godwin himself joined in the merriment the entire company exploded into roars of derision.

Cedric stood alone, mortified, rage rising in him like a welling sickness. He summoned up his courage, and bellowed to be heard above the row.

'My lord!' he shouted, pointing to the dragon standard with a trembling hand. 'I am not jesting. The last time I saw that banner, it was bloodied and disgraced in a way that shames us all!'

His own boldness astonished him, and in the sudden silence he felt he had gone too far. Under Godwin's withering stare, he could have sworn he was shrinking within his own body. For the second time that evening he was tempted to flee, and hide.

'Pardon me, lord,' Cedric went on softly, 'but I am in earnest. Only by killing Olaf can I gain back my honour. I led a hundred men to their deaths, and they still lie unavenged. Since that time, no one in the shire but my own family has spoken to me. They point accusing fingers, asking why I came home untouched. That is the chief reason I have come to you, my lord, to ask where I can find Olaf, and to ask your consent to my mission. That is another reason why it has taken me so long to get here. All winter I have been trained with sword and axe by my uncle, preparing for the day when I meet Olaf. I have sworn to slay him or die in the attempt.'

Godwin nodded, but his face told Cedric nothing.

'A good speech, boy,' he said. 'And a good boast, well meant. You made it just in time to save yourself getting stuck with this knife. Tell me, how old are you?'

'Sixteen.'

'Aha. And how many men have you killed?'

'None yet,' admitted Cedric, hastily adding: 'But I come from a warrior family, sir. My father was Cedric, Alderman of Reading, and my uncle is Oswald, Shire-Reeve of Berkshire as his father was before him. My father and uncle fought with King Canute in Sweden, and my father died there.'

'I know your family, boy,' Godwin said. 'I, too, fought with Canute, beside your father and uncle. I knew your father, and he died bravely, as Oswald has no doubt told you. But shall I tell you who else was there? Olaf Ericsson, the greatest of them all.'

'Olaf was in the battle where my father was killed?'

'He was. That was twelve years ago, when Olaf was still a young man, when we were all young men. We were all brave, but he most of all. With my own eyes I saw him walk alone into the enemy and cut down three or four men before the rest of us closed in. All together that day I suppose he slew, oh, ten or a dozen, the best of Earl Ulf's army. So, what do you think of that? Do you think you are good enough to fight a man who has been the greatest warrior in England for twenty years and more?'

'Perhaps not. But I am honour-bound to try.'

'Oh, you are, are you? Then presumably I cannot stop you throwing your life away, if you must. But answer me this; do you owe loyalty only to the dead Prince Alfred, or are you a loyal subject of King Harold, too?'

'I am loyal to my king.'

'Then how can you kill his captain of housecarls? That would be a treason against him.'

Cedric was tired and confused, much of his ardour had died here tonight.

'Are you telling me I may not fight Olaf?'

'Boy, I don't care if you fight the Devil himself,' Godwin told him. 'It's none of my business. All I am advising is that you forget Olaf, Prince Alfred, and anyone else you met at Guildford. It is done, finished. Alfred is long buried, and Harold Harefoot is king. You are moping about in the past, lad, picking over things others have long forgotten, and I shall certainly not let you go running off in my name to pester the king's highly valued servants. Here, come and fill your belly with some good food. You may sleep in this house tonight, and in the morning you had best get back on your horse and go home. Well, are you going to eat or starve?'

This was not at all what Cedric had expected. He would have understood if Godwin had shown anger, or admiration, but this careless dismissal of the matter was yet another slap in the face. Despite his resolve, he had been treated like a troublesome child, and laughed at again. The very man who had committed him to the trials he had suffered, the lord he had tried so hard to please, had waved him away with little more than a sneer.

Cedric sat at the feast, humbled and unable to eat. The more he was ignored, the lower his spirits sank. He would go out into the night and find lodgings, he decided, rather than spend another minute in Godwin's hall, and shortly after taking his place at the table he got up again and made for the door.

'Goodbye, my lord,' Cedric mumbled in Godwin's direction.

Godwin briefly raised his head and nodded; he was deep in talk with Sweyn. Cedric strode out of the hall, itching with fury. He was halfway across the yard towards the stables when Harold caught up with him and grabbed his arm.

'Hey, you can't go yet! Where are you going to sleep, under a tree?'

'I don't care,' Cedric snorted. 'I don't care if I don't sleep at all. I'll ride all night if I have to.'

'Why, are we so objectionable? Come on, don't be such a sour-face; stay awhile. We can have fun. Take no notice of father. He's a sore-headed old bull, but it's easy to keep out of his way. What are you so upset about, anyway? He was really impressed when you said you wanted to fight Olaf, I could see. He admires that sort of thing more than anything. Otherwise he wouldn't have invited you to stay; he'd have just cuffed your ear and sent you on your way. Honestly!'

Cedric stopped. He wanted to believe Harold. 'Really?'

'I swear it.'

'I thought he was making fun of me.'

'No, that's just his way. He never shows his feelings – at least, not the good feelings. I think he likes you.'

'He has a funny way of showing it,' Cedric said, some of his pride restored.

'You haven't seen anything yet. Wait till he wants to prove he's fond of you. He'll belt you halfway across the room and challenge you to a fight. I know. I've got the bruises to show for it.'

They laughed together, until Cedric remembered the errand that had led him to this strange house, and became serious again.

'Harold,' he said cautiously. 'I'm sorry to ask you this, but it's important to me. Did your father order Prince Alfred's death? Did he have my men killed?'

Harold was about to be angry, but he saw the need in Cedric's eyes and relented.

'No,' he replied firmly. 'He did not. My father is a hard man, sometimes ruthless; but he is not a cowardly murderer. Prince Alfred's death was an accident; it was never meant to be. Some fool panicked, or the housecarls got drunk on blood that night. Neither King Harold nor my father wanted Alfred dead. Will you accept my word on that?'

'Thank you, Harold. I am proud to stay at your house,' Cedric said.

Harold put his arm around Cedric's shoulders and led him back into the hall, and there was a knowing between them that they were friends.

'Now, this is my family,' Harold announced, making a broad sweeping gesture with his free arm. 'The riotous crowd of people who make my life a penance . . .'

He had five brothers and two sisters. Cedric had met Sweyn, and next of the sons after Harold came Tostig, a dark and moody boy of thirteen whose only greeting to Cedric was a sullen nod. Following Tostig were Gurth, aged twelve, and Leofwine, a year younger, two happy and boisterous boys rarely out of each other's company. The youngest brother was six-year-old Wulfnoth who was presently engaged in teasing his four-year-old sister Gunhild. Finally, Harold took Cedric to meet his mother, Gytha, and his sister Edith.

Gytha, Cedric soon discovered, was almost as frightening as Godwin. She was a Danish woman of the true Viking blood, big in stature and powerful of voice. She was still vigorous in her motherhood, though her body had been ravaged and widened by almost eighteen years of child bearing. Only eight of her babies had survived infancy. Her last two pregnancies had produced still births, and since she had now gone two years without conceiving she had concluded that her days of giving birth were over at last. So, she had become even more doting towards those of her brood she had left. Like a huge she-bear, she would gather her cubs about her and tell them endless stories of Danish heroes and all their mighty deeds, gently beating into them a sense of tradition and obligation.

Gytha was related by marriage to the Danish royal family, and in her heart she had never left her homeland. Her brother, the rebel Earl Ulf, had been married to Canute's sister Estrith. Therefore Canute's nephews, Sweyn, Osborn and Bjorn Estrithsson, were also Gytha's nephews. At this very moment Sweyn Estrithsson and his brothers were contesting the Danish throne with both Hardicanute and Magnus of Norway, and it was Gytha's greatest hope that Sweyn would one day rule the Danes.

'I tell Harold that he must go to Denmark and help his cousin win the kingdom,' Gytha boomed at Cedric within moments of meeting him. 'My son Sweyn must go, also. Together they must go, and learn to fight like Viking warriors!'

'But father doesn't think that would be politic,' Harold smiled at Cedric, as if asking his guest to have patience with his warlike mother. 'It isn't his way to back one side against the other until he sees which way the coin will fall, if neither one man nor the other means much to him. Granted, the Estrithssons are his nephews, by marriage, but he feels he has already done Hardicanute harm enough by helping put Harold on the English throne. And Hardicanute could be king of England yet.'

'Your father, afraid of the puppy Hardicanute?' Gytha chided Harold. 'Bah, this I cannot believe. He fears no-one, so why should he fear to send you to Denmark to fight for your cousins? A father who has himself fought beside the Danes should be proud to send his sons . . .'

In her excitement she dropped the garment she had been helping her daughter to sew, and she turned crossly on her daughter, scolding her: 'Edith! Hold still, please . . . !'

Cedric had hardly noticed Edith until then. The girl had been partly hidden behind a wide oak pillar, quietly working by candlelight. Now, seeing her for the first time, how beautiful she was, Cedric's heart almost stopped. She was soft and pale as a lily, with shy, innocent blue eyes in an oval face. Her sunny golden hair was braided with silver rings and hugged by a white hood, as a wrapping of silk clings to a fragile gift. Cedric could see nothing but her lovely face and small hands, but these modest glimpses were enough to give him an idea of the tantalising sweetness that lay beneath her modest blue gown.

He fell in love with her, at once and completely. Never in his life had he met a girl who stirred within him such an urge simply to be close to her.

'Edith,' said Harold, who had observed the dreamy fascination that had overcome his new friend. 'This is Cedric. Say something to him, before he faints away.'

Edith gave Cedric a shy smile and lowered her gaze to her needlework, scarcely opening her mouth as she inaudibly spoke her welcome. Cedric thrilled to her maidenly charm more deeply still, and fought for words.

'Greetings, Edith,' said someone inside his head.

'Thank God,' grinned Harold. 'At last you look as if you're glad to be here!'

CEDRIC dreamed that the house was burning, and that Earl Godwin had locked him inside. He shouted through a crack in the door, calling to Harold for help, but all Harold would say was: 'Are you going to fight me?' Cedric awoke in a hot sweat, sleepily lifting his face out of a sticky mess of breadcrumbs and slopped ale on the table where he had fallen victim the evening before to the too generous hospitality of Earl Godwin's household.

There *was* a smell of burning, Cedric realised, as he groped for water to wash the mess from his face. It did not come from the fire pit, for it was early morning and there was only a pile of white ash in the hearth. Smoke seemed to be wafted in on the wind through the open doors, and the excited shouting that he could hear from the village confirmed that something out of the ordinary was happening. Even as he pieced these thoughts together, Harold came to his side and shook his shoulder.

'Wake up, man!' Harold demanded. 'There's a house on fire!'

Cedric leapt up and followed Harold out. Everyone else had already left the hall. The stricken house was in the centre of the village next to the blacksmith's forge, and it was blazing furiously. Its timbers and thatched roof crackled loudly in the heat, and huge flames were shooting out and threatening the neighbouring houses. The entire population of Bosham was in the street, forming long bucket chains down to the waters of the creek or, if they could find no place in the line, running about in a panic. Old women stood in their way, wailing and wringing their hands. Children, dogs, chickens and goats scattered in all directions, terrified by the sparks and billowing gusts of smoke.

A roaring like evil laughter came out of the blaze, as if the fire was bellowing contempt for the feeble dashes of water thrown at it. Then, just as Cedric and Harold arrived, the roof of the forge also exploded into a great pyre, and another howl of despair went up from the crowd.

Godwin was standing in the middle of the pushing throng, angrily trying to impose some order on the fire-fighting. Beside him the owner of the burning house was shouting to be heard above the din and actually tugging at the earl's cloak in his anxiety, as though it were in Godwin's power to stop his home being destroyed.

'Save my house, for the love of God!' he was begging. 'It was Wilfred did this, do you hear? Wilfred, the smith, it was! I know it was him!'

Godwin had no time to be patient with the man. The fire was a danger to the whole village, and the people were doing little to help. He bellowed at the man to shut up, and sent him staggering away with a resounding slap to the head. Then he grabbed three men who were clogging the nearest bucket chain and pulled them out, practically throwing them towards another one.

'What happened, father?' Harold called. 'What started it?'

'I don't know,' the earl testily shouted back. 'This fool says the smith did it deliberately . . .'

'He did, he did!' the owner screamed, returning foolhardily within range of Godwin's mighty arm. 'He said he would, and now he has. Look, my house is all burned! I'm homeless! Everything has gone!'

'Do you think he did it?' Harold asked Godwin.

'Who knows?' his father snapped. 'I do know he's run away, though. He's over there somewhere, in the woods. Start the hue and cry, will you? Take the housecarls.'

Harold whooped joyfully at being given such a delicious task. Taking Cedric in tow, he raced back to the hall and ordered the soldiers to mount up. They were as eager as he for some sport, but Harold was the first to gallop out of the stables, and the first of the riders to reach the woods. He spurred his horse through the trees and clinging undergrowth at a mad pace, yelling at the top of his voice for Wilfred the smith to give himself up. A few men from the village had already arrived there and were searching on foot for the smith, and to Harold that made it a contest to be first to the quarry. His face was flushed bright with excitement, his eyes glowed with the thrill of the chase, and he appeared not to notice the branches that tore at his clothes and whipped the cap from his head.

'There he is!' Harold shouted, pointing ahead, and it was indeed Wilfred he had seen. His impulsive charge had succeeded where the villagers had failed, a quality in him that Cedric would observe many times in the years to come.

The smith had broken from cover, and was making a dash across a clearing to a better hiding place. Harold charged quickly in pursuit, riding as if to run the man down. He called to Wilfred to stop, and reined in sharply almost on top of the fugitive. Wilfred, panic-stricken as the prancing horse came near to trampling him, snatched at the reins in a bid to keep it off him. The horse reared away, and Harold was thrown.

He hit the ground with a dreadful thump that caused all who heard it to wince. For some seconds he lay absolutely still, staring at the sky, his mouth wide open in a long, deep gasp for air. Cedric was first to his aid, leaping down from his still-galloping horse and running to where Harold had fallen. He knelt beside Harold and carefully lifted his friend's head. He gave a cry of despair when he saw the vacant look in Harold's eyes and felt his head loll. Wilfred, convinced Lord Godwin's son was dead, flung himself to his knees and began gibbering to all the saints to save him. By that time the housecarls had arrived; they roughly snatched hold of their prisoner and pinned him helpless between them, landing a few hefty kicks and blows while they were at it.

'Harold,' Cedric was pleading. 'Are you all right? Can you speak?'

Harold recovered sufficient breath to groan, and tried to sit up. Then he howled in agony, and clutched at his arm in an effort to hold it still as Cedric caught hold of him and prevented him from falling back.

'My arm, ah, my arm!' he choked, rocking in pain.

'Is it broken?' Cedric asked.

'How in God's name am I to know?' Harold snapped. 'It hurts like the Devil's own touch, that's all I know.' He caught sight of the captive smith, and his temper flared. 'You, you damned fire-raiser!' he snarled at Wilfred. 'You'll hang for sure, and I'll be glad to see it!'

'Please, my lord,' Wilfred sobbed. 'I didn't mean to make you fall . . .'

He was speedily silenced by a smashing blow in the stomach with the butt of a spear.

'That's right, shut him up!' Harold raged, gritting his teeth against the hurt. 'Get him out of my sight. We'll hear what he meant to do when he comes to trial!'

Cedric helped Harold up and, with the aid of the villagers who had gathered round, got him up on to his horse.

'Damn it to Hell, this leg has gone, too,' Harold groaned. 'That idiot has crippled me!'

All the way home to Bosham he clutched at his left arm and swore whenever the ride jolted him. Back at the house, he was eased on to his bed and fussed over by his mother while Godwin sent to the monastery for a physician. Amid all the hubbub, Cedric tried to explain what had happened, but Godwin practically ignored him. The earl had not only his injured son to attend to, but also

the matter of the captured Wilfred, who was still under the guard
of the housecarls while everyone argued about what should be done
with him.

While all the commotion was raging, the monk Godwin had sent
for arrived. The fire having been extinguished, all the villagers were
now at Godwin's door clamouring for justice. As the priest was let
into the hall they followed him in a stumbling mass, overturning
one of the tables in their eagerness to see Harold's wounds and
Wilfred's punishment. Godwin flew into a violent fury. He roared a
stream of obscene curses and, backed by Sweyn and the housecarls,
whipped the crowd into order with the flat of his sword. When he
had some quiet at last, he sorted out the logical order of things.

'Now, brother,' he called to the monk. 'What of my son?'

'I do not think his arm or leg are broken, my lord,' the physician
answered. 'But they are badly swollen and bruised. I will make a
salve and bind the limbs to keep them still . . .'

'All right, don't cackle about it; do it!' Godwin commanded,
and returned his attention to the sulking villagers. Pointing to the
sorry figure of Wilfred, he asked: 'Now, who accuses this man?'

The man whose house had been burned down was Otha, a
shoemaker. He was still close to despair at the loss of all he had.
He pushed his way to the front of the crowd.

'I accuse him!' he whined, pointing a shaking hand at Wilfred.
'He threatened to burn down my house, and that's what he did.
He did it on purpose!'

'That's right; he did!' Otha's wife put in, and a score of their
friends took up the shout.

'Quiet!' Godwin ordered, raising his hand. 'You say he did it
purposely?' he challenged Otha. 'If that is so, it's a crime he'll die
for. You know that purposely firing a house is a crime as grave as
treason, murder or rape? The law of England provides for no
punishment less than death for these crimes. So be sure how you
wish to speak, or the punishment may fall on you if you accuse
falsely. You could have the tongue cut from your head!'

Godwin's words silenced Otha. Yet, after a brief pause and a
glance around the room at the measure of his support, he kept to
his oath.

'It's true, my lord,' Otha insisted, tears of self-pity welling to
his eyes. 'He has hated me ever since we became neighbours. He
has done everything to make my life miserable, with his boasting
about being blacksmith to Canute – God rest the soul of that good
king. Only last summer he threatened to burn my house. He came
out to me with a hot brand, and waved it at my house, and said

he would burn it to the ground. Now he has. Oh merciful God, I'm homeless . . .'

'Yes, well never mind that now,' Godwin rapped, and he turned to the smith, asking: 'And what do you say to all this?'

'It's not true, my lord,' Wilfred pleaded, to a chorus of jeers from the crowd. 'I didn't do it, I swear. It were an accident. The wind blew a spark out through the door, and it caught the hay beside Otha's house . . .'

'But you did say you would burn his house down,' Godwin reminded him.

'Well, t'was only in jest, my lord, believe me. It's true we've always argued, but that time I was only wanting to frighten him . . .'

'And you did run away, which would suggest guilt.'

'I ran because I was afeard. Otha and the others, they would have hanged me straight off!'

'Liar!' Otha screamed. 'He's lying! He ran because he knew he had done wrong!'

'Silence!' Godwin roared again. To Wilfred he said: 'Well, it is clear you will have to be tried. In attempting to escape you have badly injured my son, and that also would seem to point to your guilt . . .'

'My lord, I accuse him too,' interrupted a new voice from the crowd. 'He's a warlock, a master of the black arts! He made my goats sick, with spells in the night . . .'

'Will you be quiet?' Earl Godwin angrily shouted back, disturbed by this talk of witchcraft and the thought that he might have to deal with a warlock. 'We can't hang a man twice, so shut up about this. . . . this witchery!' Confronting Wilfred once more, he continued: 'Now, Wilfred; the law says that you can prove your innocence by bringing to court a certain number of helpers to support your plea. They can be friends, or even kinsmen, but they must be honest men. If you fail to find the right number, or if you make any fault in the procedure laid down for bringing your oath to court, you will do yourself much harm. Do you understand, Wilfred?'

'Yes, my lord.'

'Now, it is a serious charge, so I think you'd need – oh, at least thirty reliable witnesses. Whom will you name as your oath-helpers?'

Wilfred sagged in the housecarls' grip, and looked up at Godwin with a sad and cynical smile of resignation.

'My lord; I'd be hard pressed to find three among these who'd speak for me, let alone thirty,' he said. 'I ain't never been liked here; they bin trying for years to be rid of me. I'm not of their kind, and they were shamed by King Canute bringing me here, because there was no-one in Bosham skilled enough to shoe his horses and mend his hunting spears. Otha has his people here, but I have no-one.' He gazed round the multitude of faces in the hall, until his eyes fell on Cedric. A faint ray of hope brightened his face. 'Except the young master, Cedric Cedricsson. He's of Berkshire, he should know me. You know my nephew, sir, Elfric, in Reading. You'd speak for me, sir, wouldn't you?'

Cedric indeed knew Elfric, and was about to say that he would gladly support Wilfred's oath, when there came a shout from Harold, who was still lying on his cot, his arm and leg tightly bound in a mulch of herbs and lotions.

'Cedric will not swear for you!' he snarled. 'Not after what you have done to me! I'll take an oath myself, by all that's holy, and it's this: if you've crippled me for life, I'll hang you myself!'

'But, my lord,' Wilfred begged, 'it weren't done a-purpose . . .'

'Not done on purpose?' Harold echoed bitterly. 'You cause my horse to throw me and perhaps lame me forever, and all you can say is *"it weren't done a-purpose"*. Ha! Small comfort that would be, even if it were so!'

Wilfred saw that Harold would accept no argument. He turned to appeal to Cedric, who in turn shifted his gaze back to Harold.

'Well, will you swear for the man who has crippled me – I who have taken you into my house, offered you my friendship?' Harold spat at Cedric.

Cedric found himself torn between loyalties. Certainly he wanted Harold's friendship, but the young man's unforgiving fury shocked him. He could not bring himself to behave like some latter-day Judas and deny Wilfred, whose family he did indeed know well.

'He has craved my help, and I must give it,' Cedric declared. 'It is not to offend you, Harold; it is my duty before the law.'

'Damn you, then!' Harold lashed out. 'Befriend the wretch, then! He'll make you a fine companion. You can go and talk to his bones on the gibbet!'

Cedric was deeply hurt by Harold's anger, and humiliated by the raucous laughter of the crowd, but it would not be long before he learned that he had made the right decision. Nothing impressed Earl Godwin more than loyalty, whether that devotion was given to him or to his enemies. In that moment, Cedric had raised himself high in the esteem of both Godwin and, though the latter would not have admitted it, of Harold.

'Very well,' Godwin was saying. 'You are the first of Wilfred's oath-helpers. Are there more to stand with Cedric Cedricsson?'

Not one voice spoke up from the sullen crowd.

'None,' moaned poor Wilfred. 'I thank ye, master Cedric, but it's no good. You're the only one here with a good Christian heart!'

'Well, that settles it,' Godwin decreed. 'You'll have to undergo trial by ordeal instead. Are you willing?'

A howl of approval went up as Wilfred nodded weakly, but Otha the shoemaker was not satisfied.

'It must be by water!' Otha yelled. 'Wilfred is a blacksmith, he knows too well the feel of hot irons. That would be no ordeal for him!'

'For the last time, hold your tongue!' Godwin roared. 'I shall decide, and I'll take no advice from a stitcher of leather.'

The earl was thoughtful then, carefully considering Wilfred's fate. If Wilfred were tied in a sack and dumped in a stream, Godwin reasoned, he might prove his guilt by floating on the surface, but at the same time it might also prove that he was a warlock, as had been claimed. Godwin did not relish having a proven warlock on his hands, so he made up his mind to try Wilfred either by getting him to plunge his arm into boiling water to pick up a stone, or by making him carry a hot iron. Godwin preferred the last method. It was the more rigorous trial, and to avoid further trouble he had to satisfy the thirst of his village for vengeance.

'You will carry a heated iron a distance of three yards,' he told Wilfred. 'If after three days your wounds are clean, you will go free. If your wounds fester, you will be hanged.'

VI

THE trial was held in Bosham Church, and the witnesses were Earl Godwin and his two elder sons, the Shire-Reeve of Hampshire and the Alderman of the Hundred, the village priest, the chief accusers and Cedric. Custom demanded that for one day before the trial these men fasted, and had no bodily contact with women, so that their minds and souls would not be tainted with desires of the flesh.

'Is it his trial, or ours?' Godwin grumbled for a full twenty-four hours.

As the time for the trial approached, the witnesses formed two lines up the aisle along which Wilfred must pass. Cedric took his place alongside Godwin's family, but spoke to no one. He was sickened by the thought of what he would see happen to poor Wilfred, and afraid that his voice would betray the cowardly crawling in his guts. Already there was a tense atmosphere in the church, and the others were conversing in low mutters, getting said all they had to say before the priest came with Wilfred, when all talk other than prayer or instruction would be forbidden, in case the solemnity of the occasion should be tarnished.

Harold nudged Cedric and whispered: 'What's the matter with you? You look as if you've got belly ache.'

Cedric felt that Harold was looking forward to this harrowing event.

'What is there to laugh about?' he answered sourly. 'Would you like to see a friend of yours go through this?'

'I've never seen it done before.' Harold rejoined easily, as if that explained everything.

'Nor have I, and I'd rather not see it today. Perhaps when you've seen as much suffering as I have, you won't be so keen.'

'God's word, you can be a bore!'

At that moment, all conversation ceased abruptly as the monks of the monastery entered the church.

The door to the chancel opened with a boom like the thunder of judgment day as the procession of clerics shuffled in, their tonsured heads bowed, chanting in Latin. The leader carried before him Christ's Rood, and four lay brothers followed with a brazier of glowing coals and two small anvils. The monks divided into two files and took their places at each end of the aisle to complete the avenue of witnesses. The brazier was placed before the altar, with one anvil beside it, the other nine feet away. While the rood-bearer continued to intone prayers, a three-pound rod of iron was placed across the brazier. Two monks blew life into the coals with bellows to heat up the iron, and placed tongs ready to pass the iron to Wilfred when the trial began. Once Wilfred came into the church they would stop fanning the flames. Cedric, watching the iron gradually blacken and turn red, silently offered up a prayer that Wilfred would come in soon and get this awful thing done.

It seemed an age though before the trembling blacksmith was led in by a priest, and mumbled his way through the prayer which the priest prompted him into speaking. His eyes were fixed on the iron as it burned red, and his face was deathly pale. As Otha had said, he knew only too well the feel of blistering iron.

'Are all men here fasting this day, and all laymen abstinent from their wives and innocent of all sins of the flesh this night?' the priest called in English.

'We are,' came the response.

'Then we commit this man, and ourselves, to the divine judgment of Almighty God. Let the trial begin!'

Then the priest walked along the lines of men and sprinkled each of them with holy water. The monk with the Rood went with him, giving the image of Christ on the cross to each man to kiss. After they had leaned forward to touch their lips to the crucifix, the witnesses made the sign of the cross upon themselves and kneeled in prayer. Last of all it was Wilfred's turn, and Cedric saw that the little smith was almost on the point of collapse.

A monk took the tongs and pulled the iron from the coals, dropping it with a clang on the anvil. Wilfred's frantic gaze met Cedric's, and Cedric tried hard to smile encouragement, but Wilfred's eyes had already fixed themselves on the glowing iron.

'Wilfred the smith,' the priest was saying. 'If you are guilty, I charge you now to confess it, and to repent, before this thing is done. Is your conscience clear, or do you fear the outcome of this ordeal?'

Wilfred mumbled so softly that many of the witnesses had to strain to catch his words.

'Then God be with you. Take up your cross now, and bear it as our Lord Jesus Christ bore his, bravely, with humility, and with faith in God our Father.'

The redness had faded from the iron, leaving it smoking black. Wilfred stepped up to it; he had stopped shaking. He took a single deep breath, stretched out his hands, paused but a second as his sweating palms sensed the heat of the thing, then made a determined grab. A shudder of pain ran through his body. He did not cry out as he staggered between the witnesses towards the far anvil, but his mouth opened wide as if in a scream that would not break free. He shook the rod from his seared hands on to the second anvil, groaned, and fainted face down on the stone floor.

All the witnesses hurried to the fallen smith save Cedric who was rooted to the spot. His legs were weak and his own palms wet with sweat; he felt them burn as if it was his flesh and not Wilfred's that had been scorched. He had believed that nothing could affect him thus, after he had witnessed the carnage at Guildford, but now he discovered he was not yet hardened to the anguish of others.

Otha the accuser was hovering at the edge of the crowd, eager for a sight of the victim's wounds, and Cedric's temper snapped. He strode up to Otha, snatched at the man's shoulder and spun him around, his body rigid with anger as he restrained himself from hitting the shoemaker.

'Are you satisfied?' he raged. 'No, you wouldn't be, not yet. You won't be satisfied until you see his burns festering! You accused him falsely! What a pity you can't be proved a liar, and have the tongue torn from your head!'

Cedric slammed out of the church, not realising that Earl Godwin was watching him with some amusement and interest. Back at the house, the earl and his sons sat down to a huge breakfast to make up for their fast, but Cedric was still queasy and distressed, and could not eat. If it had not been for the lovely Edith, Cedric would have fled the dining-hall. Her delicate beauty held him spell-fast, and he knew Earl Godwin must notice that he could gaze only at her, and that he reddened and stuttered whenever he spoke to her.

'Cedric!' Godwin boomed, shattering his dream. Cedric knocked his wine cup but caught it before it toppled over.

'My lord?'

'Eat, boy! The man who holds back when he's fasted is a fool. What's the matter with you?'

'I'm sorry, my lord. I'm not hungry.'

'Not hungry? Nonsense. You can't go a whole day without food and not be hungry. If the smith's trial turned your stomach, then you're a fool, and soft at that. The trial is a fair one, in accordance with the law of the land and in the sight of God. What is there to mope about?'

'I don't like to see suffering, that's all,' Cedric said weakly. 'I've seen too much of it.'

'And you'll see more; that's one promise this life will keep.

You'll cause some, too, if you're worth the work I'm thinking of giving you.'

'My lord?' Cedric instantly feared that he was going to be called upon to perform another treacherous errand. 'What work is that?'

Godwin dipped his fingers into a bowl and rubbed the grease from them, still munching noisily on a hunk of beef.

'I like you, lad,' he announced, still chewing. 'I've been watching you. You're honest, loyal, and you have a sense of honour. That's good. Those are the things I look for in my thanes, but they come rarely. I need a collector of taxes and feorm in this part of the shire. You know about feorm, don't you? My tenants pay me rent in pigs and potatoes. The post is yours if you want it; it's an important one, too. You'd have equal rank with the aldermen and reeves of the hundreds, and it takes a hard man and shrewd one to deal with them! They're not all honest; some of them are downright villains, thieves and cheats. You have to be quick-witted to know a cunning scheme when you see it, and before now a tax agent has had to take the flat of his sword to the devils. Well, do you think you can do it?'

'I'm greatly honoured, sir' Cedric said. 'I shall try . . .'

'There's no "try" about it, boy; not with me,' Godwin growled. 'You either do it well, or back you go to Reading. I'll see that you're well trained, don't worry. Later you'll be in charge, but first you'll go out and learn for yourself where the taxes come from – and what they should amount to when they get back to the town halls.'

'Yes, sir. Thank you. I promise to do it diligently.'

'Good. You can start when we have this tedious trial done with.'

Cedric cast a look in Edith's direction to see if she had been listening, but she appeared not to have heard a word. She was busy showing her little sister Gunhild how to make a cat's cradle with a length of twine. Cedric was disappointed; most of the time it seemed she did not even know he was in the house. When this wretched trial is over, he thought, I will get to know her. He was afraid that, if he did not do so soon, someone else would come along and snatch her out of his grasp.

On the third day following Wilfred's ordeal, Cedric went with the other witnesses to the monastery where the blacksmith was being held and cared for – the monastery that was, ironically, dedicated to his namesake, St. Wilfrid. They found the smith sitting up on a spartan pallet in a tiny cell, his face drawn with worry as he waited to learn his fate.

The men crowded into the cell behind Godwin and the priest, who each took one of Wilfred's hands and unwrapped the bandages.

The soggy bindings smelled sickly-sweet and everyone who had pressed forward so eagerly to see Wilfred's burns now turned up their noses and tried to take a step back.

'This hand seems clean,' Godwin said in mild surprise.

Cedric's heart leapt joyfully at that, but then he heard the priest declare seriously: 'Ah, but there is apparently a festering here on this one . . .'

A murmur hummed among the witnesses, who pushed forward once more, keen to see the evidence of evil in Wilfred. Godwin snatched the other hand from the priest.

'Where?' he demanded.

'There, see?' the priest replied, pointing to the scorched valley between thumb and finger.

Godwin looked hard, but was obviously puzzled, as though unable to decide whether the blister was a festering or not.

'Well, I don't know,' he said at last. 'If it is a festering, it's very small . . .'

'Small evil is enough!' Otha the shoemaker piped up. 'If it's festering, he's guilty!'

'One more offer of advice from you,' the earl snapped back at him, 'and you'll be getting more than your fingers burned!' He glared at Wilfred's hand again, sighed then smiled: 'Well, Wilfred, I can only come to one conclusion – you are a little bit guilty, but not much. I will not hang any man on the evidence I see here, that's for sure.'

'Perhaps he is guilty enough for banishment?' the priest suggested.

Godwin chuckled, and slapped the shoulder of the trembling blacksmith.

'As God is my witness, smith,' he rumbled. 'I don't know what you did to make yourself so disliked, but if I were you I'd go back to where you came from. Look, it seems to me that you did not deliberately fire Otha's house, but wanting it so made you careless enough to bring it about. In that you are at fault. Your punishment is that you shall rebuild Otha's house by your own efforts, stone by stone and beam by beam. Then, for the love of Christ, go home to Berkshire!'

Wilfred sobbed his gratitude, much to Godwin's embarrassment. The rest of the witnesses dispersed, many of them grumbling in the manner of people who had assembled for a great spectacle only to have the doors closed upon them. Cedric, childishly gleeful at their disappointment, could not help laughing in Otha's angry face as the shoemaker rudely brushed through his neighbours in his haste to be out of there.

'We have seen the work of God today,' Cedric said to Harold as they left the monastery. 'St. Wilfrid really did take Wilfred the blacksmith under his protection. It's enough to inspire a man to faith! Your father is a great man, and a wise one, Harold. I was wrong ever to doubt him. From now on I am his faithful liegeman; I shall follow him to Heaven or to Hell.'

Harold, still limping and carrying his left arm awkwardly in a sling, snorted at Cedric's high-flown words. He had got over his rage at Wilfred, but he still resented what the man had done to him.

'And what about me?' he complained. 'I suppose I deserved to get this, did I? That damned wretch can atone for his sins by building a house for Otha, but can he mend my arm and leg?'

'You will be well in a few days,' Cedric said briskly. 'Then you will forget all about it. You don't really think a man should pay for an accident with his life, do you? Besides, it might teach you a useful lesson: not to be so headstrong. My uncle Oswald taught me that the charging bull will sooner or later bash out its own brains. The slow, slinking cat will live longer, and make more kills.'

Harold leaned against the monastery gate, gaping in mock astonishment at Cedric.

'Christ's blood,' he exclaimed, 'you're a conceited, pompous ass! I've known you but a few days, and I've had more advice and philosophy from you in that time than in sixteen years under Godwin's roof. And I thought no one was more perfect than my father, lord and master Godwin! The Devil take you, Cedric. It's purgatory enough hobbling about like a legless beggar. I don't want to be told I'm a brainless bull as well!'

'I didn't mean to insult you,' Cedric laughed. 'But you must admit, you are a little rash. I discovered that the first moment I met you. I believe you will be a great man one day, if you learn discretion.'

'And you might live to be an older man if you stop annoying me,' Harold growled.

VII

CEDRIC plucked up the courage to raise the subject of Edith one day when Harold accompanied him on a tax-collecting trip. They were riding across Hampshire heathland gently washed in November mist, silent but for rooks cawing in the tree-tops, while trailing some distance behind them were a couple of supply carts carrying the feorm and a bodyguard of half a dozen housecarls. They had been watching for a large band of outlaws that was known to be in the district, and for a long time no one had spoken a word.

'Have you ever loved anyone?' Cedric began, carefully.

'Girls? Yes, several,' Harold grinned. 'Why, haven't you?'

'No, not like that. I mean *really* been in love with one, so that you cannot bear to be away from her.'

'Good Lord, no. I don't believe in all that! Bed them and leave them happy, that's what I do!'

'But surely there was one you felt something more for?'

'There was one I went scurrying back to whenever I could raise the energy,' Harold boastfully admitted. 'My oath, she was a temptress; one of the serving girls at the house. But father found out and gave me a hell of a belting, and sent her off to one of his other estates somewhere. He likes to keep them all for himself, you see, greedy old goat. What are you trying to tell me, that you're lovesick for some little heifer?'

'I wouldn't put it quite like that . . .' Cedric murmured, his resolve faltering. He did not want to risk offending Harold, for they had grown very fond of each other and every day, when Cedric could escape his duties, they went hunting, hawking, or riding races along the sea shore. Other times they went out fishing with the little boats of Bosham, or explored the wide Wessex forests. They often slunk off to the ale-houses of Chichester, got drunk on ale or mead, fought mock duels, or chased the village wenches, delighted in games of duck the fool and dare the witch, and on wet days became absorbed in games of chess or dice.

Best of all were the days when they would go with Godwin and his vast retinue of riders and beaters after hart and boar, days when the mighty forests would echo with shouts and the crashing of men and horses through the undergrowth, the baying of the hounds and the squealing of the frantic quarry. In the quiet dusk the hunters would ride home dusty and bloodied, laughing and boasting as they led in the bearers with the game lashed to poles, returning like a conquering army to the women and children who ran out to applaud the spoils. Then Cedric would strut his horse about the yard and take his victor's cup of wine, and hope that Edith was there among the womenfolk to see him. They were wonderful days, particularly for Cedric, who had never known such companionship before. He did not want to ruin it all by stepping out of his place, but he knew he could not go much longer without confessing to someone, and Harold was the obvious mentor.

'It's someone you know very well,' he eventually blurted out. 'It's your sister.'

Harold checked his horse so violently that the animal shied and danced.

'*Edith?*'

'Yes, Edith. I'm in love with her.'

'You're mad,' Harold said harshly.

'Why? Is it so strange for a man like me to be in love with a nobleman's daughter? I swear I fell in love with her the first day I saw her. I think I want to marry her.'

'Impossible. You'd better forget all about it.'

'But why? She doesn't dislike me, does she?'

'Whether she likes or dislikes you has nothing to do with it,' Harold told him shortly. 'She'll have very little say in whom she marries. She will marry whoever father tells her to, and you can be sure that her husband will be someone of note.'

'And what am I?' Cedric responded indignantly, 'A serf, a beggar?'

'No, but you aren't a nobleman, either. Look Cedric, I don't want to hurt your feelings, but you must understand that Edith's a high prize and her marriage will be a political one. She will marry the son of an earl, or even a prince . . .'

'The law allows her to refuse a chosen husband,' Cedric argued.

'The law might, but Godwin doesn't. Listen, will you? It's the same for Sweyn and me, and all my brothers too. We would be fools to go against father's will and marry whoever we please. He'd cast us out, and we'd be little better than nithings for the rest of our lives. Stripped of everything, as though we'd committed some appalling crime!'

'Your father!' Cedric sighed, bitterly. 'Does he rule everyone?'

'Yes, he does. He's a great man, remember? You said so yourself. He rules everyone except the king, and sometimes even that is a matter of opinion. Godwin is as close to God on earth as you are likely to meet, so you'd better learn that his word is Holy Writ.'

'You're blaspheming,' Cedric was shocked.

'I'm trying to make you see sense! Don't ever go to Godwin with a proposal for Edith's hand, for the love of God, or at least not until you are Earl of Mercia at least. Forget Edith. I can't understand what you see in her anyway, she's only a scrawny brat. I can get you girls if you want them – good, buxom, eager, *wicked* girls. There's an ale-wife I know in Chichester. She'll let you have one of her serving girls any time you have a couple of mancuses to spend.'

'I don't want whores!' Cedric snapped. 'I certainly wouldn't waste two mancuses on some dirty ale-wife's bitch. Good lord, sixty pence would buy me a pair of oxen!'

'You have your oxen then, if that's what you prefer,' Harold chuckled. 'I'd rather have the girls. Anyway,' he added, pointing ahead, 'here is one of your ports of call. You'd be well advised to keep your mind on your work, or the great Lord Godwin will have you married to the whipping post.'

They had arrived at a partly cultivated clearing on a gorse-covered hillside, where the remains of a small barley crop struggled feebly with the weeds; a few bony hogs and sows rooted amid the lank growth. Surrounding the field was a fence of entwined brush and thorn held by log pegs, and alongside the track was a lowly hovel where a swineherd lived with his family.

The home, if it could be flattered with that description, was a shelter about thirty feet long, hardly tall enough for a man to stand up in, made of branches lodged against a log spine and cemented with mud and turf. Thick smoke from a cooking fire inside the hut escaped through a hole in the roof, through the cracks in the damp turf walls, and out through the open ends of the hovel, which were covered only with rough sack curtains. The whole rickety structure looked like a smouldering bonfire, in fact. The place wallowed in mud and pig slime and was filthy with the litter of years – broken pots, bones, discarded sacking, rotten firewood, the remains of pigskin clothing and, foulest of all, human and animal excreta.

Of the ignorant folk who scratched out an existence here there was no sign, for they had all scuttled into the shelter at the first sound of strangers. Only when Cedric halted his procession outside was he able to see the man of the family nervously peering out through fraying strands of sacking. It was a filthy face, almost completely overgrown with uncombed hair and matted beard, a thin and hungry face, gaunt and animal-like with its cowed expression and dull, smoke-reddened eyes, and it was an ageless, toothless face lacking in hope, lacking even the spark of reason. Cedric, sickened by the smell and disturbed by the haunted look of the man behind the sacking, took his lists from his bag and quickly shuffled through them. He found the place on one of the sheets, and surveyed his surroundings to compare them with the written description.

'Are you Gryf?' he called. 'The swineherd who lives beneath the two oaks on the hill west of the Miller's Ford?'

The face at the cloth vanished. Cedric waited for an answer, but the vile heap that Gryf called his house was deathly silent.

'I have come to collect your feorm!' Cedric shouted.

Still no reply came from the bonfire.

'Then I suppose I must come to you,' Cedric said impatiently, and he dismounted.

'I wouldn't go too near if I were you,' Harold recommended. 'If you think it smells bad from here, wait till you get closer!'

'What else can I do, if he won't come out?' Cedric retorted, but he soon discovered the truth of Harold's words.

Carefully picking his way through the muck, Cedric went and pulled aside the curtain. Never had he seen a scene such as greeted his eyes then, nor encountered such a stench of rotten humanity. In the depths of the dark smoke-filled den, the swineherd and his half-dozen children crouched like cowering rats in a pile of rags and pigskin, surrounded by a formless mess of food remains, filthy pots, lice-ridden straw bedding, little mounds of uncooked root vegetables, decomposing carcases stored for the winter, and a soggy mat of rushes scattered across the wet earth floor. His wife was a trembling hag, pressed back behind a branch support by one wall in a pathetic bid to hide herself. The children were black with dirt and clothed in tatters, deformed with rickets, covered with running sores. The eldest girl was pregnant – possibly by her own father since incest was rife in these miserable isolated huts, and it was unlikely that any other man would come here or want such an unclean girl. Her reaction to Cedric was the most frantic of all; she wrapped her skinny arms around her head and screamed.

Behind the family was a partition, and from the blackness beyond came the shuffling and snorting of more pigs. Like most geburs of this lowest class, the swineherd shared his abode with his animals, leading to yet further degradation. Ugly fat flies hummed in swarms around the food and the filth, and all manner of insects scratched in the walls.

All this Cedric took in at a glance, and within seconds he was driven out by the horror of it. It astonished him that anything, let alone human beings, could live in a hideous pit such as that, and he staggered away nauseated. The thought passed through his mind that the swineherd must have buried somewhere twice the number

of infants as were still alive in there. Perhaps they were beneath
the floor of the hut, adding to the evil of the place, for it was still
the custom in a few of these hovels to dispose of the dead thus.

'Come out!' Cedric angrily yelled at Gryf through the gagging
in his throat. 'Come out, or these men will burn down your filthy
hole!'

He could hear Harold hooting uproariously at him as he shouted,
but he could not see the joke himself. He was about to repeat the
command when Gryf appeared, shuffling slowly out of his home
on hands and knees. He was bent almost double, garbed in a bundle
of verminous sackcloth, and his skin was pocked by some dreadful
disease. So monstrous was he that Cedric, having called him out,
was then moved to get well away from him.

'Got no feorm,' Gryf mumbled, his gaze fixed on the ground.

'What do you mean, you have none?' Cedric consulted his list.
'Four live piglets and four sacks of barley every year; isn't that
what you pay?'

'Aye, but I got none.'

'Oh? And whose are those pigs in the field there?'

Gryf did not look up.

'Them's all that's left,' he muttered. 'Swine fever done for the
rest. If I gives you any, I don't have none next year.'

'Nonsense. How many sows do you have?'

'Sows all dried up. No more piglets.'

'How many sows, I asked you?'

'Three left.'

'Then you'll have more piglets.'

'No, sows all dried up.'

'I don't believe you. Come on, fetch those young swine, and let
me get away from here.'

The defeated Gryf raised his crooked shoulders and let them fall
again in resignation, and laboriously scuffled away towards his little
herd. There was no more protest he could make, for he knew of
no other way to make the young lord understand.

How could he, with his few words and slow mind, explain to
this well-fed youth what it meant to be a nithing, a gebur, to scrape
a living from the harsh soil with his poor deformed hands? How
could this well-dressed nobleman know the trials of fighting wind
and rain, hail, snow, frost and drought, with so little to protect his
meagre possessions? No one but he could know how, year after
year, he struggled to grow a crop in stony soil, to keep the swine
fed, to contend with the ravages of thieving outlaws, to fight off
vicious wolves and wild dogs and herds of wild boar that sometimes
broke in to steal the feed and couple with the sows, in order to

meet the claims of landlords. Gryf would not have known how to tell another what it was like to see so many babies die, to watch those who lived ail and grow crooked with starvation and disease. This year, on top of all that, there had been the swine fever, a merciless scourge which had reduced his pigs to a tenth of their former number.

No, though he might stand there and argue all day, Gryf would never be able to make Cedric understand. He had tried before, with a succession of young Cedrics, and had failed. It was easier for him to fetch his precious piglets and let the youth have them, so that at least he could get on with his thankless life in peace. One by one, four squealing beasts were thrown up into the carts with the crates of chickens and geese, the tethered goats and sheep, and the piled sacks of corn, beans, shallots and the other fruits of men's labours.

'What about the barley?' Cedric inquired.

'There be barley.' The swineherd pointed to a dozen slackly-filled sacks against the wall. Barley was in short supply this year, too, because Gryf had spent so much time trying to save his pigs, but he knew it was useless to argue with Cedric. Four bags were prised out and manhandled into a cart, and the collectors rode away without a word of compassion for Gryf's hardship. The swineherd stood like a bent and ragged dwarf beside the track and watched them go, thinking nothing, because his poor mind was too tired to think.

'What a vile place,' said Cedric, feeling as if the stench of it clung to him still.

'You do your work well,' Harold told him. 'Perhaps a little too well?'

'What do you mean?'

'Oh, it's just that father is always prepared to give way a little if people have had a bad year. He would have taken nothing from that wretch back there, on the understanding that next year he gives six piglets, and then another six the year after. Father always says: take it from those who have it, leave it with those who need it, and make those who want it wait, and in so doing, earn the respect of all of them.'

Cedric was still smarting at being branded a lesser citizen earlier.

'So now Godwin is a saint as well as God,' he sniped. He instantly regretted it, seeing a look of hurt in Harold's eyes, and he fully expected the wrath that resulted.

'Don't speak about my father like that, you ungrateful pup!' Harold railed. 'He's given you enough, hasn't he? I'll tell you one thing, Cedric, if I can be half the man Godwin is, I shall be proud of it!'

'Harold, I'm sorry, truly I am,' Cedric repented. 'I didn't mean to be rude about your father. It's just that . . . well, with a man like him, what can I do?'

'About what?'

'About my love for Edith.'

'Mother of God, are you back to that again?' Harold sighed. 'I've told you what you can do. Pretend you never met her.'

'It isn't that easy. Lord, it wouldn't be so bad if I could speak to her just once, alone, without your mother or her women there.'

'Ha! You'd as likely get a word with the Virgin Mary.'

'I know,' Cedric conceded. Hopefully he added: 'Couldn't you arrange it for me? You don't have to leave her alone with me, if you're worried about her virtue. You could be nearby. I'd just like to talk to her, only for a few minutes, that's all.'

'For pity's sake, man,' Harold groaned. 'What good would it do? Have you heard nothing I've said to you?'

'Please, will you do it? It's all I've ever asked of you as a friend.'

'All right, damn you, if you must be so stubborn. But it will be just once, and then only for as long as I think wise. I'll do it when we get back home today. And Lord help us both if father finds out!'

Harold kept his promise. Upon their arrival in Bosham, he went into the hall to lure Edith out, while Cedric waited nervously behind the stables, trying to compose a simple speech for his meeting with his beloved but finding it beyond him. From one of the upstairs rooms came the voices of Harold's four younger brothers chanting a prayer in Latin. The monk who taught them was making them work late. Cedric found himself repeating the litany as if in the hope that it would help him say the right things to Edith. Was it only such a short time ago that he had been an innocent schoolboy, Cedric wondered, droning half-learned teachings into the echoing stillness of a winter afternoon? It now seemed an age, an age in which he had all too easily learned harsher lessons, about the brutality of man and the cruelty of the world. He had had enough of that kind of schooling in the last year, and he craved for some teaching in the gentler arts. Edith was the girl with whom he wanted to learn tenderness and affection – indeed she was the first girl ever to make him aware that he wanted to, and despite all that Harold had said, he refused to believe that she was really out of his reach. A wise and just man like Earl Godwin must also be a reasonable man, he thought. All he had to do was make sure that

Edith liked him, and then in time they could surely ask Godwin to allow them to marry, without fear of his wrath.

He was still unprepared when Harold came, his arm thrown protectively around the slim shoulders of his sister. The gesture was one of pride and affection, but even so Edith looked as if she would have run away had Harold not been there to hold her. She was wrapped in a long cloak and her face was half-hidden in a white hood. Only her shy smile was visible as she gazed at Cedric, wondering what all this could be about.

'Here's Cedric,' Harold said casually. 'He wants to talk to you.'

Cedric's throat went suddenly bone dry.

'Talk to me?' Edith whispered. 'What about?'

Cedric tried to signal to Harold that it would be nice if he would move away, just a little way at least, but Harold chose not to understand. Cedric cleared his throat manfully and tried to make the best of it.

'Well,' he tried, 'Just. . . . things. You know.'

'It's too cold for "just things",' Harold jeered. 'I'm not going to stand out in the cold all night. Get on with it!'

'Harold,' Cedric implored. 'Do you think you could be quiet?'

'I will if there's anything to listen to,' his friend replied. 'But someone's got to say something.'

'Someone tell me, please.' Edith appealed to Harold. 'Why all this secrecy? What am I doing here?'

'Please Edith, don't worry,' Cedric quickly urged. 'I only wanted a chance to talk with you, that's all. It's never possible at the house, and . . .'

'All right,' said Edith. 'I'm here. What do you want to say?'

She looked at him, he looked at her, and Harold looked from one to the other of them, and waited.

'Oh, never mind,' mumbled Cedric, 'let's go in, shall we?'

Harold took pity on Cedric at last, seeing tears of desperation about to start in his eyes. He smiled and gave Cedric a slap on the back, and walked off to pay unnecessary attention to his horse.

'Hold on, I'll be with you in a moment,' he called back. 'I think my mare has a tick.'

Cedric smiled sheepishly at Edith. What little confidence he had had at the outset had dissolved in the presence of both Harold and Edith, and now he was more tongue-tied than ever. Edith saw that she must follow her brother's example, and help him.

'You and Harold have become very good friends, haven't you?' she said sweetly. 'He acts roughly with you, like father does, but he thinks a lot of you.'

'That's nice,' Cedric managed. 'I'm very fond of him, too. Of all of you, in fact . . .'

'Thank you. It's a pity you and I cannot spend time together, as you and Harold do. But we cannot, can we?'

She blushed and looked down. Cedric was astounded to find that she felt that way and that she had expressed it so kindly. He thought it must be the most gentle message of rejection any man had ever received.

'No, we cannot,' was all that he could say.

'You could come and talk to me at any time, in the house,' Edith continued, in the same sweet manner. 'Mother won't mind, honestly. You need not be afraid of her – she seems fierce, but she's quite nice really. We could talk about anything, anything that we could talk about out here.'

Cedric knew only too well what Edith meant. She was telling him that they could talk about the weather, or their horses, about hunting, tapestries, tumbling clowns, poems or heroes, but never about love, neither here nor anywhere else, never at all. His heart suddenly felt leaden, and yet the charming simplicity with which she said it only made him desire her more deeply than before.

'Yes, thank you,' he said, looking at the wall, 'I'd like that very much.'

She gave him a last smile.

'I must go,' she apologised. 'I have enjoyed talking to you.'

Cedric watched her slim form drifting back towards the house as silently and gracefully as mist, and realised only after a while that Harold had rejoined him.

'She's not interested in me,' Cedric confessed mournfully.

'She knows it would serve no purpose,' Harold consoled him. 'Edith cannot allow herself to grow attached to anyone, my friend. She knows it's true, what I told you: that her life is not her own to do with as she pleases.'

'It's not fair,' complained Cedric.

'It may be, or it may not,' Harold shrugged. 'Most women of her standing seem content with their lot. Think about it. She will never have to fight and bite and scratch for power and position as we will. One day she will just walk into it. A great home will be waiting for her, everything she wants will be handed to her for the asking. All she need do is her duty.'

Cedric said nothing, but went to fetch his horse, and went riding off on his own.

As he rode he cursed all women. He cursed Edith for being so far out of his reach yet being close enough for him to love; he cursed his mother for telling him nothing of women and how to court them. It must be his mother's fault that he lost every battle, he reasoned, for in the absence of his father, it was Constance who had brought him up, who had taught him compromise and tranquillity of soul, instead of the ways to power and dominance which he might have learned from his father. Now he must unlearn all those lessons, he thought. He must stay here, learn to demand, command, to overcome and succeed. He had no doubt that Godwin and Harold were the most able teachers he could find.

VIII

ANY and varied were those who came to Godwin's hall, and
M Cedric never tired of watching the pageant. Most frequent
were the common folk, people who came to ask the earl to settle
disputes with neighbours, or petty criminals brought to him for
punishment. There were noblemen too, young thanes like Cedric
offering service to their lord; there were couriers from the king or
from Godwin's fellow earls, travellers seeking a meal and a roof for
the night, merchants from distant lands bringing gold and precious
stones, spices, silks and ivory, skilfully-wrought weapons and
exotic clothes and ornaments. Churchmen came to discuss land
grants and titles or financial help for their parishes, and foreign
ambassadors sometimes paid courtesy calls on their way through
Bosham port, and talked about subjects such as import duties and
the wars in Europe. There were travelling minstrels and jugglers,
magicians, tumblers, acrobats, freaks, dancing bears and cock-fight
circuses, strong men and wrestlers, dwarfs and giants. In addition
to these, of course, came many personal friends of Godwin, and
high-placed relations such as Sweyn, Osborn and Bjorn Estrithsson,
nephews of Canute and, by marriage, of Godwin, come from
Denmark to recruit men for their wars against King Magnus of
Norway.

All were welcome for however long they wished to stay, and
none was sent away without food, shelter or justice. Many were
the nights when Cedric, marvelling at their strangeness, would
share a fireside and a flagon of wine with them and listen enthralled
as they spoke of the wide and exciting world they knew.

One day there came a quiet grave-faced man in middle age,
who gave his name as Gospatrick Uhtredsson, younger brother
of Eadwulf Uhtredsson who had recently been created Earl of
Northumbria south of the Tyne. All Cedric knew of Eadwulf was
that he was part of the vast Godwin clan, having married a cousin
of Godwin's wife Gytha, and that he had been with Godwin at
Guildford. It therefore came as a great surprise to Cedric when
Eadwulf's brother seemed to know all about Cedric and his family.

'Your mother was mother also to me, Cedric, during the Danish
wars,' Gospatrick explained. 'You were but a baby when I last saw
you, so would know nothing of all that. Dear Constance, she was

so good to me, and so were your father and uncle. I remember them all with the greatest affection.'

'How did that come about?' Cedric asked.

'Your mother was waiting-woman to my stepmother, Princess Aelfgifu . . .'

'Oh yes, I know that. She's always going on about those days!'

'And well she might; they were glorious times for all of us. Well, when my stepmother was sent to Normandy with the rest of Ethelred's family I was given into Constance's care. We were taken into your father's house in Wantage. Constance met your father there and married him, and you were born. I can tell you that it was a terrible loss to me when your father was killed in Sweden. He was one of the kindest and most generous men I have ever known.'

'Thank you,' said Cedric, 'it is kind of you to say so. And your stepmother – Princess Aelfgifu – is she well? Mother often talks about her. She would like so much to hear news of Princess Aelfgifu. Do please go and see her.'

'Yes, I will do that. My stepmother is very well, thank you,' Gospatrick answered, 'though in exile still. I visited her in Brittany once, ten years ago now, and I haven't seen her since, but she regularly writes to me that all is well. You can tell your mother that, or I will when I call on her.'

'But will the princess never return to England? Surely she no longer has anything to fear? It's a long time now since Englishman fought with Dane.'

Gospatrick paused; he had to be careful how he answered in the presence of Earl Godwin. Only three years ago, when Aelfgifu's half-brother Edward led an invasion force to England, Gospatrick had been on one side of the fence, supporting Edward's cause, while Godwin had been on the other, backing the claim of Harold Harefoot. Gospatrick did not dare let Godwin suspect the intrigues that were still being carried on across the Channel, where even today Gifta was tirelessly working to have King Harold replaced with Edward, or to have Edward chosen as king when Harold died.

For years Gospatrick's correspondence with Aelfgifu had been conducted under code names, he giving her all the information he could glean about the various factions in England, and she telling him whom she had met at the seats of power in Brittany, Normandy and Rome, and to what effect. Gospatrick had had one close escape at the time of Harold's accession, and if news of his spying on behalf of Edward leaked out to Godwin or King Harold, he could yet end his days on the block or the gallows.

'I suppose she is content with her life abroad,' he said casually, 'and feels that there is not really any reason for her to come back.'

He swiftly changed the subject then, and turned to Godwin with the business that had brought him to Wessex.

'My lord,' he began earnestly. 'I come to you on behalf of the northern earls, chiefly my brother Eadwulf and Leofric of Mercia. They want to know if you are disturbed as they are at the activities of certain of the king's men . . . ?'

Godwin knew at once what Gospatrick meant, but he feigned ignorance.

'What activities? What men?' he asked calmly, pouring wine for his guest. The earl never allowed discussions of serious matters to proceed until he had his visitors well into their cups. It was a ploy which enabled him to retain the upper hand at all times.

'Has Wessex not been plagued with raids by bands of housecarls, lightly disguised as outlaws?' Gospatrick inquired. 'The northern shires have suffered badly, particularly Northumbria and Mercia, and I had heard that they have roamed at least as far south as the Thames.'

Godwin hid a sardonic smile. He possessed at least as much information about the raids as did Gospatrick, if not more, but he could hardly admit that the reason they had not ventured into Wessex was that King Harold had expressly ordered them not to do so. Godwin was the favourite of Harold, just as he had been the favourite of Canute, and his territory was sacrosanct.

'I think I did hear that you were having some trouble up there,' he said. 'Is it bad, then?'

'Bad? God's truth, that is hardly the word for it! These men are little better than scavengers. They ride in great numbers, heavily armed like the old Viking pirates. They raid farms, villages and churches: they murder, pillage and rape, all across the country. Harefoot's tax collectors, we call them in Northumbria.'

'Are people so sure that the king sanctions all this?' Godwin inquired.

'They don't *think* he sanctions it,' Gospatrick snorted. 'They are convinced he even orders it. They believe their money and provisions finish up in the royal coffers and granaries.'

'You speak dangerously,' Godwin observed.

'But perhaps not without justification,' Gospatrick persisted. 'The story goes that a certain Reeve of Lincolnshire had occasion to call on the king at Northampton, and was served his meal on a silver plate that had been his own a few weeks before.'

'That's strange,' Godwin grinned. 'I heard the same story about a Yorkshireman who went to the court of Hardicanute at Durham. You cannot believe all you hear, Gospatrick, my friend.'

'Well, since you speak of Hardicanute, they say he's so frightened by King Harold's mode of government, that he has fled to Denmark to save himself from his half-brother's wrath.'

'It would not surprise me,' Godwin sighed, 'if timid little Hardicanute fled his own shadow, not to mention his own kin. But what is it your brother and Leofric are asking of me?'

'They ask you to support a petition to the king, urging him to act against the raiders. He listens to you more keenly than to anyone else; your name would lend great weight to our entreaty. There would be nothing in it to say we think it's his doing.'

'The suggestion would be there,' Godwin said critically. 'And if he is as guilty as you believe he is, I can see him flying into a mighty rage at the very mention of these raids. As you say, I do know him very well. I'll wager my entire stable that Harold would deny all of it.'

'My lord,' Gospatrick implored, 'it is not my place to preach to you . . .'

'Aye, that's true.'

' . . . but do you think it right that a son of Canute, whom you so much admired, should rip that great king's realm apart as Harold appears to be doing? The North is near to revolt, my lord. The people have had enough of these barbarians. That is why Eadwulf and Leofric are determined to do something about it. Won't you help them?'

Godwin did not often find himself cornered, and when it happened he didn't like it. His fraying patience snapped at that point. He stamped up from his seat, and slammed his goblet down hard on the table.

'No, I do not like to see Canute's memory abused!' he growled. 'I like it no more than any other man. No one knew Canute better than I. No one worked harder to help him shape the kingdom he wanted, and succeeded in building. But because I loved Canute, neither do I like to hear his son accused without a scrap of evidence. Harold Harefoot is not a perfect king; everyone knows that. But a common murderer? Thief? Outlaw leader? Those are treasonous accusations, Gospatrick. What proof do you have – not hearsay now, I mean proof – that King Harold is to blame?'

Gospatrick remained steady in the face of Godwin's rage. He was the son of an equally great earl, a man who for many years had been deprived of his inheritance by the Danish invaders Godwin served, and he refused to be cowed by this self-appointed master of the English.

'It is proof enough for me,' he answered sternly, 'that as often as not, the raiders are led by Olaf Ericsson, King Harold's axeman, the man I have sworn to destroy if it takes me all my life.'

'That is no proof against the king,' Godwin pointed out.

At the mention of Olaf's name, Cedric could not stop himself interrupting.

'You are sworn to kill Olaf? Why? What quarrel do you have with him?'

'Quarrel!' Gospatrick exclaimed. 'The most passionate quarrel of all: revenge! Twenty-two years ago this very month, Olaf Ericsson treacherously slew my father, giving him no chance even to draw his sword. I would have sought out Olaf then, but King Canute forced me to promise not to take up arms against him. Now that Canute is dead I no longer feel bound by that oath. On the day I meet Olaf, I shall fight him to the death.'

'You will have to meet him before I do then,' Cedric bragged. 'I, too, have sworn to kill him, ever since he led the swine who murdered Prince Alfred and his men.'

'Aye, many are the crimes that burden the soul of Olaf Ericsson,' said Gospatrick grimly, 'and still his lust for blood is not quenched. He has escaped justice far too long. Will you join us, Earl Godwin? Will you raise your hand against Harefoot's axeman?'

Godwin knew that to refuse would be to sacrifice the confidence of the rest of the English lords. He conceded defeat, this once, but determined that he would keep a closer watch on this irksome Gospatrick in future. He was too virtuous, too courageous, and on the wrong side.

'Tell Eadwulf I will sign his petition,' he barked. 'But tell him also not to blame me if we feel Harold's fury!'

'Thank you, my lord,' Gospatrick smiled. 'It is all in a good cause. If we do nothing, King Harold may soon feel the fury of the English.'

Gospatrick left, assuring Cedric that on his way home he would stop at Reading and tell Constance that her son was faring well. Within the week, however, Gospatrick was back in Bosham, looking graver than ever. He spoke privately with Godwin first, then Godwin sent for Cedric.

'I have just given Lord Godwin sad news, Cedric,' Gospatrick said. 'It's sad news for us all . . .'

'My mother?' Cedric cried.

'No, not your mother; she is in good health. It's your uncle Oswald. Last week he caught a chill, which developed into a fever. Cedric, I'm sorry to have to tell you . . .'

'He died two days ago,' Godwin finished, relieving Gospatrick of the burden.

Not a word came from Cedric.

Gospatrick stooped down and took from his bag a long bundle wrapped in a cloak. He uncovered it, to reveal Oswald's sword. It was a splendid piece of workmanship, with a two-inch-broad carved blade, hilt and guard inlaid with amber and silver.

'Your mother and I were with him,' Gospatrick gently told Cedric. 'He asked me to bring you his blessing, and this sword. You probably know that it belonged to his father, and to his grandfather before that. Tell Cedric to use it well and justly, he said. Tell him that it has never been raised against the innocent or the helpless. He said he knew that in your hands it never would be, and that was why he wished you to have it.'

The tears rolled unashamedly down Cedric's cheeks as he took the sword in both hands and clasped it to his breast.

'I won't disgrace him,' he choked, 'or his sword. . . .'

'Of course you won't,' Godwin confidently declared. 'Oswald taught you well, I can see it in you. Steel yourself, lad. Don't weep for a man who led a fine life and faced death bravely. Now Berkshire needs a new Shire-Reeve, and I can think of none better than the nephew of the man who has done the work so well these many years!'

Cedric was speechless again. He was amazed that the earl was prepared to hand such high office to an unproven youth barely eighteen years old, but to crafty old Godwin it was by no means an ill-judged move. Godwin had seen how committed Cedric was to Harold. Loyalty to Harold meant loyalty to Godwin, and it was an emotion of which Godwin knew how to make good use.

'Berkshire is your home, and you've watched Oswald at work; you are the obvious choice,' Godwin went on, irritated at the boy's dumbness. 'You'll have an income from the estate taxes, and a new grant of land. It's time you went home, anyway. I've had you under my feet long enough.'

'It's a great honour my father is doing you,' Harold eagerly told Cedric. 'Think of it, you'll be the most important man in the whole shire, answerable only to the king and to my father.'

Cedric nodded, searching for something to say. He had grown accustomed to the restlessness of the Godwin family, yet still he was overwhelmed by the speed and command with which they caused things to happen.

'Aye,' he murmured, 'and to think that not so long ago I dreamed that one day, in the far distant future, I might become Alderman of Reading!'

IX

THE day he received the petition from his earls, King Harold
had been in a state of delirium. These days he was often driven
to it by the torture of his swollen glands, his ulcerated face and
genitals, and he would rave for hours. For a while after each return
from the gates of Hell he would be quite passive, but later his
moods would turn dangerously unpredictable.

When the letter was handed to him, he slumped back in his bed
and stared at it for an hour or more, as though it held not the
slightest interest for him, then suddenly he leapt up in a paroxysm
of hate and ripped it to shreds.

'Godwin has betrayed me!' he screamed. 'Godwin, my friend,
dares to put his name to treason! Is he mad?'

His cronies waited, knowing that something interesting would
happen while he was in this state. There were fewer of them than
in the early days, for Harold's violent fits had been the downfall
of some and had driven away others, and the longhouse which once
had rocked to the sounds of laughter and drunken song had fallen
silent, yet still there were followers enough to carry out his crazed
bidding. And those who remained were those who asked the fewest
questions.

'It seems that he and the other earls plot against you, my lord,'
one of them mischievously suggested.

'Yes,' Harold whimpered. 'Even Godwin plots against me now.
All these years I have left him to rule like a king in his own right
down there, giving him all he could wish for, and now he's turned
against me. He must pay dearly for that! Show him that I will have
my way! Go on, show Wessex the torch and the sword!'

So the dark riders went south, eager for blood. They crossed
the Thames at Oxford and passed like a gale through Abingdon,
Dorchester and Wallingford, ravaging village and town, looting and
wrecking, and cutting down any who tried to bar their way.

They were laying waste the country around Streatley before news
of it reached Cedric at Wantage. Cedric, worried about the safety
of his mother and all the people he knew in Reading, quickly called
out the fyrd and began a day-and-night march eastwards. He had
little more than two hundred farm lads at his back, many of them
armed with nothing but sickles and clubs and making their way on

foot, but he kept hurrying on to meet the enemy at the earliest opportunity rather than waiting to recruit the most skilled old soldiers and the best horsemen from further afield.

At Reading, he found no trace of the raiders. Word came that they had veered off down to Whitchurch, so he took up the pursuit in that direction. By the time he reached Basingstoke, the raiders were reported to be back in Wallingford. Cedric's men, weary and sore from days of useless trudging, were forced to go north once more, complaining and threatening to go home as they hobbled along. They were packing up a makeshift camp on the wild downs near Blewbury early one morning when Cedric's scouts reported that large mounted armies were converging on him from both west and east.

Cedric chose a high ridge on which to make his stand. As soon as he had bullied his quaking forces into position, he was able to watch the approach of the riders. They appeared first as dust clouds far away across the bare and shimmering hills, then as colonies of ants pouring purposefully down the slopes, making directly for his sorry little fortress. Some of his men panicked and ran, and had to be beaten back to their places. Cedric himself felt like making a swift retreat, but valiantly held himself and his company in check.

Soon he was glad he had, for as the two sets of horsemen came nearer he saw that one was led by Earl Godwin and the other by Earl Sweyn. Feeling foolish he trod down the steep incline to meet them.

'You're a plucky one, Cedric, I'll grant you that,' Godwin roared with laughter at the sight of Cedric's ragged following. 'I wouldn't take that bunch of ragged-arse simpletons out against a flock of geese! God's word, look at them! Shaking like weeds! What did you think they'd do against Harefoot's warriors? Fart at them?'

'They were all I could find, my lord,' Cedric mumbled. 'I thought speed was the main thing.'

'Speed!' Godwin guffawed, 'with those plodding plough-pushers! Well, you didn't catch the king's men, for all your speed, did you? Well, don't worry about it. They've gone. I caught them at Pangbourne, and we sent them scuttling across the river so fast they hardly got wet. The heads of two dozen of them are on poles on the north bank of the Thames now, as a warning to their friends not to come back!'

'And I missed it all!' Cedric said, with a grin of relief. 'I've been very foolish. I wish I had your experience in these things, my lord.'

'You'll learn,' Godwin said charitably. 'You've learned one lesson, for a start. If you don't know where your foe is, go where he is bound to appear sooner or later, and use the time to make your arm strong. The raiders had to make their way back across the Thames at some time. I covered the few points where they could do so. I sent Harold to London, patrolled Pangbourne to Wallingford myself, and got word to Sweyn to move down on Oxford. If you hadn't left so hastily, you'd have got an order from me telling you to join my men.'

'I'm sorry . . .'

'Never mind this time. As it happened we didn't need you. Next time, though, make sure you're where I want you, or you'll be the shortest-lived Shire-Reeve that Berkshire ever saw!'

Cedric went home feeling chastened and silly, but after a while he tried to put his humiliation out of mind.

For the first few weeks of his reign as Shire-Reeve it had been easy for him to play the part without seeing the other side of his position. Having his own hall – one almost as grand as Godwin's – had gone to his head like strong wine. Being the master of all he surveyed, hundreds of acres of lands populated with tenants, servants, slaves and livestock, made him feel as if he had earned a crown instead of having been entrusted with an administrative appointment. He behaved exactly as he felt too, giving petty commands to men three times older than himself, sending trivial missives to Earl Godwin on every subject he could think of, and dealing with the most trifling incidents as though he were Solomon giving judgement. He spent extraordinary amounts of money, without looking too carefully into the depths of his purse. He bought over-rich jewellery and weapons, a thicket of hunting spears, good clothes, the best leather saddlery, and horses and hounds befitting a man of leisure, cattle and sheep worthy of a great land-owner. Trying to equal Godwin, he entertained lavishly. Reeves and thanes of lesser rank were summoned to his hall in great numbers, to be told how Cedric expected the affairs of the shire to be run.

Gradually, however, work took over from pleasure, until he became so deeply absorbed in his duties that he found scant time for the delights which he had thought to be among the chief prerogatives of a landlord. His days were spent supervising the fixing, collecting and distribution of taxes, tolls and feorm, providing protection for the collectors. He had to settle the complaints of the taxpayers, see to the repair of roads, bridges, fords and dykes after storms and floods. He attested the sales of livestock, saw that farms were not neglected, ensured that the terms of disputed wills were properly met and acted as guarantor for the safe passage of travellers, merchants and artisans working away from home. He conducted courts and dispensed justice, made certain that claims for wergild – the sum of money paid in compensation to the family of a murdered man – were honoured.

They were not easy times in which Cedric was given his burden of responsibility. His first summer at Wantage was long and hot. A terrible drought combined with disease to destroy crops throughout England. It was a pestilence brought about by the sins of King Harold, men declared, as the shortage of food worsened.

The price of a sester of wheat reached four shillings and seven-pence – the highest in living memory – and that aggravated the problems of local leaders like Cedric. Townspeople who could not afford the price reacted angrily against farmers, millers and bakers, who could do nothing about the dearth of supplies. Resentment was rife against greedy merchants who scoured the country, buying and selling, forcing prices ever higher, satisfying the rich and depriving the poor. Riots threatened in every town, and it was the odious job of the aldermen of boroughs and hundreds to enforce the peace. As winter approached, with the prospect of empty granaries, the townsfolk became frantic. Near Abingdon, outraged villagers burned down a watermill when its owner appeared to be hoarding grain for his own profit. In Reading a wheat merchant was thrown into the river and his carts ransacked, and close to Newbury a granary was raided and pulled apart from roof to foundations. Meanwhile, animals starved or were slaughtered because their owners could neither sell them nor afford to feed them.

Each night, Cedric returned home an exhausted and troubled man, who drank heavily to ease his cares and induce sleep. That was how the girl Gwendoline came into his life.

She was the daughter of a wealthy cloth-maker. She came to Cedric's house several times with her father, a frequent guest at the young shire-reeve's banquets, and one evening, in an ale-washed stupor, he took her to his bed.

He was surprised to find her there the next morning, and became indignant when he discovered that she had set her sights upon being his wife, and had to a certain extent planned her own seduction.

'If I am with child, you will have to marry me,' she blandly told him, as she sat coyly on the edge of the cot, combing her long fair hair over her naked breasts, adding: 'I have never known a man before. Father will be very angry. . . .'

'Oh, really?' Cedric grunted. 'Well, I shall decide whether or not we marry. You're not the first I have known.'

That was true enough, for he had been to the whore-houses of Chichester a couple of times with Harold, but never before had he woken in his own house with a strange woman beside him. His bluff speech was really an attempt to conceal a growing panic, for he was by no means sure of the outcome of a confrontation with an aggrieved parent.

Cedric pulled his cloak around him and got up, breaking his fast with cold chicken, high-priced bread and ale warmed with a fire iron while he thought about his predicament. If the girl were to deny that she had been willing, the law would be very much on her father's side. The man could kill Cedric almost with impunity, and could certainly sue him for a large amount of money. Cedric had learned the first expensive lesson about the disadvantages of power – the lengths to which some people would go to use his own standing against him.

'If I give you some money, will you go away and find yourself another lover?' he asked.

'You treat me like a common whore, my lord,' Gwendoline pouted, 'and I am not that. I told you this is the first time I have known a man. I am in love with you.'

'God's word, are you?' Cedric laughed, 'And what if I tell you that I am in love with another?'

'Who?' demanded the girl, jealousy flaring up within her.

'No one you would know. A noble lady, and I shall marry her one day. I am a man of ambition, and destiny. I am only eighteen yet already I am Shire-Reeve of Berkshire. One day, in a few more years perhaps, I could be an earl, and fit to marry an earl's daughter. Until then you may be my mistress if you wish, or I will give you ample property to compensate for your lost maidenhood, but marry you I cannot.'

Gwendoline could do no more than gape at the pompous youth to whom she had hopefully surrendered up her virginity. She dressed hurriedly, and left the house in tears; but she returned to his bed that night and on many nights afterwards. To her Cedric represented the prospect of improving her social position, but to him Gwendoline was a pleasant enough diversion from the cares of office, something to boast about when Harold came to see him.

Harold rode into the yard late one evening, the most welcome guest Cedric had seen for a long time. Godwin's son was in a high state of exhilaration, and could hardly pause to gulp down a goblet of wine before blurting out his news.

'The king is dead! Haven't you heard? King Harold is dead!'

'Christ's blood!' exclaimed Cedric. 'At so young an age? He was no more than twenty-three! How did he die?'

'Oh, there's talk that he was poisoned, as there was when his brother died,' Harold reported. 'But father says it's more likely he died of his filthy pox – riddled with it he was. He was in fearful agony at the end, they say. The physicians couldn't do anything for him. They tried bleeding, leeches, exorcism, everything. He was a disgusting sight too, by all accounts, covered with sores and swellings, and he'd gone blind and quite mad. They had to tie him down, he was so crazed. He would have killed anyone who went near him.'

'Well, he's no loss,' Cedric pronounced. 'What's to happen now? Who is to be king?'

'That is what we are to decide, you and I, my friend,' Harold told him. 'We are joining the Witan, at Oxford, for the election. We have to leave at first light tomorrow. Isn't it exciting? We are going to help elect a king for the first time. Hardicanute is one candidate, Edward the other. My cousin Sweyn Estrithsson is also eligible, being a direct descendant of the Danish king, but father does not give him much chance of success. Too few people in England know him.'

'I don't know any of them, except that Edward is brother to the man I led to his death,' Cedric said worriedly. 'I shan't know which one to vote for.'

'Father will soon tell you where your vote goes!' Harold laughed. 'If he can't get Sweyn on to the throne, I think he'll plump for Hardicanute. He still favours the Danish line over the English.'

'But I thought he was opposed to Hardicanute?'

'Yes, but then there was another choice. This time there isn't. I can't wait to get to Oxford. Anyway, that's all for tomorrow. It's good to see you again, you old rogue. What have you been doing all these months?'

'Ho, what haven't I been doing!' Cedric responded with a bold chuckle, slapping his arm across Harold's back. 'Working more hours than I realised a day contained, mostly, but I've had my fun too. Wait till you see the prize heifer I've got in my stall . . .'

'Why, you sly devil! Been serving some little wench, have you . . . ?'

'Aye, and a beauty at that, you'll see. She'll be here later, then you can cast your longing gaze over her. But, knowing what a lecher you are, I warn you: keep your hands to yourself!'

'So, you've taken my advice, and forgotten about Edith?'

Cedric's broad smile faded.

'No,' he said emphatically. 'I haven't forgotten Edith. Edith I love, and always shall. Gwendoline is just a girl to bed, that's all.'

'Fool. You'll never learn. This Gwendoline, what is she? Servant? Serf?'

'Merchant's daughter. Her father makes and sells cloth, here in Wantage. Ah, damn it, I have to be honest with you, of all people.

To tell you the truth, I don't know what to do about her. The cursed girl wants to marry me.'

'God's mercy,' Harold guffawed. 'You don't intend to, do you?'

'No, I don't. But it isn't funny, you know. She won't leave me alone now. One of these days her father is going to find out what's going on, then there'll be trouble. She keeps saying she'll tell him, anyway.'

'Crafty little cat,' Harold said. 'She's trying to force your hand. Send her packing. There are hundreds of women like her, Cedric my old friend, always waiting to ensnare men like you and me, men they think can make them rich and comfortable. I warn you, if you've had enough of her, send her off before it's too late. You haven't been baking a little loaf in her oven, have you?'

'I don't think so. Not yet.'

'Then be rid of her before you do. Give her a baby, and you're stuck with her. Once they're cradling a brat in their arms they can truly soften you up, believe me.'

'Oh Lord,' Cedric groaned. 'Don't talk about it, please. What about you? What have you been up to lately?'

'Ah, you needn't think you are ahead of me,' Harold grinned. 'There's one of the village wives, a firebrand of a woman . . .'

'A wife? You fool! Whose wife?'

'A fisherman's. Her husband is away for days at a time, and she gets lonely. Ye gods, how she can love then! He almost caught me once. I went to the cottage, and there he was at the door. I pretended I'd come to buy some fish from him, but you should have seen the look he gave me! Well, can you imagine it? Harold Godwinsson going out to buy fish for his supper? I had a close escape there.'

'And you called me a fool,' Cedric chuckled. 'You're playing a more dangerous game than I am.'

'Oh no, there you're wrong. If mine blows up like a windy cow there's someone else she can blame. Is there anyone to point to but you, when yours swells out for all to see? That's why I warn you: be careful.'

Harold's warning came too late, however. That very evening, Gwendoline whispered to Cedric that she was indeed with child. She mentioned marriage and begged him to change his mind, but Cedric met her pleas with a stony resolution not to be bullied. He told her that, while he was away at Oxford, she must tell her father what had happened, and say that Cedric would discuss the matter fully upon his return. The girl was terrified at the thought of facing her father alone, but Cedric sent her home before she could start to make more of a fuss.

Next morning, on the way to Oxford, he rode up beside Harold.
'You know what you were saying, about babies?' Cedric grunted.
'Oh no, she isn't!' Harold cursed.

'Yes, she is. Now what am I to do?'

'The same as I told you yesterday. Send her home. You don't want to be burdened for the rest of your life with a woman you don't want, do you?'

'But, the law . . .'

'The law!' Harold said scornfully. 'Have you forgotten? My father is the law here, and Earl Godwin looks after his own. Don't worry, he likes you. He's heard good reports about how you have done your work, and he likes what he hears. No, you don't have to worry about some little merchant with a deflowered daughter. Just give him a good purse for his damaged goods, and tell him to keep her locked up in future.'

'But it will be my child, won't it?' Cedric argued miserably. 'It may be a son – my firstborn, my own flesh and blood.'

'All right then, keep the brat if you must. Rear it yourself, if you like, and keep its mother in comfort. You still don't have to marry her.'

'Is that what you'd do?'

'I'll let you know,' Harold promised lightly, 'when my little flounder spawns. If the thing looks like me, I might keep it. If it has a fish tail, I'll throw it back in!'

X

GODWIN had commandeered the house of a thane at Oxford, close to the big moot hall where the Witan would go into session as soon as a quorum had gathered. When Harold and Cedric arrived there they found the Earl of Wessex in a rare state of agitation, like a blustering wind trapped in a ravine, because some of the reeves and thanes from the far shires of his earldom had yet to appear. It was vital to Godwin that he should have them all there for such a crucial vote, but he was still waiting for the leaders of Kent, Dorset, Devon and Cornwall. The northerners had had earlier warning of the meeting, having been the first to hear of King Harold's death, and the moot hall was filling with a crowd of Mercians as well as many of the members from Northumbria and East Anglia.

Godwin, however, was calmed by being given his first grandson, Haakon, brought by Sweyn from Hereford to be shown proudly to his grandfather for the first time. The baby was motherless, as Sweyn's woman had died in childbirth, but his future was assured, since he would share in Godwin's limitless ambitions for his family. Sweyn was robbed of his son from the moment the delighted Godwin set eyes on the baby. Time and again Godwin would go and take Haakon from his wet nurse, sit down and dandle the baby on his knee, then hand him back to the nurse. Whenever he was not giving his full attention to his grandson, Godwin would stamp about the house, ranting about the succession.

'I knew I should never have put that useless weed on the throne!' Godwin roared, pausing in his pacing to kick at the rushes, as though they represented the broken body of the late king. 'Three years, then he gives up the ghost! And to think that scruffy, mange-ridden little dog was a son of Canute! Now what do we have, eh? Two pups from that Norman bitch, Emma, one of them a brat that Canute should never have fathered, the other a puny left-over from Ethelred's crop who hardly knows what England looks like!'

He took up the baby again, fuming still. Little Haakon burped loudly and started to howl.

'You are upsetting him, my lord,' the wet nurse told him.

Godwin looked at Haakon as though he had forgotten what he was holding.

'Eh?' he challenged, 'oh – here, give it the tit and stop it bawling, will you? Holy Cross, where are those damned idiots from Kent and Devon? How much longer will it take them to get here? Ah, Harold,' he went on, as his second son came in. 'And Cedric! At least you two have managed to get here. Come and see your nephew, Harold. This is Haakon. A fine boy, eh?'

Harold feigned disinterest as he inspected the baby, but Cedric could tell that his friend was proud to be an uncle. Seeing the woman with the baby at her breast caused Cedric to wonder how Gwendoline would look with their child when it was born. Suddenly the prospect of becoming a father pleased him, and he wanted to ask Sweyn about it, but Sweyn was busy with the more serious business of the day.

'Well, father,' Sweyn was saying, 'I know who I'm going to propose. Who better to be king than my cousin Sweyn of Denmark? Why bother with Hardicanute or Edward at all?'

He was soon to learn, though, that his high office had not earned him the independence he thought he had. He considered himself his father's equal now that he, too, was an earl, but Godwin had different ideas.

'You'll propose and vote for whomever I tell you to,' Godwin snapped. 'Or you'll lose that earldom faster than you got it. I mean it, boy. As it is, I'm not at all happy with what I've been hearing about the way you run it.'

Sweyn's face darkened at this public verbal thrashing.

'What do you mean, the way I run it?' he demanded. 'What's wrong with it?'

'You know what I mean,' Godwin bellowed. 'Harsh taxes, confiscation of land, evictions, the bullying of the serfs; you'll have a rebellion on your hands if that goes on, my boy, and I'm telling you to put a stop to it. Any leader with a pennyworth of sense knows that power isn't held without the respect of the people, and if you throw away the earldom that I sweated to get for you, you'll answer to me. Do I make myself clear?'

'Yes father,' Sweyn mumbled sulkily.

'Good. So, Sweyn Estrithsson for king, you say? Well, certainly I would like to have a nephew of mine crowned king of England, but we have virtually no chance of success. Sweyn has no influence here. If he had taken the Danish throne from Magnus it might have been different, but as far as England is concerned he's untried, unknown and unliked. He has no hope against Hardicanute or Edward.'

'Then who will you vote for?' Sweyn taunted Godwin. 'You

say we're to do as we're told, but you have yet to give us any instruction.'

Godwin was about to lay into his son again, but checked himself. He sat down and gathered three empty goblets before him, moving them like chessmen, each goblet representing a candidate.

'Here's Edward,' he said, pushing forward one goblet, 'son of Ethelred and Emma, still skulking in his Norman lair. He has strong support, especially from the Church, but can he be sure of his welcome after what happened to his brother Alfred at Guildford? Anyway, I have always believed a return to Ethelred's line to be a step backwards.' He tipped the goblet over, and moved out the second, continuing: 'Here we have Hardicanute, son of Canute and Emma. Feeble, but a son of Canute at least, and easily handled, even if he does bring back his hag of a mother with him.' He left that cup in place for the moment, and shoved the third alongside it, saying: 'And now Sweyn, Canute's nephew, son of my wife's brother, a king without a kingdom, a pawn which I think we can sacrifice to good effect . . .'

His audience waited for him to go on.

'Well,' Sweyn pressed, 'which?'

'I shall nominate Sweyn Estrithsson,' Godwin announced.

'Just as I said!' Sweyn said scornfully.

'But you will not vote for him, any of you,' his father ordered.

All of them stared at Godwin as if he had gone mad, which amused the earl immensely.

'Here is another lesson in politics for you,' he beamed. 'How to make your enemies work for you. Yes, Hardicanute is the man I want, but my support would be disastrous for him. None of the northern thanes here today can forget how their lands suffered under Harold's tyranny, while Wessex stayed free. They blame me for making Harold as powerful as he was. If I nominate Hardicanute, or anyone else for that matter, the votes will swing against him as surely as if he were named Devil incarnate. I shall put forward Sweyn, because they will all be expecting me to do so. Then one of you will suggest Hardicanute and – you'll see – Hardicanute will at once become the most popular man ever named in a moot. He will be a compromise that even supporters of Edward will be willing to accept, rather than have a nephew of mine on the throne.'

'But when Hardicanute is king,' Harold put in, 'will he not remember that you appeared to favour Sweyn? He already accuses you of the murder of Alfred. This will do nothing to improve his liking of you.'

Godwin nodded, noting not for the first time that Harold discussed these matters more intelligently than did his elder brother.

'That doesn't matter,' Godwin said. 'I can persuade him to my way of thinking later.'

'If you can get him away from his mother for long enough,' Harold laughed.

'Yes, Emma is a necessary evil if we make Hardicanute king,' Godwin agreed, 'She hates me so passionately. But,' he added, with a wicked gleam in his eye, 'there is one advantage I have which I know how to exploit. She is a good deal more afraid of me than I am of her!'

Cedric, quietly keeping to the background, was astounded by this glimpse into the devious workings of Godwin. He was disappointed that his was merely to be a raised hand directed by Godwin at this, his first election, but he could not help admiring the earl's determination to be the most powerful man in England, no matter who sat on the throne, and the manner in which he went about achieving his aim.

But if Cedric's eyes had been opened at that first meeting, they were to be opened wider still when, a few days later, he walked at last into the massive moot hall and the awe-inspiring dignity of the Witan. There, beneath a soaring roof of mighty oak beams and a canopy of thatch that would have covered a small field, all the titled and mitred men of England had assembled. Their cloaks made a rich display of colours and their bright jewels shone like many-hued stars in the light of the central fires and the wall torches. There were well over two hundred of them, including not only all the earls and reeves, but also the Archbishops of Canterbury and York, the bishops of all the sees, and the abbots. Moving among them were housecarls to guard them, clerks to record the proceedings and servants to fetch food and drink. Sets of benches two and three deep formed a great square around the hall, the north side for the Northumbrians, the west for the Mercians, the east for the East Anglians and the south for Wessex and South Mercia. Near the centre of the floor was a separate bench and table for the presiding archbishops and members of the royal family, although on this occasion there were to be no kings or princes present. Among the benches, waiting for the business to begin, crowds of men debated and argued and theorised and laughed among themselves, their voices echoing like thunder around the timber columns and the wood and plaster walls, so that it was difficult to hear a close neighbour unless he shouted.

These powerful citizens of England fully recognised the opportunities and hazards that faced them this day. For the advocates of a return to the Anglo-Saxon lineage it was an unexpected chance to renew a struggle fought only three years before, and for the Danish faction it meant that the victory they thought they had won had to be consolidated once more. The air buzzed with ambition, anxiety, even hostility.

'Cedric, don't you feel proud to be here?' Harold breathed. 'Do you realise, today we are more important than kings!'

Cedric hardly heard. He was watching Godwin stride through the throng, confident of his superiority in intellect and stature.

Godwin was smiling serenely, but his mind was working like that of a cat stalking its prey. He was counting his allies, weighing up his enemies and their numbers, forming strategies, balancing the chances for and against success, and missing not a face nor a name from his calculations. Knowing that he could count upon all his Wessex reeves and Sweyn's South Mercians, Godwin was giving most of his attention to those whom he could sway in other earl-doms – Earl Eadwulf of Northumbria and Bishop Lyfing of Worc-ester, both of whom he had implicated in the ill-fated abduction of Prince Alfred. If he could win them over, they would naturally bring all their followers into his camp. But he was not so sure of Eadwulf's brother Gospatrick, an awkward one, as he had proved on his recent visit to Godwin's house. Gospatrick just then stepped out to speak with Cedric, asking the boy how he was faring as Shire-Reeve. For the moment Godwin dismissed Gospatrick, and turned to his known chief opponent, Earl Leofric of Mercia.

Leofric had agreed with Godwin on the election of Harold Hare-foot as King, but had regretted it ever since. Harold had all but ripped apart Mercia like a wolf let loose among carefully tended sheep, causing deep divisions between former allies with his intrigues and his irresponsible attitude to kingship. Leofric was sick of Danish rule, and this time was coming out strongly in favour of Edward, as was the Church. Therefore the clash of wills between Godwin and Leofric would doubtless be a battle of giants for the two men were of like nature and strength, and Godwin relished the prospect. Even as he and Leofric came face to face in the crowd, Godwin was deciding that he would engage his enemy even before the fight began, and try both to unsettle him and to score points off him.

'Ah, Leofric my friend!' Godwin greeted his rival easily, as though he had not a care in the world, 'what a sad event brings us here – the death of our king, God rest his soul!'

'Sad for you, I'm sure,' Leofric sneered, 'but it is a happy occasion for me. As for King Harold's soul, if he possessed one, I imagine it is burned to a cinder by now.'

'Ah yes,' Godwin conceded wisely. 'He did have his faults, I must admit. But he could be very generous to those who treated him well . . .'

This was a deliberate reference to Godwin's acquisition of South Mercia for Sweyn, and Leofric recognised it as such.

'Merciful God, what conceit!' Leofric bawled, and the whole room fell silent as their argument became public. Leofric added: 'You have the gall to speak of Harold's generosity, while everyone knows that Wessex was spared while the rest of us suffered the worst privations a king can impose on his people!'

'Oh, Wessex had its trials, too,' Godwin shrugged, still perfectly calm. 'The difference was, we did something about it. Have you not seen my signposts along the Thames, friend? One head per mile for twenty-four miles, that's the way to deal with your raiders.' Adopting a mischievous grin then, he went on: 'You should be more courageous, Leofric, like your dear wife. Tell me, is that really true, that the lovely Godiva rode all through Coventry, naked as a babe? Why, I'd have given half *my* earldom to see that!'

Leofric was speechless with rage as the entire Witan broke into lewd laughter. He reddened as if gripped by apoplexy, shook and stammered. Whatever the truth of his wife's infamous ride he had been taunted about it too often, and to have Godwin make coarse reference to it before this noble gathering was more than he could stand.

'God, I should kill you for that!' he finally managed, grasping his sword hilt. 'Slanderer! Liar! How dare you insult my wife!'

Leofric's friends were holding him back, and some of Godwin's companions were urging him keep quiet. It was Eadsige, Archbishop of Canterbury, who eventually intervened.

'My lords, please,' Eadsige begged. 'Your conduct shames you. We are here for a serious purpose. Please stop this unseemly bickering!'

At last all the members were persuaded back to their seats. All the while Leofric glared across at Godwin muttering threats, and Godwin continued to provoke him with a benign smile, and so it went on until Eadsige and the other churchmen began chanting prayers and reminded the gathering of the business in hand.

'Now,' the Archbishop began. 'We must name names, and with God's help truly speak our minds.'

Godwin was the first to leap to his feet.

'I nominate Sweyn Estrithsson,' he called, and sitting down again he cheekily added: 'My nephew, of course.'

Leofric was on his feet immediately.

'Of course he nominates Sweyn!' he bellowed angrily, 'nothing would please Godwin more than to have a relation of his crowned king. That is his only motive for putting up the name of his nephew – personal advancement!'

'Not at all,' Godwin said with mock hurt. 'He happens to be the natural choice.'

'How so?' Leofric demanded. 'What claim has he?'

'He is a son of Estrith, sister of Canute.'

'And does that give him more right than Hardicanute, Canute's own son?'

'No,' Godwin smiled: he had tricked Leofric into making first mention of his own candidate. 'But he is better fitted to be king. He is stronger, more decisive, more. . . . *regal!*'

'Nonsense!' Leofric spat. 'If he were all that, he would be king of Denmark now.'

'Leofric is right,' yelled Sweyn Godwinsson, jumping up at a nudge from his father, 'I nominate Hardicanute.'

Godwin made a convincing show of being a father defied.

'What,' he cried. 'Does my own son stand against me? Damn you, boy, your cousin Sweyn is your father's choice!'

'But not mine!' answered Sweyn, who at that moment almost believed that he really was standing firm against Godwin's wishes.

'I nominate Edward, son of Ethelred,' Leofric came back desperately. 'Haven't we had enough of these ignorant Danish kings? England should be ruled by Englishmen again!'

'I agree,' said Eadsige. 'The Church is wholeheartedly for Edward.'

'Wholeheartedly, Your Grace?' Godwin queried. 'With the greatest respect, I believe you are unaware of the feelings of all the bishops. What about you, Lyfing? Did you not mention to me that you thought Hardicanute the better man?'

Lyfing coughed and only half stood to make his reply, colouring with embarrassment. He knew the stern eye of his Archbishop was upon him, yet his conscience would not permit him to lie.

'I have had certain doubts to clear up in my own mind . . .' he stuttered, and a hum rose from the churchmen as they realised there might be dissent in their ranks.

Meanwhile Eadwulf of Northumbria had risen, impatient to have his say. He was eager to appease Hardicanute, just in case he was elected, in the hope that the new king would forget that the murder of Prince Alfred had occurred in Eadwulf's territory. Of Alfred's brothers, Hardicanute was known to be more spiteful than the pious Edward. Eadwulf wanted to be heard loud and clear as a corner-stone of the Hardicanute camp.

'Godwin's nomination is a ridiculous one!' he thundered. 'Sweyn

Estrithsson has no claim at all to England, and should be discounted here and now. I am for Hardicanute. Why, if we elected Sweyn, God forbid, all of Denmark would rally around Hardicanute to make war on us, and perhaps Normandy too!'

'On the other hand,' Godwin offered, 'if we don't elect Sweyn, he may bring an army here.'

Leofric now leapt upon that sweet opportunity to hit out at Godwin.

'Aye, and no doubt he would come by way of Bosham, where he would find more allies waiting,' he snarled. 'Oh no, my friends, do not be frightened off the course of wisdom by Godwin's threats. Already he has too much power, and has an unhealthy desire for more. Let us not give him a king for a nephew. Let us choose Edward, and win the respect of Normandy and Holy Rome. Then we will deal easily with the pirate Sweyn if he comes to steal a crown.'

'Aye, Edward! Edward!' a hundred voices chanted.

Godwin could see that it was time to play his winning piece, to check his adversaries now, or lose the game.

'All right,' he shouted, arms raised in surrender, 'I withdraw my nomination. I have no wish to be the means by which an unpopular king comes to the throne. Strike Sweyn's name from the list, then. But, to all of you who call Edward's name, consider this: Leofric has said that Normandy will be happier if we crown Edward, but he is wrong. There is one in Normandy more highly regarded than Edward, and that is his mother, Emma, great-aunt of young Duke William. It is well known that Emma favours the son she gave Canute above the son she gave Ethelred. If we elect Edward in preference to Hardicanute, Emma may well turn Normandy against us, making it more difficult for us to re-establish the treaty we had with Normandy to fend off the threats of the Danes. If you cannot accept Sweyn, your choice must be Hardicanute.'

Godwin knew by shrewd observation that there was a trait in human nature – though he could not have put a name to it – which tempted men to grant a victory to one of their fellows who had already accepted a defeat. His judgment was faultless. Many of those who a few moments before had been shouting for Edward were now swayed by Godwin's humility and sound argument, and changed their allegiance to Hardicanute. Godwin had only to strike the finishing blow.

'We have spoken long enough,' he told them. 'Let us put it to the vote.'

Leofric danced up and down, yelling to be heard above the roar of assent.

'Wait!' he pleaded. 'What is Godwin trying to do now? First he attempts to scare us with Sweyn, now with Emma! It's laughable! Listen to me, we must have Edward if we want the peace and just rule we had in Ethelred's time. We must put an end to the rule of ruffian Vikings who look upon England as a treasure chest to satisfy their own greed.'

It was an impressive rally, but it did not halt Godwin, who sensed that he had the greater part of the council with him.

'Ha! Peace and just rule!' he mocked. 'The just rule of Ethelred, indeed! I ask you, which was the grander rule, that of Ethelred or Canute? Which of them ran away in the midst of battle to hide in Normandy, and which of them then governed this country with a firm and fair hand for nigh on twenty years? Not only this country, but Denmark as well. Is that the mark of a ruffian Viking, or of a strong and intelligent king? Are we going to belittle the achievements of Canute by comparing him with his pox-ridden, brainless son, Harold? Hardicanute is the more worthy son of Canute. Hardicanute is our man!'

Leofric tried to protest again, but Archbishop Eadsige declared it was time to vote. When the hands were raised there was a clear two-thirds majority for Hardicanute, and Godwin put on his broadest smile of triumph for the benefit of Leofric and Eadwulf.

Shortly afterwards Hardicanute received word of his election, and came to England as king, bringing with him Emma, wife to two kings and now mother of a third. The youngest son of Canute, however, was quickly to prove himself less grateful to Godwin than his half-brother Harold had been. Hardicanute came to the throne determined to establish himself from the outset as a strong and severe ruler, and his first act was to avenge the murder of his half-brother, Prince Alfred.

The dead should be punished as harshly as the living, Hardicanute decreed. At his orders, the housecarls went to the tomb of King Harold and dragged out the corpse, symbolically hanged it, mutilated it, then threw it into the marshes to rot.

Satisfied with that gruesome act, Hardicanute then passed sentence of death on Earl Eadwulf and Bishop Lyfing. He drew back from treating Earl Godwin and his son Sweyn in a like manner, for there appeared to him to be some doubt that those two were as guilty; and besides, the Godwin family was too powerful and popular within its own kingdom of Wessex, and too well protected. Hardicanute decided that Godwin and Sweyn would be given a fair trial.

Of the other two, Lyfing was the more fortunate. He was warned of the summary sentence against him by a clerk at the king's court who owed him a favour. As the housecarls set out to arrest him, Lyfing escaped into the sanctuary of a monastery, never to be seen outside its walls again. Hardicanute flew into a rage when he heard that Lyfing had slipped through the net, but he did not dare to raid a holy place, and accepted grudgingly that the loss of his rich see and his freedom were sufficient penalties for Lyfing to pay.

Earl Eadwulf was not so lucky. He was summoned to Hardicanute's court with no reason given. He went with trepidation, but he did not dare to refuse to go. On his arrival at Winchester he was granted no opportunity to see the king, but was taken to a small stone chamber where he was greeted by three villainous looking housecarls.

The leader was the notorious Olaf Ericsson, the Hawk of Hjorring, axeman to Viking kings for twenty-four years since the day he had blooded his axe on Eadwulf's father, Earl Uhtred. As soon as Eadwulf looked into Olaf's stone cold eyes he knew he was done for.

'Olaf,' Eadwulf stammered, backing away to the wall. 'You cannot do this! I did not kill Prince Alfred, but you were there when it was done! You are more guilty than I!'

'Ah, but I am only the king's servant. I do the king's bidding, whoever he may be. A king bade me kill your father, Eadwulf, another told me to make sure that Alfred never left Ely Isle, and now a third commands me to kill you. I have never disobeyed my king; do you really expect me to do so now?'

'Olaf! We have both served kings! You have eaten at my table! Think of my family, my wife, my daughter, my granddaughter . . .'

'I shall grieve for them,' Olaf shrugged, and he waved his men forward, telling them sharply: 'Get it done, before his whimpering angers me.'

In former times Olaf Ericsson would never have dreamed of allowing another to do his killing for him, but the years had been hard on this giant among Danish warriors. These days the warrior's horny hands and wide shoulders were often siezed with agonising, grating pain, so that he could no longer swing his dreaded axe so eagerly as he had done in the past. Today he had to be content to watch, with both pleasure and resentment, as his comrades pinned Eadwulf's arms and strangled him to death.

At the victim's last gargle, Olaf barked: 'The king says his body is to be thrown into the sea.' He strode from the room, adding: 'Do it!'

Godwin, like Lyfing, had his spies at court, and heard about his impending trial some days before he was due to be informed.

'Ungrateful little brat, he must be mad.' Godwin ranted to his family. 'Doesn't he realise that, but for me, he wouldn't be king?' He thought carefully for a time before saying: 'I'll make him a gift. Something costly. That will placate the little fool.'

XI

GODWIN gave the king one of his biggest and best warships, with the message that the present was a mark of his loyalty to the last son of the revered Canute.

Hardicanute was taken aback, but since he had already made public his intention to try Godwin, he could not be seen to submit so soon. The trial went ahead as planned, much to Godwin's amazement. Then the earl heard of the fate of Eadwulf and Lyfing, took the king more seriously and busily set about preparing his defence. On the day he and Sweyn presented themselves at Winchester they took with them more than one hundred oath-helpers, including Harold and Cedric, not one man below the rank of Shire-Reeve. They crowded into Hardicanute's hall like a small army, easily outnumbering those the king had been able to rally together to assist him in laying the charges. There were precious few men in England willing to test Godwin's temper, Hardicanute had discovered.

Godwin, noting the superiority of his position, faced his king without fear. He stood with arms folded in the middle of the hall, defying Hardicanute and Emma to do him harm. It was four years since he had last met them, here in this very room, when he had washed his hands of them both and had told Emma to leave the country. Little had changed, they all recognised, except that Hardicanute was now king and his mother could not be told to go away. Otherwise the differences between them were still vividly apparent – Godwin cool and impregnable, Hardicanute temperamental and uncertain and dominated by his mother. If anything, the king had lost strength and confidence, for over the years he had become sickly and pale, his body plagued with consumption, so that he now looked more ineffectual than ever.

'Good day, my lord,' Godwin smiled. 'I am ready to defend myself. And may I say how I regret that you should have heard such rumours about me. You know, of course, that I have always protested my innocence of the death of Prince Alfred.'

Hardicanute sulked as he compared Godwin's following with his own wretched band, comprising a few timid clerics who had escaped the carnage at Guildford and some insignificant thanes who hoped for advancement and reward. The only men of repute, apart from those brought by Godwin, were the reeves and churchmen present to judge the accused.

'Earl Godwin of Wessex and Earl Sweyn of South Mercia,' Hardicanute mumbled. 'You are charged with plotting the murder of Prince Alfred, son of Ethelred . . .'

The accusers came, one by one, speaking their parts without conviction, knowing that the result of the trial was a foregone conclusion.

'In the name of Almighty God, as I stand here freely and unbought,' they said formally, 'I saw with my eyes and heard with my ears that of which I speak . . .'

They went on to tell of that night, of how, a few hours after Godwin and Sweyn and the others had left the house, the housecarls came murdering. Those accusers who had not been at Guildford had little to say, reporting a snatch of overheard conversation here and a second-hand account there. There were fragments of information which might have condemned Godwin had more reliable witnesses appeared, but of the two principal witnesses who might have been there, one had been strangled and the other driven into hiding. All that one of the thanes could offer was the weak statement: 'I saw Earl Godwin talking to Olaf Ericsson, captain of the housecarls, some days before the crime. They looked as though they were plotting something.'

'Did you hear what they were plotting?' yawned a judge.

'No, my lord, but . . .'

Godwin listened with an air of boredom, and was sublimely calm when his turn came.

'By the Lord, I am not guilty of act or part in the crime of which I am accused,' he recited. 'My first witness is Cedric Cedricsson, Shire-Reeve of Berkshire. He led the escort which met Prince Alfred at Dover, and he was at Guildford when this terrible thing happened. Tell them, Cedric.'

Cedric stepped out, not as nervous as he had imagined he would be. Facing a king for the first time in his life was less of an ordeal than he had prepared himself for, probably because this king lacked presence, for one used to Godwin's company. Hardicanute wore a rich purple cloak and a gold crown, but beneath that he was a sick, unhappy man. Cedric felt sorry for him.

'By the Lord, the defendant's oath is true and not false,' Cedric swore with care, conscious that the slightest error or fumbling in his speech could shatter Godwin's case. 'My lord,' he continued. 'Earl Godwin and Earl Sweyn speak the truth. I was at Guildford, in the hall with the prince himself when the deed was done. It was a dreadful deed, my lord, a shameful and vicious deed, and I will carry the memory of it to my grave. But neither Earl Godwin nor his son were there when it happened. They showed Prince Alfred courtesy and hospitality, and they left long before the housecarls came. Nor were they to be seen in Guildford afterwards.'

It was a well rehearsed piece, one which Godwin himself had prepared, and Cedric felt a twinge of guilt as he recited it. In his own heart he had long ago absolved Godwin of any blame; why then should this deceit be necessary, he wondered? If Godwin was truly innocent, why should he have to stand here mouthing a prepared oath like a puppet? Silently praying that his sin was not grave enough for God to strike him dumb, he saw that Hardicanute was eyeing him with something like suspicion. His stomach began to churn.

'Shire-Reeve of Berkshire, eh?' Hardicanute mused. 'An important post for one so young. Tell me, Cedric Cedricsson, when were you appointed?'

'Nearly two years ago, my lord.'

'By Godwin?'

'Yes,' Cedric confirmed, and realised in the same moment what the king might be implying. Surely Hardicanute could not think that Cedric was guilty of complicity, that the position of Shire-Reeve was his reward from Godwin? The churning grew into a crawling sickness. Quickly he went on: 'But I am a natural successor, sir. My uncle was Shire-Reeve before me, and my grandfather before him. My father was Alderman of Reading, and both he and my uncle were well known to your royal father. They fought beside King Canute in Sweden, as did Earl Godwin.'

Hardicanute smiled, but with the corners of his mouth downturned in mockery.

'So your forebears were great warriors,' he said. 'But what did you do to earn such distinction?'

'I don't understand,' Cedric answered, growing more ill at ease as the inquisition went on. It was clear that the king was trying to trap him, and he knew he was starting to wriggle like a fish on the hook.

'The question is simple enough,' Emma interrupted sharply. 'What did you do to win the same exalted rank as they, other than command an inefficient bodyguard?'

'I don't know, lady,' Cedric shot back. 'When Prince Alfred was taken at Guildford, I made a vow that I would avenge him by seeking a fight to the death with Olaf Ericsson, who led the housecarls, and in that way purge both myself and my Lord Godwin of the disgrace we had suffered. That oath still holds good today. It may be that is why the earl has seen fit to honour me with such high office, because my vow bears witness to his innocence in the noblest way possible.'

Hardicanute and Emma were stunned, unable to find fault with Cedric's testimony. Cedric had neatly turned the king's line of questioning against him, and Hardicanute's face showed that he was both impressed and infuriated.

'Very well,' he mumbled, 'you may go.'

There was admiration in the eyes of Godwin's supporters for the way Cedric had conducted himself, but his greatest satisfaction came from the grin of approval and the huge wink which Godwin gave him as he passed by. The trial had undeniably gone Godwin's way. The rest was a mere formality, as long as no witness spoiled his oath with an error. For Cedric it was a personal triumph, a vindication of his master. God must have guided his tongue in that unprepared speech, Cedric believed, and at last he himself had no doubt at all that Godwin was as blameless as he.

But in a moment, his joy turned sour. There, framed in the doorway, Olaf Ericsson stood watching him. The Viking's cold eyes were fixed unblinking on the bold youth who had dared to challenge him publicly, and his mouth was curved into a thin smile that told Cedric he would gladly take up the challenge. He looked just as he had looked on that night in Guildford long ago, menacing and merciless. He was dressed the same, ready for battle in his long chain-mail coat, and carrying his feared weapons, the broad-sword strapped to his hip, the jewelled dagger at his belt and his bitter-edged axe in his hands. The sharp nose-guard of his helmet divided his eyes oddly wide, so that he looked like a questing snake. It all brought back the massacre at Guildford clearly to Cedric, as though it had happened last night instead of four years ago, and he saw that in exonerating Godwin he had condemned himself. He forgot all his bravery, all the hate and revulsion he had felt for Olaf ever since that night; he was aware only of his terrible undertaking. He was sickened by his sudden cowardice and his regret at having spoken out loud for Olaf to hear.

'Harold,' Cedric swallowed. 'What have I done?'

Harold had been listening to the witness who had taken Cedric's place. He saw the whiteness in Cedric's face, and followed his eyes to the door.

'Christ's blood: Olaf!' he breathed. 'Did he hear you?'

'Yes.'

'Wait, don't worry. He won't dare to do anything here . . .'

'Not here, but when this is over . . .'

'Silence!' roared one of the king's officers. Harold risked a last whisper.

'Father will sort it out, if you ask him to.'

Cedric could hardly take his eyes off Olaf through the rest of the proceedings. One moment he wished that the trial could be finished soon, so that he could face the worst and get it done with, then he changed his mind and prayed that it would go on long enough for Olaf to lose patience and leave. In that he was disappointed. Olaf seemed prepared to stand there all night, grinning at Cedric like a cat toying with a trapped mouse. The torment at last ended when Hardicanute decided he had heard enough praise of Godwin, and cut short the trial with at least half the oath-helpers still to be heard.

'Earl Godwin,' the king said, waving away the next speaker, 'it would seem that God himself is your witness today . . .'

'As He is to all innocent men, my lord,' Godwin suggested reverently.

'Don't interrupt,' Hardicanute snapped, and of the judges he asked: 'Are you satisfied?'

The presiding dignitary, after a brief consultation, signalled his assent.

'Earl Godwin and Earl Sweyn, in the sight of Our Lord, are innocent of the charges brought against them,' he intoned.

Hardicanute gave a reluctant nod, but Emma was less gracious.

'Either God is his witness or the Devil is,' she jibed. 'Time will tell.'

Godwin responded serenely.

'In my experience, lady,' he said, 'time reveals little, but conceals much.'

'Yes, and there is none more experienced in that than you,' Emma snapped vindictively, but her words were lost as Godwin's supporters crowded round him. Cedric should have been among them but he was rooted to his place by the sight of Olaf. It was not until he felt a tug at his sleeve, that he saw that one of his servants had come to him from Wantage, still hot and short of breath after his journey.

'My lord Cedric,' the man panted. 'The mistress Gwendoline; she's asking for you. When I left she was beginning her birth pains.'

'Oh, God help me!' Cedric prayed, wondering what else could happen to him this day.

Harold, who had overheard, let out a hoot of delight and gave Cedric a slap on the back that felt more like a punch.

'Well done, friend!' he cried, 'you're surely a father by now!'

At that moment, Cedric could not see much cause for joy.

'When was this?' he asked the messenger. 'How is she?'

'Just the night before this last, my lord. I came here with all haste, as she beseeched me to . . .'

'Yes, but how is she?'

'She . . . she was in great difficulty. She kept calling for you in her pain.'

Cedric, cold at heart, turned to Harold.

'How long does it take for a child to be born?' he asked, having no idea.

'She'll have had it by now, I should think,' Harold said. 'Don't worry . . .'

'Don't worry? God, I must get home at once . . .'

He had forgotten about Olaf for the time being, but Olaf had not forgotten him. The captain of housecarls had finally left his place at the doors and came striding up to Cedric, towering a full four inches over him. There was a challenge in Olaf's penetrating gaze, and his mouth was crooked with contempt. The crowd around Cedric fell silent and stepped back.

'So this is Cedric Cedricsson, the man who has sworn to fight with me to the death,' Olaf boomed, silencing the entire hall. 'Tell me, little fellow, when is it to be?'

Cedric looked to Harold and Godwin and Sweyn, but they gave no indication that they would help. Cedric was on his own, unless he appealed to them directly, and he could never bring himself to do that.

'It is true,' he admitted to Olaf. 'I have taken that oath. But it will not be today. I have just heard that my first child has been born. My first duty is to my family.'

Olaf gave a derisory laugh.

'Aye; see that they are well provided for,' he said, 'for you have slandered me before all gathered here, and now I make my oath to kill you. Where will I find you, brave one?'

'At Wantage,' Cedric replied courageously. 'I shall wait for you there.'

Cedric thought to add that Olaf could appoint any day he wished, but at that moment another newcomer stepped out from the throng. It was Gospatrick Uhtredsson, who pushed in front of Olaf to speak with Cedric.

'Cedric,' Gospatrick said earnestly, 'remember, we have taken the same vow, you and I, and I much longer ago. I ask you, let me take your place. This man murdered my father, he murdered my adoptive uncle Prince Alfred, and but a few days ago he killed my brother. Did you know that it was he who strangled Eadwulf, here in Hardicanute's palace? I have so much more to avenge, Cedric. Please, let *me* fight him.'

Certainly the temptation to grant Gospatrick's request was a real one, but Cedric's pride would not allow him to stand down. After a moment, he answered: 'No, Gospatrick. I'm sorry, but there is no turning back now.'

'Why argue?' Olaf interrupted with a hearty roar. 'When the first of you is dead, the other can try.' He swung around and stalked out of the room, calling back: 'I shall be at Wantage, soon. Whichever of you stands forward first will be the first to fall!'

'Will you not think on it again?' Gospatrick urged Cedric. 'Please, for the sake of Constance, who was mother to us both. I am twice your age, my friend. You deserve a chance to live, and I deserve the chance to justify the time I've waited.'

Cedric, looking away, shook his head. He was no longer afraid, merely numbed, as though Olaf had in those few minutes stripped him of all feeling. When Earl Godwin came and spoke to him, he barely heard.

'Why is it,' asked Godwin in feigned jest, 'that no sooner do I find myself the best oath-helper a man could wish, than he picks a fight with the most feared warrior in England, in Denmark too come to that.'

'Never mind that, father,' Harold chided him. 'What are we going to do about it?'

'There's not a lot we can do,' Godwin shrugged. 'Young Cedric's burned his boats. The least I can do is see that it's a fair fight. A fair fight, but not an even one. That is beyond my power.'

Harold, less hard-hearted than his father, gently put an arm across Cedric's shoulders.

'Come on,' he encouraged, 'I'll go home with you. Let's go and see this cub of yours, shall we?'

They rode hard for Wantage on a relay of horses; there was no time for talk. There was no comfort that Harold could offer Cedric anyway, and Cedric did not attempt to fake bravery knowing that Harold knew him too well to be fooled. They spurred on their mounts grimly over the long miles across Salisbury Plain and the Berkshire Downs.

At the journey's end they found Cedric's house ominously still even for the time of night. The stables held no horses of guests come to see the new child at the first opportunity, and nor was the hall bright with torches and feast fires, as Cedric had expected. There was a gloom about the place; Cedric could feel it. Once inside, he was met, not by scurrying servants, bustling midwives or joyful friends, but only by a single, tired freedman with downcast eyes.

'What is it?' Cedric barked at the man. 'What's wrong?'

'The child, my lord . . .'

'Well?'

'The child was stillborn.'

'Was it a boy?' he whispered.

'It was; yes, a boy.'

There was no more Cedric could say. Harold asked the questions for him.

'The mother, how is she?'

'She lives, but she grieves deeply. She will not eat, nor speak to anyone. Will you go to her, lord Cedric?'

Cedric bowed his head and went to Gwendoline's chamber like a man in a trance. He pulled aside the curtain hesitantly, unwilling to go in, having no comfort for Gwendoline, not even wanting any for himself.

A solitary candle burned in there; Gwendoline lay back on the mattress, her face a white mask in the gloom, dull eyes staring at the roof. At one side of the bed sat a midwife with an untouched meal, and on the other the girl's father sat holding her hand. He seethed at the sight of Cedric, but said nothing.

'You're too late,' Gwendoline said listlessly, turning away.

'I know. They told me. Are you all right?'

Gwendoline looked at him with loathing then, knowing she had lost more than her baby. There was nothing to bind him to her now, nothing to induce him to marry her, and she knew he would never take her to his bed again. Her dreams of being the Shire-Reeve's lady were shattered. He had won, and for that she hated him.

'Do you care?' she hissed.

In the silence which followed, Cedric desperately searched for something else to say. All he really wanted was to go away and forget, but he could not leave without offering Gwendoline some consolation, if indeed there was any he could offer.

'You are welcome to stay here, if you wish,' he said, meaning to be kind, but it sounded just like the rejection she had expected.

'Stay for what?' she retorted. 'To be your whore? No thank you. I have no wish to see you or your house again. I shall go back to my father's house, if he will have me.'

'Very well,' Cedric said tersely. 'Perhaps then I can give you something to help . . .'

'You have given me enough; you have given me *nothing!* Let that be an end to it.'

Cedric nodded, and wondered why he felt so little for the girl or for his dead child.

'Leave when you are well, then,' he mumbled, and left the room.

He returned to the main hall where Harold poured two goblets of wine.

'As God is my witness . . .' Cedric started to say, but he never finished. Gwendoline's father, his face bright with anger, strode across the hall towards Cedric.

'Seducer! Evil seducer!' the man ranted, choking over his words. 'You ruin my daughter; you kill her child with the wickedness in you; then you cast her aside like a dirty rag! Lecherous swine!'

Cedric went to meet him with hands stretched out to appeal for reason, but the man was in no mood to listen. His arm shot upwards, and too late Cedric saw the gleam of a knife in his hand. Harold yelled a warning, but Cedric had already leapt back with his left arm thrown up to protect himself as the deranged man lunged. It was a vicious thrust, and Cedric would surely have died had he been struck fully. But by good fortune, the man was too enraged to judge his distance. The knife point ripped through Cedric's cloak, tunic and shirt, and most of the force of the blow was spent by the time it cut a gash in his chest, four inches below the throat. Cedric gasped with pain and staggered back, clutching at the burning wound as blood soaked his torn clothes. Harold, with a fierce cry, leapt forward and grasped the man's hand, and struggled to wrest the knife from him. Some servants, who had been sleeping around the embers of the fire, were awakened by Harold's cries, and came running. It took only a moment or two for them to subdue Cedric's attacker.

'Get some rope, quickly!' Harold ordered. 'Bind him. Damn him, he'll hang for this . . .'

Cedric collapsed on to a bench, his wound ablaze and throbbing.

'Harold, no!' he gritted. 'Leave him. Help me, please!'

Harold winced as he examined the cut, and tore a corner from Cedric's linen shirt, soaked the wad in wine and pressed it against the bloody gash.

'You'll need a physician,' Harold said as he helped Cedric to sit up, faint from shock and loss of blood.

'Then get me one, for the love of Christ.'

'You!' Harold snapped at one of the gawping women. 'Is there a physician here?'

'Yes, my lord. He do live but half a mile away . . .'

'Then fetch him!' Harold bellowed, and to the people holding down the captive he shouted: 'And you, what are you doing? I told you to get a rope!'

'No, Harold, please,' Cedric insisted. 'Just let him go. Let him go home . . .'

'Let him go? Damn him, I'll hang him myself.'

'No. I cannot blame him for this. He's Gwendoline's father, he's suffered enough. For God's sake, just get him out of here!'

Cedric almost passed out completely at that point. Harold laid him on the bench, and held a cup of wine to his lips. Cedric battled hard against oblivion, fearing that if he closed his eyes he would never awake again. When the healer monk came his gentle manner helped calm Cedric, and when the wound had been cleaned and dressed he felt better. The flowers of St. John's wort were pounded then boiled with olive oil to produce a blood-coloured mixture which would prevent further bleeding by acting as a substitute for the very fluid of life, a magical concoction indeed. Iris leaves, red and blue like bruising on the skin, made another poultice to soothe the angry swelling around the cut.

'You will live,' the physician assured Cedric, as he applied the salves, and bound up Cedric's chest. 'I have seen more deeply wounded men recover.'

The work done, he helped move Cedric to his bed and gave him some mead mixed with camomile to help him sleep. Waiting only long enough to collect a few silver shillings from Harold, the healer monk went back to his cell. Cedric's house was quiet once more, as if nothing had happened. Harold alone sat awake beside him on the edge of his cot.

'Harold, am I evil, do you think?' Cedric asked wearily.

'Evil?' Harold laughed, 'why?'

'I must be, to be punished so. First Olaf Ericsson took up my challenge, then my son died; now I've been wounded. Merciful God, what else can go wrong? Is it because I did not marry Gwendoline? Or is it that I helped your father's oath?'

'Oh yes?' Harold snorted. 'Are you suggesting that my father was guilty after all?'

'I don't know. I'm suggesting nothing, I'm seeking answers. The biggest question is, how can I fight Olaf now, like this?'

'You're not seriously contemplating meeting him still? You're mad! He's worth two of you even when you're fit. In that state, you haven't a chance!'

'But he's coming here for me!'

'Perhaps you'd better come back to Bosham with me, then. He couldn't touch you there.'

'I won't do that!' Cedric protested. 'Run away from him! Be branded a coward for the rest of my life?'

'No, knowing you, I don't suppose you would. Well, I don't know; we'll have to think of something else. My father could arrange something. . . .'

'No. If I have to meet him, it will be in an honest fight, man to man. I'm no man at all if I cannot fight my own battles.'

'And not much of a man if he chops you to shreds,' Harold observed, but Cedric was no longer listening. The mead was taking its effect, and he was slowly drifting into sleep.

XII

IT was four days later, early in the morning, that Olaf came to Wantage. Harold brought the news to Cedric as he sat at breakfast.

'He's here, Cedric,' he said. 'He's brought some friends with him, too.'

Cedric did not speak at first, for fear of betraying his dread. Sickness crawled again in his belly. Cedric went to the chest that held his uncle's battle armour. Lifting the creaking oak lid, he pulled out the heavy leather coat sewn with iron rings, the helmet with its leather mask to guard the face, and the round wooden shield overlaid with bronze. The shield, embossed with circlets of studs and with a handsome ram's head at its centre, was dented and scratched from many battles. There were cuts and scuffs in the chain-mail as well. The armour had been in Cedric's family for generations, and it was said that it had been worn in a fight alongside Alfred the Great. Cedric laid it out upon the chest and took off his cloak and tunic to try it on.

'He's got a lot of men with him,' Harold repeated. 'Let me call out the townsmen . . .'

Cedric shook his head as he struggled into the coat.

'No,' he insisted. 'Too many good Berkshire men died at Guildford. I won't have any more of them killed. This is my fight!'

'You're asking to be killed.' Harold snorted. 'Why? Is this some kind of penance?'

Cedric tied up the leather thongs of the coat, and put on the sword harness over it. He picked up the shield and the helmet and struck a heroic pose, despising himself even as he did so.

'Do I *look* terrifying, at least?' he asked.

'How's your wound?' Harold countered.

'I'm all right.' Cedric insisted.

'All right!' Harold snorted. 'That cut's about to open up again, and there you are stepping out to face the Hawk of Hjorring as if you were the fittest man in England. Damn you, Cedric. I've got used to you, you know.'

'Harold,' Cedric said, quietly but with rock-like resolve. 'I wrote my will last night . . .'

'The Devil take your will! Do you think I care?'

'I want you to see that everything's done right. I've made sure that my mother and Gwendoline are well provided for, but I'd like you to have my horses and my sword . . .'

'Cedric!' Harold shouted. 'Listen to me! Fight if you must, but don't go out there expecting to be killed. Olaf won't let you down, *and* he'll laugh as he cuts you to pieces. You're always grumbling on at me because I always win, and you always lose. For the love of God, go out *knowing* that you can beat him, and there's just a chance you might. Pull yourself together, man. You're wearing the armour of a respected warrior. Live up to it, or take it off and run. Which is it to be?'

Cedric was amazed; he had never heard Harold speak with such urgency. He was immediately angry but realised after a second or two that Harold was absolutely right.

'I'll live up to it,' he said at last.

'Then God be with you.'

In the compound, seven mounted housecarls dressed in chain-mail waited just inside the gates. Olaf was there with them, his infamous axe strapped to the saddle. His horse fidgeted, as though sensing danger.

'Cedric Cedricsson!' Olaf called, as Cedric and Harold came out. 'The time has come, little man. I hope you have said farewell to your family.'

Olaf looked very large, and formidable. Wild Viking blood ran in his veins, and in his eyes the red fire of the old berserkers burned. Cedric took a deep breath, his stomach churning, as he walked out with measured strides into the rain. It was a dismal day, grey with cloud, and Cedric thought briefly that this was the right kind of day on which to die. It must be very melancholy, he thought, for a man to see the sun as his eyes closed for the last time.

Behind the housecarls, a crowd was gathering at the gates. Was Gwendoline there, he wondered, avid to see him die? He did not have time to search the crowd for her; he did not care whether she was there or not.

'I have no family,' Cedric answered. 'My son is dead.'

'All the better,' Olaf answered. 'I shan't be making him an orphan today, eh?'

Olaf turned to the housecarls, who obliged him with coarse laughter. Grinning, he got down from his horse, took a few paces forward and, taking the axe in his right hand, stood with feet apart, shoulders back and head held high.

Arrows of pain shot through his shoulders and arms and he cursed the damp weather which stiffened his joints. His right hand was knotted and lumpy after a lifetime of combat and it was an

270

agony to straighten his fingers in the mornings. Yet Olaf Ericsson showed no sign of suffering. Stronger than any pain, lust for battle was stirring in his blood. Let the young puppy bare his teeth! Let him strut in his father's armour! Even after twenty years, Olaf Ericsson was still the mightiest and most feared warrior in all England, and battle his greatest joy.

He hefted the axe to his left hand – he could fight with it just as well as with his right – and felt the sinews tighten under the stout bronze and leather bands he wore on each wrist.

'So, young puppy,' he called. 'Let's have done with it . . .'

The clatter of hooves from outside the fence interrupted Olaf. The crowd at the gates hastily moved aside as the unmistakable voice of Earl Godwin was heard bellowing: 'Out of the way! Get out of my way!'

'He's here!' Harold exulted, 'I knew he wouldn't let you down!'

Cedric was not sure what Godwin could do to help him, but it was enough to know that he had come. It gave him no small comfort to see Godwin and Sweyn ride in at the head of a score of soldiers, all well armed.

'Father, Sweyn!' Harold greeted them. 'We're very glad to see you!'

Godwin, reining in, acknowledged his son. He quickly surveyed the scene, nodded to Olaf and, without a word, placed his riders around the housecarls. His spearmen, walking their horses without fuss or hurry, surrounded Olaf's companions. They scarcely looked at the men, yet their grim presence warned them not to act rashly.

Olaf's eyes narrowed with suspicion.

'Godwin,' he called. 'I welcome you, friend and old comrade!'

'You look surprised, Olaf,' Godwin said blandly. 'And so you should. I left within an hour of hearing that you had gone. We kept you in sight nearly all the way, you know! You are not as watchful as you were when we fought together for Canute, my friend and old comrade. You came here with all the stealth of a stag in the rutting season.'

'I know when to be watchful, friend,' Olaf replied carefully. 'I can smell out an enemy when I need to, and you have never been an enemy of mine. I am surprised that you should go to so much trouble to watch our humble contest.'

'And it surprised me,' Godwin said no less carefully, 'when I heard you were bringing so many of your bullies, merely for such a . . . humble contest.'

'The roads are thick with outlaws, as you well know. A man must protect himself when he travels. Don't you trust me to fight fairly, then?'

'Olaf, the day you fight fairly will be the day I fart the scent of roses,' Godwin scoffed. 'That is why you are still alive, and so many of your foes are dead. Good luck to you for that. But, you see, Cedric Cedricsson is one of my most reliable reeves. I don't want your hounds sinking their fangs into his back.'

'I don't need any help to deal with this brat!' Olaf snarled angrily. 'I've killed fifteen better than him in a single fight, and you have seen me do it.'

'True, I have,' Godwin agreed. 'But I have also seen you stamp the life out of innocent men – aye, and women and children too – like beetles. So you can be sure of one thing. If one of your mob so much as rests his hand on his axe, you'll have twenty of mine to deal with. Aaahh, this rain is making me wet! Let's get on with it . . .'

Harold realised that his father was prepared to let the fight proceed.

'Father, wait!' he urged. 'Cedric is not fit to fight. He is already wounded. He was stabbed the other night.'

'Harold, don't!' Cedric protested.

Godwin dismounted and walked over to Cedric, pulling open his coat and shirt to see the mess of salves, rags and dried blood.

'Christ's suffering, boy. You don't do things by halves, do you?'

'Cedric's son died,' Harold explained. 'The girl's father did that.'

'Isn't one enemy at a time enough for you?' Godwin laughed gruffly. 'Well, I'll stop this if you want me to . . .'

'No, my lord,' Cedric answered firmly. 'I have to do it sooner or later. It may as well be now.'

'Don't be a fool, Cedric,' Harold pleaded. 'Put it off until you are better prepared.'

'No! I want it settled. I am fit enough to fight.'

Godwin nodded his acceptance and returned towards his horse apparently deep in thought, but no one saw his hand move beneath his cloak, slipping its dagger from its sheath. Olaf was completely unready for what happened next, for as Godwin drew level with him the knife flashed out, and slashed across his right arm just above the elbow.

Olaf gave an indignant shout and raised his axe to Godwin. Sweyn swiftly spurred his horse out between the two men, and Olaf suddenly found Sweyn's sword at his throat.

'That should make it more even,' Godwin declared. 'Now fight!'

Furious, Olaf raised his axe and shield high and began to roar out his boasts.

'I am Olaf, son of Eric Longaxe,' he thundered. 'The Hawk of Hjorring am I. Many are my years but more are my conquests.

Still I am strong as the bear, terrible as the wolf. How many have I slain? Count the leaves that fall from the trees; count the stars on a winter's night; for those are the numbers that have fallen to my blade. Aye, and many more will fall yet, for I am Olaf the Unvanquished, Olaf the Fearless, Olaf the Hand of Odin! Quake, little fellow! Today your time has come!'

Harold saw that Cedric was spellbound by the Viking's words. He nudged him hard.

'Boast,' he whispered hoarsely. 'Go on! Make your boasts!'

Cedric shook himself, and took a step forward.

'I am Cedric, son of Cedric,' he began. His voice sounded too high, and he fought to steady it. 'I have killed none, but I have no fear of Olaf. I have no wish to slay hundreds; Olaf's is the only death I want!'

'Not bad,' Godwin grunted under his breath.

'Have you ever heard such a mighty boast?' Olaf inquired of his followers, leading a chorus of derision. '*I am nothing; I have done nothing?* What is this sorry pup that challenges me?'

'Yes! I am nothing! I have done nothing!' Cedric shouted. 'But I am not afraid to face one who calls himself a great warrior, yet murders unarmed servants and clerics as they sleep!'

The mirth of the housecarls died away. Olaf, furious, could not believe that Cedric would insult him so. No-one had ever dared to before. Cedric knew that nothing would stop Olaf now. Even if he ran away, defended by his friends, Olaf would not rest until he had sought Cedric out, to wipe out that insufferable slur. The fear that Cedric felt before was nothing to the numbing cold he felt now, as Olaf's rage caught fire.

'Insolent whelp!' Olaf snarled. 'I'll stop your yapping!'

They circled each other like cats with hackles raised. The only sounds that Cedric heard in the hush were the beat of his own heart, the patter of the rain, and the sucking of their feet in the mud. Axe and sword blades revolved, gathering speed like shining wheels, taking the men out on a journey from which there might be no return. Watchful eyes gleamed from the shadows of face-guards, each man afraid to blink in case the other should choose that very split second in which to pounce. The crowd had fallen deathly quiet, frozen into place like statues.

'Eeee ha!' Olaf screamed, and he swung into the attack. His massive arm threw the axe far back and hurled it forward again directly at Cedric's head.

Cedric was ready. He lifted his shield squarely into the path of the blow, but he was beaten to his knees by the stunning force of it. It was the hardest knock he had ever taken in his life, and it deadened his hand, his arm and his shoulder, while pain scorched through his whole body like a torrent of burning blood. He jumped up; he had no time to think about the pain. Olaf was coming at him again; this time the axe was hissing through the air sideways, aimed below his shield at his vulnerable left side. Cedric, accurately judging the curve of it a second time, brought the shield down to block it. Hardly had the shooting agonies of the first blow faded before the second crash jarred his bones and sent him back on his heels, sliding in the mire, with a yelp. Olaf, firm on his feet, ridiculed him.

'Ha! The little puppy squeals! Are you feeling so brave now, little puppy?'

'Braver,' Cedric panted, 'now that I see how weak-eyed and soft-sinewed you have become, old man!'

'Yaaahh!' Olaf roared, and charged. He whirled the axe up and over and down as if to split a log. Cedric put his shield up over his head and planted his feet solidly wide. The impact came so violently that he thought his arms and legs were broken. Tired of being treated as a nail to be hammered into the earth, he tried to make an attack of his own, but Olaf was already barging in yet again. He feinted with a blow to Cedric's knees, but changed direction and thrust at neck height. Cedric, having dropped his guard from head to knee, had to jump back, but slipped, and saw the flashing edge thud into the ground a scant inch from his head. He rolled, and leapt up fighting for balance in the cloying mud. Olaf followed, the great axe whirling murderously, and Cedric ran to a safe distance.

'Ah! Now who's the coward?' Olaf taunted. 'Look at him run! But there's nowhere to run to, little puppy. Come back and be beaten!'

Cedric stood panting, and thought furiously. His shield arm was throbbing, and he could feel wetness running down his chest but could not tell whether it was sweat or blood from his wound. Olaf was wearing him down, he realised, making use of his greater strength to batter Cedric silly, striking hard and often to soften and demoralise him for the kill. He had to change the course of the battle and change it quickly, before Olaf's axe found its mark. The only thing in his favour was his agility, and he would have to use that against all Olaf's strength, ferocity and cunning.

Cedric unstrapped his shield and threw it down. He took his sword in both hands, whisking it to and fro before Olaf like a scythe. Harold was horrified to see what he was doing, but Godwin muttered:

'Good lad. That's right. Do it your way!'

274

Olaf saw his chance to end the fight easily. Teeth bared in a grin of satisfaction, he crept closer, eyeing Cedric's swinging blade and the younger man's unshielded body. One cut would do it now, he was telling himself, one hard, well-placed cut, slicing through iron rings and leather and flesh like the tenderest meat.

He charged in, shield held before him like a battering ram, as his axe swung out humming at arm's length. But Cedric, unencumbered, chose his moment well and leapt back out of range. Olaf, missing him, turned himself half around with the force of his swing. Cedric moved in, his sword cutting with a merciless backhand sweep at Olaf's chest. Olaf staggered sideways out of reach with a hair's breadth to spare, shocked by Cedric's tactics. Recovering, he brought his shield around in time to guard himself as Cedric attacked again, chopping right and left, first high and then low, each time smashing the sword on Olaf's bounding shield and giving the housecarl no time to use his axe as he was driven to retreat for the first time in his life.

Yet finally Cedric had to rest, unable to find an opening through Olaf's determined defence. For a moment the two men stood panting, glaring at each other with hatred, drenched in rain and sweat, and exhausted.

'How do you like that, old man?' Cedric taunted. 'More fun than killing sleeping men, eh?'

Olaf chuckled and ended by coughing.

'You're a plucky little pest,' he croaked. 'It's a shame to kill you, but I will, I will.'

'So you said, but I still live.'

'Not for long!' Olaf rasped.

He lunged at Cedric afresh, but with a head-high swing which fell short of its target. Cedric was surprised that he was able to back away without difficulty, not realising that the miss was a deliberate feint. As Olaf completed the sweep, he nimbly came within reach of his opponent and brought the axe around in a tremendous back-hander, aimed to crack Cedric's head with the blunt side. Cedric, caught off-guard, knew a split second of terror as the heavy axe hurtled at his head. He could not slip back out of range this time.

Without thinking, he ducked and thrust his sword upwards to fend off the axe, which smashed into the sword and broke the blade in two. The broken piece went spinning across the yard, leaving Cedric holding a useless, jagged stump. His arms were numbed yet again, but he found strength to scramble away before Olaf could strike again. Completely defenceless, he watched Olaf gathering all his energy for a final assault, and knew there was nothing he could do to save himself.

But unexpected help was at hand.

'Sweyn!' Earl Godwin barked, and Sweyn understood at once what his father wanted. He galloped across the yard and tossed his sword to Cedric as he passed.

'Curse your luck, boy!' Olaf swore, and stormed into the attack once more. Cedric, newly brave with a good sword in his hand, let Olaf come at him. At the last moment he whirled neatly aside like a dancer, and laughed as Olaf stumbled and missed. Shrieking with rage, Olaf rushed him again. This time Cedric stood his ground, sword held out at arms' length with the point at Olaf's throat. Olaf was forced to halt and shield himself. Then Cedric pounced, striking out right and left as before, first at Olaf's legs, then at his body, to keep the older man backing off as the sword clanged against his shield time and again.

Then the Viking made a fatal mistake. Turning from one of the blows, trying to get into position for a renewed rally, Olaf slid awkwardly in the mud and went down. In that very second Cedric had brought down his sword in a two-handed smash at Olaf's head. The blade missed its mark, but carried on down to slice deep into Olaf's leg, scything through leather, muscle and bone.

Olaf roared, his eyes clouded with pain and fear as he crawled away on axe and shield, dragging his leg behind him. He would have given no quarter to an enemy in a situation such as this, and he expected none. He looked up at Cedric, who followed him with raised sword, and waited for the death blow. He never once thought of asking for a chance to live.

'Kill him, Cedric!' Harold cried, and the shout was taken up by Godwin and others.

'Aye, finish him, boy!' Godwin commanded. 'And quickly, for pity's sake!'

'Kill! Kill! Kill!' chanted Godwin's supporters, crashing spears upon shields in a noisy rhythm.

All the hatred suddenly drained out of Cedric as though he had never felt it. He could remember in every detail the torture and humiliation of Prince Alfred, how Gilbert de Bernay had all but drowned in his own blood and the stench and groans of men left dying. Yet here was Olaf, the Hawk of Hjorring, reduced to the same pitiful state; and here was Cedric Cedricsson with the prize of vengeance within his grasp. Yet he could not strike.

'Kill, kill, kill!' the crowd roared. Women and children ran round the walls to get the best view; fatherheld babies high on their shoulders, and the very oldest jostled and shoved their way to the front. No-one wanted to miss Olaf's death-blow, or the chance to tell their children's children that they had been there, had seen with their own eyes an untried boy fight to the death the most feared warrior of the age.

In his distaste for the behaviour of the mob, Cedric had taken his attention off Olaf, and Olaf had seen his last chance for survival. He hauled himself up on his shield, and with all his remaining strength threw his axe hard at Cedric's legs. Cedric observed the move almost too late, when the weapon was already twisting and humming through the rain towards him. He jumped aside with a little squeal of alarm, but the end of the handle cracked into his right shin just below the knee.

Olaf was on his knees, dragging his sword from its sheath. Cedric scrambled to his feet yet again and lashed out in rage and panic, slashing Olaf's arm. The Viking fell, his face contorted with anguish as he rolled on to his back.

An uncontrollable anger took hold of Cedric then, a primitive blood-lust born of fear and pain and loathing, of the howls for death. Rage took possession of his mind and soul, and guided his arm. He hacked at Olaf again and again, to the chant of 'Kill! Kill! Kill!' His sword thrashed at Olaf's chest, shoulders and neck, sometimes screeching against chain-mail, sometimes biting into unguarded flesh. And he went on hacking and smashing and flailing, long after Olaf's body had ceased to twitch or squirm.

At last Cedric finished. He stood there, sweating and sick. He had not simply killed Olaf; he had chopped him like meat on a butcher's slab. He could not believe that this was the man he had hated for so long, the man he had even hesitated to kill. Nor could he believe that the berserk slayer of Olaf Ericsson was Cedric the loving son of Constance, the friend of Harold Godwinsson, the simple boy whose bravest act so far had been to walk alone into the Shin Field. He would never meet that Cedric again; he had killed him as surely as he had slaughtered Olaf. The cheers of the crowd thundered in his head, but he ignored them. He ripped off his helmet, and threw it down into the mud with his sword. He limped into the house, and, shaking, poured wine for himself, gagging as he drank it. His stomach was heaving, his flesh crawling. He had won. He had survived the greatest test of his life. Now the sweet taste of vengeance was fouled with the stench of blood. At the core of him was an ice-cold void, which seemed to suck him inward so strongly that he felt as if he were in danger of collapsing like a burst bladder.

He slumped on to a bench, and groaned; 'God help me!'

'He did,' said Harold, sitting down beside him. 'Are you all right?'

'In a moment,' Cedric whispered. 'In a moment.'

'You've gone white!'

'Is that so surprising? Dear God, I will never take a sword in my hand again, never!'

'But you won, man! You killed Olaf Ericsson. You'll be the most famed warrior in England!'

'I don't care! All I want to do is forget it.'

'But what is it like, to kill a man?' Harold persisted.

Cedric shut his eyes. 'One thing I know: my uncle was right. Long ago he told me it would solve nothing. I've taken the revenge I swore four years ago, but the horror of that night in Guildford is nothing to this . . .'

'You're just shocked,' Harold said, laying a hand on his shoulder. 'After all, you were nearly killed. God's teeth, you had me worried! But you won! You fought like a demon, and you won!'

'And very well he won, too,' said the voice of Earl Godwin at Cedric's back. 'Here, warrior – take your prize!'

Cedric turned, expecting Godwin to hand him Olaf's axe or shield. Instead he found himself looking into the broken, filthy, staring face of Olaf Ericsson, held up by the hair and dripping crimson black from the neck. He closed his eyes tightly, gulping back the bile.

'Put out your hand, Cedric Cedricsson, and take it from me,' Godwin said sternly. 'You came to me once, asking for the head of Olaf. Today you have earned it. I always pay my men what they earn: remember that. Look at it! Look at it, and know the price of asking! He was the greatest warrior this land has known in my lifetime, but now you are the greater. You are not a frightened little boy; you are a proven warrior, Cedric Olaf-slayer. Open your eyes, warrior! Take your prize in your hand!'

Cedric drew a rush of air into his lungs. The bloody head stared back at him. It knew him. Facing Olaf alive was not as bad as facing Olaf dead, parrying his blows not half so hard as stretching out to take the blood-matted hair from Godwin's grasp, the weight of his great axe nothing to the weight of his hanging head. . . . Cedric flung the foul thing from him.

'Send it to Gospatrick,' he coughed. 'He has coveted it longer than I have.' Then, remembering his manners, he added: 'I thank you, my lord Godwin. I have you to thank for my life this day. I shall not forget it.'

'Thank me with a hot dinner and a dry cloak,' Godwin suggested lightly. 'I think you owe me a few of those, too.'

XIII

THE new warship rested on the mud of Bosham harbour, smelling of fresh wood and pitch. For weeks past it had been a skeleton of curving beams, slowly taking form as the clinker planks and mast were put in place, but now it had come alive, as only a fierce longship could. She was a fine craft, sturdy and broad in the beam, with a graceful dragon's-neck prow topped with a tiny devilish head whose scarlet tongue appeared to be licking eagerly at the salt air. Earl Godwin was justly proud of her, and he took a large following out with him for the launching. All his family were there, with the exception of Sweyn who was chasing Welsh raiders on his Mercian border. Among the guests were Cedric, the famed warrior Shire-Reeve of Berkshire, and Godwin's nephew, Bjorn Estrithsson, youngest brother of the other Sweyn who looked to the throne of Denmark. They and a hundred others clambered all over the ship like excited children, inspecting every joint, smoothing their hands over her polished gunwales and testing everything from ropes to rudder until the ship rocked and creaked under their weight.

'She's magnificent, father,' Harold told Godwin with all sincerity. 'The biggest and best I've ever seen. Think what it must be like to take one of these into battle!'

Godwin's grin was wide as he strode from port to starboard, gazing along the hull.

'An impressive gift, don't you think? Tofic should be pleased with her.'

Tofic the Proud was an old and revered Viking warrior who had been standard-bearer to Canute and who was soon to marry the daughter of an English nobleman. He was a good and trusted friend of Godwin, and together they were regarded as the last of Canute's great leaders. For a quarter of a century they had warred together, feasted, got drunk and wenched together, and in Godwin's estimation nothing was too good for Tofic. He was determined that his gift was to be the most magnificent. He did not care a spit that King Hardicanute would be speechless with jealousy when he saw that Tofic's ship was far superior to the one he himself had received from Godwin.

The difference did not escape Harold either.

'Any man would be overjoyed with her,' he assured his father, and with a mischievous smile he added: 'Indeed, you might call her a ship fit for a king?'

'That brainless flea Hardicanute can do what he likes about it,' Godwin laughed. 'This will serve to show what I think of him!'

Harold's younger brother Tostig was eyeing the vessel more critically. Now that he had reached manhood he was forever striving to assert himself, in a family of strong-willed individuals who were quick to put him in his place, and his manner was contrary more often than not.

'A beautiful ship,' he admitted grudgingly. 'But what good is she to Tofic? He's too old to go to war any more.'

Godwin almost choked.

'Too old,' he echoed. 'Watch your tongue, weed! Tofic will still be twice the man you are ten years from now! Listen, boy; he'll be bedding a girl half his age soon, but I wager she'll need to be a fit little filly to satisfy him. Tofic could row this ship back to Denmark, and lay that wench of his several times on the way! Aye, she's a fitting gift for him, all right. But this isn't the end of it. I'm going to fill her with everything she can hold – gold and jewels, horses and harness, weapons, everything – before the captain sails her to London. And God help you, captain, if you let her sink. If you do, you and your crew had better not come ashore!'

This caused much amusement at the expense of the ship's captain, but Tostig chose to think that the ridicule was directed at him. He felt he had to get his own back, where Godwin's wiser sons would have held their tongues.

'Taking a wife doesn't prove a man is still a man,' he scowled. 'He's doing it for what he can gain, isn't he? I'll take you up on your wager, father. Will you bet twenty shillings? I'll pay up when Tofic's woman produces a child to show that the old goat is still butting!'

Godwin was outraged. No son of his had ever talked back at him, let alone insult his dearest friend. Had he not been in such a good humour before Tostig's rudeness he would surely have struck the boy down.

'Go home!' he barked. 'Get out of my sight, before I take my belt to your back!'

Even Tostig knew when to retreat. With a shrug that was meant to be careless, but which only looked timid, he climbed over the ship's side and made for the house. Godwin watched him go, almost shaking with anger.

'Shame muddled his tongue, father,' Harold offered. 'He did not mean to be rude.'

But Godwin's temper was beyond soft words.

'He'll have no tongue to trip over if he talks like that again,' he said grimly. 'Ah, you young men! You think a man is dead at forty, yet you would not test it with men like Tofic and me, eh? Great God alive, when I look back at what Tofic and Canute and I did, and see that son of mine sulking like a table wench . . . well, sometimes I think Tofic is lucky to have no children, and Canute was lucky he did not see what became of his! How do you think he would feel today if he could see Hardicanute, who by all accounts couldn't do anything with a woman even if he had one? Poor old Canute! He thought his line would last down through the ages!'

'Well, it looks as if it won't last much longer unless Hardicanute marries soon.'

'I'm well aware of that,' Godwin replied. 'Don't think I haven't tried to talk sense into the king. That's one thing on which his mother and I agree, that he must take a wife. He's a sick man. I think he will die young like his brothers. It's becoming urgent.'

'Have you suggested a bride to him?'

Godwin leaned upon the ship's gunwale, looking down to where his wife and daughters were daintily stepping along planks laid for them across the mud so that they could carry out their own inspection of the new ship.

'No,' he said. 'But lately I have fancied the idea of your sister Edith as queen – and a grandson of mine as king. Don't you think that interesting?'

Harold, before answering, glanced quickly at Cedric. As he had expected, Cedric looked as if a spear had struck him hard. He was gazing at Edith with the same old longing. In all the years he had known her, and watched her grow from a shy child to a mature and regally poised woman, he had never forgotten his desire for her. The thought of Edith in the bed of the vile Hardicanute was too much to bear. He wanted to shout out against it, but dared not say a word.

'Interesting, yes,' agreed Harold. 'But I can't see Hardicanute taking up the offer. He's too suspicious of you as it is. And Emma would certainly protest, most violently!'

'Aye, I know,' Godwin sighed, 'but I may try it anyway, one day when I catch him in a good mood. God's word, we have to get him married to someone while he's still capable of naming an heir! I think he's getting as sick in the head as he is in body. He doesn't seem to know what he's about. First he makes this treaty with King Magnus, that the first of them to die should leave his kingdom to the other, and then he brings Edward over from Normandy as if to groom him for the throne. Who does he want to follow him? He doesn't seem to know, and no one else does. I don't think we should leave the choice to him.'

'You've never liked Magnus, have you?' Harold said.

'What, the man who has denied my nephew his throne all this time?' Godwin fumed. 'I'd get short shrift from him if he became king of England, simply because I'm the uncle of Sweyn who has put up such a fight for the Danish crown. No, I will do nothing to further the interests of that usurper!'

Bjorn Estrithsson grinned at his uncle. He was a good-looking and friendly young man, about the same age as Harold and Cedric, but with a depth of sadness in his young eyes. He had spent most of his youth fighting beside his brothers Sweyn and Osborn, and bore many battle scars on his strong brown arms. His long, plaited hair was bleached yellow-white by many campaigning summers both on land and at sea. Harold admired him enormously, and felt a greater affection for him than for his own brothers. Indeed, Harold felt that Bjorn and Cedric were his best friends, and the three of them had had some splendid times together since Bjorn came to England to rest from his warring.

'Then you should help make my brother king of England, uncle,' Bjorn blithely urged Godwin. 'Why don't you?'

Godwin growled and slapped the mast in frustration.

'I've told you, boy,' he said. 'Much as I regret it, Sweyn could never be accepted here – not now, with so much opposition to Danish rule. I nominated him once, but if I so much as mentioned his name in the Witan again it would be enough to start a war.'

'So let us have war,' Bjorn shrugged. 'We would be good at war together, the Estrithssons and the Godwinssons. Look, here we have the noblest warriors of England and Denmark! You, uncle, who fought alongside Canute. I, Bjorn Estrithsson. My brother's men say I was following them into battle before I could be seen behind a shield, I was so small. And we have Cedric, the man who slew Olaf Ericsson! Do you know, in Denmark he is known as Cedric Olaf-slayer, though some call him Cedric Shieldless, because he won without even a shield on his arm. You must not call yourself Cedric Cedricsson any more, my friend. You must let the men of Denmark honour you with one of these noble titles. It is their tribute to you for felling their greatest warrior.'

'They are good names,' Cedric agreed. 'I think I like Cedric Shieldless best. It has a good sound. What do you think, Harold?'

'I think you should mind your head,' Harold muttered. 'If it grows much more, you'll hit it on that cross-tree.'

Cedric laughed, thinking his friend was joking, but suddenly he realised that Harold had spoken out of intense jealousy. He was glowering at Cedric and Bjorn as if they were hated enemies, because they had proven themselves in battle and he had not. There could be no greater humiliation and it showed in his face like the livid scar of a sword-cut.

Cedric was at first amazed, but then he understood. How difficult it must be for Harold, he thought, forever living in the shadow of Godwin. The earl, in his constant quest for political advantage, was always playing one man against another, and when he was not doing it out of necessity and sheer cunning he was doing it through habit. He did it even with his sons, pitting one of them against the other to see which of them would prove victorious. He had even tried it with Harold and Cedric, whose friendship he had encouraged for his own ends and from which he had benefited at his trial. Cedric could remember a day when Godwin had tried to goad him into a fight with Harold, simply for his own amusement and to satisfy his curiosity as to which was the better man. No wonder Harold was so restless, so set on being best, so determined to get out from under the influence of Godwin and make his own way in the world. Small wonder, too, that he resented the successes of others, even his friends. For Harold, as for his brothers, life was a continuous struggle to lead the field. It did not matter whether it was in the hunting down of animals or men, in the winning of a race or of a favoured place in the hall, all those who clustered around Godwin were fired by his burning energy and pushed to the same thirst for power. A man had to be extraordinarily strong in spirit, and tireless in body, to keep up with Godwin.

With a constrained laugh, Cedric said: 'See, it is Harold who keeps my vanity in check. He has seen me in my less glorious moments. Did he tell you of our wrestling match, Bjorn? He had me chewing dirt that time!'

'Aye,' Bjorn agreed tactfully. 'Many's the time I've wished you could come to war with me. What a team we would make! Hurry the day, Harold. We will make the world take note of us, ya? It is not right for such as you to be kept from war. Battle makes a man come alive; it fixes his friendships as solidly as rock in the earth. Days spent fighting beside his friends are the days he remembers. Did I tell you of the night when Magnus's men surprised us at Svendborg? My brother Sweyn was in bed with his woman. When the alarm was sounded he came running out. He had his helmet, his shield and his axe; he was shouting orders to everyone. But do you know, he had no trousers on! Nothing but his boots! We were all laughing so much we could hardly fight!'

Harold laughed as easily as the next, and his outburst was forgotten. Yet for some time afterwards he took every opportunity to prove to Cedric and Bjorn that he was better than they, pressing himself to the limit in the process. He wrestled with them and would not rest until he had beaten them; he took hair-raising risks in horse races. His insatiable need for victory was still devouring him when the time came for Godwin's retinue to make its way to Lambeth for Tofic's marriage. In a long train of horses and mule-carts they went first to Godwin's estate at Southwark to meet Earl Sweyn, his son Haakon, and Sweyn's friends and in-laws. Everyone was eager to know how Sweyn had been faring against the Welsh.

'We've killed scores of them,' Sweyn boasted to his father. 'We've chased them so hard these months past, they've forgotten how to sit down! Some of those we caught on our side of the border we sent back without their tongues. So there are a few less Welshmen gabbling insults at me now in their crooked Greek!'

'Well done, my son,' Godwin beamed, but Harold greeted his brother's words with something close to a sneer.

'Why not send them home without something else?' he said. 'Stop them breeding!'

'And what would you know about it?' Sweyn responded icily.

'You're wasting time and effort, waiting for them to come across to you,' Harold told him. 'If I were you, I'd take an army into Wales and burn the swine out.'

'Ha! Listen to the great general!' Sweyn scoffed. 'All these years I've been culling the Welsh, and now I have to listen to a conceited, unblooded boy telling me how to do it!'

'Stop it!' Godwin commanded. 'We've come here for a wedding, not a war. I'll not have ill-feeling here, or by God I'll show the pair of you how I make heads sore!'

Cedric had seen some marvellous feasts in Godwin's house and on occasion had tried to match them with banquets of his own, but never had he seen anything to compare with the revelry in the house of Tofic the Proud at Lambeth.

Tofic was one of the most respected of Anglo-Danish thanes and also among the wealthiest. He held lands stretching across London, Middlesex and Essex, and chests full of gold and jewels that were his spoils of war and his rewards from three Viking kings, and he had spared no expense for this day. He was marrying a daughter of Osgot Clappa, another notable thane, and it was necessary that he should make a lasting impression on the five hundred guests who included all the most noble and powerful men in the land. Certainly the splendour of it impressed Cedric, who spent the first hours of the three-day feast goggling at his surroundings like a child in a treasure cave.

There was barely a foot of space to spare in the big hall as hordes of guests, entertainers and servants crowded in. Smoke from the cooking fires and torches drifted in a pungent fog about the enormous room, yet even this failed to dim the brilliance of the richest jewels and velvets in the kingdom.

Tofic sat with his bride at the high table. Next to him sat King Hardicanute, Emma, the king's mother, and his half-brother the pale and quiet-mannered Edward, lately returned to England after nearly thirty years in Normandy. Then came the bride's family, the bishops and the earls. Everyone else had to find what seats they could in the swaying, jostling, shoulder-to-shoulder mass. The tables were arranged around the walls, but still there was hardly enough room for the guests to squeeze in or for the servants to push through, and many were the timid requests or angry demands for someone to move aside. The mighty blackened beams and rafters resounded with the echoes of a thousand voices; minstrels strummed their harps; hounds barked for scraps; feet shuffled and benches scraped, and above it all there was the crash and clatter of plates and knives, bawdy jokes and laughter, shouted toasts and songs, and the squeals and giggles of bottom-pinched wenches. In the centre of the hall there blazed not one, but two large fires, each with a full-grown ox spitted above the flames on massive turning irons. Around the fires poets and jugglers fought with the scurrying servants for a clear spot in which to perform, and kicked and tripped over hounds who foraged underfoot for bits from the tables. Musicians played and sang to the noisy and inattentive audience; tumblers and clowns and magicians got hopelessly lost in the throng. Few of them had more than abuse and bones thrown at them for their troubles.

Cedric, who at first had shown decent restraint, was soon following the example of everyone else and snatching some of everything within reach. That was by no means easy, for he was crushed and battered by the people on either side of him and his arms were so confined he could scarcely use his knife or get his hands to his mouth. Beside him, a thane's lady was begging her husband to get her some trout, but he was too busy grabbing half a pigeon and two whole sparrows for himself. At the bridegroom's table the clergy were still chanting prayers, their gaze flickering covetously from one dish to another; their voices were drowned anyway by the laughter of Tofic and his friends as pitchers of ale and wine were poured again and again. The king was endeavouring to cut himself a slice of venison and at the same time retrieve a loaf of bread that was about to vanish down the table. A flagon of mead fell to the floor and smashed, soaking the reeds in a sticky mess, while two men argued over a loin of roast beef that was almost buried beneath cuts of pork, hare and pheasant. A servant was spitefully tripped by an angry juggler whose act had been spoiled, to the loud approval of the crowd; and a boar's head decorated with apples and herbs went bouncing across the floor, causing a savage fight among the hounds for the pick of the meat.

Cedric reached for a leg of duck, narrowly missed having his fingers severed by someone else's knife, and settled for a piece of rabbit. Harold had half a partridge in one hand and a fistful of bread in the other, and was complaining with a full mouth to Bjorn who had taken the cherries he had been eyeing. Men and women fought for the best of the salmon and the veal, cakes, honey, cheese, eggs, shallots, beans, garlic, grapes, mutton, lamb, hedgehog, chicken, crab, nuts, leeks, mussels and raspberries, while trying to keep hold of the wine jars and ale jugs.

In time, more room was made at the tables. People soon became drunk, and left the hall in a steady procession to relieve themselves, or to vomit, or even to fornicate. Some simply rolled under the tables and lay there, tripping up the servants. Others, their hunger sated for a while, began gambling with dice while some lewdly made bets on how long it would be before Tofic disappeared into the bower with his bride. A few guests started squabbles which had to be broken up by their friends, and the more cheerfully inebriated stood up on their benches and sang songs which few bothered to listen to. Servants manhandled the dogs out of the hall to make way for the wrestlers and fighting cocks.

Later in the evening, a performing bear was brought in, but the entertainment went seriously wrong when the beast became frightened by the noise and the fires and began to rage round the hall. Its keeper, striving to control forty stone of maddened bear, was flung on to a table which promptly collapsed, covering the screaming guests with broken plates, food and wine. The sight was too much for the well-intoxicated Tofic, who laughed so hard he fell backwards off his bench, and choked until his face turned purple. A number of people, his new wife among them, carried him from the hall.

'There they go!' cried half a dozen gamblers. 'I've won the wager!'

'That doesn't count! That's not what they're leaving for!' the losers protested, and yet more dishes were shattered as a scuffle broke out.

Cedric giggled like a child as he tried to tell Harold about it, but Harold had been outside to be sick, and was too sombre in his drunkenness to appreciate the joke. He set about filling his empty stomach with a chicken leg and a stick of celery, which he washed down with yet more wine. Cedric's mirth died away. He suddenly felt very ill; the vigorous laughter had been too much for him. He got up and staggered outside to the vomit-spattered wall, and disturbed the fattest rat he had ever seen from a pile of straw. Painfully, he swayed back into the hall. Just inside the door, he slumped against a beam, slid to the floor and went to sleep.

He was woken in the middle of the night by servants running about in a panic because embers from one of the fires had set the rushes alight. But Cedric merely closed his eyes again, and when next he awoke it was early afternoon. Then he suffered the full consequences of the night's excesses. His head pounded and swam, and his stomach lurched; his whole body ached from the awkward position in which he had been lying. He tottered to his feet, feeling terrible, and was surprised to find that the banquet had continued apparently without respite.

Harold, like Cedric, had just come out of a deep sleep. Godwin had hardly rested at all, and neither had Sweyn, simply out of a determination to keep up with his father. Both were drunk and tired and Sweyn was on the point of giving up, but Godwin looked good for a few more hours yet, and was joyfully boasting of his superior staying power. Meanwhile Tofic and his bride had not reappeared in the hall, which inspired more coarse jests. Many others were still missing, but Hardicanute was at his place; he looked white and drawn, and not really aware of what was happening. Edward and Emma, with their more refined Norman ways, had eaten and drunk only moderately and continued to view the proceedings with disdain, if not completely soberly.

Some late arrivals were filing into the hall to fill the places left empty, and yet more quantities of food were being brought in to replenish the tables. The two fires, encircled by dusty rakings of ash, had been stoked up once more. A third ox was being turned above one, and a stag complete with antlers on the other. Servants were clearing plates cluttered with crumbs and half-picked bones, bringing new dishes of hams, bacon, beef and mutton, goose and quail, fresh-caught whiting, shrimps and cockles, casks of wine and flagons of ale, loaves, parsley, pumpkins, onions and radishes, raw eggs, cream and cheeses. All these were added to yesterday's less sought-after dishes, the wilting lettuce, dry beet and watercress, cabbage and corncockles, scrawny half-baked thrushes and black-birds, and mouldering apples, so that the tables were a jumble of scraps and overflowing trenchers, dirty cups and fly-crawled slops.

Cedric regarded the mountains of food, and wondered if he could so much as think about eating again for a week.

'You look awful,' Harold grinned, although he too was grey in the face. 'Why don't you try some raw eggs mixed with milk? I ate some sage. Sage is good for stomach ills.'

The thought of raw, slimy eggs was too much for Cedric, who slumped back into his place at the table and reached for a wine jar.

'I think I'll just drink myself back to sleep,' he groaned. 'God's teeth, I've never felt so bad!'

'Me too. Lord, look at that father of mine,' Harold said enviously. 'How does he do it? You'd think he'd only started an hour ago.'

'He's going to talk to the king,' Cedric observed. 'What do you think he's going to say?'

'I don't know, but it looks as if Hardicanute wouldn't hear anything now if our Lord Jesus Christ himself came down to speak to him. I should think he wants to discuss the matter of the king's marriage. Crafty old devil, trust him to wait until Hardicanute is half stupid.'

Cedric's gaze instantly flew to Edith. She was sitting with her mother and sister Gunhild, both of whom had fallen asleep over the table. Edith, despite all the debauchery around her, managed to remain serene, and Cedric was filled with admiration for her. Again his love for her tore at him.

'Hardicanute won't marry her,' Harold said. 'You needn't worry.'

'I need to know that she doesn't want to marry him,' Cedric muttered, getting up.

'And if she doesn't?'

'Then, by God, I'll take her away, somewhere far across the sea.'

'You wouldn't reach Dover!'

Cedric went to Edith and leaned over her shoulder, blessing these rare moments when her watchdogs slumbered.

'I have two fleet horses waiting,' he said in a jesting fashion. 'I think it's time I rode away with you, my lady.'

Her eyes thanked him for his flattery, softening her refusal.

'But sir,' she played along with his make-believe, 'I cannot, I dare not.'

'Would you marry the king?' he gently asked her, letting his smile fade.

'What do you mean?'

Cedric nodded towards Godwin, who had edged himself in on the seat beside Hardicanute, and was virtually leaning on the king's shoulder in his bid to be heard; there was loud laughter on the other side from Leofric of Mercia and his wife, the fabled lady Godiva of Coventry.

'What do you suppose your father finds it so important to talk about, Edith?' Cedric challenged her. 'Why don't you ask to marry a man of your own choosing before it's too late? For the love of God, do not let yourself be married off without at least letting Godwin know your will.'

Edith was sitting more stiffly now, and staring straight ahead.

'My father acts only for the best, whether for himself or his children,' she said tonelessly. 'I have never opposed him, and I never shall. Besides, you do him an injustice, it is not me he is talking about – it's you.'

'Me?'

'Yes, he is asking the king to listen to a singer who has made a song about your triumph over Olaf. He thinks it will remind Hardicanute how his innocence was proved beyond all doubt when you slew Olaf. It was a sign from God, he is telling him. After that, they may get to the subject of a marriage.'

Cedric went back to his place cursing the ever-scheming Godwin, but also himself for the clumsy manner in which he had used his precious time with Edith. He settled himself down just as Godwin silenced the hall with a loud shout, and bade the singer begin.

The singer strummed his harp, and music and words rang sweetly through the cavernous hall, telling Cedric's story:

> Have you heard how Cedric Shieldless
> fought the mighty Olaf,
> Hawk of Hjorring?
> Aye, Olaf was a fearful warrior,
> Denmark's champion,
> strong as the oak, swift as the raven,
> slayer of many . . .

'Is this a song about me, or about Olaf?' Cedric whispered to Harold.

'Be quiet, you oaf,' Harold hissed, 'and listen. Be thankful someone sings your praises. I wish it would happen to me soon.'

The tribute went on:

> But Cedric Shieldless stood his ground.
> The thunder of axe on sword
> like a dreadful storm
> was heard in every corner of the town –
> aye, in all the land.
> Cedric defied his awful foe,
> casting aside his shield,
> daring the great one with a laugh!

Then Cedric brought down Olaf
with a blow like iron descending,
like avenging lightning,
and slew the killer of thousands.
Cedric now wears the mantle
of Olaf's might and skill at arms.
Hail Cedric, Olaf-slayer,
Cedric Shieldless,
tall among men!

It had woven true, that fabric of a dream Cedric had dreamed, six years and an eternity ago in Berkshire's summer woodland. He was the hero he had wanted to be, recognised as such by all the nobles of the land, and even by the king. The glittering array of guests at Tofic's wedding applauded generously as the song was finished, banging their goblets on the tables, cheering and clapping the hero and the singer. What a shame, he thought, that it should happen to him now, when all that mattered was his unrequited love for Edith. Many a woman in that hall would have come to him at the crooking of a finger, and he knew it as he stood to acknowledge the shouting and saw their eyes upon him. He knew he was handsome, with his fine clothes and strong bearing, his flowing hair and long moustaches, but what good was it if Edith made herself blind to it? Once he had believed this was all he wanted, this worship, but tonight he would have forsaken it all for one hour alone with Edith.

Even Godwin was joining in the applause for Cedric, though he was making a mental note to reduce the singer's pay for failing to make a single mention of his own part in the battle. Pleased with the effect he had produced Godwin turned to the king to see if his latest attempt to get on the right side of the man had succeeded. He was about to ask if Hardicanute thought the song a fitting tribute to Cedric, but when Godwin saw how the king looked he halted with mouth still open and stared.

While the ballad was being sung Hardicanute had been sitting droop-shouldered, his face white and his misted eyes fixed upon some vague point in the middle distance. His lips had been moving, ever so slightly, as though he were holding a silent conversation with himself. Emma had looked concerned, but had not dared suggest that he go and lie down, because she knew only too well her son's rage if he was fussed over too much, especially in public.

But now he had emerged from his trance, his behaviour stranger than before. He was gazing about wildly, and he was having mild convulsions like one in the first throes of a fit. His face had changed from white to ghastly grey. Shivering from head to foot, he slowly stood up. His whitened fist clenched his wine cup so tightly that it looked as if he were trying to crush it. Suddenly everyone was watching him. The entire hall was silenced, and a chill of fear ran like a wind through everyone there, for surely they were seeing a man possessed by some terrible demon.

'My son!' Emma cried, and hurried to him.

'Attend me,' Hardicanute pleaded, his voice a harsh gargle. 'Help me, please . . .'

Then he fell, crashing onto the littered table. He slid to the floor limply as though all bone and muscle had been sucked from his body, and slumped in a heap between table and bench.

Emma threw herself upon him, sobbing, screeching for someone to fetch a physician, but few thought a physician could help. The clerics at the high table were already making the sign of the cross and preparing to speak the last rites. Of all those watching, stunned, Leofric was the first to come to his senses. He knelt beside Emma, his hands feeling for Hardicanute's heartbeat, then he lifted his head to make the announcement all were expecting:

'The King is dead.'

They had to prise Emma away from the body of her favourite son. While the ladies escorted her to a bower, the men covered Hardicanute's head with his purple cloak, and carried him away so that the ugly contortions of death could be erased from his features, and he could lie in state with dignity. For the rest of the people in the hall there followed a time of bewilderment and drunken incomprehension, of muttering and disbelief, and for some a stealthy return to gorging while there was still time – for the wedding celebrations would have to end as soon as Tofic and his bride were given the news.

For Godwin, there was more than grief. For him there was an inner rage at this untimely end to yet another reign, the sixth he had seen and the third he had helped to establish. For once he had left it too late. The king had died before Godwin was ready for him to die, and Godwin was left like a warrior stranded without weapons in the midst of his enemies, like a fox in the open field with no cover to run for.

Earl Godwin looked at Edward, and in Ethelred's son saw the future he had fought to prevent. That thin, slight figure, that pale face, that calm and pious manner, these were the shape of the future. This last surviving son of Emma and of Ethelred, brother of the murdered Alfred, who had spent most of his life in exile, this was the next king of England, and there was nothing Godwin could do about it. Every thane in the country would rally to

Edward's standard this time. There was no one else; the frail Edward had outlived them all. The last of Canute's ill-fated line was dead. The Viking legacy had been lost; the spirit of Ethelred had crept out from the shadows like a ghost. The golden dragon had woken from its sleep, had shaken off its rusting shackles, and the black raven of the North had flown.

Godwin went to Edward.

'My lord,' he said humbly. 'We grieve for the king your brother. I wish to assure you of my loyalty in the difficult times that lie ahead of you – as king.'

Although Edward's face still bore signs of shock, a quiet and secretive humour began to flicker in his eyes as Godwin spoke. Edward recognised the future in Godwin, just as Godwin had seen it in him. Here before him stood the Earl of Wessex who had ruled much of England in all but name since the death of Canute, the famed English Viking whose dress and fine jewellery outshone those of any monarch, the great overlord who could dominate lesser men by sheer force of will. Here was the man Edward must rule, if he were to rule England. Yet how did one begin the task of mastering a man who was used to making and breaking Kings?

Godwin's humble words did not fool Edward. He was too shrewd a judge of character to be easily misled. He had lived a long time in Normandy, but Godwin's reputation had not been bounded by England's shores. Chief among the many snippets of knowledge which he had acquired concerning the Earl of Wessex was that not all the stains had been washed from Godwin's hands after the murder of Alfred. In Normandy, where Alfred's death had been mourned more deeply than in England, little credence had been given to the trial which had supposedly cleared Godwin's name, nor to the 'miraculous' defeat of Olaf Ericsson which, many claimed, showed God's own hand in the matter. Most Englishmen may have accepted those signs as proof of Godwin's innocence, but to the Normans Godwin was still a treacherous killer. Edward was of the same mind, and would continue to regard Godwin with suspicion, and handle him with caution. He had to be wiser and stronger than this man if he was to survive.

'Thank you for your kind words, Earl Godwin,' he said politely, 'but isn't your declaration of loyalty a little – premature?'

'I don't think so, my lord,' Godwin answered. 'You will be king now, if it is your wish to regain your father's kingdom. The Witan will support you to a man.'

'Because there is no other choice?' Edward queried craftily.

'No, there is another choice. I'm sure you know that Hardicanute made a pact with the Norwegian usurper Magnus – without the consent of the Witan, I might add – which gives England into his hands after Hardicanute's death.'

'But the Witan will help me overturn that treaty?'

'Without a doubt.'

Edward nodded, and fell silent. He was studying the dark and smoky hall as if it were England itself, containing all that was English and representing all that England was. His nostrils twitched, suggesting that its smell was the smell of England, and one he found not quite to his taste.

'I think we could do with some fresh air in here,' he said.

XIV

A ND in that year of 1042, when Edward became king, it was
like a gentle English breeze returning, blowing away the black
clouds that had come with the Northmen thirty years before. The
blood-red leaves of the Viking autumn were fluttering away,
revealing the cleansed earth where the soul of Ethelred could rest
in peace at last . . .

Godwin considered it bad enough that he should have to travel all
the way to London to hold counsel with the King. To have to
move his entire household from Bosham to Southwark made the
journey doubly tedious, and that the trip had to be made in the
worst of the year's rains put the final edge on his bad temper.
Godwin, soaked and mud-spattered, rode beside the leading cart,
too proud to join Gytha under the cowhide canopy of the vehicle;
that was the place for women and servants. It was painfully slow
going as the long line of heavily-laden carts lurched and slithered
in the mud, for the struggling horses and oxen found it harder than
a man walking, but Godwin obstinately kept to his saddle. His
head bowed beneath his drenched cloak, he vehemently cursed the
rain and the showers that cascaded down upon him from the
blowing trees.

'Why in God's name does he have to choose London, of all
places?' Godwin raged for the twentieth time, as the sorry cavalcade
crossed the last fields and copses and farm lands south of the
Thames. 'Winchester was good enough for Canute. It was even
good enough for that idiot Hardicanute. Why does Edward have
to pick London? Of all the out-of-the-way, useless places . . .'

'Edward is not Danish,' Gytha answered, with the simple logic
of a patriotic Danish woman. Then, in deference to her husband,
she quickly added: 'There is not even much English about him.'

Godwin grunted a dismissal of his wife's explanation. He
suspected the true reason for Edward's choice of London as his
capital, though he was loath to voice it.

Edward, wary and perhaps even afraid of the English earls, was
trying to assert his own rule from the first. In Winchester he would
appear to be in Godwin's pocket, anywhere else he would be too
close to Leofric or another. He might truly believe London to be

the right place for England's capital city but it seemed more likely that he had gone there to be as far away from all the Vikings' warlord earls as he could get. That knowledge rankled with Godwin but, wary and ambitious himself, he understood Edward's reasoning and could even find some respect for it. Godwin was at least within closer reach of Edward than anyone else, but for him that had not been good enough. Putting aside his own comfort and convenience, he had resolved to follow in Edward's footsteps, leaving behind the house and the part of the country he loved best.

'All for a monkish bookworm who should never have come to the throne,' Godwin grumbled aloud. 'Lord, if only the sons of Canute had been men enough to have sons!'

'They say there was a son of Harold Harefoot,' Gytha began gossiping. 'They say Harold coupled with a she-wolf and the child runs wild in the Northampton woods, a dreadful thing, half man and half beast, which eats people.'

'An admirable heir for his father,' Godwin remarked acidly. 'Look, woman, I'm not interested in idle rumours. I have to speak with the king, and I won't dawdle in this damned rain any longer. You go on to Southwark, and have a good dinner ready for me when I get home. I'm going to the king right away.'

Godwin took a dozen housecarls with him, leaving as many again to protect his family, servants and property. He rode to London Bridge, glad to be rid of his cumbersome train, and within half an hour had traversed the last of the swampy fields that stretched south of the river to the forests of Kent and Sussex. His small escort clattered behind him between the crumbling stumps of the Roman towers and across the rattling wooden planks of the bridge and through the southernmost gate, into the city he hated, a city he thought of as a stain upon his beloved England. It carried no weight with Godwin that London was one of the country's largest, busiest and wealthiest sea ports, and that merchants came there from all over the world. London's port collected a fortune in duties from the hundreds of ships that brought in Italian glassware, oriental silks, linens and papyrus, jewellery, preserved fish, African bronze, copper plate and ornaments, French wines and many other luxuries. When they left port again, the ships took with them England's salt, iron, tin, and timber. The fleets of merchant ships were there for Godwin to see today, crowding the river as they wallowed in the broad reaches of tidal streams and mud banks, loading and unloading at crowded wharves outside the city's old walls, yet the sight of them did little to lift his spirits. London might be a money market, he was thinking, but that did not mean that he had to have anything to do with the place. To him, it was an ugly, crawling mass of people, a huge bad-smelling open sewer. It was a jumbled collection of run-down wood and thatch houses jostling too tightly together in a hopeless maze of streets, where ten thousand people lived cheek by jowl. There were a few big houses, and some neat little stone churches among the shattered monuments of the Romans, but in the main it was a sprawling mess, ripe for burning, and a side of England that would be better hidden. One-tenth of its population was blind, crippled or disfigured by disease, and reduced to begging for a living. Everywhere one saw the legless, the one-armed and the filthily poor, belying the riches the city possessed. North of London, well into the Epping Forest, there was a leper colony which the city was capable of keeping supplied all by itself, and there were more hospitals here where the victims of various ills went to die than in any other part of England. The River Walbrook, running through the centre of London, carried all manner of foulness into the Thames. The streets were not much better, for many of those were uncovered drains. In London it was the rats and bugs that lived best, and Godwin was more than happy to leave the city to them. The moment he was inside the walls amid the crush of people and wagons serving the docks, he stopped the first man who would listen to him.

'Where does the king build his palace?' he asked.

'Out of town, to the west,' the man replied, pointing across the Walbrook. 'Hard by Canute's old palace.'

'Well, at least he has that much sense,' Godwin muttered, and signalled to his men to ride on.

They went across the wooden bridge over the Walbrook, past the little church of St. Paul's, and left the city by the Ludgate. After crossing the Fleet River, they cantered out into the fields and marshes, through the villages of Strand and Charing, until a mile outside London they came to Thorney Island. This was a tract of land bounded on the south by the Thames and on the west and east by two tributaries which forked through the marshes, and it was there on that island that a great surprise awaited Godwin.

The small church of St. Peter, which some called the West Minster, was as he remembered it, and so was Canute's timber hall. But between those buildings, like a great mountain of creamy stone, Edward's new palace was rising out of the earth, presenting a sight such as Godwin had never seen before. An army of artisans and labourers filled the cluttered space within the growing walls, and there were as many again outside and all over the island. The noise of hammers and chisels was deafening, the rasping of saws grated on the flesh like a hair shirt, and the racket of voices was such as might have been heard at the building of the Tower of Babel. Gangs of workers strained to lift blocks of limestone on big, creaking tripods. Architects argued over parchment plans while their assistants walked the incomplete walls with plumb-lines, and on the ground paced out distances with measured strides. Carpenters sawed and planed, masons cut and dressed stone, mortarmen mixed cement, labourers pushed the mighty blocks into place, few of them resting from their tasks for long. Carters drove through the midst of them splattering mud and shouting curses, and whipped the oxen as they urged their squealing, shuddering wagons on to the site, through whatever narrow gaps they could find. The carts, loaded with immense, uncut rocks from Lincoln, from Oxford and from the Dorset coast quarries, were bogging down in the muck under their tremendous weights and nearly bringing down the specially-built bridges. More timber cranes unloaded the wagons as they rolled in on ramps of planks and rubble until the boulders formed an untidy ridge.

Godwin rode slowly through it all, bemused.

'This is madness,' he grunted at last. 'What is he trying to build, a whole city?'

There were more surprises in store for him when he went into Canute's old palace. Equal in size to any three grand thanes' halls, it could still not match Edward's great undertaking. Canute's timber palace was in fact a series of large thatch-roofed chambers, like several halls joined together, and each of the big rooms was overflowing with people. Among them were scholar monks from Normandy, France, Germany and Italy, invited to England to bring with them the culture that Edward had known in exile. They were as busy as the labourers, unpacking crates and sorting piles of books and parchment scrolls ready to establish Edward's libraries when his palace was complete. There were women there too, unfurling tapestries and silks. Servants were handling weapons and hunting spears, shields and harnesses, mail coats and helmets, furniture and ornaments. Kitchen slaves fussed over cooking utensils; men staggered under exquisitely carved chairs, and other furniture. The whole place resounded to a jumble of languages. In one corner, an Italian physician who had been trying to lay out his surgical instruments shouted angrily at a woman who had got her cooking irons mixed up with the equipment on his table. A donkey had wandered into another room, and was being chased out by frantic monks who feared the damage it could do to their precious papers.

'He's brought Normandy with him,' Godwin declared, as he squeezed through the throng.

At last, he found King Edward in one of the smaller, quieter chambers, sitting at a table with three men whom Godwin did not know. One wore the vestments of a very senior churchman, the second was an elderly monk, and the third a young Norman nobleman, expensively but soberly dressed in the style of Duke William's court, with only a modest show of jewellery and none of the flamboyant decoration affected by the English.

The meal on the table was equally moderate. Indeed, to Godwin's way of thinking, it was hardly a meal at all, consisting merely of raw eggs, cheese, bread, grapes, slices of chicken, herbs and fruit, with wine and milk to wash it down. What puzzled Godwin most, however, was that it was all neatly laid out on a pure white cloth with not a crumb or wine stain to be seen anywhere. It looked to him more like some religious ceremony than a breakfast, and his stares amused Edward. The king could see that Godwin was out of his depth.

'Well, Earl Godwin,' Edward said warmly. 'I was not expecting you, but you are welcome. Will you eat with us?'

'Just some wine, thank you,' Godwin replied, but he did not sit down. Edward presented his three companions to Godwin.

'This is Robert Champart. Until recently he was Abbot of Jumièges, but he is here to be my Court Chaplain.' Next he indicated the monk, adding: 'Father Herman from Lotharingia, who is to be my Chancellor.' Finally he nodded at the young knight and said, with pride: 'And this is Ralph de Mantes, son to my sister Godgifu and Drogo of the Vexin. He, too, has chosen to come to England with me. We have yet to find him a suitable position.'

So Edward was already surrounding himself with foreign followers, Godwin thought, as he inclined his head in greeting. Two Normans and a Lotharingian in prime positions at court, not to mention all those foreigners out there supervising the building of the palace. A fine start! And what position, he wondered, would this Ralph de Mantes be given? Standard bearer, perhaps, with all the power and responsibility. And how many more Normans did Edward intend to ease into high positions without even consulting the Witan?

'My lord,' Godwin said to the king. 'I would speak with you privately if I may. It is an urgent matter that brings me.'

'It must be urgent,' Edward mused, 'if you cannot pause to get dry, or refresh yourself.'

'Yes, my lord; it is.'

Godwin had the feeling then that they had all been discussing him earlier, as if Edward was silently saying to his companions: 'You see? This is the man I was telling you about.' But the king's bland smile gave no clue as to the course the conversation had taken, and he was still outwardly amiable. He stood up, and ushered Godwin out of the room.

'I expect you have seen my new palace?' Edward said. 'Let me show it to you while we talk. What do you think of it?'

'Very fine,' Godwin condescended. 'But . . .'

'But?'

'Well, it's your right, of course, my lord, but I wonder why you are going to such trouble and expense. This one has years of good life in it yet, I would have thought. It's big, and dry . . .'

Edward was smiling his dark smile, gazing round Canute's old hall as he stepped through the crowds and the jumble.

'Ah yes, this one,' he said, like a man politely rejecting a bad apple. 'I have made up my mind about this one. It will do very well as stables and servants' quarters.'

Godwin halted in mid-stride, his mouth dropping open ready to challenge what struck him almost as sacrilege, but he stifled the words in time. Canute's palace, where some of his happiest days had been spent: was it really to be turned into stalls for horses and donkeys? The glories of Canute's reign to be buried beneath piles of horse dung? Ah well, he reflected then, perhaps it was only to be expected of Edward, who had been flung into exile by the coming of the Danes, whose kingdom and heritage had been stolen, and whose family had been all but destroyed during Canute's time. This was a small revenge for him. Godwin could see in Edward's eyes a quiet triumph that Ethelred's line had survived Canute's, just as Edward could see in Godwin the suppressed indignation. No longer would Godwin dare praise Canute, not to this king anyway, if he wanted to find favour at court.

'Of course, my lord,' said Godwin. 'They'll be the finest stables in the land.'

Edward held back a chuckle. They had reached the main doors, and stood looking out at the rain-lashed building site and the palace that was rising like a solid rock out of the mud.

'And there,' the king murmured, pointing to the little church of St. Peter, 'there I see an abbey, a beautiful abbey, a monument to the glory of God such as England has never built before. It will be the Abbey of West Minster, the most glorious in all England.'

'Yes, my lord, that will be splendid,' Godwin said guardedly. 'You obviously intend to do a great deal of good for your kingdom, and we thank God for it – and that more or less brings me to the matter I came to see you about . . .'

'Oh dear, forgive me, Godwin, I digress,' Edward answered benignly, raising his hands in self-admonition. 'Do tell me what you had to say.'

'Thank you, my lord. You see, the sad truth is, for many years now England has been so unstable . . .'

'True, too true,' Edward sighed.

' . . . because the succession to the throne has been so much in doubt . . .'

'Yes, very true.'

' . . . and,' Godwin persisted desperately, cursing the king's irritating vagueness, 'I think I speak for all men when I say that we would dearly love to see peace and settled rule here now. We want to dispense with the doubts and troubles that have plagued us for so long. You are the first ruler since – ' he had been going to say 'since Canute,' but he quickly said instead: ' – the first ruler in many years to earn such widespread support from his subjects. This at last gives us an opportunity for stability and continuity . . .'

'Ah, continuity,' Edward interrupted, with a knowing lift of his head. 'You are saying, are you not, that I ought to marry and father heirs to the throne?'

'Yes, precisely that,' Godwin confirmed, relieved to have got so quickly to the point. He waited hopefully then, hesitating for a decent interval before pointing out that the best choice for queen would be his own daughter, Edith. It was a suggestion that he would put most carefully when the time came, but he knew he must not press too hard. Edward, however, appeared to have lost track of the conversation altogether, for he had gone back to staring at the walls of his new palace. On his face was the unearthly expression of tranquillity that often accompanied his passing into this kind of trance. It was a smile that meant nothing to anyone but Edward, so ambiguous was it, so enigmatic.

'My lord?' Godwin probed, but Edward remained deep within himself for a while longer, and the earl resigned himself to waiting.

'I have a paradox for you,' Edward said eventually. 'We are as figures in a tapestry. Of our own will we form the pattern our life is to take, and yet at the same time we are part of that pattern and helpless to change it. We are shaped by the stitches; we are caught within the borders of the work; yet it is we who hold the needle and move the threads. Sometimes we work knowingly to God's great design; but at other times we stray from the course we know to be right, and have to unpick what we have done if we can. We are the weavers, and we are the tapestry.' He shuddered, as if chilled by his own wisdom, and seemed to come awake. 'Look at me,' he addressed Godwin directly. 'Here am I, King of England; yet who would have believed, when my father ruled this country, that it would come about? I was the last of his many sons but for my poor brother Alfred, the one least likely to inherit his crown.

I did not expect it, did not work towards it, yet here I am, the last of many sons, returned to regain the kingdom my father lost. Can there be continuity in such a world, Godwin? Only if God wills it, I would submit.' His expression changed again, grew grim, and he continued: 'They say King Magnus has plans to invade, to take England back into his Scandinavian empire. Is this true, do you think?'

Advancing age had not slowed Godwin's wits. He still thought as quickly as ever, still knew an auspicious opening when he saw one.

'There is a way to stop Magnus before he starts, my lord,' he told the king. 'Send an army to help my nephew Sweyn take Denmark. That will ensure a peace between English and Danes for generations to come.'

Edward laughed, more with cynicism than with amusement.

'Godwin, I had always heard you were swift to sieze an opportunity,' he said. 'Now I see you are all I had been told. Would I really be more secure with your nephew ruling Denmark than I am now?'

'No nephew of mine would turn against you,' Godwin insisted.

Edward did not reply. In the look he gave the earl, though, there was the faintest hint that he would trust a kinsman of Godwin no further than he would trust Godwin himself.

'No,' he decided. 'I cannot help Sweyn. I will not become involved in a fight that does not concern me. Personally, I feel that Magnus will not invade. I think he has enough to occupy him, what with Sweyn bidding for Denmark, and his own uncle Harold Hardrada coming back from Byzantium – some say with the intention of conquering Norway. But I shall be prepared, all the same. I am having new fleets of ships built, both here in London and at Pevensey. The coasts will be well guarded.'

Godwin did not pursue the point; he could return to it later. First he must do all he could to get Edith married to the king.

'You are building well,' he praised Edward. 'If you could build a family with as much determination, the future of all of us would be assured.'

'Ah yes, we are back to the succession. Certainly I shall have to think over what you say. But there is so much to be done to improve the English way of life, and I want to start upon all of it as soon as I can.'

'But what could be more important than an heir?'

'Many things, many things. There is the question of the church. We must introduce canon law here, as have other countries. We cannot go on having church matters dealt with in secular courts.

We must end the autonomy of the bishops, and the multiplicity of sees and offices. All of that drags the administration of Holy Mother Church down to the level of a common brawl. I know the Pope wishes to see the English church restored to dignity.'

Godwin paced about restlessly while Edward rambled on, himself not caring a pip for the church and its troubles although it did occur to him that the reforms Edward had ennumerated might lose him his influence over certain church men.

'If you'll pardon my saying so,' Godwin growled, 'a wife in your bed at night is not going to stop you attending to these matters by day.'

Now the king was deeply offended.

'Godwin, such remarks border on the insolent!' he snapped. 'I will not tolerate them. Whatever familiarity you engaged in with Harold and Hardicanute, even Canute, do not think you can do the same with me. I represent a line of English kings going back five hundred years.'

'Pardon me, my lord,' Godwin quickly entreated. 'I had not meant any insult.'

'It is forgotten.'

Edward turned to go into the old palace, then looked back over his shoulder to say, almost mockingly: 'Did you, by the way, have any particular bride in mind for me?'

Damn the man, Godwin thought, can he see through me so easily? Does he have magic powers?

'There are a number of ladies in England fit to be your queen, my lord . . .' he began afresh, but Edward gave him no chance to finish.

'I'm sure there are,' he said. 'You must let me have a list, with your own recommendations at the top, of course!'

Godwin went home to Southwark in a foul temper, and dealt brusquely with Gytha's eager questions about Edward's possible interest in Edith.

'Almighty God, *you* try talking to the man!' Godwin laughed bitterly. 'I tried to, and got nowhere. All he did was gabble on about getting tangled up in his own tapestry. I think he's as mad as the last two fools we've had on the throne!'

Gytha could not be sure that she had heard aright, that her husband's scheme had failed. And God forbid, she thought, was there a suggestion in his surly manner that he was losing some of his confidence? If that were the case, what an extraordinary man this Edward must be – and what a dangerous king!

'Have you given up, then?' Gytha demanded.

The earl had been chewing on a piece of bread. He had an

unfortunate habit, when unjustly accused, of shouting in his own
defence without emptying his mouth. It happened again now.
Crumbs filled his windpipe, and he coughed and spluttered so hard
that Gytha had to beat him on the back and pour him two cups of
wine.

'Given up?' he choked, when he could speak again. 'Me? Give
up to a puny, woolly-headed king who ought to be in a monastery?
Watch your tongue, woman! There is still none fitter to decide the
destiny of Godwin than Godwin himself. I'll have to think again,
that's all!'

XV

WHEN Godwin did get around to suggesting his daughter as a bride for Edward, the king was remarkably receptive. Despite his earlier coolness towards the lord of Wessex, Edward seemed inclined to offer a truce to Godwin. In doing so he went against the advice of English as well as Norman advisers, and he went too far for his own good. Not only did he accept Edith as his wife, he also made Harold the third earl in Godwin's family by handing him the rich domain of East Anglia. Other thanes gasped at this enormous increase in the power of the Wessex clan and predicted that only evil could come of it, but Edward was content that he had handled the man who could so easily be his greatest enemy in the best way possible. Cheerfully, he married Edith at Canterbury on Wednesday, the twenty-third day of January, 1045. Harold became Earl of East Anglia later the same year.

Cedric was overjoyed at his friend's advancement, but even this could not diminish the pain he felt at the final loss of Edith. Alone and lonely, the forgotten warrior hero who had shone for such a brief time went back to the obscurity of Wantage and threw himself into his work as Shire-Reeve with more energy than ever before. He shunned the company of women, and he drank himself to sleep at night.

He heard nothing of the Godwin family again for more than a year. Then, going to Reading to see his mother, he found her closeted with Gospatrick, whom she still regarded as an elder son.

'Gospatrick brings grave news, Cedric,' Constance told him. 'It's about Harold's brother, Sweyn. He has done a terribly wicked thing.' She made the sign of the cross.

'Aye, he's in bad trouble,' Gospatrick affirmed. 'He's violated an abbess.'

'Merciful God! Tell me about it.'

'Sweyn was on his way back from Wales with his army. They stopped at Leominster for food. I don't know how it came about, but Sweyn apparently abducted the abbess, carried her off to his house and ravished her. So far he's ignored the pleas of the church and the thanes there to let her go.'

'He will bring God's wrath down upon us all,' Constance declared.

'The fool! I always thought he had a touch of madness in him. What is being done about it?'

'A court has convened in London to try him. His father and Harold are there pleading for him, but Sweyn – well, he must be mad, as you say – he's still in his house, barricaded in. He has refused to go to London as the king ordered.'

'He'll destroy his family and throw away all their power and wealth,' Cedric said. 'I must know how it turns out. I'm going to London.'

'At least stay long enough for something to eat, and to tell us your news,' Constance begged.

'I want to talk to you as well,' Gospatrick said. 'I have to thank you for bringing Olaf to justice. You avenged not only Prince Alfred, but also my father and brother. My stepmother, the Princess Aelfgifu, asked me to thank you for her, too. In a letter not long ago she said you must be the last of England's great warriors. Oh yes, she means that sincerely. It was something I wanted to do all those years, but never had the courage for. You did. And Gifta and I will always be grateful.'

Embarrassed, Cedric shuffled his feet.

'It's all in the past, Gospatrick,' he smiled. 'Olaf is long dead, most of his housecarls dead with him. Let them all lie buried. We live in different times now, though God knows, it looks as if these days will be no less troubled.'

The second trial of Sweyn Godwinsson was still in session when Cedric reached London. Godwin and Harold were closeted with the nobles and church leaders who had been brought together to give judgment, so Cedric could only wait to hear the latest news from them. He paced through Edward's magnificent stone palace, marvelling at its proportions and style of architecture. With time on his hands, he studied with awed gaze the soaring pillars, the vaulted ceilings, the extravagant tapestries and banners, the deep stained-glass windows colouring the sunlight, and the statues of saints and past kings. To him it was more like a cathedral than a house, and he felt small and humble. The loneliness and emptiness of it disturbed him, and finally he left a message for Harold that he would be with Edith. In the queen's quarters, Edith greeted him more like a long-lost brother than as an old friend. She shooed away her hand-maidens so that they could converse privately, but appeared anxious to talk about anything other than Sweyn's awful crime. The warmth of her welcome delighted Cedric. It almost made up for his sorrow at having to regard her now as completely untouchable. It was difficult for him, because she was even lovelier than he remembered. Her natural beauty had been enhanced by the regality and dignity she had taken on with marriage, as surely as the girl had blossomed into womanhood. She was graceful and sedate, gracious and charming, as though she had been born to be queen, yet she had lost none of the simplicity that Cedric remembered when she had been a shy girl sheltered in her father's house. Even then her dress had been rich, but now it was of gorgeous luxury. She wore a gown of pale green, caught at the waist with a thin chain of gold, and a flowing overmantle of dark green satin trimmed with fur, with bracelets of gold and silver and necklaces of turquoise and emerald. Her pale face was framed within a wimple of shining white silk, her long plaits caught in clasps of gold, and her crown sparkled with gems. Her radiance thrilled Cedric, but hurt him too. Just then he hated his king with all the passion of the defeated and cheated lover he considered himself to be.

'Queen Edith,' he mused, standing back in admiration. 'I always knew you were a fine lady, but I never dreamed it would come to this. I don't suppose you did either. I only pray that you are happy.'

'Thank you, dear Cedric,' she smiled. 'I am as happy as any person has a right to be.'

'I'm not quite sure what that means.'

Edith rested in her alcove window-seat and looked across the silent marsh to the broad blue river and sky. She resembled a caged song-bird then, safe and well-nourished and chirruping its tune of contentment, yet perhaps wondering what it would be like to fly.

'I have not much to pray for,' she explained. 'Those who can say that must be happy.'

Cedric eyed her thoughtfully and said: 'But I get the feeling there *is* something you pray for.'

'A son,' she admitted. 'A son and heir for Edward. It is my duty. It's why he married me.'

'There is time,' Cedric said kindly. 'It is only a little over a year.'

Edith uttered a small, sardonic laugh. Her sadness was gradually creeping to the surface, but so was her relief at being able to speak after so long with someone she could trust.

'There is time,' she agreed. 'But only if there is something else as well.'

Cedric gawped at her.

'You mean . . . ?'

'I mean that the king has yet to come to my bed. I am a virgin wife, Cedric. And God have pity on me, I don't know how to tell my father, with all the troubles he has now. Poor father, he has been watching like a hawk to see my belly swell. I feel I have failed him terribly. How shall I tell him?'

What a shameful way to treat this woman, Cedric was thinking angrily. He had loved and desired her so much! He felt such biting hunger when he looked at her, yet her useless husband had her for the taking and rejected her, like a sated man at a banquet. Somehow the knowledge that her virtue was intact made his torture worse. In time he might have been able to accept that she belonged completely to another man, but now he never would.

'I should say nothing to Godwin for a while,' he counselled. 'See if Edward can yet prove himself a man. Oh, Edith! I told you once that I would sacrifice everything to ride off with you. Today I feel just as inclined to do that . . .'

'Don't you start,' came the voice of Harold from the doorway. 'We have enough trouble with Sweyn.'

Cedric and Edith both leapt up, and heaped Harold with questions.

'Banished,' Harold announced glumly. 'All his property confiscated, and he banished from England indefinitely. The king has sent the entire force of housecarls to Hereford to see that the order is carried out. Lord, it was close, though. There were shouts for the demon in him to be burned, and he with it. Under any other king, such madmen might have had their way. I'll say this for Edward, he is a just man.'

'How is your father taking it?' Cedric asked.

'Very, very badly. I have never in my life seen him so distressed, so much at a loss. He thinks he can hear the mocking laughter of every thane he has ever triumphed over in the past. Worse, he believes that this act of Sweyn's has swept away all the goodwill he has been building up between him and Edward.'

There Godwin had misjudged Edward again. Many of the king's advisers urged him to use this disgrace to crush Godwin's family once and for all, but Edward continued to go his own way. Within hours of the sentence, the Confessor called Godwin before him, treated him to a humiliating lecture on the need to exercise tighter moral control over his offspring, then proceeded to hand out unexpected favours. He wished to show his trust in his father-in-law, he told the perplexed earl, and therefore it was his intention to leave the earldom of South Mercia in Godwin's family. Sweyn's former lands would be divided equally between Harold and Bjorn. Godwin could scarcely credit his good fortune. Bjorn had become an ambassador of higher importance, and a stronger ally of Godwin, since his eldest brother Sweyn had won the kingdom of Denmark upon the death of King Magnus, and the new King Sweyn Estrithsson would surely regard his uncle Godwin more kindly with the grant of English lands to Bjorn.

Harold and Bjorn were jubilant, too. They celebrated with a scorched-earth war west of Offa's Dyke. Taking with them a large band of riders, they swept like a forest fire through a dozen Welsh villages and a hundred fields of crops, setting homes and barns ablaze. Harold killed his first men there, encouraged by the experienced Bjorn. At a feast in one of Harold's houses at Oxford, they proudly boasted of their exploits to their chief guest, Cedric Shieldless.

'Next time, Cedric, you must come with us,' bellowed Bjorn, still glowing with the thrill of battle and the telling of deeds. 'Did I not say that we would all go to war together one day? Aha, now the world trembles when it hears that the Godwinssons and the Estrithssons are coming. We hold England and Denmark in our grasp, and next it will be Wales!'

'Conquer Wales, and you will indeed make history,' Cedric chuckled. 'It has not been done before.'

'I think, my friend,' grinned Harold, pouring wine, 'that that is our destiny – to make history. If my family cannot do it, no one ever will again. I give you a toast, cousin Bjorn, friend Cedric. May the three of us stand together, like the warriors we are, until there is no one fit enough to feel the edge of our swords!'

They were still at their feasting in Oxford when a messenger came from Godwin, bidding them all gather their men at once and go to Bosham. Knowing that some trouble must have arisen for Godwin to make such a call on them, they instantly obeyed, and travelled south with all speed.

It was a haggard Godwin who greeted them at Bosham, where he had formed a fair-sized army even before the arrival of his son's and nephew's reinforcements. The Earl of Wessex had aged suddenly. His features were tired and jaded, his body wracked with stiffness, and much of his old energy had gone. Cedric remarked to Harold that in all the years he had known Godwin he had never seen him look so dejected, and Harold agreed that neither had he.

'Sweyn is back,' Godwin told them grimly. 'The stubborn fool! He has raised a fleet in Flanders, and now he's raiding along the south coast – trying to force the king to give him back his lands. Edward has sent his own fleet and the housecarls out against him, but I want to find him before they do. Do you understand? Only Godwin will deal with a son of Godwin, here in Wessex. The latest news I had today was that Sweyn was near Pevensey. That is where we will make for first, and by God you'll all feel my anger if we don't catch him before Edward's men!'

'What will you do with him, father?' Harold wanted to know.

'To be honest, I'm not sure,' Godwin growled. 'But God's word, whatever I do, I'll make sure the fool regrets this. Raiding his own father's land! Defying his king!'

'This is a war I would rather not fight,' Harold said to Bjorn, as they went out to remount.

The young Dane put an encouraging arm across his cousin's shoulders.

'All will be well,' he assured Harold. 'We are the fastest and best in England, remember? We will get to Sweyn first.'

They saw a few dying fires when they reached Pevensey three hours after dark. The town was silent, its inhabitants having either fled or stayed cowering in hiding. Stray animals roamed aimlessly, a sheep here, a cow there, a dog slinking through the gloom. In the distance a house or hay-rick crumbled in flames, but the larger part of the town, though ransacked, had been spared the torch. Riding to the beach, they found no sign of Sweyn's fleet. Black waves hissed softly on the shore, and the sky was obscured by gathering storm clouds. A low wind blew the salt spray into their parchment-dry faces, like teasing whispers that they were too late.

'He's gone,' Harold said needlessly, as the riders slid down from their horses and slumped on the shingle, aching with fatigue yet knowing the night was not yet done.

'But where?' Bjorn wondered. 'West, or east?'

'In this light no one could tell, even if they'd had the guts to come out and watch him go,' Godwin grumbled. 'We must split up. Harold and Bjorn, you go east. I'll go west. We'll send men ahead of us, to get ships. We must chase him by sea as well as by land.'

'Can you still go on?' Harold asked him.

'As long as you can, boy!' Godwin snorted.

Ships were easy to find but willing sailors were not, in the dead of night along that terror-stricken coast. The crews had either made themselves scarce, or flatly refused to go out against Sweyn's pirates. Harold, Bjorn and Cedric and their men reached Hastings in the early hours of the morning before they succeeded in commandeering three vessels, which even then were undermanned. While the ships put out to sea, the exhausted travellers fell asleep on the hard decks. It was daylight when they were woken by the captain, and they found themselves back at Pevensey. The cunning Sweyn had made a false retreat from the town, and had spent the night there fully aware that it had already been searched. Eight of his warships now lay at anchor off the beach, and the shore was crowded with several hundred men all watching the new arrivals.

'Well, we've found them,' observed Cedric. 'But now what? They outnumber us two to one.'

'We'll go ashore, just the three of us, for the time being,' Harold declared. 'Let them see we come in peace.'

They were surrounded by hostile pirates as they waded up the beach. Only Sweyn could prevent the mob from pouncing upon them, eager to stab and beat them to death. Sweyn pushed his way to the front, yelling at his raiders to hold back, but there was little welcome in his manner for his brother, cousin and friend. He stood with hands planted firmly on his hips, waiting for them to speak.

'Well, Sweyn,' Harold said gently. 'You gave us the Devil's own run, trying to find you.'

During his long absence from England, handsome Sweyn had become an unkempt pirate, and had dulled both in looks and spirit. His beard, once neatly plaited, now sprouted long and tangled like a thornbush, hiding much of his weathered face. His sunken eyes gleamed like ice from dark wells, his hair fell lank and unclean from under his helmet in a greasy, stringy mess. Gone were the finely woven cloak and rich jewels, which he had sold to help raise his force. In their place he wore a shaggy bearskin cape, which made him look like some big, mangy beast. He was clearly aware of the deterioration in his appearance, for he regarded the finery of his three former companions with a seething disdain.

'I'm surprised you bothered,' Sweyn sneered in answer. 'You and father did little enough to help me when I needed it most. I hear that you and Bjorn have profited well by my land. Why have you come? To make sure I don't get it back? You'll need more than that laughable little bunch of sea-borne farmers!'

'You are being unreasonable,' Harold told him. 'There's more than these after you. The whole English army is scouring the coast for you right now. That's why we have been riding ourselves into the ground all day and night, trying to get you to a truce before it's too late. We're not against you, Sweyn. There was nothing we could do to save you from banishment. It was all we could do to save your neck.'

'What touching concern,' Sweyn said bitterly. 'But don't worry about me. I've an army here that can match anything the king sends. I've come for what is mine, and I mean to take it.'

'This is not the right way.'

'Oh? What do you suggest I should have done? Perhaps I should have written a polite letter to King Edward, begging to come home?'

'It might have been favourably received. Certainly more favourably than what you've done here.'

Sweyn uttered a short, harsh laugh.

'Horse-dung!' he snapped. 'Pious King Edward has made it plain what he thinks of me. The sword is all that monkish little runt understands, and that's the only word I have for him. Go to him if you like, and give him that message.'

'Speak to father first,' Harold said earnestly. 'He's just down the coast. Let's mend as much damage as we can before Edward's men get here.'

'So father's running after me as well, is he?' Sweyn laughed. 'Well, don't expect me to quail at his anger, brother. Father doesn't frighten me any more. No one does. One thing I have learned from exile is that there is no place in this life for the meek. Only the strong survive, and there is none stronger than I.'

Harold sighed; it was impossible to argue with Sweyn while he was in this stubborn mood.

'We might discuss it better on a full belly,' he said. 'Can we at least eat together?'

'Did I ever refuse you hospitality?' Sweyn chided him. 'A meal you are welcome to, but I have nothing else to offer you unless you want to join my fight. Nor do you have anything to offer me.'

They sat down at the raiders' camp fire, chewing on the roasted pig that Sweyn's men had thieved, washing the food down with stolen ale.

'I think I do have something to offer,' Harold tried again.

'My own earldom?' Sweyn said sourly.

'No, it's not in my power to give you that . . .'

'Even if you wanted to!'

'Sweyn, for the love of God, do you really think we have no feeling left for you? Listen, I'll gladly do anything I can to get you pardoned. Father will too. Just give us a chance to talk to Edward. But you'll have to call off this army while we do it.'

There was a dangerous mutter of discontent from Sweyn's band of Flemish and German warriors.

'You see what they think of that,' Sweyn told Harold. 'They have been promised rich rewards for helping me get what's mine. They are not going to be satisfied with a few cattle and a bit of church plate.'

'You fool,' Harold shouted. 'You've almost burned your boats! What do you think you'll be able to give them – an earldom each?'

'I'll give them anything I can force out of Edward.'

'Edward will not be forced. He may be swayed, but he won't be forced. It can only end in disaster if you insist upon war. How many men do you have, all told? A thousand? Edward can raise five times as many in a few days.'

'But in those few days I can bring him to his knees.'

'No, you can't. You're reckoning without our father. If you

311

continue to raid his lands, he'll be angry enough to come against you himself. He'll strike more quickly, and harder, than Edward.'

'Has he said he'll do this?' Sweyn demanded.

'No, but you know he will. He'll probably do everything in his power to help you, if you stop now. But defy him, and he'll destroy you. Do you see him giving up everything he has, for your sake or anyone else's?'

Sweyn stared into the fire, tortured with indecision.

'Let us speak to the king,' Harold prompted.

Looking around at his men, Sweyn knew that they would swiftly slit his throat if he dropped a wrong word. Their stern gaze warned him against betraying them.

'Talk to your damned king,' Sweyn snarled, boldly adding: 'Tell him we give him this day and tomorrow to meet us with an acceptable offer. If we hear nothing by sundown tomorrow, we will take to the ships again and burn every town on this coast.'

There were some mutters of dissent among the crowd, but most of the raiders seemed satisfied to take two days' rest, as long as there was still the prospect of booty at the end of it.

'I'll find father,' Harold agreed. 'We'll go to the king together.'

Before leaving on a borrowed horse, he took Bjorn and Cedric aside.

'I've got to race like the devil now, to reach father and get to the king,' he told them. 'But I'm afraid to leave Sweyn with this bunch of cut-throats. If they get impatient, they may force him to start the fighting again. It might help him hang on if he has friends with him. Will you stay with him while I'm gone?'

'Of course,' both agreed.

When Harold had left, Cedric and Bjorn drew Sweyn away from his soldiers and tried to cheer him with talk of former days. Sweyn' though, was slow to respond. He had withdrawn deep within himself, as though all he wanted was solitude. He drank steadily and spoke little.

'It's a long time since we were all together last, in Bosham,' Cedric tried. 'Or was it Tofic's wedding? Lord, that was a time, wasn't it? Do you remember, how that great bear scattered the people under the table?'

'And how Tofic fell off his seat laughing,' Bjorn chuckled. 'Did we ever see him again after that? There was so much fuss about Hardicanute dropping dead in the middle of the feast, I never did hear what happened to poor Tofic!'

They were walking along the beach as they spoke. It was a cool, windy day, and the waves were high, causing the ships to bounce about like little wooden bowls. Seagulls fought the breeze and failed, drifting backwards overhead, and great black hills of cloud were piled upon the horizon. Sweyn stopped, coldly surveying the grey-green seascape as if seeking something of interest out there in the swell, anything to ease the boredom of waiting. He took a long pull from the flagon of ale he carried, drained it, and spat the dregs into the sand, then hurled the empty jar far out into the sea.

'Don't talk to me of good times,' he growled. 'Times past are of no more importance to me. Today is all that matters.'

'Of course, you are right,' Bjorn said soothingly. 'But don't worry, all will be well . . .'

Sweyn turned upon him fiercely.

'I'm not worrying!' he snapped. 'Do you think I'm scared of the monk Edward? Or Godwin? Well, I'm not. And no prattling preacher king is going to take from me what is rightfully mine, and he knows it. These men are good enough for him. Even so, I can get more if I have to. There are thousands more like them, waiting across the Channel, and I could fetch them now if I had to. I can smash Edward, and I will, if he doesn't give me what I want!'

Cedric and Bjorn were worried. There was a madness in Sweyn, they saw now, the madness of a once-valued man deprived of all he possessed and humiliated beyond endurance. The raving simmered in him as in a pot coming to the boil; a few more flames might bring it all out in a scalding torrent.

'Yes, you're right,' Cedric humoured him. 'Edward is a troubled man. He did not imagine that you would return like this, to test him.'

'But your father is good at handling him,' Bjorn added eagerly. 'I don't think you will have to fight more. It will be all over by this time tomorrow.'

'You are playing me along,' Sweyn softly accused them. 'Like poachers teasing a trout out of a stream.'

'No,' Bjorn protested. 'We are with you, Sweyn!'

'You are playing for time, keeping me here while the king brings his army! Is that what Harold was whispering about? Was he telling you to delay me while he fetched Edward's men?'

'That is not true, and you know it!' Cedric said with contempt. 'Can you not trust even your own family and friends? Do you not trust me, Sweyn, even though there is a bond of gratitude between us? You saved my life when I fought Olaf. And remember that I helped defend you at your first trial.'

'Harold has nothing to gain by helping me, and neither does Bjorn,' Sweyn argued, pacing restlessly. 'They both have plenty to lose, though; they have my earldom to lose. They've divided my earldom between them, haven't you, Bjorn? And never once, in all the time I've been rotting in Flanders, have I heard an offer of help from you! Why should you change your minds now? Damn you, I will not wait on this beach to be trapped! I am going to my ship. I'll fight in my own time, not Edward's or my father's.'

'We will come to your ship with you, then,' Bjorn said casually. 'That will show that you can trust us. What could we do to stop you leaving then?'

'Come if you wish,' and Sweyn waded out into the tugging waves.

He struggled up over the gunwale of his flagship and slouched in the stern under a rough canopy, drinking again and becoming more miserably drunk. Cedric and Bjorn, sitting close to him, could not think of any way to bring him back to his senses. He was trapped in his own dark mind, one moment confident and full of daring, the next withdrawn and plagued with doubt. He appeared to have no idea what to do next, yet when his own men asked about his plans he dismissed them as if they were stupid to ask. He was a lonely man, a frightened man convinced of his bravery, a disturbed man suspecting the sanity of everyone else.

'I'm going to Bosham,' he drunkenly announced, late in the day. 'Make for Bosham, captain. I am going to avail myself of the hospitality of my father's house. Will you join me, cousin Bjorn? It will be just like those old times you were talking about.'

'No, Sweyn, not Bosham,' Bjorn pleaded, anxiously watching the sailors get under way. 'Don't make trouble at your own father's house. That would ruin the last chance you have!'

Sweyn's anger flared instantly.

'Very well, then,' he slurred. 'We will not go to Bosham. We will go to your house, shall we? Your house that was my house! You will not object to having me in our house, will you, lord Earl Bjorn? I trust you found the wine to your satisfaction, the bed comfortable and the wenches willing?'

'Sweyn, please,' Bjorn said sadly. 'I did not want to take anything from you . . .'

'And my son, Haakon!' Sweyn raged. 'Who has my son?'

'His grandfather cares for him . . .' Cedric began.

'Ah, you see? You've all got something, haven't you? Sweyn's home. Sweyn's blood, divided up like spoils while Sweyn festers in Flemish fleapits! Oh yes, I saw you all standing there on the wharf the day I was thrown out by the housecarls, all weeping for me as I sailed away, never to return – you hoped! Where were you all? Were your spirits there at the quayside? With me in spirit, were you? Never mind, Bjorn. I know how busy you were, moving into my house!'

Bjorn knew that Sweyn was mindless with drink, but could no longer contain his own wrath.

'Stop your whining, you fool!' he shouted back. 'Blind, self-pitying fool! Damn you, I doubt that anyone can help you. You cannot even help yourself!'

Bjorn turned away, leaving his cousin shaking with helpless anger. That final insult from Bjorn brought Sweyn's mind to the breaking point.

'Traitor!' Sweyn screamed, and leapt up tearing his sword from its sheath.

Bjorn heard the blade being drawn and swung around, his hand flying to the hilt of his own sword. Cedric jumped to his feet. They were both too late. Sweyn took two lurching steps forward, and swung his weapon with all the strength of the madman he had become. The blade sliced deep into Bjorn's belly.

The young Dane doubled up, agony and astonishment twisting his face into a ghastly white mask, but he uttered no sound. Sweyn, suddenly sobered by what he had done, pulled out the sword and stepped back. Blood spewed from Bjorn's torn stomach in a torrent, washing the deck with red and splashing Sweyn's feet. Bjorn's head went back, his eyes rolled; he spun once and crashed lifeless to the deck.

Cedric and Sweyn stood facing each other, motionless as statues; it seemed an eternity. It was Sweyn who broke the spell as he drifted back into the protection of the madness from which he had briefly emerged. His face became calm, and he turned the bloody sword upon Cedric, pointing it at his throat.

'Are you going to fight me, Cedric Shieldless?' he asked, nodding towards Cedric's sword hand.

Cedric had not even realised that he had drawn. He looked down at the blade and sheathed it, shaking his head.

'You are Harold's brother,' he answered, his voice unsteady. 'I cannot fight you. But, by God, I swear, if you were anyone else, I would cut you to pieces for this!'

He kneeled beside the body of his murdered friend, reached out and closed Bjorn's eyes. Tears welled up and the beat and wash of the sea against the rolling hull sounded like thunder in his brain.

'Oh, dear God,' he moaned. 'Why?'

Sweyn had stood the point of his sword on the deck, and was watching the blood trickle on to the planks as a child interests itself for long minutes in the meanderings of a tiny stream.

'The king is mad,' he said thoughtfully. 'He gave away my land; he should have known this would happen. He'll have to give it back to me now.'

Cedric, feeling sick, got up and went to the shoreward gunwale. 'Put us off,' he begged. 'I must take Bjorn ashore.'

'I should kill you, too,' Sweyn said, matter-of-factly. 'You came here to spy on me. You said you would help me, and now look what's happened. I ought to kill you.'

'Kill me then. I don't care. God knows it would be better than having to tell Harold what you've done.'

Sweyn scowled, thinking it over. For a moment he surfaced from the depths of drunkenness. He shook his head, as he might do to rid himself of the memory of a bad dream, and peered down at Bjorn as if for the first time. Bewilderment crossed his face, to be quickly followed by remorse and muted rage. He looked at his sword, and his blood-stained clothing, wiped the blade on his cloak and almost reverently pushed it back into the scabbard.

'I have killed Bjorn,' he whispered.

'Yes.'

'I did not mean to kill him!'

'Put me ashore,' Cedric repeated. 'For pity's sake, let me off this cursed ship!'

Sweyn called to the captain to make for land. The vessel was steered in close to the beach, and Cedric leapt over the side. He struggled to keep his head above the water, and saw Sweyn and the crew watching him flounder. They could have been considering whether they ought to let him go, to tell what he knew, but none of them spoke or moved.

'Give me Bjorn,' Cedric demanded.

Sweyn nodded to his men. Three of them picked up the body and heaved it over with a splash, pushing it towards Cedric with oars. Cedric grabbed it and guided it towards the shingle. The indignity of this, for one who had been his friend, brought all his anger flooding back. It was like heaving the carcass of a drowned calf out of the river.

'Now go to hell, madman!' Cedric yelled. 'Go and burn in hell where you belong!'

He never saw the ship leave, or the fleet that followed it. Reaching the beach, he laid out the dead man as carefully as he could, and covered the face with Bjorn's own cloak. He sat beside his friend, soaked and shivering like a dog that refuses to leave its master, until his own ships came and his men came ashore.

'Go and find Earl Godwin, or Earl Harold,' he ordered them. 'Tell them what has happened and show them where to come.'

Well into the night Cedric stayed with Bjorn. In the long wait he stared at the sea, or the sky, or sometimes at Bjorn, but more often at the patch of sand and stones between his feet. He longed for the others to come, yet dreaded it. He had no idea what to say, and was afraid of the grief he would have to witness. Once he thought that he would simply walk away when they came and leave them to mourn alone, but he recognised that as cowardice and dismissed the idea with self-contempt. Face up to it, he commanded himself; re-learn the lessons you have learned so many times before. See again the ravages of ambition, the cruelty of men and the price of power. Stay here with death, and see again how death touches the living, as you saw it do at Guildford. Stay and see Harold learn what you learned then: how easy it is to give one's friends up to death, how weak and useless is a man's hand when he tries to stay death, hold it away from those he loves.

Prince Alfred and Gilbert de Bernay, Eadwulf Uhtredsson, Hardicanute and now Bjorn Estrithsson; he had seen so many come to an untimely end.

When Cedric heard the sounds of horsemen, he started to his feet as if he himself had been caught in the act of murder. Both Godwin and Harold were galloping at the head of their men and Cedric's body went cold in anticipation of their wrath. They hardly noticed him, however, but reined in sharply and ran to the body. Wild-eyed, Harold went down on his knees, and with trembling hand reached out to remove the cloak from Bjorn's face. He broke down, wailing as he threw himself across the corpse:

'Bjorn! Oh, Bjorn!'

Godwin stood over him; his ageing frame shook with fury and shame.

'How did it happen?' he asked, through clenched teeth.

Cedric opened his mouth, found no voice, and had to try again.

'Sweyn killed him, my lord,' he said with difficulty. 'He was drunk, and possessed by demons. It happened so suddenly that neither Bjorn nor I could prevent it.'

'But why, damn him, why?' Godwin roared, his face purpling with anger. He raised his arms with fists clenched, as if beating at a spectre of Sweyn that only he could see, and cursed on: 'The stupid, mindless fool! Has the Devil taken his senses? Why, why, why!'

'My lord, I cannot tell you. I was there and I saw it, but if I live a hundred years I will never know why. Jealousy, drink, rage, fear – who can say? One moment they were talking; the next Sweyn was plunging his sword into Bjorn as if he were his most hated enemy. I could see no reason in it then, and I can see none now.'

Godwin was breathing hard, clutching at his chest.

'His own cousin,' he groaned. 'The son of his mother's brother! And one who loved him, who would have followed him anywhere!

Oh God, how could he do it?' he pleaded, then lowered his voice and added with a growing malevolence: 'May the man be damned to Hell! He has destroyed a nephew of mine, and he has destroyed a son of mine too. Sweyn is no son of mine after this. Let it be as if he had never lived. From this day on his name will never be spoken again, lest I cut out the tongue of him who speaks it. He is a nithing, and I myself will see that he is declared so. I myself will pay the reward to the man who kills him. Were he here before me at this very moment, I myself would cut him down!' He turned to his men then, and pointing to Bjorn's body, told them: 'Take him to my house. Lay him out there with all honour.'

They had to lift Harold away from the body, but after that he helped carry the stiffened Bjorn and strap him across a horse. Suddenly in his frustration at having no foe at whom he could hit out, he turned upon Cedric.

'Could you do nothing?' he cried. 'You, Cedric Shieldless? Were you so helpless you could do nothing to stop him?'

'Harold!' Godwin barked. 'Calm yourself, man! You are a son of Godwin, not a bleating woman. Now you are the elder son of Godwin. Behave in a fitting manner!'

Having said all he had to say, the Earl of Wessex stumbled off. Godwin took his defeats as he had taken his victories, shouldering the burden alone as he had collected the prizes and praise; no one would ever know what he felt like inside. Deep in that fortress of a man, a consuming blaze of grief might be gutting him, but no one would ever see the damage. All that he had built in a lifetime had been shattered; his standing and influence among the lords of the land and the church had been severely tested; his bid to gain himself a prince for a grandson had failed; all the favour he had won with King Sweyn of Denmark was now lost forever; and his already-disgraced eldest son had turned murderer; yet not even those closest to him would hear him whining in self-pity. Godwin would grieve silently and alone, confounded and embittered at the very last, and there would not be a further ounce of compassion or regret left to spare by the time Sweyn died in exile, two years later. Not even his death was spoken of in Godwin's hearing.

' "*Know the price of asking,*" your father said to me the day I slew Olaf,' Cedric muttered. 'It seems the price of wanting is the same. You see what ambition costs? We have been presented with its account today, more ruthlessly than we have ever seen it written before. And never have we paid so dear a fee.'

'I have a feeling you are preaching to me again about my family's ways,' Harold snarled.

'If that is the way you hear it,' Cedric answered coldly.

'In other words, if the cap fits wear it!' Harold hissed. 'By God I swear, this is the worst time you have ever chosen for your cursed moralising, Cedric. I have lost a brother and a cousin; if you insist that I lose a friend as well, I should be well prepared to bear it. I've told you before: get away from us if you don't like our ways. Go where you like; I'm not stopping you. Go back to the farm you came from. I still have the stomach for the life we live, despite all this. I wish you well.'

He stormed away to his horse and rode into the darkness without another word. Cedric shook off the weight of grief then, and only a burning resentment remained. He took his sword, dashed the blade against a rock until it shattered, and hurled the hilt far out into the sea.

'Die, Cedric Shieldless!' he shrieked. 'That's the end of you, Cedric Olaf-Slayer! Mighty warrior! *Die!*'

THIRD BOOK
The Day of the Leopard
1052–1066

I

C EDRIC might have passed by Brithnoth the herdsman without a second glance, but for the man's strange behaviour. Brithnoth was standing alone in the middle of the field, a few hundred yards from his poor cruck-built home, going through some ritual. The old man had a lighted candle on the ground beside him, although it was noon and a bright sunny day. He had taken a pad of dried cow dung in his hands, and was throwing it up into the air, catching it, and tossing it again. Finally he let the dung fall to the earth. Then, singing softly, he picked up the candle and carefully tilted it three times, each time letting the tallow drip on to the dung.

Filled with curiosity, Cedric reined in his horse and paused to watch, and the words of the herdsman's song came quite clearly to him across the field:

'Bethlehem was the exalted town where Christ
was born,
it is famed all over Earth.

So may this deed be known of men notorious,
per crucem Christi.

The cross of Christ was hidden and has been found.
The Jews hanged Christ,
they did to him the worst of deeds.

They concealed what they were not able to conceal,
and never may this deed become concealed,
per crucem Christi.

When the song was finished, Brithnoth put the candle down again and stood up as straight as his crippled back would allow, facing east.

'May the cross of Christ bring it back from the east!' he shouted. Then he turned about. 'May the cross of Christ bring it back from the West!' He turned to the south and to the north with the same chant. Then he saw Cedric watching him. He hung his head, as Cedric rode through the field towards him.

'What in the name of God are you doing, Brithnoth?' Cedric laughed.

'Aye, in God's name it is, master,' the herder mumbled. 'It's only He can help me find it.'

'Find what? What have you lost?'

Brithnoth was a sorry sight in his childish reluctance to answer, bent with age, white-haired and thin of limb, dressed in a single rag shift tied at the waist with string. Through all his hard life in this tiny corner of Berkshire he had never possessed more than the minimum of food and clothing necessary for his family to survive. Cedric's family had bought Brithnoth, his wife and children from a harsher master many years ago. He had not been beaten since that time, yet still behaved as though he would be soundly thrashed whenever he did something wrong.

'The cow, sir,' he eventually replied. 'I weren't trying to be deceitful, master. Honest. I were going to tell you . . .'

'You have lost one of my cows?'

'Not lost, sir. It weren't my fault. Her were stolen, last night. It was getting dark as I were getting them in, and her were left over by yon copse. I heard a noise like her being chased, then her were gone.'

Cedric could not help smiling, despite the loss of a valuable animal. It was not the old man's anxiety to avoid punishment that amused him, though. He was thinking in that moment how small were the troubles in his life these days. How insignificant was the theft of a single cow, he reflected, compared with the troubles he had had to deal with when he had been Shire-Reeve of Berkshire, lord of the county's affairs in peace and war, and faithful liegeman of Godwin, Earl of Wessex. He had mingled with the highest lords of the land in those days, even with kings and queens, bishops and warlords, and he still found it difficult to get used to being a mere farmer. He was thirty-one now, and led a life of peaceful ease, so peaceful that sometimes he longed for the old excitements he had known with Godwin and Harold Godwinsson.

'And this is the way to get her back?' he teased Brithnoth, pointing to the candle and the dung.

'Aye, that be a sure charm, master,' the old one said eagerly. 'You'll see. Her be back afore nightfall . . .'

'I doubt it,' Cedric shrugged. 'She probably made a good dinner for some hungry outlaws, or she's been sold at a market somewhere.'

'No sir! Her will come, you mark my words. This charm at the noon-day cannot fail, 'tis been taught to us by our fathers for many a year. The thieves'll lose her, or be caught, and back her'll come.'

'All right, if you say so,' Cedric conceded, admitting to himself that he knew no more of the ways of God or of magic than these simple serfs, who lived so close to the earth. 'Don't worry about it,' he added kindly. 'Just try to watch them more closely in future. I cannot afford to lose many.'

'Aye, sir, I will. You be a good master. God been good to me, giving me a master like you.'

Cedric glanced at the herder's house, a rickety shack of rotting timber, turf and more dried dung, and recognised an irony in the old man's pitiful gratitude. He had lived among men who would cut the throats of their own kin for greater wealth and power, and he had feasted in rich halls where that hovel of Brithnoth's would not have made even a roasting fire. Yet here was an ancient herdsman, who had struggled every daylight hour of his life in this miserable field, watching his children die of starvation or disease, thanking Cedric for not striking him down. Well, thought Cedric, being a farmer at least taught a man a thing or two he would never have dreamed of in the halls of the mighty, where they would waste more beef at a single meal than Brithnoth had allowed to stray.

He plucked a silver shilling from his purse, and held it up for Brithnoth to see.

'Have you ever held one of these?' he asked the old man.

'No, sir,' Brithnoth chuckled. 'T'aint for the likes of I to hold silver.'

'What would you do with it, if you had one?'

Brithnoth searched his dull brain for an answer, and could find none. His food came from a share of the crops he helped to grow for Cedric, and his milk from the cows. His clothes were made of animal hides, and any meat he ever ate was that left over from the slaughtered cattle after Cedric's table had been filled. His winter fuel came from the woods, as did the materials for his shelter. There was nothing on which he would spend money.

'You could buy a good woollen cloak,' Cedric told him, putting the coin in his hand. 'Indeed, cloaks and blankets for all of you. Wool is warmer than hide or sack-cloth; it will make next winter's nights a little easier. Good luck with your charm. If the cow comes back, she's yours. You have earned her.'

He rode away, smiling at the speechless Brithnoth, who could only stare from the shilling to his master and back at the shilling again. It felt good to have been so generous, and Cedric sang all the way home to Reading. Dismounting in the yard, he convinced himself that he was content to have left behind the Reeve's hall at Wantage, to come back to the house of his birth and childhood. He watched his boys, his stepson Cuthbert, a lad of eight, and his own son Harold, playing chase among the chickens and dogs, and was pleased that Brithnoth had this day helped him understand the truly good things in life. As Cedric walked to the door he swept the younger child up into his arms and held him high.

'There, now he can't catch you, can he?'

Cuthbert stamped his foot in a sulk.

'You always help him,' he complained. 'It isn't fair. You never give me a chance to win.'

Cedric let Harold down, and tousled Cuthbert's hair.

'He's only two,' he explained. 'Little boys need help, men don't. You'll be a man long before he is, so I have to help him keep up with you.'

'You like him best because you're his real father!' Cuthbert scowled. 'If I had a real father, he'd help me.'

The child's words pained Cedric. He had tried to treat both boys equally, but all his efforts apparently could not overcome the resentment that Cuthbert felt for his half-brother. Cedric guessed that Cuthbert, having found a new father after the death of his own, had thought before the birth of Harold that he would again have that father all to himself.

'Don't let jealousy rule you, Cuthbert' he told him gently. 'I have seen men destroy themselves, and the people they loved and who loved them, and all for jealousy. It isn't worth it. I promise you.'

Cedric went into the house, remembering the day three years earlier when Sweyn Godwinsson had murdered his cousin Bjorn, an act which had led to the final disintegration of poor, mad Sweyn, who died in exile and disgrace. It had brought about the downfall of Earl Godwin, and it had smashed the close friendship that Cedric had shared with Sweyn's brother, Harold. Harold had blamed Cedric for Bjorn's death and Cedric had not seen Harold since. So much had been torn apart in one moment of madness, and yet it happened time after time, one generation after another made the same mistakes and never learned. Would it be like that with Cuthbert and little Harold?

Later he sat and talked with Ingrid, who sat rocking baby Gwendoline to sleep in her arms. 'Peace and contentment! A dream, an illusion. Do you know, the only contented man I have ever seen is a man who has known nothing but hardship and poverty all his life? Why is that, do you think?'

'Not so loud, you'll wake her,' Ingrid said, pulling a shawl over their daughter's head. 'What is the matter? Have you had a bad day?'

'No. It's just that Cuthbert is terribly jealous of Harold. I'm not sure what to do about it.'

'He will get over it. He's very young.'

Cedric poured a cup of wine, and contemplated the shield and sword hanging on the upright beam behind his place at the table. The shield was the one he had thrown down the day he had fought and killed Olaf Ericsson, earning for himself the name of Cedric Shieldless. The sword was his third, and was still unblooded. The first had been broken in the battle with Olaf, the second he had deliberately shattered and thrown away at his parting with Harold Godwinsson. Should he teach his children to use them, he wondered? Should he tell them of the war and death he had seen? Perhaps not, he thought, turning his gaze to Ingrid. She was a soft and gentle woman, who had come into his life, like an angel, Cedric always told her. Despite her own suffering and loss, she still possessed warmth and serenity, and Cedric had come to love her very much.

'We lost a cow last night,' he said.

'Oh dear,' she said calmly. 'Is there no hope of finding it?'

'Brithnoth thinks so. He dripped candle wax over its dung and sang a prayer.'

'Oh yes, I've heard of that.'

'I hadn't. Does it work?'

'I don't know. I've only heard about it from the country people. Gwendoline has a slight rash, look.'

'Call the physician, then.'

'I'll try a herb balm first.'

Cedric was restless. He wasn't really bored with the homely conversation, but something deeper than that was troubling him. It was as if Brithnoth's peculiar rites in the cow field had stirred within him a dark foreboding that changes must be made, that nothing was still down in the nether world where men's fates were always forming and re-forming. Getting up to look at Gwendoline's rash, he spilled some wine on the floor, and suddenly it was the blood of Bjorn that he saw drifting into the rushes.

'Cedric,' whispered Ingrid with alarm. 'You are shaking. Are you all right?'

Cedric neither saw nor heard her. He was having an awful waking vision. It *was* Bjorn's blood that was spreading at his feet. Suddenly the horror released him, leaving him cold and sweating even in the warmth of the fire.

'I need some fresh air,' he mumbled, threw down his cup and went outside.

An ox-cart he had not seen before had drawn up in his yard. A large cowhide canopy covered it; the carter was lashing down a corner that had come loose, as if to further conceal what was inside from prying eyes. At the sight of the cart, Cedric felt the shivers

327

running through his body once more. Another waking dream came to him. He knew that whatever, whoever, was in that cart would change the peaceful life he had made for himself. He shook himself awake, and went to greet the puzzled carter who had limped up to the door.

'Be you Cedric Cedricsson, sir?'

'I am.'

'There be someone here to see you, then. In my wagon.'

'Who is it?' Cedric demanded suspiciously. 'Why don't they come out?'

'It's as I were told, sir. The lady asked for you to go to her, there.'

'The lady?'

Cedric clambered up on to the cart, and dragged aside the curtain. A nun was sitting inside; she had a familiar face, and yet it was a face Cedric felt he had never seen. It was several seconds before he recognised her.

'Edith!' he gasped.

'Dear Cedric,' the Queen of England said with a wan smile. 'Please do not speak loudly. God knows what will happen to me if I am discovered. Getting here was the most arduous task of my life.'

Cedric climbed in beside her, and took her hands in his, open-mouthed with disbelief.

'But, why the secrecy?' he asked, 'And why are you dressed like this?'

Edith raised a hand to hush him, before he could ask more questions than she could answer.

'I have dressed this way since Edward sent me to a nunnery, a year ago, when my father and brothers were banished,' she told him. 'This is my punishment for my family's sins.'

'But why? It was none of your doing!'

'Edward hates my father,' Edith shrugged. 'He wanted all trace of Godwin removed. He also thought that in a nunnery I would be out of harm's way, unable to act as my father's spy in his court.'

A forgotten contempt for King Edward came flooding back. Cedric's dislike of him had been born the first day he had looked upon Edith as the bride of Edward, learned to accept that he could never have her. Now here she was, her beauty wasted and rejected, her lovely body smothered in a coarse grey habit and she herself locked away like a criminal because she was Godwin's daughter. It had hurt him enough that someone else should take her, but to see that the other man had cast her aside and yet retained possession of her, like the proverbial dog in the manger, was unbearable.

'Will you come into my house?' he invited her. 'It must be a long time since you enjoyed any comfort.'

'No. Thank you, but I dare not stay long or be seen.'

'But why have you come?'

'Harold asked me to.'

'Harold! But he's in Ireland!'

'Yes, but he sent a travelling monk with a message, and one of the sisters brought it to me.'

'And he asked you to come to me? Why?'

'He wants your help, Cedric. No, let me put it more strongly than that. He *needs* your help, and your friendship.'

'He wants me to go to Ireland?'

'No, please hear me out. Much is afoot. He and my father are planning to come back. My father is in Flanders with Tostig and Wulfnoth, raising an army there. Harold is in Ireland with Gurth and Leofwine. They will both start their raids at the same time, father at Dover, Harold in Somerset. They will strike all along the coasts until they meet, calling Wessex men to their side as they go, then together they will march on London.'

'Merciful Lord,' Cedric groaned. 'War with the king again! May God help them. They didn't do too well last time, did they?'

Cedric was remembering that the final rift had come about because Godwin had argued with the king over who should be appointed Archbishop of Canterbury. Godwin had favoured an Englishman, a kinsman of his, but Edward had had his way and had installed the Norman prelate Robert of Jumièges. Godwin, infuriated by the appointment of yet another Norman to one of England's high offices, had irritated Edward at every opportunity. The hot blood had simmered between them for a year, and then had boiled over when Edward's sister Godgifu, and her second husband Count Eustace of Boulogne, visited England. At Dover the couple claimed to have been insulted by the townspeople, and a fight between their bodyguard and some of the local citizens had ended with a number on each side being killed. Edward had seen fit to punish both Godwin and the people of Dover by insisting that the Earl of Wessex himself should deal severely with those responsible. Godwin had rudely refused. This time their argument grew so heated that they met each other with armies at their backs. Godwin, however, had been severely humiliated. His inferior numbers meant an ignominious retreat, followed by the sentence of banishment for himself and his five sons.

His fall had been the most resounding England had known since King Ethelred had been dethroned by the Vikings. Godwin had virtually ruled the country throughout the reigns of Canute, Harold

Harefoot and Hardicanute, and now he had fallen like a lightning-struck oak. Many were the lords of equal ambition but lesser ability who rejoiced at his disgrace, and who would lend the king all the weight they could muster to prevent his return.

'He was hasty last time, over-confident,' Edith argued. 'He will not fall again, Cedric. You know him better than that, and you know Harold, too. Will you go to Harold, at least to talk with him? He regrets to this day that he acted as he did and lost your friendship.'

'He did not lose my friendship. He still has it.'

'Then go to him, Cedric, please. He needs you at his side again. He has great respect for you, as well as love. I know he feels that your support will help him as surely as his own courage in what he has to do. You are worth a hundred men to him, his message said.'

Cedric chuckled ruefully. How could he help but put his head in the noose? Being Harold's friend had always been like that. For the last three years Cedric had been a devoted family man, a conscientious farmer and every minute of it had bored him, he had to admit to himself now. Of course he was deeply attached to Ingrid and the children, but he was still a warrior, and he longed for Harold and his adventures, his mad breathless race through each and every day.

'You know,' Cedric answered, 'long ago I used to think, in my innocence, that loyalty was a simple thing. I believed that a man could be loyal to his family, friends, his overlords and his king, and live with an untroubled conscience. Now I know that's impossible. Loyalty is a matter of choice. One friend or the other, one lord or the other, friend or king. You choose rightly, or wrongly, but by God, sooner or later you *have* to choose. It's been the same for you, hasn't it? Husband or father, that is what you have had to decide. Yes, I'll join Harold, and be damned for my sins if need be.'

'Thank you, Cedric,' Edith said sincerely, taking his hands in hers. 'You will make him so happy. And he is right; one Cedric Shieldless is worth a hundred others. That name alone will warn England that Godwin and his sons are coming back!'

'You flatter me,' Cedric grinned, 'And I like it. Where does he want me to meet him?'

'Take what men and ships you can, and sail west along the coast until you meet him.'

Cedric nodded agreement. Then they fell into an awkward silence. Cedric suddenly longed to talk about more personal matters while they had these minutes together. They had never been alone long enough to talk freely about what was in their hearts in all the years they had known each other, and it was no easier now. He was married to Ingrid, and she was a Queen of England who had also taken on the mantle of a nun. They might as well have been in the midst of a crowd for all that they could confess to each other.

Cuthbert and Harold ran past outside, shouting.

'Are they yours?' Edith asked, looking out past the curtain with the wistful interest of a childless woman. Long ago she had told Cedric that she was a virgin wife. Rumours at court had contradicted this, saying either that she was frigid, but only with Edward, or that Edward was impotent. Cedric did not know the truth, and he did not want to.

'Yes,' he confirmed. 'The elder is my stepson. The little one is named for Harold.'

'They are fine boys.'

'Thank you. I have a daughter too, just six months old.'

'You must be very happy. And your mother, how is she?'

'She died, last year.'

'Oh, I am sorry.'

'I miss her a great deal,' Cedric admitted. 'But you grieve and go on living. The king recently lost his mother also. I suppose you heard about that?'

'Yes, messengers came to tell me Emma was dead,' Edith replied, and with a grim smile she added: 'Edward sent them with instructions that I was to go into mourning. Perhaps he thought I would be rejoicing! But enough of death and mourning. Let us think of happier days to come, shall we? Help my father and brothers win back what is theirs, and then I shan't have to rot in those dreadful cloisters any more. We can all be together again. I pray for it, Cedric. And I am so grateful to you for what you are doing.'

She surprised him with a kiss then, and his old desire for her flared up suddenly. He acknowledged to himself that he would have done anything for her even if his friendship with Harold had never been.

'We will meet again,' he answered her, 'if I have to break down the door of your cell myself!'

Cedric stood in the yard to watch the cart out of sight. When he went into the house it was as a warrior, his head and heart racing with a yearning for battle and an impatience to be reunited with his best friend. He put all thoughts of treason and danger aside, and reminded himself of Harold saying that the game was not worth playing unless it was played to be won. He looked out his mail-coat and helmet, and took his sword down from the wall, and for the first time in three years became Cedric Shieldless in spirit as well as in memory.

'What are you doing?' asked Ingrid, alarmed. 'Cedric, what has happened?'

'The charm has worked, my love,' he told her. 'My sword was stolen from my hand, but today it is mine once more. It's war, wife. And I must go.'

'You can't!' Ingrid cried, distraught. 'What of your home? What of the children? You said you had finished with war!'

'I meant it when I said it, but it's Harold who calls for me. Don't worry, my love, I'll be back. And if not, my will is made . . .'

'I don't want your will! I want you,' Ingrid protested, trying to hold him back. Cedric kissed her, and held her at arms' length; he spoke to her kindly but intently as he would have to his children.

'Ingrid,' he said, 'if a man is born a warrior, he can be nothing else. He cannot be a monk, or a farmer, or a potter or a wheelwright. All my life, I have been led to battle as surely as if God himself had taken my hand to guide me. It happened when I reached the age of manhood at fifteen; I was at Guildford when Prince Alfred and his company were slaughtered. It happened again when I was chosen by God to avenge that murder by killing Olaf Ericsson. It is happening now. There is nothing I can do about it. If I put down this sword and stayed at home . . . well, it's simply impossible for me to do it, that's all. It would be like Edward denying that he was destined to be king – or Godwin and Harold accepting defeat. Such things just cannot be.'

Cedric caused quite a stir in the sleepy town when he rode out to raise fighting men for Harold. He paraded his horse about, his sword held high, calling the citizens out.

'Remember Cedric Shieldless?' he bellowed to the gathering crowd. 'I am he! Cedric Shieldless is going to war. Who will follow him?'

Excited boys whispered among themselves, old fighters talked of former glories; children fought mock battles; wives called their husbands back to their homes. Mothers dragged eager sons away, while brothers nudged each other to be the first to volunteer. In the midst of the throng, Cedric sat his mount like a giant from the old legends, drunk with the admiration of the crowd.

'Well?' he demanded, 'are there any warriors here, or is Reading full of basket-weavers and tailors? Will Cedric Shieldless's own town let him go to war alone?'

'I'll go with you!' shouted one, and after that the shout was taken up by a score of others.

They were all committed to Cedric's service before it occurred to them to ask the enemy's name.

II

Six tall-prowed ships could be seen through the mists, no more than a mile away. They came with sails furled and oars pounding, and Cedric watched them keenly from his place in the bows of his flagship. The newcomers outnumbered his own company by two to one, and he prayed that they were Harold's fleet and not the King's. Cedric's three ships had crossed the Bristol Channel two days before, and had since been hugging the south coast of Wales, and he was afraid that, in cutting across the broad reaches of the channel, he might have missed Harold. Now his men were on the alert, and only the beat of oars and the wash of the swell disturbed the tense silence.

'If they are the king's ships, turn and run!' Cedric advised the captain.

'Turn and run?' the older man scoffed. 'Some sailor you are! Have you ever tried to turn one of these against the wind? It's like flogging a team of dead oxen uphill!'

'Then we meet either welcome company, or death,' Cedric shrugged.

The six ships came on, deliberately making towards them. Armed soldiers could be seen at the gunwales, prepared for battle as were Cedric's men. White spray spat up from their glistening oars, and bright water creamed around the squat bows.

'Do they look like Irishmen?' the captain asked.

'I don't know what Irishmen look like,' Cedric retorted. 'Do you?'

Even as he spoke, however, he caught his breath and leaned forward, peering at the nearest of the ships. At the helm stood a tall, well-built man in chain-mail and helmet, a man of noble stance with long moustaches; it looked very much like Harold. As their vessels ploughed to within a few hundred feet of each other, Harold's voice carried across the sea, calling:

'Cedric Shieldless!'

It was more than a greeting. It was also a call to his men, and a cry of triumph at having his most trusted friend back at his side.

'Harold Godwinsson!' Cedric yelled back.

Then the men of all nine ships exchanged greetings and war cries. Oars were raised like standards, glinting wet in the pale sunlight, and axes were crashed against shields. Lusty and heroic songs were struck up as the two flagships bumped together, almost nose to nose. A plank was thrown across, and Cedric bounded over to meet Harold. They hugged and laughed and thumped each other vigorously, while Gurth and Leofwine laughed to see their brother dance such a jig of comradeship with the legendary Cedric Olaf-Slayer.

'You soft farmer!' Harold good-humouredly abused his friend. 'Three years you've been stalking in your hayfields! What were you trying to do, make me feel like a leper?'

'You stayed away from me as long!' Cedric reminded him. 'Is it my fault you went vagabonding off to the far ends of the Earth?'

'No, nor was it mine,' Harold chuckled, 'I do believe Edward had something to do with it. Let's go and ask him, shall we?' His face suddenly grew serious, and quietly he went on: 'Cedric, my dear old friend, the last time we saw each other I called you a coward. I must have been mad. Will you forgive me?'

Cedric put his arm across Harold's mail-clad shoulders.

'There is nothing to forgive,' he said. 'I know you didn't really think I could have stopped Sweyn killing Bjorn. You were mad, with grief, and with anger. Any man would have been. A more dutiful friend would have stayed by your side at such a time, no matter what you said. You have no more to be sorry for than I.'

'God's truth, I swear it's going to be as good as before! Now I know we can win! Look,' Harold said with a sweeping gesture at his ships, 'I have a thousand warriors here, all good fighting men of Ireland. And now you have brought me more . . .'

'Not really all that many to go against the king,' Cedric observed.

'More will join us in Wessex,' Gurth interrupted eagerly. 'We've had promises of support.'

'And my father has a bigger force still,' Harold put in, 'mainly Flemish, thanks to Tostig's brother-in-law, Count Baldwin. He is as interested as anyone in seeing Godwin's family get back its lands. And as Gurth says, more will rally to us from Wessex when they see how strong we are. We will have three thousand or more by the time we march on London. A few more weeks, and the numbers would have been even greater.'

'Then why did you not wait?' Cedric asked.

'Father is anxious to move swiftly,' Harold explained. 'Have you heard that Duke William has been to London to see Edward?'

'I have, yes. But what is so important about that?'

'It's very important. The rumour going around Normandy – all around France, in fact – is that Edward is going to name his bastard cousin William as his heir! Frankly, we don't believe it, because

334

Edward has much closer kin than a first cousin once removed whom he hardly knows. But we cannot take any chances. We want to be back in the Witan again in time to vote against any suggestion that William may succeed. I ask you, what true Englishman wants to be ruled by a Norman? There are too many damned Normans in office in England already. That is why we're sure we can call plenty of Englishmen to our banner.'

'It will be good sport,' laughed Leofwine. 'Tossing a few Normans out of the Witan.'

'What are your plans then?' Cedric asked.

'Father and I will raid along the coasts until we meet. We'll gather all the men we can on the way, then face Edward again. And we shan't back down this time, as we had to at Tetbury.'

'But you'll be making war on your own people of Wessex!'

'They can always choose to join us first.'

'But what a choice,' Cedric mused. 'Defy the king, or risk the wrath of Godwin.'

'You made it quickly enough,' said Harold. 'You have no doubts, do you?'

'Doubts? Now that I stand here among warriors again? My friend, the most exciting thing I've done these last three years was to fetch the midwife when my wife was in labour. That's no place for a man, I can tell you. Let's get on with your war, Harold Godwinsson!'

He had cause to remember his words many times in the days that followed, for when Harold's fleet reached England's shores they found themselves making war on the weak as well as on the strong. They landed first at a Somerset village where the inhabitants had heard wildly exaggerated tales about the strength and purpose of the warriors from Ireland. Many ran to hide in the hills, but those who stayed presented Harold with a gruesome offering of peace. They had clubbed to death the alderman and two of his kinsmen who had urged them to resist the invaders, and the corpses were displayed on a cart ready for Harold when he led his men up the beach.

'What place is this?' Harold raged at the waiting villagers.

'Minehead, my lord,' came the humble answer.

'Well, people of Minehead, I am Harold Godwinsson, once Earl of East Anglia and southern Mercia, and here beside me is Cedric Shieldless.' Harold paused to let that sink in, then went on grimly: 'We are fighting to restore my father, Godwin, as your rightful Earl of Wessex. Will your young men join us?'

There was a short consultation among the villagers.

'We respect you and your father greatly, my lord,' one of them said at last, 'as you can see for yourself. We dealt with these fools who told us to rise against you. But we are poor, simple folk who cannot tell which lord is right, the king or Earl Godwin. All we want is peace.'

'There is no peace for the doves when the hawks hunt,' Harold said sharply. 'Do not worry your heads with the right or wrong of it. Just remember that the king is in London, and can't hurt you. We are here, and can.' He made a quick estimate of the size of the village and added: 'Give me fifty of your men and some provisions, and we will leave you unharmed. Defy us, as those wretches would have done, and you will share their fate.'

Given no choice, Minehead surrendered its men and food, and the people were relieved to see the fleet depart with no injury or damage done. Harold had a price to pay, however. News of his arrival and his purpose spread rapidly along the coast, and he soon found that other ports were going to be less submissive. The very next town was ready for them, and a rabble of some three hundred fyrdmen gave the ships a hostile reception as they sailed into the harbour.

Harold's ships went into the wharves like angry swans among yapping dogs; they splintered small fishing boats and thundered into the harbour walls. Scores of warriors teemed ashore. Townsmen and raiders met on the muddy waterside and in the narrow streets, with shouts and groans and the hammering clash of steel on iron. Harold and Cedric were at the head of their men, cutting and hacking mercilessly at the defenders as their superior strength slowly pushed back the fyrd. Some of the town's fighters deserted and ran into the fields. Men at the rear of the invading army smashed in the doors of houses and shops for plunder. In one a brand was snatched from the fire and thrown spitefully into the wall hangings, and within minutes the house was blazing. In other dwellings, women were dragged from their hiding places and raped, their menfolk killed if they dared interfere. More houses were fired from the first. The wood and thatch town began to burn like a yardful of log piles, and families ran shrieking from their homes into the very hands of the foe. At the spearhead of the attack, too busy to know of the slaughter in their wake, Harold and Cedric still advanced with bloody axes and swords swinging.

The rout took less than an hour. The last defenders having fallen or fled, the two pirate leaders walked, breathless and bemused, back through a town of torn streets and crackling smoke. Dead and mutilated men lay in pools of mud and blood, amid litters of unwanted loot. Weeping women clutched bawling children, and the old people watched aghast as the pillaging continued unchecked.

Some of the raiders were getting drunk on stolen wine and ale, and others were turning upon their own companions in fierce arguments over booty.

'We have taught Wessex a hard lesson today,' Harold said with some remorse, as they returned to the dockside. He caught his brother Leofwine by the arm, asking: 'Have we lost many?'

'A few,' Leofwine reported. 'We were far too strong for them. I would think we lost no more than six or seven, and one or two are wounded.' He pointed across the street and said: 'There's one badly hurt there. I think it would be kind to put him out of his misery. There's nothing we can do for him.'

Cedric saw a man lying doubled up on his left side, moaning weakly and clutching at a spear that had penetrated deeply between his ribs. He was Guthrum, a man Cedric had known all his life. Cedric gave a cry and ran to him, he knelt beside him and gently turned his head to look into the contorted face. Guthrum's glazing eyes were those of a man betrayed.

'Damn you, Cedric!' he wheezed. 'Damn you and your boasting! Come on, great warrior, prove your courage again! You end it for me, if you have the guts . . .'

The man was in terrible agony, and he began to sob and writhe. Cedric, numbed by his bitter words, slowly pulled himself up straight, taking his sword in both hands. Guthrum himself had laid on him the obligation to release him from his torment, and deep in Cedric's mind lived the knowledge that there was no turning away from the task. Later he would be amazed how easy it was. He raised the broad blade and dashed it down with all his strength, mercifully severing Guthrum's throat.

'You knew him?' Harold asked, coming to Cedric's side.

'Since we were children,' Cedric nodded. 'Before you, he was my closest companion. Do you know something, Harold? The day I killed Olaf Ericsson, I did more than rid the world of a murderer. I breathed in his evil spirit as he died. His soul lives in me. One demon is born as another is slain. Perhaps Guthrum knew that. Perhaps that's why he cursed me.'

'Nonsense,' Harold told him. 'Pain robs a man of his reason. So does knowing he's dying. He'd even have damned the priest who came to give him the last rites.'

Cedric was surprised how readily he accepted Harold's explanation, and with what little charity he now regarded the corpse of Guthrum. Coldly, he said: 'He chose to come, didn't he?'

Gurth came up to them, pinch-faced with indignation. He had brought some men with him to carry the body of a young woman. She had been stripped and savagely slashed to death.

'Look at this!' Gurth raged. 'Was this necessary? We came to fight men, not women and children. What are we, warriors or wolves? This will do our cause no good at all, in the sight of man or God'

'Who did this?' Harold demanded of the crowd.

'Wild Brian,' an Irishman replied, as if it should be obvious.

'He always kills his women,' another snorted.

'Find this Brian and bring him here,' Harold ordered.

Wild Brian appeared without protest, a look of puzzlement on his face. He was well-named, for he was a big man, bull-shouldered and mad of eye, and his brute features were almost entirely covered with a tangle of wiry red hair. He presented himself before Harold as though he expected some sort of reward for his day's labours, but could not understand why he had been singled out.

'You killed her?' Harold asked him.

'Killed her,' Brian grinned. 'Yes, me.'

Harold did not waste any more time. He turned to Gurth.

'Take the pig,' he commanded sharply, 'and hang him.'

Brian's temper erupted then with frightening force, and it took a dozen strong men to drag him to the tree. Some of the wild man's kinsmen and friends fought to free him, but were quickly beaten out of the way. Gurth showed no hesitation. A rope was tied around the madman's thick neck and looped over the stoutest branch. Brian was hauled up, kicking and choking, without any hearing. His friends watched in seething silence while Brian the Wild thrashed about in his final throes.

'Go back to Ireland, if you cannot stomach his punishment,' Harold told them. 'And I swear before you all, any man who touches a woman or child from this moment on will suffer a like fate. I will keep that vow if I have to hang one of you on every tree from here to London.'

'It's going to be a difficult journey,' Cedric muttered, watching the signs of discontent, 'if it's going to be like this all the way.'

'We won't always have such trouble,' Harold said confidently. 'There will be plenty who choose to join us, especially when the news of this day gets around.'

At the next town he was proved right. There, upwards of two hundred armed fyrdmen cheered Harold's fleet in to shore, pledging their loyalty. They showed him two more ships ready to sail with him and, more important, were able to warn him of what lay ahead.

'Most of the towns round these parts are with you,' the leader of the fyrdmen told Harold. 'Not Ilfracombe; they're waiting for you there. They've set booms across the harbour to trap your ships, and there's a large band of the Devon fyrd lying in wait.'

'How many?' Harold wanted to know.

'It's hard to say. Possibly five hundred. Men have been going there from all over the shire at the king's orders.'

'Pass it by,' advised Cedric.

Harold thought for a minute.

'No,' he decided. 'We have to show we can deal with anything Edward sends against us. We will attack them tonight, but not in the way they expect.' He asked: 'How far is Ilfracombe?'

'By land? Five miles along that road. By sea it's . . .'

'Right, then we will go along that road with the main force,' Harold resolved. 'Gurth, you take the ships and make as if to attack the town. But keep clear of the harbour. Be there an hour before midnight, and make all the din you can to draw their attention. We will strike from their rear.'

'It could be a trap,' Cedric whispered. 'This may be just what they planned.'

'I think not,' Harold argued. 'But we will go carefully, all the same. If it does turn out to be treachery, our new friends here will be the first to die.'

The men of Ilfracombe were dozing at their watch fires when Gurth's ships rose up like shadows from the starlit water. Gurth and his men loudly gave voice to insults and war cries, and beat upon their shields. The startled town guard snatched up their weapons and ran down to their beached boats, ready to row out and hurl firebrands the moment the ships became ensnared in the waiting tangle of logs and chains.

When Harold and his army came rushing through the streets behind them, it took a moment for them to realise that they had been trapped with their backs to the sea. Flaming torches and bright steel were reflected in the black waves, and shouts and the clash of arms rent the night. Fighting superior numbers and with no room to move, the defenders were gradually pushed out from the shore. They battled gamely first in ankle-deep surf, then went deeper as the fight went against them. Men died, and floated amid the living all along the crimson beach, until at last the frightened fyrd surrendered and begged Harold for mercy. Harold called his warriors back, and the defeated ones staggered out of the water, leaving a hundred or more for tomorrow's tide to throw up on the sands.

'Now fight with us,' Harold offered. 'I can promise you better leadership, if not better fortune.'

Better leadership was what most of them chose, and Harold's army grew still stronger. Tales of his victories were carried through the south-west. He found some communities deserted as he went, the inhabitants having decided that they would die neither for the king nor for Godwin. Other places contested him and were subjected to fire and the sword, but still more greeted him as a hero and added men and ships to his forces. He sailed to the meeting with Godwin with twenty vessels and more than twenty-five hundred soldiers.

Once they came upon a squadron of the king's ships, rowing hard against a stiff wind about a mile to starboard. Harold's rebels jeered and laughed as they cruised past. By the time Edward's sailors had turned their awkward boats and set sail, Harold's masts were vanishing over the horizon.

Then, one morning in September, Harold's and Godwin's armies came together. On a lonely windswept beach whole sheep and pigs were roasted among the dunes, and some five thousand men drank and joked and danced, wrestled and sang raucous songs. With Godwin were his other sons, Tostig and Wulfnoth, and Haakon, Sweyn's thirteen-year-old son. Godwin, now over sixty years old, laboured these days under the toll of age and stiffness, but today his heart was once more that of a lion, and his eyes twinkled with youthful eagerness. He regaled Cedric and Harold with tales of his own campaign.

'Ah, you should have seen it!' he roared, 'I swear I doubled my forces that day we put in to Dover. Never did you see such a welcome! The people remembered the humiliations Edward and his damned Normans subjected them to. There were some poor French and Norman merchants unlucky enough to be in the port when we arrived. The townsmen picked them up bodily and threw them in the sea, and all their goods with them. We made bonfires from their wine barrels. I knew we could not fail then. I knew it would be like this, and by the Lord, just look what we have to show Edward now!'

'Aye, we're back, right enough,' Harold said. 'What are your plans now?'

'We march directly to London. Edward's army is in confusion. He's got the fyrd running here, there and everywhere, scattered like a flock of frightened crows, either trying to find us or trying not to. I've had some reliable reports from my thanes who have been in London recently. The king could not get Earl Leofric to help him because he's too old and sick; Earl Siward neither, because he's being troubled by the Scots. All Edward has huddled around him are a few Norman toadies and the housecarls, and they're going to be no problem for an army like ours.'

'That's grand news,' Harold told him. 'Why don't you rest for a few days? You're looking tired, and we have time on our side.'

'Rest?' Godwin echoed. 'Now? When it's nearly all over and

Duke William's bragging to the whole of Europe that he's to be the next king of England? This is no time for rest. The saints preserve us, boy, what more do I have to do to prove that I'm still as tough as my sons? Shall I wrestle with you, or run a race?'

'No, no, you don't have to prove anything to me,' his eldest son placated him, laughing yet wondering how many other men over sixty possessed the energy of his father. 'I just think that a successful army is all the better for refreshing itself while it can.'

'Aha!' Godwin bellowed. 'So it's you that wants to rest, and you use my age as your excuse! Gather your rabble together, my son. We are setting out for London this very day, and I'll bet my sword I'm still in the lead when we get there.'

'He still has the vigour of a man half his age,' Harold told Cedric, as they began sorting and rounding up their men. 'But I think he believes time is running out for him now. He can't wait to make good his losses. You watch him on the march. He'll keep going now, if he kills us all!'

They did watch the old man, and Cedric saw that Harold was right. Godwin was strong enough in spirit thanks to the success of the summer campaign, and he was urged on by his impatience for a confrontation with Edward the Confessor. Yet though he marched determinedly, it looked as if his legs occasionally threatened to give at the knees, and his neck sometimes seemed incapable of holding his head as erect as he wished. Even when they got a horse for him, the strain of the journey showed in his sagging back and bleary eyes. His thoughts came slowly now; his orders were sometimes confused, and he mumbled to himself during the day and slept badly at night. When he caught his sons eyeing him he snapped at them to mind their own business, and for a while afterwards made all the more effort to push himself harder than he could afford to go. He drank too much, and once or twice was violently sick. Yet still he refused to rest, and they reached London in an astoundingly short time for a man of Godwin's age and condition. On the fourteenth day of September they faced Edward with only the width of the Thames between the two armies. Godwin had to be helped down from his horse. He sat on a tree stump, swaying slightly, trying to make out distant details that were beyond the range of his eyes.

Edward's throne had been brought to the north bank, and he sat there surrounded by his court. He had with him, too, a larger following of soldiers than Godwin had been led to expect, though it was by no means an overwhelming force. They stood, deathly quiet, in a peaceful green field before the white walls of Edward's palace and the rising height of the new West Minster Abbey, while

341

from down the river sounded tuneless peals of bells in older London churches, celebrating the feast of the Exaltation of the Holy Cross. Ecclesiastical intervention came in the rotund shape of Bishop Stigand, an ambitious churchman who had basked in the patronage of Edward's mother Emma, who was sent across the river at the head of a delegation from the king. Stigand was seeking a new benefactor and he did not mind whether Edward or Godwin proved victorious, as long as he could be friend to the winner.

'The king has appointed me to mediate,' announced the pompous Stigand.

'I'm not surprised,' Godwin answered gruffly, 'since you have the ability to look both ways at once. What suggestions have you to make?'

Stigand kept his temper. He could tolerate a great deal in order to advance his own interests.

'First, before I am able to offer you anything,' he said, 'the king wants you to disperse your army.'

'Impossible. I am here to obtain all the titles and lands my family had before we were exiled. This army stays in the field until I get them.'

'Then you will have to come across the river and talk to him yourself, but with no armed men.'

'That I will do, but my soldiers can soon follow me over if need be.'

Godwin took all five of his sons and his grandson on the ferry, but he left Cedric in command with orders to tear London apart if there were any hint of trickery. On the other side of the water, Godwin found that the symbolic golden axe of peace had been laid on a table covered in purple cloth, ready to seal an agreement if agreement there could be. He also observed that Edward was accompanied by numerous Normans in high office, including his nephew Earl Ralph of Hereford and Robert, Archbishop of Canterbury.

'Good day, my lord King,' Godwin called, from the safety of the ferry. 'You see that I am back. The nature of my coming may be unfortunate, but there was no choice open to me.'

'Unfortunate indeed, Godwin,' the pale and monkish Edward said evenly. 'Once you refused to punish a few criminals, and forced me to bring you to trial. Now, to get your own way, you commit a crime worse than theirs, and savage the whole south coast.'

'You accused me unjustly, and ordered me to punish my own people without trial,' Godwin corrected him. 'If I have hurt anyone on my way here, it is only those who failed to be loyal to me for the sacrifice I made for them. Had they stood at my side then, we could have settled all this long ago.'

'Can any man be loyal to two masters?' Edward argued. 'You have sorely injured men loyal to me. It is I who first commands the loyalty of Englishmen, Godwin, whether they be from Wessex or Northumbria. Or do you place yourself above your king?'

'I place myself in the place I believe to be mine, that is all,' Godwin replied. 'You know what place that is, my lord, so what I have to ask of you will come as no surprise.' He turned to Stigand, telling the Bishop: 'You had better get on with the work he gave you. I'm tired of shouting at him!'

Stigand, hands clasped before him in a pose of wisdom and humility, went before Edward and quietly repeated Godwin's blunt demands. Edward nodded as he listened, as if this were merely confirmation of what he had expected. He glanced in Archbishop Robert's direction, and saw a stoney fear in the prelate's face. Edward's Norman friends felt particularly vulnerable at the return of Godwin, and with good reason. Following the treatment of the Normans in Godwin's Dover raid, stones had been thrown at Norman houses, and threats made against their owners. Rumours that Edward intended to make Duke William his heir had not helped. Few English relished the prospect of rule by a foreigner with no interest in the country nor any legal claim to it other than being a cousin of Edward. With Godwin back in a position of power, the Normans domiciled in England knew the feeling against them would be deliberately heated up to boiling point. Godwin and his clan had vowed not to let William near the throne. William was not even a close relation of the Confessor as was Edward's nephew Ralph, who might have been more acceptable to the English despite his Norman birth, since he had already lived in England for some years. But Ralph appeared to have fallen from grace with the king lately. In looking about for a successor, Edward and his Norman court were also ignoring the king's nephew-in-exile Edward, son of his half-brother Edmund Ironside, and Edward Edmundsson's baby son Edgar. Ralph, Edward the Exile and Edgar were all more eligible than William. Besides, Englishmen argued, it was not too late for King Edward to take back his wife, and for her to give him a son. They feared that a Norman monarchy might be being forced upon them for no better reason than the profit of the Normandy Edward had loved for most of his life.

'I cannot advise you to reinstate Godwin as Earl of Wessex, my lord King,' Robert said earnestly. 'Knowing the man for the Devil's disciple that he is, I fear he will bring only sorrow to this kingdom. You could try offering him a bribe to take his army and go away.'

'A considerable bounty that would be,' mused Edward, eyeing the gathering on the south bank.

'With respect, my lord Archbishop,' Stigand interrupted, 'I am sure that would not satisfy Godwin. He does not intend to go away. That much is plain.'

'Then let him live here, but with limited property and power,' Robert pleaded.

'How can I tell him his powers are limited, when he has five thousand soldiers glaring at me across the Thames?' Edward sighed.

'But, Uncle,' Earl Ralph contributed. 'You surely cannot consider letting him come back unconditionally? He would start treating you as contemptuously as he did before!'

'Not unconditionally,' Edward assured him. 'Certainly not; though I have scant defence against his threats.' He thought for a moment, then told Stigand: 'Go to Godwin and say this to him. He and his family shall be fully restored to their former estates, but only with these provisions; he shall disband this army immediately, sending back the foreigners to wherever they came from with whatever reward he cares to give them. Further, he shall give up to me two hostages as proof of his goodwill and as surety against another uprising. One shall be his youngest son, the other his grandson. These two shall live with Duke William in Normandy with my guarantee for their safety and comfort until such time as I consider Godwin can be fully trusted.'

Stigand took the message to Godwin.

'What!' Godwin bellowed his contempt. 'Is that lily-faced monk still dictating terms to me . . . ?'

'I would think about it more carefully, if I were you,' Stigand counselled him. 'You must allow him some small victory. He cannot step down completely under the eyes of his men. The only choice is war. And that will lose you a lot of support, after he has gone so far to meet you.'

'He's right, father,' Harold said. 'We have in our grasp what we came for. Let's not throw it away.'

'That's all right for you to say,' Wulfnoth cut in vehemently. 'But why should I have to go away to Normandy, while the rest of you take the prizes here?'

'Shut up, boy; you'll do as you're told,' Godwin snapped, while he thought it over. 'We can get you back soon enough, once I have Edward in my hand again. Yes, you are right, Harold. I think we must agree to the king's conditions . . .'

Godwin stepped up to the table. He picked up the ceremonial axe and carried it to the king's chair, where he bent low to lay it at Edward's feet. A jarring pain struck at his back like a lance thrust as he tried to straighten up. His heart was beating painfully fast; he gritted his teeth and pretended to be still bowing to the king until he was able to rise. If Edward noticed, he gave no sign of it. He rose from his throne, took the axe and laid it before Godwin. Then, like two distant cousins making a show of affection, the two men exchanged the kiss of peace.

A half-hearted cheer went up from the troops on either side of the river. Few were really pleased by the apparent reconciliation, and some less so than others. Wulfnoth and his young nephew Haakon, both feeling betrayed and used by both Godwin and the king, stalked off to tell the ferryman to take them across to Godwin's old house at Southwark, where they would have a good grumble, and sulk and get thoroughly drunk.

Meanwhile, Archbishop Robert hurried away. He and many of his countrymen decided they would not stay out the day in England, but went to their houses and packed all they could take with them, and sent messengers ahead to Harwich demanding that ships be made ready. Late in the evening Robert, William Bishop of London and Ulf Bishop of Dorchester, together with a company of clerics and personal bodyguards, formed up in a large body and rode hard for the East Gate, but news of their flight had gone ahead of them, and they found a dangerously playful mob waiting at the gate to stop them or make them run the gauntlet.

The Archbishop's company charged through, hacking right and left with staves and swords. The crowd scattered, and a number of people were left lying injured in the street as the fleeing dignitaries galloped out into the dusk and made for the coast.

III

'And what of the mighty lands that Thorfinn Karlsefni and his people found to the west?' the story-teller asked his enraptured audience. 'Lands as far to the west as Jerusalem is to the east. Lands of great mountains and forests, rivers so full of fish that a man may scoop them up with his hands. Lands so vast that, even from the tallest mountain, a man cannot see across them. These lands are peopled with naked savages, and strange beasts, half horse, half bull. The seas around them are alive with monsters bigger than the whales that Greenland and Iceland know. Those who travelled with Thorfinn say that there is no end to these lands. It cannot be true that the world ends in an ocean-fall over the edge, as the ancients have it. The brink of the world is a precipice of rock, falling into Hell. And in these lands, that is where·the sun goes down at night, through a hollow mountain, leaving the rock encrusted with its fire. If we could learn the tongue of those savages, perhaps they could tell us where that mountain lies. Aha, Thorfinn the Icelander was a brave adventurer, but it would be a braver man still who would go in search of that dreadful chasm where the sun burns down in the depths!'

The gathering of nobles and thanes and their ladies sat murmuring in wonder, considering these things, and for a while even the generously-laden tables were forgotten. Few purported to have the answers to the extraordinary questions posed by the story-teller, and most looked to the wisest among them for their opinions. They looked to King Edward, who was believed to have some visionary powers because of his saintly aspect and his proven ability to heal the sick by the laying on of hands. They turned to Stigand, the new Archbishop of Canterbury. But at the high table, the thoughts of the leaders of the land were taken less with the mysteries of the new world than with the trials of the old.

Since the reinstatement of the rebel earls, this spring feast at Winchester was the first meeting between Edward and Queen Edith, and Edith's father Godwin. There was a tension in the air that could be felt, despite all efforts to forget the trials of the past. Edward and Godwin still remembered the differences that had wasted valuable years for them both, and both were still inclined to blame each other rather than themselves. Godwin still found himself opposed to everything Edward the Confessor stood for but, whereas in the old days he would have challenged this or any other king with conviction and swagger, he now did so with the bitterness and blunt indiscretion of old age. Edward, in turn, saw that he could do nothing to please Godwin, and had decided that he would never again try. There was also unease between Edward and Edith, that of an estranged couple brought together out of necessity rather than desire. Finally, Edward regarded Archbishop Stigand with distrust and dislike; he felt that his friend Robert had been deposed and replaced by a charlatan. Small wonder that, to the four most important people at the banquet, the magic of the West was as trivial as the unsolved riddle of why flies disappeared in winter. They were all too occupied in trying to make the best of their enforced closeness. They were all in a prison of their own making, and they were beginning to realise how much they were going to regret it.

'These beasts,' asked a listener. 'These half-horse things you spoke of, what manner of animal are they?'

'Devilish monsters,' the story-teller replied, 'such as no man here has ever seen. There is another that is half bear and half man, as tall as the rafters of this hall, and with the strength of a team of oxen. One of Thorfinn's men saw such a giant uproot a full-grown tree, and toss it easily as far as the best warrior here could hurl a spear. In the sea there are fish so huge that they could bridge the waters between England and Flanders, and in the mountains there are cats as big as wolfhounds. Other beasts there are with teeth so sharp that they can eat through trees; they build enormous dams across rivers wider than the Thames . . .'

'Beavers!' scoffed a more wordly man. 'I have seen such creatures in France!'

'Ah, and so have I,' said the story-teller quickly. 'But in Vinland the trees are three times higher and thicker, and so are the creatures that fell them. More, there is an evil in the air there, which can steal the mind of a man if he is careless and forgets to devote himself to prayer. Among Thorfinn's people there was one such man called Thorhall the hunter. He climbed to a high place and later was found quite mad, babbling to the rocks.'

'Then any man would be mad even to travel through such a land,' declared another, 'let alone walk to the edge of the world and look down into Hell.'

There was a silence then. No-one felt quite bold enough to gainsay that opinion. But Cedric had been drinking steadily, and now he jumped to his feet.

'I would go,' he boasted, 'if other men would follow me. If

ignorant savages can survive there, then good English warriors can. I would walk to the brink, but I don't know if I would look over. I have no wish to know what Hell looks like – yet.'

Laughter and applause greeted his words.

'Good old Cedric,' laughed Harold, 'a dreamer still. One of these days you really will go off on one of these ridiculous adventures of yours. I remember when you wanted to go to Byzantium, to join the Varangian Guard. Now it's the edge of the world.'

'Why not?' argued Cedric. 'No warrior should grow fat and bored, sitting at a table doing nothing but gorging. If there are no wars to fight, he should go out and find dragons to slay. Hey, story-teller, how long must one sail to reach these lands?'

'Thorfinn and his company journeyed many weeks,' was the answer. 'They sailed westward past Greenland through mountains of ice, until they reached the Stoneland and the Land of Wood that Leif Ericsson found before them, and then many more weeks to the south. Thorfinn stayed three winters, and upon their return he and his people defied anyone to live longer in that place. It is wild and cruel, he said. The winters are so harsh that there is nothing to hunt, and even in summer no crops will grow there. Also there is a distance between Earth and sky that makes a man feel lonely in himself, and too small in the order of things. It can drive him out of his mind. It is as if God forbids us to live so near to Hell.'

'Ah, now there I should think you have come close to a truth, my son,' said Archbishop Stigand wisely. 'Curiosity is a sin when one inquires into evil things, and there can be no more sinful curiosity than to seek the very lip of Hell. The Church could not sanction such a journey, Cedric.'

'Unless, of course, there were gold in the new land to bring back for the Church.' Godwin contributed sourly, referring to Stigand's well-known love of wealth, a guarded joke which caused some titters as Godwin added: 'Is there gold in these western wilds, story-teller?'

'Yes, there is gold in the trees,' the entertainer answered, causing gasps of astonishment around the hall.

'Gold, growing in the trees? How can that be? Surely Thorfinn would have returned with more riches than any man had ever carried before!'

'It grows only in the autumn,' the story-teller smiled, 'when the leaves die. Thorfinn's people said that never before had they seen such an incredible glory of colours than in the new land's wide forests. I'm afraid that is the only gold to be found there, my friends.'

It was an amusing way to end his tale, and his audience laughed good-naturedly at the jest he had made at their expense. They clapped and cheered, and paid him generously with a shower of coins.

'Most interesting,' acknowledged Stigand. 'I could build a sermon upon it for Easter.' He turned to the king, asking: 'What do you think, my lord?'

'Preach what you will, Stigand,' Edward said carelessly. 'I shall not hear it. I can attend no service held by you.'

Stigand was shocked.

'And why not, might I ask?' he gasped.

'Well might you ask, though you seem oblivious to all counsel. Pope Leo has refused to confirm you in your appointment. Therefore I cannot be seen to patronise you, nor to endorse your appointment either. That is the plain and simple answer.'

Stigand felt cruelly crushed. It was true that Rome had scorned him, for as far as the Supreme Canonical Court was concerned, the absent Robert was still Archbishop of Canterbury. Stigand's appointment, brought about by Godwin before Rome's nomination could be known, was unlawful. Pope Leo IX had refused to invest Stigand with the Pallium, the ultimate badge of office, and Stigand had made matters worse by simply acquiring the Pallium left behind by the fleeing Robert. In the eyes of the Church he was an imposter, but he had no intention of stepping down. He knew there was nothing Rome could do about his holding Canterbury in defiance of their wishes, short of sending an army of monks to bring the reluctant Robert back into England and drag Stigand out of the cathedral.

'If the Pope does me an injustice, need my king do likewise?' Stigand asked petulantly. 'How can they demand that Robert be Archbishop, when he chose to leave and refuses to come back? And was I not elected in the proper manner, with the approval of the Cathedral Chapter?'

Edward nodded wearily. He had to admit that the election of Stigand had been done with precise attention to form, unlike a previous occasion when Godwin had made an arrangement of his own in an effort to get a kinsman into the office, but that did not alter the fact that the Pope would not give his blessing. To Edward, the Holy Father's word was law. He would not oppose Leo on Stigand's behalf, especially as Stigand was Godwin's man. Edward had in fact tried to have the Chapter's decision reversed but Godwin and Stigand between them had too many friends in the Church. Now Edward's kingdom was the seat of a religious scandal that was being discussed throughout the civilised world, and nothing could have hurt this monarch more.

'You must examine your own conscience in this matter,' said Edward. 'It matters not who approves of you and who does not. It matters only that you be aware of the opinion of the Pope, the Church and your king. It is for you to recognise the right thing, and to do it.'

Stigand understood. He was being politely told that, if he had any sense of honour at all, he would save the king and the Church a great deal of embarrassment by resigning. The hint was a humiliation, but one which he was prepared to suffer. He would not give up anything, not after devoting his life, to God certainly, but also to reaching the greatest heights he could achieve.

The Church had not been his choice, after all, and he had borne much to make the most of it. It had been forced upon him as a child, when at the age of seven years his parents had given him into the service of God. It must have been in those dreadful early years, he was thinking now, when he had first determined to profit somehow from the fate that had been decided for him, and that old resolve had never died. In those cold, hard, spartan and hungry cells of the monastery – that was where his awareness of the need to survive must have been born, gradually hardening into an obsession, like the water in his bedside cup had hardened into ice on freezing winter nights. Now the riches and the luxuries of the Archbishopric were a just reward for those cold days, he considered.

Stigand saw in his memory the boy he had been, the confused and frightened child watching those gigantic gates crash closed on the outside world, on affection, on freedom, and on warmth. It was as if he had been sentenced for some crime he could not recall committing. Suddenly he was a muted child with tonsured head, wearing itchy coarse cloth shift, learning with an awful shock the harsh disciplines of monastic life. The lessons were learned quickly, because the beatings for disobedience or misunderstanding were felt like knife cuts for many days afterwards. Even the less severe punishments were an effective education, he remembered, feeling the hard stone floor where he had lain prostrate with face pressed to the rough pavings. He had spent hours like that, summer and winter, praying for forgiveness for breaking wind at the wrong moment, or some such trivial thing. Oh yes, the lessons were learned fast, yet the hardships had continued, year after endless year.

They were boys who had started out with normal, playful minds and limbs, but they had soon been whipped into a humble submission. Soon they had become little apostles of utter silence and motionless bodies, released only for devotions or work. A summer's day was a whole summer long, spent in prayer and chant and back-breaking labour. A winter's day was a black numbness, a cold paralysis of brain and body, which nevertheless had to be made to function as it was instructed, even on two frugal meals.

It was difficult to determine, even now, which of those seasonal routines had been the hardest to bear. Both, in their own ways, had been tortuous for their unchanging order, their relentless demands on physique and soul.

A winter morning meant leaving a bed which was a hard bench and thin straw mattress, and not enough blankets to keep out the chill, and stumbling out in the icy blackness before dawn with unfeeling feet fumbling for sandals on the stone. It was prayers on an empty stomach, walking in draughty corridors, and menial duties until pale daylight crept down the bare walls. Breakfast was a mouthful or two of tasteless porridge, a lump of bread and a cup of water, all taken in silence. Then followed more devotions, more work, and tedious studies, until the blessed night. Supper was bread and honey and a mess of boiled vegetables, after which came exhausted sleep.

Summer brought one or two more meals a day, but ages more of study and muscle-aching labour in the gardens. Summer days began at one-thirty in the morning for nocturnes, and went on and on towards distant night with matins and prime, tierce and vespers, confession, psalms, litanies, High Mass, service upon service and prayer upon prayer.

Oblates did not speak to each other, touch each other, make signs or smile, and no one but their masters spoke to them. They possessed nothing, they spoke only when spoken to, they went nowhere unless accompanied by a master, and they never left the monastery confines unless some errand made it necessary. Even then a master usually went with them. They read nothing but the Bible and their lesson books, the monastery rules or approved religious works. The slightest hint of boyish behaviour was punished with a beating, or abstinence from what little food they were accustomed to having.

Disciplines changed little when they became monks. Stigand and all his little dumb companions were twenty years old before they escaped out into the fresh air again as priests. They were reasonably free then, as long as they did not want to better themselves. But if they wanted to do well in the Church, there next came the years of bowing and scraping to people like Emma and Godwin, who blatantly used the influence the clergy had over the ordinary people to their own gain. Such people virtually preached their own self-advancing sermons from the pulpits, and used their own pretences at devotion to salve their consciences as they followed the gospels of power and wealth. And, dear Lord, thought Stigand, what hardships had they ever known?

Those were the prices that Stigand had paid for his high position, and only now was he able to consider them worth paying. He reckoned that he had earned what he had acquired now in those first thirteen years in the monastery, never mind all his efforts since. He could no more tear up his papers of appointment than he could have torn up those documents with which his parents had signed away his life.

'I am Archbishop of Canterbury,' he said firmly. It sounded like defiance of the king, but it was no more than re-assurance that he spoke the truth.

'Then I don't know what we can do about it,' Edward said blandly. 'Perhaps I should convene a meeting of the Witan. They can, if necessary, over-rule the Cathedral Chapter.'

Stigand had been expecting that, and had an answer ready.

'But my lord,' he said, with mock alarm, 'is that not the very thing you have been endeavouring to put a stop to all these years – secular interference in Church affairs?'

The king could hardly contain his anger at that, and his white cheeks turned a livid pink. He did not care to be slapped in the face with his own principles.

'Mother of God, you are a fine one to speak of secular interference!' he hissed. 'You, who won your office chiefly through that!' Turning to Godwin, he went on: 'And you: you wasted no time in taking up your old ways, did you? You make a hopeless trial of my life, Godwin!'

The old earl had been amused until then. He started to say something in his own defence, but was seized by a hacking cough. It had been a bad winter for him. Crippling pains and chills had confined him almost constantly to his bed, and he had been too weak to pursue his customary and well-loved plots. A failing appetite had wasted him away to half the great bull of a man he had been, and strong mead and wine had been his chief nourishment. Since last summer's wars he had had little exercise other than an occasional walk from his bed to the table and from the table to the latrine ditch. Only with the coming of the spring had he been able to raise sufficient strength even to get out of the house. The journey from Southwark to Winchester to join the king's Easter celebrations had all but finished him, and it was a clear sign of his failing health that his only achievement since his reinstatement as Earl of Wessex had been to get Stigand installed as Archbishop. In the old days, such a triviality would have been a few days' diversion for Godwin.

'Might I suggest,' he croaked, when his coughing was done, 'that you try making more representations to Rome? It seems to me that the only way to have this matter resolved is to offer the Church something it wants in exchange for Stigand.'

'Trust you to think of everything in terms of gold,' Edward said cuttingly.

'Well, right or wrong, it does rule the world,' Godwin shrugged. 'I'm not suggesting we try to bribe the Pope. I'm sure he wouldn't have it. I'm only saying it may be that we have not tried hard enough to persuade Rome of our cause.'

'*Your* cause,' the king corrected him.

'All right, we know full well you want Robert back. But has he shown any willingness to come?'

'Can you expect him to? After the treatment he received at the hands of my subjects?'

'He went in haste and fear,' Godwin scoffed. 'No one was going to hurt him.'

'He saw in the eyes of Englishmen that savagery which is the curse of this nation,' Edward argued. 'Sometimes I look at my flock and wonder if I am a shepherd to ignorant sheep, or to wolves in fleeces.' With that he lapsed into silence, longing for the days when he had been surrounded by his own kind, advised by people of refinement who had at heart his interests and the interests of Christian order. Now his mother was dead, people like Robert Champart had been forced to flee, and his nephew Ralph had become self-willed and unmanageable. What remained of his family after the ravages of the Vikings was scattered far and wide. His nephew Edward was still in Hungary, and his half-sister Aelfgifu was living in Brittany. One brief visit by his sister Godgifu had led to civil war with Godwin. He was alone again, hemmed in by ruthless people such as Godwin and Stigand. It seemed that the harder he applied himself to God's work, the more viciously he was beset by the forces of the Devil. It was a test of his faith, he understood, yet at times the testing seemed too severe for a mere mortal. The ways of God must needs be incomprehensible to man sometimes, he was fond of telling his court, yet he could not help wondering why such punishments were mercilessly heaped upon him while he was trying to do good works. His reign had hardly begun when his kingdom had been visited with the hardest winter in living memory, followed by murrain and famine and starvation. He had struggled to people his court with men of good faith and conscience, yet the bad had returned to triumph and drive out the good. In life there was a mingling of the bad with the good, like faulty threads running through an otherwise perfect tapestry, necessitating a lot of unpicking and re-weaving, but – merciful God! – must the whole of the work be destroyed time after time?

'Your subjects are English people who are content to remain English,' Godwin was saying. 'Your only mistake, if I may say so, my lord, was in trying to change England too soon, too sharply. This is an ancient kingdom. You cannot too rapidly stamp Norman ways upon it.'

'I tried to force nothing upon the English people,' Edward retorted indignantly. 'I tried to do no more than combine the English traditions of my father with the Norman refinements my mother taught me. I have respected everything English. It was the Danish invaders who did the damage, not I; the Danes of Canute's ilk who tore apart the England my father knew. You resented my changing anything, yet it was the stamp of the Danes you hated to see removed.'

'Danish England died eighteen years ago with Canute.' Godwin said impatiently. 'And all we who served Canute have known that ever since his ill-bred brats tried to take over what he left.'

'Have you really? Will you ever really admit that Canute's day is done? You tried hard enough to make another Canute of me: pressing for alliances with Denmark; fighting to retain the autonomous rule of the earls, like old Viking chieftains; trying to keep the Church submissive to secular interests, as if the Church were nothing but a pagan priesthood through which the messages of self-appointed gods are passed to the gullible peasants! I tried to trust you when I became king, Godwin. I tried to accept you as one of the elders of the realm, one of the most able and experienced men at my side. But you chose to be jealous of the friends I brought with me. You set out to unseat them, and perhaps to unseat me, too. I don't have to look very hard to see what it is you have had in mind all these years.'

Godwin was tired of the monk-king's whining, and careless of his opinion. He had proved himself in the halls of power, and he no longer worried for the future of his family, nor concerned himself with what the king thought of it. Further talk on the matter would only bore him. He ripped a piece from one of the Easter loaves, marked with the Cross of Christ, and put it to his mouth.

'If I have ever acted against the person of my lord king in any way,' he said, 'may this holy bread choke me!'

'You have never acted against my person, Godwin,' Edward said, 'but I believe it was you and your damned Danes who put me on the throne of England. How different my life would have been had Alfred not been so brutally slain . . .'

It sounded like a direct charge against Godwin. With his mouth still full, the Earl began to bluster in his usual way, and the piece of bread he had been about to swallow was sucked into his windpipe and choked him. Purple-faced, coughing and spluttering violently, he half-raised himself from the bench and bent forward, gripping the table. His chest heaved as he fought to dislodge the wad of bread and draw breath. People crowded around him, holding him steady and beating him hard on the back. Harold even tried to reach into his father's throat and prise the bread out.

It was all in vain. As Godwin gradually lost the battle for breath his strength left him. His mouth and eyes opened wide, and his contorted, beet-red face turned deathly white. He collapsed to the floor.

There was an awed silence throughout the hall as Godwin's sons carried their father away. The guests had all witnessed an act of God, a terrible and final judgment upon Earl Godwin, and the dreadful presence of God's avenging hand in their midst was a warning to all. Edward, no less shaken than his subjects, made the sign of the cross and knelt to pray. He asked for God's blessing and forgiveness for the whole assembly, and at that everyone followed his example.

'At last thou hast made known, oh Lord, the perpetrator of my brother's untimely death,' Edward prayed. 'By his own words Godwin has condemned himself, and thou hast punished him for his sins and perjuries. Have mercy on his soul, oh Lord, for by his own admission has he sacrificed himself for his wrong-doing.'

While the gathering knelt, trembling with wonder and murmuring confessions, Godwin's sons knelt to mourn the earl in his death chamber.

Edith wept on Harold's shoulder, and Cedric stood by him on the other side. The other sons of Godwin gazed in disbelief at the ruins of the man who had filled their lives, the father who had seemed as irremovable as the stars, as overpowering as the sun. Gytha threw herself across her husband's body and shrieked. It was Gurth and Leofwine who persuaded her to a more respectful stance. Grief there was aplenty in that little room, but greater than the sorrowing was the astonishment that Godwin could die. Yet there lay the white face of death. It was as if a great chasm had opened up in the earth and a huge and soundly-built house had fallen into it.

'We will never see the like of him again,' Harold declared, tears running freely down his cheeks. 'There never was a man so large in heart and body. He was hard and cunning, devious often, cruel sometimes, unrelenting and unafraid even of God, some said. But he was just, dauntlessly brave, and boundlessly generous to those who honoured him. If there is a special place in Heaven for warriors, as the Norsemen believe, then that is where Godwin stands now.'

As Harold spoke, Archbishop Stigand stood over the corpse of Godwin, chanting the last rites. Godwin, who had created kings, had created Stigand also, but that man was his last and least perfect creation. Stigand would prove to be one of the dangerously faulty strands in the tapestry that the house of Godwin had woven, one of the odd threads which, when pulled, would cause the entire work to unravel in ruins.

And at Stigand's side stood Godwin's third son Tostig, the thread of whose life his father had not handled as carefully as he should.

IV

I T was like travelling back into a dim and half-forgotten past,
Cedric thought, as he walked his horse into Bosham on a wet
summer morning. In that past, before meeting Godwin and Harold
for the first time, he had been an innocent who believed in honour
and honesty, who had believed the world to be a place where the
doer of right would prevail against the worst of evils, and never be
tainted by sin. How many men had he killed who did not deserve
to die, since those days, and how many crimes had he committed
out of loyalty to Godwin?

Yet so little of the town itself had changed. The townspeople
going about their tasks untroubled by the problems at Edward's
distant court looked the same; the house of Godwin still loomed
like a stern father over the little port. Did it matter that kings had
lived and died and left their marks upon the land, or that lords had
warred against each other for gain, only to pass into oblivion in
their turn? The sleepy harbour of Bosham and countless other little
English towns changed very little; people were born, built houses,
had children and died, and only by that much was any change
made. Was there, somewhere haunting this place, the spirit of a
fifteen-year-old Cedric who still believed that good was good and
wrong could never be right?

He rode on through the stockade gates of Godwin's hall, which
now belonged to Harold, who had become Earl of Wessex in his
father's place. He dismounted before the big open doors, and halted
in amazement.

The place was empty. It was nothing but a cavernous, black-
ribbed barn, cold and bare and smelling foully of animal droppings.
Bales of straw were heaped untidily where the great Lord Godwin
had sat in splendour at the head of his table. Cattle pens and horse
stalls, littered with dung and hay, stood where the curtained cots
had been. Milking cows munched from troughs where the most
high lords and ladies had feasted on rich foods, and where bright
and welcoming fires had roared, there was only a thick mess of
hoof-marked mud and cowpats. No brilliant shields or hunting
trophies or axes gleamed on the walls. There was nought but naked
wood, crumbling wattle and daub decaying like the damp dirt sides
of ditches, and crawling with beetles and spiders. And on the far

wall, where the magnificent golden dragon banner of Wessex had hung, there were only hangings of dusty cobwebs.

Cedric grabbed a cowhead by the arm.

'What in the name of God has happened here? Where is Lord Harold?'

'Ah, you thought to find him in this old place, did you, sir?' the man chuckled. 'No; it's all different now. Do you know the stables as used to be? You go along there – you'll see.'

Only when Cedric walked round to the ancient Roman granary did he understand. A team of workmen was being directed by Harold himself, who was poring over parchment plans with the master-builder. The stables had been ripped out of the ground storey, and new brick walls were being built between the Roman columns. An outside wooden staircase had been built up to the old offices on the floor above, and a doorway cut out at the top. Harold approached his friend with a broad grin.

'Well, what do you think?' he asked, with a proud gesture.

'I don't know yet. What is it you're doing?'

'What does it look like, idiot?' Harold laughed. 'This is the modern hall of Bosham. No longer a draughty old barn, but a real palace for the new Earl of Wessex. Not quite as good as Edward's, I'll admit, but I'm content to live more modestly!'

'But you've turned your father's hall into a cow byre!' Cedric cried.

'Yes, I know,' Harold laughed. 'He's probably raging at me somewhere up there, poor old fellow. Perhaps he's considering sending a thunderbolt to strike me dead. But I've decided this is the way it must be. Times are changing, my friend. We are not living in the dark age of the Vikings any more. I always said King Edward had a lot of good ideas about the way life should be lived, and if it's good enough for him, it's good enough for me. Come on, I'll show you around.'

Harold led the way up the fresh-smelling staircase and into the still musty maze of rooms on the upper floor. Some had been made into sleeping-quarters, others were to be used as studies, teaching rooms, servants' quarters and kitchens. Clean rushes covered the flagstone floors, and the furniture consisted mainly of the tables, benches and cots from the original hall. In the open windows Harold had had inserted some of the best coloured glass from Italy and the East, which made the hall look like a church, Cedric thought. On the walls, the faded Roman paintings of country scenes and gods and goddesses had been covered with tapestries or trophies of war, boar and stag heads.

In the biggest of the rooms, despite all the sawing and hammering down below, Harold's family was already installed. His mistress, Edith Swanneshales, greeted Cedric kindly as they entered. His mother, however, acknowledged him with a curt nod and went on with her weaving. Quite obviously, Gytha was less than pleased with her new home, and showed it by grumbling at Harold's four young children, Godwin, Edmund, Gunhild and Gytha, who were running about playing noisily.

'I'll have to make a hole in that roof to let out the smoke before we light a winter fire in here,' Harold was saying, pointing through the wreckage of the ceiling to the rafters and tiles. 'I can't understand why the Romans themselves didn't do it. Otherwise it makes a grand but comfortable house, don't you think?'

'A grand tomb,' the black-garbed Gytha commented drily before Cedric could answer. 'If God had meant people to live in rock holes, he would never have led them out of the caves. May your father forgive you, Harold; God rest his soul.'

'Mother doesn't like change,' Harold smiled. 'But she'll get used to it. You like it, don't you, Edith?'

Edith glanced quickly at Gytha, working up the courage to voice an opinion of her own. In six years this quiet woman had borne four children for Harold and now was pregnant with a fifth, but she was as lovely as Cedric remembered. She was called Edith Swanneshales – Edith of the Swan-neck – because of her graceful long, white neck. Harold had fallen in love with her at first sight. He could not marry her because she was a fairly close cousin, a grand-daughter of his mother's cousin Hilda, but he had defied all conventions and scandal by determining to live with her whether or not the Church would agree to wed them. Cedric remembered also that her late grandmother, Hilda, had been wife to Earl Eadwulf of Northumbria, the man summarily executed by Hardicanute for the murder of Prince Alfred. Eadwulf's younger brother Gospatrick was stepson to King Edward's half-sister Aelfgifu. When Edward's family had been exiled in 1013, Gospatrick had been brought up by Cedric's mother, and was almost like an elder brother to him. Now here was Edith Swanneshales, Harold's second cousin and the great-niece of Cedric's foster-brother, forming another piece of the pattern of their life-long friendship.

'You have made me a home a woman can be proud of, my lord,' Edith told Harold, finally daring to gainsay Gytha. 'I am grateful to you.'

'Indeed, it's very fine,' Cedric nodded, but to placate Gytha, he added: 'But changes take a lot of getting used to.'

'There is one more thing I have to show you,' Harold said

mysteriously. 'The most important, as far as you are concerned. Come with me.'

He took Cedric to the small work-room where women servants did much of the domestic needlework. Two girls were there at their duties now, weaving a cloth big enough to cover a bed. Cedric, stepping closer, saw that it was in fact a banner bearing a device in bright red, an armoured warrior of fierce countenance, holding axe and shield.

'The fighting man,' Harold explained. 'This is my own banner, to be carried alongside the golden dragon of Wessex . . .'

'Excellent!'

' . . . and it is also to be your badge of office.'

'What?'

'It will be carried beside you wherever you go to carry out official duties for me,' the earl told him, with a smile. 'I have a new post for you, my dear old friend. Nothing so humble as Shire-Reeve of Berkshire this time, but a position I have created especially for you. I am making you High-Reeve of the Wessex Shires. You will be my second-in-command, my right hand in matters military, civil, financial, or anything else. Next to me, you are to be the most high-ranking thane in Wessex, with my authority to command or over-rule any other reeve from Dover to Land's End.'

Cedric knew of no answer to give.

'You're not saying no, are you? You weren't planning something else, like sailing off to the lip of Hell, for instance?'

'Of course I'm not saying no. And I'm not going farther west than Land's End. I just can't believe it, that's all. A thousand thanks, my friend. I only hope I can live up to your trust.'

'You've never let me down yet. I don't know where I could find a man more loyal and trustworthy. Of course, it means you'll have to bring your wife and children to live here, with us. We'll have good times, just like the old days!'

'Certainly we'll come. And it will be different, living in a house of stone. Like being in church all the time.'

'Not if I have anything to do with it!' Harold grinned. 'All right then, come and see your new home. You can have the downstairs half.'

As they stepped carefully through the mess of masonry and carpentry on the ground floor, Harold slipped and nearly fell. Seized by sudden pain, he clutched at his left arm, and then sat down to rub at his left leg.

'What's the matter?' Cedric inquired.

'That time I was thrown from my horse, years ago, remember?' Harold gasped. 'I think it never properly healed. Both arm and leg hurt like Hell's own torment when it's wet, like today. By God, it hurts . . .'

'Shall I send for a physician?'

'No, leave me. I'll be all right.'

Harold vigorously rubbed his arm and leg, took a deep breath, and appeared to be willing the pain out of his body. Then he got up again, a look of relief slowly smoothing the lines from his face.

'You should rest if it is bad,' Cedric advised him.

'There's no time for rest. These are busy days, Cedric. I want to get this building well under way before I return to court.'

'What's the hurry?'

'There are too many people I don't like, sneaking too close to Edward.'

'And you think to scare them away?'

Harold smiled: Cedric had learned little about the different approaches to politics, despite his close connections with the highest in the land.

'I am not Godwin,' Harold said patiently. 'His methods are not mine. Father had one great failing, you know,' he went on casually inspecting a beam, a flagstone, a new stand of brick. 'He was stubborn. He resisted change like a mule fights against the shafts. He knew he must be shackled with it in the end, but his obstinacy could not let him admit he was wrong. But for that one serious fault, he could have been even greater than he was. I learned a lot from my father, Cedric. There were things he taught me knowingly, but yet more things he never realised he was teaching me. One of those lessons was not to fight change, but to use it to advantage. You can't influence people like Edward by opposing them. But if you appear to do what they want, but do it your own way, and then convince them you are right, then the outcome is satisfaction for both parties!'

'So, tell me of your plans.'

'Well, they are vague as yet, but they will harden as time goes by. One thing is certain: Edward, good king that he is, needs guidance. I intend to be the one to guide him. He likes me and he is growing to trust me, which is something father could never claim.'

'And what will you guide him to do?'

'To be a little more decisive about the succession, for a start. Edward has kept very quiet about it. He won't say anything, even to his closest companions, about William's claim that he is to be Edward's heir.'

'And you are as strongly opposed to William as Godwin was,' Cedric suggested.

'Definitely. Would you like to be ruled by a Norman King?'

'Edward is half Norman,' Cedric shrugged. 'I don't see the difference.'

'But he's half English, too. William would be different. He would try to make England nothing more than a province of Normandy. We have already seen what happens when Normans get too much power here. They are an arrogant race. So sure that they are right in all things, and that we English are nought but ignorant serfs.'

That statement led Cedric neatly to a subject he had been waiting to broach.

'Harold,' he said seriously. 'Is there going to be anyone left by the time Edward dies? You know the court is in mourning again . . . ?'

'Aye, for Edward the Exile. Is it not strange that King Edward's nephew should die so mysteriously within days of landing in England for the first time since he was sent away as a tiny babe? No wonder his poor wife scuttled back to Hungary with little Edgar; she must have been terrified that, they, too, would die in their sleep. Even our own wise men are asking why it should be that the king was not allowed to see the face of his kinsman, and why it is that the kinfolk of King Edward are still dying the moment they set foot back on English soil.'

'Certainly everyone is peering about at everyone else at court.'

'Are you saying that I am suspected?' Harold asked grimly. 'Do you suspect me?'

'Certainly not! You may be nearly as ruthless as your father, but I would never think of you as a poisoner! But it makes me wonder; if Edward the Exile did not die naturally, who could have been responsible? I thought you might know.'

'Who can know?' Harold returned lightly, as if it mattered not a whit. 'Who can know but the one who did it? His cousin Ralph, perhaps? An agent of William? Such are the only people likely to benefit.'

'Well, all I can say is, if you are setting out to advise the king as to who his heir should be you had better think very carefully about it.'

Harold sat down again on a block of undressed stone. He was very thoughtful, seeing a vacant throne, a crown without a head; and stirring deep within him were feelings which he could not himself explain, let alone voice. It was as though he never could visualise a face to fit beneath that crown. He knew that there must be one to be found somewhere, yet he could not think whose it would be. Certainly it was not that of Edward's nephew Ralph, nor his cousin William.

'I would hope to see a child of my sister's, even yet, upon the throne,' he said. 'It is not too late for Edith to give Edward a son, as long as a miracle occurs.'

'You're hoping for another Immaculate Conception?' Cedric asked wryly.

'Don't jest with me, Cedric. It's a serious matter. I don't know who there is, not yet, but I'm not going to wait for miracles. All I know is, I shall strive to ensure that it is not William the Bastard.' He stood up, like one snapping out of a dream, and became full of resolve in the old restless way that Cedric knew so well. He could not sit still and brood for long, but had to do something even if it was only pacing about.

'That,' he continued firmly, 'is why I must get Wulfnoth and Haakon back from Normandy as soon as possible. While William holds so much power over me, I cannot hope to sway Edward. I will not have my brother and nephew used as barter tokens in the battles to come.'

'Battles? Against whom?'

'Ah, now your eyes light up, Cedric Shieldless!' Harold laughed. 'Yes, we're going to war again. But not against Edward this time. We, my friend, are going to buy him with a prize that every English king has coveted for the last five hundred years. We are going to cut off the head of the Welsh dragon and give it to Edward on a platter!'

V

THE army lay coiled around the hillside like a silvery snake waiting for its prey to pass, a segmented serpent of men basking without warmth in the pale sunlight. The steel cold of their armour was all but welded to the iron cold of the earth where the frost had hardened patches of snow into ice, trapping the bodies of the soldiers in cold shells, as if they had taken the freezing ground and wrapped it around themselves. They were tired and hungry men, exhausted by weeks of hard campaigning in the unyielding and unforgiving Welsh mountains. High on a scarp slope, they stared numbly to the north along a steep-sided valley of stone and coarse grasses. In the floor of the valley a narrow river trickled through broken layers of ice. To the east of the stream ran a rough track, the only route north for several miles around. It was this track the snake-like army watched, while over their heads the banners of the golden dragon and the fighting man of Earl Harold hung limp in the cold, as if infected by the weariness of the men who followed them.

'Are you sure they'll come this way?' Cedric asked Harold, peering into the eye-watering distance.

'They must,' Harold said with confidence. 'It's the only way Griffith can reach his stronghold. And that's where he'll make for when he sees the size of Tostig's force. We have him trapped this time. North or south, he cannot squeeze out.'

Cedric stamped his feet and beat his arms about his body. It was useless to pull his cloak about his mail coat, for it seemed to enclose the cold rather than keep it out. It was better to keep moving, though it was not possible to move far when lying in wait for an enemy who might appear at any moment.

He looked at the men, and saw trouble in their eyes. They were mostly housecarls since Harold was working to build up a standing fighting force and depend less on the rag-tag fyrd, but although they were trained and regular warriors, they were close to the limits of endurance. War in spring or summer was taxing enough, but this new idea of Harold's for winter strikes into Wales meant ceaseless hardship. The crippling cold ate up a man's strength after a few miles' march, and if he then had to go into battle he did so with leaden limbs and an empty belly. As a result Harold had lost many men, and not so much from combat as from such causes as hunger, broken bones, frostbite and the flux.

Last night Harold had forbidden his followers to light fires because of the nearness of King Griffith's army, ordering them instead to stay awake all night in whatever cranny they could find out of the wind. Three men had fallen asleep, and had been found frozen dead in the morning. The ground had been too hard to bury them, so their bodies had been left under cairns, which had given rise to a grim joke. So far, at each victory over the Welsh, Harold had had such cairns erected with the legend: 'Here Harold conquered,' a warning and an insult to the native warriors. Now, over the shallow stone tombs, one of the housecarls had written: 'Here Harold conquered three Englishmen.' The culprit had not been discovered, but his bitter words, and the protection he enjoyed in the ranks, were clear pointers to the mood of the men. It showed just as surely in their faces. They were drawn faces, clench-jawed and sombre. Only the weary eyes bore any expression, and they were full of resentment, yet still concealing the true depth of that feeling.

Some sat, shivering and gazing at nothing. Others stood, to gaze with hate at the hostile hills. A few chewed slowly on precious pieces of tough meat or stale bread from their meagre rations, while several polished shields and spears, over and over again, in the hope of keeping warm. Most were too weary even to move, but curled up under rocks where the snow had not reached, wrapped in cloaks or blankets, longing for sleep yet fearful of the sleeping death that might overtake them.

In all of them there was a dullness born of fatigue and nagging fear, desire simply to start walking and not stop until they reached England. They were unlikely to desert, however. Even if a man were prepared to face the dangers of the Welsh mountains on his own, the awful punishment if he were caught was enough to make him think very carefully about trying to sneak out of camp. Harold considered desertion a heinous crime, especially among professional soldiers, and had made his opinion well known. A man who left his comrades to fight without his help was a coward, Harold said, a thief of other men's lives, and a traitor. He deserved to lose the feet that had carried him on his way, just as a thief deserved to lose the hand that stole, or one who gave false witness deserved to lose the tongue that lied. There had been one deserter, early in the campaign. The luckless fellow had been mutilated before the assembled company, and Harold had pointed out that he was being merciful by severing only one foot. There had been no desertions since. The men accepted Harold's fierce discipline, followed him obediently and had fought well, but with each new day they seethed with discontent. That was all they had to give them warmth in this cold wilderness.

'They cannot take much more,' Cedric told Harold.

'They won't have to,' Harold replied. 'They'll be going home soon. It will be finished by nightfall. Today is the last day of King Griffith's rule in Wales, I swear it.'

'I hope so,' Cedric said. 'There can be no worse place in the world to fight a war than here, God-forsaken land that it is. No wonder the Welsh are always spilling over into England. Sometimes I pity them, having to live here.'

'You may pity them today, then' Harold answered gravely. 'They will be deserving of it . . .'

A rider was hurrying along the valley, guiding his horse cautiously along the jagged path.

'It is our messenger,' Harold announced. He stood tensely, his breath like smoke on the icy air, his eyes alight. His fingers curled slowly into fists and spread out again, as if he was attempting to draw the rider more quickly towards him. When at last the messenger arrived, stiff and breathless in the saddle, Harold demanded his report with only a snapped 'Well?' He would not let his voice betray his anxiety.

'They are coming, my lord,' the messenger gasped, sliding down from his mount like ice melting from a roof. 'King Griffith's army has met your brother, Lord Tostig, and takes flight this way as you expected. Lord Tostig is chasing him hard, as you ordered.'

'How far off?'

'They will be here within the hour.'

'And Griffith is with them?'

'He was when I saw them start to retreat, my lord.'

Harold joyfully slapped fist into palm.

'I knew I would have him this time,' he muttered, then raising his voice, he called sharply to his commanders: 'Station your men as I told you,' he told them, 'and let there be no mistakes. If they want to start for home tonight, they'd better fight like demons!'

The soldiers leapt up willingly when the orders were given, glad that their bone-freezing vigil was at an end, eager to start the fighting they had been trained for. Warming, too, was Harold's suggestion that this might be the last day of this foul war.

The silver snakes wriggled into new positions. Half of the army, with Harold and Cedric and the banner bearers at its head, formed an armoured dam across the valley floor, making a solid and formidable shield wall in the path of the approaching Welsh. The other half divided itself evenly on either side of the valley, trudging up through the rocky slopes, spreading out and concealing its numbers high in the rocks and snow, forming the walls of a tunnel into which Tostig would herd the enemy. Harold watched with critical gaze from his position behind the shield wall, and occasionally shouted to a commander whose arrangements were not quite to his liking. He timed everything calmly, determined not to have one spear-point out of place even if it meant re-forming right up until the last moment.

'If all goes as you expect, it will be the first time we have ever dealt the Welsh such a blow,' Cedric observed. 'Edward will be overjoyed.'

'He'll be more than that,' Harold grinned. 'He'll be in my debt for a long time to come. I will have equalled my father's achievements, Cedric; that's the important thing. I'll be as indispensable to Edward as Godwin was to Canute. The house of Godwin will regain all its old power and glory, running this country's affairs with the king's approval, the most powerful voice in the Witan, the one voice no one will dare try to hush.'

'Your family should have been born of royal blood,' Cedric laughed. 'You would not have to work so hard to rule England then.'

'If we were of royal blood,' Harold said boastfully, 'we'd be ruling the British islands and all Scandinavia by now. Besides, I am almost of royal blood. I am a cousin of King Sweyn of Denmark, remember. And had it not been for my stupid brother Sweyn murdering his brother . . . well, who knows what we might have achieved together? But let's not dwell on that. Let's attend to the job in hand, shall we? I don't want the Welsh to hear us before we see them.'

He need not have worried. The Welsh army was too intent on fleeing from Tostig's forces to be listening to sounds in the mountains. Completely disordered in their retreat, the warriors of King Griffith came along the valley floor like a huge flock of mountain goats, limping on bruised feet, stumbling over stones and over each other, fighting among themselves for a place on the track. Some had even cast aside helmets and shields. When the first of them saw the English shield wall silently waiting, they came to an awkward halt and shouted back warnings. This caused panic in the pressing mass behind. For a few moments indecision and fierce argument reigned; some were all for pushing on through Harold's ranks, while others insisted on turning back and trying to get out of the valley before Tostig caught up with them. Their leaders could hardly make themselves heard above the excited voices echoing along the ravine.

Harold did not give them time to solve the problem.

'Battle horns!' he yelled, and with hoarse war cries, screeches of triumph and the deafening blast of the horns, the housecarls rushed on the crowded Welsh. They ran into the attack as fast as they could, keeping their wall intact as much as they were able to over the jagged slate underfoot.

Some of the surprised Welsh immediately resigned themselves to fight, and bravely went to meet the housecarls. Those to the rear broke away towards Tostig's soldiers, and still more tried to make their escape straight up the hills, either by climbing directly up from the track or by splashing through the shallow waters of the stream and attempting to slip around the edge of the English trap.

They did not have far to climb, before Harold's men jumped out and bore down on them, trapping them with their backs to the crush of battling warriors below. In a few minutes, Harold had the Welsh rabble completely enclosed, leaving them no choice but to stand and fight his far greater numbers. They were hemmed in with barely enough room to swing a sword or thrust with a spear, and all up the floor of the valley the housecarls savagely jabbed and cut and thrust at a slowly shrinking bunch of Welsh struggling against each other for space to move. Harold's army pushed forward over the bodies of the dead and dying, and the Welsh warriors fell back against comrades who in turn shoved them forward again. English and Welsh blood flowed in rivulets in the freezing stream and on the slippery slopes. Englishmen smashed down cruelly at Welshmen who had to strain as hard to keep their balance as to strike with blade or staff, and all through the valley the screams and shouts and the clash of steel and cries of despair echoed back and forth among the rocks, as if a hole had opened up from the screaming depths of Hell.

And hell on earth it was, for few of the wounded came out of the battle. If they were not despatched immediately with steel, they were crushed to death beneath the feet of those still fighting or hacked to pieces by those who followed. Welshmen went down by the dozen, then by the score, then in their hundreds, and those who managed to slip out through the tiny chinks in the ring of English armour could be counted on one man's fingers. Within an hour, the battle was done. The survivors leaned tiredly on axe and spear surveying the carnage; they counted one dead Englishman for ten Welsh. Corpses were piled high wherever they looked. A strange quiet descended on the place, as though, with no word spoken, a respectful silence had been ordered, and the day was no longer cold. Those warriors left living had been warmed with the blood of the slain.

Tostig joined Harold then, riding at the head of his army after tidying up the stragglers at the other end of the valley. His soldiers pushed before them a clutch of about sixty prisoners, who carried before them a man's body on a rough litter of poles and cloth. They laid it down as if it were an offering to Harold.

'You did well, Tostig,' Harold cheerfully hailed his brother. 'Now tell me that is Griffith you have there, and I will say you have worked wonders!'

'The Welsh pigs say it is their king,' Tostig answered. 'Cowardly traitors! When they saw they were trapped they turned on Griffith and killed him. They brought him to me in the hope of saving their own skins.'

Harold studied the body with interest, noting the quality of the clothing and armour. The dead man – mutilated with several axe and sword cuts – had been tall, well-built and black-bearded, as Harold had been told. Here, Harold hoped, lay the greatest victory of his life. It was only one dead man, but for years that man had been a painful thorn in English flesh, with his harrying raids all along the border.

'Can they prove it is Griffith?' Harold asked.

'We have only their word for it,' Tostig admitted.

'Well, I'm not prepared to take the word of a Welshman for anything,' the Earl of Wessex declared. 'We will make sure. We'll take this mess to Griffith's palace, and show it to his family. Then we'll know if this is the king of the Welsh.'

'Right back into Wales?' Cedric questioned. 'I thought we were finished with this war.'

'We are strong enough,' Harold told him. 'We have broken their back here.' He nodded towards the prisoners, his own and those brought by Tostig, and added: 'The only question that remains is, what do we do with these men? Walking into the jaws of the enemy I don't mind, but taking them some teeth is a different matter.'

'Then we must kill them,' Cedric said coolly.

Harold looked hard at his friend, once the gentlest and least warlike person he had ever known.

'Just like that?' he mused. 'All these unarmed men?'

'It is the only way,' Cedric replied. 'It's what they would have done to us had we been captured. We must show that we can be as ruthless. We can't free them, or they will gather new forces and attack us again. Anyway, they are worthless traitors for the most part. They murdered their own king! They don't deserve mercy.'

'You've changed, Cedric,' Harold said, not as a criticism, but as a matter of fact. 'You have changed so much I feel I don't know you.'

'Life changes a man, in time,' Cedric replied to that. 'But war changes him more quickly, more surely. Like a sword being forged. He begins raw and unshaped, uncertain in the heat of the coals. When the fire cools, he is either worthless and breaks, or he is formed to a hard edge, a living blade. There is no other kind of warrior.'

Harold nodded, acknowledging the truth of Cedric's words, remembering that once upon a time he had urged Cedric to be more warlike.

'Tell your men to dispose of the prisoners,' he commanded, turning back to Tostig. 'Mine are too tired to lift an arm.'

Screams and frantic protests rent the winter air once more as Tostig's men moved in and methodically hacked the prisoners down. Harold prepared to move out even as the butchery continued. He had his horse fetched to him, ordered some men to carry the body of Griffith, and instructed his officers to form up their companies for the march. At the head of the armies flew the golden dragon and the fighting man, proudly proclaiming the might of Earl Harold. Neither did Harold forget to have built the usual stone tribute to his own conquest, as if the spread of broken bodies across the valley were not evidence enough.

It was less than ten miles to Griffith's headquarters. The stone and slate-roofed village lay deep in a hollow in the mountains, spoked with a maze of passes which would have afforded the king numerous ways of escape had he made it back there. The villagers knew of Harold's approach long before he arrived just before dark, but they made no effort to flee or resist. With Griffith's army dead or scattered, there was little they could do to defend themselves, and they had nowhere to run to. They left the stockade gates open, and sent their elders out to plead for mercy. Harold told his men to guard every home, and himself rode up to the door of Griffith's hall. He summoned the king's womenfolk, and had the body dragged to the threshold and laid at their feet. Their wailing satisfied Harold that he had the right man.

There was, however, a young girl who made little display of mourning. Harold recognised her as Aldgyth, daughter of Earl Aelfgar of Mercia.

Aelfgar had given his daughter in marriage to King Griffith, to protect Mercia from Welsh invasion. She was a pretty girl, no more than nineteen years old, dark-haired and with bright, brown eyes that were only slightly misted with tears as she glanced up from the dead king to the man who had widowed her. She was saddened not so much by the death of her husband as by the fact of her wasted marriage, a virginity roughly taken, and all without purpose.

'This is your husband, is it not, lady?' Harold asked.

'It is King Griffith,' she confirmed, resentfully.

'I'm sorry to have made you a widow,' Harold told her. 'I have known you since you were a very small child.'

'You have widowed many women today' the queen said coldly. 'Do not delay in Wales to apologise to all of them, or you will never get home.'

Harold gave her a sardonic smile.

'You have a sword-sharp wit, lady,' he said. 'Of course it is foolish to say sorry to a woman when you have just killed her man. I shall be seeing your father on my way to London. I will take you with me, if you wish.'

Aldgyth was not long making up her mind. She looked once more at the dead king, and nodded.

'I have nothing to stay here for,' she said. 'I will pack some things, if you will wait for me.'

While Aldgyth went into the house, Harold ordered his men to take back Griffith's body. That proved to be almost as difficult a battle as they had fought with Griffith's army, for the women tore and beat furiously at the soldiers, and had to be manhandled out of the way. Even when the body had been put across a horse and was guarded by an impenetrable wall of housecarls they raged undaunted, struck again and again, shrieking insults and obscenities, until they were exhausted or led away.

'Can't you leave them even that?' Aldgyth asked contemptuously, returning from the hall with a small knot of servants, who carried her jewels and clothes.

'The carcase belongs to King Edward, lady,' Harold replied. 'I have promised him Griffith's head. Now, if you are coming, get on your horse. Otherwise stay with your Welsh friends. I don't care.'

Harold gave his army little rest on the homeward march. He made first for Coventry, the home of Earl Aelfgar, and strode into the hall without waiting to be invited. Aelfgar, son of Earl Leofric and Lady Godiva, had inherited both his father's earldom and his dislike for the Godwin clan, and Harold's victory in Wales had further angered him. It set his treaty with King Griffith at nought. Going to greet Harold with his sons Edwin and Morcar, Aelfgar was obviously trying to keep a check on his simmering anger. He was a plump, round faced little man, whose baggy eyes and long moustaches made him look like a sad hound, and he knew he was no match for the Earl of Wessex in size, power or intellect.

'Good morning, Earl Harold,' he said carefully. 'I commend you on your triumph. Edward will be pleased, I'm sure.'

'I think you lost your daughter in Wales,' Harold tartly replied. 'I've brought her back for you. She's very pretty: you'd better be careful not to lose her again. And I've also brought a friend of yours, or at least the best part of him.'

Aelfgar went to the door, which Harold held open for him, and looked out. Harold's soldiers filled the yard, and at the front of the throng two men were displaying the head of Griffith on a pole, raised like a banner. This evidence of Harold's skill, flaunted in his face, caused Aelfgar to pale. His alliance with Griffith had been more than an attempt to strengthen his borders; he had seen it as a means of winning favour with King Edward and gaining some ascendancy over those damned cubs of Godwin's, who now surrounded his lands like a band of invaders. Tostig had taken over the earldom of Northumbria after the death of Siward, and new earldoms had been carved out for Gurth and Leofwine as well. Gurth held all East Anglia together with Oxfordshire, and Leofwine all of Middlesex, Buckinghamshire, Hertfordshire and Essex. With Harold in Wessex and Herefordshire, the sons of Godwin had virtually acquired the tenancy of most of England. They were more powerful than Godwin had ever been, and Aelfgar's one great ally, whom he had been working to have admitted to the English Witan, now stared back at him with sightless eyes from the top of a pole. Aelfgar spat, as if to clear the bitter taste of defeat from his mouth, and tried to assume an untroubled air as he turned to face his tormentor.

'Yes, Harold,' he said. 'You go from success to success. Small wonder people are beginning to call you Prince Harold. What will you do next, conquer Scotland?'

'No, there are more urgent problems in England yet,' Harold answered lightly. 'But I think we have gone a long way towards solving them now. If I were you, Aelfgar, I would choose my allies more carefully in future. Your motives could be misread. If you are seeking friends, why not look eastwards? The view is more rewarding than that to the west.'

Aelfgar's calm started to crack.

'What are you accusing me of?' he blustered.

'I think Lord Harold is trying to say that you and Griffith were planning to over-run England, father,' Edwin interrupted. 'Earl Harold does not believe in allowing strangers into the Witan. It might upset the balance of power.'

'Certainly not foreign strangers who try to get in by force,' Harold agreed. 'The Welsh have been pestering us for generations, and thousands of Englishmen have died trying to keep them in

Wales. I can't see the Welsh changing their ways now, whether or not your father tries to smuggle them in through the back door!'

'Bah! You and your noble ambitions!' Aelfgar stormed. 'What do you care about the Welsh borders, when you can make yourself comfortable hundreds of miles away in Edward's court? I'm the one who has to live next to the Welsh, and because I try to settle the troubles with an honest alliance, you make me out to be a criminal! Glory is all you went to Wales for, Harold. Glory and more favours from Edward! Don't pretend to be high-principled about the menace of the Welsh!'

Aelfgar spoke more rashly than he would have cared to had he been able to stay calm, but Harold took the insult with indifference.

'Are you really so lonely out here, then?' he challenged mockingly. 'I said you ought to find some English friends. This daughter I have returned to you is young and nice-looking; why don't you try finding a good English husband for her? I'll tell you what: just to show how willing we are to take you into the fold – I've got two unmarried brothers with rich earldoms to offer. I'm sure Gurth or Leofwine would be delighted to marry the lady.' He looked Aldgyth up and down, and was not altogether jesting when he added insolently: 'Come to that, I'm still unmarried myself. She could easily take my fancy.'

Aldgyth blushed deeply and turned her back on him. But despite the impudence of him, a man who openly lived with a cousin-mistress and a litter of bastard children, she was not unflattered.

Her father, though, was shaking with rage.

'Get out of here!' he shouted at Harold. 'Get out, and take your filthy prize to Edward. And I hope it haunts you both out of your wits!'

Out in the yard, as they mounted up, Cedric asked,

'Did you mean that, about marrying Aldgyth?'

'Why not?' Harold laughed. 'Daughter of the Earl of Mercia? She's the most marriageable widow in England. Imagine it. I am already brother-in-law to the king, and then I would be son-in-law to the only remaining earl who isn't my brother! The Godwinssons would have a holding in every shire, as well as at court. Yes, I must think more seriously about it.'

'But you wouldn't cast Edith aside after all these years, after all the children she's given you?'

'Who said anything about casting her aside? Can't a man have a wife and a mistress?'

Tostig then joined in with a derisive laugh.

'My big brother,' he told Cedric, 'would become an infidel, if it would give him more wives and more earldoms. The only reason he does not, I do believe, is that he would then lose the confidence of enough churchmen to fill Canterbury Cathedral.'

'You should be glad to have a big brother to look after your interests,' Harold said carelessly. 'Who persuaded the King to let you have Northumbria, eh?'

'Our sister, that's who!' Tostig answered scornfully. 'Don't pretend you wanted me to have Northumbria, Harold. It's even bigger than Wessex, and you didn't like that at all. I wouldn't have been made earl if Edith hadn't worked so hard on Edward. You only agreed because the other choice was to let it go to Waltheof Siwardsson.'

Suddenly there was between them a rift that had lain hidden for years, ready to crack wide at the first strain. Harold and Tostig, sons of Godwin and joint conquerers of Wales, were fingering their sword hilts again, and this time the war looked like staying in the family.

'Well, now that you have it,' Harold said frostily, 'I should do your best to hang on to it. Take the advice I have just given Aelfgar. Know your friends!'

Cedric suddenly saw in his mind's eye a morning long ago when five young men went riding forth together like knights to adventure. Their names were Sweyn, Bjorn, Harold, Tostig and Cedric. Then Sweyn had murdered Bjorn in a drunken, jealous rage, and had died in exile and disgrace. Now Harold and Tostig were facing up to each other as if they, too, could easily lash out in hate, and Cedric could only watch in dismay the crumbling of another great comradeship.

What men we have become, thought Cedric. How does the zest for life change to greed, boldness turn to bloodlust, and a man's own self become a slave to covetousness. But he was not the only one who had changed.

VI

CROWDS of cheering people greeted Harold's entry into London, though few Londoners cared a snap for the Welsh border, or would know where to find it. They wanted a hero and a spectacle to break the boredom of Edward's blessed and tedious peace, and Harold did not disappoint them. He deliberately chose a route that would take him through the city on his way to Edward's palace, and the citizens turned out in their thousands despite the biting cold and the snow flakes that flurried in the wind. They packed the narrow streets from the northern gates to the western precincts, men, women and children all shouting themselves hoarse with cries of: 'Hail Prince Harold! Death to the Welsh! Hail Cedric Shieldless, hail Tostig! Long live King Edward!' They scurried out of the path of the leaders' dancing horses, gazed with awe at the fluttering banners of the golden dragon and the fighting man, pushed in on the ranks of tired and bearded soldiers to touch their mail coats, shields and axes, but most of all they gawped like wide-eyed children at King Griffith's gruesome head, raised high on its pole. Some even took to throwing rotten vegetables and stones at the head in a bid to knock it off until they were chased away by the housecarls. Most, however, were content to gaze upon the battered trophy and wonder at the strength and skill of Harold, who, it was rumoured, had slain Griffith in single combat. Here was the Welsh King with fearsome magical powers, who had eaten English children alive, had sliced ten English warriors with a single blow, had raped every woman of an English village in a single night and had burned whole towns with their inhabitants trapped inside, according to the stories. Now he was nothing but a head rotting on a pole, and proof of England's might, and cause for wild celebration. Gifts were offered to the soldiers as they passed, effigies of Griffith were burned in the streets, and women ran out to hug and kiss the victors.

There were broad grins on the faces of the men, despite their fatigue, for they could see they would have no trouble taking the girls of their choice tonight. Especially favoured would be those who could show a stump where a hand had been severed, or a vivid scar from a Welsh spear. They would be treated to all they could drink in the ale-houses while they told tales of brave deeds, of heroic fights and incredible hardships, of how they had survived without food or water in the winter mountains, and yet had over-powered enormous bands of savage Welshmen.

'I have never heard such acclaim,' Cedric told Harold. 'You must be the greatest English hero since Edmund Ironside.'

'A doubtful honour,' Harold smiled. 'English heroes have a tendency to be on the losing side. I think I'll trust more to the Danish half of me!'

Cedric, the pure Englishman, answered only with a tolerant smile, content to allow his friend his moment of arrogance.

They left the city and rode westwards to the palace and the abbey, where more adulation awaited them in the tiny township of Westminster. Edward and Edith and their court stood at the palace doors, their faces alight with welcome. Harold, his helmeted head held high, halted his army and rode slowly to the steps. He bowed from the saddle, and turned to point to the head of Griffith.

'Greetings, my lord King,' he said grandly. 'There you see the prize I promised you. The Welsh will be quiet for a long time now, for there is their tongue.'

'You have served me well again, Harold,' Edward acknowledged. 'But come inside, so that I can thank you as you deserve. I am too old to stand out in this dreadful weather.' He gave one more look at the head of Griffith, and added: 'Have your men mount that over the Ludgate. I don't think I want it in the palace.'

In the great hall, Harold, Cedric and Tostig thankfully drank their first good wine in months as the court jostled to applaud them. Edward allowed the racket to continue for a while, then called for quiet. As the babble of voices died down, the king went to his throne and gestured for his brother-in-law to approach him.

'Harold, Earl of Wessex,' Edward said solemnly, 'your victory in Wales has proved yet again your devoted service to your king and his people, and we praise God for your success and your safe return. Such bold exploits cannot go unrewarded. When news reached us telling of your victory I called a special meeting of the Witan. With the sanction of that noble body, I now confer upon you an entirely new honour in recognition of your conquest of the Welsh. From this day forth you shall be known as Dux Anglorum, General of the English.'

Edward reached into a casket and beckoned Harold to him. From the box he took a gold medallion and chain.

'This I had cast for the occasion,' he explained. 'It is my seal on your appointment as my supreme military leader, an office greater than Staller, which appointment I thought not good enough for you.'

The medallion bore the golden dragon, and the words: 'Harold Dux Anglorum, by the grace of God. Awarded in the name of Edward, King of England.'

'You confounded those who said it was a foolhardy venture,' Edward concluded, 'who said that a war in Wales in winter was impossible.'

'A war when the enemy least expects it is a war half won,' Harold smiled. 'But you honour me hugely, my lord. I have not words enough to thank you. I am proud to fill this great office for you.'

'Thank you,' Edward said. 'They are calling you Prince Harold these days, perhaps because I have said that you are more like a son to me – which indeed you are. Well, a prince I cannot make you, but this much is well deserved.'

'It is more than enough,' Harold said, but still he liked the sound of the title Prince Harold. He was thinking that from Dux Anglorum to Edward's heir might be but a short step now. Even in this dizzying moment of glory, no new heights were too lofty for Harold to contemplate. In his mind he was adding: 'Certainly it is enough for the present.'

Edward had turned his attention to Tostig and Cedric.

'You, too, have served me well under Harold's command,' he beamed at them. 'I must consider rewards for you, also. New lands, maybe, or treasures . . .'

'My lord,' Harold politely interrupted, 'If I may make a suggestion, on behalf of Cedric at least . . .'

'Yes?'

'The Welsh wars have shown the value of an army relying more on housecarls than on the fyrd,' Harold told him. 'We should keep recruiting housecarls, making up their strength as much as we can, until we have five thousand, perhaps six thousand, well-trained men always on call. Cedric is always preaching to me about how the Romans divided their legions into cohorts, and their cohorts into centuries, and organised the best standing armies ever known. He has studied military matters, and is himself a proven warrior. I would like to suggest that he be made commander of the housecarls, and be given the task of building up the force. The name of Cedric Shieldless alone would be enough to draw bold young men to join his ranks.'

Edward looked interested.

'Has Harold spoken of this with you?' he asked Cedric.

'He has, my lord.'

'And you would consider this ample reward?'

'I, too, will be honoured to serve my king as he wishes,' Cedric confirmed.

377

'Then I shall put it before the Witan,' promised Edward, and that meant that it was practically done, since Harold held the greatest sway in the assembly. Cedric was overjoyed, yet he experienced a curious sinking sensation which at first he failed to understand. Then he realised that he had come full cycle; he was actually stepping into the shoes of the first man he had ever killed. It seemed he would always walk with the ghost of Olaf Ericsson. He had gradually taken on every quality of that long-dead Viking, from his remorselessness in battle to his position as commander of housecarls, as if he really had breathed in the soul of the man at his dying. But thoughts of his future prevented him from being too downcast, and one look at Tostig was enough to jolt his thoughts in quite a different direction.

Tostig was most definitely displeased, and it showed clearly.

Not only had Harold and Cedric stolen all the glory, in Tostig's view, but also Harold had put in a word for his friend before his brother. And, by having Cedric made commander of housecarls, Harold had assured Cedric's place as second-in-command of the whole army in all future wars, ousting Tostig from his position as Harold's chief lieutenant. Tostig knew enough of Harold's plans to realise that in future the army and the housecarls would be one, with fyrdmen merely making up numbers. It was as if Tostig had been publicly humiliated instead of honoured. He was mutely furious. Before anything more could be said, he abruptly excused himself from the king's presence. He left the hall, asking Edith to go with him with the excuse that he had news to give her of their sister Gunhild, though everyone knew that there were times when only the queen could deal with her petulant little brother.

It was a shaming moment for Edward, Harold and Cedric. They had been slighted before the entire court, and it was left to the king to smooth over Tostig's rudeness.

'He must be very tired,' Edward shrugged, and to Harold he went on: 'Will you come to my quarters, please? I have many important things to discuss with you.'

When they were alone in the veritable library of work which Edward set for himself, the king sank limply into his chair and rubbed at his lined brow, fumbling with one hand for the papers he had kept out for Harold's return.

'I know you must be very tired, too,' he apologised, 'and I shall not delay you longer than I must, but truly, Harold, I know of no one other than you I can turn to. Problems have been closing in on me of late, plague, the hard winter, threats of Danish raids . . . it's all too much for a man of my years to handle alone. There is the growing worry of our finances, too. The treasury funds are diminishing at an alarming rate, and the decline must be halted. And yet you are talking now of paying a larger army. First to Church matters, however. The new Church Council has agreed an order of ethics, and a charter must be drawn up giving them authority for the changes they plan. I want you to witness that before you go back to Bosham. And, of course, there is the question of the dedication of your Abbey at Waltham . . .'

'Yes,' Harold nodded, 'and the matter of who should conduct the dedication service.'

'Quite!'

'It should be the Archbishop of Canterbury, of course,' Harold said, with commendable piety. 'But I don't want Stigand's name associated with my abbey while Rome still refuses to ratify his appointment.'

'Of course not!'

'It would be seen as an endorsement of his position,' Harold continued, 'and I could not embarrass my king like that. I would invite the Archbishop of York instead.'

'You are wise,' Edward complimented him. 'But Stigand and his followers will put up fearful objections.'

'Ah, but I do have an olive branch to hold out to him,' announced Harold. 'I have been thinking it over during the cold nights in Wales. Have I your consent to make a pilgrimage to Rome?'

Edward appeared surprised.

'Well, naturally. But we were discussing Stigand . . .'

'Yes, and the pilgrimage will serve a twofold purpose. Apart from demonstrating my devotion to my faith – the first consideration, of course – it may help us resolve the problem of Stigand. It was something we were never able to settle in the reign of Pope Leo, but Pope Nicholas may be more amenable. I shall ask for an audience, at least with the Cardinals, and try to show them how anxious we are to have an unblemished church in England. I shall see if we can at last get the Pallium for Stigand. If I tell them of the hard work we are doing for our religion here, as exemplified by the dedication of yet another new abbey, we might just succeed.'

'Do you honestly believe there is a chance of it?'

'I can but try.'

'Ah, you are so unlike your father, praise be to God,' Edward declared. 'I do not wish to malign the dead, believe me, but I can hardly credit that you are his son. Sometimes it seems you should have been mine. What a shame he misguided you so in your youth, although it is the simplest of tasks to forgive all that now.'

'Then there is just one more favour I would ask of you, my

lord,' Harold said humbly. 'When I get back from Rome, may I make one more journey abroad?'

'Where to?'

'Your kind words show that you have learned to trust me. Grant me this, then: that I may go to Normandy and bring my brother and nephew back from exile.'

Edward bent his head in self reproach, as if he had forgotten all about Wulfnoth and Haakon long ago, and should have thought of sending for them himself. He laid a hand on Harold's arm in the manner of one pleading for forgiveness.

'Of course you may,' he murmured. 'They have languished there long enough. The need for hostages is long past. By all means, bring them home.'

'Thank you, my lord. I shall always be grateful,' Harold said. Then, casually, he added: 'And, I would submit, the most important thing we must talk about, my lord, is the question of who is to succeed you – though God stay the day when you are no longer with us, I pray . . .'

But Edward had already slipped into a private world, as though the very mention of the succession induced deafness in him. He smiled his benign, enigmatic, infuriating secret smile, and gave the slow nodding movement that informed the world that he would speak when he was ready. Edward locked away thoughts like a miser hid away treasures, it had been said, and certainly there were subjects on which he simply would not be drawn. The nomination of his heir was one of them, and to Harold the most annoying. Did this strange man consider himself immortal, Harold wondered? Did he think England would nestle forever beneath his guiding hand? Or was he incapable of taking such a decision, fearing to offend one hopeful if not the other? It was not as if many choices were left open to him. Recently another had vanished with the death of Earl Ralph, son of his sister Godgifu. Now the only two being generally discussed were Duke William of Normandy, Edward's cousin, or Edward's great-nephew the little Edgar, grandson of Edmund Ironside.

Harold, stifling his anger and frustration, excused himself from further business that day. Later he and Cedric walked together beside the river.

'A pilgrimage to Rome?' Cedric questioned. 'Those who want to be seen to be truly devout go barefoot all the way, in sackcloth.'

'They'll see me start out that way,' Harold smiled. 'But I'll make sure there's something more comfortable waiting for me across the Channel. I'm not that pious!'

'Then what is this all about? Harold, I know you too well after all these years. Why this long journey just at a time when you're high in Edward's favour? It isn't to do Stigand a favour, and it certainly isn't to cleanse your soul!'

Harold remained quiet for a time. He plucked a reed and idly twisted it into knots while he walked, staring thoughtfully at the broad expanse of river and the snow-patterned fields to the west of the Abbey.

'Yes, you do know me well, don't you?'

'I do.'

'Then I will tell you, Cedric my old friend. Do you realise how important it is to clear up this business of Stigand, the false Archbishop of Canterbury?'

'It would halt all criticism of the English Church,' Cedric shrugged. 'So?'

'It would do more than that,' Harold informed him. He stooped down, placing his broken reed on the water and pushing it gently out into the current, adding: 'It might change the course of English history.'

'How so?'

Harold continued to gaze into the river, as though seeing the future reflected there.

'Edward still will not say whether he has made any firm promises to William, but meanwhile William knows full well that to be Edward's heir, even if he is, is not enough. A king may nominate his heir, but it is the Witan that elects the king. So William is finding himself an ally stronger than the Witan. He is pressing home the point in Rome, and all through Europe come to that, that Stigand is an example of the shocking state the English Church is in, despite Edward's reforms. He is striving to convince Rome that only one man can put matters right after Edward's death, and that that one man is the bastard Duke William of Normandy. He is starting a landslide of opinion that not even the Witan will be able to resist. And that landslide will be started by one small stone: Stigand.'

'Then what do you hope to gain by going to Rome?'

'The Pope's belated blessing on Stigand's appointment. I shall put it to the Pope that it is the one great reward he can bestow upon that dedicated servant of the Church, King Edward, who has worked so tirelessly for its betterment. That will stop William's scheming.'

'Well, I wish you luck,' Cedric said. 'But it seems a great deal of trouble to go to. Why not simply arrange for Stigand to be kicked out of office? The result would be the same. You would get the credit for ridding us of a scandal, instead of William.'

Harold shook his head.

'No, you still can't see the whole picture, can you?' he teased.

'What are you talking about?' Cedric asked crossly. 'If you painted a clear picture in the first place, one might be able to see it more plainly.'

'I need Stigand as much as he needs me. False incumbent he may be, but still most of the members of the new Church Council are his friends. With them and a large part of the Witan behind me, I would command opinion here. Then, when I go to Normandy to bring home Wulfnoth and Haakon, the last hold William has over me, it is I who will be in a position to bargain with William. I can show him an English Church purged clean without his help, and a Witan largely in favour of Harold, Dux Anglorum, a Witan which will not endorse Edward's choice of heir if that choice happens to be William!'

For the first time, some astonishing suspicions were crossing Cedric's mind.

'Just who are you thinking of as Edward's successor?' he whispered.

'I think you know,' Harold laughed. 'Who else but the man who practically runs the country for him already, the man he has come to regard as his son, the man they are calling Prince Harold?'

'You. . . . king?' Cedric gasped. 'You can't! You're not of royal blood!'

'Is William?' Harold intervened. 'He is Edward's first cousin once removed, that's all, descended from Emma's side of the family, not Ethelred's. Does that entitle him to the throne of England?'

'But he is at least related to the king, as all Europe will be quick to point out.'

'Does it matter? I can claim family connections with Canute's line, if necessary. I am cousin to King Sweyn of Denmark, Canute's nephew. There was a rumour at one time that Harold Harefoot was Godwin's son, not Canute's. That would make me the brother of a former king. Anyone can seek out royal kinships if they try hard enough. William has no greater claim than I do.'

Cedric was still trying to recover from the shock of hearing his friend declare himself a contender for the throne.

'I need time to work all that out,' he said. 'But my oath, Edward was right when he said you were nothing like your father. If only he knew! Even Godwin never contemplated making himself king!'

'Well, that's the way it's to be,' Harold determined. 'Are you with me, or not?'

'Do you need to ask?'

'Good, I knew I could trust you, as always. Please, don't breathe a word of this to anyone while I'm away, will you? I will make my intentions known in my own good time.'

'Then I can't come to Rome with you?'

'No, there's other work I need you to do. Most of all, I want you to keep a very close watch on Tostig, and on Edith here at court.'

'Oh, merciful God, what now?' Cedric sighed in exasperation. 'Watching Tostig I can understand, but your sister? What has she done to deserve your mistrust?'

'Nothing, yet. But I have my suspicions. She and Tostig exchange a great many confidences, which means that Tostig probably knows a good deal more about the thoughts of King Edward than I do. Tostig has some schemes at the back of his mind, I'm sure, because I know that little brother of mine extremely well, and today's sulks are typical of his behaviour lately. If he tried to involve anyone in his little machinations, it will be Edith. I must take precautions. With so much important work to do, I must have my back guarded.'

'So I must spy on Edith.'

'I know how you still feel about her, even now,' Harold said with understanding. 'But don't think of it as spying on her, rather as preventing Tostig drawing her into a conspiracy either to undermine my influence on Edward, or to urge Edward towards some act that will affect the succession. In that case it is for her own good, isn't it?'

'If you say so,' Cedric agreed reluctantly, and as they started back towards the palace he decided to treat Harold to some of his much-scorned philosophy, saying: 'You had better make your journey to Rome more than a political one, Harold. You had better make it as much a proper pilgrimage as you can, while you have the chance. God and the Devil still lead the greatest armies, no matter what power men acquire. And with what you're planning, you may need some Divine assistance.'

'I'll be the model of a Christian pilgrim,' Harold promised, without sincerity. 'Don't worry, I shall be praying every step of the way, even if I'm not barefoot in sackcloth. I'll have the Pope himself be my confessor, if I can.'

'Then why don't you marry before you go?' Cedric suggested, still worried by the sins his friend carried. 'You want to be king, and you want the blessings of the Church to help you achieve it. They might look upon you more kindly if you make your children legitimate, and make your bed respectable for Edith Swanneshales. It won't give William any moral advantage over you because you wed a kinswoman. He married his cousin in defiance of the Church, too.'

Harold was eyeing his friend like one constantly persecuted by those he loved.

'You know,' he said patiently, 'The occupation of matchmaker is one most unbecoming to a commander of housecarls. Please just be the warrior you are, Cedric, and I won't be frightened to have you near me.'

VII

CEDRIC regarded the suggestion of intrigue between Tostig and
Edith with scepticism, but he did as Harold asked and had
them both watched. Tostig was the most difficult to spy on, for
Cedric knew no one in the North. He had to rely on conversations
with merchants and thanes who had been to Northumbria and were
ready to gossip about the mess that earldom was becoming, and
how people there were coming to resent Tostig's hard rule.

Keeping an eye on Edith was much easier, though distasteful to
him. He instructed one man in each change of guard to pay
particular attention to the various comings and goings of people
around the queen's chambers, and to be doubly sure he ordered
another man to watch the first, and check the accuracy of his
reports.

One night, several weeks after Harold had left for Rome, one of
Cedric's young housecarls came to his quarters in the palace
barracks. The commander of housecarls was admiring his reflection
in a hand-mirror of polished silver, and the young soldier hesitated.

'Speak, man!' Cedric barked, but he did not take his concentration from his own features. He was smoothing the long, fair
moustaches that drooped below the line of his jaw, wondering why
the Normans shaved their faces smooth, thus depriving themselves
of a very warrior-like decoration. Cedric thought his own mousta-
ched countenance, framed within its chain-mail hood, as fierce and
overbearing as any warrior could wish.

'Sir,' the housecarl began nervously. 'You told me to report
anything unusual directly to you . . .'

'Yes?'

'Well sir, it may be nothing, but . . .'

'Tell me.'

'Well, there were two of us detailed to the queen's chambers
tonight. I was at the door of her private apartment, and the other
guard at the head of the passage, when the messenger arrived from
France with the queen's letters . . .'

Cedric put down the mirror, impatient with the man. There was
nothing out of the ordinary in what he had heard so far. Queen
Edith, in helping Edward with foreign affairs, often received missives from abroad. The soldier had paused again, however, as though

afraid either to make a fool of himself, or to get a comrade into trouble.

'When the messenger left the queen,' he continued cautiously, 'he went along the passage and stopped to talk to the other guard. They whispered a few words, and the messenger handed over a sealed parchment. When the messenger had gone, the guard moved away, casually, as if going for a stroll. I thought that was a bit odd, so I went to the end of the passage. Do you know the little door to the gardens beside the chapel? He unlocked that and passed the letter to someone outside.'

'Did you see who it was?' Cedric demanded, disturbed by the idea of secret messages passing within the palace.

'I believe I recognised him, sir, but I cannot be sure; it was dark. It looked like a certain deaf-mute slave who often acts as a courier for the Northumbrian thanes.'

'Lord, I hope you are right, boy. If you are, you have done well tonight, and I'll see you well rewarded. Quickly now, do you know where to find this deaf-mute?'

'No, but there are soldiers here who do. Sometimes they get him to take their letters home to northern parts.'

'Find those men, and bring them to me. Tell them to be armed and ready to ride at once. Be discreet, though. I want no one else in the palace to know what is happening.'

Cedric's heart was pounding and his mind teemed with questions as the young housecarl left.

Had Edith sent out a secret message? If so, to whom? Tostig? That seemed unlikely, for she could always reach her brother without incurring suspicion. To someone else in the North, then? Or could it be that the letter had nothing to do with Edith at all, that it was mere chance that the exchange was made near her quarters? In that case, who was using the palace messengers for their own purposes? It would have to be someone with quite strong court connections.

Cedric was itching to know the answers, even if they reflected badly on his beloved Edith. He would do his best to protect her if necessary, but this mystery had to be resolved. When the young housecarl returned with a dozen of his comrades from the northern shires, Cedric questioned them swiftly and discovered that the deaf-mute messenger always slept at one of three ale-houses when he was in London. He wasted no more time. Taking the men with him, he rode to the city at the gallop.

It was a bright moonlit night, eerily still but for the distant howl of a lone dog and the pounding of a dozen horses along the hard mud road. The riders left Westminster and went by the moon-washed fields and through the silent villages of Charing and Strand, into a city where hardly a light shone anywhere. Scavenging cats and dogs were the only living things to be seen. The streets were no more than narrow slits in jumbles of shadowed timber piles; grey-faced houses bent thatched heads over a litter of leaning stables and workshops, silent shops, and cold-walled churches rising like stone monuments in the midst of wooden crosses in a poor grave-yard. London had gone to sleep, but Cedric was in a mood to waken all of it if need be.

At the first ale-house they tried, the owner was still about; he told Cedric that he had not seen the deaf-mute for months. They found the second in a filthy side-street, strewn with rubbish and stinking of urine. The house, like its neighbours, was dark and quiet. Cedric dismounted and tried the door, and found it firmly locked.

'Is there a way out at the back?' he asked one of his men who knew the place.

'Yes, sir, there is.'

'Take four men and guard it. Let no one by.'

Cedric gave them time to get round to the back, then hammered on the door. There was no reply, so he drew his dagger and rapped on the stout wood.

'We are closed; go away!' came a muffled voice from inside.

'You will open,' Cedric shouted back, 'in the name of the king.'

'I will open to no one at this hour!' was the angry reply.

Cedric turned to his housecarls.

'Bring those axes,' he ordered. 'Cut it down.'

Two soldiers set into the door vigorously, their gleaming blades crashing into the solid oak, splintering and vibrating it violently. After a second or two muffled cries of alarm were heard from inside, hysterical screams from the women, shouts of indignation and fear from the men. Cedric did not give them a chance to open the door, but signalled grimly to his men to keep working.

The door gave way and collapsed, swinging crazily on its bottom hinge. Cedric strode in, followed by his men. The main room of the house was lit by a single torch, held unsteadily by the white-faced innkeeper. His wife huddled quivering at his side. It was not surprising they were terrified, Cedric thought, for he knew from his own experience what it was like to have a force of fierce, chain-mailed housecarls come bursting in from the night, axes at the ready. He had no time for pity, though.

'If a deaf-mute came here from the palace tonight,' Cedric snapped, 'fetch him out!'

'You can't do this,' the owner protested weakly. 'I'll see the Alderman . . .'

'I am here on the king's business,' Cedric said menacingly. 'I am Cedric Shieldless. You well know that all the aldermen in England cannot frighten me. Now, if you have my man here, fetch him out, or I take you instead.'

The miserable innkeeper shuffled away with not another word. He went to a curtain that hung over a large alcove, and hastily pulled it aside. In the dim torchlight, the pale faces of nine men peered out from the squalid cots arranged around the walls.

'Is he there?' Cedric asked his informant.

'Aye sir, that's him, the thin-faced one there.'

Cedric grabbed the man by his coarse cloth shift, just below the throat, hauled him out of the cot and dragged him to the middle of the room. He threw him sprawling on the floor.

'So,' Cedric said harshly, 'let us see if you really are a deaf-mute, shall we?' He siezed the slave's hair and pulled his head back, and held his sword close beneath the man's chin, saying: 'I am going to cut off your head. Tell me why I should not!'

The slave rolled his eyes, whimpering. He tried to plead, but could only make a gurgling sound.

'Yes, it seems you may be,' Cedric nodded, lowering the sword. To his housecarl he said: 'How do you talk to him?'

'With signs, sir.'

'Make your signs then. Tell him I want the letter that he took from the palace tonight.'

At first the slave grunted and shook his head vehemently, but when Cedric placed the tip of his sword at his throat he scampered away and produced the letter from beneath his bed cover. Cedric snatched it from him. The seal was plain, and gave away nothing. He ripped it open, and looked first for the signature and the name of the person to whom the letter was addressed.

It began 'Dearest Goose,' and ended 'your loving Butterfly.'

The rest of the letter told him little, for it consisted of little more than light gossip about people Cedric had never heard of, probably because they were also referred to by code names, but one paragraph in particular stood out from the rest as the most cryptic of all.

'Be assured, dear Goose, when the Good One is gone the Little One will be ready to fly, Mine and Yours has told me so. We must do all we can to help the Little One, for the dangers will be many. Not all of the black ones have flown home, and I have no doubt they are as ruthless as ever . . .'

There must be a meaning in that for someone, Cedric reasoned.

Could it refer to some sort of plot against the king – the Good One? He looked up, rubbing his chin with the edge of the parchment as he stared thoughtfully at the slave. Quite unexpectedly, memories began to stir deep in his mind. For a moment the knowledge he knew was there would not make itself clear, but then there came to him the memory of his mother speaking fondly of days gone by.

' "*Goose,*" ' he repeated, almost inaudibly. ' "*such a sweet little name she always had for him . . .* " '

Cedric knew who Goose was. He thought he might have the real name of Butterfly, too. The race of his blood quickened and brought a flush of excitement to his face. He read the letter briefly once more, then pushed it into the pouch at his belt. He pointed the sword at the deaf-mute again.

'Ask him,' he told his housecarl, 'who owns him.'

But the slave shook his head, and mournfully gazed at the floor as if resigning himself to his fate.

'He's faithful to his master, whoever it is,' commented the soldier. 'And you can't torture it out of a wretch who can't even scream. They say there's no better servant than a dumb one. But look, sir, he has a slave mark.'

Cedric took the slave's arm and studied the mark. It was a scar from a branding iron, in the shape of an axehead. He did not recognise it, and neither did anyone else.

'We'll find out,' Cedric said, 'though I could make a very shrewd guess, anyway. Take him to the palace, and keep him locked away. If anyone asks why, say that he was caught stealing, and nothing else. Is that understood? Any man who tells of what happened here tonight will answer to me. I believe we have uncovered a plot against the king. That is all you need to know.'

He suffered agonies of impatience waiting for Harold's return. There was no one else he could talk to about what he knew, though the news was bursting to leave him. The day he heard that Harold was back, and had sailed into Bosham, Cedric put off everything else he had to do and rode hard for the coast. It was a welcome chance to see his own family again, anyway. At Harold's house he ran to his own quarters, kissed his wife and children and swiftly exchanged news with them, then dashed up the stairs to his friend's apartments. The two men embraced each other like long-lost brothers, and Harold poured wine for Cedric.

'Well, how was Rome?' Cedric demanded.

'Too damned hot,' Harold grinned. 'And full of foreign-speaking people. Never has my Latin been so severely tested, and they don't speak it properly themselves. Bah! You can have warm countries.

I have never felt so fondly towards England as when I set foot back here again.'

'And the journey wasn't fruitful?'

'No, it was thoroughly wasted. I wasn't allowed to see the Pope. It took me long enough to get an audience with some pompous Cardinal, who told me in no uncertain terms that there will be no Papal blessing for Stigand. So Canterbury still has a false archbishop. Still, perhaps the fact that I took the trouble to go there will do some good one day.'

'I have some important news for you,' Cedric interrupted. 'Something that will astonish you. Shall we go outside to talk about it?'

They strolled down to the harbour, and Cedric handed to Harold the letter he had taken from the slave. Harold read it carefully twice, but shook his head.

'It means nothing to me,' he admitted. 'What is it?'

'It was found on a slave who sneaked it out of the palace with the help of a messenger from France. When I tell you who Goose is, and who I believe Butterfly to be, you will begin to understand.'

'Then, for the love of God, tell me!'

'You know Goose very well, and so do I,' Cedric told him. 'I remembered my mother telling me how he had been given that nickname. "*Goose*," she said to me one day, "*such a sweet little name she always had for him*." She was speaking of Gospatrick Uhtredsson, and his stepmother the Princess Aelfgifu.'

Harold read through the letter again.

'Gospatrick, the great-uncle of my Edith? Yes, your mother took him in, didn't she, when Aelfgifu went into exile? Then this is . . .'

'A coded letter they want no-one else to understand. There is no doubt who Goose is, Harold. I made inquiries about the mark on the slave. That brand has been used in Gospatrick's house since the time of his father, Earl Uhtred.'

Harold gripped the parchment tightly as he studied every word of it.

' "*Be assured, dear Goose*," ' he repeated slowly, ' "*when the Good One is gone the Little One will be ready to fly, Mine and Yours has told me so. We must do all we can to help the Little One, for the dangers will be many. Not all of the black ones have flown home, and I have no doubt they are as ruthless as ever . . .*" '

' "The Good One" must be Edward,' Cedric suggested.

'Aye; you've found a treasure here, my friend. By God, do you realise what a service you have done me? Let us put this riddle together, piece by piece. Here we have Aelfgifu, Edward's half-sister, writing from Brittany to her stepson in England; I know Aelfgifu is in Brittany, because Edward has told me so. What is she writing about? What happens when Edward dies, that's what. "The Little One" can only be Edgar, the great-nephew of Edward and Aelfgifu. He will fly south from Hungary, where both Edgar and Aelfgifu have strong ties.'

'So this letter speaks of a plan to have Edgar succeed Edward.'

'Quite. And we are the black ones, Cedric, my brothers and I: half Danish, and, in Aelfgifu's mind, the black ravens of Denmark! Clearly she expects trouble from us!'

'And "Yours and Mine" must be Ealdgyth, Aelfgifu's daughter, and Gospatrick's half-sister. She is married into the Scottish royal family. Do you think the king knows about this?'

'To judge from all this secrecy, I very much doubt it. Perhaps they know he wants Duke William to succeed him.'

'But why should they be so afraid to come out into the open? They are the king's own kin!'

Harold laughed.

'They feel they have good reason to be afraid. Look at the history of Aelfgifu and Gospatrick. When the Danes conquered this country they killed Aelfgifu's husband and brothers. She saw the kingdom stolen from her father, and she was forced into exile. She never forgave her stepmother Emma for marrying Canute. Harold Harefoot was responsible for the death of her half-brother Alfred, and Emma's son Hardicanute had her stepson Eadwulf executed. No doubt she believes that her nephew Edward was poisoned, too. It was the same for Gospatrick. His father was killed by the Danes; his elder brother Aldred was murdered by Englishmen who sided with the Danes, and his other brother Eadwulf killed at the orders of a king who was at least half Danish. They believe they cannot have young Edgar openly nominated as Edward's heir. For them nothing has changed. They fear for Edgar's life, yet they are determined to have this last male descendant of Aelfgifu's father made king. All these years they have corresponded in secret, and waited. Now they want it all back. Aelfgifu wants to see the last English prince on the throne, and doubtless Gospatrick would like to win back his father's earldom of Northumbria. Perhaps the Scots would be asked to help too!'

'It's a dangerous game they're playing,' Cedric nodded. 'It could be construed as treason against King Edward. I'm sure Duke William would see it as such. What about you? What are you going to do about it? I'm sure I don't have to remind you that Gospatrick is kinsman to us both, in a way. And Aelfgifu is the king's half-sister.'

Harold inclined his head in agreement, but was silent for a long time.

'This slave,' he said at last. 'You still have him?'

'In prison,' Cedric confirmed.

'He must stay there. Gospatrick must not know we have his letter, not yet.'

'Then you have no intention of helping Gospatrick, or Edgar. You still see yourself as the next king.'

'You think I should change my mind?'

'It's for you to choose. I merely thought that since there is a plot under way to provide someone other than William . . .'

'That I should lend it my support? No, Cedric. To me, Edgar is no better a choice than William. One belongs to Hungary where he has lived all his life, the other belongs to Normandy. I belong to England and England belongs to me! My father worked for it, I have worked for it. Look, my friend, I know this is as great a division of loyalty for you as it is for me. Gospatrick is the great-uncle of my Edith and, since she is also my cousin, he is, as you say, a kinsman of mine. But he is closer than that to you. Your mother fostered him; he grew up in your home. He is like an elder brother to you. If you want time to decide whom you should support, I will bear no grudge . . .'

'Just tell me what you're going to do! You know who commands my loyalty, now or at any other time!'

'Thank you, my friend. Of course I shouldn't have doubted you,' Harold said. 'I must act swiftly, I still have to go to Normandy, but will have less to bargain with now, since I have not been able to get Stigand's appointment ratified. Now I must go to William with an offer that will benefit both of us.'

'An offer? Of what?'

'I'm not sure. That is something I shall have to think about. This new plot changes a great deal. My only hope now lies in some sort of alliance with William. There is certainly no gain for my brothers or me in Edgar's claim. Edgar would over-run England with Scots and Hungarians, just as Edward tried to over-run it with Normans. I have no wish to start all over again at the bottom. Cedric, will you come to Normandy with me?'

'Gladly, but is that important?'

'I think so. You will come as my military commander and as England's greatest champion. I want William to understand that any offer I make him will be as much a guarded threat as a peace offering. Apart from which, of course, how could I do without you? I set you the simple task of watching my sister and brother, and look what you uncover! You are invaluable to me. Have you learned anything more about Tostig and Edith by the way?'

'Only that Edith is as loyal to you as she is to Tostig. You have no need to worry about her. As for Tostig, well, you knew what he was up to in Northumbria before you went away, and it's getting worse. He's like Sweyn, Harold. I hope he doesn't go the same way. I'm told there's hardly anyone in the North who has a good word for him.'

'Aye, there'll be a revolt there soon enough. That's another reason I must get to Normandy and back quickly. I shall have to see the king first, but with any luck he won't keep me dallying long.'

Harold started back for the house, with such long strides that Cedric almost had to run to keep up with him.

'Harold,' Cedric said urgently. 'Are you going to give yourself enough time to think this over? This is a good deal more hasty than anything you've done before; and by God, that's saying something! What are you going to say to Edward? Are you going to tell him anything at all?'

'Not yet,' Harold determined. 'When he wants to know, I'll think of something to tell him. Damn it, does he ever tell me what's going on in his devious little mind?'

'No,' Cedric conceded drily. 'The way he treats you, you'd think he ruled the country.'

VIII

.

ALL his life Harold had been ambitious and purposeful, but he
had never been so rashly confident as to ignore the signs that
Heaven chose to send him from time to time. Even now, when he
was reaching for the richest prize of all, he tried to heed them.
When his ship ran into the most violent storm he had ever known,
he became more conscious of the possible significance of the
tempest than the danger it presented. He fought as hard to convince
himself that it was a perfectly normal squall as to keep his balance
on the wildly pitching deck, but he could not fully dismiss his
doubts.

'You don't think this means anything, do you?' he shouted
at Cedric, barely making himself heard above the howling and
crashing.

'It means we may not live out the day . . .' Cedric began, but
was taken with a painful retching before he could say more.

The storm had sprung up quite suddenly as they approached the
Norman coast, and such was its fury that, within the hour, they
had no idea where they were or in which direction they were going.
It was noon on a summer day, yet the sky was as black as night
with rolling clouds that clashed in bright, hissing sheets of white
and deafening bursts of thunder. The sea had turned to a heaving
black and white, now rising high above the tall prow, now plunging
down again over the deck, leaving the vessel wallowing hopelessly
in a trough or suspended sickeningly in mid-air. The rain lanced
down in torrents, blotting the horizon, hissing into the waves and
washing from decks and crew the salt water that crashed over the
gunwales.

Trying to stand upright was like struggling to stay on a madly
bucking horse. The high head of the ship dipped into watery
chasms, vanished into the waves, reared up, spun to the left or to
the right and twisted crazily beneath the pounding that came first
from the port side then from starboard.

Crew and passengers clung to slippery wet ropes, to the mast,
to the rowers' benches, to anything solid that was not likely to be
dragged away by the sea, and could do no more than pray. One
crewman had been swept over the side, almost before his cry of
despair had left his lips. Next some of the horses had gone, breaking

loose in their panic and nearly trampling the men as they slithered off the deck. Now, with the fate of the ship taken out of their hands, the men waited, some with eyes closed, some wide-eyed with fear, to know if God would destroy them or grant them mercy. Harold and Cedric, as passengers of noble rank, had been given the safest position near the mast, but they were as exposed as any other to the wind and waves. The heaving sickness took away much of their strength and resolve. They clutched at each other as well as at the mast, and the captain tried to protect them further by wrapping himself around them as far as he could stretch.

'It's not necessarily a bad sign,' Harold yelled. 'It could mean that if we survive this, we can come through the worst that faces us . . .'

Cedric was not impressed.

'You mean this is not the worst you are expecting?' he moaned. 'If this is a sign, it means that soldiers should stay on dry land, and leave the sea to those who like it. God, what a way to die!'

Hardly had the words left his lips when the ship struck something solid; the impact shuddered through every timber and joint, shaking everyone loose like fleas and throwing them heavily on the hard deck.

'We're beached!' they heard the captain call as they went down.

'Jump sirs, jump over the side now!' the captain beseeched his passengers, and indeed, some of the crew were already scrambling across the gunwales to take this one slim chance of reaching land safely.

Harold inched back to the mast, and lay with his arms round it, hugging it like life itself.

'Jump into that?' he bellowed back. 'I'll be damned if I will!'

'Please, my lord. It is your only hope! The ship will be smashed to splinters at any moment!'

It was soon plain that the captain was right. The vessel was hurled on to the beach a second time and, as well as the jarring crash of the hull going aground, they clearly heard the sharp cracking of timbers. So steeply was the ship canted over to one side that men slid helplessly down the streaming deck and piled into the rough-edged coaming, while some went right over into the water. Huge waves poured over the side and sloshed violently across the deck as the ship righted itself, catching up more men and pounding them from side to side before tossing them into the sea. Even Harold was not prepared to go through that again. He and Cedric took the captain's advice and rolled over into the crashing waves. They pushed blindly for the shore; they knew they would be crushed if the sea picked up the great hull looming over them and dashed it down once more. Their feet touched sand for an instant, but then the undertow snatched them back and they had to wait for the next inward rush of the tide to send them back on to the swift-sliding shingle.

Cedric, weighted down by his mail coat, could scarcely move, and within seconds had given himself up for dead. But suddenly he found himself on hands and knees in waves no higher than his chest. For a while he could do no more than kneel there and regain his breath, but finally he managed to stumble up the beach.

They lay in the sheeting rain, exhausted, listening to the booming of thunder and ocean and thanking God for their deliverance. Everyone was alive, as far as they could tell, but no-one had the strength to take a tally. They watched the ship spin like a leaf in the wind and smash itself to pieces between land and sea, and were amazed that they had escaped.

'Well, where are we, captain?' Harold grumbled. 'I can see nothing but dunes. We could be miles from any kind of port.'

'The Norman coast, sir, I think,' the captain offered.

'The Norman coast,' Harold repeated sourly, shaking with cold. 'That's very helpful, thank you. I had been worried that it might be Africa.'

'Wherever we are, I suggest we try to find some people,' Cedric cut in. 'I have the strength to walk, if you have.'

'Walk on,' Harold said, getting up. 'I can still match Cedric Shieldless pace for pace.'

'My lords,' the captain nervously interrupted. 'My lords, there is the unpaid passage money . . .'

'Money?' Cedric shouted indignantly. 'Christ's blood, man, I'll say it's unpaid! You destroy our horses, you nearly drown us in your rotten ship, you land us miles from anywhere – and you have the effrontery to ask for money?'

'But sir!' the captain protested, 'I have lost everything, my ship, my cargo . . .'

'And your passengers,' Cedric said harshly. 'We're going!'

'Wait!' Harold cut in, and he took some gold coins from his purse. 'Here,' he told the anxious seaman, 'here's your fare, and some besides. I am willing to believe it is partly due to your skill we are still alive, and I did charter your ship before you were fully ready to sail. I regret the loss of her. I hope you make it good soon. If not, come to see me when we have returned to England, and I'll do what I can to help you.'

'Thank you, lord Harold,' the captain said humbly. 'And God bless you. You are truly the prince they say you are!'

'It does no harm to treat people kindly when they are in need of it,' Harold chided Cedric, as they trudged away through the sodden dunes. 'I think you must have forgotten all those lessons you used to try to teach me, long ago. Damn it, man, once I would have hanged a fellow for knocking me off my horse, and it was you who stopped me. What has happened to you?'

Cedric stumped along in silence.

'I don't know,' he confessed at length. 'it may be that I live with a constant feeling of fear these days. Can you wonder at that? You're just as much to blame. Your plans become more and more ambitious; your hands reach higher and higher. I wake up at nights wondering how far you will go before you destroy yourself . . .'

He stopped short, realising that Harold was no longer with him. Looking back, he saw his friend doubled up with arms clutched tightly into his stomach, and limping painfully. The lameness down Harold's left side had taken him again, and Cedric went back to him.

'Can you walk if I help you?' Cedric asked. 'We've got to get you somewhere dry and warm.'

'Don't stand there talking about it, then,' Harold grated. 'Give me your arm!'

But before they had taken more than a few steps, Harold stopped again. He pointed into the dunes nearby. 'You see?' he said hoarsely, 'now there's an omen for you!' In the wind-blown drifts, flapping like a torn brown parchment, was Harold's favourite falcon. He had brought her with him knowing that Duke William loved to go hawking above all other sports, but the last he had seen of her was on the ship when she had been fluttering wildly, chained to her perch, battered by the storm. Somehow she had broken free and, drenched and bedraggled, had flown or been washed ashore. Harold pushed free of Cedric and hobbled down the beach to pick up his pet and stroke the water and sand from her feathers.

'Nothing can beat down the bird of prey for long, Cedric Shield-less. This pretty pet has come through the storm and will soar again for the kill. Would you tell her how high to fly?'

'No,' Cedric admitted, as he helped disentangle the knotted jesses. 'But then, she knows from experience.'

'And experience comes from daring,' Harold replied. 'Doesn't it, my lovely one?'

They noticed then that a small band of mounted soldiers had ridden down the beach to talk with the sailors, still huddled in the rain where Harold and Cedric had left them. They saw the captain point them out, and the riders approached them at a casual trot.

'I have heard these coasts are swarming with pirates and wreckers,' Cedric said, his hand moving to his sword hilt.

'There's not much we can do about it,' Harold shrugged. 'We're on foot with nowhere to hide. No, leave that blade of yours where it is, my friend. There is a chance they could be friendly, you know.'

The soldiers reined in a few yards short of them, regarding their bedraggled finery with interest. The leader smiled and spoke to them in French, but Harold and Cedric could only signal that they were hopelessly lost, cold and anxious for direction. The commander grinned, and motioned for them to climb up behind two of his men.

'Well,' Harold commented. 'We may be in luck.'

'Maybe,' Cedric conceded. 'But I hope you have another of your omens ready in case they intend to cut our throats.'

The soldiers carried them for a mile or more through marshy coastal reaches, and their fears were somewhat allayed when they saw a huge motte and bailey loom up ahead of them. The leader pointed to it and, with another grin, gave a name to its owner.

'Le Comte Guy de Ponthieu.'

'Who's that?' Cedric called across to Harold. 'Have you heard of him?'

'The name has a familiar ring to it,' Harold frowned. 'But I can't say I know why.'

When they were escorted into his grand hall, Count Guy seemed genial enough, a big, rotund man, concerned and hospitable, yet after a few minutes Cedric and Harold both sensed beneath the outward amity an almost indefinable hint of treachery. The Count gave them good clothes to change into, warmed them by his fire and was generous with his food and wine, but all the while they had the feeling he was watching them as a money-lender watches time multiply the interest on his investment, and soon they were to be proved right.

'A most unfortunate accident for you,' the Count gushed, while his guests ate hungrily. 'But it is an honour for me to entertain such exalted Englishmen as Prince Harold and Cedric Shieldless. You were travelling to see Duke William, you say?'

'We were,' Harold confirmed.

Guy waved expansively at his stone hall, with its high vaulted roof and impressive tapestries neatly hung between carved pillars, and the massive central chimney where two men could have quite comfortably stood roasting a whole ox on the iron spit.

'Well,' he sighed, with mock humility. 'This is not the palace of William, Duke of Normandy, but I trust I can make you as welcome as he.'

'Thank you; you are most kind,' Harold responded. 'But we

will not impose upon you longer than necessary. I'm sure you understand; we are eager to keep our appointment with the duke.'

Something changed in Guy's face then, something all but unseen yet real enough. It was not the smile, for that remained fixed, nor the benign satisfaction of a host watching the enjoyment of his guests, nor the ease of a master secure in his own fortress. It was something else, a change in the eyes from false warmth to true coolness. Whatever it was, it was felt immediately by his two guests as surely as if a door had been opened to let in a cold draught.

'Yes, of course,' Guy said. 'But that is something we must discuss when you are well rested.'

Harold and Cedric exchanged glances, their instinct for danger working like a single shared nerve. Both surveyed the hall with scarcely a turn of the head. The doors were strongly guarded, they observed, considering they were but two harmless travellers.

'I think we are flies in a web,' Cedric whispered.

'Aye,' Harold returned, 'and I believe I remember now where I heard this man's name.' Returning his attention to Guy he calmly asked: 'Discuss? Does our journey present you with some difficulty, then? We will gladly buy horses from you, if you have them to spare . . .'

'Oh no, it's not a question of horses,' the count laughed jovially. 'Good Lord, I have plenty of those, and you may have your choice. No, it's more a little matter of the law, really . . .'

'I'm sorry, I don't understand,' Harold said frigidly. 'What law?'

Guy's geniality faded. He remained polite, but with the time for play-acting past, he regarded his guests as a tutor would look upon slow pupils.

'The traditional law here regarding shipwrecks,' he told them. 'It plays a large part in sustaining the income of my estates. You see, it states quite categorically that all vessels washed up on my shoreline become my property, together with their cargoes. But more to the point, in your case, it gives me the right to ask a price of your families or overlords for ensuring your safekeeping and return.'

Cedric leapt to his feet.

'You dare hold Earl Harold for ransom?' he raged. 'This is intolerable!'

Guy was undisturbed. He indicated the soldiers at his command, and fixed Cedric with a warning glare.

'Please sit down and calm yourself, Cedric Shieldless,' he requested. 'Even here in France we know of your reputation, but I am sure you can see it would be foolish for you to challenge my powers here.'

Cedric made to argue again, but Harold restrained him.

'Sit down, Cedric,' Harold agreed, his own anger held in check. 'The count is perfectly correct. We cannot fight him. But we can repay his hospitality by pointing out to him the foolishness of his scheme. I wonder if you realise, Count, that we are emissaries of King Edward to the court of his cousin, Duke William? As such, we are entitled to the courtesy and protection afforded to official ambassadors, and I am certain that neither William nor the King of France would approve of you holding us here against our will. I ask you to reconsider.'

'Duke William, the King of England, the King of France,' Guy shrugged. 'None of them knows you are here, so their shadows do not startle me at this moment. As I say, I am within my rights. All I need is a written contract with you, authorising that a certain sum be paid for your release, and I can go to King Edward without a care. Not even he can argue against a signed agreement between you and me. Whether or not he wants to pay it is a different matter, of course. But I have no doubt that he will, for his Dux Anglorum.'

'And how much is this certain sum?'

'Oh; shall we say, for the two of you, five thousand pounds of silver?'

'A ridiculous price! You're asking for the treasury of England. What if I refuse to sign this contract?'

Guy spread his arms in a careless gesture.

'Then you are my guests for as long as you wish to stay,' he said, with feigned magnanimity.

'This is indeed intolerable,' Harold snarled. 'You are holding us imprisoned. Five thousand pounds of silver is a king's ransom. Edward's entire estates must scarcely be worth that much. You had better think it over again.'

'No, it is you who have to think it over, lord Harold,' persisted Guy, 'in as much time as you wish to devote to it. Myself, I have all the time in the world. Perhaps you would like to discuss it in private? Let me have you shown to your rooms.'

'He has us pinned down very firmly, damn it,' Harold admitted when they were alone. 'There's nothing we can do about it!'

'Edward will never pay that much, that's certain,' Cedric groaned, 'not even for you. He can't. We could try to escape.'

'From this fortress? We have no chance. He could have us murdered and our bodies disposed of. No one would ever know we had been here.'

'But he won't. He's too greedy. You can see the silver gleaming in his eyes.'

Harold started wandering around their chamber, which adjoined an untidy little library where litters of documents were gathering dust. It looked as though Guy had taken these papers from countless messengers unlucky enough to be shipwrecked in his territory. The seals were broken on some of them, but others were tossed into piles unread, and Harold began to sift through them curiously.

'The greedier the man, the more ruthless,' he was saying. 'He'll kill the goose rather than let it go. That's probably what happened to some of the bearers of these letters. No, we must play for time, try to persuade him to ask for less. We can only hope that Edward hears what's become of us, when the captain returns home. Incidentally, how wise I was to pay him! God's word, look at all this! He must have been collecting it for years. I wonder if there are any more of Aelfgifu's or Gospatrick's letters here? Perhaps we could spend our time finding out more about them and their plans.'

'By the cross of Christ, I swear, Harold, if you're going to start telling me this is all for the good, all part of your good omen, I'll throttle you . . .'

'Easy, friend, I was going to say no such thing,' Harold laughed. 'But wouldn't it be more commendable than spending the hours moping and hoping for release? Just think of it! Somewhere here there may be plans for a Scottish invasion, a Hungarian invasion. . . .'

'Just now I've lost interest in what they're plotting,' Cedric said with contempt. 'So should you. We may get home – one day – to find Edgar king, Gospatrick Dux Anglorum and Duke William commander of housecarls.'

'Not while I live,' Harold vowed. 'No upstart little wrecker like Guy is going to keep me here long enough for that! Don't worry. If no help has arrived here within a few days, then we'll have the fight you're spoiling for. We'll get out of here or die in the attempt, but the Devil take me if I'll sign any contract with that fat hog!'

Count Guy remained confident and patient, however, and even began to lord it over Harold and Cedric in the face of their passive resistance. Indeed, he started to boast about his future in a manner which suggested they would have no future to look forward to without his mercy.

'Duke William and I are good friends, as it happens,' he told his hostages. 'I have known him since he became master of Normandy, at such a young and tender age. I had good counsel for him in those days, and he has always been grateful for it. Once you are a friend of William you are a friend for life, I can say that for the man. I am one of the few people to whom he has promised estates in England, when he becomes king of your country.'

'He is so sure he will be king?' Harold inquired, giving little credence to the man's bragging.

'Has not King Edward made him his heir?'

'So it was rumoured. Edward has never confirmed it.'

'It is well known on this side of the Channel,' Guy said loftily. 'No one here doubts that William will be king.'

'In England we elect our kings.'

'But only from heirs nominated from within the royal family. There are no other candidates, are there?'

Harold was not prepared to discuss with the Comte de Ponthieu what he knew of Gospatrick's plot, nor was he ready to announce to the world that he himself had ambitions for the crown. Cedric was still the only person who had been entrusted with that knowledge.

'There may be, before Edward dies,' he replied. 'William shouldn't put his hand out for the crown yet – it will be humiliating for him if he has to withdraw it again. Nor should you count your English acres too soon, dear host, even though you are already asking Edward for all he owns in exchange for us!'

Cedric burst into a mocking laugh, and Guy coloured with indignation.

'We will see how much your king is willing to pay for you,' he retorted. 'And as for your obvious dislike of Duke William, I should be careful not to make it known to him, should you ever meet him. When the duke sets his mind on a goal, nothing is allowed to prevent him reaching it. And just as he is most generous to his friends, he is most unforgiving towards his enemies. Oppose him now, and you may find yourself not so highly placed when the crown is his.'

It was Harold's turn to scoff.

'It seems there are plenty like you, eager to take Englishmen's places the moment William steps in. Do you think we have not heard the list of those waiting for favours from William? His brothers, Odo and Robert, his wife Matilda, his children, his friends Eustace of Boulogne, William Fitzosbern, and so on. All we have yet to hear is how much the English nobility will be allowed to keep, if anything.'

'Oh, don't worry yourself so, Lord Harold,' Guy smirked. 'I am sure you will still be a rich man under William's rule, if you give him your support now. Look, since you seem so concerned about your future in England, I'll show our goodwill by making my demands for your return a little more modest. I'll ask not five thousand pounds, but one thousand for you and five hundred for Cedric . . .'

A disturbance at the hall doors interrupted him. A guard from the outer gates came hurrying in breathlessly.

'Emissaries from Duke William, my lord,' he told Guy. 'They are at the gates with a large company of soldiers, demanding entry by authority of the duke.'

Guy paled, realising at once that the sudden appearance of this force could only mean that he had over-stepped the mark, but he tried to retain his composure.

'Well, of course, they must be admitted, you fool!' he stormed at the messenger. 'Do you think the duke's emissaries are to be kept waiting outside my house? Show them in at once!'

Harold and Cedric smiled at the pricking of the man's pomp, and Guy saw their amusement.

'This changes nothing,' he muttered. 'I am within my rights, and Duke William will be the first to recognise that.'

'Naturally,' Harold grinned. He could not imagine that they would kick their heels in this castle much longer now. Guy knew it, too, and was desperate to conceal the inner quaking he felt. Now it could be seen how heavily the shadow of William lay over Normandy.

Two young knights breezed into the hall, and announced themselves as Roger Fitzwarren and Hugh d'Evreux, direct from William's court. Fresh-faced and cheerful, hardly into their twenties, and considerably outranked by Guy de Ponthieu, they nevertheless showed much confidence in themselves and by the manner of their bearing treated him as an equal. They were only too well aware that they came with the invisible yet palpable weight of William's might behind them. They greeted Count Guy with brief courtesy, and turned immediately to Harold and Cedric without giving the count a chance to ask them their business.

'My lords, Earl Harold and Cedric Shieldless,' Roger began, 'we are pleased and honoured to meet you, and overjoyed to find you safe after your ordeal. Duke William has heard of your misfortune. He sends his sincere good wishes, and says he is eager to meet you.'

'Thank you; you are most kind,' responded Harold, instantly liking the two young men, and with a significant glance at Guy, he added: 'We are also anxious to see him.'

Guy, annoyed at being ignored in his own hall, pressed himself into the conversation.

'If you come as the duke's emissaries to me,' he blustered, 'perhaps you would be good enough to pass whatever message my Lord William sends with you . . .'

'Oh, indeed, we shall, Count,' smiled Hugh d'Evreux. 'Duke

William thanks you for caring so well for his guests, and says he is pleased to be able to welcome them himself at Rouen, where we shall escort them.'

There was respect enough in the way in which Hugh delivered the words, yet there was also a firmness, even a veiled threat, which Guy could hardly miss. He had been left an opening through which he could have escaped his own stupidity, gracefully, but even with his back to the wall he was as obstinate as a dog who will not relinquish his hold on a juicy bone.

'Well, of course,' he said, with a careful, oily smile. 'I would not wish to delay our noble English guests a moment more. But I must crave the duke's indulgence while I exercise my rights under the law . . .'

'No, Count,' Hugh stated flatly, his smile and deferential manner vanishing. 'The duke has made it plain to us that you may crave nothing! He orders us to return to Rouen with his guests as soon as they are ready to leave, and without conditions. To tell you the truth, he is rather annoyed that they should have been detained so long.'

'Damn your impertinence!' Guy gasped, making a last effort to salvage both his pride and his anticipated riches, 'Not even William has this right. I act within the law!'

Neither Hugh nor Roger were shaken by his words. They grinned at each other, and at the men they had come to rescue, and Roger said:

'Yes, our Lord William expected you to say as much. And he asked us to put this to you. You may deliver your hostages to us here and now, or prepare to receive him personally. Do reconsider, Count. The duke will be extremely displeased with all of us, won't he, if he has to make the journey himself? As for the law, well, you know what the Duke is like about changing laws which impede him. He has, in this instance, waived the law of shipwrecks.'

'Oh, has he? And does King Philip of France know of that?'

Roger shrugged.

'I feel there is a very good chance,' he said patiently, 'that you will be arguing the matter with William long before you can take it to King Philip.'

Harold and Cedric had watched with astonishment, and admiration for the young couriers. In England, no mere messenger would dare to be so insolent to a nobleman, no matter whose word he carried. It was not unknown for disrespectful emissaries to have their tongues cut out, or to be sent back to their masters in a shroud. Yet here were two tail-wagging pups pushing themselves into a count's castle as though they owned it, and not only giving him orders but offering him threats in his own home.

Roger and Hugh knew they courted danger, despite the size of the army they had brought with them, but their peril was no greater than Guy's. They came with William's might at their command. They were his devoted servants, and they leapt at the chance to prove themselves like hunting hounds straining at the leash. They were expected by William to convey not only his order, but also the authority with which he intended it should be received. As the emissaries of William, they were William in the absence of William himself. Such boldness might astonish the English, but it did not surprise Guy. When his temper cooled, he had no choice but to accept that to strike down these brash youngsters would be tantamount to taking a gauntlet and slapping William in the face with it.

Finally speechless, Guy expelled air like a bladder deflating. The challenge of a direct confrontation with the bastard duke had hit home hard. He ignored his tormentors, and turned to Harold.

'You may go whenever you wish,' he scowled. 'I have too much respect for Duke William to quarrel with him merely over your presence here.'

Harold nodded, feigning gratitude.

'Thank you, Count,' he said, 'for valuing us so highly. If ever you come to England, I promise you there will be a price on your head that not a monarch in the world can afford.'

On their way out, Cedric muttered: 'I think I'm going to like Duke William. He does things our way.'

'That,' said Harold, 'is why I am not going to like him!'

'I hope you will not think that all Normans are like Guy de Ponthieu,' Hugh said, as they set out on the journey to Rouen. 'He is one of those stubborn men who try to resist change, the kind of men the duke has little time for. Duke William has asked us to apologise for your treatment at the Count's hands.'

'You have more than made up for it,' Harold assured him. 'It was a delight to see how you handled Guy. We are indebted to you.'

'We are honoured,' said Hugh, glowing with pride. 'And more so since the praise comes from such a great warrior. We have heard of your exploits; how you fought King Edward to win back your lands and titles, and how you warred with the Welsh. We heard that you slew King Griffith in single combat, struck his head from his shoulders with a single blow – and him a giant of a man standing half again as high as any other. Was it truly so?'

'Well, these tales lose nothing in the telling,' Harold confessed with a smile. 'But it was the toughest fight of my life, I can swear to that.'

'And you, Cedric Shieldless,' Hugh went on. 'They say that you are the most feared of England's warriors. We have been told that some of your weaker soldiers run away, claiming that you train your men by making them run across trenches spiked with spears. Is it so?'

Cedric saw Harold wink at him, and realised that Harold wanted to keep these legends alive, probably in order to raise their reputation to its highest level here in Normandy, where it mattered most.

'Yes, but they are blunt spears,' answered Cedric, straight-faced. 'And the trenches no wider than a man can manage with proper effort.'

If Hugh was taken in, his friend Roger seemed to suspect that they were being gently teased.

'Duke William would approve of such methods,' he said with equal seriousness. 'He, too, believes that an army should consist only of the toughest and most courageous men. Each day his men are made to run beneath a bombardment of rocks and burning pitch from the catapults.'

Hugh's mouth dropped open at this scurrilous lie, but then he noticed Harold and Cedric shaking with silent laughter.

The mirth burst out from all of them then, echoing across the broad green fields of Normandy.

English and Normans were traditionally suspicious of each other, but it did not seem strange now that Harold was able to strike up a friendship with these young Normans so quickly. Since he was half Danish, they came from the same stock. Language and culture might have grown widely different, as the Northmen had settled in different lands, but for the first time, Harold was beginning to feel that these Normans were not such arrogant fools after all. It was as if a door had been pushed ajar, and both Normans and English were able to peep through at each other with growing interest.

It led Harold to think that a satisfactory arrangement with Duke William was not out of the question, and he rode on more cheerfully.

IX

NEVER had Cedric felt so out of place as at the Ducal court at Rouen, not even the first time he had mingled with English princes and earls, and never had he been made to feel such an object of curiosity. Now he thought he knew how it must feel to be a wild beast brought from a far country in a cage.

As soon as they arrived in the enormous banqueting hall of William's castle, Cedric and Harold were hemmed in by the court – counts, viscounts, knights and their ladies, bishops and abbots and captains, ambassadors, artists and architects who gloried in the patronage of the Duke – and it seemed that in all the babble of foreign voices and crowds of faces there was only one topic of conversation, the Dux Anglorum and his friend. Everyone was keen to press forward for the best view, or a touch or a word from the newcomers. The giggling women were fascinated by the long fair hair and moustaches of the guests, and their rapt attention was highly flattering, yet for Cedric also disturbing. The men stared covetously, jealous of the Englishmen's excessive display of jewellery, and the children gaped in awe of these two famous warriors who were said to have eaten newborn babies while campaigning in Wales. It was hardly dignified for men of such rank to be put on show and whispered about and, Cedric suspected, made the butt of jokes, as though they were a fresh consignment of court jesters. Harold looked well enough at ease, doubtless because he had been to other palaces, but for Cedric it was painful, and he was thinking he would rather face a hostile army than this crowd of gawping idiots. He fully expected them to start prodding and poking at him as if he were a performing bear at a fair.

'What's the matter with them?' he grumbled to Harold. 'Have they never seen English men before?'

'Why should you mind?' Harold chuckled. 'You are being admired by some of the loveliest women in France. Don't you realise that many of them have come here especially to see us? You can have your choice of those beauties, you know. They are aching to know what it is like to bed with a bad, bold Englishman.'

'I'll be glad to show them, if we ever escape this crowd.'

'Well, do as I say. Pick your fancy, and I'll bet you a pound of silver you can have her. Only don't try to make off with mine, the black-haired heifer with the udders – see her? Any other is yours.'

Cedric replied with a snort, not so much in mockery of Harold's confidence as because of impatience with all the fuss. He could find comely women without going through this, he was thinking, and he looked longingly but without success for a way out of the hall. The noise of idle chatter deafened him, and he was grateful for a proferred cup of wine.

There was no mistaking the moment when Duke William arrived. He was not announced, and yet a hush slowly spread across the throng before him to muffle the sounds of revelry. Harold and Cedric were aware of the crowd falling back and becoming quiet some seconds before they caught sight of the duke, who approached them with all the deference due to his important visitors, but with no more show of respect than if this meeting were a quite ordinary one.

William was burly and brusque, with the simple authority of the hard-fighting politician he had been all his life. He came trailing his noble retinue like a chain of dogs, every inch a self-made man, the hated bastard son of a duke and a tanner's daughter who had whipped the warlords of Normandy to heel and had kept them there through nearly thirty years' reign. He towered above his underlings both in stature and force of will. At just under six feet William was a tall man, equalling Harold in size, but more sturdily built, his big body gradually going to fat. His largeness was further exaggerated when, as now, he was accompanied by his tiny wife Matilda, who was a mere four feet from slippers to coronet. In fact, all around him became small, including his half-brothers, Bishop Odo of Bayeux and Count Robert of Mortain.

This, then, was William, supposed heir of Edward the Confessor of England, and even Harold could not help but be impressed by this legendary Norman warrior lord. William then proved himself an able diplomat as well as a cunning warrior by singling out which of the two Englishmen was Harold with not a hint of hesitation. He had taken the trouble to have Harold described to him in the finest detail, so that he might avoid a mistake no matter how many Harold brought with him. Thus two of the greatest leaders in Europe came face to face as if they had known each other all their lives, each as assured as the other. The people tensed with expectation, aware that they were to witness a meeting of giants, one that could decide the future of nations. Everyone there knew that these two men ruled their respective domains without hindrance, and would tolerate none. The crowd was silent, but the air hummed like a hot summer field. It was as though two wrestlers were sizing each other up and deciding whether to engage in a battle to the death, or to acknowledge their mutual strength and fight instead side by side against all comers. Perhaps it was admiration, or perhaps amusement at the eagerness of the crowd, but Harold and William began to regard each other with real pride and liking. William extended his hand, Harold grasped it firmly, and they exchanged the kiss of peace.

'Lord Harold, you are welcome in my house and in my dukedom,' William said. 'Long have I looked forward to this moment.'

'And I, Lord William,' Harold responded. 'Already your hospitality warms us deeply.'

More compliments were exchanged. William quickly inquired after the health of his cousin King Edward, and then became more serious.

'Your first experience of Norman hospitality was an unfortunate one, I'm afraid,' he said. 'I offer my most sincere apologies for the ill-mannered actions of Guy de Ponthieu. He is a vulgar pirate, no more.'

He spoke in the precise manner of one unsure of himself in company, a man aware of the more educated people surrounding him. As he carefully chose each phrase, he would glance challengingly from one companion to another, as if seeking confirmation of his words, or defying anyone to disagree. This surprised Harold, and he read it as a lack of assurance. Later he would find that, for the first time in his life, he had underestimated his man quite badly. When William sounded ill at ease, it was only because his mind was active with other plans.

'Your welcome has atoned for his more surely than any words,' Harold told him. 'Your knights Hugh and Roger deserve high praise. They made Guy look more like a sly poacher than a pirate.'

'A poor poacher, that one,' William laughed. 'He set his traps for prize stags, and caught nothing but a chill!'

The whole court bellowed uproariously at that, and their mirth sealed the new friendship between the Dukes of Normandy and England. William laid an arm across Harold's shoulders.

'And now, my Lord Harold,' he said. 'Let us not forget the purpose which brought you to Normandy . . .'

Harold would not have recognised Wulfnoth and Haakon if William had not pointed them out to him. Both had grown older, of course, and Haakon had changed from a young boy to a man of twenty-five years, but quite apart from the changes the years had made, Harold would not have known them for Englishmen, let alone members of his own family.

They were in Norman dress, their hair short and their faces shaved clean. It shocked Harold that his brother and nephew should have drifted so far from English ways. Haakon, however, had not seen the disdain in his uncle's eyes, and he ran to Harold with arms outstretched.

'Uncle Harold!' he cried, 'It's so good to see you again! Is it true, can I really go home with you?'

'You can indeed, nephew,' Harold laughed, putting aside his outrage at the young man's appearance. 'King Edward himself has given his blessing. When I return to England, so will you.'

He detached himself from Haakon's eager hug and turned to greet Wulfnoth, and was at once chilled through by his youngest brother's coolness. Wulfnoth politely held out a hand, a contrast with Haakon's welcome that was little short of insulting.

'Well, Harold,' Wulfnoth said blandly. 'It's been a long time, hasn't it? The day I heard that father had died I thought it might be quite a while before anyone remembered me. I must admit, though, I didn't expect even you to leave us here twelve years. I hear that you have done very well for yourself in that time. I congratulate you.'

Harold said nothing for a few seconds which seemed to pass like minutes. His jaw was working as if he were biting hard upon his anger.

'I'm here now, Wulfnoth,' he managed at last. 'I have spent these years working for my brothers, as well as for myself. Tostig, Gurth and Leofwine will all tell you that. There is plenty awaiting you in England.'

'Is there?' Wulfnoth answered bitterly. 'A pity, then, that England holds nothing to tempt me any more. Twelve years ago it did, perhaps even five, but not now. I have a Norman wife, a Norman home, Normandy and Duke William have treated me well. I have forgotten England. Take Haakon with you; he wants to go. But don't worry about me, not any more.'

Harold was astonished and deeply offended. He could not believe his ears. For a moment he suspected a Norman plot, thinking that his brother must be speaking under duress, but one glance at Duke William and his advisers showed that either William was innocent of any conspiracy, or he was a commendable actor. He and his family looked as shamed by this exhibition of rudeness as did the rest of the court.

'Stay if you wish, then,' Harold told Wulfnoth coldly. 'The choice is yours. I'm pleased to hear that you have found happiness here.'

Bishop Odo leaned towards Duke William.

'The English dogs are beginning to snarl over the bone,' he murmured. 'Did I not tell you it would be so? You cannot keep so many hounds in one kennel; they'll always start to scrap among themselves.'

William nodded, brushing his brother aside, and took it upon himself to ease the silence. He took Harold's arm and, ordering his retinue to remain with the other Englishmen, he began walking with Harold towards his private apartments.

'If you are well enough refreshed, Lord Harold,' William said, 'I wish to talk with you alone. There is so much we must discuss . . .'

Harold immediately put his brother's sourness out of his mind, and became the professional politician again.

'King Edward asks me to convey his sincere affection,' Harold said, when he and William had been left together in a small ante-chamber, sipping wine. 'He also expresses his gratitude for your many years of faithful friendship. He will never forget the kindness he was shown in Normandy, and he assures you that there is no small place for you in his will.'

It was a diplomatic way of telling William that Harold personally neither believed in nor cared for the supposed promise of the crown to the Norman duke. William saw the statement for what it was, and was amused. The ghost of a smile played around his lips as he replied.

'Kind sentiments, for which I thank him,' William said. 'But let us pray that the conditions of his will are not to be fulfilled too soon. He is a saintly one, my cousin Edward. It will be a great loss to the world when he passes on.'

'Quite,' Harold shrugged. 'But he grows old. He is fifty-nine years old now, which is a great age for any man. We must prepare.'

William's grin finally broke out.

'Yes, we must,' he conceded, 'and I believe you do not want to beat about the bush any more than I do, Lord Harold. Allow me to flush out the hare, then. I am not unaware, you know, that you do not share my cousin's wish that I should inherit his crown.'

Harold was taken aback by the duke's directness, but he soon recovered. Now he had no choice but to be as candid as William, he decided, and he drew a deep breath, ready to test the duke's hospitality and friendliness to the full.

'Rather let us say, my lord Duke,' he began cautiously, 'that I hope there is plenty of room for a happy partnership between us, should you be as willing as I am to contrive something.'

William contemplated that for a moment. The same thought had occurred to him, but he was not sure what he and Harold had to offer each other. His wife Matilda had suggested that perhaps

Harold could be given one of their daughters in marriage, but that did not please William. He abhorred loose morals, a repulsion born of the taint of bastardy against his own name, and the prospect of a daughter of his being married to a man who casually lived with a mistress and had illegitimate children by her did not please him at all. Besides, while it might be a good match for Harold, it offered William little more than an ambitious son-in-law.

'I would be only too happy to strike up some mutually beneficial agreement with you,' William said sincerely. 'And let me assure you, I wish to take nothing that you presently hold. So let us start from there. What can I do for you, and what can you do for me?'

'Well, I am not a selfish man, but one of simple wants,' Harold beamed, draining his cup and holding it out for more. 'So let us put aside what you can do for me, for the time being. There is much I can do for you.'

'Oh?'

'Yes, there is. And the first thing is that I can rid you of a spy you may be unaware of. A well-established spy, someone who was at this court long before you or your father became Duke. She was here in the time of your grandfather, Duke Richard.'

'She? You intrigue me.'

'I thought I would. Have you never heard of the Princess Aelfgifu?'

'Edward's half-sister? Daughter of Ethelred by his first marriage?'

'The same. She was brought here by your great-aunt Emma, with Edward, when Ethelred's family was sent here during the Viking invasion, more than fifty years ago.'

'And you are telling me that this ancient exile is spying on me?'

'Ancient, but still very active,' Harold nodded. 'Let me explain. She lived in this court for many years, made many powerful friends, kept in touch with what was left of the English royal family, and – because of all that she lost, because of all the cruel things that were done to her family – lived by the vow that one day Ethelred's kingdom would be restored to the descendants of Ethelred. While Edward has been king, that has been brought about, but now she sees a danger of Ethelred's line being snuffed out once more. She and her followers are determined that the crown shall go to the last pure descendant of Ethelred, and that is his great-grandson Edgar, Edward's great-nephew. Edgar is ready to come from Hungary as soon as Edward dies.'

William finished his wine, and put down his goblet. It had been his third of the day, and his temperate nature limited him quite strictly to three.

412

'I see,' he said. 'Princess Aelfgifu keeps Edgar informed of all that happens in Normandy?'

'All the alliances, all the plans for alliances, all the enemies you have, how they may be used against you, everything. Not only in Normandy, but in France, Flanders, Hungary, Rome, she has built up a circle of well-informed friends over half a century. And just as she knows the nobility of Europe possibly better than you do, so her stepson Gospatrick Uhtredsson knows every noble in northern England who will rally to Edgar's cause when the time comes. They are well organised, Duke William, and well prepared. If we do not want Edgar to be king, we would be well advised to catch up with them.'

'You suggest there is much to be gained by – removing this woman?'

'Time, and advantage over your enemies. If you cared to remove her, as you put it, I could quickly dispose of Gospatrick once I returned to England. Edgar's two most able supporters would then be lost to him, and with them much of his following.'

'And you, no doubt, can tell me where to find her?'

'I can.'

William waited, and his wry smile reappeared when it became clear that it was now his turn to lay down a sacrifice to the god Avarice.

'Your price?' he inquired bluntly.

'As equal partners, we have twice the strength of Edgar,' Harold calmly pointed out. 'I have heard, William, that you do not care much for any place other than your beloved Normandy. Why leave it, when you can profit as much by staying here? Suppose you and I ruled England jointly: myself in London, you in Rouen?'

'I as king, you as regent?'

'Rather as joint kings, I was thinking.'

'You are a man after my own heart, Harold,' William chuckled. 'Quite blandly you ask me to descend suddenly from the greatest height I could ever reach. Half a kingdom, instead of a whole one? And all to know where to find an ancient crone, whom I could find in a short time anyway? Could I not strike a bargain with Edgar as easily?'

'I think not. Since we discovered the plotting between Aelfgifu and Gospatrick, we have taken a good look at them and all their kin. They want no half measures this time. They want the next English king to be a pure Englishman. No Normans, no Danes, no foreigners, no broken lines of descent. They want the loss of Ethelred's kingdom wiped from England's memory forever. Edgar does not need any nomination, and he has all the allies he needs north of the Humber. He believes that once he starts to march south, every man of pure English blood will rush to his side.'

'So you have nothing to gain from Edgar's reign, either?' William said.

'Nothing. Remember, my family was supposed to be responsible for the murder of his great-uncle Alfred, and various other crimes which Edward has forgiven. Gospatrick wants Northumbria, the earldom held by my brother Tostig. My Earldom of Wessex has probably been promised to one of Edgar's Scottish or Hungarian friends.'

'I must confess,' William acknowledged, 'that this is the most interesting conversation I have had for a very long time. But you are forgetting one thing, Harold, my new-found friend. Edgar does not have Edward's promise of the crown, whereas I . . .'

'William,' Harold interrupted gently. 'Shall we continue to be perfectly honest with each other, now that we have started so well?'

'Certainly. Say what you wish to say.'

'Few people in England set much store by that "promise," and Edward's silence would seem to indicate either that he did not intend it as you believe he did, or that he has since changed his mind. It is not only in England that Edward's royal brethren have died untimely deaths, is it? Didn't his nephew Walter of the Vexin die here in a Norman prison, where you put him? No, don't be offended, Lord Duke. I am only telling you the thinking of the English. They find it hard to accept that he would have promised you the crown thirteen years ago, anyway, because there were so many other possibilities then. First, he might have had sons of his own – and still could, come to that. Would he have denied them their inheritance for the sake of a cousin once removed? At that time his nephew Edward the Exile was still alive, and after him came Edward's son Edgar. Next there was his nephew Earl Ralph of Hereford, a favourite of his in those days. Ralph and his brother Walter were both quite suitable, being sons of Edward's sister. Several putative kings, my lord, all with a greater claim than you.'

William was shaking his head, like a man perplexed by a new idea and trying to come to grips with it.

'Do you know,' he sighed, 'I would never have believed that any man would come into my castle and call me a liar, let alone make me like him while he was saying it!'

'I am not calling you a liar,' Harold assured him. 'I think you were led astray by Edward's dithering, as many of us have been. No one can be sure what Edward intends, never mind what he thinks. We cannot rely on him to make the decision, William. We must make it for him, and quickly.'

'Joint kingship?' William repeated, thoughtfully.

'Yes, King William and King Harold.'

'It seems to me that you have most to gain.'

'No, I would gain no more than I have. I rule England now in Edward's name; you know that. In the same way, I would lose no more than I already hold. But you would acquire estates, wealth, a voice in the Witan, even greater power, higher rank and respect in Europe. You would become King Philip's equal, at Philip's own threshold.'

'You have a persuasive tongue, Harold, especially as I have no wish to war with you. Will you allow me time to think it over?'

'Of course. Though we should not delay settling the matter of Aelfgifu.'

'It is not my way to have old ladies smothered in their sleep,' William warned him.

'Nor mine. There is no need for that. It would be sufficient to lock her up somewhere, let her live the rest of her days comfortably where she can do no harm, and, most important, where she cannot receive news from her family and cannot give them any information about what is happening here.'

'On what pretext would I imprison her?'

'That is quite easy. Ever since she came to Normandy she has lived in sin with a man of the cloth, a monk called Theobald. He has not only broken his vow of celibacy, but has ravished a woman of royal blood, the stepdaughter of your great-aunt Emma, no less. And as for her, well, she has encouraged him in his sinfulness. Isn't that enough, in this devout land of yours?'

'And this wicked pair,' William said with a sardonic smile. 'Are you going to tell me where they live?'

'In the town of Dinan, in Brittany. Theobald is curator of the church library there, and they live in the library apartments as brother and sister.'

'Ah,' William breathed. 'Then that presents us with another problem. Count Conan rules Brittany, and he refuses to recognise me as his overlord.'

Harold shrugged again.

'Doesn't that give us an excuse to go there?' he asked.

William got up and paced the room, studying Harold closely, thinking what a formidable foe this man could make were he not a cunning ally.

'I could take an army into Brittany to subdue Conan,' he stated at last. 'France is quite accustomed to seeing me go on such adventures. And, as my honoured guest, naturally you would be invited along for the sport.'

'And,' Harold smiled, 'we could be sure to call in at Dinan . . .'

' . . . where, as it happens, Conan has one of his strongest forts. Lord Harold, you are a most extraordinary man. I know now how you rose to such power. Just answer me one more question. What if King Edward hears what we have done to his sister? Will he not disown both of us? Will he not have you sent into exile again, or worse? And who then is left for him to nominate as his heir but Edgar?'

'Edward need never know. Who will know, if we say nothing?'

'We would be deceiving Edward,' William observed. 'He has always been good to us. He does not really deserve treatment of this kind.'

'Sometimes it is wiser to be deceitful with good but indecisive men,' Harold argued, 'to ensure that the right course is taken. Come now, Duke, do we have any choice? Can we let Edgar the Stranger walk in and take all that we have worked for?'

William spread his hands in a gesture of resignation.

'I will send Count Conan an ultimatum, which I know he will refuse,' he promised. 'If by some chance he does comply, however, we shall have to find some other way to get this Aelfgifu in our grasp. That may prove difficult, and I may decide to leave her alone, rather than risk discovery and the loss of Edward's confidence.'

'Then you agree to my proposal?'

'Of joint kingship? I still want time to consider that. Just let me add, however, that I prefer to have you as a friend than as an enemy, Harold Dux Anglorum!'

Wulfnoth and Haakon were showing Cedric the quarters which he and Harold were to occupy when Harold rejoined them. Cedric was marvelling at the splendour of the rooms and the beds, for the silken covers and velvet cushions were as fine as anything in the king's palace in London.

'Look at this! I've never been so well stabled!' Cedric greeted Harold. 'Maybe I will be tempted to stay here, too.'

Harold saw Wulfnoth scowl at Cedric's thoughtlessness, and turning to his brother he said soothingly: 'You must forgive Cedric; he's spent too long in his Berkshire farmyard. Wulf, listen to me, will you? I can understand your anger, but can't we both try to forget? Think hard for the next few days, and if you do decide to come back to England, even if not immediately, you can be sure we'll all welcome you with open arms.'

Wulfnoth looked as if he regretted his earlier rudeness. He laid a hand on Harold's shoulder, but shook his head.

'Thank you,' he said. 'But I do believe I shall stay here. I would by lying if I said England meant anything to me now. Perhaps some day I will have a yearning to see it again, but not while Edward lives. That so-called saint condemned me to spend years in exile, and I'll make the best of it rather than go back to serve him. Send me word when Edward goes to his glorious reward in Heaven, and I might reconsider then.'

'So be it,' was all that Harold could say. After Wulfnoth and Haakon had left he sat on his bed, rubbing the grime of the journey from his fingers. He said nothing until Cedric jogged him out of his gloom.

'So, what has come of your talk with Duke William?'

'I have chanced all and put the bait before the bear.' Harold sighed. 'Now I must wait to see if it will gore me or let me put the collar around its neck.'

'The moment I saw the man I wanted to warn you not to trust him,' Cedric said. 'But it sounds as if it's too late now. He's as resolute as you, that one. Two such men cannot live in harmony for long.'

'So you think I'm losing my touch?' Harold growled. 'I look back on a succession of failures. First I fail to get Stigand recognised; next I fail to get Wulfnoth home; now I reveal all my secrets to William without getting a firm promise from him. What has gone wrong, Cedric? I won't go on losing now, will I? I couldn't live with that.'

'What was it you used to say to me, when we were not much more than boys? If you believe you will lose, then you will? I've never seen you like this before, Harold, and I pray to God you'll snap out of it soon. Stand or fall, it's what you are going to do here in Normandy that will determine your whole future; you don't need me to tell you that.'

Harold made a visible effort to regain his old assurance. He bounced up off the bed, pulled off his cloak and shirt and thoroughly doused himself in a bowl of rose-scented water as if to wash off the black clouds that had suddenly gathered around his head.

'You're right,' he gasped, shocked by the cold water. 'The Devil take William. If I can't be king with his help, then by all the saints I'll be king without him! God's word, what is this stuff? I smell like a flower bed!'

'How should I know?' Cedric retorted, 'There were no such sweet scents in my Berkshire farmyard!'

X

THEOBALD was past seventy, possibly the oldest man in Dinan, and age had treated him harshly. His thin, frail body could hardly carry him up the stairs. Bracing himself precariously with a hand against each wall, he would urge a foot to move on upward, then watch in despair as it hovered midway between steps while the pains of effort cut all through him. Beads of sweat ran tickling down his ancient pate – the monk's tonsure had spread outwards with the passage of time until all traces of hair had gone – and tears of frustration ran with them over the bone ridges from which his cheeks had sunk. Once, long ago, it had been a moment's journey between the library where his life's work was done and the loft quarters where he lived with his beloved Gifta. Now those stairs were a formidable toil on their own, more taxing than the studies which he insisted on pursuing as long as he could move at all.

It was a long time since anything had made him try to hurry the journey, however. He was accustomed to allowing himself all the time he needed, taking one step, resting, regaining his breath, contemplating the next, and hoisting himself on once more. This day, though, was different. Today he was urged on by the sounds of panic in the town, and by the thundering fear in his breast. His anxiety made no difference, he knew, and perhaps even hampered him more, but he could not help but struggle to make the ascent with more speed than he was capable of. After all this time, so little time was left. Each time he was forced to stop he listened through his own hoarse panting to the noises from outside, and heard the people shouting, crying and running, boarding themselves up in their homes.

Theobald had seen Conan's army in full flight, galloping in across the river and into the castle, where they had shut themselves up to prepare for a siege. He had seen the catapults trundled up to the walls, the moat gate slammed shut, and the ramparts begin to bristle with spears and bows. Then he had seen the outriders from Duke William's force rein in on the hills across the water, take in the lie of the land and wheel about to report back to their leader. He had seen the unprotected townspeople and the country folk snatching up what few possessions they could carry and scamper for shelter, streaming into the town across the bridge or scuttling away into hiding places in the hills, and then he had waited to see no more. For the first time in all his years as librarian, he had discarded pen and parchment and scroll without regard for blot or rip, and had pushed his aged form into the stiff, shambling semblance of a run.

Gifta had also seen what was happening. She went to the top of the stairs, saw Theobald's plight, and carefully descended to help him the last few yards. She was of great age too, sixty-eight last birthday, but a little more nimble. Though slight of figure and plagued with the aches of advanced years, she was able to lend Theobald support on the climb. She eased him to his bed, hushing him as he laboured to speak to her, and propped him up there so that she could give him wine to sip while she wiped his brow.

'It is as we heard, my love,' Theobald hawked, the wine dribbling from the corners of his quivering mouth. 'It is William's army, and doubtless Earl Harold is with him, as they said.' He clutched at his weakening heart, as the will to resist seeped away from him, and whispered: 'Dear God, we should have gone away. Now it's too late. After all these years, it's too late . . .'

Gifta was trying to be calm for both of them. She tried not to forget her royal blood, although it was fifty years since she had been permitted to live as a princess should. She straightened up from tending to Theobald, and walked with dignity to the window, where she stood with small chin defiantly raised, and watched Conan's timid soldiers jostle each other on the ramparts. On the far bank of the Rance, the woods were alive with the bowmen and horsemen of Normandy. They tramped down through the woods to the bridge quite unhurriedly, like huntsmen and beaters seeking a likely spot for a day's sport.

A horn sounded on the summer air, thin as the piping of a distant bird. William's men halted then, and stood and stared at the enemy fort in deathly silence. Somewhere out there, Gifta imagined, the grand Duke William and the grand Earl Harold would be riding among their men, hearing the opinions of their commanders and surveying for themselves the strength of Conan of Brittany.

'There was nowhere to go to,' Gifta murmured. 'We always knew that this would be the last place for us, my love. Let us thank God we were given so much time. So many others were not.'

Theobald attempted to get up to join her, but fell back weakly. His eyes closed tight as he rubbed at the pain in his chest.

'Gifta . . .' he pleaded.

She sighed and went back to him, fondly, but thinking that he had never been strong of spirit, this dear quiet lover of hers. She looked into his agonised face as she helped him to another drink, and she reflected that her husband Uhtred had possessed grit enough for ten men such as the mild monk Theobald. Poor Uhtred, so long in the grave where the Danish murderers had put him. How different her life would have been, had he lived. She would have lived like the lady she was born to be, in the land she had loved. But God had willed it otherwise, and she had been given Theobald, who was kind, faithful and loving to the last, and she had no right to complain nor wallow in regrets.

'Quick now,' she soothed him, her hands working to revive the heart and soul of the man. 'We do not know yet that they have come for us. We have only been supposing.'

Theobald's head made a feeble nodding motion.

'It *is* so,' he said. 'Don't you remember the dream I had when we first came here, many times repeated?'

'It was a dream. Nothing more.'

'It was a truly prophetic dream. I always knew it, and now it is plain to see. Merciful God, such a dream! It began with a terrible wind blowing through the house. Don't you see, that wind is the army that will rage through this town? Then, the door crashed open and in came two dreadful creatures. One was a cat – the Norman leopard, Gifta! – the other was half bird, half dragon, and who could that be but Harold, half Danish, half English Harold? They came in with a fierce fire that consumed all the books and '. . .'

'I remember!' Gifta interrupted shuddering. 'They dropped the body of Gospatrick from their bloody mouths. Be quiet about your cursed dream, Theobald, for pity's sake! Don't you think I have worried enough about my stepson, living in the shadow of those vile Danes all these years? Oh Lord, if only I could know that he is all right. I would not care then what they did to me.'

Theobald gripped her hand tightly, and lay with his eyes closed as if praying silently.

'What is happening out there now?' he asked.

'Are you sure you want to know?'

'Yes. I am trying to prepare myself.'

Gifta returned to the window.

'There is something going on in the castle,' she related, reaching up on tiptoe to make it out. 'Ah yes, they are going through the ritual of surrender, I think. The keys are being handed out on a spear-point to William's emissaries. It seems Count Conan has had all the fight he wants.'

'Then it will not be long before they are here. Gifta, my love, I am too old and weak even to leave this bed now, but if there was somewhere you could find to hide, they could not torture it out of me . . .'

'I have told you, I cannot and will not run,' she replied. 'No, damn them to Hell. I should not have run away from them fifty years ago. Uhtred did not run from them, nor did my father or my brothers. It would have been more honourable to die with them than to spend a lifetime cowering like a mouse in a hole.'

'No, Gifta, no,' Theobald rasped. 'We would not have had these fifty years. . . .'

Gifta looked ashamed. She sat beside him once more and took his hands in hers.

'I regret nothing,' she placated him. 'Nothing at all, I promise you. It's only that I feel I should have been a warrior, if I had not been born a woman. I do love you, Theobald. I have always loved you, and my life with you has been good. If I have a regret, it is only that we never married, so the world could see us in our happiness.'

'That was my fault, too. I refused to forsake my vows.'

'Oh my dear,' Gifta smiled. 'How you punish yourself for your goodness! I understood then, and I still do. If a man has to choose between loyalties, he does not choose, but lets his loyalties take him where they will even if they split him in half. Be at peace, my love! I am proud to have lived with you, proud to have shared your bed, though all mankind might despise us for it. There is nothing more I could have asked for, nothing more I want. Only,' she added, with a deep sigh, 'to know that all will be well with Gospatrick, little Edgar, my daughter, my grandson . . .'

'Ealdgyth and your grandson will be all right. They will stay safely in Scotland. And Edgar, well, he will be the next king of England, and will erase all the dark crimes of the past. It may be that William and Harold can rid themselves of helpless old people like us, but they cannot alter the will of God!'

Gifta hugged him to her.

'Ah,' she whispered, weeping, 'In moments like this I feel that you are a good deal braver than you let me think, holy man. You do love me still, don't you?'

'I love you more than my life, as I have always done.'

The town had fallen quiet, as though everyone had gone away and left them there alone. It was a pleasant thought, that they might be left in peaceful solitude for the rest of their days, but as they sat and listened to the silence they knew it could not be. Nevertheless, the calm raised their spirits, but in a melancholy way, as a brilliant dawn or a birdsong might encourage a condemned prisoner to thoughts of eternity. Theobald thought it was a pity he could not finish the particularly interesting manuscript on which he had been working, and Gifta let her gaze wander around the room, recalling the happy days when Ealdgyth and Gospatrick had been there with her. Suddenly their faces and voices were there with her again, like phantoms, and she smiled at them as if they could see her.

'Gospatrick is well,' she breathed, thinking aloud. 'I can feel it.'

'Of course.'

'Aye, you are not the only one to have visions, Theobald. I have had some, too, in my time. I remember when the Danes came, in a dream I saw the filthy carrion ravens of the North pecking at the dying English dragon . . .'

'Wounded, not dying. Did you see it actually dead?'

'No . . .'

'There you are, then. It lives on in Edward, its wounds slowly healing, and in young Edgar it will grow strong and prosper.'

'Yes, but they say Harold carries the Wessex dragon now, presumptious spoiler that he is!'

'Edgar will free it . . .'

In the library below, they heard suddenly the harsh tramp of feet and loud voices shattered the stillness. Next came heavy footfalls on the steps, thumping like a drumbeat on the creaking timber, and there appeared before the old people's gaze the gleaming helmets, the grim faces, the arrow-head shields, and the spears and the chain-mail of William's men. The soldiers stopped at the head of the stairs and peered at the ancient monk and the lady, then one of them turned to shout down:

'My lord, I think we've found them!'

'Aye, my lord,' mumbled Gifta, as she put her arms round Theobald, 'I think they have found us. So many years, but they have found us now.'

More footsteps, more faces, drifting in and out of range of weary old eyes which would insist on clouding. Theobald stayed lying down, but Gifta rose gracefully, like a queen receiving visitors, and stood with back straight and head raised. She viewed William Duke of Normandy, Harold Dux Anglorum, and Cedric Shieldless, commander of housecarls, and left no doubt in their minds that she regarded them all as upstart commoners.

'Good morning, my lords,' Gifta said stiffly. 'We have been expecting you.'

William tiredly removed his helmet and brushed dust from it with a corner of his cloak.

'Princess Aelfgifu,' he replied, with a measure of respect. 'My father spoke of you, I recollect. I believe you knew him well?'

'I enjoyed the hospitality of Duke Robert in Rouen. And that of your grandfather, Duke Richard.'

'Such a pity you left there,' William grinned, though with little humour. 'I could have been as well acquainted with you, without having to fight all through Brittany for the pleasure.'

'I would not have asked you to fight a war for my sake, Lord William,' Gifta said icily. 'We have lived here quite at peace with the world.'

The Duke looked out at hushed Dinan, pretending to be studying it with the interest of a traveller.

'But not quite removing yourself from the progress of its affairs,' he suggested calmly. 'That is why I had to see you, princess. I must ask you who it is that has been passing you information from my court. Spying is a most unsavoury trade. Will you tell me?'

'Spying?' Gifta scoffed. 'What would I have to gain by spying on you?'

'The English crown, perhaps!' William snapped, rounding on her. Then, reverting to his former politeness, he added: 'How is your great-nephew, Prince Edgar?'

Gifta realised from that that they knew everything. If they knew that she was helping Edgar, they would know that Gospatrick was too. If they had not already dealt with her stepson, it was for his sake that she must continue to play the innocent. She struggled not to let her fears show.

'If you wanted to inquire after the health of my great-nephew,' she said loftily, 'you could have fought your way to Hungary. The last time I heard, he was quite well, thank you.'

William had plenty of time to be patient. He walked to the bed and stood over the nervous Theobald, not menacingly, but with blatant curiosity.

'And you must be Father Theobald,' he said, with exaggerated prurience. 'My father spoke of you, too. He always thought it rather shabby of you to break your vow of chastity – though Almighty God knows, he was hardly the man to moralise!'

'Please, my lord,' Theobald begged quietly, 'Chide me if you must, but do not insult my lady Aelfgifu. She is too good to merit such lewd jests.'

'Don't worry, Theobald, I am not offended,' Gifta said. 'I told you that our living together has been a matter of pride to me.'

'Father,' said William, addressing Theobald again. 'You are a very old man, and a sick one I think. You will die soon. I will have a priest sent, so that you may make your confession and prepare yourself in the proper manner. First, however, I would like you to confess to me that you and the princess have spies in Rouen. And I would like to know their names. Do not delay making your peace with God, father, for your own sake.'

'Leave him alone,' Gifta snarled. 'Is this what the great Duke of Normandy has sunk to, threatening old men?'

William made a gesture of helplessness and turned to Harold.

'You were right,' he said. 'They do not wish to help us.'

That was Harold's signal to confront Gifta, and he did so with as much forbearance as the Duke.

'My lady,' he began quietly. 'We know that you are advocating Edgar as the next king of England . . .'

'And why should I not? He is the only rightful heir.'

'Then why hasn't your brother Edward nominated him as such? Do you go against Edward's wishes?'

'Edward has nominated no-one. He will do so when he feels the time is right.'

'Duke William believes that he has Edward's promise.'

'Then Duke William is wrong.'

'Has Edward told you this?'

'That is a personal matter, to be kept within my family.'

'My lady Aelfgifu,' Harold said, in a stern, warning voice. 'There is much we know. We know that, just as you have been passing information to Edgar from Normandy, so has your stepson Gospatrick been doing from England.'

Gifta felt faint. She sat down on the bed and pressed a hand to her brow. Harold poured her a cup of wine, and waited while she sipped it, eyeing him as the trapped hare eyes the circling hawk.

'For the love of God,' she whispered, 'Leave Gospatrick in peace. He has lost father and brothers, friends. He has suffered enough. Why should he suffer more for what I am supposed to have done?'

'You need not fear for him, if only you tell us what we want to know.'

'Damn you, Earl Harold!' Gifta spat. 'Do you think I could trust a son of the murdering Vikings? Yes, you! You are no better than your mother's people, for I have heard of all your deeds. You have the Viking bloodlust in you, and the treachery! It showed when you rebelled against Edward and helped murder his kinsmen.'

'I have murdered none of Edward's kinsmen!' Harold hissed, keeping a check on his temper with difficulty.

'Your family has, and your kinsmen who are also the kin of Canute. My father, my husband, my brothers. Ethelred, Uhtred, Edmund Ironside, Eadwig, Alfred, Edward the Exile and his brother Edmund, and Gospatrick's brothers, Aldred and Eadwulf. The list of those who died before their time, murdered by the Vikings and their English allies, is endless. And you, Duke William. You helped, by letting my nephew Walter die in your dungeons! You are ruthless, selfish, killers all! I will tell you nothing! Kill me, as you have killed all my family! No doubt you will kill Gospatrick, too. But there is one you cannot reach, short of making war with Hungary, and that is Edgar. And may God give him the strength to snatch England away from your bloodstained claws!'

Harold and William glanced at each other, perplexed. It was the Duke who next took up the questioning.

'Princess Aelfgifu,' he said firmly, 'I think you are making more of this than is necessary. No one need be killed. Why can't there be a treaty between us? Suppose, for instance, you were to write to King Edward, simply asking him to confirm that I, not Edgar, am his chosen heir . . .'

This was a move which William had not discussed with Harold, who looked sharply at William as if to remonstrate with him for putting his own interests to the fore. He need not have worried, though, for Gifta's answer was bluntly derisive.

'No, my Lord Duke, you are not!' she stormed. 'Your family gave my family shelter when they needed it, and for that we were grateful, but the English crown is not the price we will pay for it. You have not a drop of Ethelred's blood in you. Edgar does; he is purely of royal English blood, and he is the one and only rightful heir! Please do not again do me the discourtesy of asking me to betray my family!'

'Very well,' William said. 'I think we have given you time enough to be reasonable. I will ask you once more, princess. Will you give me the names of your spies in my court? I shall find them anyway, and it will be the worse for them if I have to hunt them out.'

Gifta stood up to help stiffen her resolve. She took Theobald's hand, to draw courage from it.

'I have no spies in your court, or at any other court,' she declared. 'Now do with us as you will.'

Duke William drew himself up then and took a deep breath.

'There is no doubt that you have committed crimes and sins you must atone for,' he told them. 'You came from England as guests, yet you have dishonoured the trust of my grandfather and father. More seriously in the eyes of all Christendom, you have lived here together adulterously – you, a princess of the blood royal, and a holy man who has continued to wear the habit of his order. Aelfgifu, you will be taken from here to a nunnery, and you, Theobald, to a monastery, where you will be kept from each other and from all others for the rest of your days. I can be no kinder than that.'

Gifta and Theobald held each other close, crying softly, as William and Harold made to leave.

'And you, killers of princes!' Gifta screamed after them, 'How will you atone for your crimes? Do you think the Lord God will close his eyes to your sins? May He have mercy on your souls when your time comes!'

Cedric stayed behind. The two old people were sobbing in each other's arms. All his life he had been curious to see the princess his mother had adored, but he wished he could have done so in other circumstances than these.

'Princess Aelfgifu,' he said, carefully. 'Forgive me; I know you must hate me as much as you hate the men I serve, but there is something I must tell you. I am Cedric Shieldless, Cedric the son of Cedric and Constance. I know you were fond of her, and I wanted to tell you that until the day she died she spoke of you with pride and affection. She always hoped to see you again. She would be sad to know that such misfortune has befallen you.'

Gifta wiped the tears from her eyes, and regarded Cedric, uncertainty, mistrust, flickering in her gaze, until she remembered.

'Cedric,' she repeated, 'Yes, Constance wrote of you. So, you are her son. Then you know my stepson, Gospatrick?'

'Yes, I know him.'

The aged princess placed a supplicating hand on his arm.

'Of course you do,' she whispered. 'For is he not like a brother to you? Was he not cared for in your mother's house?'

'Yes, he was. My mother regarded him as a son.'

'Then please, Cedric Shieldless, by your mother's memory, promise me that you will let no harm come to this brother of yours, if it be in your power. Will you grant an old woman that one wish? Promise me that, and I can bear what is to come.'

Cedric raised the withered hand to his lips, and kissed it.

'If it is in my power, I pledge it,' he told her, and meant it.

When Gifta and Theobald had gathered a few belongings together in blankets, Cedric escorted them downstairs. Harold and William were waiting outside; they watched the two ancient lovers being put up into a cart.

'You look unhappy,' Harold muttered to Cedric, with no note of real triumph in his own voice.

'Perhaps because we have not made war on old age before.'

'I know. I wish it did not have to be so.'

William, meanwhile, had beckoned to one of his captains.

'There must be no trace left of Princess Aelfgifu and Father Theobald,' he instructed. 'When they have gone, burn this place down, manuscripts and all. I want nothing left.' To Harold he added: 'We must also tell Count Conan that no one in this town is ever to mention what has happened here today.'

The Earl of Wessex and the Duke of Normandy had given each other plenty to reflect upon. They had seen each other in battle, dealing with common enemies, and each had been forced to acknowledge that the other was no mean handler of men. They had seen more than that, however. On the march south, at Mont St. Michel, William had watched in astonishment as Harold had risked his life to rescue two soldiers who had wandered on to the quicksands. With not a moment's hesitation, the Englishman had thrown his shield to one man, snatched the other by the coat, and had bodily dragged out both of them before anyone else thought to move. Was it done naturally, William had wondered, or merely to impress his hosts? Or was it, perhaps, due to the impetuous and reckless nature of the man. Did he always act first and think afterwards?

If the journey had been enlightening for William, it had been much more so for Harold.

'Are we going hunting?' Harold had asked, the morning they set out from Rouen, for he was amazed by the large company of archers who were to accompany them.

William uttered a laugh of delight.

'They are warriors enough, you will see,' he told his guest. 'You English have forgotten – if you ever knew – what a good fighting force bowmen make.'

Harold and Cedric had indeed been impressed by the skill of the archers once they had engaged with Conan's men, but they had been astounded by watching William send mounted men into battle.

'They fight on horseback,' Cedric had gasped. 'And God's word, watch them cut through those ranks!'

Harold was still watching, now that the warring was done. He was watching the organisation and discipline of William's men, observing how they obeyed orders promptly and without question, and he was envying the duke an army of that quality. There would be some changes when he got back to England, he vowed. He would talk to Cedric on the way home.

'Well, Harold,' William boomed, as they rode out of Dinan. 'A rewarding expedition, I would say.'

'Doubly so for you,' Harold smiled. 'You've not only removed a thorn from your flesh you hadn't known was there, you've also subdued Conan.'

'Quite, and I have you to thank for it. Now is the time to show my gratitude. We will ride now to Bayeux, where Odo is arranging a special ceremony. I intend to honour you with a grant of arms, make you a knight for your services to me.'

'I am greatly honoured,' Harold said, 'But is it wise? Won't people want to know why? Not for just pulling two soldiers out of a bog, surely?'

'No, but the fact that you fought at my side is reason enough, if I say so. But there is something else that will remain secret for the time being . . .'

'Yes?'

'I have thought over your proposition, as I promised I would. And I agree.'

'We are to be joint kings?'

'Yes, joint and equal kings of England on the death of Edward. We will not say as much, but we will strongly imply it at the ceremony. We will both of us swear on holy relics that neither of us will impede the other in his designs. We will know the true meaning of that oath, if no one else does. When we are ready, we will announce our decision to the world. What do you think?'

'I trust you.'

'Naturally,' said William. 'We trust each other.'

XI

THEIR families came running to greet them when the ship docked at Bosham. Edith Swanneshales stood, eyes aglow, surrounded by her bastard brood. There were six of them now – Godwin, Edmund, Magnus and Ulf, and Gytha and Gunhild. Haakon, who had not expected to see so many cousins the moment he set foot in England, stood amazed. Cedric saw his wife Ingrid and their children in the crowd; he was just as proud to see how his son and daughter were growing into fine, healthy children. His stepson, he noticed, was not there.

'Are you going to tell her?' Cedric asked Harold, nodding towards Edith.

'Tonight,' Harold confirmed. 'I must tell her before we go to London.'

'Poor Edith. It will break her heart.'

'Damn you, Cedric! It's hard enough without your preaching!'

Harold left it until late in the evening to tell Edith of her fate. They were alone beside the fire, and she was gazing contentedly into the flames, so there was no one to see him opening his mouth and closing it again before he could get started.

'Well, Edith,' he began at last, 'do you think I will make a good king?'

'I can still hardly believe it,' she giggled, leaning against him. 'King Harold!'

'And King William.'

'Ah, but he will be in Normandy, and you will be here. You will be the real king.'

'I'm glad you are pleased. I was worried that you might think me prideful and ambitious.'

'Who could ever think that of you? You are England's greatest lord.'

He cleared his throat, still dreading what he must say.

'But the thing is, you see,' he mumbled, 'I shall have to have a queen . . .'

A chill of fear troubled Edith for the first time in all the years she had shared his house. She eased away from him and looked into his eyes, searching for the one meaning to his words which she feared to discover.

'A queen?' she repeated, 'Harold, are you telling me . . . ?'

'I'm not telling you that I intend to cast you off,' he quickly assured her, but her face turned pale, and she sprang to her feet as if burned.

'No! Don't jest with me like that! Dear God, that's what it does mean. How could you live with a wife and a mistress? You do want to cast me out, the mother of your children!'

Harold went to her with arms outstretched, but she slid away from him and turned her back, head bowed on her long white neck. She was shaking with shame, and sobbing.

'Edith!' Harold pleaded. 'Please listen to me. Haven't I always told you? Our love is true, but marriage is no more than a political game. It doesn't make people love each other as we do! You know, as truly as I stand here, that I would never cast you aside, never! This house is yours . . .'

'This house?' she choked, 'This house without you in it? Do you think that is all I want? I want you. You are all I have ever wanted, you and my children! Oh, blessed Mother of Jesus, I have never cared that you did not want to marry me, but . . .'

Harold was trying to be gentle with her, but his own shame was stirring up his anger.

'It is not that I did not want to wed you!' he snapped, 'You know that it was not possible . . .'

'It would have been possible, if you'd wanted it enough. Everything else has been possible for you. You can even become a king, but to marry me is impossible because we are cousins and the Church frowns upon it. That's nonsense, Harold. You know that's nonsense. I'm just your whore. . . .'

She broke down then, and Harold stood helpless, thinking how much easier it was to face an enemy in combat.

'Edith,' he whispered, kneeling before her, taking her slim hands, 'I love you no less, and I'll always love you. There is rarely any pleasure or satisfaction for me in the things I have to do; there is certainly none in this. But no king ever held the command and respect of his subjects without a queen, to give him sons to succeed him. If I could take you as my queen I would be overjoyed, but . . .'

She was trying to regain her calm, but a shuddering sigh shook her.

'But I am a common whore,' she said icily. 'A tarnished woman, incestuous lover, mother of a clutch of bastards . . .'

'Edith!'

' . . . And what of our sons, Harold? Will they be disowned too, by your legitimate heirs?'

'I do not betray my own kin, woman! No more than I would forget you . . .'

He halted as he saw the scorn in her eyes. It told him without words that she wanted no false promises, neither for herself nor for her children. She would rather he said nothing at all than that he perjured himself to her.

He gave up trying to console her, and returned to the fireside, where he angrily tossed logs into the flames.

'Your queen,' she said coldly. 'Who will she be? Or have you not decided yet?'

'Aldgyth, Aelfgar's daughter,' he muttered. 'It's no more than a political match, as I said. Her family's earldom of Mercia is the only part of England I do not control.'

Edith uttered a bitter little laugh.

'Oh, Harold,' she taunted him. 'How smoothly you steer your own fate. You make a widow of a queen, then take her as your own. I could almost believe you planned this from the day you began your Welsh campaign!'

'You were right,' Harold admitted to Cedric the following day, as they rode to London, 'she is *disgusted* with me!'

'What did you expect?' Cedric asked. 'You shame her, cast her off. You can hardly expect her to be wild with joy. You always do things the difficult way. As if dealing with Edward were not enough, you look for yet more battles.'

'Edward holds no fears for me,' Harold growled. 'After William, there is no one else in this world I can possibly be afraid of.'

Edward obviously considered that Harold should go to him with some degree of humility, however. Looking much older and more frail since their last meeting, the king received his adopted prince with an air of displeasure which Harold had not seen since their conflicts of earlier years. He gave young Haakon only a cursory greeting, then quickly dismissed him and Cedric, and even sent his queen away before Edith had had much opportunity to welcome her brother home. Once they were alone, Edward slouched on his throne, his thin old body trembling slightly, and eyed Harold in the manner of a man badly let down.

'Harold, Harold,' he tutted. 'I thought the time had long passed when you treated your privileges like unlimited licences. What possessed you in Normandy? Do you think it is not obvious to everyone what you and William are plotting between you? Have you so little respect for me that you undermine my authority in this way, try to steal from me my right to choose my own heir?'

Harold assumed an air of contrition, but he was only relieved that Edward had apparently heard nothing of the fate of his half-sister Aelfgifu.

'No one is trying to take that from you, my lord,' Harold lied glibly. 'All that William and I have done is try to establish some sort of security for your realm. My lord, I have begged you to act, but time and again you have put off deciding who is to succeed you. England must know your intentions before every pretender in Europe starts scrapping over the bone!'

'Now it appears you would decide for me. Could you not have asked me before you went to William?'

'If you will remember, my lord, I did; many times.'

Edward shifted to a more upright position, smoothing at his white hair with an unsteady hand. He seemed to be trying to make something straight in his mind, something that kept escaping him before he could tether it firmly. Later Edith would tell Harold that the king was frequently like that. All his life he had been vague and secretive, but now his secrets were lost even to him. He was no longer able to make a decision. In Harold's absence, affairs of state had been conducted by Edith, Tostig, Aelfgar, Archbishop Stigand or anyone else to hand, and the confusion was becoming intolerable to all.

'You bully me, Harold,' Edward complained, having given up the search for his line of thought. 'Your insistence, your haste – they worry me. You and Tostig, you are both the same. I have given you both so much, but your appetites grow greater. You have given me much joy, but at times you give me so much pain, more than your father ever did. At least I knew where I stood with him . . .'

'You never trusted my father!'

'No, I did not, and that was why I knew where I stood with him. I knew when it was safe to let him have his head, and when it was necessary to draw sharply on the reins. That is something I have never known with you. One day I believe you are acting only for my good, the next I learn you are plotting against me . . .'

'If you don't want William and me to secure England's future,' his brother-in-law snapped impatiently, 'what *do* you want us to do? What do you want *me* to do? Tell me.'

Edward apparently had not heard. He was staring, not at Harold, but over his shoulder into the past.

'I had so many good friends I could trust, rely on, discuss things with,' Edward murmured. 'Robert Champart, Herman, Ulf. Oh, what fine conversations I had with those men. Such plans we had!'

'My lord,' Harold sighed. 'Is there anything further you wish to say to me, or do you wish to be left alone with your memories?'

The king came out of his dream, eyeing Harold reprovingly.

'You see?' he said, in tones of bitter disappointment. 'You have little respect for me, Harold. You have seen me grow old and less able, and now I do believe you cannot wait for me to get out of your way. Harold, my son, I have been king for twenty-two years. I came here to find a barbaric circus in which men tore at each other's throats for gain, and I turned it into the Christian kingdom my father left behind. That beautiful abbey out there is the symbol of my reign, Harold, not the murder and plunder and the destruction that marked the times of Canute and Harold Harefoot and Hardicanute! I have made this realm one where the devout can worship and serve God in peace, where no man should fear his neighbour. Is that not true? Do you think I don't care what happens to it when my time is done? Do you think I want to die fearing that all will slide back to chaos and bloodshed?'

'And you believe that is what I am working for?' Harold challenged.

'No, you are more of my ilk than of Canute's, I know that. I know it is not what you would deliberately do, but it is what I am afraid will happen unless men like you – well-meaning men, but ambitious – curb your desires. It's a dangerous game you are playing with William, and it hurts me that you chose to play it without my knowledge.'

'Then for the love of God, tell me what you want, tell me who you see as the next king,' stormed Harold, and he almost wept with frustration as he saw Edward's head drop hopelessly into his hands.

'I don't know,' Edward groaned. 'Dear God, I wish I did know. I have prayed hard enough for guidance! Why does the knowledge evade me, Harold? Why?'

'Because you think no one as holy as yourself!' Harold rapped out, before he had time to think what he was saying. He made to leave the chamber.

'Harold!'

'Yes?'

The earl paused at the door and turned back. The king was rigid with fury, and it was some moments before he could release his voice from the tense grip of his throat.

'Bully me all you want, hurt me if you must,' he managed finally. 'You will not press me into a decision I am not ready to make – not a decision as important as this. And Harold, I may be aged and slow in my wits, but I am still no fool, and I advise you to think on this: the man who shakes hardest at the tree cannot see who waits to steal the fruit.'

Harold smiled despite himself. He returned to Edward with humility in his manner that was not entirely for show.

'Forgive me, my lord,' he said. 'I was rude, and I have treated you without the respect you deserve. You are, without question, the greatest king this country has known. You could have no worthy heir – there could be none worthy of you – so perhaps God has acted for the best in leaving you without one, so that you may choose from among the best of men. But my lord, I implore you, choose soon and let everyone know your intention before it is too late. I no more want to see all your good work destroyed than you do. Yet the destroyers are waiting, hungry for your death. They are always there, waiting.'

'I know,' Edward nodded. 'You are speaking to one who has seen the spectre of the evil one lurking in dark corners since the last days of Ethelred. More than that, I have seen even more often than you have those I thought most good change into something wicked. That is why I take my time, and why I shall continue to take what time the good Lord leaves me. Make me one promise, Harold, my son . . .'

'Yes?'

'On the day I speak my last words to you, will you heed them? Will you serve me in death as you have served me in life?'

Harold hesitated only a second before responding: 'I know of no other man I could serve, in life or in death.'

Such a vow committed him to nothing, Harold felt. It did not prevent him going ahead with his own designs, nor did it trouble him that Edward had taken his words as a binding agreement. Harold was quite sure that he could make Edward's dying wishes fit his own plans, so that whatever happened, he would never need to feel guilty about taking that pledge. Edward's most fervent wish, obviously, was that England should remain a peaceful and devotedly Christian realm; that was more important to him than the name of the man who was to rule. As long as Harold toiled to put Edward's religious reforms and improvements into effect, the king could never suspect him of any selfish motives.

Meanwhile, there was plenty which Harold wanted done to ensure his way was well prepared. Some of it, like arranging his marriage to Aldgyth, he undertook himself. Most of the more difficult secret duties, however, he assigned to Cedric.

'First, we must put a stop to Gospatrick's plotting,' he told his commander of housecarls.

'That will not be so easy as it was with his stepmother,' Cedric warned him. 'No one saw Aelfgifu disappear. Gospatrick has many friends in the North.'

'I know that. I'm relying on your skill to deal with them. You have built up your own web of spies, Cedric. Put it to work at once. If Gospatrick has made one mistake which will enable us to get him exiled or imprisoned – preferably exiled – I want to know about it at the earliest opportunity.'

'And if he hasn't?'

'Then, by God, we'll have to invent something.'

'I want no harm to come to him,' Cedric declared. 'I gave my word to Aelfgifu that no harm would come to him.'

'There is no need to worry, my friend,' Harold assured him. 'All we need do is undermine his authority, so that his efforts for Edgar come to nothing. And since he is not one of the great and powerful thanes of the land, it should not be too difficult to achieve. He's an irritation, that's all, but one that could spread like a rash. Scratch him for me, Cedric. Scratch him off my back. But do it soon. There is more important work I want you to do for me.'

'I know. Strengthening the housecarls.'

'Right. I want you to build up their numbers as high as they will go. But that isn't all. I want archers trained for battle, just like William's, and I want others taught to fight from horseback. I was greatly impressed with his army, and I do not want it to be better than mine.'

'The trouble is, there is no one who can teach them,' Cedric reminded him.

'I know, but you've seen it done in Normandy. Just do your best for me.'

Plans for his marriage were to be no easier, Harold soon discovered. He sent off his proposal to Aldgyth's family, but at first was answered with a long and ominous silence. He did not mince words in his second epistle, and demanded, rather than asked, that Aldgyth should be sent to him. Matters of state kept him too busy to make journeys of courtship, he pointed out, so if Aldgyth could not come to London, he would have to leave the discussions until the next time he needed to travel northwards, with an army on a military expedition. This time he got a letter back promptly. Aldgyth was perfectly at liberty to visit him, it said, and whether or not she accepted his proposal would also be up to her.

When she arrived at his home in Southwark, one hard frosty night, Harold divined that the widow queen had been well prepared. Her proud face was a mask, but the easy manner in which she shed her outer wraps of wool and beaver suggested that she was already making herself at home. Harold guessed that he had just won another victory. He set before her his best table, but the wooing had been done long ago, in Wales.

'You flatter me, Lord Harold,' she haughtily told him. 'Now I see for myself the enormous arrogance men speak of. First you kill my husband and take me from the land where I was queen, and now you ask me to marry you!'

'I took a lot away from you,' Harold lightly admitted, 'but I can give you more, much more than Griffith ever could.'

'I was his queen.'

'Queen of a pile of cold, wet slate!'

'No, of a lovely land, full of gifted and kindly people. You could have seen that, if you had taken time away from the slaughter to look at it.'

'All I ever saw of the Welsh was the burning English villages and the orphaned children they left behind.'

'I'll wager I have seen more Welsh orphans than you have seen English.'

Harold laughed, enjoying the banter.

'My, you are a strange breed, you women of Mercia,' he teased her. 'I suppose if any woman would happily go to such a windswept place, to be queen of the goose-pimpled, who would it be but a grand-daughter of the famous Lady Godiva?'

Aldgyth blushed and slammed her goblet down on the table, pushing it away as though rejecting his hospitality.

'So now you are going to insult my family by dragging up that old tale!' she spat. 'I must say, Earl Harold, you have a most strange way of courting!'

'Well, better than Griffith's, from what I hear,' he retorted. 'They tell me his idea of courting was a rope and . . . no, I suppose I should not speak of such things to a queen . . .'

'Why not? You have insulted me enough already.'

'All right, shall we call a truce?' he chuckled. 'That is, after all, what this meeting is about: a truce between my family and yours. My father and your grandfather would never have believed it possible, but . . .'

'A truce,' Aldgyth repeated with ill-concealed contempt. 'Is that all a marriage means to you? Is it to be nothing more than a contract, an alliance, an arrangement between us? And you speak so scornfully of Griffith! At least he had the courtesy to make me feel he desired me as a bride.'

'But that was an alliance, too, was it not?'

'Is a woman like me ever taken for any other reason?'

Harold viewed his bride with satisfaction. It pleased him that she was so spirited. The docile Edith Swan-neck was a warm and agreeable companion, but his queen would need to be more, more than a lively bedmate and willing mother. As well as bringing him

436

a sound interest in the Mercian lands, thus consolidating his hold on England, she would have to be a queen of intelligence, wisdom and loyalty, and Aldgyth seemed to possess those qualities. In addition, she had already been a queen. He congratulated himself on making the right choice. There remained only one point to be clarified.

'If you give me sons,' he told her, 'you must understand that, where my will and favours are concerned, they will be treated equally with the sons I have by Edith.'

Aldgyth made a tiny upward movement of her small shoulders.

'I should imagine you have plenty for all of them to share quite happily,' she said. 'You presume that I have accepted, then?'

'Have you?'

'I believe we are bound by destiny, Lord Harold,' she smiled. 'The day you brought my dead husband to me, I hated you; yet somehow I knew that was not the end of it. Something told me that I was to be bound to you as surely as poor Griffith was lashed to your horse. Strange, is it not, that we can see into the future, if we heed the knowing of our minds?'

'We have much in common,' Harold nodded. 'I, too, believe in fate and destiny. I think we will make a good match.'

'And the wedding feast,' she asked later, when the heady wine had brought out the eagerness in her. 'Will it be grand? At my wedding with Griffith we were on the run before your army! All we had for banquet was a few half-cooked rabbits!'

'It will be a feast the like of which England has never seen before,' he promised. After all, for Harold himself, it would have to be. He could not have it said that any celebration in living memory surpassed his. If the grandeur of a feast signified a man's importance, then all of Europe would know after supping at Harold's table that he was already King of England, the most absolute monarch in the nation's history. This marriage was his declaration to the world that now no man could match Harold Godwinsson acre for acre, treasure for treasure, or sword for sword. It was his triumph, and his statement of intent. It symbolised not only the union of man and woman in wedlock, but the ability of one man to take a country and force it cowering like a nervous virgin beneath his cloak.

Everything about Harold's wedding had been planned to display immense confidence. He ordered a bridge of warships to be placed across the Thames, leading to his Southwark house, so that the feeble old king would not have to travel all through London to reach the festivities. The ships would be lit with hundreds of torches, and the whole causeway would be guarded by housecarls. It was more

437

than a novelty and a convenience, it was a demonstration of might. Similarly, more housecarls were brought in to stand watch over the caskets of gold, silver, jewels and furs which the bride would receive as wedding gifts, and armies of men were recruited to hunt down herds of beasts and flocks of fowl, and to catch baskets full of fish. Harold invited not only all the nobility of England and much of Ireland, but also the greatest houses of Europe, including the powerful family of Tostig's wife Judith of Flanders, his cousin King Sweyn of Denmark, and Duke William of Normandy. He was not surprised when the Danish king refused to come, for he knew that Sweyn had never forgiven the Godwin family for the murder of his brother Bjorn, but he was puzzled when Duke William replied that he would not be able to attend. Was William truly enmeshed in delicate politics at home, Harold wondered, or was the duke, for reasons best known to himself, allowing their friendship to cool?

Harold did not agonise over the question for long. William's presence would have helped proclaim his status, but there would be plenty of other rulers to make up for his absence. All his schemes were proceeding extremely well, he thought.

But the Earl of Wessex was shocked out of his cheerful complacency when Gurth and Leofwine arrived in London shortly before the wedding day with disturbing news about what was happening in the earldom of their brother Tostig. They had come laden with wedding gifts, but in a black mood better suited to a funeral. The whole of Northumbria was about to flare into armed revolt, they reported. Already there had been violent attacks on Tostig's own house, and on those of the thanes who supported him.

Harold stamped about shouting curses on his brother. Not even his closest companions had ever seen him in such a frightening rage, and brave men though they were, they were moved to stay well clear of him.

'Now!' Harold raged, slamming his fists on the table, 'Now, of all times, he does this to me! God damn the man to Hell, what has he been doing there? What has been happening?'

'You know Tostig,' Gurth shrugged. 'He has always ridden roughshod over people as if all Northumbrians were born to be his slaves. It has been simmering for years, now it has simply boiled over. Apparently there were two thanes who had always opposed him. A few days ago they were found under the walls of York with their throats cut. No one needed to be told who ordered it. Within hours, mobs were forming all over Northumbria. If there isn't a civil war there yet, there very soon will be.'

Harold slumped in the high chair at the head of the empty tables, fighting down the fury that tore at him.

'Does the king know of this yet?' he inquired hoarsely.

'I believe so,' Gurth said. 'What are you thinking?'

'I am wondering if I should wait for his orders to take an army up there, or if I should do it on my own authority.'

'Go against Tostig yourself?' Gurth queried.

'Wait, Harold,' Leofwine interrupted. 'You have not heard everything yet . . .'

'Dear God,' Harold groaned, 'what more can I hear?'

'We hear that Gospatrick is on his way to London,' Leofwine said, 'to see the king . . .'

'Gospatrick?' Harold breathed, as if hating the very sound of the name, 'Why him? How does he come into this?'

'Very significantly. The two men who died were old friends of his. It is quite possible that it is Gospatrick who has stirred up most of the anger against Tostig. Now, with the king's help, he's going to ensure that it continues to boil.'

'By the holy cross of Christ!' Harold exclaimed like one witnessing a revelation, and for a while he fell into careful thought. He beckoned to Cedric. 'What have you learned of him, anything?'

'Nothing like this,' Cedric admitted. 'If Gospatrick has been plotting an uprising, he has done it with admirable secrecy. My men have not been able to find a mark against him.'

Harold was silent again for a long time. He got up and resumed his pacing around the hall, but more calmly, more purposefully, measuring each stride. It was a long wait for Gurth and Leofwine, who wanted to know if they were going to be ordered to make war on their brother; their apprehension showed in their fidgeting. Harold, though, dragged out every minute as far as he wanted it to stretch. He would not speak until every detail was clear in his mind. This was one of those occasions when he would seek the opinions of his lieutenants only after he had made his decision.

'It is the first move,' he stated eventually. 'Gospatrick is making his first move for Prince Edgar and the throne. That is why he is coming to London. Now he can show the king how untrustworthy the Godwinssons are, and how wise Edward would be to adopt Edgar as his heir at once. The Devil take the man! If only we could have got rid of him as easily as we rid ourselves of his pest of a stepmother!'

'Do you think Edward will listen to him?' Gurth asked.

'Yes, unfortunately,' Harold replied tersely. 'Because he has a great deal to offer. He can point to Edgar as a means of securing peace, just when Edward has been losing patience with me and

Tostig! Damn Tostig, damn him! Does he know what he's done to me? Does he care, the blundering idiot? God's word, I'm going to have to tread very carefully if I'm to forestall Gospatrick. And I may have to sacrifice Tostig to save the day.'

'What do you mean?' Leofwine was anxious to know.

'I must quell these uprisings myself. I must go north and try to reason with Tostig, and with the Northumbrians. If they will not listen to me, then Tostig's earldom is forfeit. I shall tell him to get out of it, or be put out of it – by me. It's the only way I can beat Gospatrick at his own game. I need time, though. I must get this done before Gospatrick sees Edward. Cedric, I want Gurth and Leofwine to come with me, but I need you here. I don't care how you do it, but make sure that Gospatrick does not talk to the king before I get back. Do you understand? He must not even get a message to the king! Can you do it?'

'I'm not sure what I can do,' Cedric said doubtfully, 'short of binding the man and throwing him in the cellars.'

'Then bind him and throw him in the cellars, if you have to. But don't let him speak one word to Edward. Go, and ring the palace with guards now. Tell my sister what's happening so that she can help you. Don't worry, you won't be left alone for long. I intend to be back in time for my wedding.'

XII

Gospatrick did get into the palace. He might have achieved it with a bribe or by a ruse, but the first Cedric knew of it was when a messenger came from Queen Edith urging him to go at once to the small chamber off the main hall.

'She says there is a man there who must be restrained, sir!' the soldier explained, and Cedric realised immediately what was wrong. He ran through the great stone corridors, buckling his sword harness over his chain-mail coat, fearing that it was too late to aid Harold's cause now. The one hope was that King Edward would still be in his bed at this hour, and that Gospatrick could be spirited away before Edward awoke.

He found Edith and Gospatrick in a state of high agitation. The queen had two housecarls with her who were keeping a firm grip on Gospatrick, and her face was red with anger and anxiety. Gospatrick Uhtredsson, a man of sixty-three years, was normally of placid nature, but today he was as irrepressible as an unbroken stallion. His face was livid, and he stamped about before the guarded door as if prepared to batter his way through with his fists. When he saw Cedric, son of the woman who had fostered him through much of his childhood, Gospatrick made an effort to check his temper but his body continued to shake in defiance of his will.

'Cedric, this is an outrage!' was his greeting. 'I am the king's adopted nephew, and I claim my right to see him – as kinsman, as subject and as speaker for the people of Northumbria. . . .'

'Gospatrick, please, calm yourself,' Cedric requested quietly. 'Queen Edith is only doing as she has been asked . . .'

'By whom? Her high and mighty brother? Who is ruling this land, Cedric? Is it still King Edward, or is it self-crowned King Harold now?'

'I am asking you to put off talking to the king until Earl Harold gets back, that is all.'

Gospatrick stood with feet spread wide, arms folded across his chest and features dark with a challenge for the younger man.

'No, Cedric, I will not,' he declared. 'Harold and his brothers have had the bit between their teeth these past years, and it's time someone slowed them down a bit. My business with the king is urgent. All of Northumbria is in turmoil, and . . .'

'And Harold will deal with it!' Cedric snapped.

'In his own interest, not ours!' Gospatrick raged. 'Cedric, listen to me. I have not come all this way to be pushed into a corner and told to wait my turn. Too often in the past I have been cowed: never again. I am going to tell Edward exactly what is happening in Northumbria, how good men are being murdered in his name by that unscrupulous savage, Tostig. But I want more than that. I want to know what has happened to my stepmother, and I don't doubt that he will want to know what has happened to his sister, when I tell him that she has disappeared!'

Cedric had not been prepared for that. That Gospatrick knew of Aelfgifu's fate, or at least suspected it, shattered his composure and left him speechless.

'What do you mean?' he said at last. 'Who says anything has happened to your stepmother?'

'I know something has,' the old Northumbrian stated flatly, 'and I am determined to discover what. I think you may know, Cedric. Will you tell me, old friend? Is she dead? Has she been murdered, like most of her family before her? Why can my messengers no longer find her, Cedric?'

Cedric wished he could answer, but he could not betray Harold's trust. He fought to quiet his own conscience, realising that all hope was gone of persuading Gospatrick to be silent, that he must steadfastly oppose the man no matter how long there had been friendship between them. He hated himself for it, but his first loyalty was to Harold as always, and as always he was willing to sin, lie and cheat in order to let that be so. It was difficult to look Gospatrick in the eye, but he managed it.

'She is not dead,' was all he said.

'I want proof.'

'I cannot give it. You must take my word.'

'That is not good enough, Cedric. If she is not dead, where is she? In prison? Dying? Under torture? I will know.'

'I ask you again, wait until Harold returns. Then you can speak to the king.'

'No,' Gospatrick insisted. 'Now. You will not stop me, other than with force.'

'Gospatrick, I ask you for the last time. Unless you give Harold a chance to settle the North, the whole of England may fall into civil war again.'

'That is Harold speaking, not you. That is how the Godwin clan have always ruled, deviously, with cunning, with honeyed words and hidden dagger. I insist on seeing the king, now!'

'And I repeat, you cannot,' Cedric said, indicating the soldiers at his command. 'Will you come to my quarters, and talk quietly?'

'I will talk with the king, no-one else.'

Cedric drew his sword, ready to move in and make an arrest.

'You leave me no choice . . .' he started to say, but to his astonishment Gospatrick took a step back, and unsheathed his own blade. The two guards behind Cedric started forward, but Cedric raised a hand to stay them. 'Gospatrick,' he went on, in a tone that was both a command and a plea, 'You are being foolish. You cannot fight every housecarl in this palace. Please . . .'

On Gospatrick's lined face there was an expression of both regret and suicidal resolve. He had dropped into a fighting stance, and was covering Cedric and the two guards with his sword. He really did not care if he had to fight to the death. All through the Viking wars and the northern feuds that had killed his father and brothers, and Gifta's family, he had remained passive, submissive. Only once had he warred, long ago after the death of Canute when he had tried to help Edward take the throne, and that had ended in abject failure. He would not step down again. He might fail again, but no more would he be humiliated, left to mull over his shortcomings on many a sleepless night, to rage mutely at the dark. Gospatrick had seen a lifetime of frustration and defeat. At last, the time had come to prove his worth.

'I will fight you if I must, Cedric, but I pray God you will not make me. We are brothers, you and I. Your mother took me into her home before you were born. Your father was a father to me. You won your championship by slaying the swine who murdered my own father and brother, and for that alone I shall be eternally grateful to you. Now I beg of you, step aside. Let me do what I must do . . .'

'Cedric!' Edith cried. 'Let the men take him!'

Cedric Shieldless answered her with a slight shake of his head. He could see that Gospatrick would fight to the end, and he would not stand by like a coward and see the job done by two of his men. This was his obligation, the most terrible he had ever faced, but undeniably his. He would make one last attempt to reason with Gospatrick, as they circled each other like two scarred old fighting cocks, but both of them would understand that it was no good.

'You can do your cause no good by dying here,' Cedric suggested softly, eyeing Gospatrick's poised blade and watching for an opening despite his unwillingness to strike, like the practised warrior he was. 'I do not want to kill a man who wishes to serve the king. Live, Gospatrick, and serve him!'

'If I cannot serve him now, at this moment, I cannot serve him at all,' Gospatrick panted. 'Yet still I may serve him, with my death, unless you are going to throw my body in the river. Be warned, Cedric; when Edward hears that Gospatrick Uhtredsson has died in his palace, he will know that the old treacheries thrive still. Forsake Harold, Cedric. It is the only way to save your soul!'

'Kill him!' screamed Queen Edith. 'Be done with it!'

Her bloodlust incensed Gospatrick. She was no better than the rest of the Godwin brood, he told himself in a sudden surge of anger. If he must kill Cedric then she would be next. He raised his sword high with both hands and leapt forward, bringing the blade down at Cedric's head. The commander of housecarls dodged aside and easily parried the blow, and the shocking ring of steel reverberated around the stone walls as the two men broke away and began their careful stalking anew. There could be no more talking then, no more trust, no more pleas or striving for goodwill. The bloody die had been cast, the friends and brothers of many years were now made deadly foes.

Gospatrick attacked again, this time lashing out backhandedly with the cruel edge, and Cedric had to skip backwards out of range with arms thrown out for balance like a great bird. He was still regaining his balance when Gospatrick rushed in once more, sweeping left and right as if mowing corn. Cedric set himself squarely on the flagstones and thrust away the gleaming blade with a screeching, scraping clash that sent shudders through both their bodies. Now, tired of being on the defensive, Cedric barged Gospatrick into a stumbling backward trot, and went after him. Gospatrick ducked, and Cedric's sword hummed inches above his balding crown.

They paused, both out of breath, crouching feet away from each other, waiting, watching. Gospatrick, nearly twenty years the elder, knew that he was at a disadvantage the longer this contest continued. Already his breath was coming in harsh gasps and his heart was pounding painfully, but he would not give up. He had to finish the fight quickly, or die, yet his limbs were weak and leaden. He backed away, seeking time, knowing that Cedric could not allow him to take it.

And Cedric did not. He leapt forward again, hacking out for Gospatrick's chest as the older man flailed madly, parrying some blows, slipping out of reach of others. Then Gospatrick's back was to the wall, and time after time he was desperately blocking Cedric's sword with his own while sliding awkwardly from side to side against the stone. With one last lunge, Gospatrick deliberately risked Cedric's blade to throw himself forward, and both men went down in a scrabbling heap on the floor.

Cedric was the first up. Gospatrick scrambled on hands and knees. Cedric struck down at him and missed. The old man appeared to be praying when at last he stiffly pushed himself to his feet. There was little strength left in his legs and arms. He stood, rocking slightly and, still with a double-handed grip, made one almighty strike at his enemy. It fell short, and the force of it whirled him around into a vulnerable position. His left side was exposed; it was an irresistible opportunity. The famous sword of Cedric Shieldless thudded between his second and third ribs like a cleaver into meat.

Gospatrick sagged and collapsed heavily, pitching forward on to the floor. The sword, still wedged in his side, was snatched from Cedric's hands. Gospatrick's breath soughed out of him like a passing breeze. He rolled over, his face white and tightened with shock. His lips moved slowly, but whatever he wished to say was never heard, for he died with it unspoken. No words of blame were necessary, for Cedric had words of his own, unvoiced, ringing in his head. He was hearing himself promise an old woman, far away in Brittany, that he would try to keep her stepson safe. No one else's accusation could have been as telling. He had destroyed his friend, the nearest he had ever had to a brother, and he had destroyed a little more of his own soul. When he looked up at Edith, whose pale face showed no pity, he acknowledged that he had also destroyed the love he had felt for her ever since he was a boy of fifteen. He had destroyed it, or she had – it made no difference. It was gone, washed out of him by guilt and blood. In that moment all his hate and despair was turned against the slender girl whose beauty had helped bind him to the House of Godwin, who had urged him to slay a brother.

He bent down and yanked the bloody sword out of Gospatrick's body, and threw it clanging at Edith's feet.

'Know the price of asking, your father once said to me,' he told her, the sound of it close to a sob. 'Now you see the price of demanding without pause for compassion. Harold I still serve, because he does not demand it. But as God is my witness, I will never again serve you, Queen Edith!'

Cedric ordered Gospatrick to be buried with the honours due to a warrior. He offered to go before the king himself and confess to the killing of his kinsman, but the frenzied Edward refused to see him and, according to the reports of the few people allowed near him, declared that he would see no one but Harold, the moment his wayward brother-in-law got back to London. Harold returned the following day, as it happened, and Cedric waited at Southwark with Gurth, Leofwine and Haakon to hear news of Harold's audience with the king.

Long after nightfall Harold arrived at his house, worn out by a day of angry argument. His wedding was but a few days away then, but no man ever looked less like a bridegroom. He was red-eyed, mudstained and subdued, but he still thought to go first to Cedric and lay an arm across his friend's shoulders.

'Cedric, old friend,' he sighed. 'I wish for your sake it had never happened.'

'It's done,' said Cedric. 'And it's no one's fault but mine. How have you fared?'

Harold took long draughts of ale before reporting on the meeting.

'He's practically insane with rage,' Harold told them. 'It was like trying to talk with a maddened dog. We're lucky not to be banished again, all of us.'

'And Tostig?' Leofwine asked.

'He is banished.'

The judgement did not surprise them, but it silenced them for a while.

'That settles it?' Leofwine wanted to know next.

'Aye, that's enough to satisfy poor, feeble old Edward,' Harold confirmed. 'I told him that Gospatrick's death was a direct consequence of Tostig's actions, Cedric. It has diverted his fury away from you. I told him that none of us would oppose the banishment of Tostig, if it would restore peace. I had to sacrifice Tostig, as I said I might have to. You must all understand that. He could have brought us all down with his stubborn stupidity, just as father did.'

'From what I saw of Tostig's mood, he will not go quietly,' Gurth guessed.

'He has little choice. The housecarls will be on their way north now. In a few days Tostig and Judith will be back with her family in Flanders, I expect.'

'Tostig and Gospatrick, both sacrificed,' said Cedric expressionlessly. 'They have followed Sweyn and Bjorn and Wulfnoth just as surely as if they were all bound together by some rope of evil. How many more friends, Harold? How many more brothers?'

Harold, with a quick look at Cedric, could see that it was not meant as a real challenge, only as an expression of mourning, but he had no answer anyway.

'He's right, Uncle,' contributed Haakon. 'It seems all the dice fall against us, again and again. Are you still going to press for the kingship?'

'This is no time to let superstition dissuade us,' Harold declared, 'nor to indulge in self-flagellation for deeds that were not of our making. There is no turning back. Fate has taken us by the hand, and is rushing on; it will not release us, so we had better ride with it as boldly as we can. Should we let William step in, after all that we have done? He is starting to cheat us, you know. Haakon has heard from friends in Normandy in these last few days that lies are flying thick and fast to bolster William's cause, and he is doing nothing to refute them. It is being said that the only reason I went to Normandy was as Edward's messenger, to confirm Edward's promise of the crown. What nonsense! Can anyone imagine me being so meek? The Normans are also making much of the pledge I made to William, and little of his to me. William is even encouraging the ridiculous rumour that his whore of a mother, Herleva, was the illegitimate daughter of Edmund Ironside, making him a direct descendant of Ethelred! Really, how much further is the man prepared to go to worm his way out of our agreement? I will not bow to the bastard duke – will you?'

'We are with you; you know that,' said Gurth. 'We have suffered some setbacks, but that doesn't make any difference to our loyalty to you.'

'Aye,' agreed Leofwine, 'if William wants a fight, we'll give him one. We've always won at the finish, and we're good enough for him.'

'Better than he is,' Harold corrected, 'for all his fancy horse warriors. Let's see him swim them across the Channel. He won't find that so easy as sneaking across a border!'

For all his brave words, Harold continued to be a picture of gloom all through the three days of his wedding feast. He, who should have been the merriest, was the gloomiest man there, so busy was he with planning what must be done to restore him to the king's trust and esteem. Yet the wine and ale flowed, the banquet was eaten and the ribaldries resounded from table to table.

His younger brothers forgot they were grown men, and resorted to the boyish antics for which they were notorious, so that when Cedric went out to check his duty guard, he found Gurth and Leofwine coming ashore in a small boat, giggling like children. They had cut adrift a large section of the ship causeway, sending fifty furious housecarls floating helplessly down the river.

Cedric, hearing his men shouting to be brought back, started to be equally angry; but he was soon affected by their mirth as they rolled drunkenly out of the boat, sliding in the mud and covering themselves with ooze.

'Don't worry, Cedric,' Gurth cried, 'They're only going to Normandy to bash old William!'

'They volunteered!' Leofwine hooted, falling flat in the morass. Cedric, grinning broadly, helped him up.

'Well, now you'd better get them back for me,' he said. 'I think I might need them here soon.'

XIII

I T was Thursday, the fifth of January, 1066, and King Edward the Confessor was dying. The candles that had been prepared for Epiphany Eve were now being lit to illuminate the way to Heaven for the soul of a saintly man. He lay on his narrow bed, his thin, white face shadowed by the great purple canopy of state, and his gaze wandered for the last time about this corner of the wonderful palace he had built.

Beyond the posts of the bed he could just make out the arched window of his chamber, and the gently swirling snow outside, and although he was covered by a wealth of furs, the sight sent shivers running through his tired old frame. Nearby, the fire hissed and smoked on green wood, and he saw no comfort there either. It was as if the flames were flickering out along with his fading life. Only when he looked up at the golden dragon banner over his head, and the holly and the ivy and the mistletoe that had been put up in celebration of Christmas, did he feel cheered. The banner was a mark of his triumph, for he had restored it to dignity, and the greenery was the symbol of life everlasting. Such was Edward's fate, he was sure.

His eyes turned to the people who surrounded him. His queen, Edith, was there, and so were her brothers, the earls Harold, Gurth and Leofwine, their nephew Haakon and Harold's wife Aldgyth, heavy with their first child. There were also Stigand Archbishop of Canterbury, Ealdred Archbishop of York, and Edwin Abbot of West Minster. Of these, Edward was thinking, only Edwin was truly his friend. The rest were but users of his power. If he could have been granted one last wish, he would have asked to have by him his friends and family. But his friends had all been frightened away long ago, and all but one or two of his family were dead, murdered or harried to an early grave. His consolation was that he would soon be reunited with them. They were calling to him, those beloved faces of times past.

Edward raised a limp hand to draw their attention.

'I must tell you, I had a vision once,' he said, in a weak, croaking voice, but before he continued his story he broke off to speak a prayer: 'Eternal God, if those things which have been revealed to me come from thee, grant me strength to tell of them. But if they are no more than vanity, let my sickness prevent me speaking of them . . .'

Edith took his hand.

'Rest, my lord,' she whispered, thinking that he was rambling again, but he rolled his head in protest.

'No. It is important that you hear me,' he mumbled, 'for I feel God give me the strength I asked for, so it must be His wish that I speak. In this dream two monks came to me. They foretold woe for England, if those in high places were not the good men they seemed to be. After my death, they said, a curse would fall upon this country. It would be given over to fire and sword for one year and one day. Nothing could stop that happening, not even penance . . .'

Edward, suddenly anxious, struggled to sit up, his arms reaching out towards Harold, who went to him, helping Edith to lay him down.

'My lord?' inquired Harold, knowing that the king had something to say to him.

Edward closed his eyes, seeking within himself the strength to go on. He laid his hands on those of his queen and prince.

'Harold,' he murmured. 'In God's name I beg of you, be of clear conscience. Do not let this land of mine waste beneath the torch and the blade . . .'

'Easy, my lord. It shall not be so.'

The watering eyes opened once more. The king's fading regard was fixed upon Harold. When next he spoke, it was in a voice so soft that everyone had to lean forward to distinguish one syllable from another.

'This woman and all my kingdom I commend to your charge,' Edward was saying. 'Serve and honour her faithfully as your queen and sister as long as she lives, and do not rob her of any honour received from me . . .'

Harold and Edith looked at each other, not understanding why he should think that Harold would rob Edith of anything. Harold caught the eye of Archbishop Stigand.

'He has named you his heir,' Stigand nodded.

'My lord?' Harold urged. 'Is that your meaning?'

But the old body was still. The last gargling breath had left the colourless lips. Edward, last surviving son of Ethelred, who had lost the kingdom fifty-three years before, was dead. Abbot Edwin sprinkled holy water, intoning Latin over the corpse. Soon, when the news had been passed to the waiting city, the bells of London would begin to toll.

Harold stood up. Edward's last bequest had made him King of

England. He kept his thoughts to himself, for he was thinking: 'You old fool! What trouble you could have saved us all, if only you had spoken that wish before!'

'You are king, Harold,' Edith said, stunned.

'We are all the witnesses you need,' agreed Stigand. 'The Witan will acclaim you to a man. But you must summon them quickly, before others try to change their minds.'

Harold looked at the crown, and stretched out a hand to it, then drew it back as if fearing some sharp-jawed trap within its circlet of gold. Why could he not snatch it up as joyfully as he wanted to? Through long years and many trials he had worked for this prize, the greatest goal of his life, the final victory, the fulfilling of all ambition. Nothing, no one, stood in his way. No one would offer even the mildest rebuke if he picked up the crown now and placed it on his head himself, so why this dread of a simple act of triumph? He did not doubt that he deserved it; he did not doubt that he could keep it. No longer did his treaty with William mean anything. He would never have considered such a pact if he had known Edward was to favour him so. Why then, why was he afraid for the first time in his life? He gave voice to the reason almost before he realised he knew it.

'The King's vision, his dream,' he said. 'What of that?'

'He was sick,' replied Stigand firmly. 'It means nothing.'

'If he was clear enough in his mind to hand me the kingdom, he must also have been sure about that,' Harold argued, wanting to be wrong.

'Does it matter, even so?' Stigand answered. 'He said fire and the sword would scour the land if men in high places were not as good as they should be. You are not an evil man, Lord Harold. Gurth, Leofwine, Cedric – none of them are evil men.'

Harold was reassured. He took up the crown, and turned it slowly in his hands, delighting in its beauty and all that it signified.

'Very well then, Archbishop,' he smiled. 'You have work to do! Tomorrow there is to be a funeral – and a crowning.'

As they were leaving Edward's death chamber, Harold met Cedric, who was commanding the guard, and told him the news.

'Stigand left out one important person when he was speaking of evil,' Cedric said, 'and that was himself. He's a cuckoo in the nest, Harold. You aren't going to let him conduct the coronation service, surely?'

'I can do nothing about it,' Harold sighed. 'The ceremony is the prerogative of the Archbishop of Canterbury. Like it or not, he's the only Archbishop of Canterbury we've got.'

'But Rome will not accept you as king!' Cedric insisted.

'I doubt whether they will, anyway. And since when has Rome crowned England's king? They must put up with it.'

'Please, think again. William above all others will use this against you. Please, Harold, find someone else. Send for the Archbishop of York, anyone but Stigand!'

'Cedric, old friend, there is no time! Stigand was perfectly correct when he said others will be trying to influence the Witan against me as soon as they hear Edward is dead. The most dangerous is Edgar, who will lose no time trying to sway every northern thane he can reach. He may have some success, and that I cannot risk. I will be king tomorrow, Cedric, no later than that. And no-one will be able to do anything about it then, not the Pope, not William, no-one!'

Later that night Gurth and Leofwine also tried to talk Harold out of acting too hastily, but he was set on his course. The following morning, even while Edward's funeral procession was forming, Harold went before the Witan and rapidly put his claim. Their verdict was unanimous, and after the vote Harold cheerfully invited them all to see him crowned that afternoon. Then they went to the Abbey to bury the late king.

There was feverish excitement in the streets of London and around West Minster. People garbed in sackcloth and ashes wailed and wept as Edward was borne to his tomb. Eight nobles carried the coffin on their shoulders, flanked by lines of black-robed Benedictine monks. Housecarls struggled to hold back the crowds, but again and again mobs broke through to harangue the procession, as though it were their fault that Edward was going to his last resting place. It was as if a terrible fear had swept through the nation with the passing of the man who had been their spiritual saviour and peace-maker for nigh on a quarter of a century, and yet in other quarters some remarkable events held to be connected with the death of Edward were greeted with a joyous delirium. The blind shouted that they could see again, and cripples hurled away their crutches to run screeching through the throng. As news of these miracles spread, the very air of London seemed to crackle and no one knew whether to be afraid or happy. Knots of citizens gathered at the roadside to go down on their knees and praise the Lord with chants and prayers. Seeing Harold, they eagerly cheered him and asked him to join in their exultations, and to be sure to continue the good work of Edward the Confessor.

Harold felt a renewal of hope deep inside him.

'Surely, Father,' he whispered to Abbot Edwin. 'This must mean that the signs are good?'

'It means,' Edwin answered sagely, 'that God is telling us of his

452

love for Edward, and of his acceptance into the Kingdom of Heaven. That is all I can be sure of, my son.'

The mood of celebration, quickly replacing the earlier dread, continued through that cold, bleak day as Harold returned to the Abbey to be crowned. The splendid church that Edward had created was packed, and thousands more fought for a place at the doors to watch the hastily organised ceremony. Once more the battered housecarls had work aplenty, pushing and bullying the crowds into some semblance of order.

Nervously walking up to the high altar between his brothers and two bishops, Harold was surprised to see that Stigand had, at the last moment, stepped aside and allowed Archbishop Ealdred of York to take his place.

A rapid but intense discussion among the elders between the funeral and coronation had persuaded Stigand to surrender ground yet again for Harold's sake. It was agreed that it would be Ealdred who actually conferred the crown upon the new king, while Stigand would lead the devotions. Stigand was visibly offended, but he was becoming accustomed to the humiliations caused by the uncertainty of his tenure of office.

'This should please everyone,' murmured Gurth to Harold.

'I doubt it,' Harold grunted. 'The fact that Stigand is even present will be enough to annoy Rome, I shouldn't wonder. If we're going to fly in the Pope's face, we might as well do it boldly.'

He had to admit afterwards, however, that all was done in splendid style. No stranger would ever have guessed that he was a commoner, not of the blood royal, the first king for five hundred years who could not claim descent from the Wessex, English or Danish monarchs. He looked like a Viking, or a descendant of Cerdic, as he strode proudly to his place. Humbly, as would a son of Ethelred, he bowed before the altar, and removed the ordinary gold circlet from his head. He prostrated himself before the Host in the tabernacle while Ealdred and the choir sang the Te Deum, then rose at the bidding of the bishops as the last echoes died among the mighty stone pillars.

The abbey fell silent, save for a tiny shuffle, a single cough. The crown was held high above Harold's head.

'People of England, make known your will!' Archbishop Ealdred boomed. 'Is it right that Harold Godwinsson, Dux Anglorum, Earl of Wessex, shall by the grace of God this day be made Harold the Second, your lord and king?'

For Harold the pause between question and response lasted an age.

'Aye, aye, aye – long live King Harold!' the people roared, and a long sigh escaped him as he felt the crown touch his head.

The consecration that followed, the anointing of his head with holy oil, the singing and the acceptance of the ceremonial axe and the sceptre and the sword of state, all passed as if in a dream. He took his vows and received the investitures, and when Ealdred gave his blessing and offered the Body and Blood of the Lord, Harold scarcely heard him.

'Last night a commoner, tonight a king,' he mused an hour later, as he presided at a noisy banquet in the great hall of the palace. 'Nothing feels real any more. It seems a week since we stood at Edward's death-bed, days since I got ready to go to the Abbey. God's word, I'll tell you something, my friend, I've never shaken so much in all my life as I'm shaking today. Could it be that I'm. . . . *frightened?*'

'I would be,' Cedric laughed. 'The burden must be terrible. Rather you than me, that's all I can say. There's one thing I'll wager you haven't thought of yet – there's no one to turn to any more. The whole of England looks to you, and you are as alone as a hermit on a mountain.'

'No I'm not,' the king corrected him. 'Because you are coming up the mountain with me. I'm making you Staller, my right-hand man. I want you to remain commander of housecarls as well. And together, we are going to build an army such as England has never seen. We'll get the fyrd regularly trained and ready to move for war, if I have my way. Damn it, what am I saying? I *will* have my way! I'm king now, aren't I?'

'You are,' Cedric chuckled, with goblet raised high, 'By God, you are! And every time you take a step up, you haul me up with you. There are times when I pray you'll let me down to the ground again.'

'The ground is for farmers. The heights are for hawks, such as we. Fly, my friend. Spread your wings, and fly with me. We are going to work wonders!'

There was yet a nagging fear in Cedric's heart.

'Must you speak of wonders?' he gently chided his king, who was drunk more on success than on wine. 'We saw wonders today, awful wonders, a tribute to Edward from Heaven itself! Has any man seen such miracles since the time of Christ? You have much to live up to, if you will be as true a king as Edward.'

That soured Harold's mood a little. He did not like the suggestion that he would not be as worthy as his predecessor. Only Cedric could have spoken those words with impunity.

'Yes, Edward was a pious ruler,' he admitted grudgingly, 'but there's more to being a King than fasting and praying. There was plenty he left neglected, Edward was so busy being holy, plenty that I have to attend to, as I always did. But now it will be done as I wish. I will decide our policies of trade and commerce, and taxes and agriculture, and war and treaties of peace. I will choose our ambassadors, especially to Rome, and I will show every one of our neighbours, from the tip of Norway to the shores of Africa, that no one treads on England's toes any more. And besides all that, my dear Cedric, if you'll sleep the easier at hearing it from me, I'll keep paying my due respects to the Lord. There, does that make you feel better?'

'And what will you do if Rome announces to the rest of Europe that you are a false successor?'

'You think they will?'

'With pressure from William and his uncles, they'll be sorely tempted. I'd wager my house on it.'

'Damn you, was ever a man so good at spoiling a feast? What do you suggest I should have done?'

'For the love of God, get rid of that man,' Cedric pleaded, pointing to Stigand. 'Go through the coronation ceremony again with an untainted Archbishop of Canterbury. It's not too late.'

'It is too late,' Harold snarled. 'I'll be damned if I'll let the Pope or anyone else dictate to me!'

Cedric was soon proved right, but even he had not anticipated the severity of Rome's vengeance when it came. Within weeks of his crowning, Harold received a letter from the Papal offices. Accusing him of wrongfully claiming to be the Confessor's heir, and thus "stealing" the English crown, it stated that the punishment was to be excommunication both for himself and Archbishop Stigand.

The missive arrived the day after the birth of Harold's first legitimate son, also to be named Harold. He was still at Aldgyth's bedside when the messenger came, shattering the mood of jubilation. Harold, enraged, stamped about the chamber brandishing the parchment, defying everyone to discover an ounce of justice anywhere amid its haughty Latin phrases.

'William!' he screamed. 'This is the Bastard's work, right enough!'

'He has pledged that he will take this kingdom,' Leofwine reminded him. 'Now he has all he needs to embark on a holy crusade. It will bring adventurers flocking to his side like suckling pigs to the sow. We had best prepare such an army as we have never turned out before, Harold.'

Harold ceased pacing and for a moment fell silent, his brooding stare fixed upon Aldgyth and the swaddled babe in her arms. He did not say a word, but it was plain to all that he regarded little Harold as his heir, his future hope, and that the baby's birth had served only to strengthen his already rocklike resolve. There would be no more disputed heirs to disrupt the continuity of the English royal line, Harold had decided. There would be no more dog-fights whenever a king died, as there had been these fifty years past. Harold II would be succeeded by Harold III, and the sons of Harold Haroldsson would go on with the work, staunching the long-bleeding wounds of England.

'We will,' he said softly, in answer to Leofwine. 'We will send the Norman bastard home with a bloody nose, never fear. I don't care how great a rabble he brings with him; we'll sweep the offal into the sea!'

He threw the letter down, and stormed out of the palace, down to the low-lying fields where Cedric was attempting to turn some of his housecarls into horsemen and archers. What he saw there gave him further cause for despair. The housecarls could sit their horses well enough, but being unused to wielding weapons from the saddle, and having no one to train them properly, they were making a sorry mess of the charge and the strike.

Posts bound with straw had been hammered into the boggy earth. The riders were attacking the stakes with vigour but little skill. As Harold went to stand beside Cedric, four of the horsemen were spurring out from the ranks, two with spears, one with an axe and one with a heavy club capped with iron. Halfway to their targets, the clubman cut across the path of one of the spearmen. The cursing spearman reined in too late, the horses crashed into each other, neighing and threshing madly, and the spear impaled the clubman's shield arm and dragged him from his horse.

Howls of derision came from the ranks, though Cedric's face was dark with anger. The other two soldiers galloped on. The first lunged for the post with his spear, then swiftly drew his arm back as if fearing he might break it, and rode on without making the hit. The second, not so cautious, took a mighty whack at the stake with his axe and suffered the fate the first had feared, leaving the weapon to clatter to the ground while he galloped away yelping and clutching at a strained wrist.

'Clods!' Cedric roared. 'Slow-witted, useless fools! Can you never get it right?'

'Am I seeing the worst of them?' Harold asked hopefully.

'I can only think of about half a dozen better,' Cedric sighed. 'This doesn't come easily to men trained to fight on foot. The best we can hope for is that William's cavalry will fall off their horses laughing.'

'What of the archers?'

'A little more success, but not much. You can teach bowmen to loose off a volley more or less in unison, and hit a standing target, but you can't force them to stand firm in battle. We had a mock fight, archers against cavalry. When they saw the riders bearing down on them, a good two hundred yards off, half of them scattered and ran!'

'Then forget it. Let them get back to training for battle as they know it. We have no time to waste on this.'

'The invasion will be soon, then?'

'It could be. Cedric, my dear old comrade, I have to admit that I should have listened to you. I have been excommunicated . . .'

'Dear God!'

' . . . and my brother Leofwine is right in what he says: it means that William will be coming here with the Pope's blessing on his banner, followed by every crusader from here to the Holy Land. He will come this summer, there's no doubt about it.'

Cedric laid his hands on the king's shoulders.

'Harold, God himself has brought you to the throne of England.' he declared. 'He will not desert you now!'

Harold, with a wry grin heavenward, answered: 'Then let us hope He'll over-rule the Pope, eh?'

It seemed that that was not to be, however, for the next blow came in the form of a sign that appeared to come from the very hand of the Creator. Ever since Harold had defied the Mother Church and taken Edward's crown in the presence of the false Archbishop Stigand, all Europe had been watching nervously for some sign of divine disapproval. It came just after Easter, when for the first time Harold wore his crown in public at the Abbey. That night the sky was lit up unnaturally, as if the moon had risen at the wrong time. People rushed into the streets, and cried out in anguish and fell to their knees in prayer when they saw a fiery sword hanging there brilliantly, subduing the stars. The wailing that had accompanied the funeral of the Confessor now began again. The churches were crammed with chanting, tearful people, again in sackcloth and ashes, but many hid indoors, waiting for the awful apparition to be gone.

They were to be disappointed. The sword, with shining hilt and glittering blade, stayed on night after night; sometimes it could even be seen in daylight. It surely foretold the end of the world, the seers said. And while the lamentations went on, a number of terrified citizens abandoned their homes and went hurrying into the countryside with cartfuls of possessions, only to find the dread portent pursuing them. Others formed an angry band and marched on the palace, shouting to Harold to repent, and beating at the doors until they were driven away by the housecarls. Seeing that Harold was going to do nothing, a few of the frantic crowd threw themselves screaming into the Thames, or cut their own throats.

There was nothing Harold could think of to do. Deep down, though he put on a brave face, he was as terrified as any of them. He stood for hours at the window, staring up at the fearful cross.

'An amazing sight,' he breathed to Cedric. 'A wonder of the universe. Have men ever seen such a thing, before our time? What does it mean, Cedric? What does it mean?'

Cedric had recently come from his London house, where he had gone to reassure his family. Ingrid had been close to panic, being a woman of deep-rooted superstition who believed the prophecies of Armageddon that were being repeated. She had wanted Cedric to stay with her and the children until the sky-fire descended and swallowed them up, so that they could all face their Maker together, and when he had insisted on going back to the palace she had screamed abuse at him.

'One old man says it was seen just so in the time of his father, a full five and seventy years ago,' Cedric shrugged. 'Evil raged through the land then. Perhaps it will again. How should I know?'

'Then it's not thought to bode evil for me alone?'

'By no means. Stigand says it's William who should be repenting, for giving false witness to the Pope. Merchants have brought word that it can be seen just as clearly in France as here.'

'It's difficult to decide,' Harold said thoughtfully, 'whether it's the blade that is turned towards me, or the hilt. Come on, Cedric. You of all men can be honest with me. How would you say it lies?'

'I honestly don't know. But I cannot help remembering that dream of Edward's you spoke of. What was it? For a year and a day after his death, the land would be given over to the fire and the sword. Perhaps this means that all England lies waiting on God's anvil, not you alone. Who can say which man – you or William – must atone for us all?'

'Cedric, you are quite an able sage, for a soldier,' said Harold, feeling better.

'For a farmer,' Cedric chuckled.

'Well, you have the last laugh now, the farm boy from Berkshire who counsels the troubled king in his palace! Aye, we've come a long way, Cedric. The journey was hard, but we got here, you and I. And I'm not going back down that road, not even if it was William himself who had that fiery cross hung up there!'

Cedric brought him a cup of wine.

'Why is it,' he asked wearily, 'that whenever I reassure you that you can still bestride rivers, you immediately start trying to leap oceans?'

'Are you afraid?' Harold challenged him.

'Of a fight? No, not I. If I am afraid it is for our souls, not our skins.'

'So, because of this light in the sky, you think I should try diplomacy rather than war?'

'Consider it, at least,' Cedric shrugged.

'I have. But it is William who has girded up for war. It is he who has turned all my waking thoughts to war, when all I wanted was to reign in peace. And he's the one who has to leap seas, not I. Let him come. Whether or not there be a sword of vengeance on high, I shall meet him without fear.'

He meant every word. He was troubled in spirit, but his assurance was growing stronger once more, and he forced himself to ignore the things that were going wrong and set about reassuring his people. First he announced that he would attend a special mass at the Abbey, at which prayers would be sent up for England's salvation and at which he would do penance for any sins he might unknowingly have committed. By chance – though Harold would not have admitted as much – the fiery cross vanished almost exactly on that date, which won him back a great deal of support and confidence. Freed from his religious obligations, and much calmer at heart, Harold then turned to making a stand against William.

He set a watch on the south-east coast, and put men to work on strengthening the fortifications of the larger towns. In London the fleet was kept in a state of readiness; all through the shires the fyrdmen were ordered to be on call, and Cedric was quite needlessly instructed to keep his housecarls hard at their training. While all these preparations continued into the summer, tales of William's preparations began to flood in from merchants, seamen and spies. The Norman shores were alive with activity, they reported. William was building a massive fleet of ships wide enough to take horses and siege engines. His soldiery was flocking to him eagerly from far and wide, hundreds of men every day: reports of their numbers varied between ten thousand and thirty thousand. The Pope had indeed given William's leopard banner his personal blessing, and it was even said that a company of soldiers from Holy Rome was joining the Norman army. William was promising his men exceedingly rich booty for a successful invasion, and the word from the court in Rouen was that the duke's friends were already marking out which English lands should be theirs, and had told their families to be ready to join them as soon as the fighting was done.

Harold listened to it all with interest and made jokes about the scores of disappointed Norman wives who would have to unpack and start looking around for husbands, but although outwardly he treated the news lightly, he took careful note of every detail that came to his ears. He passed on his information to Gurth, Leofwine, Haakon and Cedric, and made sure they knew what would be needed when the day came. First of all, they would try to prevent the invaders landing, he told them, but if that failed then their choice of ground would be all important in dealing with the Norman cavalry and archers. They were to render the siege engines useless by drawing the battle away from the fortresses into the coastal forests where they knew the ground like foxes. They would soon make William regret ever venturing into England.

Everything appeared to be going well, until the long-awaited messages came announcing an assault on England. Then King Harold learned that the fates had dealt him a cruel blow, for the attack came not from the south, but from the north, and not from William, but from an entirely unexpected quarter.

Early in September, Cedric took Harold intelligence from his northern scouts. A large army of Norwegians had landed, and after a fierce battle at Scarborough had advanced on York.

'It's Tostig,' Cedric told Harold. 'He has brought them here.'

But for a burning regret in his eyes, Harold's face said little of the feelings that boiled within him. He had been drafting some important new laws, but at Cedric's words he shoved pen and parchment aside as though they no longer mattered.

'Tostig,' he repeated softly. 'Is he with them?'

'He's with them, and fighting as fiercely as any, by all accounts. They captured some English thanes at Scarborough. Some they tortured to death, flaying them alive, but a few they set free with a message for you. Tostig wants his earldom back, and he'll fight until he gets it. It seems since he was banished from England he has been trying everywhere for allies. First he went to his wife's family in Flanders, then to your cousin Sweyn in Denmark. None of them was prepared to help him. Finally he got what he wanted from Harald Hardrada in Norway.'

'And what does King Harald want?'

'A share of England. He reminds you that when his nephew Magnus was king of Denmark, he made a treaty with Hardicanute that one would inherit the other's crown. Harald says he has come to see the terms of that treaty fulfilled. He says it is still in force and that he is entitled to Magnus's inheritance.'

'Oh, does he, indeed?' growled Harold. He pushed himself up from his chair and strode easily to the carved oak chest where he kept his chain-mail coat and sword harness. 'Then we will have to show him that flaying my Englishmen and raiding my land is not going to win him a penny from me.'

'You will fight Tostig?'

Harold rounded on Cedric, face ablaze as though deeply insulted, but his anger quickly subsided.

'Do I have a choice?' he shrugged. 'Do you think I want to fight with my brother – again? But, God's word, what am I to do? Oh Lord, what a time he chooses, damn his hide! How soon do you think William will come?'

'He could come any day. The summer is fading. He will either come now, or wait until the spring.'

'Well, what does it matter? We'll have to go north and settle with Tostig first. We must pray that William holds off a while longer. Move swiftly, Cedric. Get word to Gurth, Leofwine and Haakon at once. Tell them to gather all the men they can in the time it will take us to reach Cambridgeshire, and to meet us there. Send out to as many of the southern shires as we can reach, and bring in the fyrd. Tell them not to waste time making for London, but to head for the same meeting place as soon as they can. We will start out with housecarls and as many men as we can muster in London . . .'

A messenger nervously interrupted them at that point. He had ridden day and night from Northumbria, and was almost too fatigued to get his words out. He was one of a constant stream of horsemen who would be galloping south with tidings over the next few days.

'My lord,' he gasped. 'York has surrendered. Lords Edwin and Morcar beg you to pardon them. They put up what resistance they could, but the city was overwhelmed by the Northmen . . .'

Harold nodded sharply. One more setback was the least he expected.

'So my brothers-in-law let me down, too, do they?' he hissed. 'And where was Hardrada's army when you left, occupying the city, or moving south?'

'Neither, my lord. They were pulling back to a camp by the Derwent, where they say they will wait until you have had time to answer their demands.'

Harold turned to Cedric with a savage grin.

'Have someone go to them,' he commanded. 'Tell them I am thinking it over, and they will get my reply very soon.'

XIV

SPEED and surprise had always been the most important consider-
ations in Harold's campaigns, and this time was no different
despite the daunting two hundred miles he had to cover. He was
aware that in this battle he must use caution, however. Tostig knew
his tactics, and would have to be treated very differently from the
foes Harold had encountered before. On the rapid march north,
therefore, Harold took time to gather numbers of men at least equal
to the reports he had received of Hardrada's strength. He also
promised himself and Cedric that he would control his natural
instinct to go rushing into the fray the moment they reached York,
and pause to decide whether he could spare yet more time for
further reinforcements to come up.

That extra time seemed unlikely to be granted to him. Reports
reached him as he entered Northumbria that Hardrada and Tostig
were growing impatient for his answer, and were rampaging
through the country east of York. They must have guessed that
Harold was on his way, even if their scouts had not sighted the
column. But were their actions intended to goad him into a battle
too soon, or were they merely keeping their bloodthirsty Vikings
amused? Harold endeavoured to learn the answers before leaving
York to engage them. He drew his army up before the city walls,
and ordered that Edwin and Morcar should be brought to him.
The two brothers came out trying to retain an air of dignity, but
looking somewhat shamefaced and not a little fearful.

'We fought well, Harold,' Morcar said, without being asked.
'But we hardly had time to get our men together before they were
here. They are at least five thousand strong.'

'So I've heard,' Harold snapped, dismissing his explanation.
'Have any more joined them in the last two weeks?'

'I don't think so. I don't know . . .'

Harold, still astride his horse, was tiredly rubbing at his left leg,
which had siezed up again, and caused him agonies on the long
ride. He was in no temper to suffer fools.

'Do you mean to tell me,' he snarled, 'that you have not even
bothered to find out for me exactly what I face? My God, when I
married your sister I thought I was buying myself some allies. She
might as well have brought me a herd of sheep as dowry!'

'It has not been easy for us here, you know,' Edwin cut in hotly. 'It's we who have had these Northmen on our doorstep these weeks past, slaughtering, and sacking town after town! If we had not made some kind of pact with them, the whole of Northumbria would be in ruins by now.'

'It is in ruins, fool,' Harold retorted. 'And so will you be, if we don't quickly patch up the damage you've done. Where are they now? Can you tell me that much?'

'This morning they were back at Stamford Bridge.'

'And where's that?'

'It's on the Derwent, eight miles east of here.'

'Open country?'

'Mostly, yes. Some of the land between here and there is wooded.'

'Give me someone to guide me,' Harold said, and turned to talk to his brothers and Cedric.

'If they have chosen their ground, it could be a trap,' suggested Gurth.

Cedric was worried about Harold. The king's eyes were watering with the pain of his leg, and he kept working his jaws as if silently willing himself to stay on his horse.

'Why don't you rest here, and let us do it?' Cedric asked.

'No! Sit here and wonder what's happening? I'll let this damned leg-fall off first. Tell me what you think, Cedric, about Tostig's position and ours.'

'They appear to be waiting for us. They must have their reasons.'

'Leofwine?'

'I say let's get it done with. Much as I dread meeting Tostig, I want no more of this delay.'

'And so say I,' Harold nodded. 'We march.'

He rode at the head of his men, as always, with Cedric Shieldless on his right with the fighting man banner, and Haakon at his left with the ancient golden dragon. His fyrdmen were footsore and his housecarls weary of the saddle after more than two weeks of travel, but Harold went on in the certain knowledge that they would follow him until they dropped.

They moved at a steady pace, not so fast as to tire out the foot soldiers, but at speed enough to cover the distance while it was still morning, leaving enough daylight for battle. The day looked clear for some miles along the winding track and open countryside, but the low hills towards Bridlington and the coast were obscured by a watery mist and the occasional brief squall. Harold, having ordered his scouts to work well in front and out on the flanks but never to lose touch with the main column, kept a continuous watch on them, peering intently into the distance. But for the strain of his continued suffering, he might have been a huntsman waiting for beaters to flush out a quarry. He did not speak, and he never once looked behind. Nor did he complain of his pain. When Harold was at war, nothing but the next engagement occupied his mind.

Seven miles from York, as the army was approaching the silent village of Gate Helmsley on the ridge above the shallow Derwent Valley, Harold saw two of his outriders galloping back, waving to indicate that they had come upon the enemy. Harold called a halt.

'We saw the Northmen, my lord. A dozen or more, foraging, or spying out the land. They made off down the slope towards Stamford Bridge.'

'Did they see us?' wondered Harold, raising himself in the saddle to stare into the valley.

'They must have. It's no use, my lord, you cannot see the river from here. Another half mile or so, and we will surely sight them.'

'Send a company ahead,' Cedric advised. 'Be certain of Tostig's exact position before we go on.'

'No,' Harold argued, 'if we have any advantage left, any more delay will wipe it out. We must do battle now.'

'And so must Tostig, God's mercy on him,' breathed Gurth.

'Aye,' grated Harold. 'Let's get this last damned mile done with, then!' He spurred his horse forward into a trot.

Down the long incline they went to where the road ran almost parallel with the river, hurriedly now, the horsemen gradually stringing out ahead and the fyrdmen jogging along behind.

There was a stillness in the damp autumn air and in the grey-green valley, as if earth and sky and time had all stopped to let Harold's army pass by. The men heard nothing but their own heavy breathing and the tramping of human and animal feet in the mud, the slap and jingle of weaponry and harness. Many of them faced agony and death, and the silence hung about them like a waiting shroud. Already they were as much ghosts as men, ghosts of those who had marched this same road against the same foe fifty years before; one hundred, two hundred years before. Whether old or young, whether they were the sons of those who had marched with Ethelred, or were born but fifteen summers past and knew little of those times, it now seemed they had always known that one day they would come to this place and this time.

Then, suddenly, a few hundred yards above the Derwent, they stumbled to a standstill. Below them, on the west bank of the river, north of the wooden bridge, the valley was alive with men, their helmets and mail coats and axe and sword blades glistening in the pale sun, like the scales of a huge dragon. The Norwegians were dousing their camp fires, readying themselves for battle. As the English appeared on the hill, they sent up derisive shouts and thrust weapons and shields up in the air, again and again, like the breaking of waves. Then they clashed blades on shields with a thunderous roar, enough to strike fear into all but the most experienced warriors even before a charge.

'God our Saviour, look!' whispered Haakon. One man stood by far the tallest amid the throng. 'Is that Harald Hardrada?'

'That's him,' confirmed Harold, who had had the Norwegian king described to him. 'That's the man whose name has spread terror across the world. And I'll pay his weight in mancuses to the man who slays him!'

It sounded a generous offer, but it would be an awesome task. Harald Hardrada, Harald the Ruthless, stood head and shoulders above any other man in the field, and was of frighteningly massive build. He was a giant in both size and reputation, indeed, for everyone knew the story of his thirty-six years warring from Norway, through Poland and Russia and on to Byzantium, the Holy Land, North Africa and the Mediterranean lands. His prowess and his cruelty were legend, and it was said that he was endowed with magical power. At his first battle, fought at the age of fifteen beside his brother King Olave the Saint, the sun had suddenly darkened and the land was cast into blackness at mid-day. Olave had been killed that day at Sticklestad, and his enemies had taken the darkness as a sign that their cause was just. But Harald had escaped to go adventuring around the world, winning great riches and a mighty name for himself, and then had returned to take back the kingdom of Norway. He shrugged off the heavenly portent that preceded the downfall of his brother, and prospered more than any other who had witnessed that wonder. Harald Hardrada defied any man's gods, just as he stood defying the English army today, his mocking laughter rolling along the valley like a death knell.

'Any man who can cut him down,' Cedric smiled grimly, 'will deserve to go home with his riches. Some ten or twenty had better conspire to share the prize . . .'

'Harold, look!' Gurth interrupted. 'It's Tostig! He's coming to meet us.'

Tostig had walked his horse out from the Norse ranks. He approached slowly, pausing to see if he would be allowed to draw nearer. When Harold gave him a brief sign, he came on. He rode almost to within arm's length of Harold, Gurth and Leofwine, looking both uneasy and resentful at having to face his brothers in such circumstances.

'Greetings, Tostig,' Harold said easily. 'It's fine company you've brought us.'

'You know what it is to be banished, Harold,' Tostig answered. 'I am no less eager to return now than when I fought by your side for the same purpose.'

'And you can. There need be no fight between us.'

'You would give me back my earldom?' asked Tostig, taken by surprise.

'Today, if we can agree terms without fighting.'

Tostig glanced at each of his kinsmen in turn, suspecting that Harold was jesting, but saw in all of them only a willingness to welcome him back.

'What are your terms?' he inquired of Harold.

'Send home this army. That is all.'

Tostig sighed.

'I brought them here,' he said. 'I cannot send them back empty-handed. What will you offer Harald Hardrada?'

'Nothing,' his brother stated flatly.

'But that's no good,' Tostig protested. 'You'll have to offer him something!'

'All right,' Harold replied. 'I'll be generous. He's a bigger man than most. My offer to him is seven feet of good English earth.'

Harold's men laughed, but Tostig was struck speechless with anger.

'Is that your final word?' he demanded icily, at last.

'For Harald Hardrada, yes. But Tostig, there's time for you to think again. I meant what I said.'

'It's no good, Harold,' Tostig shouted, wheeling his horse about, 'I will not betray the friends who have followed me here.' He began to ride away, but after a few yards he turned about with a brave grin, calling: 'We are truly Godwinssons, we four! Though we meet as enemies we part as brothers. God be with you!'

'God be with you, Tostig,' Harold responded sadly, but hardly had he spoken before he was starting to issue his instructions. The Norwegians had been busily preparing while Tostig and Harold were talking, and started moving into battle order as soon as they saw Tostig ride in.

Hardrada had ordered his Vikings to hurry across the bridge, to put the deep river between themselves and Harold's force, and then to move up to the high ground above the east bank where they could make a better stand and gain time for their reinforcements to come in. The Northmen were streaming over the river by the time Tostig rejoined them, and horsemen were being sent out to bring in outlying bands of Vikings.

'We need that bridge!' Harold growled, ignoring his lameness as he leapt down from his horse and drew his sword. 'Quickly now, battle horns!'

Saxon trumpets sounded down the valley. Shouts of 'Holy Rood!' rose up from the English ranks, and a wave of men washed down to the Derwent. The last of the Norwegians were making the jostling run across the bridge, but a huge Norse axeman had taken up a position halfway across, ready to meet the attackers alone. He was nearly as big as Hardrada, and utterly fearless. Cheered on by his comrades, he swung his immense blade as though it were no heavier than a broom, smashing right and left at the oncoming fyrdmen.

The first two spearmen to reach him were brutally dealt with, spread on the timbers like slaughtered sheep. Another Englishman leapt over their bodies and was as swiftly despatched and tossed carelessly into the river. Half a dozen javelins were thrown, and the Viking guffawed contemptuously as he batted two of them aside. He brushed off another that barely penetrated his tough leather coat, and watched the others clatter harmlessly about him.

'Come, puny English piglets!' he bellowed. 'See, one Norwegian is good enough for a whole army of you!'

They rushed him, but in disorganised groups of two and three. The Viking stepped back hardly ten paces while meeting them, man after man. His arms were tireless, his aim deadly as the lunge of a snake. Ten men fell, horribly mutilated, then another ten, and another. Beneath his feet the timbers were soaked with blood and gore, and the piles of dead and dying mounted like so many discarded sacks, until he was fighting on top of a barricade of corpses.

'Merciful God!' breathed Harold. 'He'll defeat us by himself . . .'

'We're wasting men and time trying to take him on the bridge.' Cedric snapped. He had seen a large swill tub that had been left by a swineherd on the bank beneath the bridge. He snatched a spear from one of his housecarls, and ran down the bank. Pushing the tub into the water, he stepped into it and shoved it out awkwardly, going hand over hand from one strut to the next, out to midstream. Directly beneath the Norwegian axeman, he reached up to wedge his spear between two planks to hold himself there while he thought about what to do next. He could not wait much longer. The blood of some forty Englishmen was raining down into the river. Every minute that giant stayed there the Viking messengers were riding closer to their distant reinforcements.

Cedric took aim, and thrust upwards with all his strength. The spear point shot up between the Viking's legs and pierced deeply

467

at his anus. The fighter screamed, and let his bloody axe fall as his hands went down to the source of the pain. Another English spear was plunged into his stomach, and then a sword sliced into his neck. He fell at last, although Cedric did not see it. He had lost his footing and fallen into the river. He clutched gasping and spluttering at a stout wooden pillar.

No one realised that Cedric had almost drowned. His housecarls were swarming across the bridge and into the meadows beyond, engaging hand to hand with those detachments of Norwegians left holding the slopes while Hardrada gathered the main body of his men on the ridge. Harold himself led the attack, the pain in his arm and leg forgotten. When Cedric at last crawled out of the river, he saw the English pressing slowly but surely up the hillside, overwhelming the desperate outposts one by one. He raced into the ranks of his housecarls, yelling at them to hold back.

'Let the fyrd do this!' he commanded. 'Form up, keep to the rear,' and pointing with his sword to the formidable shield wall on the crest, he added: 'There is your work, housecarls. Save yourselves for that!'

His trained troops marched in the wake of the steady massacre, eager of hand and taut faced, plodding up the hill as they waited for each obstacle to clear. English fyrdmen and Viking warriors went down together in a score of murderous skirmishes, yet the housecarls did nothing to aid their struggling countrymen. Foot by foot, yard by yard, through the mess of broken bodies, tuned like bowstrings at full stretch, they slowly reached Harald's fighting men. Harold, panting harshly, streaked with sweat, blood and grime, sought out Cedric. He nodded towards the Norwegian shield wall, now no more than one hundred yards away.

'Can your men handle that?'

'That and as many again,' Cedric Shieldless yelled. 'Or all my efforts have been in vain.'

'Then go to it now! Break that line for me! I will bring on the fyrd after to widen the breach.'

Cedric shouted 'charge,' and the bowstring was loosed. The housecarls shrieked their war cry and broke into a headlong run, swords and axes high. Their mailed mass crashed into the ramparts of round Viking shields like waves bursting upon rocks. The clash of steel, iron and wood was deafening.

The housecarls were the more disciplined force. They held their lines and scratched like terriers for weaknesses in the Norwegian defence. Their blades were bright hammers raining upon the Norse anvil; they chopped and hacked mercilessly at that tight wall of armour until the first sign of a breach. Then came a renewed onslaught to prise through the slight gap. Men dropped, howling curses and supplications to the heavens. Others pushed into their place, and were struck down. Suddenly the whole line went down, and the housecarls coldly set about choosing their prey, isolating it, worrying and savaging every yard of the line, killing without pity every man who faced them.

Hardrada's infamous Landwaster banner vanished beneath the dead. The proud raven of the North had been crushed in an hour, by the fierce English dragon that had waited half a century for its revenge.

In the unearthly silence that follows the din of war, the English lords stepped reverently through the ranks of the dead, seeking to identify just two of the fallen. Soon the first of the bodies was brought to them by the housecarls, who laid it gently at their feet.

'It is your brother, my lord,' one mumbled to Harold.

The king looked down, then averted his gaze. A housecarl's axe had split Tostig's helmet in two before cleaving through his head, and he was scarcely recognisable. Gurth and Leofwine came to see what Harold had seen, and it was a while before any one of the Godwinssons could speak.

'Bury him with all honour,' Harold commanded, and he made no attempt to stop the tears.

The second body was brought shortly afterwards. It was that of the invincible Harald Hardrada, warrior king of Norway, slayer of hundreds, conquerer of lands from one edge of the world to the other. A spear had pierced the stout neck, and the head was turned fully to the right, the sightless eyes still seeking the marksman who had done the impossible.

'I promised him seven feet of good English earth,' said Harold. 'Let it be known that King Harold keeps his word.'

No victor ever felt less like celebrating his triumph, but Harold was obliged to hold the customary feast for his men that night in York. He sat at the high table with Gurth and Leofwine, Cedric and Haakon, and supped a single cup of ale while watching without interest the carefree excesses of the revellers. Few words passed between them, for there was little that could be said. It was a bitter victory they shared. They did not need to remind each other of times past, when Tostig had come adventuring with them, and had sat with them at the same high table. Their silence was their tribute to a friend and brother lost forever.

Late in the evening, a messenger from the south came to them, shouting to make himself understood above the racket.

'My lord,' he panted. 'Duke William's army has landed at Pevensey. They are attacking and burning towns along the coast.

It's a vast army, my lord; some say thirty thousand at least. They have been bringing ashore men, horses, machines and supplies. There is no one to resist them.'

'What foul misfortune,' cursed Leofwine. 'Just when we are helpless here!'

'Not misfortune,' Gurth corrected him. 'His spies must have known when we left for the north. He's chosen his moment perfectly.'

All looked to Harold.

'We are not helpless,' he stated. 'We march again at first light.'

'Harold, your men are exhausted,' Cedric protested. 'They may look all right now, full of food and drink, but they have nothing left. They need time to rest.'

'We have no time to give them,' Harold answered. 'Tell them to get their sleep while they can.'

'Thirty thousand!' Gurth was saying, shaking his head. 'If we can muster half that number after our losses here today, we'll be doing well.'

'And that,' Harold said emphatically, 'is why we must face William while he still thinks it impossible for us to be there so soon.'

'I'd say it's why we must wait, and get more men in from the shires,' Cedric persisted.

'That will take weeks.'

'Then let us take weeks.'

'No!' Harold rasped, pushing himself up from the table. 'William would never have landed on that South Saxon shore had I been there to prevent it. But I can prevent him taking more. And I will.'

XV

With leaden tread, heads bowed, they scuffed through the fallen gold of beech and oak woodland, over damp-matted barriers of leaves that pulled cruelly at weary feet. It was a brilliant day – the kind of day when the sun surmounts dark storm clouds and shines with breathtaking luminosity on yellow and crimson, setting them glowing against the brooding dark of the sky – but the ragged files of men on foot or horseback had little regard for the splendours of nature. They were fatigued to the limit, neither knowing nor caring where their labouring trudge would take them. In not much more than five weeks they had tramped two hundred miles north, had fought a fierce battle, and plodded two hundred miles south again. They had started out early in warm September, and now, on the thirteenth day of cool and rainy October, it did not seem to matter how many more days or miles or battles there were to go. Marching had become a habit, the fight for survival inevitable, and they would simply continue until their legs collapsed beneath them, as had happened to some of their companions, or until an enemy blade sent them into oblivion, as had happened to many others. They shuffled on through the fallen leaves, through the huge and majestic stillness of the Sussex forest. The slap, slap of their feet on the dead carpet was no longer a sound of their own making, but echoed back from the woods like a mockery.

'We'd put up a poor fight if we were to meet William now,' Cedric told Harold, trying not to sound down hearted. He had argued that they should stay in London for a few days more, both to rest the men and to wait for reinforcements from the far shires such as Warwickshire, Worcestershire, Somerset and Devon, but Harold had over-ruled him. The king was determined to choose his ground, as he had always done. He would not be caught and besieged in his own capital, he said, to be cooped up there for months and finally starved out. Furthermore, he would not allow William to take one yard more of his beloved English soil.

So they had said farewell to their families in London, and had gone forth on what many felt would be their last journey; this time the farewells had been spoken without the carefree merriment that had prevailed before the march north. Harold had bade his queen take their baby son into hiding, and that may have been an indication of his fading confidence. His eldest sons, Godwin and Edmund, had wanted to join him on the campaign against William, but Harold had forbidden it and had told them to wait their turn. He had, however, permitted Gytha, his old mother, and the two Ediths – his sister and his faithful mistress – to be camp followers on this occasion. Cedric was sure that this was because Harold wanted some of his own women at hand to enshroud him properly upon his death.

Cedric himself had been plagued with doubts as he left Ingrid and their children. He had given his wife his will, begged her to be brave, and had left her weeping. They were a tired and outnumbered army, the signs were against them, and they had little hope of victory. Such thoughts had obviously filled Harold's mind when he had stopped off at his Abbey of Waltham to pray, and to give more gold to the brothers there.

Harold suddenly reined in his horse.

'This is the place,' he declared.

The land sloped steeply away before them into a valley of scattered clearings. The arms of the ridge spread out to right and left on either side of the road from Hastings, seven miles away. It was a good place, Cedric had to admit. Positioned all along that ridge, they would have the advantage of height over William, who would have to take the ridge if he wanted to move on to London. Neither his foot soldiers nor his cavalry would find it easy to come at the English uphill. At this moment, thought Cedric, it looked so beautiful, so peaceful. The sun was sinking down behind black, fire-tipped clouds, and the birds had fallen silent.

Cedric nodded and asked: 'When do you think he will come?'

'He left Hastings this afternoon,' Harold answered. 'But the ease with which he moves suggests he is not looking for a meeting tonight. He will camp somewhere near. Tomorrow will be the day we decide it.'

'Not enough time for all our fyrdmen to catch up.'

'Not all, but enough.'

The women's cart, escorted by Gurth and Leofwine, had pulled up beside them. Harold got down from his horse and helped his mother out. Old Gytha was complaining about being dragged on such a journey. She, for one, was nowhere near conceding defeat for her sons.

'You could have let the Normans come as far as London,' she chided Harold.

'Never mind, mother,' Harold laughed, 'you're here now. Look, here's a place for you tomorrow, just under this oak. You'll have a fine view. Down there, that's where the battle will be.'

Edith Swan-Neck climbed down next, and Harold took her aside. Last came Edith, the former queen, as cool and aloof as ever. Her gaze met Cedric's, but she looked away too quickly. Cedric's hopeless love for her, which for a time, after the slaying of Gospatrick, had turned to hate, had since warmed to a sad longing for what might have been, and she knew it. She took a step towards him, and he jumped down from the saddle to greet her.

'I wish you good fortune tomorrow, Cedric,' she said. 'Harold is well able to look after himself, yet I always feel he is safer with his champion, Cedric Shieldless, at his side.'

Cedric recognised this as forgiveness for his harsh words to her the last time he had spoken to her.

'Thank you, my lady,' he murmured. He wondered if he dared to add what he wanted to tell her, and decided he could not let the opportunity pass. Carefully, he went on: 'My lady Edith, as well as Harold, you have been a lifelong friend of great value to me. There was a time when I wished we could have been . . .'

She smiled and, quite unexpectedly, interrupted him by lightly kissing his cheek. In her eyes were the words 'I wished it also,' but they remained unspoken.

'Come now,' she told him. 'You talk as if all is done. It is not. Tomorrow we will ride back to London in triumph.'

Later the golden dragon and the fighting man were planted side by side on the shadowed ridge, and a thousand evening fires glowed in the darkened woodlands. Harold and Cedric strolled through the camp, inspecting their men. Some were quaffing ale, turning meat on spits made from spears, raucously exchanging jokes to belie their exhaustion and their fears. Others were sleeping soundly on the wet turf. Yet more were straggling into the camp from far-flung places, to throw themselves down in the first empty patch they could find. Those who could not sleep were drinking themselves into a stupor, blotting out the fear of tomorrow as well as their aches. Harold regretted treating them so roughly.

'I had to, Cedric,' he said quietly, more as an explanation than an apology. 'You must be weary of having your good advice fall on deaf ears. But you know it isn't that I don't value it. You've always given me the soundest counsel. Yet there are times when I can act only as I think best. I must take the final responsibility. It has to be my decision, in the end.'

'We have been friends for thirty years, Harold,' Cedric grinned. 'Do you think, if I could not stomach your way of doing things, I would be here with you today?'

'Aye, thirty years,' Harold whispered. 'Thirty years since you came creeping out of those woods near Bosham, such a frightened little farm boy . . .'

'To get a beating from an arrogant little lord.'

They laughed loud enough to distract the drinkers.

'We've had some great times, my friend,' Harold went on, in a gentle voice Cedric had rarely heard before. 'God's word, we've had some times, when you think back. It seems we were forever fighting, or feasting, or womanising, or fighting again. Were there ever quiet days – days when we did nothing?'

'I suppose there must have been. But who wants to remember them?'

'Aye, you're right. No one remembers days when nothing happened. Perhaps it is that man is by nature a wild thing, and cannot be tamed. He keeps hunting until the greater hunter cuts him down, or until he has killed all there is to kill.'

'As you have?' queried Cedric, hearing a hint of discontent in Harold's tone.

'Yes, I suppose I have. I have gained all I set out to gain, and I look at it now and long for the days when I still had such an aim. Talking of old times has reminded me, suddenly, that it's all work and little fun being king. We have not had so many of those good times lately, have we? Not since I put on this cursed crown. When this is done, we must try to find them again.'

'Of course we will,' Cedric told him, and prayed that it would be so. He smiled to himself. They must be thinking the same thoughts about the day to come, yet even after all these years they could not bring themselves to speak of it, to confess their fears. 'When this is done, we'll have all the time in the world.'

Only when the words were out did he realise how cryptic they sounded.

They came to the fire where Gurth, Leofwine and Haakon were eating and gratefully took a platter each of mutton bones and some ale, muddy after being brought over rough roads, but good enough.

'Did our scouts see the Normans?' Harold asked Leofwine.

'They did,' the younger man confirmed. 'They are camped not more than a spear-throw away. Haakon went out there, too. Ask him.'

'Thousands of them,' Haakon nodded, munching casually. 'All through the trees, everywhere you look. I couldn't have counted them if I'd stayed all night.'

'And their temper is good, I should think,' Harold suggested.

'They seem quite settled,' Haakon shrugged. 'Occupied with their devotions, though, as I've always seen them before battle.

Everywhere there are priests, taking confessions and saying the mass. It's like being in a church over there. You can almost smell the incense from here!'

A smile touched Harold's lips as he looked around at his own soldiers, laughing, singing, jesting, swearing, drinking, albeit wearily.

'A prayer or two might not go amiss here,' he said.

'These are Englishmen and Danes,' Gurth said with pride. 'They do their praying in church, their fighting in the field, and their wenching and gorging in between. I'd rather keep this company than be with those monkish Normans tonight.'

'Aye,' Leofwine agreed. 'If you must die, you must live first.'

It was the first time that any of them had mentioned the possibility of death. There was a heavy silence.

'I know of no reason why we must die,' Harold said. 'We have a duty to live through tomorrow and defend what is ours, as we have always defended it.'

'I'm sorry,' Leofwine mumbled. 'A man can speak too carelessly at times like these. Sometimes it is better if he holds his tongue.'

'Hold that tongue?' Gurth teased him, 'You'd make easier work of holding a greased pig!' and they all laughed, grateful to have something to laugh at.

They slept little that night. They dozed for a while now and then, but always within a few minutes some tiny sound or thought would snap them awake again. Then they would shift uncomfortably into new positions, and wonder if they had done all they should do before the new day, and discuss it among themselves until the subject was as worn out as themselves. Then the black silence of the forest would crowd in on them again, and they wrapped themselves in their cloaks and tightly closed their eyes knowing that rest would be as elusive as before.

When the dawn came, its light hurt their sore eyes, the chill penetrated more sharply into their marrow, and the shrill cheerfulness of the birds was a cruel mockery. Painful, too, was the fresh beauty of the woodlands in the early light. The rising sun burned gold through a transparent haze, the grass was strung with bright dew, and the leaves blazed in a dying glory of red and yellow.

'We should be going hunting,' mused Cedric.

'We are,' Harold growled.

They took a last gulp of wine, and made their way to the ridge where the standards of England hung wet and limp against their poles.

Around them, twenty thousand men stumbled from the trees

and the mist to take up their positions. The quiet of daybreak was shattered by the tramp of feet, the shouted orders, the clanking of armour, blades and shields.

The duke's men rode or walked out with no more hurry than the English. They were greater in numbers, but looked strangely small down there in the hollow of the land, as if they could be no more threat than a band of children. Harmless they were not, however, and the English knew it. They were the best fighting men, not only of Normandy, but of Brittany, Flanders, France and many other nations, and they were fresh and full of vigour. Their proud banners and pennants were as colourful as the autumn and as many as the branches through which they were dipped and raised.

'God pity us now,' was Cedric's unvoiced prayer, and to that he added: 'And you, Aelfgifu and Gospatrick, if you are watching. Pray for us.'

His prayer was interrupted by Harold, who came stamping up to stand beside him.

'These fyrdmen of mine have never faced such power,' said the king, looking right and left at lines of armed farm boys. 'They worry me of a sudden, this morning. Will my housecarls hold steady, Cedric?'

'The housecarls will stand here as long as I do,' Cedric told him, 'and I shall stay until you leave.'

Harold nodded, sure it would be so if Cedric said so. He took one last look behind him, up to the oak where his mother, his sister and his mistress sat among a small knot of women.

'Well, I hope they don't decide to take a hand,' he smiled, and paid them no more regard.

The English began to shout insults down at William's soldiers, urging to come and get the business done. Some waved swords in the air, others beat them upon shields as the Viking warriors had done at Stamford Bridge such a short time before. They called out 'Holy Rood!' or 'Rood of Christ!' and after a while struck up bravely with songs. They were ancient melodies, these battle hymns of the English, older than the hymns of Christianity, songs of a darker time long since glossed over with the new godliness, songs to the Old Gods which did as well for the one all-conquering God, songs from the long night of their history, songs from the memory of their pagan forefathers.

Under the ridge, the ranks of the Normans stirred. A single horseman, a soldier-minstrel, rode out ahead of them, leading them with a clear, piping tune of his own that sang up to challenge the chanting. It was a fresh song, lyrical and light and born of an awakening spirit – a song of the morning.

THE END OF THE WARRIORS OF THE
DRAGON GOLD

EPILOGUE

THE cream of the old English nobility died with King Harold II at the Battle of Hastings. His brothers Gurth and Leofwine, his nephew Haakon, many other lords and his band of fierce house-carls, all stood beside him to the last man. The commoner who had taken it upon himself to become a King had proved himself a true leader, one who can inspire those about him to fight to the death for a cause already lost.

His cause had been lost for more than half a century. It had been lost years before he was born, when Ethelred the Unraed had taken his Norman wife Emma, and the life of the sister of Sweyn Forkbeard of Denmark, in one and the same year. Nothing could change the destiny of England then, not even the troubled reigns of eight kings – Ethelred, Sweyn, Edmund Ironside, Canute, Harold Harefoot, Hardicanute, Edward the Confessor and Harold Godwinsson. Powerful men, they were all nevertheless the helpless victims of such King-makers and King-breakers as Earl Godwin, Emma of Normandy, Sweyn and Tostig Godwinsson, Aelfgifu and Gospatrick, Archbishop Stigand and Harald Hardrada.

The only one of Harold's five brothers to survive after 14th October 1066 was the youngest, Wulfnoth, still exiled in Normandy. There he remained until after the death of William the Conquerer in 1087, by which time he had spent 35 years away from his homeland.

As for Edgar, great-grandson and last male descendant of Ethelred, he never was to take his rightful place on the English throne. But sons of his sister Margaret became Kings of Scotland, and one of her daughters, Edith Matilda, married William's son, Henry I.

Perhaps only then did the spirit of Gifta rest.